GALAXY WAR

THE SKYWARD SAGA BOOKS 4-6

A.R. KNIGHT

ORATUS

A SKYWARD SAGA SHORT STORY

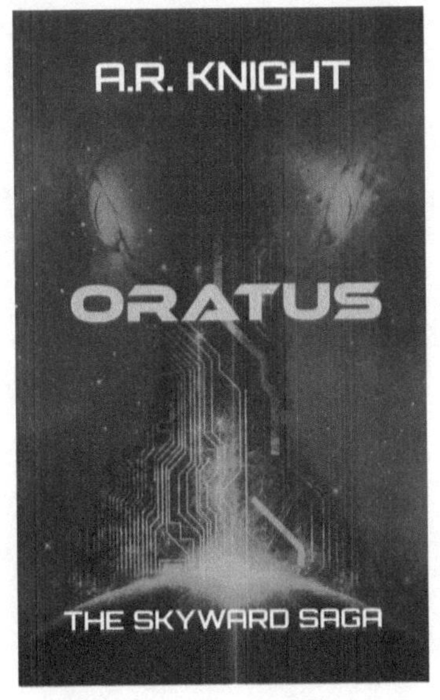

She begins in luminous blue. It's wet, cool. There's electric twitches as her muscles begin to activate, as the tips of her claws curl. The first breath comes filtered. Clean, ecstatic air. Life floods and flows through her.

She opens first one eye, her left. White everything, a black line in the middle. Then her right. What they see is a membrane holding her massive form. The light, she realizes now, comes from the outside. Smell is only the barest tickle, and even that is purified. She moves one of her arms, of which, she realizes, she has four. It snaps and crackles, shifts as molecules and muscles stretch in ways they've been designed for, and yet have not experienced. She meets resistance; the water. The name for it comes to her almost without thinking, from some reservoir of knowledge with depths she can't explore here.

Because the feeling consuming her growing consciousness is that she is trapped and she must *GET OUT*.

Fortunately, she is a weapon.

Her head darts forward, her mouth full of tearing teeth.

They grab hold and rip at the edge of the membrane even as her four arms and their claws shred the same. It's not thick —the skin isn't meant to hold her. At least, not once she's awake.

She spills out, falls from the sac onto hard-packed dirt. The sand sticks to her as she tries to stand. At first it's a wobbly affair, her legs not used to bearing her weight, her talons not used to the concept of balance.

But she's being watched, so she gets herself under control. Digs those claws into the ground. Looks.

The creatures watching her are not her own. They are smaller, scurrying around other sacs like the one she came out of. Brown, black, and gray fur covers their bodies in all manner of patterns. They chatter to each other in words she cannot understand. They ignore her. Don't meet her eyes. They surround the sac she's just left and begin tearing the rest of it apart and carrying it into the shadows.

Small halos dot the floor, which, she notices, come from slight holes in the cavern's rocky ceiling. The light's enough to bring her attention to another sac, one twisting and shaking like her own must have. There's a rip, a rush of fluid, and something comes out. Four arms ending in claws, a head atop a neck, deep red scales and a long tail... but its legs. Unlike hers, which stand strong and firm, this new one's are twisted and shriveled, bent at wrong angles.

The creature pulls itself from the sac, falls onto the floor, and struggles to right itself on its four arms. She takes a step towards it—a mix of curiosity and compassion pulls at her—then stops as five of the small creatures rush by her. They surround the struggling one, and she rises up on her legs just in time to see a bright blue flash and a sharp hiss that extends to a dying sigh.

She moves fast then, following lights leading away from

the sacs. She doesn't want to give those furry things a chance to evaluate her, find her wanting. Apparently this place does not deal in mercy.

A steel door slides shut behind her—she must have passed through it without noticing. As the door closes, a long, featureless hallway illuminates in soft yellow ahead. Standing in the middle of it is another thing that looks like her, bright blue-scaled and with its four arms crossed.

She pauses. Her muscles tense. Is this thing going to try and kill her?

"Oratus," the creature says, its voice a deep hiss. "You have been made. What you are, what you know has been given to you. A debt you must now repay."

It doesn't wait for a reply, but turns and strides down the hallway away from her. There's nowhere else to go, and this thing seems like it's not going to kill her, so she follows, her talons clicking soft on the dirt floor.

The blue one leads her to dazzling brightness. One not artificial, she notices. One that hangs high in the sky and casts an orange glow upon the deep green and pink covering. Giant arcs of glittering black rock stand over the lush gardens, sparkling and monstrous and scattered as far as she can see. Hanging from these arches are bulging rock bulbs. All suspended on large, thick cables hanging from those black arches. And then she realizes where she stands, too, is hanging. A massive boulder carved out and strung up.

Summoning her voice takes effort. She calls upon an instinct within her, natural and not, to make her throat move in such a way as to create a rasping hiss that pours forth words she's only just beginning to understand and yet has always known.

"Who am I?" She rasps.

The blue one says nothing at first, only orients back to her. Its is a look of pride, coupled with expectation; she has come so far and has so much further to go.

"Oratus, that is what you must discover."

The blue one points down, and she approaches the edge and looks.

"You will leap from here and find your way to that Mountain's peak. Survive, and you will take the first step to learning your name, and who you are meant to be."

The blue one says nothing more, and only stares at her. She looks first to the Mountain, off away from the glow and rising like a spearhead on the horizon. The drop is far, and deep beneath the vegetation is a darkness she cannot see. Sounds barrel up from it, a cacophony of roars and whistles, rattles and shakes.

She hesitates but senses that every second she remains upon this platform is one she is judged for. That no questions will be answered here.

She makes the leap.

The fall is swift, and as she plummets, she sticks her four claws and two talons out in front of her, looking to grab the first thing she encounters. Which happens to be a large pink flower shooting up from a thick green trunk. She strikes a soft frond that does nothing to slow her fall, but provides the barest hint of a grip. With her left foreclaw, she digs into the core of the flower and swings herself, nearly breaking her arm in the process, into the cluster of blossoms and petals, some of them as large as her. She bounces and rolls, desperately trying to keep her grasp, and she's moving, falling off the end of the petal and towards the ground. Only this time, the trunk runs along her back and she's able to turn with her claws, reach out and slice through the bark. It splinters and shatters as wet green wood flies out.

But she slows.

Eventually, she reaches the forest floor.

It's a soft landing on all sixes. Because, she realizes, it's not dirt or rock she's on, but a cushion of leaves and fallen petals. They litter the forest floor, covering everywhere in their fading greens and pinks except for the shoots of other plants—greens and blues, mostly—trying to make their way up to the far-off sky. The air hits her next, as the vents lining her chest open up and take in a thicker scent than what blew across the hanging rock; she finds it invigorating, sharp and bright. Even opens her mouth to see if she can taste it, lick up the flavor, and only gets a piece of falling flower for her efforts.

Beyond the undergrowth, however, the forest is crowded and dark. Orange light beams down at random, and the shafts move with the breeze above, so that she feels as though she's fallen into some mystic riddle. A place not too unlike the membrane that gave her life, except here, if she's careless, the forest might take hers.

So she's ready when there's a rustle, then a sudden thrash behind her. Swinging her tail, she uses the momentum to twist on her talons, bringing up her foreclaws towards the approaching noise. A gray-scaled creature, similar to the blue one above and, she believes, to herself, tears through a sprawling fern and rolls by her. Her eyes follow it, catching the glistening red of fresh wounds sprinkled across its back. The creature settles on the ground, unmoving.

But the thrashing isn't done. A moment later, following its prey, a bronze-scaled Oratus, larger than her, Blue and Gray strides into the small copse where she fell. Like Gray, Bronze shows signs of fighting, though by the size of the cuts, it's obvious who's winning this struggle. Bronze stops as he catches sight of her—she can tell his sex from the way Bronze smells, a pheromone hovering on the edge of her senses.

"Another one?" Bronze says. Then he seems to

remember a plan, clasps his strong four arms in front of himself, and nods towards Gray. "Welcome to our momentary world. I march towards the Mountain."

"And him?" She points to Gray.

"One whose journey is over." Bronze spares Gray a glance, it's not a merciful one. "He protested my leadership. He failed."

She watches as Bronze moves to stand over Gray. Bronze raises a claw, looks back towards her, and opens his mouth as if to say something, when Gray bursts from the ground. With two, then four claws, Gray scales Bronze as the latter hisses, flails, and misses as Gray leaps from Bronze's shoulders. As Gray flies, his tail snakes around Bronze's neck, circling tight and, with Gray's momentum pulling it forward, drags Bronze over and slams the creature onto his back. Loosening his tail, Gray wheels around, raises a talon and hovers it above Bronze's head.

She cannot deny the thrill rising in her, the power pulsing in her veins at the fight, the primal urge to join in and tear with her teeth, her claws. It doesn't even matter who, just that she is a part of the carnage. And she cannot resist. This, this is her calling. What she *lives for*.

Her jump carries her into Gray, knocking him away from Bronze. Gray, though, uses her own momentum against her and, rolling with his talons pushing against her own, kicks her off so that she flies on into the forest. Bounces off one of the trunks and lands on the plant floor. The shock jars her mind, clears the rage, though it lingers and she feels she can reach out, grab and wrap herself in its fiery cloak...

A pair of hissing roars snap her eyes up to see Bronze and Gray circling each other, eyes locked and claws sharp. They are so like Blue. Like her.

She leaps in between the two monsters, hissing as she does so. Both Bronze and Gray dart back, avoiding what both must think is an attack aimed at themselves. She winds up alone, with plenty of space to circle and stare at the other two, as they stare at her.

"Do you go to the Mountain?" She asks, turning her head from one to the other as she states the question.

"I do," Bronze says, and she sees confusion in his eyes. "I told you that a moment ago."

"I do, but not with that one," Gray hisses. "If I wish to die, I'll do so on my own terms."

The two burst into another fight, though this one, at least, is waged with words. Insults and accusations fly too fast for her to catch, with names of places and strange things tickling her mind but being interrupted before clarity can struggle through. What's clear, though, is that both of them have been down here longer than she has. A deficit of knowledge she must correct if she's going to survive long enough to make the Mountain.

So she roars again. This time louder, more confident. A guise, and one that works. Again, Gray and Bronze stop and stare at her.

"I come from above," she admits. "And I do not know where I am."

A risk, but she hopes they forget their feud to focus on her. Even if they tear each other to shreds in another moment, she wants to learn what she's able to first. Get what she can from these two so much like her before they vanish, either into the forest or the cold whisper of death.

"You came from the last arch?" Gray asks, looking up towards the canopy.

Bronze says nothing, and by his questioning eyes, he's as interested in the answer as Gray.

"A blue one of us told me to leap," she replies. "I landed here."

"Then you are the missing piece," Bronze says. "The third one to our trio."

"Our trio?" Gray replies. "I'm not going with you."

"No choice," Bronze says the words as if describing stone. "Three arches, one of us from each. That is the design."

She doesn't understand what Bronze is talking about, but Gray's anger seems to dissipate at the words. He looks at the shredded scales on his skin, at the crimson blood seeping from them towards the floor, and closes his eyes. She looks over to Bronze, who, sporting his own scratches, stares hard back at her.

"What design?" She asks.

"I'm from the first arch," Bronze replies, as if that says everything. She cocks her head so he knows that's not the case. Bronze takes a breath, his chest swelling with the intake. "This one is from the second, and you are from the third. The three of us are meant to join together, as it takes three to complete the Mountain."

"Why should I listen to you?" She asks. Distrust trickles through her senses. Her instincts warning her that the wrong allies can be just as fatal as enemies.

"You shouldn't," Gray hisses from behind her. "He wants your help for his own ends."

Bronze hisses, glares at Gray. "This one would go alone. Would abandon you in a moment if he thought it would help him. You need companions, pink. You must have help, or you will die out here."

Bronze casts his claws wide, calling her attention to the noise coming from the jungle around. All those unknowns lurking in the shadows behind the trees and thick blue and purple leaves, floral smells mingling with an undercurrent of rot and fresher kills. Bronze likely isn't wrong—this is a place full of predators, and a loner makes for easier prey. Survival isn't something she needs to learn.

"I'll go with you," she says and Bronze nods, as if he had expected no less.

"A mistake," Gray hisses. "But he's right about one thing; you'll die alone in this place. You have your trio, Bronze."

Now Bronze bursts into a toothy grin. "Then we have nothing more to wait for. Assuming you're not hurt too badly, let's go."

"As if he could hurt me," Gray rasps softly behind her.

She thinks about pointing out the wounds, the bloody scratches, but stays quiet. Even now, only a short time after hatching, she already knows what buttons to press and what to leave alone.

B ronze chatters endlessly as they climb between trees and branches, over small ponds and wading through a rushing river—she is thankful for her talons and the way they cut footholds in the rocky floor. They brush aside ferns and endless amounts of small, pestering insects intent on clogging up her breathing vents. Yet always, always Bronze talks, and because the only alternatives are the jungle noises, which quickly blend into an indistinguishable miasma, she listens.

Bronze lays out a parade of theories. Guesses and questions about what might happen on the top of the Mountain. What lies beyond the sky above, because they, Bronze asserts, did not all come from here. He wonders if this is all a game, if there are people deriving entertainment from their struggle. Or if this is some sort of strange military exercise.

When Bronze asserts that the whole thing might be an illusion, a mental trick, she can take it no longer.

"Bronze, what are you talking about? I hatched, and a blue one shoved me off a cliff and into the forest. He told me nothing," she says as she steps over a wide, triangular purple leaf.

Bronze holds up his left midclaw, points to a green ring around his forearm that she has, up at this point, assumed was a piece of jungle plant or maybe a scar.

"This tells me. It whispers in my mind, answers every question. I've barely begun to dig through what it holds," Bronze seems to lose track of reality even as he says this. "It's like an ocean, one I can keep swimming forever."

"Tell her where you found it," Gray says.

Bronze looks away, off towards some distant forest point. As if by not meeting her eyes, he won't have to face the horror of what he's about to say.

"I took it," Bronze hisses. "The owner didn't need it anymore."

"And tell her why," Gray continues. "Tell her why the owner was so free to give up this holder of all knowledge."

Bronze ignores him, "We need to keep moving. If we don't find a tall group of trees to camp in before nightfall, it will be treacherous."

This is a sloppy evasion, and one she catches easily. Yet, Bronze is larger than her, and, with Gray wounded, conflict doesn't seem like the best course of action. Not here, not when the likely result is a fight and then being either dead, or down one or more of their small team.

"When I hatched, only one thing in my arch wore one of those. Watched me get up, scattered a bunch of those furry things, then she took me right to the edge. Told me to find my name." Gray is saying the words, and she's catching tone. He's leading on to something. "And you know what I didn't do? I didn't slaughter her."

"Neither did I," Bronze stops as he speaks. "It was a

struggle. He thought I wasn't fit for it. He thought wrong. I did nothing more than claim what I earned."

She moves between the two. Slaps her tail against the ground. It's a wet thwack, the force of her muscles pressing plants, scattering dirt, crushing bugs. But it gets their attention.

"I don't care," she says. "I don't know where I am, I don't know who either of you are, and I don't trust you, but I need you. Whatever you both did before you got here doesn't matter. What does is getting to the top of that Mountain."

Gray hesitates a second, then lowers his claws. "Fine. Until we get to the top."

"I'll be ready," Bronze replies. Then he turns and points, high up, where several trees are bunched. Their green, scaly branches all looping together in a sprawling tangled knot. "That's where we'll spend the night."

Not that she plans on sleeping.

With four claws and talons, the climb up to the tangled, woody mess takes little time, and it's a big enough space that Bronze and Gray find their sides and stake their territory with glares and quiet, simmering eyes. She has no time for this, and anyway, it's her first night in the forest. Not something she wants to waste with a pair of brooding fighters. Thankfully, it's not hard to find where she can go: Up.

The trees continue above, stretching towards the canopy before exploding into the wide purple and pink flowers she saw from the arch. That she fell into. Now she climbs to them, and it's a softness that her claws bite into when she gets there. Tearing through the bright color almost feels wrong, but the sky, now that she can see it clear, pulls her further until she's above. That's the only word that can describe what she's looking at—a world spread out before her. One that she saw from the arch, yes, but that's when everything was new.

Now she knows it. Understands what she's seeing, the sounds she's hearing, and the smooth smothering of floral scent that flows into her vents with every breath. In one direction, striking against the burnt orange sky as twilight takes its due on the day, are the black arches. Definitely three, and they're much farther away than she would have expected. Bronze had kept them moving, and she supposes it's a good thing, because the sooner they get to that mountain, the sooner she can get rid of them.

As she watches, the arches seem to glow. Only for a second, though, and then the lights refocus into tiny points along the arches. Like glittering blankets. She wonders what Blue is doing, whether he's pushing another hatchling off the edge, or if, like her, he's looking across the jungle treetops and wondering about the world beyond.

The thought turns her the other way, towards the mountain that occupied a sharp triangle on the horizon when she left the arch but that now dominates more than half of it. The mountain isn't quite the perfect shape she thought it was from afar—it's lopsided to the right, and the sides are jagged in parts and curved in others. Shaped by nature, and not by more purposed hands. She glances at her own claws, shadowy themselves in the last gasps of light. Razor sharp, but there are nicks. Chips here and there from rocks or deep cuts during the run. The imperfections are calming—maybe she's natural too.

A trilling cry starts and stops quick above her, and when she looks up and catches—for an instant—the black line with wide wings that made it, she as quickly forgets it in favor of what dominates her view.

The daylight is gone, and in its absence, the stars have come out to play.

She doesn't know what they are, these bright sparkles flaring. There are countless numbers of them, some in clusters and others spread alone, as if choosing to walk their own paths. Patches of the dark shift in color, with bluish-white slashes cutting behind as if a shallow scar has been cut through the universe. In an instant she is made small, a tiny nothing against the vastness of the cosmos, and for a moment the wonder she's feeling threatens to slide into panic.

Instinct helps her here. She's a hunter, a survivor, built for murderous, efficient purpose, and she knows that what she *doesn't* know is the greatest threat to her existence. She has to fill the gaps, understand what she's seeing. Know what to avoid, to find, to use and, if necessary, to kill.

That thought slips her towards Bronze, and what he's wearing on his wrist. Bronze said knowledge lived inside it. A vast amount. Enough, maybe, to tell her what's going on up there.

She descends face first, looking for any sign her two companions might have murdered each other while she was stargazing. No blood greets her return to the tangle, only a pair of sleeping... and that's when she realizes she doesn't even know what they are. What *she* is. Words and names have come flitting through from... somewhere, telling her to call these things trees, to call those lights in the sky stars. But there's holes.

There's nobody to answer the why. But there's something that might.

She takes a cautious step towards Bronze, her talons resting on their points, keeping things quiet. Even so, she figures the noise of the night—the hoots and howls of things on the prowl and the panicked cries of their prey—would cover anything she does. Another step, keeping her tail off the ground, her midclaws spread, ready to reach down and slip that emerald bracelet off of Bronze's wrist.

"You can't have it," Brown says as she starts to reach

towards him, without opening his eyes. "This belongs to me now. It's mine, forever."

"You took it from its owner," She replies, covering the shock and frustration with a question. "I only want to look. To ask questions."

"If you're lucky, someday you might find your own. Now sleep. Got a long way to go tomorrow."

And just like that her questions remain unanswered. She gets another first—failure. The feeling saps her enthusiasm, lets the day's efforts in, and she slumps back to her own side of the platform. Curls up, resting her head on her tail. Sleep comes cloaked in mysteries and whisks her away.

When Grey announces he's hunting for breakfast, she's says she's going with him. Gray doesn't answer, just leaps from the branches towards the forest floor, though when she follows, Gray greets her landing with a steely stare.

"I'm not doing this for fun," Gray says. "I'm doing this for food. I don't want to take care of you."

"We're supposed to work together to survive, right?" She replies. "If I'm no good at this, how can I help you?"

She's hoping the logic might drive a wedge in Gray's attitude, but he just shakes his head. "If I need your help, I'm already lost."

But Gray doesn't object when she follows him. When he bursts into a fast run, she does too. Her talons catch deep into the dirt and propel her along, diving after Gray between the trunks and dodging vines as they move. Until, suddenly, Gray stops.

"We'll never catch anything with you making all that noise," he hisses. "Don't move. Watch."

She looks as Gray starts to bound. She notices something; His claws, rather than dig into the ground, ripping and tearing, land lightly. As if the tips of the claws themselves are the only things that hit the earth before Gray springs up again. When he passes by tree trunks, as he goes in a large circle around her, his foreclaws reach out and gently guide him from one tree to the next. His tail, rather than dragging on the ground like her own, stays rigid behind them. It swings through the air without a sound, providing balance.

"You're quiet," she says when Gray stops back in front of her.

"It's called hunting," Gray replies.

"Let me try," she says, and doesn't wait for an answer.

It's hard. She has to measure her weight, has to battle her own balance and lean forward into her momentum. She keeps her claws, and tries to only extend them when she's making a sharp turn, or needs to steer herself through close bunch of trees. These things come quick, but the tail is the hardest part. It wants to sink down; it's heavy and not used to being taut. This will, she realizes, take time.

But it's a start.

When she circles back around, Gray doesn't wait for her to settle, but breaks off. She recognizes the chase for what it is and keeps after him, though now she's hearing the rushing air as they move, the startled cries of creatures caught underfoot, and the gurgle of flowing liquid, which grows into a roar. Until, stopping himself hard against a knot of trees, Gray stays still. She's going fast too, and the sudden halt isn't something she's ready for, so she digs her talons in deep, her head jerks forward and she's about to pitch past Gray into the ground when his tail whips out in front of her like a bar and keeps her steady.

"Water source," Gray hisses, and she has to strain to hear him over the churning rush just beyond. "Stay quiet."

As if he has to tell her that. Gray nods one way, then points at her and the opposite. The meaning's not hard to parse, and so, one talon at a time, her fore- and midclaws out and ready, she circles left. The brush here is thicker—the constant water giving them plenty to grow on—and it's hard to move without pushing aside wide leaves and thick stalks. In between the green and purple vegetation, though, she catches glimpses of the swirling rapids beyond and the pool into which they pour.

As bodies of water go, her limited experience makes this the largest one she's ever seen. The pool is larger than the branch nest they slept in the night before, wider than the groves they've come across, and its deep sapphire color stands in contrast to the brighter pinks and greens of the flowers above and ferns nearby. She briefly considers the pool as a source of peace, rest, even, but instinct smothers that feeling quick as she catches sight of the pool's already-present members; there's a pair, and she realizes why it took a moment to pick them out of the foliage; because they are like what surrounds her.

Like large rocks, only coated in hundreds of slippery emerald vines that sink down and pool on the ground around them, though with a decided majority angling towards and dipping into the pool, the creatures seem to be resting. The only sign that they're not the very plants they imitate comes from small clouds of yellowish dust that puffs from the tops of their sloping bodies every few seconds. The dust falls back down on the creatures, and when it coats the vines, they glisten.

"Do you know what they are?" she hisses, softly, at Gray.

"No," Gray replies. "But they taste good."

Her confused face asks the question.

"Bronze taught me what I taught you three nights ago," Gray admits, and by the huffing of his vents, its clear he's not thrilled about it. "I think he's been running around here longer than he admits. Told me that I'd need to know how to catch my own food, but after our first day moving, I didn't have the energy. So he had me watch."

"Watch what?"

"This." Gray slithers by her, moving quick and soft along the wet bank towards the two creatures.

They don't move. Don't even react to Gray's presence as he closes in on them. She focuses. Waits for the creatures to run, or maybe attack. But they don't. Gray gets real close. Stands over the nearest one, then turns back to her. Even from here she can see the sad glint in his eyes, the lost chance at a thrill. Then he turns back, opens his mouth, and the claws begin to tear.

No natural predators. That's what Bronze says when they get back to the nest. The creatures, which Bronze claim are Mossox, are delicious. Juicy and tangy, and she eats more than she thinks she can. Apparently running through the jungle gives her an appetite.

Bronze partakes too, and though he did none of the work, he eats the largest portion. Even ushers the two of them to eat faster. She waits for Gray to protest, but the hunter says nothing. Barely speaks during the meal.

"Is it hunting if the prey doesn't run?" she asks Bronze, mostly because Gray had seemed so excited and now no trace of that murderous gleam could be found.

Bronze holds up his left foreclaw, the one with the bracelet, "You find it, kill it, eat it. That's a hunt, according to this."

"Then that makes you a hunter," she says to Gray, who pauses for a second and glares at her.

"She's right, little one." Bronze is grinning too wide while he says this. It twists the nickname into an insult, and, when Gray bares his own teeth back, she tenses. "There's not much I've found that'll give us a chance to really test our skills. Best be happy with this. At least till we get to the mountain."

"And when will that be?" Gray hisses.

Bronze looks towards the mountain, though it's almost impossible to see through the thick brush. Turns back to Gray and turns all four of his open claws up. Gray huffs at the gesture, then goes back to the meat.

As if answering instead of Bronze, a snap-crack wind gusts through the grove they've claimed, and she looks up to see pure-white bolts splitting a darkening sky.

Just because everything she can see is a swirling mix of rain and falling foliage doesn't mean they don't run. If anything, she thinks Bronze is moving faster today than before. Their leader is leaping high over muddy pits, and using his claws to tear apart brush in front of him rather than avoid it.

At first Bronze's change in tactics are a curiosity, soon she gets worried.

"What are you doing?" she asks during one of the rare moments they pause to catch their breath.

The forest, though it must be the middle of the day, is almost pitch dark around them. The trunks press in close, and even though she thinks she's the deadliest thing in this forest, a fear she might be proved wrong shivers with the cool storm wind.

Bronze, though, doesn't answer her question. He gives her a wide-eyed look, then bounds on, his talons tearing up chunks of mud that splatter the trees.

"He's afraid," she says to Gray, who's staying back with her.

"Of what?" Gray's as confused as she is, which makes her feel better.

Though maybe it shouldn't—as Bronze is getting ahead now. She bursts after him and hears Gray hissing curses behind her. How does she know they're curses? Only because the words trigger some deep twitch in her, a recognition that such things should be said in the most desperate of times.

She risks a glance back to confirm that Gray is not, in fact, in such dire straits, but instead of his flashing form, she only sees black jungle. No sign of him. No sound either.

She's kept her legs pumping through the trail of Bronzes' wreckage out of instinct, but now she falters. Bronze isn't getting closer anyway, and it's either wait for Gray or continue on alone.

Wait for Gray. That assumes he's coming.

She looks around her and notices that the trees are thinned. The forest gradually breaking up into grassier land, lit up in blinks from overhead. She opens her mouth, catches some of the rainwater and embraces the ice cold rivulets running down her throat. Her vents lacing her chest inhale the fresh scent of nourishing growth... and the rank stink of fear.

It's coming from her right, back towards the thicker forest. She can't see past the ferns bleeding into the grasses, but there's something back there. It might be Gray, or it might be prey. Either way, Bronze is gone and there's nowhere else to go.

So she raises her tail, treads lightly and lopes towards the smell. Goes around the first batch of trees, blinks away the raindrops, and hears something beyond the sounds of the storm; growls, ones she know, and they're being answered by whistling hums and wet thwacks.

She slides her head around a trunk, and in the next flash of lightning, sees Gray flying through the air, but he's facing the wrong direction. By the time she forms the word how, Gray collides with a tree and falls to the ground. She looks back the way he flew and there, crashing through the brush, is a whirling wall of vines writhing and stretching towards Gray's limp form.

There's a click of recognition—the thing's a Mossox, only one far larger than the pair they'd eaten at the start of the day. And unlike the two docile ones, this Mossox is moving with a vicious speed, and its vines slice through the air towards Gray.

Indecision strikes for a second. She's safe behind the tree, and the Mossox doesn't look like it's noticed her. She could run, pick up Bronze's trail, and probably catch up to him sometime later. At the very least, this thing wouldn't eat her.

In that hesitation, the Mossox's emerald tendrils reach Gray, wrapping around his claws and legs. Lifting him from the ground. Lightning-lit, the Mossox lumbers closer, and she sees the horde of vines encircling its front peel away, like water from the head of a fountain, and beneath their cover spins a rocky maw. The Mossox's teeth, unlike her own, are black and crumbled, stumps jutting forth from a dirt-ridden wreck of something that may have, in some distant past, been flesh.

She has no doubt those stumps are going to tear Gray to pieces. Would tear her to pieces too.

Gray's eyes snap open as the vines pick him up. He struggles, but the vines have him taut. Those claws, wet and ready in the rain, can't move. He tries to lash his tail and it bounces off his living manacles. Which leaves Gray with one option—his own mouth.

His teeth are razors, and they act as such. Gray's neck is long enough to get him within snapping distance of the vines holding his foreclaws, and with a couple of quick, tearing bites he gets part of himself back.

That's all she needs to see. Gray's fighting, and she's not going to stand here any more and let him die.

The Mossox sends another batch of green forth, a twisting onslaught of leafy doom, but before it reaches Gray, she leaps in between, her four claws, two talons, and one mouth enacting a visceral demolition that covers her in sticky plant juice, her scales sporting a borrowed emerald skin.

Without really trying, she's managed to cut Gray free, a fact becomes readily apparent when her friend—the term slides through without her stopping it—jumps past her straight at the Mossox's still churning grinder.

Gray, though, times his leap right and jumps up and over the rocky teeth, landing instead in another nest of vines. Here, though, the length of those tendrils works against them, as by the time those long green hairs manage to orient to Gray's position, he's cutting them down by the forest-full.

Whether through panic or anger, the Mossox rears up, its root-like legs visible now that their vine cover is gone, and she sees the mottled pink underbelly of the creature. Where, just hours ago, she's carved herself breakfast. This one makes for a big target, and it's not one she's going to miss.

She takes a quick two-talon step, then leaps into a four-claw grip on the beast's underside, setting to work like Gray taught her—with reckless abandon. This works for all of a second before the Mossox calibrates to its precarious position and plunges its front back down. She doesn't know if

Gray's still on its back, but she's coming real close to the ground.

The Mossox's front legs hit with a bone-rattling shake, and now she's tearing not to kill the thing but to survive. Either she gets through, or the Mossox, sinking lower into the ground, is going to crush her into nothing. Her tail feels the pressure first—the unrelenting solid earth. This certain death drives her into a frenzy, a red-hued state of sheer twitching muscle and frothing anger that sends all of her pushing, raging towards her own survival.

Daylight came back in strips and slashes. A dull gray glow filtering through the greasy wet coating her eyes, her scales, her everything. Except her vents, which gulp in the bits of fresh air that flow through the offal to her, and this gives her strength to move again. This hurts, and there's snaps and creaks as her bones and muscles realize that they're not quite dead yet, but they're awfully *close*.

"Are you alive?" A voice she doesn't expect, but, after a second's hesitation, welcomes.

"Bronze," she hisses. "Here. Underneath."

That's all she has the air for, but that's all she needs to say. The tearing intensifies, and soon she's seeing eight sets of claws ripping away the dead Mossox's remains. It feels similar to breaking out of the sac, like being born, only this time she emerges barely alive instead of fresh and ready. Gray has to help her stand in the middle of the great beast.

The storm, having decided to plague other parts of the planet, leaves a glistening sheen on everything which, in the afternoon light, makes the forest appear golden. Mist rising from the ground as it warms back up, and where the fog catches the light, haphazard rainbows form. It would be enchanting if she had the mind for such things. As it is, though, she's twitching her claws, her talons, her tail.

Some are chipped, all are sore, but being pressed flat against the ground hasn't ruined her.

Gray notices her examination and offers up a light hiss, "You didn't need to come back for me."

"I know," she replies. "I did it because we need you."

She says this last part loud enough for Bronze to catch; the big Oratus is prowling around the edges of the Mossox, occasionally snapping bits of thick hide and sticking it into his mouth. Foraging their kill. He ignores her, which sparks a snarling fire in her gut.

"Why did you run?" she lurches towards Bronze, though whatever intimidation she's going for stumbles along with her left leg, and Gray has to catch her. Still, her vents work, her mouth moves, so she keeps going. "You didn't even turn back. Not once."

"I'm here, so clearly I came back," Bronze replies, tearing at another scrap of flesh. "I knew we were being pursued, and expected you both to keep up with me."

"You ran."

Now Bronze looks back at her, and she sees the same dangerous glint Bronze had when she first met him fighting Gray. The Oratus has pride, and she's able to wound it. As she's considering this, she feels a tap on her tail. Gray. She catches him in her left eye and sees caution on those scratched, cracked scales.

Neither of them are up for another fight. Coward or no, Bronze could tear them apart if he wishes.

"I scouted ahead. Not my fault you're not as fast," Bronze replies, but leaves the end of the sentence hanging, an opening for her to cut in a reply. To swing the argument over the edge.

She closes her eyes for a moment. Those flaring coals inside her still want to push forward, consequences be damned, but no. It's not her right to push Gray into this, and there's a kernel of very real, very sharp fear deep inside. She's not ready to die yet, not after she's just come back. So she allows her vents to breathe out her own anger.

"Just, next time, wait?" She offers.

A peace offering. Keeps her pride and his intact.

"I will," Bronze accepts the exchange.

They relax, and, the immediate hazard of the moment passing, the three of them set gorging themselves on the feast they've made for themselves.

"How did you know?" She asks Bronze as they finish. "You were running differently before it attacked?"

"This." Bronze again shows his bracelet. "After we ate the small ones, I searched for them. Found that they tend to travel in groups, with larger ones protecting, avenging their young. And if you had listened, beyond the thunder, you would have heard it coming."

"So you knew, and didn't tell us?" Gray counters, getting a bit of fire back.

For the first time, Bronze falters. His mouth hangs there. His vents suck in some air, but no words come out. Until he glances towards the bracelet again, "This thing is hard to describe. It's like a fog that covers your mind. Once I'd found what was after us, I kept digging, trying to learn how to get away, what it would do if it caught us... and I started to run. I only realized you weren't with me when the storm broke away."

She's thinking that, perhaps, Bronze couldn't be trusted with the bracelet if he can't keep himself under control, but before she can put that thought to words, Bronze turns his back to them and gestures onward. Says they ought to get moving if they want to make some progress before real nightfall comes again. She stores the thought for later, but she's going to take a second look at everything Bronze does from now on.

The going is slow now, what with her and Gray shambling rather than loping along. Every step sends twinges from myriad places racing up and down her nerves; tiny aftershocks from the quake her body endured. As the anger at Bronze fizzles away, the adrenaline goes with it, leaving her struggling to keep going as the daylight shifts more and more towards that purple orange pastel.

At least the scenery changes here at the edge of the jungle—the ferns make a gradual shift to long, wavy grass as the covering trees add spacing and then vanish entirely. She sees why—behind them, the jungle's wide valley is visible, but here the plateaus slant down into a wide plain. The wind is picking up, blowing cool air against her scales. Fluttering insects hop from stalk to stalk, while darting, leather-winged creatures snatch others for dinner. Batches of woolly-pink seedlings drift along the air, and she sets her foreclaws to the task of keeping her eyes and vents clear.

The Mountain juts up without interference in front of them. The plain doesn't go far before rising to its foothills, and then the peak—now obscured by some remaining storm clouds. They're close. Up there, on that gray monolith, waits her name.

And she's going to get it.

They spend the night around a pool of muddy water. It's not elevated, but the grass is tall enough to provide some cover and Bronze, checking his bracelet, doesn't think there's many predators out here. At least, none that would tangle with three Oratus. She's grateful for the rest, and when dawn comes, she's reluctant to move. Until she sees Gray pointing to the distance, towards the Mountain.

"Today," Gray hisses. "Today we make it up to the top. Today we earn our names."

"Do you think it'll be that easy?" She says. "The climb? Then we're done?"

Gray doesn't have an answer. She doesn't press him. They're still sore, hungry, and she doesn't care to start an argument. But she keeps an eye turned up there, to the peak touching the cloudless sky, as she stretches out. Bronze declares it's time to go and, with nothing to pack up, they leave.

Without the snarl of trees and ferns, the run goes easy

and hours pass as they roll through the plain and up into the foothills. Up to where the grass gets shorter and the ground rockier. Where the purple flowers and white-tipped stalks give way to a darker scale. The bugs and leather-winged things disappear.

They keep going; their destination too close to stop now. She feels the Mountain looming, its bulk curling towards her every so slightly, so that it seems as if the peak is directly overhead.

It's what she's staring at when her talons hit something that's not ground. Something hard, that shrieks an unnatural sound as her right talon slides along it. The noise makes her look down in the dirt at the slab of faded yellow metal that she's landed on. The rocky black dirt is busy reclaiming the thing, but the corner she struck is still making a play for the air. The tip is oranged-over with rust, and there are charred streaks mingling with the yellow paint.

"Where do you think that came from?" She asks Gray and Bronze.

"I would talk with the bracelet, but I don't know what to ask," Bronze replies.

He's unsettled. Tense at the sudden twist to their plans. She wonders if he'll run again, like with the Mossox.

She looks at Gray and pauses. There's something moving up his back, a bright blue circle crawling up his spine, traveling towards the back of his head. Gray, though, has his eyes on the metal plate, as if he recognizes it. She can't ignore the circle, though.

"Gray," she starts as the circle centers on the back of Gray's head.

"Let's see what's beneath," Gray says and lurches forward towards her, crouching towards the plate. In the same instant, there's a high-pressure whine and a brief flash. The ground behind Gray glows hot white before the rocks themselves melt into sludge.

There's no hesitation.

All three of them scatter. Instincts take hold, call for her to take cover, to find somewhere to hide. Except the only thing here are slate rocks and cliff edges. A steep slope and nothing more.

The sparse cover goes for the shooters and she sees them now; they've crept around the bend, a small group of four things, and one of them has an awfully long, metal weapon, but other than the fact that it's aiming her way, she's not sure what it is. She spots the blue circle tracking towards her, and she jumps as it gets close. There's another flash and more molten splotches appear where she stood a second ago.

"We have to close," Bronze roars and the big Oratus begins to jump and claw his way up the Mountain.

For once, she agrees with Bronze. She pushes with her tail as she jumps, the extra push adding another couple of meters to the move. Her claws scrabbled as she lands, gripping into the hard soil and pulling herself the mountainside towards the foursome. She hears Gray behind her, skittering on the rock.

It hits her that this is first time she's actually hunting. Chasing after prey, and even if these things are deadly there's no doubt in her mind that they are just that: prey. A thrilling flurry flickers through her muscles. She accelerates the climb, keeping her eyes locked on the target. The one holding a long weapon, the one now angling towards her. As she gets closer, out of the shadows she can see its mottled brown and red skin, with scraggly feathers sticking out from its arms and body. One bright green eye looking up from its bulbous head, the spot where its second should be only a tan-scarred gash.

As fast as she's going, though, there's still no cover. The creature has her zeroed.

A rock flies hard and fast and strikes the creature in its right arm. It drops the weapon, its harm hanging limp, as the rock bounces back down the Mountain. She doesn't hesitate —she'll thank either Gray or Bronze later. No sense in giving her prey a chance to recover. Another quick lunge with her talons and then she gathers her legs and leaps up towards the outcropping where the foursome waits. As she swings over the top, she keeps moving her tail and bashes the first one back in the cliff wall behind them.

The other three creatures look at her. She's alone up here, even through Bronze started further up the Mountain. Where is he?

She banishes the thought in favor of instinct, as the creatures are moving. She presses on to the one that'd held the weapon and shoves it to the ground. She sees, in its face, a sad defiance. She hesitates. She should be sweeping through the prey without a second thought. Yet this one, and the one she's pinning to the rock with her tail, is pitiful. Up close it's clear these things are sick, weak and struggling.

These are pieces of meat, not creatures worthy of her efforts.

The other two, the ones she thought Bronze would handle, are cowering now. Sinking back against the cliff wall and holding each other. Gray catches up to her then, and she can see two other rocks in his claws ready to release. He lands in front of the fearful pair and they, like the one beneath her, make him pause.

"What are you?" She says to the one under her talons.

"We are the last trial," the scene speaks in a raspy, dry voice, and then breaks into a broken-hearted laugh.

"The last trial?" She asks. Bronze and Gray never told her anything about trials.

The creature slides one eye towards her claw, the one pinning him to the rocks. She lifts it, slightly. Adjust its points to angle right towards the creature's thick throat. No uncertainty as to the consequences of an escape attempt.

"Were the last trial," the creature croaks. "We used to be all over this mountain. Fortifications, squads and gear all set up to give you monsters what you deserved.. To prove that we were better."

"Better than who?"

"Better than you," the thing replies. Then it laughs again. "You want to see what your quest gets you? Look at us. Every one of you that succeeds sends more of us to lives like this. Every name you earn strips one from us."

She glances at Gray, whose returning the same confused look. No help there. She turns back.

"I don't know what you are, but you tried to shoot us. Why?"

"Because they think you're perfect now, so they've forgotten about us. There's nothing left to do but die slow and take as many of you with us as we can."

She's too far gone into thought, doesn't catch it right away as the creature rolls out from under her claw. Plunges towards the rifle. But she's too fast, he's too slow. Too weak. She doesn't want to kill, but she can't stop herself. It's an instinctual strike; her claws make a quick slice and now there's some red rocks on this mountain. The other three rock back, somehow pressing themselves even deeper into the rock.

"I don't know," Gray hisses, apparently unconcerned with her casual murder. "If we leave them alive, they might come after us."

She looks at the trio. They seem about as dangerous as dirt, but she agrees with Gray, so she takes the dead creature's weapon. Bends it, breaks it with a creaking crack. Splits those halves smaller with her claws, then throws the tiny pieces behind her down the mountain.

"Now they are no threat," she says to Gray. "We can be better than animals."

Gray doesn't object, though he does give one last dead stare back at the three creatures before the two of them begin climbing on the ledge and up the Mountain. Bronze is nowhere to be seen. He must've gone straight up, not even waiting a moment for them.

"When we find him, he's mine to kill," Gray says as they climb.

"I won't stop you."

It's still a gentle grade up. Lots of chipped rock, and in shadowed clefts of soil small plants struggle for light. A trail comes out of the rubble, smooth, crushed rocks more well trod, and it leads to an opening not far above them. A cave that heads down into the mountain. Not up, towards the peak.

"Should we scale outside?" She asks.

Gray glances up. The mountainside gets steeper and steeper until they would be straight climbing, depending on their claws and soft enough rock to keep going. "I don't see Bronze, which means he went inside," Gray says.

Suppose there's that too. For her part, she'd like to carve a piece of the coward as much as Gray, but she also wants to find out why he left. What's the point of joining up with them only to leave every time they get into a conflict?

Pursuing Bronze takes a temporary precedence over the peak, and the two of them step into the cave. It's not all that dark; small glowing lights are embedded in the walls. They emit a soft yellow that glistens off the smooth insides, which are far too clean and rounded. Nothing natural. She sees more metal as they move, supports built to keep the tunnel up. After spending a couple of nights in the jungle and plains, it feels strange to be back among more artificial things. Yet everything she sees tickles her senses, knowledge on the edge of her mind.

She *knows* these things.

"How far away was the second arch?" She asks Gray as they move down the tunnel. "How far did you travel with Bronze?"

"Far enough for him to make me angry," Gray hisses. "It wasn't even a whole day. They pushed me out in the night, and after I crashed through the canopy, Bronze found me. Told me we had to move."

"You went with him?"

"I didn't know what was going on, like you. I knew enough to realize being alone was a risk."

That certainly seems to be true.

"So when you found me, what were you fighting over?" She says. "That he killed his protector to get that bracelet?"

"I wanted to lead," he replies, and there's not a hint of regret in his voice. No shame or chagrin. "Thought I'd be better than him. Bronze disagreed."

"You nearly killed each other over that?"

Gray pauses, there in the tight tunnel, looks over at her. "I trusted my instincts. They told me that Bronze would get me killed. He almost has, twice."

She can't argue with that one.

The tunnel broadens and then shifts from circle to square. The dirt stops being, well, dirt and switches over to the sleek steel of an artificial shelter. Immediately in front of them is what looks like a door, but it's been broken ajar, with one of the two sides hanging askew. She can see part of a word, scratched and faded, and it says *One*.

"Those things down below, they said they were the last trial?" She says. "This could be the first?"

"If it is, it's not in good shape," Gray says as he ducks beneath the door slab.

She follows him inside a single room, no, a ruin. Broken parts of many things cluster together. Slashed white tubing snakes through clusters of broken and smashed debris. Glass, metal, and things she doesn't know litter everywhere. Pools of strange liquids occupy divots in the floor where something large fell.

The only light comes from a pair of flickering globes, themselves unstable and hanging off the walls they once called home. Her vents burn as they inhale the fumes, and her eyes water at the same. The only exit she can see through the blur is at the back. A large closed door. The word *Two* emblazoned on it in bright yellow.

"I think we're not the first ones here," she says.

Gray, though, seems more perturbed. He's inspecting the tubing, brushing aside piles of scrap with his tail. "What happened here?"

She picks up a thing on the ground near the entrance, it's long and thin like the barrel the of weapon used further down the Mountain. Jagged edges show where it was cut. "I don't think this trial is working."

"If we don't pass the trials, then we don't earn our name," Gray replies. "This isn't the deal."

He picks up a piece of scrap, throws it at the far door. It clings off, leaves a dent and a scratch but nothing more.

"You still think that's true? That If we make it to the top, will get our names?" she says. "After all this, I think the only thing we'll find is dust."

Gray glances back at her from the refuse. "Do you know what my guide, the one who greeted me when I hatched, told me?"

Obviously she doesn't.

"He told me that our names are everything. If we don't get them, if we don't earn them, then we are nothing."

She hasn't seen Gray this angry since that first fight with Bronze. He turns and whips another chunk of metal at the door. It bounces off, leaving a shiny scar on its surface.

The dead moment gives her a chance to reflect. She's done plenty; killed, saved, seen the stars. Proven herself, at least in her own eyes. That only leads to the bigger question —*who was she?*

She'll have to answer that one herself.

"We can't control what happened here," she says to Gray. "But we can keep moving. Bronze has to be up ahead somewhere. We can make the peak, name or no name."

She goes by Gray to the door he's been whacking with debris. Unlike the first one, this door seems put together. It's tightly shut; a thick pair of steel walls pressed close together. No sign of a forced opening. If Bronze came through here, then he did it nicely.

"See anything?" Gray still sounds a little miffed, but she thinks he'll come around if she can find a way forward.

If.

"Nothing," she says, inspecting. "It's just the door. Shut tight."

Gray ambles up beside her. They both stare, trace the letters *Two* with their eyes.

She leans in closer. Looks at the line where the two slabs bind together. A black coating covers the gap; a seal. She sticks her foreclaw against it, presses. The material gives way, with her claws sinking as though sinking into fruit. And, she realizes, it gives her grip.

"Do the opposite of me," she says and doesn't wait for Gray to acknowledge.

She takes both of her foreclaws, digs them in the central seal. Then turns to the right, digs her talons into the floor, and gets ready to push. Gray stares at her. Adopts the opposite stance and sinks his own claws in.

"Ready?" She says, staring directly into Gray's face,so close to hers.

"Of course."

As soon as she feels Gray start to pull, she pushes, digs her talons in with all the strength she. Presses her tail back against the edge of the wall beyond the door, pushing even while Gray, in front of her, backs his talons against the ground and pulls hard with his foreclaws, and then he digs his midclaws in to the center of the door and pulls with those two. First there's nothing, and she hears a creak and a crack as the seal begins to rip away.

It's fast then; the door shoots into its slot alongside the

exit. Gray stumbles back, hits the wall and she flies forward into him, and both of them wind up on the floor in a tangle of scales and claws. But the door's open.

After extricating themselves, they move on.

What greets them is a long shaft leading up. A cylinder of rock and metal with a long blue glow coming from a distant top. There's no elevator, there's no ladder. Not that they need one.

"I'll go first," Gray says, and he leaps up, catches the rock with his claws and talons and begins to ascend. She jumps to the opposite side, and clamors up to meet him. Together they begin to scale up the shaft towards the blue light.

"For the second trial, this isn't hard," Gray says.

"You mean I don't even get a thank you?"

"For what?"

"For getting us out of the room," she's goading him, but Gray's too serious for his own good. He needs to relax. She's afraid he'll fly into one of his rages again, or lose himself in some serious mania.

She doesn't believe this is the whole trial, and she'll need Gray cool and calm when the real challenge comes.

"We got out of there together," Gray says. "Though I suppose you did find the door seal. Thank you."

She doesn't bother hiding her teeth when she returns the grin.

The climb is long, and they can't move fast because sections of the tunnel are made up of those metal plates, which are too hard to dig in while supporting their weight. So they scuttle around, occasionally making small jumps taller parts of the cylinder to get around them. Until, gradually, they reach a section where entire shaft is metal. Up above, she can see the rock returning, talon and claw holds. Too far away to reach. To jump to.

Alone, anyway.

"I'll throw you," Gray says even as she says she'll throw him.

"No," Gray argues. "I have the better grip. You'll go."

She's about to protest, when she realizes he's right about his position. He's got the most rock, and his four claws and two talons are biting into it. She's only got her talons, with her midclaws making what they can of a spiky section of hard brown rock.

"And when I get up there? What will you do?" She replies.

"Hope you find a way," Gray says.

There's not an ounce of doubt in his voice. He believes her. Just like, she realizes, she believes him.

"Ready?" She asks.

He lets go with his foreclaws, crouches on his talons, and waits for her.

She jumps, presses off of the rock and her talons land, just so, in his foreclaws. Then he pushes, sends her flying up. As she goes, she reaches towards the rock, passes the metal band, and strikes. Claws bite in, but as she scrambles up she feels a sharp yank on her tail. Her claws slide down the rock, gouging up pieces, and she makes a quick glance downward, sees Gray hanging from her tail. Careful not to let his own claws dig in too far, though she's feeling those points pierce her scales.

"I lost the hold," Gray says. "When I pushed you."

She looks back towards her foreclaws. They're already numb, hurting. The only thing that's keeping her up is that her claws have lodged themselves in the rock. In a moment, they're going to tear away. Which means there's only one option.

"Climb me," she hisses to Gray.

"What?"

"Climb me," she hisses again. "I'm going to fall."

Now Gray registers what she wants. He doesn't waste a second. Every one of his claws digs into her as he clambers up her tail, her back and then over her head and, standing on her shoulders, he easily grips the rock and pulls himself off of her. A thousand stings shout, and she feels little cuts from him bleeding down her back, but she's escaped death. She's not going to fall now, especially as Gray offers his tail for her to help pull her up past the metal band. They stay there for a moment, resting on the sides of the tunnel.

"I'm sorry," Gray starts.

"Don't," she replies. "We needed to survive. You can't apologize for that."

Gray nods at her. He understands. There are places for compassion, for apologies. This is not one of them.

Once her muscles are stable and the twinges in her fore-claws die away, she gives a slight hiss and Gray takes a signal. They climb to the top of the shaft and the broad blue lamp lighting it, get over a small ledge and then crouch through a tighter tunnel. It leads out to an opening, with the series of steps leading away around the outer bend of the Mountain.

The daylight's slanted to orange purple twilight now, and she stops for a moment to breathe in the fresh air. To look out over the plains and the jungle and those three black arches in the middle of the vast, tree-filled canyon. Some-where down there are more Mossox, more flowers and bugs, the leather-winged things. She's so far above them that, for the first time, she feels a real taste of accomplishment. Her first real achievement.

"Beautiful," she says.

Gray, beside her, doesn't say anything at all.

Eventually, they move on. There's no sense in climbing the Mountain after dark, even if there is a trail. They don't have to go long. The peak's not far above them, and when they get up there, amid the ridges and the cold wind blowing, there's a simple flat circle of rock. In the middle of it, to neither of their surprise, stands Bronze.

All four of Bronze's claws are crossed in front of his vents as he stares at them. There's no sign of the cowardice, the uncertainty that Bronze so often cast upon his face before. Instead, there's purpose. A rigid poise in his straight-backed stance, his tail pooling around his feet. This is a different Oratus than she knows.

It shakes her. Is this a race? Did Bronze, beating them here, earn his name while both she and Gray failed somehow?

She hears a hiss from her left. Gray, who's clearly not following her line of thought. He steps forward, claws out and ready.

"Coward," Gray says, more spitting the words than speaking them. "You left us."

Bronze doesn't reply except to narrow his eyes towards Gray, ever so slightly. He lets Gray come another two steps before he opens his own claws and drops into a wide stance, and the two face-off.

She knows she should help Gray. It should be two against one. But there's an emptiness here on the peak, a void where she expects a grand parade to be. A shower of success. A name and a new purpose delivered. But there's only the rocks, the wind and the cloudless night descending with starlight. The sheer emptiness of it pulls over her.

What's the point in fighting if there's nothing to gain and nothing to lose?

"What do you believe?" Bronze says to Gray. "Do you think I left you there? Do you think I guided you all this way just to ditch you the moment of our triumph?"

As Bronze speaks, they circle one another, and she stays on the outside. Watching.

"Seems just like you," Gray replies. "Always quick to take advantage, always quick to remove yourself from danger."

"Why?" Bronze shoots back.

They complete a full circle, keeping their distance from one another, waiting for their moment. Bronze's words strike her as odd. Why doesn't the Bronze attack when he could overpower Gray, especially here in this tight spot where the smaller Oratus has no room to move? Why is Bronze playing word games when he never has before?

"Because you're a coward," Gray says. "You've always been. You are no warrior."

With that insult, Gray's negotiations are over. Gray feints a sidestep, then lunges forward, closing the gap to Bronze in a microsecond. Yet even that is enough time for Bronze to spin and sweep his tail at mid height, smashing into Gray. The impact flings Gray off to the side of the circle, where he bashes into rock and bounces back onto the floor. Gray rolls with the impact and gets up on his talons, looking at Bronze and hunting for weakness.

"Predictable," Bronze says. Even his tone is different now; no longer the curious, wondering leader but a dispassionate teacher. "If you want to claim your name, you'll need to think. You need to do more than be your instinct."

Bronze has his back turned to her. She feels she could try a quick swipe, maybe catch him off guard. But then, what if she succeeds? What if she brings Bronze down? Then she'll never learn what he means.

Gray's not interested in waiting. He lunges again, and this time Bronze meets Gray straight up. Their claws link and they push and strain at each other. With their mouths, they dart and snap, narrowly missing each other's necks. Bronze tries to sweep his tail around, but Gray twists his talons away, dodging the tail. So Bronze tries something else.

The big Oratus squats, keeping his claws linked with Gray, then leaps into the air. Gray tries to release, his eyes going wide, but he can't extricate himself. Bronze twists in the air, swinging Gray beneath him. Gray lands flat on the ground, Bronze on top of him, pinning her friend's arms and legs against the rock floor. Bronze opens his maw wide— Gray squirms, but there's nowhere to go but to that endless sleep.

"Don't," she hisses suddenly, staring at Bronze's back as the larger Oratus keeps her friend down. "There's no reason to."

When Bronze twists to meet her eyes, it's not the same. He's cold, distant. Vicious and uncompromising.

"You either earn your name, or you don't deserve it," Bronze replies.

"What are you talking about? You are with us," she replies.

Bronze glances at his bracelet. "I am beyond you. I am what you hope to be."

She doesn't understand, but she does know one thing:

once Gray is dead, Bronze will come for her next, and she doesn't want to face him alone.

She breaks into a run at the larger Oratus, who turns as she comes, plants a talon on Gray's throat.

Which leaves Gray's own legs free.

"Just like before," she shouts she closes.

Gray gets the message, and she jumps, sweeping her claws towards Bronze's face. The big Oratus is ready for the frontal assault, his claws ready to meet hers. What he's not ready for is Gray's talons as Gray catches her feet and pushes, launching her over Bronze's head. She whips her tail as she spins over Bronze, circling its end to catch Bronze around the neck and pull him with her.

She yanks Bronze off of Gray and they both collapse. She's on her back, with her claws facing the right direction and her tail pinning Bronze against her. Bronze tries to push with his own tail, but her grip is tight. She could kill him, but she's after something else.

Her left claws grab hold of Bronze's left foreclaw, and she digs for the bracelet. It's not like loose clothing. Taking the bracelet off rips Bronze's scales with it, but then it's free. It springs off of Bronze's foreclaw and rolls along the ground. All the knowledge, all the secrets waiting there for her to take.

As if the bracelet kept Bronze going, he stops struggling once it's free, instead leaning his head back to look at her and Gray.

"Together," Bronze says. "I am impressed."

Gray rolls himself back to his feet, and is about to launch for Bronze when she frees the larger Oratus and gets between the two males.

"Impressed?" She asked before Gray decides to go through her. "Impressed by what?"

"By you. I did not think it likely," Bronze says as he leans back against the rocks, massaging is for claw with the bracelet once was. "You are together. You formed the bond that is the whole point of this journey."

Now even Gray's confused. "What bond?"

Bronze gives them a side smile, brighter than ever before.

"You are a pair."

A pair?

Gray beats her to the asking.

"What you mean, a pair?" Gray says. "I thought we were three."

Bronze is still sitting, and the look he throws Gray is one of soft amusement. "I am your guide and also your judge, assigned to watch and make sure you both grow as you should. To make sure you're ready for the trials and, if you fail, to know why so the next Oratus will be better."

"That doesn't explain why you're calling us a pair," she says. Though it does explain a lot of Bronze's actions. Why he has the bracelet, why he left whenever danger approached. Why he didn't kill Gray in that first jungle fight.

"Being a pair means that the two of you will always work together. You will be inseparable, and will be able to face challenges one of you alone would never pass, but both of you will conquer," Bronze says.

His voice has the slant of ritual to it. A speech given many times before.

"The trials were broken!" Gray protests. "We were supposed to earn our way up here, but those creatures said—"

"Things change," Bronze interrupts. "The Vyphen, those that you encountered, are lingering remnants. Part of older trials left to wither, as most of their species has done. If you dispatched them, then you have done them a favor. Regardless, you survived. You triumphed."

Gray doesn't look convinced. For her part, she's not sure what's going on. Decides to wait and see because it's clear Bronze isn't done.

"Having made it here, you must both name one another," Bronze says. "You have earned your first letter."

"Letter?" She asks, realizing she's never had to consciously spell before.

Bronze points to the bracelet. "Slip on the Cache. It will guide you."

She moves over to it, Gray watching. Picks up the bracelet—the Cache—and, the moment her claws close on it, the bracelet changes. It glows bright green, and tendrils spring out. The Cache breaks apart as it encircles her left foreclaw. Then the tendrils reform, close together into a new, perfectly-fitting bracelet. With a single flash, the green glow dims.

And she's lost.

It's like diving from the arch—only this a rush of knowledge instead of air. An infinity of terms, places, people, species and thoughts. It's so much that she almost collapses until she hears Bronze, in the back quiet of reality, telling her to focus. To think of what she wants to find.

Names. Oratus letters.

There they are. As if she's standing in a vast room surrounded by words, only not just text—which she's never read before—but whole ideas. Gray, rendered into emotions and surreal images. They shift as she looks around, and gradually the ideas compress into individual letters. Large ones hanging in the gray infinite around her.

She tries to point at one, though she has no claws, no form. Yet the Cache registers, and the letter floats down in front of her. S. The sound of it wisps through her mind, and it's followed by impressions, images and definitions. An Oratus that bears this letter is strong, fast, yes, but also aggressive and perilous. A force to be reckoned with, and to watch.

A perfect fit for Gray. So perfect that she wonders if the Cache, in fact, took what she knows about her fellow Oratus and guided her to this choice.

The reasons, though, do not matter if the decision is the right one. She speaks the letter aloud to Gray, who only looks confused.

Bronze, though, accepts this. Asks her to remove the Cache.

She doesn't want to, but at the same time, she's afraid she'll drown if she keeps it on. So with her right foreclaw, she begins to tug at the bracelet, which dissolves into a thin wire frame eager to find a new target to wrap around. The Cache slides off and she hands it over to Gray who slips it on just like she did.

She watches his eyes. They, like hers must have, grow wide as the Cache connects. As he dives into the endless pool.

"B," Gray says after some time in silence.

Bronze nights again. "Fitting choices."

"Now what?" Gray, S, says.

"Now?" Bronze points up, and she notices a quartet of

bright white lights descending from the night sky. "Now you wait for what comes next. Welcome to your lives, Oratus. Welcome to the galaxy."

CREATOR'S END

THE SKYWARD SAGA BOOK FOUR

Earth. Home. The pale blue sphere looms in front of us, dominating the view and, at the same tearing at my heart.

This should have been a moment of triumph. Happiness. Instead all I can see are the long lines, the blots against the white clouds and sapphire oceans that show the presence of the Sevora. That show who's come to take my home away from me.

"We go in." I issue the command because somebody must.

Three of us on this ship and, of them, I'm the only one labeled an Empress. The only one given a direct, divine responsibility for a people I'd left behind.

Not anymore.

"You know that's a whole lot of enemies between us and where you're wanting to go," T'Oli replies.

The Ooblot has its white, liquid-like self spread between a number of terminals and controls at the front of the ship. By rapidly thawing and freezing parts of itself, T'Oli flies the craft in a lazy arc towards the Earth, trying to get away from the Sevora ships, to find a path through the atmosphere that doesn't involve a suicidal gauntlet.

"We've already survived a planet full of them," I come forward, stand next to T'Oli. "You can get us through."

I have no idea if that's true, but I say it anyway. Because I hope, and sometimes that's all I've got.

"Then you're going to want to sit down," T'Oli says. "Because once they realize we're not friendly, things are going to get real exciting."

As we get closer it's clear that in front of us isn't just a motley collection of spaceships—not that I know what I'm looking at when it comes to these things—but a formation. The Sevora have arrayed their craft in a grid that moves along with the Earth itself.

"Orbit," T'Oli says when I mention it. "They've matched the speed of your little planet there, so they can stay above the same spot while doing whatever it is they're doing."

I put aside my momentary blown mind—Earth has a speed? Why does it spin?—in favor of more important issues like, "What *are* they doing?"

"Turning us all into slaves, probably," Viera says.

The Lunare is slumped back into her netting, arms folded and wearing a look that would reduce most people to gibbering apologies if she directed it at them. I know why she's looking that way, but I'm trying not to think of it. Mostly because if I remember Malo now, if I remember how I left him lying there in a crumbling cavern infested by the enemy, I'll fall apart. Which is something I can't do right now.

Later, though. Later I'll give Malo the grief he deserves.

There's a crackle, then a strange voice, flubbery like a

Whelk's, comes bubbling out of the speakers, "Approaching shuttle, identify yourself."

"And that's not what you want to hear," T'Oli says. "They're already guessing we're foreign. Must not be transmitting the right codes for this."

I have no idea what T'Oli's talking about, but I wave for the Ooblot to let me speak anyway, and at a dual-blink from T'Oli's twin eyestalks, which rise up from its gray puddle of a body like reeds from a muddy riverbank, I start.

"Sevora, this is Kaishi, Empress of the Charre people. I demand you stop your incursion into my territory. I demand you leave my home, and never return." I'm more confident than I thought I'd be, and my voice sounds strong.

I earn silence.

Then bright points begin to appear across the grid of Sevora ships, each one appearing as a lumpy sliver across Earth's backdrop.

"What is that?" Viera asks as the same question forms in my mouth.

"Your response," T'Oli says. "They're targeting us now, and they're going to follow up with energy weapons in a moment. Think miners, but bigger. If that fails, they'll send up smaller fighters to roast us up close. We're dead, basically."

I point behind me, down towards the shuttle's lower deck. Where we came in and, if I'm right, where we'll be going out.

"There's another way off this ship right? For emergencies?" I remember the Oratus shuttle having one, and the space station *Cobalt* had things called escape mods.

"It's a defenseless ball, but yes, technically," T'Oli replies. "Good if you don't have any other options."

"Do we have any other options?"

"Seeing as we'll be in range of their cannons in about five minutes, after which we'll be reduced to something close to molecular bits by a frenzy of laserfire, and you've already said no to running—"

"We get it," Viera interrupts, shakes herself out of the nets. "But even if we jump ship in the escape mod, what's preventing them from just shooting that out of the sky too?"

"A decoy," I say. "Something big and bright to distract them. T'Oli?"

"The shuttle's only going to explode if they hit the right parts," T'Oli, I think, does the Ooblot equivalent of a shrug. "They miss, it'll just pop holes in everything and our ship'll disintegrate when it hits Earth's atmosphere."

"Earth's what?" Viera asks.

"Can you make it explode?" I trump Viera's question.

T'Oli swivels one eyestalk to Viera and one to me. "I suppose I could push all the energy we have into the engines. It'll make this shuttle go way too fast, but if the batteries overheat, it could ignite the oxygen we've got—"

"Do it," I order. "Then meet us at the mod."

"Okay," T'Oli says.

Viera blinks, then follows me down to the shuttle's lower deck. A second later, T'Oli's fix goes in and we lurch forward as if we'd suddenly fallen off a cliff. Then we start to float, our feet raising off the ground, my hair poofing out around me.

"Forgot to say that this takes power away from every-thing else," T'Oli announces as it flows to meet us, its hard-ened body looking like milk. "Better get inside before the panels go dark too."

"Does anything ever phase you?" Viera says as the Ooblot wanders over to a panel in front of a small arched door.

"No." T'Oli sends part of itself up the wall, over the control panel, and then hardens it.

A light above the panel blinks green, and the door opens to a cramped space with two long gray-metal benches. Benches set far too low for human height, but that, if we bend over and crouch, we can use. T'Oli, for its part, flows in behind us as the shuttle's lights flicker out.

The mod doesn't make a sound as it disengages from the shuttle. A set of lights around the hatch blink from green to red, and the viewport out the back swivels as the mod points itself to Earth—something T'Oli says the thing does automatically.

"So there's something else," T'Oli says as we settle in, which involves Viera and I bending around each other and T'Oli puddling up beneath the viewport.

"Something else?" Viera says. "Other than the exploding shuttle and the fact that we're now plummeting towards Earth in a tiny pod?"

"We're heading to the other side of your planet," T'Oli says.

"The other side? Why?" I've never been to the Earth's other side. Don't know what's there, but I do know my people won't be.

"Because if we kept going with the shuttle, we'd run right into the Sevora ships," T'Oli replies. "You sounded like you wanted to live, so I changed the trajectory. At our angle, it's going to be hard for them to see us with the explosion, even harder to shoot us."

I stare at the Ooblot. Confusion is melting away to anger. "Earth isn't like Vimelia, T'Oli. There's no tubes to fly people around. No way to get from one side to the other quickly."

"Oh," T'Oli says. "Well, it'll be a long walk then."

We glide around the Earth for what seems like a long time. T'Oli spends the journey educating Viera on the finer points of astronavigation and I tune them both out. Take the cramped, dull interior of the escape mod and vanish inside my own mind.

We'd all been there, on Vimelia, at the edge of our escape. Ignos had shown up, with a new host—why does that bother me?—and even though Viera had blitzed them down with a showy display of miner accuracy, the Sevora had decided to crash their own ship into our route to stop us from getting away.

Why, I keep wondering, are we worth so much to them? Why commit so many forces to stopping us?

Why kill Malo, when we didn't have the weapons, the numbers to threaten them?

Plenty of my tribe had vanished during my childhood—hunters departing on raids never to return. Others dying of disease or animal wounds. It's a part of jungle life—appreciate the time you have because it might run out at any moment.

Malo, I realize, is the first human to die off of Earth. He'd probably laugh at the thought, before remarking that falling in service to one's kind or something makes the sacrifice worth it.

Not to me.

There's only one way I can think of to fill the void where Malo's presence used to be, and that's by taking what we have, rallying my people, Viera's people, all of them to stand up against the creatures that took Malo away. That will take us all away if we let them.

We won't.

Coming into Vimelia, I stood in the cockpit with a calm Sevora voice in my head telling me everything as it happened. Explaining what was going on, what was worth worrying about and what, crucially, was not.

As the escape mod begins its rough-and-tumble turn towards Earth, as our viewport becomes a blinding glow of orange-red fire, my only options for solace are a white-faced, fists-clenched Viera and T'Oli, an alien whose primary mode of being is obtuse bemusement.

"Hitting the air pressure now," T'Oli announces as the fire grows hotter. "You've got a thick atmosphere on this one. Congratulations."

My eyes feel so wide that they're going to burst out of my skull. The novas blowing around the capsule are incredible, though I'm less excited by the heat seeping through the walls of the escape mod. My back is warm, even my feet, covered by ill-fitting Flaum boots, feel like they're stepping in desert sand. I remember to breath only when spots start flitting in front of my eyes.

"You'll want to use the handles," T'Oli says. "Going to get bouncy for a while."

The mod rumbles hard, shaking and rattling us around. I manage to grab onto the edge of the seat while Viera holds the handle on the hatch door, turning her face away from the viewport. She's closed her eyes now, but I force mine to stay open. Because the fire's starting to die away now and what I see morphs my mind.

From space, I'd recognized my corner of the planet. The browns and greens, even interrupted by Sevora ships, that marked my homeland. Even if I didn't know exactly where Damantum sat, the colors and arrangement fit. What I see here though is a spidering swath of blacks and blues. A mass of tendrils against the huge oceans, and most of that land is the color of ash, with patches of browns, greens, and one large orange oval towards the center.

"This isn't Earth," I say.

The mod's settled itself enough that my fear of death isn't quite enough to conquer my curiosity, my wonder at what's happened to the other side of my planet.

"Definitely is," T'Oli replies. "Though I'll admit the differences between the halves of your planet are striking. Not what I expected."

We continue our hurtle down, and things transition wildly in temperature, from hot to cold to warm again as the black expanse draws closer and closer to us. I'm noticing too, now, that T'Oli is still fiddling with controls by the front of the mod, making subtle changes in the direction of our descent.

"Where are you aiming us?" I ask.

"Towards one of those green patches," T'Oli replies. "Statistically, that's the most likely place to have things we need. Food, water, lack of deadly remnants."

"Deadly remnants?" Viera asks.

"What we're looking at," T'Oli says. "I'd guess, is a ruin. Something's gone wrong here. We want to stay as far away from it as we can."

"But we're landing in the middle of it." Viera's reply has a tint of resignation—of course we're going to wind up right in the thick of a new problem.

"No," I say. "Looks like, if we go to the west, the land continues around the horizon. Maybe we can get home that way?"

"Maybe," T'Oli says. "Going to need a lot of luck either way."

Viera shoots the Ooblot her dagger eyes. "You keep talking like this, I'm going to kill you before long."

"If you don't position yourselves for impact," T'Oli replies. "You won't get the chance."

I can't see the oceans anymore, or the orange lake. The viewport only has gray and black rock, and it's rushing up at us fast, too fast. I start to scream when the mod jerks, judders as flames appear around the edges of the viewport and our crashing speed slows.

And we settle on the unknown world I call home.

Criminal. Rebel. Fighter.

Traitor.

Useless words. Unable to capture the depth of feeling swarming through Sax as he stands, with Bas, on the bridge of the *Mobius*. Plake herself is at the controls, her skin only visible on her head, with everything else covered by rainbow feathers. She's orienting the *Mobius* now, pointing it towards a mustard-yellow planet whose surface swirls with passing storms.

"This is your idea of a place to hide?" Bas asks as the planet comes into view. "Rathfall?"

"When was the last time you heard of the Vincere coming here?" Plake replies, that burble of hers tickling Sax's ears.

Vyphen always sound like they're underwater.

"Rathfall won't have what we need." Sax flexes his claws. They're still not moving perfectly, and he's worried the heavy stunning might have done some permanent damage. "Evva won't be here, and we won't be able to find passage to the Chorus this far on the outer edges."

"The Chorus?" Plake laughs, then turns to the red slug-like creature at the back of the bridge, the eternally armed Agra-Red. "You hear them? They're traitors and they want to go to the Chorus!"

"I think it's true—Oratus without the Vincere just want to die," the Whelk says.

"That's—" Sax can't finish the words before a buzzing alarm cuts him off.

The sound's the same no matter the ship. A signal to find your crash netting and get situated, because you're about to hit atmosphere and going from zero air to lots of it makes for a bumpy ride. None of them have to move far; panels in the ceiling above them pop open and the black, padded stripes fall down to connect with magnetic loops in the floor. Making himself safe is as easy as falling backwards and getting caught.

Sax doesn't bother restarting the conversation, because it's too late. The view outside is entirely swirling yellows now, and the *Mobius* is already rattling in its descent. Plake wouldn't change course this deep. After they land, Sax and Bas will have to find another way off-world, back to where they need to be.

Entering Rathfall's atmosphere is a visual treat, once Sax decides the *Mobius* is well-built enough to handle the turbulence. The planet is the product of hyper-pollinating plants and the giant, mindless insects that swarm from each flower to the next, scattering so much of the pollen that the planet's covered in the stuff. Ordinarily, the shading of starlight would have resulted in a super-cooled atmosphere, but the plants dealt with their own problem, burrowing deep into Rathfall's soil and rock to release heat from the planet's core.

The plant's practice was quickly co-opted and refined

by those who found Rathfall's natural cover a perfect opportunity for businesses the Amigga didn't want in the open. With guidance, the plants now keep Rathfall's temperature equalized, and with that balance, trade flourishes.

Outside, the pollen scatters and bursts as the *Mobius* plows through pockets. Some sticks to the windshield for a second, exploding out against the pressure in grainy-yellow patterns. Flames appear as the ship hits the harder parts of the atmosphere, flicking in whites and blues along the edges of the glass. Sax thinks he can make out larger shadows flitting in the distance—the bugs about their work.

When they get beneath the upper pollen cloud, into the pocket of pressure that splits Rathfall's canopy with its floor, it's as if the *Mobius* is suspended for a moment in between worlds. Sax can see clear to the left and the right, with the windy tendrils of pollen above and the roiling, thicker mass of it below.

Plake pulls the *Mobius* out of its dive and settles into a streak across the surface, heading towards, Sax has no doubt, one of the Spires.

"What will you do?" Bas asks now that the rough-and-tumble part of the entry is over. "Leave us and run?"

"You promised me a way to get back at the Amigga," Plake doesn't hesitate before replying. "We're seeing it through. I want those ugly things knocked down as much as you do."

"So you trust us."

"I trust what I can see," Plake replies. "The Vincere want you dead, which means there must be a reason. You two aren't smart enough to be thieves, so my guess is that you're a threat."

"We are always a threat," Sax says.

"Yeah, yeah," Plake sticks up one feathered arm, waves

away Sax's words without looking at him. "I get it. The posturing. Oratus always have to be the deadliest ones in the room."

"Even when they're not," Agra-Red says from the back.

On the edge of the horizon, a dark pole appears, jutting up from the clouds beneath and its wide, flat top stopping well below the upper canopy.

Sax pushes away tempting thoughts of carving Agra-Red to fine, jelly bits and instead focuses on Plake.

"So you will not take us to the Chorus, even to hurt the Amigga?" Sax asks.

"Prove to me that's what we need to do and I'll think about it," Plake replies. "As it is, we're low on cash and I've still got all these supplies. You failed hard in that respect, Sax."

"Not our fault," Bas replies.

"Guess who doesn't care." Plake ruffles her feathers, then her long tongue wicks out of her mouth and brushes a few of them that didn't fall back into place. "Here's the plan. We'll dig around on Astre's Spire for a bit, see if we can't find out something on your missing commander. Agra-Red'll sell the supplies and the Engee can make sure this ship isn't going to fall apart after the hits we took getting away from *Scrapper Station*."

"We're not much good at digging," Sax says. "It's not, as you say, what Oratus are for."

"Oh, I know," Plake replies. "That's why you'll be staying on board. Guard the ship, so that when Coorvin and I figure out where to go, it'll still be around."

"Guard it from what?"

Scrapper Station was lawless enough. How all these places continue to exist on their own, without the Vincere enforcing basic rules, makes no sense to Sax. Then again, if guarding the ship means he can spend the time threatening smaller, more pathetic species, he'll at least be entertained.

"How should I know?" Plake presses a hand on the terminal to her right and, immediately, the windshield covers the visible area around the growing Spire with diagrams, statistics, and news. "Read up, everyone, because in ten more minutes, this is going to be our new home."

Landing in Astre's Spire means doing some light dodging around the mess of cargo drones coming and going, ferrying raw materials to much larger ships that would break apart if they attempted to enter the atmosphere. Plake doesn't seem the slightest bit concerned as she weaves around the blocks and their big engines, and she settles the *Mobius* in with a half-dozen other passenger craft. Almost immediately after, the captain and her crew disembark, leaving Sax and Bas alone with Engee, the Teven who prefers her endless experiments and her lab to interacting with the two Oratus.

At first, it's annoying being left behind. Sax burns to move, to get *going* after being stuck for so long. After an hour of watching ships come and go, and waving off the occasional robot asking if they have cargo to sell, Sax finds himself settling in, finds himself falling into a long conversation with Bas as the two of them stand at the base of the *Mobius'* entrance ramp. It's the first time in a long time they've been able to just be with each other for hours, and the time begins to whirl by as they walk back their memories.

Yet even when Rathfall goes through its deep night, with Astre's Spire lighting itself up in a bright blue glow to be more visible against the yellow murk, there's no sign of Plake, no sign of Agra-Red or Silver and Black, the two Flaum that vanished with them.

"Do we go after them?" Sax asks as Rathfall edges towards daylight, and their own exhaustion weighs heavy on their eyes. He's sad to ask the question, as it signals an end to what they've had, a return to the harsher realities of now.

"Plake said it might take a while," Bas replies. "And this is a large Spire. There's been no word of a fight, a kidnapping or anyone trying to take a ship who's captain has met a sudden end. Another day, then we look."

They wait one more round of shifts, another night under the halo lights in the bay as Rathfall's skies grow dark. In the morning, though, there's a sense that's something's definitely not right. Not a soul's returned to the ship, and nobody's tried to lower the ramp or yell for help.

"Doesn't make sense for them to pay for rooms in the Spire," Bas says what Sax is thinking. "Not when their quarters are here."

"But for all of them to vanish at once?" Sax replies. "That would mean a concerted effort. Who would care that much about a few worthless transporters?"

Bas punches the button to lower the *Mobius'* ramp. "It may not be Plake and her crew that are the target."

The two Oratus descend the ramp, claws out and ready, miners attached to tight holsters meant for smaller bodies. Sax wishes they had functioning masks, but such things are hard to come by without a Vincere operation behind you. As it is, they'll have to rely on their scales and a faster draw than anyone after them.

Outside, Astre's Spire continues apace. Ships come and go and various species mill back and forth through the docking bay. Nobody spares the *Mobius* a suspicious glance.

"Maybe they're all on a sudden vacation? Celebrating a

successful sale somewhere?" Bas wonders after no threat presents itself. "Too much to take, and they decided to stay in the Spire?"

"Can you imagine Coorvin doing that?"

The Flaum, who'd spent a very long time in crippling service to an Amigga, was both old and careful, not one to take his consciousness and throw it in a trash bin for kicks. Even if Plake and Agra-Red wanted to blur out their stress for a night, Coorvin would have brought them back safe.

There's a scrambling noise behind them, and both Oratus whip around, claws at the ready.

"Whoa, hey!" Engee, the short Teven, stands at the top of the ramp.

Her carapace is covered in small hooks, from which hang a cascade of tools and devices. Engee herself pokes her eyes out of a couple of holes near the top, while her padded feet emerge at the bottom. Apparently she's nervous, as her arms stay protected inside the shell.

"Want to say that there was a message waiting for us this morning. Sounds pretty strange! You want to hear it?" Engee practically hops as she finishes the sentence. "Vocal signatures don't match the records either, so it's a new species or someone wants to keep themselves a secret!"

Sax glances at Bas, then they both clomp back up the ramp, shutting it behind them—no reason to give stowaways or thieves easy access—and they head to the cockpit. There, blinking on a large terminal, is the yellow indicator saying something's waiting for them.

"Engee," the message starts, and it's a synthesized voice, mechanical and distorted. "It is unfortunate that you did not come into the Spire. I know you still have what I need, and you will give it to me. I've waited long enough. Come to the Wildfire, and make good on your promise, or you will never leave this place."

The two Oratus look at the Teven. "That was the most straightforward and dull threat I've ever heard," Bas finally says. "Who are they and what do they want?"

"I don't know!" Engee pips. "I'm as confused as you are! I don't know anyone who would threaten me!"

Sax blinks. "Then what could they be talking about?"

Engee's arms pop out and wrangle themselves together. "I don't know, Sax. Maybe they want something on the ship? Something I have?"

Sax glances at the message. Plays it again. Listens hard for inflection, for background noise and gets none. Whomever left it is taking care not to give themselves away.

"It's probably a trap," Sax says. "If they know where you are, and that you have what they want, then they would come here and get it."

"The *Mobius* does have some defenses," Bas replies. "Perhaps they're afraid."

"Regardless, they gave us a choice," Sax hisses. "Either we answer, and go to this place, or we stay here and wait for them to act on their threat."

"Engee, the voice spoke to you. It's your choice," Bas says.

The Teven doesn't look like she wants to decide. She scampers a bit back and forth around the cockpit, then stops. Turns towards them.

"I'll go. But someone should stay and watch the ship, in case this is a trick to get us away."

"You watched the ship on *Cobalt*," Sax says to Bas. "I'll take guard duty here."

Bas touches Sax's tail with her own in thanks. Neither of them wants to stay here, and they both know it.

"Perfect. Bas and I!" Engee announces. "Before we leave, though, we should probably get some gear. I'm not going to be caught unprepared like on Scrapper!"

Back on that station, the Teven had found herself accosted and unequipped with any defenses. Sax had stepped in, but before he'd needed to use his claws, Agra-Red had annihilated one thug with a hard blast from the Whelk's miner. Unnecessary, messy, and something Sax had quite enjoyed.

Wearing masks, which coat Sax's skin like light cloth, is second-nature. Wearing what Engee gives him, which amounts to a vest with four holes cut for his arms, feels heavy and strange. The vest itself is made from woven chrysalis fibers, a not-very-rare insect product from Dellis, and it's a silver-blue color that would be beautiful were it not marred by a thousand little gadgets.

Sax may be exaggerating, but that's what he thinks when he looks down at it. Each node dotting the vest ties to a specific sensor, linked by pinprick needles to Sax's nerves, and each of those sensors tie into the *Mobius*. Engee describes the vest as a connection to the ship itself—if Sax is frightened, or nervous, then the ship will engage various defenses and use Sax's own mind to target threats. To eliminate them.

The problem, as Sax sees it, is that he doesn't get nervous. He doesn't get afraid.

Bas laughs at this. "You might not say it, my pair, but you feel it. We all do."

Sax doesn't dignify that with a reply, and after a quick touch of tails and claws, the Teven and Bas depart for the Spire, leaving Sax alone with the *Mobius*.

This begins an even more boring exercise of watching ships come and go. Sax replays Engee's message a few times and hears nothing new. Then resorts his attention to scanning the news, hunting for signs of Evva. There's word of major Sevora military moves, but they're not heading towards the Chorus or any known world, so the Vincere aren't trying to stop them.

A Flaum on an old space station accidentally triggered self-destruction protocols and prompted an evacuation. A poison gas leak on a ship required an emergency landing. The Amigga are introducing a new version of the Fassoth, said to be more dependable and less aggressive.

All standard stories. All boring.

This is not the life Sax wants for himself. He ought to be on the front lines, in perpetual fights and dealing death with his claws. Or, failing that, somewhere like Nova, enjoying beauty with Bas. Not here in this dull cockpit, watching the little freighters play out endless monotony.

Sleep doesn't announce itself, but when Sax is leaning back in crash netting with nothing happening, when the boarding ramp's closed and the alarms are set, there's not a lot of reason to stay awake, so Sax drifts away staring at Rathfall's yellow sky.

And wakes up later to another blink from the message terminal. Outside things are deep dark. He's slept too long, then remembers the only thing he's doing is waiting. He reaches out a claw, presses the button for the message, expecting some sort of status update from Bas.

The filtered voice comes on again.

"Engee, you missed our meeting. I'm not playing games anymore. Not again. This ends tonight."

The message cuts there, leaving Sax looking at the blank terminal. Not again? Missed our meeting? If Bas and Engee didn't even make it to the Wildfire, then what's going on?

Sax jerks himself up from the netting, retracts it into the

ceiling, when the *Mobius* bursts into harsh noise. Alarm lights in the ceiling flash orange, and the terminals in front of Sax swap into camera feeds from around the ship.

Looking at the gray-scale images, Sax expects certain types of intruders. The common species for break-ins and threats. He doesn't expect this.

Scattered around the ship are cargo robots, ones with sleds attached to help with the moving of large goods. Their magnetic coating lets them hover above the surface, and now they're sitting outside the *Mobius* like metal ghosts, silently ringing the ship.

The intercom next to Sax crackles to life, bringing the same filtered voice into the cockpit.

"Engee, are you inside? I hope so, for the sake of your ship, for the sake of your own life," the filtered voice announces, and instead of anger, Sax hears sadness, frustration. "I've sent some robots to gather what you owe me, and I expect you to deliver it. Or I will have the Spire's own guards take it by force. You have thirty seconds to respond."

What would Engee possibly have that would require a dozen cargo robots to move? Sax doesn't recall seeing anything of that size here. He wouldn't mind a fight, but starting a struggle against a force of Spire guards, who might decide to just blow the *Mobius* apart from afar, doesn't seem like a great idea.

So Sax hits the button to reply.

"Engee isn't here. She went to meet you at the Wildfire. I'm only watching the ship, and don't know what you are looking for."

Straightforward. Peaceful. Bas would be proud.

There's a moment's wait before the intercom crackles again.

"No games, whoever you are. I know the Teven landed

with this ship, and I know she never appeared at the Wildfire. So I will take what's mine. What's owed to me."

"What is it then?" Sax tries. "I don't even know what you're looking for."

"Engee promised me a dozen crates of Ceres Crystals. They must be on your ship somewhere. Find them. Now."

Ceres Crystals? Sax hasn't ever heard of those before, but then, the Oratus don't need to be versed in commodities without military application. If the Vincere doesn't need it, Sax doesn't need to know about it.

Until, of course, he does.

The escape mod settles on its side and Viera, at a sign from T'Oli, presses against the handle and twists it open with a screeching thunk. The door swings out, and I breathe the air of my home for the first time in what feels like forever.

And it's terrible. It feels, tastes like I'm breathing in rocks and wood chips. The air scratches at my throat, makes me cough before I've even stepped out. My eyes water as they burn, and when I look at Viera to see if she's experiencing the same thing, her eyes are blood red, her nose is running, and she looks like she's about to throw up.

Even T'Oli, normally a creamy white, has splotches all over its skin. Yellow and blue-black spots spatter across its form. The Ooblot's eyestalks shrink down and nearly close.

"This is quite the hostile environment," T'Oli says, before scurrying back into the escape mod.

"This isn't our home," I manage. "At least, not what it should be."

I'm trying to cover my face with my hands, and I hold cloth up to my mouth and wish I still had the mask. After the fight escaping Vimelia, our masks were fractured and broken, and we left them on the shuttle. As it is, I stumble back against the escape mod, try to stuff my face into my loose, makeshift robes, and know that we'll never survive any kind of journey in this air.

"Here," T'Oli announces, coming back out of the mod. "There's filters in the mod. They're adaptable."

The Ooblot's holding—in hardened grips of itself—a pair of what look like translucent spiderwebs. Viera and I don't hesitate. Even if this things are meant to kill us, breathing this air seems a more terrible way to die than anything these filters could do.

They're cool to touch at first, and slightly wet, as if grabbing a damp rope. I hold it up to my face as T'Oli says they belong over where we breath. As if sensing my intention, the filter squirms in my hand, reaches out and grips my cheeks, my chin and my forehead. Pulls itself to me, then flattens against my face.

I can't see what it's doing, so I look at Viera, and over where she breathes—her nose and mouth—the filter glows bright white for a moment, and when the glow recedes, there's a solid pearl coating. The filter feels like wearing paint, but it works; I'm breathing in and out and there's no scratch, no choking weight of decay and ash.

The filter glosses my eyes too, at first making it seem as though everything is now just a shade lighter than it was—the black ash now looks gray, and T'Oli is closer to the snow I've seen on the tops of far away mountains than the milk it used to be.

"How are you handling this?" I ask the Ooblot.

"We breathe through pores in our skin," T'Oli says. "It's about calibrating myself to catch the particles I need and kick the others."

Already those yellow spots are shrinking as T'Oli does what it needs to do. I suppose if an Ooblot can harden itself, it might be able to do that on such a fine level as to block out the same things the filters do for us.

Turns out Ooblots are hardy creatures.

Now that we're not dying as we breathe, I actually take a look around where we landed. The foggy ash makes it hard to see far, but what's there looks like the aftermath of a fire. A vast plain coated in the flaky stuff.

During dry summers, I'd seen fires tear through the plains west of the jungles—their devastating journeys given away by the massive plumes of smoke—and my father had taken me once to see what they left behind. This scene matches those childhood memories, but what's confusing to me is that life comes back after a fire.

Ignos renews, after all.

Here, though, there's no sign of that. No plants poking back up through the grit, no weeds trying to make a start. It's as though life here has given up.

"What happened?" Viera asks the air and, so far as I can hear, she receives no reply.

"Let's go west," I announce. "That's the way towards our home, even if it's going to take us a long, long time."

"There are rations in the escape mod," T'Oli says. "Don't know how long they'll last for humans, though."

More nutrient goop, and the packets come in a variety of flavors with names I don't understand. We haven't eaten since Vimelia, since leaving the Clarity's Dawn hideout deep beneath those pipes, so Viera and I take a moment to devour packets of chalky slime.

The filters, as if sensing the motions of our mouths, peel back their layers while we suck down the goop. T'Oli, for its part, smears a packet on its skin and, like water disappearing into a cloth, the Ooblot absorbs the meal.

"You're really weird," Viera says to T'Oli.

"I get that a lot."

"Are you, uh, typical for your species?" Viera continues.

"I don't know," T'Oli replies, its eyestalks twisting into a slant. "I've never met another Ooblot before. I think I was the only one on Vimelia."

"You didn't grow up with any?" I can't help but ask.

"Grow up?" T'Oli does that weird Ooblot laugh, with its skin slapping against itself. "I was grown, Kaishi. Made right there in Vimelia off of Sevora samples. They tried to host me, but I'd just melt away any openings when they tried. So then they threw me away."

"That's awful." It's all I can think of to say. "No wonder you wanted revenge."

"Revenge?" T'Oli laughs again. "I just wanted purpose. Something to do, something with meaning. After slinking around the tubes for a long time, I found Clarity's Dawn and they offered me a job. That's all I wanted—to feel worthwhile. Don't need more than that."

We climb through the ash westward for hours. There's nothing much we see, aside from the odd two and three-meter black pole. They stand as silent watchers, and while at first I think they're trees—long dead, but still—when we happen to pass near one I take a closer look, brush away the thick grime coating it.

"Metal."

T'Oli, who's turned gray-black as the ash sticks to its flowing form, just blinks at the discovery. Viera, though, gets what I'm after.

"People lived here, once," she says.

"Something did, anyway," I reply.

But there's no further answers waiting in that single pole, so we move on. Keep going until the ground dips and the ash, if anything, gets even thicker. Up to my calves now, and I'm noticing that it's not all soft flakes. There's bigger chunks brushing by my legs, and I slip every now and then when my foot lands on something not quite broken down, like stepping on a log hidden by forest leaves.

After the pole, Viera keeps her miner drawn, her head on a constant sweep around us. When I ask why, she says it makes her feel better.

Makes me feel better too.

Especially when we see the shadow in front of us. More a swirl of disturbed ash than anything, the distant cloud marks a line ahead, a trail where something passed.

"Could be a small breeze," T'Oli says.

"No breeze is that small." I start moving towards the trail. "Come on—if there's something out here, I'd rather find it while it's still light out."

Viera agrees and the two of us break into a stumbling run, chasing the line of falling ash. I hope T'Oli's following, but the Ooblot doesn't make much noise, and it's so much slower that I don't even try to wait.

We're kicking up so many of the gray flakes that T'Oli shouldn't have trouble following anyway.

The trail leads us to a pit. Or a crater. It's large enough, either way, for the far edges to disappear behind the fog's obscuring mists. But we can see plenty of what's below.

"Well there's your proof," Viera says, and we stare for a long moment at the alien structure nestled in the ash.

From what I can see, the building sprawls out in rounded fashion. A front portion angles towards us, with enough ash dug up to provide something of a stair from the pit's edge down to what might have been a door once but is now a rusted portal to who knows where.

Beyond that opening, the building billows out, approaching and disappearing into the edges of the crater, though the ash covers so much of the structure that it's hard to know how much of it is simply mounds of dirt.

Put simply, I think it's huge. Bigger than the Vaos. Taller too. And it had clearly been the target of someone's wrath.

The walls and ceiling we can see are pitted with rust, with chunks blown apart or missing altogether, as though bitten away by sharp teeth. Or burned off by a miner.

"Who do you think made this?" I ask.

"Being an expert on all things alien," Viera says. "I have no idea."

I crouch, give my legs a breather after the run. We don't have unlimited rations. Taking the time to explore the building would put us even more at risk for getting anywhere habitable before we starved.

"Well that's certainly unexpected," T'Oli says as the Ooblot flows up behind us. "More and more mysteries. Have to say, this is all much more interesting than Sevora sewers."

"T'Oli." I brush off the Ooblot's meandering words like a fly. "How long do you think it would take us to make it halfway around a planet Earth's size?"

"At the speed we're going?" T'Oli blinks its eyestalks. "We'll be long dead by the time we get close to where the Sevora are."

I nod. That's what I needed to know.

"Then we're going in there. Might be something we can use."

"Might also get us very dead." Viera shrugs. "Then

again, I've been expecting my sudden demise for so long now that it's not even scary anymore."

"Happened to Malo," I reply without thinking.

Viera only nods at that. I shut my eyes for a second. Take a slow breath.

Now's not the time.

"Let's go."

So I jump off the edge, land on the ashen slope and skip along, feet remembering what it's like to find holds and lose them again in a moment. There's a certain joy to moving fast under my own power and it's been too long. Even here, in this gray desolation, I manage to crack a smile and forget all the awfulness behind and ahead.

Only for a moment.

Viera yells for me to be careful, but I'm in my run and to the door before she's started her descent. I look back, flash a smile, then wave for them to come down. Nothing's jumped out of the door to scare me yet, and inside is only deep dark, so it's obviously safe.

Or maybe, at this point, I just don't care. T'Oli's saying we're going to starve long before we make it home, and everything around me is ruin, so I decide that I'm going to spend my last days smiling, laughing, trying to dig up what joy I can.

Malo would want that, I think.

T'Oli follows Viera, using the rivets made by the latter's feet as pools to guide it slime-run towards me. Eventually, the three of us form up again outside the door, a rusted, bent thing that's lost any element of security it once provided to this place.

"How about next time we go together?" Viera says. "There could have been something waiting here."

"Then I would've taken care of it," I reply, holding up

my hands. "I know how to fight."

Viera pats her miner. "Trust me when I say shooting's much more effective."

I shrug. "As the Empress, I declare my opinion correct."

Viera rolls her eyes, but doesn't argue the point.

Sometimes, authority has its benefits.

"Anybody have a light?" I ask, staring into the deep entry. "I don't think Ignos is going to get much beyond that door."

The great god isn't doing much for keeping this side of the world bright anyway—the gray fog covers most things, and it's been getting steadily dimmer as the day goes on. None of us are under any illusions that we'll be spending the night somewhere in this blasted land, and all of us—T'Oli possibly excepted because Ooblot minds are, well, different—are hoping there'll be somewhere in this building we can use for shelter.

But nobody's eager to embark on a pitch-black chase after an unknown creature.

"I'll lead," T'Oli says. "I won't be able to see any better than you, but I'm very hard to kill."

Viera snorts, but we give T'Oli's plan the go-ahead and the Ooblot doesn't make anymore words about it, and slides into the door.

As the Ooblot moves, T'Oli describes the surroundings, remarking on the cold flat floor, the constant broken shards of glass, swept-in ash, and evidence of long-dead devices now taking up their decaying places along the sides.

Viera and I—with me in last place—step slowly behind the Ooblot, following its directions as our sight gradually decreases until all I've got is a right-hand grip in Viera's own to guide me.

The sheer darkness calls me back to the moments

before Ignos entered my mind for the first time, and I almost laugh at the contradictions. There, then, I was expecting to meet a god or his gift, find a way to save my people or bring them prosperity. Here, I'm marching with fatal determination, moving forward because staying still means a slow, pointless death.

"This remind you of home?" I ask Viera, remembering that the Lunare came from beneath the mountains.

"Our tunnels aren't dark," Viera replies and her voice sounds loud in the quiet hall. "We plant glow-worms, and feed them. The way their light reflects off of the rocks and pools of water is beautiful, fascinating. I miss it."

As if responding to Viera's remembrance, we turn a corner and notice wisps of light in front of us. Blue curls coming out of a round door not far ahead, ones that silhouette T'Oli's twin eyestalks and make it seem as though we're walking towards some portal to a dark beyond.

A person stands in the middle of the domed room. They're the source of the glow—or rather, a sapphire light beneath them is. It's a man, wearing what seems to be a series of striped bands all across his body. Because everything is in that blue color-scheme, I can't tell if the man's outfit is supposed to be a rainbow display or a black-and-white affair.

Which is good, because there are other things I ought to be focusing on. Namely, why the man's right eye seems to have slid down his face, so that it rests just on top of his cheek. He only has one ear—the left—though I don't see any evidence of a scar. Thick hair covers his head, unmoved by the subtle breeze slipping through the place.

"If you aren't the ugliest man I've ever seen," Viera announces as we head into the room.

She's already drawn her miner, aimed and pointed it at

the man. I think she's happy we're facing, for once, another human. An enemy she knows.

"Hello," the man says, speaking in the same universal language as everyone else. "Welcome to my home."

Malo's Charre lingo, apparently, didn't make it to this side of the world.

Otherwise, the man's voice is an even-keel, though it fuzzes at the edges, as if someone ran the ends of his words through a rushing river.

"Your home could use some cleaning," I say, stepping into the room around Viera, who's slips me a 'stay-back' look that I ignore.

The man doesn't seem to have any weapons, doesn't look aggressive with his smallish hands by his sides. And with Viera covering him, I can't imagine anything he could do that wouldn't end in his smoking corpse on the ground.

Until I notice that his feet aren't on it. The ground, I mean. The man's floating a little above the floor. I check his shoes—but his feet are only wrapped in those same bands. None of the magnetic flying boots used by the Flaum back on Vimelia.

"It's an image," T'Oli says. "This thing isn't really here. Which, all things considered, seems like a smart decision."

The man's head swivels towards the Ooblot, and his face shifts into a sad, if disturbing, smile. "I haven't really been here in a very long time."

Behind the man, spaced out around the room, are piles of broken equipment. Shattered glass and bent, burnt metal couple with deep grooves in the stone floor to tell a story of disaster. The filter keeps me from knowing what it smells like down here, for which I'm thankful. Wreckage like this usually means death, and bodies left to rot tend to make unpleasant finds.

There are, however, two other doors splitting off to parts unknown.

"Looks like you're here right now?" Viera's asking.

"It's like Nasiya," I say. "Just a picture. The real question is, where are you?"

"Dead," the man says. "I've been dead for far longer than you've been alive."

There's a brief second of silence, before I bust out a long sigh. "Of course, after everything we've seen, why not a ghost too?"

Ignos, my god, supposedly casts reflections at times, sends back past relatives to glimpse the present, to meet with their chosen family and pass along wisdom. Not something I'd ever experienced, but seeing as the priests claimed Ignos sent these visions along in times of need, getting a ghost for myself now would make sense.

"A ghost?" the man shakes his head. "No. Merely a recording. For any who survived the cancellation."

"You're throwing terms out there without a lot of context," I say.

"You don't know?" The man doesn't put any shock into his voice, but I gather he would if he could. "You are not survivors?"

"We are," Viera says. "We'd like to stay that way, too."

"Then you should know that this place is not safe," the man replies. "You are at risk, here. And you should leave."

I gesture at the other doors leading further in, "We need supplies. A way to get to the other side of the world. You have that?"

"My data has been corrupted, survivor," the man says. "I have no inventory to give you. If, however, you helped me, I could perhaps find you a way."

Being told by a shimmering, distorted mistake of a creature that our survival depends, maybe, on helping it is not on the list of things I want to hear. I'm the one, no, we're the ones that need help, not some avatar that freely admits it's dead.

But what choice do we have? Say no? Venture back into the ash lands and starve slowly in the choking gray?

"What do we need to do?" I ask, T'Oli and Viera apparently deferring to me for once.

The ghost turns and gestures with its right hand, and from it leaps a series of small stars stretching forth to the closer of the two doors. The line hovers at my eyeline, their blue sparks twinkling motes of fire.

"Follow them," the man says. "Find the core, and open the vents."

"Well, if that doesn't clear things up," Viera mutters, and we start off.

The blue line peters out at the edge of the room, not even lasting us past the door. I glance back at the man, wondering if the ghost realizes his guide-posting is rather lacking, but all I get is a blank stare back.

"Guess this is what we have," I say and down we go, once more into the dark.

T'Oli again assumes its leadership role, courageously descending us along a wide, flat ramp that curls, every so often, back against itself as it winds further and further. Viera remarks that stairs would take up less space, and I'm inclined to agree.

"Not every species can step." T'Oli makes the observation in the same slap-tone it always does, as if unaware of what it's saying.

T'Oli's remark, though, cracks a certain code. I'd not thought of another alien species making it to Earth until that moment. That one might have been here far earlier, might have made this whole structure answers and creates questions at a rate that threatens to overwhelm me.

So I reach out to the Cache, that all-knowing bracelet given to me by a Sevora when it first crashed outside my village, and rub the cool, hard surface. I want to check, to see if it knows anything about what's happened here, whether Earth's part in the galactic chaos comes earlier than my own dalliance with dominating parasites.

The Cache, though, is like walking into a dream. It takes all my concentration, and while reading its lines I'm going to be useless to Viera and T'Oli. In a place like this one, with who-knows-what around the corner, blasting my mind into purgatory isn't a safe move.

There's other ways of learning things, though.

"What do you think would use a ramp like this, T'Oli?" I ask the Ooblot as we continue through the dark.

On either side of me I can feel the walls close in, and I reach out to brush them every now and again. Cold metal, generally, though often pocked and scratched. T'Oli's been calling out to us whenever it hits debris that we have to blindly climb over, and a few times it's noted other doors, but I figure the ghost would have told us if the path branched at all en route to our destination.

"Like this one?" T'Oli muses. "Whelk certainly wouldn't mind it, but it's too wide for them. Or for other Ooblots, though there are other signs this isn't of our making."

"Then whose?"

"Oh, there's really only one species that would make a place like this," T'Oli says, and I can feel Viera stifling a sigh. "Amigga."

Sax glares at the intercom. Then heads out, jumps down to the loading bay and hits the button that lowers the boarding ramp. As he does so, one of the cargo robots shifts in front of the ramp, the small intercom on the thing's block-like body crackling to life.

"Where are the crystals?" the filtered voice, via the robot, demands. "I don't see any."

"Search the ship, if you want them," Sax hisses, stepping right around the robot.

The robot turns, as if it's going to follow Sax. "Where are you going?"

"Engee didn't show. My pair was with her," Sax replies, glaring back at the floating metal sled. "I'm going to find them."

As Sax walks away, though, his vest blinks red. The *Mobius'* ramp suddenly retracts, closing off the cargo bay and leaving the twelve robots without anything to do. Which doesn't bother Sax in the slightest. He's following the trails of light globes towards the Spire's center, towards one of the many doors leading inside.

He's nearly there before the entrances—wide, rectangular things with several layers—shift open to reveal a grimy airlock, coated with yellow pollen. Inside it, standing with two of small miners in its hands, is a tall Teven.

Unlike the naked carapace so many of the species wear, this one is plated over with blue steel, and a pair of helmets house the creature's eyes through holes in its sides. Its arms, or legs—Sax isn't sure what is what when it comes to Teven —leak out the top of the carapace, two holding the miners, one free, and the fourth hanging on to what looks like an energy knife.

What's more fascinating though is what the Teven's done to its base; instead of leaving it open for the creature's legs, this one's gone ahead and attached a magnetic circle to itself, allowing it to float over the floor. Useful if you live on a metal construct, perhaps, but entirely useless in the wilds.

As Sax starts into the open airlock, the Teven tilts back and, with its magnet, glides away from Sax towards the rear of the space.

"Stay right there, Oratus," the Teven says.

"Why?" Sax replies, and keeps moving forward. "You think you can hurt me before I tear you apart?"

"I'd aim for your eyes!"

Sax opens his mouth, shows off the teeth. Breathes deep through his vents and exhales in a loud hiss. "I don't need those to end you."

"But they'd help if you want to find your pair, wouldn't they?"

And there's the clue Sax needs. This is the filtered voice. Which means he's not wasting any more time. Sax digs his talons in and leaps high, over the Teven, and as he goes, Sax whips his tail down, knocking the miners from the creature's hands. As soon as the Oratus hits the ground, Sax digs in his claws, flips directions, and tackles the Teven, driving the yelling alien to the floor.

The airlock doors shut behind them as Sax looms over his victim.

"Tell me where they are," the Oratus says, making sure to open his mouth good and wide so the Teven can use the full power of his imagination on those razor teeth.

"I don't know," the Teven's voice is reedy, indignant. "They never came to the Wildfire."

"Then you have a problem," Sax says. "Because they were trying to get to you, and if something's happened to Bas, you're the one I'm going to blame."

The Teven squirms as the inside airlock seals shift open, leading to the interior of Astre's Spire. Here at the top, the walls are plastered with various terminals and vending machines for nutrient goop, water, and the various types of licenses and passes for cargo shipments. The center of the space is a series of interlocking elevators, with large ones for cargo and smaller ones for passengers.

Sax stands and hooks a mid-claw around the Teven's carapace, lifting the lightweight creature and carrying him out of the airlock.

"You don't understand," the Teven's wailing. "I wouldn't hurt her! Or her friends!"

"Doesn't sound like your message," Sax says, looking around. "You made a clear threat."

There's not many other species on this level at this time of night. A few are set up around a vending bar, where drinks and other substances are provided purely by mechanical means. A big terminal scrolls through news sources and plays soundless video. Four Flaum are tugging a cargo sled out of one of the elevators towards another airlock.

Nobody pays them any attention.

"I know, I know, but I need those crystals, and Engee too," the Teven says.

There's a flutter around the Teven's words that catches Sax's attention. He's heard that lilt before, from Bas, from himself.

"Are you and Engee together?" Sax asks.

He's not sure how Teven mate, if they mate. Sax isn't sure if they lay eggs, if they replicate, or if there's some complex ritual involved.

"Well, no," the Teven says. "Not yet, anyway. That's why I need the crystals! To earn her love!"

"You're threatening Engee to get things from her... to earn her love?"

"I wouldn't expect an Oratus to understand." The Teven squirms hard, kicks that magnet bottom of his and shoots out of Sax's hand.

The Oratus lets the Teven go. Sax can catch him again if he needs to, and without his miners, the Teven's not exactly a threat.

"I don't really care," Sax says to the Teven. "Just tell me how to find them."

"I already said! I don't know where they are." The Teven searches, sees where his miners lay on the ground, just past the shut airlock door.

Sax leaps to them first, slips the small weapons into the many holsters on his waist. Vincere principles call for leaving extra space in case of useful finds, and just because Sax isn't part of the military anymore, doesn't mean he's not going to keep good habits.

"Then you're going to help me find them," Sax says as the Teven stares at his stolen weapons. "What's your name, Teven?"

"Nobaa," the Teven replies. "And you, Oratus? Should I call you Deathclaw?"

"Sax is fine."

He, Nobaa tells Sax while they wait for an elevator, is an engineer. He met Engee when they were both in school, and, like her, he's been fascinated with self-augmentation ever since. After achieving their degrees, they both came here, until Engee declared the noxious yellows of Rathfall some sort of creative killer and left when Plake offered her a job.

"I agree," Sax says at this part, as an elevator pings open in front of them and they step into its ad-blasting confines; shifting images with Flaum hawking various restaurants, hotels, and other products on Astre's Spire.

Sax is expecting a single-button stop, right to the Wildfire, but Nobaa uses the terminal to select more than a dozen points.

"You agree with what?" Nobaa says, tilting an eye in his dark blue helmet towards Sax.

"Leaving here. It's a terrible planet," Sax narrows his eyes at the Teven. "Why did you pick so many stops?"

"You don't know where they are, I don't know where they are, so they could be anywhere!" If Nobaa's expecting Sax to do something with this statement, the Teven's bitterly disappointed. But not for long. "Engee and I worked on Astre's Spire for a while—I might as well give you a tour, and maybe we'll run into them!"

"I'm not here for a tour."

"Oh, I know. Neither am I!" The elevator dings to its first stop as Nobaa speaks, and the doors shift open to reveal a dark and damp space.

There's no walls Sax can see, and the only light comes from floating motes—likely tied to robots—drifting around in the distance. From what illumination spills out of the elevator doors, Sax sees thick green fronds sneaking into view. The air's thick with the smells of flowers and fertilizer.

"Every Spire needs a greenhouse," Nobaa says as the elevator's doors shut. "We make sure Astre has fresh food, and that nobody's starved for something natural!"

"Stop it," Sax takes a long step over to the panel, pushes the Teven out of the way, and hits the emergency stop button. "You're going to tell me what you're doing. Now."

The elevator judders to a sharp halt. Sax glares at Nobaa, whose four hands wrangle their fingers together. The Teven's eyes bounce past Sax to the terminal, something the Teven's not going to get near again.

"It's true, I swear! All of it!"

"Talk straight," Sax replies. "Tell me where they are, or I'll cut you apart right here and take my chances."

"I don't know, uh, exactly where they are," Nobaa replies. "And I'm not the reason they're gone! I wanted to meet them at Wildfire, honest!"

"You're not helping."

"Right," the Teven takes a step back, but the elevator's not large. No move is going to buy Nobaa more than a half-second of time before Sax takes his due. "See. There's a lot of money on your heads, you know? Not just you, but the whole *Mobius* crew. I just wanted my crystals before you all wind up dead."

Sax takes this in like he does everything else—with shrugging resignation. The galaxy's never made things easy for him, why start now?

"So the Engee thing was a lie?"

Here Nobaa actually looks distressed. "No, no, that's all true! Yes, I want the crystals, but Engee's a friend. I was hoping she'd come to Wildfire, and then I'd find a way to keep her out of this. With the crystals, of course."

"Such a romantic," Sax throws some extra venom into the hiss. "This Spire isn't that populated. Who here is going to risk fighting us?"

The Teven nods at the elevator panel. "Can we go? I have a place. It's not big, but it's more secure than here. People might be listening."

"If you're trying to trap me, Teven, know that I'll kill you first."

That fact delivered, Sax steps aside and lets Nobaa adjust the elevator's destinations. Takes Sax deeper into the Spire, to one of the residential levels. If Sax is calculating right, it's right in the middle of the thick lower cloud, which means Nobaa's not among the power players in the Spire.

If the Teven doesn't have resources, then Nobaa had better have information, because without it, he's wasting Sax's time.

And Sax is not a patient person.

Nobaa's apartment is little more than a single room with a food dispenser and an info terminal where the window would be, if there was anything to see other than flowing mustard-yellow gas.

"It's not much, but then, I don't need much," Nobaa says, pointing one of his small arms at the soft-box in the middle of the floor.

Full of what looks like sand, it's where the Teven would sleep. The grit keeps the Teven's carapace centered and straight, while providing a comfortable space to thread limbs if Nobaa wants.

Overall, the whole space isn't far off from what Sax would have on a Vincere ship.

"Don't care," Sax hisses. "Tell me what you know. Now."

"Sure," Nobaa says, floating his way into the soft-box. "Here's the thing. You're all wanted by the Vincere and the Chorus for an amount that's, frankly, obscene. Only there's not many on the Spire that read those alerts and fewer that can act on them."

"Get to the point." Sax folds his four arms and lets his tail curl around his legs.

"As an engineer, I did some work for the group I think took Engee, and probably the rest of your friends. A Vyphen, goes by the name of Frayk."

"He runs the the shipping around here?"

"That's the weird thing," Nobaa replies. "Frayk doesn't run anything, far as I can tell. His name isn't on any company, he doesn't show up to big ceremonies, and nobody talks about him. The only way I knew this store I was designing connected to him was because he stopped by once and you could tell, oh you could tell; there wasn't anybody in that place who didn't stop what they were doing and wait for him to stay something."

"So you think this Frayk is doing this for money?"

"I, I'm not sure," Nobaa says. "I don't think Frayk needs the money. I'd say he's doing it for something else. A favor, maybe? Get the Vincere or the Chorus to allow something?"

"Like what?"

"No idea! I'm not a detective, Sax. I'm an engineer! I make things!"

"Sure," Sax says. "How do I find the Vyphen?"

"No idea. You might be able to try the place I worked at though? The one I designed?" Nobaa waits a second. "Guess what it's called?"

"The Wildfire?"

"Wow! You're good. You're really good. I can see why the Vincere is all your species now, scary *and* smart."

Sax puts up with the Teven long enough to get the Wildfire's location, then ditches Nobaa in the apartment with a warning not to touch the *Mobius*. The Oratus heads back to the elevator, taking off Engee's vest along the way and tossing it into a trash bin. It's annoying to wear, and Sax isn't going back to the ship without his pair, without the crew that's been taken.

The Wildfire is on the fiftieth level from the top of the Spire, in the heart of the restaurant series. Sax gets off the elevator into a shifting crowd of night-cappers. It's well after dinner and the ones roaming the ring, drifting in and out of those few places still open have left sense and sensibility long behind. They barely glance at the walking array of weapons that is Sax, and those that do regard him like he's a dream.

Sax doesn't care. He's focusing on the luminous red display in jagged font screaming his destination. The name-plate sits above a broad opening flanked with billowing flames—not real ones, as fire in sealed environments can cause... problems. Regardless, there's an empty stand for visitors to check in and see available seats, unnecessary given the late hour, and past that a broad array of tables and seating areas bordered with walking isles marked by red-orange metallic paint.

The lighting in the place evokes the fires too—hitting the same color notes as the floor and doing so with strands of laser-wire hanging from the ceiling, as if it, too, is aflame.

There's a single many-armed, no-eyed robot bartender serving a half-dozen species around a central ring bar. Sax steps his way up to it, signals the robot for a glass of water and a packet of nutrient goop. Hardly an exotic order, but when a greased-up, working Whelk slides his wobbly eye over to mock Sax, the creature realizes who it's about to insult and quickly withdraws.

Sax can't see anyone else in the restaurant, and there's no visible signs of struggle. So either Engee and Bas didn't make it here at all, or someone talked them into leaving.

"Who's the manager?" Sax asks as the bartender delivers the goods.

"Currently?" the robot replies. "Or during the day?"

"Now. I want to speak to them."

The bartender turns and presses something beneath the bar. "They'll be out shortly."

While he waits, Sax glances up at the screen. There's an array of sports scores for games Sax neither knows nor cares about. Some talking-head Flaum blather on for a moment, before, at last, things shift to a galaxy update.

"The Chorus are responding to increasing unrest led by a pair of rogue Oratus, Evva and Avan, whose whereabouts are sought by the Vincere. After accusations emerged that the Chorus may be engaging in wholescale manipulation of civilized races, the First Chair denounced the assertions and laid out a long series of points purporting to show how the galaxy has improved under Chorus and Amigga control." The gray-black turns to his partner, a golden-haired, smaller Flaum. "Do you think that'll be enough?"

"It's ludicrous to go against the Chorus," the golden one says. "They've done too much good, and even if you don't agree, they control the Vincere. Anyone seriously opposing them is just going to wind up dead, so what's the point?"

"What's the point. indeed. Inspiring stuff, as ever," the black Flaum replies.

Sax looks away from the screen at the sound of approaching wheels. The manager's here.

A Belloch. Thick, yellowed, and with eight thin arms of varying lengths wrapping around its curving bow of a body, the creature sits in a concave chair tied to a pair of treads trundling across the floor. At the top end of its body, the Belloch has a bulbous eye cluster, deep red and dark, and a slit that, Sax knows, can open to reveal its goop-sucking proboscis.

Sax recoils, though, presses back against the bar with his nutrient packet in one foreclaw and his water glass in the other. Bellochs are mistakes, Amigga errors long-since stopped, but with enough lifespan to keep on going. There's rumors that the species has found a way to reproduce, but Sax hasn't seen evidence.

He hopes he never does.

"You're not what I expected," the Belloch says, its voice nasally and full of mucous. "Usually, an ask for a manager is a complaint waiting to happen. You, though, don't seem the type."

"I want information."

"Yes. Who doesn't? Perhaps I can help you, perhaps not. The question really becomes, then, why?"

This is why Sax hates Bellochs. Why, he thinks, the Amigga gave up on them. Their reasoning is always circular, always angling for an advantage. Mostly, the things talk too much.

"I'll kill you if you don't," Sax says. "Do the galaxy a favor."

"Oh yes, another threat. I don't have any choice as to what I am, Oratus. Consider that before you snap your mouth at me."

"Consider my threats mercy, then," Sax says. "I'm looking for a Teven with another Oratus. A pink one. They were supposed to be here?"

The voices on the screen go quiet, and Sax is aware of the other bar patrons staring at them, pacing their conversation. As far as eavesdropping goes, they're not trying to hide. So Sax starts to plan his attack.

"Two Oratus in one night?" the Belloch clasps all eight arms in front of it, each eight-fingered hand entwining with another. "That would have been truly memorable. So I'm sorry to say such an event has never happened here. You are the only one of your species to grace the Wildfire this evening."

Sax takes a final slurp of the nutrient goop and sets it on the bar, where the robot scoops it up immediately. He slips off the chair, keeping his claws ready, and swishes his long tail across the floor. Have to make sure everyone here knows an Oratus isn't easy to kill, isn't worth even trying.

"Do you know what happened to them, or not?" Sax hisses.

"Do I know? Why would I? I'm only a simple manager of a simple restaurant catering to fine souls like yourself."

"You must have recordings, though," Sax says. "That would show what you say is true? If so, then I'll leave."

"Alas, my security is broken at the moment. It's why I retained these helpful friends to keep things civil. It can be rough out here, as I'm sure you know."

The Belloch doesn't seem concerned in the slightest, but Sax is picking up plenty of nervous scents from those behind him. Hard to tell whether the nerves come from their boss lying, or just from an Oratus standing battle-ready.

Time to find out.

Sax whirls away from the Belloch, jabs a foreclaw towards the Whelk that was, moments ago, so unnerved by

Sax's presence. "What do you think, Whelk? Is the Belloch telling the truth?"

The alien can't even speak. The Whelk blubbers out some unintelligible garbage, stops, and takes a long sniff of the powders set in small bowls before it. The creature's color changes from a lime-green to a soft blue, and the Whelk's jelly body shivers.

"Now that you've got your courage," Sax hisses. "Try again."

"Yes," the Whelk blurts out. "Yes they were here. But not anymore, not anymore. I swear it wasn't me!"

There's a reedy sigh from the Belloch. "Whelks. Always prone to failure."

The Belloch acts first; throwing his tread-chair into reverse and zipping away from Sax even as stools topple and the Belloch's muscle makes their move. The blue Whelk imitates its employer as Sax takes stock of the opposition, squishing away from the Oratus and letting a Flaum trio, paired with a couple of ragged Vyphen missing most of their feathers, take front stage.

"Really?" Sax hisses at the group. He's not seeing weapons, while Sax himself has a couple of miners and plenty of claws ready to work. "You want to die for that one?"

"Acton pays," the center Flaum, mottled brown and white, says.

The five attempt to fan out around Sax, who keeps the bar to his back. Their eyes shift between the Oratus and each other, and it's obvious they're waiting for a signal.

Sax decides to give them one.

He springs to his left, towards a gray-black Flaum whose raised claws mean he's not caught entirely by surprise. Not that it matters. Sax catches the Flaum's hands with his foreclaws, then uses his midclaws to grip the Flaum's clothing and smash the creature into the bar. Once, twice and then he drops the limp alien to the floor.

A couple of clacks sound as the brown Flaum gets close, but a whip from Sax's tail sends that one flying into a table, denting the metal furniture. Sax pivots around in time to see the first Vyphen's strong tongue as it lashes out, grabs ahold of Sax's left leg and sweeps the Oratus' talons out from under him.

Another species might be troubled by that, but Sax catches his fall with his tail and boosts himself forward, leaning onto his claws and closing his mouth over the Vyphen's retracting tongue. Sax bites in just enough to stop, not enough to snap—eating through a Vyphen's tongue would probably mean death for the creature, and Sax doesn't want to kill.

Not yet.

The last Flaum and the other Vyphen see the stalemate and hesitate. The first smart decision they've made, and a sign that Sax can still make a deal with them. An employer that pays doesn't mean much if you're dead.

Sax thinks the Belloch's run away, which is why it's a surprise when the blue burning bolt from a miner hits Sax hard in his torso. His jaw goes numb, lax, and the captive Vyphen yanks its tongue back home. It's a powerful stun, meaning it's not coming from a handheld, small miner. Sax crumples to his side, manages to see the Belloch, holding a large assault miner and rolling back between his thugs.

"Always keep one around," the Belloch sneers. "Nobody ever checks the chair. It's remarkable, really. Thanks for not ruining my friend here. For that, I'll let you in on a little secret."

Sax tries to move, but it's like there's a stone block

between his mind and his body. No connection. No way through.

"You and your pair are only leaving this Spire one way, Oratus," Belloch continues. "In a prison prism."

The Belloch raises the miner a second time, fires it, and in a wash of blue, Sax ceases to think.

I find a wall to lean against in the black stairwell because, for the moment, I want a chance to breathe without wondering whether my next footfall will plunge me into some nether abyss.

Amigga. Of course it all comes back to them. Despite all the claims about how evil the Sevora are, the nightmares I keep having all revolve around the tests on *Cobalt*. The carousel of terrors that Dalachite subjected me to under some pretense of 'study'. As if I, and, by extension, our entire species is an experiment whose results are, as yet, unclear.

Courtesy of Sax and a miner, we cleared it up for that Amigga, at least.

"Doesn't matter," Viera says. "What the Amigga care about isn't our problem right now. It's damn dark in here, I'm cold, and we're still stuck on the slow track to starvation, so let's keep moving."

Right. Focus.

T'Oli, as usual, proceeds on in glib apathy, gliding down the ramp and calling out obstacles as they appear. Eventually the path straightens and, because my arms no longer hit hard metal when I reach out, I know we're at the bottom, and in a large space.

"Wait here," T'Oli says. "I'll scout around."

Viera and I take a seat at the end of the ramp, though I can only tell she's close by the sounds of her breath.

"This wasn't the homecoming I wanted," Viera says after a second. "Thought, maybe, I'd actually get home."

"Dumb of us to hope," I reply. "Nothing I've planned has worked out in a long time."

"We made it off of Vimelia, didn't we?"

"Some of us."

"That's how Malo would've wanted it," Viera says. "He was always looking for ways to give himself up for you."

"I never asked for that."

"That's what loyalty means—you don't have to ask."

I blink away a tear that's threatening to escape. Malo was loyal. To a fault, really. We'd left the hierarchy of Damantum, gone into an alien society where grit, strength, and knowing how to fight seemed to be the main link between life and death. That's where I should've been tossed aside—Malo, the warrior, ought to be sitting here now, ready to come back and lead our people in desperate battle against the Sevora.

"You think, if we make it back, that humanity's going to survive?" I ask.

"I'm not even worried about that," Viera replies. "You know us. We're like bugs—we'll scramble and find some way. Maybe not all, maybe not even most of us, but someone's going to make it out the other side of all this."

"I'm betting you will."

"Because I'm so good with a miner?"

I laugh. "No, because you're willing to do what it takes to win."

"It's not about winning, but about living to see what happens next. I'm too addicted to life to leave it."

There's a scuttle from the far end of the room, then a burst of orange.

The light leaks up from the apparent back wall of the chamber, central. If I'd run straight from the ramp across the space, I'd hit where those orange lines are crawling up the wall, to where they're now spidering out through the sides and up onto the ceiling.

T'Oli, shadowed by the glow, has formed up into its usual ball-and-stalk shape next to what appears to be a very crusty lever.

"Vents," T'Oli announces as we look over to it. "Simple stuff. Would've expected more from Amigga, but if you're lookin' to grab and throw heat, this works."

Viera and I glance at each other, then back at the lines of energy. They're moving slower now as they extend towards the ramp. Towards us. As the lines get closer, it's clear they're not a pure orange but instead a roiling cluster of reds, oranges, and deep yellows that swirl around and back on each other.

Like fire.

The lines, though, stop well before they reach us. Fade out, with licks occasionally popping further along before falling back.

"The thing upstairs said we had to open all the vents," I say, standing and, now that my pupils have adjusted to the shock of having actual light, following the dead remainder of the lines along the ceiling.

They keep flowing to the ramp and then up the walls alongside it, where they vanish into the dark higher up.

"If it lets us see, then I agree with the monster," Viera says, then she nods towards the circular door onward behind T'Oli. "Guessing there's more of these?"

"If I had to guess, which, cause I don't know, I have to," T'Oli muses, its eyestalks swiveling along the lines. "What we're getting now is only a trickle of what a place like this would need to run. Clarity's Dawn, down in that rusted sewer, took a lot more energy from the Sevora than this vent is giving here."

"Then we go?" Viera looks at me.

"We go," I reply.

Before we leave the room, though, I walk over to a pile of bent and broken metal. Unlike most of the other debris we've seen, this doesn't look burned but smashed. Someone deliberately beat whatever this was to pieces, but as their efforts give me a good meter-long stick of hard, splintered metal to wield, I'm not mad about it.

Both T'Oli and Viera are staring at me when I turn around, the short staff in my hands.

"What?"

"Nothing." Viera smiles. "Glad to see you'll be able to fend for yourself."

"I'm only taking this to hit you when you're annoying," I wave the stick towards her. "Like now."

"Humans are a strange species," T'Oli burbles from his corner.

"You're one to talk." I swing the staff towards the Ooblot. "Lead on, slimeball."

T'Oli oozes forth, though one eye turns back towards me, and its back half ripples out another reply, "If only I could. The best Ooblots can turn themselves entirely liquid."

"Of course they can," Viera mutters as we follow beneath the orange lines. "Why wouldn't they?"

I'm expecting another ramp but instead we get hallways. So many hallways. It's not a straight line anymore either—we've reached a basement warren. As big as the building looked from above, standing on the lip of the ash pit, it feels bigger now as we follow T'Oli through one turn after another.

Viera and I only know we're shifting because T'Oli tells us, with short 'Rights' and 'Lefts' when a turn comes because those orange lines die out a few steps beyond the room, returning us to dark. I let the meandering go for a bit before I ask T'Oli to stop.

"How are you choosing where to go?" I ask. "And I'm going to be upset if you say 'at random'."

"The energy we're unlocking comes from below," T'Oli replies, though there's something different about its voice— it's off, though I can't figure out why. "The vents control access to lines that channel this energy, and it's hot. Keep your hands on the lines and you'll feel a little more heat from the right direction, where the energy's coming from."

"But the lines are above us?"

"At first it's not comfortable, but an Ooblot can get just about anywhere, even up."

Now I get what's different. T'Oli's talking down to us from the ceiling, where it's somehow attached himself.

"Remind me not to underestimate Ooblots," I say.

"I will."

Our line-tracing continues a little longer until we reach another room—identified as such because T'Oli announces it. Viera and I take up leaning on walls at the entrance while we wait for T'Oli to find the vent. But instead of the shunting of a lever, the next thing we hear is a series of rapid clicks along the floor behind us. Clicks I recognize.

"Claws," Viera and I say at the same time.

I hear my friend draw her miner, though I'm sure she can't see anything to shoot at. The claws click again, closer, and I try to remember how many turns took us here. How many possible ways a monster could find us.

"T'Oli? The vent?" I'm proud to say my voice only jumps up a little bit.

"Working on it!" the Ooblot's reply is maddeningly cheerful.

As if she's encouraging the Ooblot, Viera fires her miner. The bolt is bright, blue, and blinds me for a second before it buries itself into a wall. The hallway back the way we came, though, is empty.

"How many shots do you have left?"

"No idea," Viera says. "Never really learned how to read these things."

"Rackt didn't teach you?" The Vyphen fighter back on Vimelia had given Viera that miner, had taught her how to shoot.

"There's a bunch of different options, Kaishi. If we need to kill someone, I'll figure it out." Viera stops talking for a second and I wonder why, until I catch the clicks again.

They're close. In the room.

I whirl and swing the piece of metal out behind me. Hit nothing, but I'm so juiced up at this point that I keep whirling and clang the bar off the wall to my right. The ringing noise echoes around the room, I wince, and then T'Oli finds the vent.

Orange bursts forth on the far side of the room and we get our first look at what's following us, what's there in the room, what's coming at me in a whirl of claws.

"Oratus!" Viera shouts, and on one hand, she's obviously right.

On another, I don't think Sax would call this thing one of his own. The same breaking orange light that lets me see the Oratus only has three arms left—the fourth, its left foreclaw, is nothing more than a shoulder stump—and less than half a tail, causes the Oratus to pause, snap its head back towards T'Oli.

Viera fires again.

She doesn't miss.

The blue bolt crashes into the Oratus' chest as the creature registers T'Oli's an Ooblot and, by the way it keeps its claws towards us, decides the slimeball isn't a threat. Viera's shot gets a hiss, a slight stumble, but the Oratus doesn't fall.

So I try my stick.

The Oratus is taller than me, so my strike heads in for the thing's waist. It notices, bloodshot yellow eyes glaring at me as its midclaws catch my metal bar, as they tear it from my hands and break it.

"Next shot kills, Oratus," Viera says. "Don't move."

The Oratus glances at her. Pauses with my bar in its claws. Opens its mouth with a long, angry hiss, "You should not be alive."

We're staring at the Oratus and it's staring back at Viera and I, claws back out and ready, though it seems less bloodthirsty than before. Maybe that's what happens when you've got a miner pointed in your face, maybe that's what happens when things you think are long dead suddenly show up again in front of you.

"You're better than you were," the Oratus hisses. "More perfect. More as they intended."

"Yeah, you keep talking in riddles like that and we're

going to get along just fine," Viera says. "How about you explain why you're hiding down here in the dark?"

Though, I think, it's not dark anymore. The roiling orange is all through this room now too, and the lines burn bright back the way we came. That whole network of hallways we stumbled through is probably all lit up now, which makes me wonder what we might've missed.

No. We're not here to explore. We're here to get home.

"It's been so long," the Oratus says, then looks at itself and shakes its head. "I was young then. My first assignment, to come here and oversee the deletion of a project."

"How about we start with your name, and then we can get into the messy details?" I offer.

T'Oli, meanwhile, has re-attached itself to the ceiling and has made it way above the Oratus. At first I don't understand why, but when the Ooblot shifts most of itself into a hard rock, it makes sense—a surprise, heavy dive bomb.

But Vee, who insists that his name is only one letter, decides he's not interested in fighting right then and instead, in a rasping, hazy voice, spills out one revelation after another.

Humans are, Vee says, simply one more experiment gone wrong. Earth, a habitable zone chosen because it would support the kind of life the Amigga wanted to grow. In fact, Earth already had most of its own life forms, plants and animals, so the Amigga didn't have to seed much at all to make it work.

Several Amigga began the project, which led to what we saw up above, a sampling of an earlier creation. Vee says he doesn't know much about what happened after the early humans were developed, but things went wrong soon after the Amigga gave us sentience.

"You're too hard to control," Vee says. "They wanted something pliable. Something more capable than Flaum, but less dangerous than us. What they wound up with had too much freedom."

Humanity pushed back. Fought against their creators for a chance at their own destinies. Which is when Vee arrived, along with other Vincere forces. They were told the Sevora had taken a species, told that humanity had lost itself and needed to be eradicated.

"The Vincere probably think they succeeded," Vee says. "I landed with another five Oratus. The whole engagement was kept secret, to keep other species from finding out what happened here." Vee snorts, laughs at this. "We were told it was to keep the fear of the Sevora in check—if the enemy destroyed a species, it might destroy others. But the real reason? To keep the Amigga's goals hidden from the rest of the galaxy."

Which is why, when five Oratus proved unable to wipe out the humans, the Vincere proceeded to obliterate the entire base from orbit. They fried everything for kilometers, burned the land to bury a species, to hide the Amigga's failure.

"Which is why I'm surprised to see you standing there," Vee says. "You shouldn't exist."

"Sorry to disappoint," Viera snaps. She still hasn't lowered her miner, and I'm not about to tell her to.

"Looks like you've got two choices, Vee," I say. "Either you prove, somehow, that you're not going to try to kill us, or Viera roasts you right here."

The Oratus keeps his eyes angled towards me, his half-tail swishing across the ground. "Do you know what it feels like to have your own people fire at you? Assume you're dead and burn the skies around you?"

"That's a hard no," I reply.

Vee laughs, but it's a broken thing. Nothing of the manic glee Sax had when he chuckled about his murderous rampages.

"It doesn't do much for loyalty," Vee replies, then gestures at himself. "I'm old, I'm breaking down. Nothing but hunting rats in the darkness and talking with that projection up there for far too long. You're offering a new life. Potential."

Something here, though, doesn't add up. What's an Oratus doing sitting here in the dark when all he has to do is flip these vents?

I ask the question. Vee blinks.

"Vents? I don't know anything about any vents," Vee says.

"Didn't the projection tell you?"

"We trade insults. I tell it stories and it listens," Vee cocks his head. "You, though, are something else. A human. Perhaps it trusts you more than the creature sent to destroy its civilization."

"Vee makes a good point," Viera says. "Why *would* we trust an Oratus?"

"I think I can help with that," T'Oli says. "If you'll stand still, Vee, I can give you a chance to prove yourself."

The Oratus starts, looks up, just as T'Oli drops from the ceiling. The Ooblot splashes onto Vee and flows around the creature's head, spine, and around his claws, becoming a robe, albeit one with a pair of eyestalks sticking out from the top, above Vee's head.

In a moment, the Ooblot hardens, locking Vee's claws out. Stiffening a hold on the Oratus' neck.

"There we go," T'Oli says. "Now, if you try and do

anything, I can break all of your arms and your neck in a moment! Pretty neat, right?"

Vee makes a choking noise and T'Oli shivers the section around Vee's neck.

"A little tight?" T'Oli asks, and Vee tries to nod. "Sorry 'bout that. We'll just have to keep adjusting till we find the perfect fit between deadly and flexible."

Vee looks more than a little upset at the situation, his vents flaring, but when he notices Viera still hasn't lowered her miner, when he tries flexing his claws and finding the Ooblot really does have a hard hold on him, Vee sighs and dishes me a resigned stare.

"Think we can work with this, Viera?" I say.

"I'm not putting my miner down."

"Fine by me." I point towards the back of the room, towards another door heading deeper. "Guessing the third vent is that way. Vee, would you lead on?"

The Oratus doesn't fight this time and, with Viera behind him and me taking up the rear, we head on towards the third vent.

What Vee's saying, about humans being a failed Amigga experiment, I shuffle into the back corner of my mind. Even if it's true, there's nothing I can do about it. And there's something deeply satisfying about knowing we're an experiment the Amigga failed to destroy.

Unlike the first two, the third vent doesn't require a winding staircase or a hallway maze to get to. It's just a straight shot along a wide corridor, a gray one with thick doors spaced evenly on either side. Each door has a dead control panel next to it, and a range of numbers plated in tarnished bronze on the surface.

"What are these?" I ask Vee as we trod along.

"I don't know," Vee says. "By the time our force arrived, they had already sealed most of this base."

"The humans?"

"The Amigga that oversaw the experiment, the one they all said was the cause of the problems. It locked everything away. The only thing we found here were traps." Vee hisses. "Almost all of us were lost when we entered. Rooms sealed around us. Gasses and fire."

"How'd you survive?" Viera says.

"I ran," Vee replies. "We realized what was happening, and it was my job to cut off the power. I wasn't fast enough."

I take a closer look at the plate of a door next to me. 50-75, it read. I trace the numbers with my finger. The grooves aren't precise. These were etched by hand, not by machine.

"Before, most of the base sat above this place," Vee continues. "I was so deep my mask couldn't send out any communication. Once the rest of the team was lost, the Vincere decided they didn't want to risk any more."

"So you hid down here while everything burned?" Viera says.

Vee twitches his stump of a tail. Doesn't reply and keeps moving.

The third vent, on the other side of the corridor, is surrounded by dark terminals. Some sort of basement control center. Vee, at T'Oli's gentle instruction, flips up the vent and sends the orange bursting up the lines along the ceiling.

Around us, all those same terminals fly to life. At first the screens display blues, reds, angry reams of text flying around that I can't read before they're gone. Then they fade to a single logo, one I recognize because I've been taught to know it all my life. Taught to revere it.

A circular star, with a halo, black against a white backdrop, though I'm used to seeing it on stone.

Ignos.

Viera sees the icon too, guesses its meaning. T'Oli and Vee, though, stare at us like we've lost our minds.

"Something interesting?" T'Oli asks.

"The icon," I say. "There in the middle. What is it?"

"No idea," T'Oli says. "Vee? You can talk now."

I give the combo Ooblot and Oratus a side look as T'Oli, with a shimmer around Vee's neck, loosens his hold on the Oratus.

"I think that it's best to keep hostages on edge," T'Oli says at my look. "A tight throat means this Oratus isn't going to forget I can crush his neck whenever I want."

"I won't," Vee rasps, his hissing even more hoarse now. "As to your question, I don't know. These designs can mean anything."

Part of me wants to dive into the Cache then and there. I've never, I realize, actually looked for Ignos in the bracelet, never tried to find anything on the god my entire tribe has believed in. When neither Sax nor the Sevora that lived in my mind mentioned him, I figured Ignos simply wasn't followed in the wider galaxy.

And yet, here he is. I know that's the same design as the one carved into the top of my tribe's Tier. I want to trace the connection, to think about —

"Hey," Viera interrupts my thinking as she moves aside the sole exit door. "Something's happening."

Vee-T'Oli goes to peer out, then turns back to me. "The doors are open."

That's not all, though. I'm hearing a noise, one that starts low and grows, echoes off the walls and pours around us. A sound unmistakable and amazing.

Humans. Screaming.

"Go," I say after a moment. "Let's find them!"

With Vee-T'Oli in the lead, the three of us head out of the room, take the first left into an open door, into an orange-lit cavern where, piled on each other like the stacked full crates of nutrient goop in a shuttle, are dozens and dozens of tubes.

Immediately inside the door, there's a ramp leading to the base of the cavern, where the tubes rise three-deep, each one almost double my own height. They're filled with a black liquid, and all of them have red lights blinking on top. And a few, the ones from where the screaming pours, are open.

"No," I say, because I can't think of another word to describe the things hanging from those tubes, their harnesses keeping them suspended in the air.

They're not human, not really. Like the project in the upper level, these things are malformed. Limbs are in the wrong places, or have the wrong number. Too many fingers, too few arms. As if some child were building figures out of clay and didn't care if they misplaced bits and pieces.

"Maybe your people were right to bomb this place," Viera says to Vee. "This, this is terrifying."

The floor at the base is coated with spilled black liquid, a puddle that grows as more of the tubes begin to hiss and burst open. More yowls, hoots and strange hollers join the growing chorus as things better left dead find themselves alive.

"Let's go," I say. "I don't like this place."

"And leave them?" Viera says to me. "They're suffering."

"Do you have the energy to shoot them all?" I reply,

motioning towards all the tubes. "Or are you going to climb to every tube and stab whatever's inside?"

"I bet we could release them," T'Oli says. "Figure those consoles back there have a way. Usually how these things work."

Release them? I look from our door across the way to the closest tube, at a thing with three eyes, no nose, and a wide mouth open in a permanent scream. It senses my glance and meets me, and in those three eyes I see six deep blue pupils.

"I...." I have to fight down a sudden surge of nausea.

"Human," Vee hisses, and though I've never seen a Oratus look sad, I can tell this is it. "Now you see."

What I do see is that we need to get out of here.

"Come on." I lead the way out of the tube chamber, back into the hallway.

The others, thankfully, follow. I'm not sure I could've turned back after them if they hadn't.

As we go down the hallway, I glance at all the other rooms—now open—as we pass. They're also orange-lit, also filled with tubes and the crying of those within them. I start to run. Anything to get away from those screams.

We head through the second vent room, then beyond to the maze of corridors. Only now, with the orange lines glowing along the ceiling, it's not all that difficult to follow them and find our way through to the smaller room with the first vent, and the way to the stairs.

With the light, though, the dark hallways become story-books, tales of horror, their walls lines with gouges, miner-caused blast marks, and unmistakable red stains. Metal junk couples with bits that look like bone, claws, or other parts.

Finally, when we reach that smooth stair up, I stop and breath hard. Then turn to Vee.

"What happened here?" I ask. "This, this... I don't understand?"

"This was not us," Vee replies after T'Oli loosens its grip. "I told you, there was a fight. A push back against the experiments here, before the Vincere were called. War leaves scars, human, on all it touches."

"You can stop it with the philosophy," I reply. "If you came after the fight, what did you find? What was here?"

"As I said. Traps."

"But nobody fighting back?"

The Oratus shakes his head. "Other than those things, those failed experiments, nothing. Only the projection."

I lean against the wall. Vee said there were multiple Amigga here. And, apparently, plenty of humans, at least of one type or another. If there was a fight, and if nobody was left here, then what happened to the winners?

"Kaishi," Viera says. "As much as I'd like rest, I think we have to leave, as fast as possible."

She's right. But we can't just run. We'll die out in the ash lands too.

"The projection told us it would help if we opened the vents," I say.

"If you can trust it," Viera replies.

"We don't have a choice."

Stunned. Again. Sax is getting real tired of this. First Gar back on *Scrapper Station,* and now the Belloch, whose name he doesn't even know. It's sloppy, it's inexcusable, and it's one more tick on the long list of people Sax owes vengeance.

But now he's in a prison prism, surrounded by three glistening sheets of pure disintegrating energy on a wet floor. The water's licking at his scales, his talons. It's moving, and in one direction, which has Sax wondering for a moment if he's been dumped in a river.

Then he gets his head around. Sees the harsh reality. He's in a waste-water basin, and what's coming down his way is all the leftovers Astre's Spire doesn't use. The smell's more industrial than natural, meaning they didn't put Sax in the sewer, but instead where all the chemicals from the Spire's factory floors run.

The prism itself consists of four diodes, three on the bottom and one above, each about three meters apart from one another. They're connected by slim silver bars that Sax could snap in an instant if the act of doing so wouldn't start a chain of unstable combustion throughout his body.

More than one prisoner's been disintegrated that way.

Looking beyond his death cage, Sax sees the trough he's in is pretty small, and from the sounds of it, there are others near him, each with their own waste-water pipe sending fluid down to the purifier. Above, there's tiny lights casting a placid white, barely enough to see the edges of his cage.

Getting up takes effort, takes time. It's a puzzle re-assembling his nerves, though every connection made is a rush as senses come back online. When Sax finally crouches on his talons, when the slime's dripping off him to join the rest in its rush downstream, the Oratus blows out his mouth and vents with a hissing roar.

The sound echoes around the chamber—Sax has no idea how big it is—and, a moment later, it's followed by second hiss, this one lighter, surprised. Instantly identifiable.

"Bas?" Sax asks.

"I'm here," his pair answers from a few troughs away.

"Me too!" Engee announces. "They took you, huh?"

Sax expects Plake, Coorvin and the others to be here too, but there's no other responses. After a moment, Engee starts dishing the details of their capture. How she and Bas went to the Wildfire as promised, how it was absolutely jammed, and how, after queuing for a table, a green Whelk came their way and offered a special setting in the back.

"I was opposed," Bas clarifies at this point. "The Whelk seemed too nervous."

"But who doesn't want special service?" Engee says. "Although, perhaps it was suspicious. They shot us not long after we sat down, then we woke up here."

"The Belloch running the place knew I'd be coming," Sax says. "How?"

"Oh, they asked where Bas' pair was. I told them you were back at the ship," Engee chirps. "I mean, was that wrong?"

Teven. There's a reason the Vincere doesn't let them near the front.

"It's not worth worrying about," Bas says after a second. "We need to find a way out of these prisms."

Sax is about to say he has an idea when a doorway shunts open above them, blindingly lit, and several silhouettes come in.

"Find a way? No, no, there's no need," says a new voice, watery and thick. "Stay here, stay comfortable. You're much more valuable that way. Yes, yes you are."

Sax plumbs the air with his vents, catches a scent beneath the chemicals. Fresh-molted feathers, the tart scent of a Vyphen's mucous layer.

"Frayk?" Sax asks the shadow, which turns to one of the others.

"How does it know my name? It shouldn't, shouldn't know that," the Vyphen says. "I don't want it talking. Not at all, at all."

There's another flash, then. Bright and overwhelming.

Sax comes to as he falls. It's a second blind panic—his muscles still stunned and the only thing around him is black and bang, Sax hits a wall. Rolls as the flood of watery chemicals slides over him, pushes him on. Sax can't feel his claws enough to try and grab on.

The Oratus rockets around another bend before his stomach falls out as he plummets long seconds in the dark, not knowing if he's going to live or die or what when *splash*. Sax sinks beneath the oily surface, and he's piecing his nerves together as he goes, gets one swing of the tail, a couple pushes of the talons and Sax is almost out when he's sucked away again.

It's a fight to keep his chest above water, to suck in the stale, briny air through his vents. Those moments come in flashes as Sax thrashes his way through the pipes.

Until, at once, it's over.

Sax catches a glimmer of dense yellow and then the pipe ends, launching Sax out into the air. The Oratus crashes down, splashing into a deep and, as he gets his head above the surface, small lake.

Thick yellow-green gas obscures a lot, but Sax can still see the lake itself is a bubbling concoction of chemicals, and it's cleared away a zone of rock around the shores. Beyond those few meters, though, Rathfall's true rulers begin.

Arcing roots and leafy tendrils swoop and dance with each other in a tight maze, the very tips of petals, larger than the *Mobius*, coming into view like blades from a massive fan.

Sax turns and swims back towards the pipe and the shoreline beneath it. He's hoping the Spire's right there, that he might be able to climb it or find an elevator, but there's nothing more than the long, thick pipe rocketing back into the undergrowth and out of sight.

Once Sax gets himself on land, he has to deal with the air. It's thick and scratchy, like breathing smoke, only the smell isn't of ash—it's pollen, leaden and stuffy. Rathfall's air by itself won't kill him right away, but the pollen's going to clog his lungs eventually, leaving Sax without room to breathe in what he really needs.

That's only one of his problems, though. Sax watches

the pipe's end, hoping Bas or even Engee's going to pop out and join him down here, but nothing comes except the endless sludge. Eventually, Sax will have to move or he'll die here, one more pile of waste.

If that happens, Sax won't find Frayk. Or the Belloch.

Can't leave a list like that unreconciled.

The only way he knows to go is along the pipe, so Sax forces himself to his feet and begins to claw his way into the wilds. The tendrils are hard and bulky, and every claw swipe that clears a root or stalk coats Sax in sticky sap. Pollen clings to him, along with bits of dirt from the ground, and soon Sax can't even see his own gray scales. He's all rotting yellow.

The pollen doesn't just affect his looks either—it keeps sticking to him, to itself as Sax forges on, weighing him down, pressing him closer to the ground until Sax has to use his tail to keep his balance. And his anger to keep his energy. Few things are better Oratus fuel than a fiery desire to end an enemy. Sax keeps hacking, keeps pressing along with the pipe to his left. One claw, then the other, then the next and the next and the next...

The wind hits Sax hard, strong. Pollen blows off of him in chunks as Sax struggles to open his eyes. They'd been covered too, in the end. All of him, every last bit stuck over with sallow golden fluff until he couldn't move anymore.

Only now it's going away, washing off his skin and floating or rolling into the plants around him. Nature taking pity on Sax, maybe?

"Look at this," says a voice that tickles Sax's mind. "Never expected to find him out here."

"Wasn't he supposed to be watching the ship?"

"Don't know what Plake told him."

That name gets Sax to open his eyes fully, to look up and see two Flaum, one pure black and the other a bright silver, staring at him through breath masks attached to full suits. Black, her name, wields a wide tube that links around to a battery pack on her suit—that's where the wind is coming from, and as Sax looks up, she blasts him in the face with it.

"Sorry, had to get that last bit off ya," Black chitters, her voice coming through a mesh filter in the mask she's wearing. "Would've looked funny with a yellow hat on your head."

Sax tries to stand up, but his muscles are weak. He can't seem to get enough air. His vents strain, cough, and Sax sees the poof of yellow-orange dust that comes out when they do.

"Rath-lung," Silver says. "Have to pump him clean."

"Whaddya think he'll do if I try? Claw me to death?"

"I bet he can't lift a single arm. But if we don't help him and his pair finds out, she'll make sure we're meat."

Black slots the tube into a notch near her waist, bends down and takes hold of Sax's foreclaws. Tries to pull the Oratus, and all Sax does is shift some dirt.

"That's not gonna work," Black says, standing back. "Any ideas?"

"We've got to bring the pump to him."

"Think they'll allow that?"

"We won't tell them." Silver points to Sax. "You think Sax won't pay us back in full? An Oratus out here ought to get us plenty."

Sax washes out of consciousness as the lack of oxygen causes the world to fuzz. He does manage to hear the soft sounds of wheels on dirt, though, and definitely catches the fizzing suction of a vacuum going to work.

Black's holding something like her tube, only smaller and targeted, with a funnel leading back to a large tank.

"You stay real still," Black says as she kneels down next to Sax. "Last reward I want for saving your life is a slit throat."

She sticks the tube up to, and then inside Sax's first vent. It hurts, it's stunning, like feeling Sax's insides roiled around inside him, but after a few seconds she pulls it away and Sax can suddenly breathe. Yet before he's had a breath, Silver plants himself next to Black and, with a tube in both hands, spreads a gray ointment over the vent Black just cleared.

"Don't wait for me," Silver says to Black. "Keep going. I want to get this done before he really gets going, so we have a chance to run if he's mad."

"You think we'd manage to get away?" Black laughs in her suit as she suctions another vent. "I need to get you off the ship more. He'd run us down and have us carved for dinner before you manage a single call for help."

Breathe.

That's all.

Breathe.

Sax opens his eyes, and both Flaum are staring at him. He must have passed out again, but now there's strength in his limbs. His mind is clear, and the blurs at the edge of his vision have passed away into nothing.

A glance at his chest confirms it; there's seals over all of his vents now, and bits of yellow dust cling to them.

"It'll keep the pollen out, though you'll want to clean

them off from time to time," Silver says. "Basically required for going out on Rathfall."

"Been wantin' to ask you," Black starts in. "What're you doing way out here without a suit? Any kind of mask?"

"Also, you smell toxic." Silver runs a glance up and down Sax's long body. "You may want to shower, or you'll find yourself with some tumors by morning."

Sax decides to give his voice a try. "Fraykt took me. Took Engee and Bas and sent me through the waste channels out here."

"Fraykt?" Black says. "Never heard that name before."

Sax gives the short version of how he made it here, and at the end of it both Flaum shrug.

"We sold the goop, but Plake said we weren't leaving for a bit, so Silver and I thought why not make some extra cash?" Black waves at the plants around them. "Bug catching's a valuable service around here."

"Only there's a condition," Silver says. "Once you rent the suit, you've gotta get enough bugs before they'll let you back in."

"And it turns out we're not very good at bug-catching." Black holds up her small claws. "These don't work so well at grabbing them, and nobody told us to get some better equipment."

"I said we should wait, think about it, but you wanted to go right away." Silver ends the sentence with a sigh.

"Enough," Sax hisses, standing to his full height. "Bring me back to the Spire. I need to find Bas."

The two Flaum look at Sax. "Problem with that, Sax, is there's no getting back to the Spire from here. Not unless we hit our quota." Black says, then she presses a button on her suit.

A blue projection springs up in front of Black, with an

image of the three-carapaced flying bugs that call Rathfall home, and a fat zero beneath it.

"Help us get the bugs, we'll help you get back in," Silver says. "It's that simple."

Sax narrows his eyes. Looks at both of these insignificant creatures. "There's no other way?"

"None," Black says. "It's kind of the thing here. If you're not digging up ore, you're catchin' bugs. They make a lot of things out of those parts."

Well, at least it's hunting, and if there's one thing Sax is good at, it's a hunt.

Sax has seen plenty of bugs; the small ones on most planets that buzz around until he swats them away, the cloud-sized ones on Alnert that glide through the atmosphere and feed on kilometer-high geysers, but Rathfall's pollen-chasers are a unique kind of ugly.

Silver and Black lead Sax to their first view of one, sitting on a flower petal, apparently catching its breath after a pollen frenzy, seeing as its shiny lime-green heads are covered in the yellow fluff. The bug itself has twin heads, each with a dark eye cluster, connected by a long, oval body over which, now, fold a pair of wide, luminous wings. Six legs jut out from that oval, each ending in a barbed single claw that cuts through the flower petal and gives the pollen-chaser its traction. Beneath each eye cluster, as if embarrassed by them, the pollen-chaser hides a proboscis beneath a quartet of mandibles. The whole thing is a couple of meters long.

"Ugly," Sax says.

"You're one to talk, Oratus," Silver replies.

Sax has to hiss a laugh at that. It's true the Oratus aren't on many lists of the most beautiful species to grace the galaxy, but then, if you're designed to be perfect for a singular purpose, is that not beautiful in its own way?

"So how do we capture one?" Sax says.

Both Flaum glance at each other, then back at Sax.

"Hoping you would have some ideas," Black says. "We've tried miners, we're tried grabbing them, but they break and fly away as soon as we get close."

"And we don't need them alive?"

"This isn't some environmental project," Silver replies. "These plants are crawling with pollen-chasers. All we need are the wings and the mandibles."

Sax could ask why, but... why? There's only one goal here, and that's getting back into the Spire. So he brushes past the two Flaum, stalks down and low, keeping one eye on the pollen-chaser. It's using the proboscis to lick the pollen off its own head, suctioning at it like a vacuum.

Sax goes under a pair of vines, keeping close to the ground until, looking back across the thorny meadow towards Silver and Black, he can tell he's beneath the bug. Straight up, Sax can see the green bits where the pollen-chaser's feet have burst through.

It's easier to harvest components from a dead creature— they tend not to struggle as you take what you want. So Sax crouches and bursts up, tearing through the thick petal and getting his claws around the pollen-chaser's midsection.

Or, at least, he tries.

Sax's sharp claws slide against the pollen-chaser's green carapace, flaking off the outer shell but not biting in. For something that can tear through metal, can even get through an Ooblot, not being able to pierce the pollen-chaser's shell throws Sax into a momentary panic, one that only grows when he finds himself being lifted off of the petal by the very bug he's trying to capture.

The pollen-chaser's legs close around him as its huge wings unfurl into Y-shaped gossamer. They catch the filtered light coming this far through Rathfall's atmosphere and sparkle it out around Sax, like he's moving through a glistening nebula. It would be beautiful, except the ground is getting awfully far away now. Silver and Black have disappeared, and the only thing Sax sees beneath him is a vast blanket of dull yellow. The wings fan floating dust against his face as they rise, forcing Sax to close his eyes.

There's no sense killing the bug now—Sax would only plummet who knows how far. So instead the Oratus uses his talons, claws and tail to find grips and hang on as the pollen-chaser carries him through the sky.

The ride goes on long enough to fade into an almost-relaxing carriage. The cool temperature mixes with the steady wing beat, the background clicking of the pollen-chaser's mandibles; it's a pleasant ride.

Until the pollen-chaser decides its done carrying the Oratus. The bug's legs open wide without warning, stretching Sax as he keeps his claws clinging. The beating wings, though slow. The breeze changes, and Sax feels the bug give in to the pull of gravity.

They're landing. The question is, where?

The pollen-chaser answers that a moment later when it breaks into a dive, angling towards a bulky mound that appears from the dust like a dream. The mound is coated in pollen and pocked with holes, and Sax sees plenty more pollen-chasers coming and going from it, like ships to Astre's Spire above.

It's a nest, and the pollen-chaser's taking Sax right to it.

As the bug nears its target entrance, Sax lets go. He doesn't know what's inside that nest, and being carried in without a chance to scout seems like a bad idea. Instead, the

Oratus drops a few meters, smacks the side of the mound, which crumples in some at the heavy Oratus impact, and Sax rolls down until his claws and tail can bring him to a stop.

The mound itself feels like thick clay under Sax's claws. Unlike the bugs, which blaze green in the yellow, the mound is a dirty, dried brown. At first Sax wonders if the bugs are actually digging up dirt, but the mound has a distinct scent as Sax hunkers close to it. Thick, loamy and with a hint of lemon.

The flowers. The mound is built on picked petals, placed and pressed down over who knows how long to create this strange palace in a pollen jungle. It's obvious too that Astre's Spire doesn't know this place exists, or they'd have attacked it already; an easy way to harvest a horde of pollen-chasers.

Silver and Blake said the wings and mandibles are the only targets, the only valuable parts. A full-grown pollen-chaser might be a difficult catch, but if Sax is right, if that's a nest in there, then he might find an easier option.

Not that going into the nest of an enemy comes without consequences. Sax goes down first, descending the mound until he reaches the very bottom where it tangles with flower vines. There aren't any pollen-chasers down here, but a few holes remain. No doubt holdovers from the mound's earlier days. Whereas the ones above are large enough for Sax to walk through standing, these are partially collapsed, tight, so when Sax picks one to use, he has to get on his stomach and crawl.

Bas would laugh if she saw him now, squirming through dirt, brushing his filtered vents against crushed flower petals like Sax is some sort of snake.

Light disappears a meter into the tunnel and Sax has to

rely on touch and the constant clicking of what must be a thousand mandibles to tell him how close he's getting. The tunnel shrinks more and more as he moves, until Sax is essentially digging his way forward. The chittering gets louder.

How sharp are those mandibles? Can they get through his scales?

When Sax manages to get his head through the last stretch of the tunnel, he has to blink for a while and stare. Yellow light pours into the mound from the wider holes above, angling down like miner blasts. The beams strike shifting hordes of pollen-chasers, their bright green bodies shifting and crawling over each other and the walls. Some skitter right by Sax without giving him the slightest notice.

Nearby, clustered along the bottom level, are large clusters of dim-red eggs. They're translucent, and Sax can make out squirming babies within. Clusters of yellow pollen sit around the hatchery, and, in the middle, looms the Queen. She's more than four meters tall and looks much the same as the pollen-chaser that took Sax all the way here, only if that same chaser had been twisted by some horrifying accident: the Queen's mandibles hang at jagged angles, and her—Sax assumes—wings stick out, bent and broken. Scars litter her darker-green shell, though the deep red egg sack hanging from her abdomen appears in good shape.

Sax can't fight this many, even he's not that confident. But there's a chance he could trade the location, give away the hundreds of pollen-chasers clustered here to the ones who would have the firepower.

Proof.

That's what Sax would ask for if someone promised him a treasure cache like this. Something that shows Sax isn't lying to get back in. A bug part wouldn't work, but—Sax notices the red eggs littered at the base of the mount—those would. The smaller ones would fit in a single clawed hand, too.

All Sax has to do is get across a swarming legion of pollen-chasers and he's all set!

The Oratus clenches his claws, gets ready to dive and run across the swarm. Grab an egg and break for one of the larger tunnels, get out and... what? Run in a random direction?

No, he has to go back the way he came, the way the pollen-chaser flew him. If Silver and Black are following, they'll be along that path. Forging through the flowers.

Sax has a direction, now he needs a plan. The bugs would crush him, grab Sax and chew him to pieces if he tries to just run across them, which means he needs a distraction. He doesn't have any miners, doesn't have any tools aside from his own body, so Sax decides to make one.

Using his claws, Sax scraps off the flower-clay from the tunnel around him and presses it together into a tight ball. It's small enough to fit into his right foreclaw's palm, about the size of a pollen-chaser's mandible. Now all he needs is a target.

Sax creeps to the very edge of the tunnel, where the nearest pollen-chaser is within a meter, its big body sitting in what looks like sleep along the mound's floor. Sax pushes himself up on his midclaws, gives his foreclaws enough room to throw, and lets loose.

The clay ball flies towards the only target big enough to matter—the battered queen in the middle of the mound. Sax's missile breaks up somewhat in flight, with nothing more than a few pebble-sized fragments streaking into the Queen's face.

It's enough of an insult, apparently.

The Queen jerks towards Sax, that abdomen of hers shifting more slowly to follow. Her mandibles click rapidly, and the resting bunch of bugs take notice. They rise, start to shift towards the Oratus, when Sax makes his move.

The Oratus scrambles the rest of the way out of the tunnel, jumps and plants his talons on the closest pollen-chaser and leaps to the next one.

It's a frantic set of hops that bring Sax smashing into the pile of eggs beneath the Queen. The eggs, with their soft shells, are at least easier for Sax to climb than the hard green carapaces and he scrambles as the pollen-chasers wake themselves up enough to care.

The Queen's huge up close, her shell riddled with cuts and dents from a thousand fights. The egg sack pulses deep red, and Sax's talons pick up the constant vibration of a thousand unborn bugs quivering beneath him.

The Oratus has a moment before he's crushed by the Queen's protection. One chance.

Sax jumps. Leaps and grapples the Queen's body, scrambles around the joint between her head and abdomen until he's on the Queen's back. Which is where the swarm catches him.

The pollen-chasers follow their Queen's order to the letter; attack and destroy the intruder, tear him to pieces. Only Sax makes himself a difficult target and uses the Queen's bulk to send the biting bugs into each other, into the Queen herself. Bugs slam into the carapace around Sax, grappling for a bite before the next diving bug knocks them away.

Sax earns one cut after another as scrabbling mandibles and claws find their marks, but the Oratus stays true to his goal; get the swarm around the Queen, get them attacking her as they attack him.

The Queen plays her part, shifting around and snapping at pollen-chasers as they bash and climb her to get at Sax. She's his own defense, driving away her defenders in a panicked frenzy to keep herself on top of the egg pile she's so committed to growing.

Sax feels a moment of chaos—when there's so many bug bodies pressing into him, smashing and biting each other more than the smaller Oratus—and enacts his escape. He's made steady progress down the Queen's body, rolling and slashing, kicking and jumping, that the large egg sack bulges out beneath him. Sax takes another three slashes across his back, feeling scales peel away, and presses through the bugs onto the sack itself.

And Sax goes through it.

Tooth, claw, and talon play equal roles in the digging, and Sax sates his own hunger in the brutal process. The egg shells form their own barrier as Sax works deeper and deeper, the broken, ruined eggs falling around him, burying him.

Protecting him.

The noise outside is terrifying; the Queen's found some way of working her mandibles into a constant screech, and the thunder of a thousand pollen-chaser wings rattles the mound. Sax only goes deeper, until he reaches the bottom of the egg pile and the hard ground beneath it. There, covered by meters and meters of unhatched pollen-chasers, he finally takes a breath. Listens to the chaos play out.

Without a target, the pollen-chasers and the Queen turn on each other, parlaying momentary slights and scratches into deadly duels that send the bugs careening into the sides of the mound and, often, into other pollen-chasers, turning two-bug slugfests into quartets of slicing, biting misery.

Sax sees it all through the smeary red translucence of the eggs, taking what breaths he can spare. Pollen-chasers who don't survive the fighting start to pile up on the bottom, on top of the eggs. A mortal tent for Sax to hide beneath.

Bas would be impressed.

Bas *will* be impressed when Sax tells her about this.

After he saves her.

The projection is waiting for us when we follow the orange lines up the ramp to its room. Its misshapen face grins as we walk in, though I wish it wouldn't. There's something about that eerie smile that suggests all kinds of unpleasant things.

"You've succeeded," the projection states. "Thank you."

Then it looks over my shoulder, to Vee-T'Oli, and here its smile vanishes.

"And you've found our intruder."

"He found us, really," Viera says. "Told us what happened here, too. Unlike you."

The projection looks towards her. Doesn't change from its flat expression. "I have parameters. My first priority is to open the vents, and to do whatever is necessary to accomplish that task. Now that it's done—"

"You'll tell us how to get back home," I interrupt. There's been enough long-winded speeches in here, and my ears are picking up a noise from below, one that sounds too much like the screams we left behind. "Now."

The projection seems to stutter, the light breaking for a

second, before it snaps back to existence in the center of the room, its blue-white shades flickering as it turns towards me. "Apologies," the ghost says. "This data is somewhat corrupted. I have not accessed it in a very long time."

"That's not what I asked for." I slide my hand to my waist, a signal for Viera to draw her miner. "Our exit, please."

If the projection notices or cares about the weapon now pointing its way, the ghost doesn't show it. Instead, it motions to the left side of the room, where a sealed door suddenly blinks to life and shunts open.

"If there is still hope for you, it lies at the end there." The projection says.

Vee-T'Oli's already moving towards the opening, taking their cue from the definitely-growing chorus of noises behind us. I'm not waiting either, and, with Viera following me, all of us dash from the room into the new path.

"Thank you!" the projection calls after us, echoing with faint malice.

I don't have time to think about why the projection wanted all those disasters freed. It's not like there's anywhere for them to go, any food for them to eat, unless Vee left some nutrient goop behind.

Of course, they could eat us.

The tunnel, though, makes it hard to speed up. Like the other paths, this one is littered with debris, though not the smashed junk piles and bones, but instead patches of caved-in walls. Broken ceiling panels hanging low, forcing us to duck and weave our way around. The damage causes gaps in the orange lighting, making the run a sprint through a gauntlet of shadows.

"What do you see?" I call ahead to Vee-T'Oli, who, with the Oratus' legs, are moving faster than Viera and I.

"Nothing so far, the hallway simply continues," T'Oli calls back. "It's a weird way to build, if I'm being honest."

"The Ooblot talks too much," Viera huffs behind me.

I find T'Oli kind of charming, a welcome respite from the tense straits tightening the rest of us, but I don't bother saying that. Instead, I jump over a collapsed beam, dance around a broken sidewall and the mound of rock and dirt that's poured through. Keep on moving, keep on moving.

Because I can still hear those screams.

The corridor goes on for a long ways—though it's hard to tell distances when your only reference point is the flashing half-tail of an Oratus waving in front of you. I'm sweating, breathing in the musty air hard with every breath, but I'm not going to stop.

"They're still coming!" Viera says behind me. "Why are they chasing us?"

All we have to go on is their voices. That endless moaning and shouting. We're moving fast enough that, to my ears anyway, the things we set free haven't made up any distance, but it's clear they're in the hallway now.

"They want to say thank you?" I reply.

"Almost to the end!" T'Oli yells from the front, riding on the Oratus. "I would say another ten seconds or so and you'll make it."

Ten more seconds of side-winding, hurdling jumps, and ducking under collapsed crud has us making T'Oli's guess come true. The question, though, is where we've gone. My first thought, coming out of the hallway, is that we've gone back to Vimelia, to the spaceport. The chamber is huge, with a strictly arched ceiling where, in several places, torn holes have let rocks crumble.

The chamber's floor is one of packed dirt, and it holds two cross-shaped shuttles. Ships with bulky, circular middles sporting four branches off of the sides. Both are painted a glistening yellow, and both bear, on their fat sides, Ignos' black design.

"I think that's our way out," T'Oli says, pointing Vee towards the closest shuttle.

Except I can't see an exit. There's one wide tunnel that, I think, was meant to be the way out, only it's entirely collapsed. Broken beams, rocks and deep brown dirt clog the way.

"Where would we fly it?" I say as I look around, hoping for an option.

"While you figure that out, we'll see if it still runs," T'Oli announces, then heads for the ship.

"Always taking the hard problems," Viera says, moving next to me. "Don't suppose you have a shovel in that pack of yours?"

I shake my head, not that it would matter anyway. "We wouldn't have time."

Viera takes a few steps into the vast space. Looks towards the tunnel, towards the ceiling. "How far up do you think this goes? Close to the surface?"

I don't know. "Probably?"

There's a hissing noise from the closer shuttle, and I look to see T'Oli-Vee bound up a lowering entrance ramp. If nothing else, maybe we could hide in there until the creatures went away.

"Come with me," Viera says. "Let's see if we can get the other one working."

"The shuttle?"

"Yes, the shuttle." Viera heads across towards the second one and, not wanting to be left to the encroaching screams alone, I follow.

From underneath, the shuttle's four wings reveal a

series of four... holes on each. Metal slats cover each of them in a lighter gray that stands out against the flower-yellow paint. I'm trying to figure out what the marks do while Viera takes stabs at a clear panel on the front of three landing struts.

"Any ideas?" I ask her, throwing a look back towards the way we came.

No creatures yet.

"We should've asked T'Oli," Viera grumbles. "I thought it would be easier."

T'Oli and its captive Oratus are still in their shuttle, and the only thing I've seen them do is turn on a number of exterior lights, popping glowing white bulbs all across the craft. Not that I'm unhappy with the extra illumination—the orange lines coating every ceiling in this place are high above here and things get dim on the floor.

"Let me take a look," I say, heading over.

Viera touches the panel as I approach—it's a little wider than her spread hand, bolted against the metal strut—and the screen flashes red at her pressure. No ideas come to me, but then, I have something on my wrist that can help with that.

"Don't let anything jump me for a minute." I raise the Cache, look at its dull green-brown surface, and focus.

There's a green flash, and then I'm inside.

I think of terms: shuttle, controls, boarding ramp and images flood the mental space around me. All kinds of different craft, terminals, and things I don't recognize flash and float. At first I'm lost in a sea of gray shapes, then I remember the paint. Take away the yellow, the black design, and look for the cross.

The Cache reads my idea and most of the ships disappear in a poof of nothingness, leaving only a few, one of which is the right shape and size. I focus on it and then it's just me and the shuttle in a vast emptiness. I bring back the idea of control panels and different sets appear, some on all three struts, some standing alone.

There's only a pair that apply to the front strut alone. I go for them, and narrow the choices to the one we're working with. From there, I think a single word.

Open.

Around me, through me, walks a generic gray Flaum. I step to the side and watch as it places its hand flat against the screen. There's a green flash and the ramp descends. Only, we tried that and it didn't work.

So the Cache starts again. Another Flaum, this one black, comes up to the control panel. This time, instead of placing its palm, the Flaum pulls out a miner from beneath its fur, sticks it against the panel. With its left hand, the Flaum turns the miner's settings to a low burn, then holds the trigger. Blue light splashes the front of the panel until the screen crackles, there's a pop and an acrid sting in my nose, but the shuttle's ramp descends.

Got it.

I shake my head, withdraw from the Cache, and blink my way into consciousness.

To see Viera, miner raised, aiming towards a growing group of monsters making their way into the docking bay, their mouths open in constant screams.

These things were frightening enough in the tubes, held back by restraints and glass barriers. Now, lurching in the open, one even crawling on three long arms, the 'humans' hit me with a combo of revulsion and fear that has me taking a step back, then another, until I run into the strut and remember what I'm supposed to be doing.

"I need your miner, Viera!" I call.

The Lunare hasn't fired a shot yet, and I think it's because the humans aren't coming towards us so much as T'Oli's shuttle. Which still has its ramp down.

"What?" Viera says without turning to me. "Why?"

"Because we need a way in!"

Now Viera gives me a questioning look, wondering, I bet, if I'm going to just shoot a hole in the bottom of the shuttle, but apparently my outstretched hand and pleading look work enough magic to get her to toss me the weapon. By some miracle of coordination, I catch the miner in both hands, turn and, twisting the power dial, jam its nose against the panel.

"T'Oli, you need to raise that ramp!" Viera's yelling as I pull the miner's trigger.

The weapon judders in my grip as its gasses ionize to their lowest temperature, as they spit electrical fire against the panel.

"Raise it, T'Oli!" Viera calls again.

Come on, come on. We don't have time for this. I risk a look to the left, see a half-dozen humans nearing T'Oli's ramp. See another three heading our way, one, leading the bunch, sporting a head with at least five ears. It would be funny if not for the mindless panic on their faces, the rattling, hoarse screeches coming from their throats.

The panel crackles, my nose gets the smell, and there's a ping from inside the shuttle. Bright and clean, followed by a hiss as the ramp comes down.

Ignos, the Sevora that took up residence inside my head, did a lot of evil things, but I still owe the creature my life several times over for the Cache alone.

"Let's go!" I flip the miner back to Viera and we both head to where the ramp's landing, when we hear a roar that cuts through all the other noise.

It's impossible not to look at what follows, at the terrible destruction of an Oratus unleashed. Vee, with T'Oli nowhere in sight, tears out of their shuttle and into the pack of grasping humans. His four claws rip and tear, his mouth bites and shreds, and the humans fall away before him. Vee, for his part, seems to delight in the melee, moving from one target to the next in a whirling, slashing tornado.

"Wow," Viera says, and I can only agree. "Sax and Bas always looked deadly, but I never saw them fight. Not really."

I'd seen Sax duel with an Amigga, but that was only one target, and the Oratus had been badly injured by then. Vee is old, Vee has scars, but Vee has had a long time to wait for this chance.

Still, no matter how many the Oratus cuts down, more of the humans pour out of the hallway. After Vee slices through the initial wave, more press on him, grabbing at his claws, falling against his scales or picking up pieces of junk to wield as clubs.

"He's going to get overwhelmed," Viera says, starting forward to help him.

She doesn't make it two steps before T'Oli's shuttle spools to life, a pyrotechnic whine filling the cavern.

I clamber up out boarding ramp as soon as it hits the ground. T'Oli's lifting its shuttle, gliding it over towards Vee, though I don't know what the Ooblot plans to do with it. At least until T'Oli rotates the craft, bringing the right cross-wing over some of the humans, where the jets bursting from those holes in the wing commence some instant cooking.

I don't bother watching that. Viera doesn't either. She's coming up the ramp with me into what is, thankfully, a familiar setting. A fat area with netting and handholds for flight, with the cockpit visible to the right.

"I'll figure out the door, you learn how to fly," Viera says to me.

"On it." I head to the forest of levers, terminals, and buttons that is the cockpit.

I'm about to look at the Cache again when something burbles, crackles and bursts through the speakers next to me.

"See you've chosen your own ride!" T'Oli's voice comes through after a moment. "How's it look over there? Our's is a bit beat up. Nothing like the Beast."

There's a big green bar beneath the speaker grille in the center of the cockpit's set of terminals, so I try a hunch, press it, and speak, "T'Oli! How do you fly one of these things?"

"You'll want to cycle the power supply first—hold on a second." the speaker goes dead and I stare around, looking for something that looks like a power supply, not that I know what that is. "Sorry, had to roast a couple aggressive-looking types. These are great ships for that, you know. Most—"

"T'Oli!"

"Ah, sorry. You're wanting to pull the big lever on the right. That'll release the emergency tank. Do you know that's the only hard fuel on these things?"

I don't know what T'Oli means by 'hard fuel', but I see the lever. There's no chairs, no objects to dodge in these cockpits other than the flying net hanging up above, so when the lever doesn't move, I'm able to stand in front of it, brace my legs, and press down on the bright red stick.

There's a shunting noise somewhere beneath me, and a brief whoosh of rushing liquid.

"What'd you just do?" Viera shouts from back near the ramp.

"No idea!" I reply. "You get the ramp up yet?"

"Don't want to talk about it!"

One of the terminals blinks to life as the bright red lever slowly rises back up to its set position. Thanking Ignos that the galaxy uses the same language we do, I read what it says. Which isn't much:

BATTERY PRIMER READY

START?

So I hit the big green triangle beneath the word, and the shuttle gets to work. I reach towards the communication panel, hit the button.

"T'Oli, I think I've got the primer going. What're you doing?"

"Seems like these things won't stop coming, so I'm picking up Vee. Then we're going to have to figure out a way to get above ground. These shuttles aren't meant, you know—"

"I know. But how?"

"Good question! I've been pondering that. Oh, looks like one of them's found a way onto the ramp. I'll be right back, Kaishi."

T'Oli cuts off, leaves me staring at the terminals, watching the one lit screen display a bar across it that fills extremely, extremely slowly. I think I've seen grass grow in my village faster than this. I tap the green triangle again, see if that makes it go faster, but no luck.

"Kaishi!" Viera calls from the back. "Help!"

As I rush into the passenger area, I see Viera take the miner in her right hand, pull back, and throw the weapon down the ramp.

"Out of power," Viera says as I get close.

Three of the humans are at the base of the ramp, which, I notice, holds more than a few motionless, burned bodies. Viera's been doing work.

"I'll take them," I say.

"You will? With what?" Viera replies.

"Myself." I take two steps onto the ramp, to the space where the shuttle's doorway keeps my left and right safe, to where the only place the humans can get near me is straight on. "Go back to the cockpit, let me know when it's ready to go. And, if you see another weapon, bring it!"

Viera's departure comes through the steel clang of her boots. Leaving me looking at a tri-armed menace loping up my way. I'm expecting to see hate in its eyes, or anger. But there's none of those things—only desperation, fear.

What would I be like, stuck in a tube, unconscious and kept alive through means I don't understand, and suddenly released into a wild world with a hundred others both like me and utterly different? If I had nobody to teach me where I was, what I was, who I was?

So instead of going for a crushing kick to the throat, I aim for the legs instead, crouch low and sweep my foot at the human's knees. Buckle them and trip the person back along the ramp, into the others until the whole array collapses at the foot of the shuttle.

This gives me a bit of time to look out across the bay, back to where Vee's taken a leap away from the swarm and, using his claws, hooked himself into T'Oli's shuttle, which is drifting our way now.

Our way.

"What are you doing?" I shout, though of course T'Oli can't hear me.

I feel a tug on my left arm—it's a vice grip, strong. Nails dig into my skin. The three-armed one is back, and I turn to its frightened face as it pulls at me, tries to drag me to its friends. With my right hand, I deliver a series of blows to its stomach and its face, pushing it away, though not breaking its grip.

"Let go!" I snarl, but the thing doesn't care, doesn't know what I'm saying.

My feet slide on the ramp and I fall back up, use my legs to kick the human off of me. It's an equal-opportunity snatcher, though, so it snags my foot once it loses my arm and now I'm in the same straits as before.

When Vee, over the approaching drone of T'Oli's shuttle, makes his entrance. The Oratus pushes his way past the other humans, climbs the ramp, grabs my attacker and throws it away to the floor. Vee doesn't stop, either—pulls me and keeps going till we're both inside the shuttle.

Then the Oratus turns, presses a claw on the control panel inside the door, and shuts the ramp.

"Thanks," I manage to say.

"Save it for the Ooblot," Vee replies. "T'Oli's making the real sacrifice."

"What?"

"We're ready!" Viera announces from the cockpit. "And T'Oli's saying it knows a way out of here!"

I leave Vee to supervise the ramp's closure and head back to the cockpit, where T'Oli's intercom voice is giving extremely patient instructions to Viera on what buttons to push, what terminals to look at, and which levers to pull.

"This is not what I'm good at," Viera says as I walk in. "Slow down, T'Oli!"

"Would if I could," T'Oli replies. "But once you put your shuttle in the air, you have to fly it. Or else things won't go well."

All the terminals are lit now with a mesmerizing

display of shifting numbers, graphs, and blinking things that, frankly, send my heartbeat into overdrive and nearly push me into a panic. How are we supposed to deal with all this?

"Kaishi's here now," Viera says as she punches at something that looks like a big circle. "Yell at her for a minute while I try to breathe."

When Viera hits the screen, the shuttle shudders. There's a muffled whine—the same one I'm thinking we heard when T'Oli took off, but here blunted by the shuttle's own walls—and I notice the orange-lit cavern start to shift as we leave the ground.

"Kaishi! How are you?" T'Oli asks.

"Been better," I reply.

"Who hasn't?" T'Oli merrily continues. "Can you press the bar there on your central screen that says 'Manual'?"

It's a red bar, and all the ones we've pressed so far have been green, so T'Oli's command makes me suspicious.

"You sure that's the right one?"

"If you don't, the computer's going to route you on an automatic path that doesn't exist anymore. You'll fly right into the wall. Which would not be good."

The Ooblot makes a convincing argument. I press the bar.

The base of the terminal pops and what looks like a tightly-wound, light gray coil shoots out, then unwinds into a tall, three-pronged stick with a number of holes along the sides.

"Something strange just came out of the terminal," I reply as both Viera and I stare at it.

"That's your flight stick! See those holes? If you had claws, or used shaping techniques like me, you'd be able to grip there. Cool, right?" T'Oli says.

"Right," Viera replies. "We're not moving anymore, T'Oli."

The cavern walls have stopped shifting. I'm guessing we're hovering above the ground. Which, at least, puts us out of reach of the things below.

"Not supposed to be!" T'Oli says. "Who wants to fly?"

Viera throws a glance my way and I remember that I'm the only one that's really worked with this stuff. Ignos, through me, piloted the shuttle away from *Cobalt*. It's not much to draw on, but it's something.

"I'll do it," I say, and step up to the stick.

When my hands touch it, the shuttle lurches to the right. Not much, but enough to get a small yelp out of Viera. I let go immediately and the shuttle settles back.

Somehow, we're not dead.

T'Oli proceeds to give me a slow rundown of the mess in front of me, rendering it from indecipherable, deadly chaos into a mushy spread of semi-coherent options. The most important thing, the Ooblot tells me, is the flight stick in my hands. The shuttle's going to go where I point that thing.

Though, right now, there's not many good directions.

"I'm working on that," T'Oli says when I point out our limited options. "Hang on just a moment, and we'll have ourselves an exit."

I'm about to ask what T'Oli's going to do when the cavern fills with a roar. I twist the flight stick rather than pull it, which rotates the shuttle to the right, giving us a broad view of the human mass teeming beneath us, and T'Oli's shuttle as it points its nose towards one of the thinner, collapsed sections of the ceiling and accelerates.

I don't have a second to protest. No time to yell. Viera and I can only watch as T'Oli's shuttle bursts up, crashing into, and through, the rock and orange lighting. Sparks shower down, followed by the gray fog clogging the air around the pit.

"T'Oli made it through!" Viera says.

Another rumbling quake follows her sentence as the ceiling around the new hole starts to collapse. The humans beneath us sense the problem and begin piling back into the hallway, back to the base from which they came.

We, meanwhile, are stuck in a floating box that's getting hammered by falling chunks of metal and debris.

"We should go!" Vee calls up from the passenger compartment.

Oh yeah. Guess that's my job now.

I push forward on the flight stick, just slightly. The shuttle's nose dips towards the floor, and when I nudge the small lever to the left, what T'Oli calls the throttle, we head forward till we're beneath the new hole. Then I try to mimic T'Oli's maneuver, pulling back on the stick until the shuttle's pointing towards the sky.

"Hold on," I say, then shove the throttle up.

The shuttle jumps like a juar, roaring up through the hole before I can even blink. The pressure should send me flying back out of the cockpit, but the acceleration triggers the netting, which drops in a flash behind me and keeps me pressed against the flight stick.

There's a long moment when we're simply churning into the sky before I take a breath. Before I tell myself that we're flying. That I'm flying.

And we're still alive.

"Yes!" Viera cries once she realizes the same. "Amazing! You didn't kill us!"

"I thought we were going to die!" I reply.

"Me too!"

The giddy moment only lasts longer when the fog parts a second later to reveal a brilliant blue sky, white clouds streaking across it like feathers. It's beautiful. Ignos, in his yellow majesty, makes me squint, but I don't care.

This is home. This is what I've been trying to find.

Until Vee brings us down with a simple question,"Where's T'Oli?"

By the time Sax crawls out of the mound, an egg in one midclaw, there's not a single pollen-chaser interested in him. Most, including the Queen, lie dead in piles while others twitch and flit about in confusion. None even spare him a glance as Sax takes the red egg and crawls out of a larger hole halfway up the mound.

Back in the yellow cloud, Sax finds the impact from his first drop and tracks along the pollen-chaser's flight path. Every so often, Sax stops, takes a deep breath from his vents, and lets loose a loud, hissing roar.

A crude way to get attention, but he doesn't have other options.

Still, progress is slow and Sax burns his energy hacking through the vines all day. When nightfall approaches, Sax crawls up into a flower, sets the egg aside, and dips in and out of sleep surrounded by long stalks coated in yellow pollen.

He wonders if Bas is stuck in that same place, talons dipping in wastewater, with nothing more than the grind of machinery to pass the time. Not that Sax is in much better straits—he has no food out here, and the only sound is the whistling wind as it cuts through the vines. That, though, is enough to bring about fitful dreams to guide him through to dawn.

Midway through the next day, not long after another hissing roar, Silver and Black crash through the vines in front of Sax. The Oratus has never been happier to see a pair of Flaum in his life. And, once they see the egg and Sax tells them what it means—that there's a horde of salvageable bodies not all that far away—they're ecstatic.

Until Sax relays the rest of his plan.

"No, no," Silver replies. "You can't tell them what you've found. They'll take it, they won't give you anything. Better if we bring it back piece by piece, ensure we get paid the whole amount."

"I don't have that kind of time," Sax replies. "They'll let me back in the Spire, or they'll never find out where it is."

"They'll just torture you," Black says. "Force you to give it up. There's a method to these things, Sax. Being out here is part of the punishment—you're not supposed to cheat it."

"What are you being punished for?"

"Greed." Black doesn't look the least bit embarrassed. "We want the money, this is what's required to get it."

Sax looks at the two Flaum. Processes the nonsense coming out of their mouths. This is some kind of game? A machination for profit?

The Vincere never once mentioned money as the reason for a raid, for an intercept or an ambush. Sax has been to dozens of worlds, never once under the guise of revenue. Survival was always—is always—the reason.

"Where's the Spire?" Sax hisses.

"There," Silver says, pointing back the way they came.

"Keep going and you should see it by nightfall. Like we're saying, though, you don't get in."

"That's my problem," Sax says.

He doesn't get more than a few steps, enough for the Flaum to realize Sax intends to do just what he's saying, before Black calls back to him.

"Hey! Where's the mound?"

"Follow my claws," Sax replies.

Then the Oratus breaks into a run, his talons chewing up the ground and his tail straight back behind him for balance. It's a freeing sprint, even with the dust clogging up his eyes. Sax holds his vents open and gulps in the filtered air, pushing it through to his muscles, juicing them for each and every long footfall. The kilometers vanish as Sax follows the trail blazed by the two Flaum, occasionally jumping over or ducking under a vine not quite cut. The pollen-chaser egg stays clutched in his right mid-claw, cradled against Sax's abdomen as he runs.

Sax makes the Spire well before nightfall, when the roiling clouds above are only starting to fade from brighter yellow to orange and dark gold. The Spire's base expands beyond what Sax can see, coating the horizon as he gets close, and the area beyond this particular entrance is heavily overgrown. He'd have to work if he wanted to circle the structure.

Instead, Sax goes right up to the wide airlock and taps at the single-button panel outside. Nothing happens. The panel doesn't even turn on, acknowledge the press. Beyond the lines of the airlock door and the heavy metal and stone construct of the Spire itself, its ridged curves rising up into the dust, nothing moves.

"Whatcha got there?" grumbles a voice from behind Sax.

The Oratus turns, making sure to keep his claws in full

view, and looks right into the small hovering camera of a microdrone. Simply a metal ball containing a battery, a camera, and a thousand tiny jets, the drone stays out of Sax's reach, but it's focusing on the egg.

"A trade," Sax says to the thing. "A pollen-chaser egg to get back into the Spire."

"We're after wings and mandibles," the voice behind the drone replies—Sax thinks it sounds like an old Flaum, but it's hard to be sure. "What're we going to do with an egg?"

"Hatch it, breed it, harvest the results," Sax says. "Or go for the hive, a couple of days that way."

Sax points, but not the way he came. Far to the right of it. Silver and Black are on Plake's crew, and the last thing Sax wants is to save Bas and find themselves stranded on this waste of a world because he annoyed their ride.

"You think I'm going to let you back in for that?" the voice says, but the drone belies the intentions, as it swings around for a different angle on the egg. "Go get a few more and we'll talk."

"No," Sax says. "You'll let me in now. For the egg."

The voice laughs. "It's like you think you've got some power here, Oratus, but your Vincere buddies aren't on Rathfall. Don't know how you put yourself on the surface, but there's a price to get in this way, and you're not paying it with that egg."

Sax turns back to the airlock panel. It's a single-button, which means it's simple. Probably been here for some time. Sax isn't an engineer, but he's broken a lot of doors, and most of the locks come down to a simple switch. Connect the right wires, or break the right thing, and the door opens.

"What're you doing now?" the voice asks as Sax puts one foreclaw up to the panel. "It's not going to let you in."

"I'm going to tear it apart until it does."

The drone buzzes over near Sax's head. "You'll be trapping yourself, and everyone else, out here!"

"You'll be losing all your profits."

The drone hovers for another second. Sax drags his claw along the metal side of the control panel, letting the shriek sound long and loud. It blinks to life before Sax scrapes a single side.

"Good choice," Sax says, hitting the button.

The airlock shudders and opens slow, with dust cascading off the doors in yellow waterfalls.

"The egg, then," the voice says. "A fair trade."

Sax doesn't reply, but walks towards the airlock instead. The drone hovers close, dropping back only when Sax begins to enter the doors. Which puts the microdrone in the perfect position for a swat from Sax's tail that sends the machine careening into the ground, where it pops and fizzles into a hundred pieces.

The little robots are annoying.

The other side of the airlock shows that the Spire's ground entrance wasn't always a profiteering mess. Sax walks into a mostly-empty ring dominated by a central cargo elevator., and a smaller passenger version alongside it. Unlike the docking bays near the top, which hold an even assortment of small and large transports for goods and passengers alike, down here there's only a single option for him.

The rest of the level is smooth stone flooring and plain white lighting. Sax is almost disappointed that Fraykt doesn't have a squad of flunkies here for him to dismember; it's so dull. The cargo elevator tries to liven things up with rushes of rumbling action every few seconds, and the floor still reeks of pollen, showing that an airlock can only do so much when everyone coming inside is coated with the stuff.

Sax makes it all the way to the passenger elevator in three long strides, egg still in hand, and taps the request button. No lock on this one. No microdrone.

But there is the whoosh of an opening door, the humpf of a big, burly Flaum emerging from what Sax thought was a stack of old shipping containers but that, looking more closely, is a makeshift control room. This Flaum, though, makes Sax hiss in laughter.

Yes, the Flaum's holding an assault miner of a type banned for civilian use. Yes, he doesn't look thrilled—Sax figures the microdrone belonged to this angry furball. But the Flaum's also sporting a deep blue dye job, one that he's not been able to redo in a long time, as bits of bright tan fur are poking through at the roots.

"Laugh again and I'll shoot you right there," the Flaum barks in response. "You crushed my drone."

"Payment for wasting my time," Sax replies.

"I'll be wasting a lot more if you don't give me that egg right now," the Flaum says.

The Flaum's wearing a look Sax has seen too many times to count. There's a squint to his eyes, a set to his shoulders, and a tensing of the Flaum's muscles that says as soon as the egg makes its safe flight his way, the Flaum's going to be exacting a price of his own with the miner.

The predictability is boring. The results are not.

Going down is far more frightening than going up. For one, turning away from Ignos means we're diving into a rippling, puffy gray expanse. For another, my stomach churns as we make the arc, the thought of that rocky ground we're now speeding towards tying my last snack of nutrient goop into knots.

Several of the terminals start to blink, displaying numbers in increasingly large and panicky sizes. I'm assuming all of them are counting down the moments till we splatter against the rocks and die.

But T'Oli's the reason we're up here, T'Oli's the reason we're on Earth in the first place. I can't just leave, can't assume that the Ooblot's fine.

"Don't crash," Viera squeaks, pressing back against her netting as we dive into the gray.

"You may want to pull up," Vee hisses from the back. "You're coming in too steep."

Pull up. Right.

I move the flight stick back towards me and the shuttle

responds, though it's hard to tell how much since everything I can see now is just varying shades of foggy gray. Some of the terminals, though, stop yelling at me, so there's that.

"How are we going to find T'Oli if we can't see anything?" I ask nobody in particular.

"Get low, to the surface," Vee's voice is so close that I twitch.

The Oratus is up from the passenger bay, apparently willing to risk the journey while I'm piloting, which seems suicidal. Yet there he stands, his claws looped through my crash netting, those bloodshot eyes of his staring at the screens.

"Use the maneuvering jets," Vee hisses. "Not the engines."

"Yeah, that doesn't help me," I reply. "You know how to do that?"

"I'm not a pilot."

As not-a-pilot Vee keeps telling me how to fly, the shuttle coasts through the gray, and I start to see a darker shade below. Apparently we're still descending, because the shade resolves itself into the ashy ground I'd hoped we'd left behind.

I keep playing with the flight stick and the throttle and find that when I lock the throttle's lever into a central notch that the main engine dies away. This results in a momentary panic as our descent becomes a plummet, accompanied by our screaming trio—Vee's wild hissing doesn't harmonize, but I appreciate that the Oratus is as certain as we are about our impending death.

Then we bounce. Sort of.

It's like landing on a pile of grass—the shuttle catches itself as we near the ground, what must be the maneuvering jets finally finding enough pressure to keep us aloft. I take a huge gulp of air, stare at the ground around us, and thank Ignos I'm still alive.

"Intentional," I say a second later. "Completely intentional."

"Next time, I'm riding with the Ooblot," Viera says.

The first signs of T'Oli come in the form of wreckage; a broken wing, a still-burning engine lying on the ash. We follow the debris trail till we find the main body in the middle of an ash trench dug by its own crash.

Now that I have a handle on the maneuvering jets, it's not too difficult to get the shuttle low enough to land. Actually deploying the struts, though, requires Viera slapping at terminals until something she hits works.

Vee takes the lead after we drop the ramp, and the Oratus doesn't bother waiting for us. He's loped through the ash all the way to the wreck before we make it to the ground.

"He makes me feel slow," Viera says as we move.

"We *are* slow compared to him."

"You're supposed to say we're just as good."

"Sax and Bas proved that's not true," I say. "At least, not when it comes to fighting."

"You think we're smarter?" Viera replies.

"I hope. Otherwise, we're going to wind up like the Flaum."

Humanity as servants, as playthings for the galaxy's more powerful species. I won't, can't accept that.

Vee's tearing away at the wreck, flinging bits of metal into the air as we get close.

"What do you think's happening on the other side?" I ask Viera. "Back home?"

"I think they're going to be gone by the time we make it

there," Viera replies. "The Sevora will either take all of us, or destroy us. I don't think Nasiya's going to accept an alternative."

"We'll stop them."

Now it's Viera who laughs. "Kaishi, when did you get to be such an optimist?"

"You told me I needed to act like an Empress, so I am. We have to have hope, Viera. If not us, then who?"

Whatever Viera's thinking of saying, it's interrupted by Vee's victorious hissing. With both foreclaws, Vee holds up what looks like a large lump of rock, complete with a pair of small stubs rising up from its surface.

T'Oli's rock skin is ash-blasted and burned, chips are missing and the Ooblot looks a far cry from the smooth puddle it often takes. The eye stalks, those two stubs, are more like stalagmites; spikes of solid black emerging from a more mottled body.

"Is T'Oli still alive?" I ask as the three of us stand over the Ooblot.

We're back in our shuttle—ramp raised to keep any roaming creatures out—and T'Oli's sitting in the middle of the passenger compartment. It hasn't thawed, hasn't moved.

"Ooblots are difficult to kill," Vee rasps, then flexes his claws. "It would take me some time to carve through one."

"Never heard a better compliment," Viera mutters, then looks at me. "We can't just sit here waiting for it, Kaishi, if T'Oli's even alive."

"You're giving up quick," I reply.

"Every minute we spend here is one that we could be using to fly home." Viera points at Vee, who blinks back at her. "There are species on this planet that want nothing more than to kill us, or take us as living bodies. We have to get back, Kaishi. We have to help them."

She's right, but I barely know how to fly the shuttle, much less how to fly it where we want to go. And if I try anyway, choose wrong and wreck our one chance to get back?

"T'Oli crashed through the ceiling to make a hole, Viera." I crouch next to the Ooblot, place a hand on T'Oli's warm rock skin. "It's the reason we're here right now. We'll give T'Oli a chance. Besides, I'm exhausted, hungry, and it's almost night. Humanity can survive just a little longer."

That argument, at least, gets some support from my cohorts. We dig into some rations from our escape mod packs. The nutrient goop, preserved in sealed bags, tastes— as ever—like the dustiest of dirts, but my stomach isn't in a position to protest. The shuttle manages to have some filters that recycle water, and, Vee says, it even pulls moisture from the air, so we're able to quench our throats.

Night falls over the ash and at first we don't notice—the shuttle's a constant bright white inside. At least until Vee finds a setting in the cockpit that adjusts the spectrum so that we're sitting in twilight purple that gradually fades to a starry black.

"Why bother?" Viera asks as the lights shift around us. "Seems like a lot of unnecessary work."

"These are meant for survival on new worlds," Vee explains as we sit around T'Oli's rock-body. "The shuttles, I mean. Land, introduce colonization steps, and live here. It wouldn't help much if the colonists lost their minds, would it?"

"After seeing what they did here, I'm not sure." Viera takes a long look at her own hands, as if coming to the same conclusion I had back in the rooms with the tubes, with the experiments. "The Lunare always figured Ignos was a myth, you know. That we never came from some mystical god. Guess we were right."

She doesn't sound too thrilled about that. Go back not all that long and I'd press her, I'd defend Ignos with everything I had, but after this, after those things, I don't really have the energy.

"Congratulations," I finally say, and that's all.

"Gods are for those who need them," Vee hisses into the silence. "They're not right or wrong, they just are."

"Do you have any?" I ask the Oratus.

"The Oratus are weapons, human. We exist to serve a purpose, not to ask questions."

"I don't know whether that's a nightmare or a blessing." Viera stands, paces around the room. "Don't you ever get curious? Don't you ever wonder what it's all about? Why you're here?"

"We know why," Vee replies. "It's clear from the moment we are born."

I'm used to mornings starting with Ignos rising from the horizon, or, lately, the blinking on of lights in whatever dark metal structure I happen to be in. This one, this time I wake up to the sound of cracking stone, of flakes and chips settling onto the shuttle's floor in soft patters.

We're all curled up in the various netting, sleeping as best we can, so it's something of a mess as Viera, Vee and I scramble up and get ourselves tangled. We're able to see T'Oli shift back to its creamy white form, though—even its eyestalks shake off the coating, blink their way back to life.

"That took a longer nap than I thought," T'Oli announces, taking the rest of us in. "Is that how you all normally sleep? It seems uncomfortable."

I wrestle myself free first—a virtue, I think, of being the smallest one—and crouch next to T'Oli. Hunt for any signs of damage, like bleeding or scars, but see nothing. It's as if the Ooblot is perfect, even though it just crashed a ship through a rock wall, a ship that then exploded and fell into the ground.

"How?" I can only ask.

"Ooblots are very hard to kill," T'Oli says. "Shooting us into space works. As does concentrated miner fire. But an explosion? Especially if we have time to prepare? Not an issue."

"He's got scales, this thing can turn itself into a rock," Viera says, getting up. "How'd we get stuck with the fragile bodies?"

"Because the Amigga wanted something they could control," Vee hisses. "Something that would not be hard to kill should it prove a problem."

"Seems like we weren't as easy to kill as you wanted," Viera replies.

Vee hisses a laugh. "We underestimated your species. And the Amigga who very much wanted you to survive."

"What happened to it? The Amigga?" I ask.

Vee shakes his head, "I don't know. It was gone, with plenty of humans, before we arrived. They used shuttles like this one, I believe. Escaped to the far side of the planet. I don't know why the Vincere did not pursue."

I wait for Vee to say more, but instead the Oratus hunts for and finds a package of nutrient goop and starts tearing into it. Breakfast is a higher priority than information, apparently. So I switch targets:

"T'Oli, we need you to fly us home," I ask.

"Can't do that for a while," T'Oli replies. "I might look good, but it'll take another day or two before I'm able to shift cleanly again. You want to travel now, you're going to have to do the flying."

"You can guide me, though, right?"

"My speaking abilities are just fine, Kaishi." T'Oli swivels its stalks towards the cockpit. "Let me grab a bite, then let's see if this shuttle's still in good shape."

This time, when the shuttle clears the gray fog, I have T'Oli beside me yammering about what each and every little symbol means. This diagram shows the shuttle's orientation, that one shows the speed, and this last thing here is the fuel, powered by batteries.

"Batteries?" I ask.

"Big buckets of energy," T'Oli replies. "These were dead, which is why you needed to release the emergency liquid fuel to kick them up. I'd say we have a few hours of flight time before you'll have to land."

"Then what?"

"Either we get some place where the light can hit the shuttle's wings and charge it up, or we walk."

So I boost the speed, turn the shuttle west, and hope we can outrun the fog. Even with the time limit, flying above a gray sea doesn't do much for my attention. It's relaxing, sure, but T'Oli pushes me to let the computer keep to the course. Diversions waste power.

I take my hands from the flight stick and look at the Ooblot puddled up on the ground next to me. Vee and Viera are in the back, both catching naps after the initial excitement of clearing the clouds wore off.

"Do you think we can trust Vee?" I ask the Ooblot. "He was sent here to kill us, right?"

"If I had to guess, he'd rather be killing Sevora. Seeing as that's where we're going, he ought to be fine." T'Oli tilts an eye stalk. "Between you and me, who'd you be more loyal to? The group that left you to rot in that base for so long, or the ones that rescued you?"

"Oratus are strange, T'Oli. I don't know what he'll choose."

"They're strange, Kaishi, but they're not stupid." T'Oli says. "One thing I'm curious about, though, what's your place here? With the humans?"

We've got the time, so I tell T'Oli the story. The Ooblot's a patient listener, and I feel like I've gone through the tale enough that I tell it efficiently. Skip over the boring bits. Though I find myself stumbling over Malo. He's only a character now. Someone that appears in memories and nowhere else.

T'Oli notices.

"Losing friends is a terrible thing," T'Oli says after I finish the bit about *Cobalt*, how we barely survived, when the Sevora in my head sent us to the place that would take Malo's life.

"I'm sure you've lost plenty." I wonder how many T'Oli's known, forgotten during the time spent with Clarity's Dawn.

"Gained plenty too," T'Oli replies. "You can't dwell on it, Kaishi. Otherwise it becomes all you are; a walking list of tragedies."

"That's what you think I am?"

"Not yet."

I laugh, sad and short. "Thanks. Guess a living puddle would know."

"Now there's an insult," T'Oli replies. "You know, I've heard that in most of the galaxy, Ooblots have plenty of power. We run things the Amigga don't care to. I might wind up running this planet when we're done, and then we'll see what you call me."

I think it's joking, but there's enough in the Ooblot's

words to catch my mind. Running this planet? Did that happen?

"What do you mean?" I finally ask. "Wouldn't we, humans, choose who's ruling us?"

"Nope," T'Oli says. "If you fight off the Sevora, the Amigga will come next. They'll give you a choice: annihilation, or joining the galaxy. And once you join, you're under their laws. Not so bad really—the Amigga mostly care about themselves and, after they've stripped your DNA of anything they want, they'll leave you alone. You understand, of course, I only know this secondhand, but everyone in Clarity's Dawn preferred the Amigga to the Sevora."

Two of the terminals are flashing by the time the mountain rises into view above the gray. T'Oli's calmly counting down the moments till our shuttle runs out of power and sends us crashing, Viera and Vee are all strapped into the netting for when that happens, and my hands are on the flight stick, holding it tight and wondering how much control I'll have when what amounts to a big metal rock decides to fall out of the sky.

"Can I land there?" I point to the mountain, whose frosted top rises out like the tip of my father's black-glass knife.

"Are there any flat parts?" T'Oli asks.

That's a no. At least, not above the cloud. The gray is thinner here—we've made progress and I'm able to see the shadowy outline of the rest of the mountain—and its shorter brethren—beneath the top of the haze. Maybe the shuttle could still get some energy under the lighter cloak?

In any case, it's not like I have a choice.

I angle the shuttle into a slow descent, aiming for the peak and hoping something resolves itself.

"If you crash us into the only thing above the clouds…" Viera says behind me.

"I'm trying to land us anywhere," I reply. "There's not a lot of options."

By which I mean zero, but I don't say that. All I do is continue sending us towards the mountain, lower until we're kissing the tops of the foggy clouds. The peak draws close, and I'm still not seeing anything.

"I would start going in," T'Oli says. "Staying up here much longer will make for a rough landing."

"Go in where?"

"Anywhere, really. Landing under some semblance of control is always better than crashing without it."

The peak is beautiful snowy obsidian and it glints in the noonday light as I start a long banking turn around it, dropping all the while. It's a magical last look at nature, something I've missed since leaving Damantum, since leaving home.

Then it's all gray. All fog.

"Push that there," T'Oli says, angling an eyestalk towards a circular icon split by various lines.

When I push it, the glass in front of me flashes and suddenly burning blue lines appear beneath us. At first I don't know what's happening, then I see a big line glowing to the left, right where the peak rises. Outlining the landscape.

"Easier than flying blind," T'Oli says.

"You could have told me about that," I reply. "I would've gone in sooner."

"But the view was wonderful."

"You need to work on your priorities, Ooblot," Viera snaps from the back, and I agree with her.

Regardless, we're now coasting over a rocky pattern of

blue. The terminals now are all showing red, and I've noticed the lights inside the shuttle are shutting off.

"Non-essential systems shutting down." says a voice, a very non-living voice, from the speakers in front of me.

"Nice of it to tell me," I say.

"Focus on finding a place to land," Vee hisses. "I just escaped from that terrible prison. I'd rather not die now."

"Then maybe you should be the one flying," I shoot back.

So far, being a pilot is a terrible experience; I'm always under attack from enemies outside or from snarky passengers inside. I'm either breaking out of a buried spaceport, or crash-landing into nowhere.

Give me legs on the ground and a long march, and I'll be happy.

As if listening to me, a section of blue lines ahead flares bright white for a moment, and then a section the lines surround shades in with that soft white color.

"Going to guess it wants me to land there?" I say.

"You're learning!" T'Oli cries. "There is no prouder moment for a teacher than when their student acts on their own for the first time."

"Uh, thanks. Now, how do I land?"

T'Oli falls into rote instruction mode, rattling off buttons to press, angles to shift the flight stick, and, finally, when to shove the whole thing into neutral and use the maneuvering jets to settle down. It's all going fine until, when I activate the struts, all the terminals flicker and blink off. The jets die, and the shuttle plummets the last two meters to slam into the dirt.

But, somehow, nobody dies. The shuttle doesn't explode. I fall into my netting, T'Oli slides around, and Vee and Viera continue hanging, useless.

"That wasn't so bad?" I offer.

"Had better," Vee hisses. "But, I am alive."

"Kaishi, I'm never flying with you again," Viera says. "But, thanks for not getting us killed."

"You're welcome."

Sax doesn't reply, doesn't clue the Flaum in except to take the egg in his right midclaw and toss it high in the air, almost to the level's ceiling. The Flaum tracks it, and Sax takes advantage. A one-two kick with his legs sends Sax flying across the floor and into the Flaum before the furry creature can react.

With his midclaws, Sax tears away the miner as his fore-claws pick the Flaum up—painfully—by the shoulders. Sax digs in his midclaws, piercing the miner's circuits and gas canisters, rendering the weapon a useless hunk of garbage. Then, glancing up, Sax swings the Flaum around.

"Catch," Sax hisses in the Flaum's face, and, to both their surprise, the Flaum actually overcomes the pain and shock to get his furry hands up and snatch the egg as it falls. "Nicely done."

Sax sets the Flaum back on the floor.

"A fair trade," Sax hisses as he turns back to the elevator.

The Flaum offers nothing in reply.

The elevator only rises a short distance before chugging

to a stop, the panel blinking orange in the universal signal for remote override. Sax doesn't doubt for a second who's actually controlling the lift now.

Fraykt, or one of the Vyphen's cronies.

But he doesn't expect the doors to open.

Level 93 makes a greasy first impression. Chunks of half-refined ore sit immediately outside the lift's doors, and the mechanisms for turning dirt-covered minerals into usable metals lay further back, behind hanging sheets and exposed walls, as if someone wanted to hide their misuse. Light comes from the floor-to-ceiling windows that, as the day dims into evening, start to glow with their own stored energy. Not solar, not on a planet as fogged as this, but wind-driven. Molecules blown around and around, giving off low light only visible when other sources go away. Old tech, and inefficient, but given its place in the Spire, Level 93 might be very old.

So why's he here?

"Bring me to Bas," Sax hisses loud.

Anyone waiting for him on this level's going to know he's here anyway, and if Fraykt is listening, then Sax may as well make demands.

"You want, really want your pair?" the voice comes back at Sax from a speaker somewhere—maybe even multiple ones—throughout the level. "Then tell me, Oratus, tell me why you left your precious Vincere for our little, little Spire?"

"I didn't leave for your Spire." Sax gets around the chunks of ore and heads back through the sheets. "We left to find the truth. To find Evva and learn why she abandoned her post."

"What truth?"

Sax hesitates, then makes a cold calculation; there's no

reason not to tell Fraykt everything. If the Vyphen is loyal to the Chorus and the Amigga, then he's probably already killed Bas, and Sax will destroy him for it. If the Vyphen's not, or has other ideas, then Sax proving he's not a follower of Chorus law—a statement that sounds weird anytime Sax thinks it—might lead the Vyphen to give in without a fight.

In that case, Sax might even show the creature mercy.

Maybe.

"The Chorus and the Amigga are after perfection," Sax says. "Control. They don't trust us, or any species. We found one on a space station Evva sent us to, and it was designing biological servants. Replacements for us."

There's quiet for a moment, then a soft laugh comes through the intercom. "Replacements. Your friend Plake surely, must have told you how it feels to be replaced? To be told, declared you're no longer useful?"

Sax has no time for Vyphen pity.

"This is not the same," the Oratus hisses as he completes a circuit of the level. "The Amigga don't want to retire us, they want to eliminate us. Remove any threats to their power, their way of life."

There's nothing on Level 93 for Sax to use, nobody for him to kill. Though by the time Sax gets back around to the lift, its doors are closed. He punches the control panel, but gets no response. So Fraykt's trapped him here.

"What is your solution, your answer to this problem, Oratus?" Fraykt asks. "Slaughter them all? Use your claws in the only, absolute way you know how?"

"That wouldn't be the worst thing."

"This Spire and all within it survive, live because an order exists in the galaxy," Fraykt replies. "That order allows commerce, allows us to profit and, if not prosper, if not thrive, to make something of our lives. Removing the

Chorus would thrust everything into chaos, disorder. Trillions would die as everyone scrambles for power."

"Better that than a slow extinction."

Sax looks up along the lift shaft to the level's ceiling. No obvious options. Except, and Sax turns to the chunks of rock, he could make his own exit.

"That's your thought, your opinion," Fraykt tries a comeback. "Some of us would prefer to enjoy our remaining lives, rather than spend them in your hellish fight."

Sax picks up the nearest chunk of ore. It's heavy, and he's using all four claws to hold it. This would have been easier if he'd kept that Flaum's miner, but Sax isn't good at planning for the future. He's much better at wrecking the present.

"Last chance," Sax hisses. "Open the lift and bring me to Bas, or I'll make my own exit."

"It's coming," Fraykt replies. "I also find it quaint you assume , you think your pair is still alive. We had the same conversation, her and I, and I have to commend you both. You're made for each other, both of you. Or were, anyway."

Sax hears the shuttling of the lift heading his way and drops the rock, makes a dash for the other side of the level, then leaps up into the crossbars from which those thick sheets hang. The lift settles into the platform and, with a chime, the doors open. As expected, two Flaum and two Whelk come out slow, miners raised and ready.

"I trust you'll let my friends continue our conversation," Fraykt announces, though Sax doesn't hear any glee in the Vyphen's watery voice. "You and your pair reached, clawed too far, Sax. Revolution doesn't need to be done in such broad strokes. Better to change the galaxy in small shifts. I am sorry, so sorry."

Sax doesn't believe Fraykt's sorry at all. The two Oratus

are just another annoyance to be removed. Sax, though, has no intention of dying. Not yet, anyway.

The quartet split into pairs, a Flaum and a Whelk in each, with the furry ones taking the lead and sticking their noses in the air. Smelling for Sax, who, no doubt, reeks of pollen dust. With one pair coming towards him and the other breaking the opposite way around the central shaft, though, Sax has an opportunity.

Those lift doors are still open.

Sax bounces from his crossbar to another, then another, each landing causing a metal rattle as the bars bang against their settings. Flaum and Whelk cry out their alarms, but Sax has one goal, and with his claws and talons pushing and grabbing in unison, he skates into the open lift before anyone can pull the trigger.

Sax's tail slaps at the door panel and a moment later the lift's closed and rising. There'll be another override coming, but the Oratus is getting higher up the Spire. Getting closer to Fraykt.

His claws can wait for that.

When the lift judders to a stop after only one level, it's not exactly a surprise. Fraykt isn't going to let Sax come riding right to his floor, not that Sax knows where that is. Right now, the Oratus is trying to get back up towards the top, because everything about Fraykt screams that the Vyphen isn't much for bottom-dwelling.

The doors, though, don't open this time. Sax doesn't feel like waiting for whatever plan Fraykt cooks up, so he springs to the lift's ceiling, using his claws and talons to forge his own handholds in the smooth gray tile. There's a thick outline for the meter-long access hatch, with a small handle jutting out from the ceiling, marked with holes for easy gripping by small Flaum hands. Sax uses his right foreclaw to do the dirty work, grasping and pulling the hatch open. It swings free of its stuck sides with a shower of dust, and then Sax climbs through into the wide shaft.

As he's making his escape, Frakyt pulls his next move and starts the lift heading back down. Standing on top of it, Sax has a great view of the entire shaft, which launches up through the Spire like some strange tunnel. Neon blue lights line the shaft at four sides, casting a just-over-dim amount of glow into the wide space. The constant squeal of brakes and the whistling whoosh of other lifts far above echo around Sax.

Who jumps.

Thankfully, the walls of the Spire shaft aren't all that thick, and Sax carves himself an easy perch where he can see his former lift descending, and stopping a level below. When he sees the Flaum and Whelk head into the elevator, Sax realizes he forgot to close the hatch behind him.

Guess that makes things more difficult.

Fraykt's thugs aren't oblivious to the new opening above them, and they look Sax's way, bringing their miners to bear. So Sax decides to take himself where they're not, jumping across the shaft towards the other side.

And landing on the rapidly rising cargo lift that, at this level, takes up the rest of the shaft. Sax hits hard and rolls, barely managing to stop himself from skinning against the shaft's sides. The pressure from the throttling rise pushes Sax into the floor. The smooth walls blitz by him, making his peripheral vision a blur.

One thing's certain though—this lift will end, and soon. The shaft breaks into different lift setups as the Spire goes on, shifting from most of the space reserved for cargo to smaller, passenger-friendly lifts. Which is why Sax isn't thrilled to see the dark bulk of another lift heading down towards him.

Using his tail and his midclaws, Sax scurries out from under the approaching lift as his ride slows and eventually stops. There's a loud shunt as the cargo lift's doors grind open, and Sax takes the opportunity to stand as the smaller, higher lift settles to its own halt before a door one level higher.

There's a couple meters between the two, and Sax makes the leap, clawing up the side of the smaller lift and over the top as it starts to rise again.

He's done with the outside.

Sax rips open this lift's emergency hatch from above, then drops into the middle of a pair of uniformed Flaum, wearing dirty full-body seals coated with dust and oil. They both press themselves back against the sides of the elevator when Sax lands between them, and the Oratus gives them a feral grin.

"Stay there," Sax hisses. "And I won't maul you."

He looks at the panel. Level 68 and climbing. Looks like this lift is heading to the 43rd.

"Fraykt," Sax says, swinging his head to catch both Flaum in the glare. "Where is he?"

"Who?" says the Flaum on Sax's left, but Sax doesn't care, because the one to his right emits a high-pitched, incriminating squeak.

"You," Sax says, turning and looming over the smaller creature. Behind him, Sax uses his tail to press and trap the other Flaum against the lift's wall, keeping the furry critter from getting any stupid ideas. "Fraykt. Speak, and you both leave this lift alive."

"I don't know where he lives," the Flaum says. "Nobody

does! But, but, I can tell you where you go if you want to see him?"

The Flaum hesitates, his small black beady eyes searching for some hope in Sax, that this nugget might be enough to earn him his life.

"Tell me, then," Sax says.

"39th level. It's a utility floor, but he keeps a shop there. In the back, near the generators."

Sax leans in close. Flaum aren't normally good liars, especially not with their lives on the line, but this one's had it rough. His gray-white fur is black-tarred and torn, one of his large ears is missing a chunk. A dangerous life breeds dangerous habits, like lying to an Oratus.

"You'll guide me, then," Sax says as the lift stops at level 43.

The doors open, showing a quiet residential level split into small apartments. No miners, no Fraykt guards waiting for him, so Sax uses his tail to push out the Flaum's friend, then, with his left midclaw, Sax punches the 39th level into the lift's control panel. The doors shut and they're off again.

"Are you fighting Fraykt? Are the Vincere finally coming for him?" Now the Flaum's got a hint of coy in his voice.

Information is as good a currency as any other, Sax supposes.

"I'm not with the Vincere," Sax says. "Fraykt has a friend, and I'm getting her back."

"You think you're getting her back?" the Flaum shakes his large head. "Even you, Oratus, aren't going to win a fight with him."

"His guards don't scare me." Sax watches the lift's counter tick down on the panel.

Almost there. Almost to Bas.

"No, not the guards. Fraykt himself. He used to be a commander, you know. Before?"

"That means nothing to me."

Sax, though, is lying as he speaks. There aren't many Vyphen commanders left. The Chorus had tried to kill them all when they removed the Vyphen from power, when the Oratus took their place as the officers in the Vincere. The culling had made sense at the time—these Vyphen knew the secrets of the Vincere fleet, of their strategies and ships.

Leaving any alive to be taken by the Sevora, even if Vyphen couldn't be controlled directly, presented a risk.

Sax, though, has never hunted one before. If Fraykt is truly an old Vyphen commander, then the fight would be a good one. If it ever occurs. Sax blinks his priorities straight as the lift opens onto level 38. He's not here to fight Fraykt. He's here to rescue Bas and, if possible, Plake, Engee, and Agra-Red.

We don't lower the boarding ramp so much as open the door. A few stones roll into the shuttle, and we actually step out and up onto the plateau where I managed to set down the ship. Aside from the usual clutter of gray and black rocks, flimsy grasses make themselves apparent too. They're light green and white, shivering in the cold wind whipping the fog around up here.

"At least there's life," Viera says as she stands next to me, keeping her hands close in to her sides.

I'm freezing too—our thin outfits aren't a match for this weather, and I'm about to suggest holing back up in the shuttle when Vee, exploring off the front end of the ship, makes a loud hiss and waves us over.

The Oratus is standing over a drop-off, though it's one I could see myself scaling if I had to; plenty of jutting cliffs and handholds. My hands ache at the thought of gripping all those icy rocks, but then, considering what we're looking at, I'll probably make them.

Because beneath our feet there's a particular orange

glow. Not like the pipes back in that Amigga horror-base, but the calming flicker of something very human: fire.

"There's something down there," Vee states the obvious analysis.

"A settlement?" T'Oli proposes.

"Too small," I say. "There's not enough food, land here. Maybe travelers, someone who's very, very lost?"

"No." Viera joins us at the edge and, by the stunned tone in her voice, I get she knows something we don't. "This is one of ours. Mine, I mean. The Lunare."

"The Lunare?" Vee's confused.

"One of your caves?" I don't have the patience to give Vee a crash course on real human history right now. "All the way here?"

"It's possible," Viera says. "We've tunneled a long way. Always looking for more resources, for a places we can expand without the Charre, without your tribes in the way. But I don't think we've gone to the other side of the world..."

"The shuttle was flying fast," T'Oli adds. "We're much closer to your side of things than we were. I'm surprised the Sevora haven't found us, really. They should have shot us from the sky, or hunted us here."

"So you're saying we need to get off this rock as soon as possible?" I give T'Oli a bewildered stare.

"Oh, yes. The longer we're up here, the odds the Sevora blow all of us to pieces goes up exponentially. They would be certain to detect the shuttle's energy."

"T'Oli, next time you know these things, please tell us," Viera says.

"Teaching Kaishi how to fly seemed the greater priority at the moment," T'Oli replies. "And after we landed, I assumed we would depart quickly. We are, however, moving slower than expected."

I shake my head. "Fine. Let's go."

We take a quick minute to dash back to the shuttle, stuff the emergency packs full of nutrient goop, and head back out. Vee offers to carry all the packs down the mountainside, for which I'm grateful, as the climb proves harder than I thought. Numb fingers, it turns out, make physical acts difficult.

T'Oli and Vee, by virtue of one being, effectively, a liquid and the other a four-armed physical freak, beat Viera and I down the cliff. I take my time, testing every rock before putting my weight on it, ignoring the constant ache in my hands until they finally go numb. It's not pleasant, but I'm making my way.

Until a cascade of red flashes splits the fog from above and an earth-rattling explosion pours over the cliff edge. Gouts of yellow-white flame followed by black smoke and flying chunks of debris follow, cascading over Viera and I.

Somewhere in there—I can't feel when—my fingers lose their hold on the rocks and I fall back, staring up and screaming as more red beams lance towards where our shuttle sits. I'm sure, certain, I'm going to bash against the bottom in a second and in that moment of certain death, I call out to the only thing that comes to mind.

Ignos.

And, despite everything I've seen, despite all the contradictions, my god comes through for me.

Vee catches me in his four arms, his legs squat down and his half-tail pressed to the ground so that I collapse into the Oratus' massive chest. Which isn't to say that the fall doesn't hurt—whatever air had been in my lungs takes the impact as a chance to flee, and my back blossoms into a new kind of pain as it crunches against Vee's bones.

The Oratus, too, gasps, Vee's chest vents blowing their

own air against my face. The Oratus stumbles back, then half drops, half rolls me onto the ground. It's cold, hard, and wonderful.

I'm not dead.

The thought repeats itself a thousand times before I get around to thanking Ignos, before my heartbeat slows enough to check if Viera's made it down safe—she has—and to actually pick myself up.

"Thanks." It's the first thing I say, and Vee takes it with a slight nod. "Really. Thank you."

"There's no need for it," Vee finally replies. "The risk to myself was slight, the benefits to our expedition of your survival great."

"That's the Oratus-talk I'm used to," Viera says, before she steps up and wraps me in a hug. "Next time, Kaishi, I'll teach you how to climb like a Lunare."

I separate, stare her dead in the eyes; "I'm never climbing again."

"I suggest we get moving," T'Oli says, the Ooblot oozing its way over towards the glow. "Those blasts probably came from a Sevora ship, and they might decide to cleanse this entire mountain rather than risk our escape."

"They'd blow up a mountain to get to us?" I ask.

"Kaishi, they would cover this planet in ash and fire to destroy you," T'Oli replies. "You are an existential threat to the Sevora. If they cannot control you, they will annihilate you. It's how they operate."

"Well, they've failed so far," Viera says.

"Let's keep it that way." I point at the glow. "Lead the way, Viera?"

The Lunare takes the charge, goes in front of T'Oli, and though we have no weapons—aside from Vee's formidable claws—Viera strides ahead tall and sure. I suppose, after surviving what we've lived through, there's a lot less to fear from a Lunare outpost.

So I catch up to her, and together the four of us leave behind the smoldering ruin of our shuttle.

The Lunare spread all over under the Earth's crust, spiderwebbing their way through rock to try and find resources, places to build cities or, the ultimate goal, to find a new surface that they could claim for their own.

"Until we found this," Viera's saying as we stand outside the tunnel entrance. "I'd heard about the fog, about how this side of the mountains was all covered in it, how everything was dead."

The cave is twice as tall as Vee, plenty wide for the four of us to walk abreast, though we haven't gone in because it's gated shut. Wood planks seal the way, with a pair of torches flickering in braziers on either side.

"Where are they?" I ask, nodding at the torches. "The Lunare who must be here?"

"I don't know." Viera walks up to the gate. There's no visible handle on this side, but she puts her hand on the boards anyway. "They might have sealed it after the explosion. Figured anything causing that kind of destruction was better left on the other side."

"Is there a way to talk to them?"

"They're listening now," Vee hisses. "I can smell them. They're afraid."

The Oratus stalks up the gate, next to Viera, and places a claw in front of her head. Then reaches with his left midclaw and taps it a half-meter to his own left. "Here, and here. I could break through this barrier and end them, if we want."

"No, no, that's not necessary." I join them at the gate, then raise my voice. "Lunare, I ask those of you behind this gate for help. We're lost, and without aid, we'll die. In exchange, we'll give you information. We'll give you hope."

There's a shifting noise from behind us, and the three of us—T'Oli doesn't turn so much as swivel—spin around to see a trio of humans rappel from the rock above. As soon as we turn, there's a creaking as the wooden gate slides up to show two more Lunare.

All of them are wearing thick fur jackets, and all of them wield the crude gray pistols Viera used to carry, the weapons I thought were the height of deadly warfare until I saw what true danger looked like.

"Hope?" says a burly man in the middle of the climbers. "How can you say that when you've brought one of those monsters here with you?"

That's when I realize all of their weapons are pointing at Vee.

"You know him?" I nod at Vee.

"Seen their kind before," the man replies. "Though not this one. Where'd you come from? Nothing lives out in the damn fog."

I think back to the strange humans stuck in those tubes. How there's plenty of them still wandering that base.

"There's more out there than you realize," I say. "And we'll be happy to tell you about it, but first, could you lower your weapons?"

"Not till I get some proof that thing won't kill us all."

Vee bares his teeth. "None of you would be worth the effort."

The man laughs. "Insults aren't going to work, creature."

"I'll guarantee it. On my life." I move to stand in front of Vee. "He will not hurt you. And you will not hurt him."

"They couldn't even if they tried," Vee whispers to me.

"And who're you to make that guarantee? A scared, cold girl?" The man doesn't know who I am.

I relish the moment.

"I am Kaishi, Empress of the Charre people, and emissary of Ignos to Humanity." I announce with all the grandeur I can muster.

A snort is not the reaction I'm hoping for. But at least the man waves at the others to put down their weapons. "Empress? Guess it's worth taking you to Avril, then. She'll decide if you're telling the truth, and then she'll probably kill ya."

After that delightful opening, the man introduces himself as Diego, declares that he's the leader of the small band in charge of this outpost, and caps it off, as we sit around their small fire a little beyond the gate, by stating we've had the misfortune of arriving at the worst place on Earth.

"I think," I say after he finishes. "That is where we came from."

"Don't know where that is, don't want to know," Diego replies. "Because if it's worse than here... well, I have too many nightmares already."

Vee and T'Oli take the hint based on the wary eyes of the Lunare and sit off to one side, Vee calmly munching through a packet of goop while spreading some on T'Oli, who absorbs it all. Whatever urgency I'm feeling about getting home hasn't passed along to the two of them, and while it should irk me, all I really feel is jealousy.

I miss coasting through life without a world weighing on my shoulders.

"We need to get back home." I turn the topic to what's important. "I know it's far, but we don't know the way, and you do. If you or one of your men could guide us?"

Diego holds up his left hand, keeps his right near the pistol. "Hold on. I know what you said. Empress, right? We'll take you to Avril, sure. But we're scheduled to run our term here for a long time yet. You want to get back earlier, you've got to give me a reason."

I take a breath. About to launch into the old story, when Viera takes over. She stands up—quick enough that Diego's men reach for their weapons and Vee drops his nutrient pack—and stalks over to stand above Diego, and stares pure heat at the gruff Lunare.

"Your reason is sitting right over there," Viera says, pointing towards T'Oli and Vee. "Your reason is back out that gate, up that cliff where the wreck that we flew, *that we flew*, is still burning! You say nothing lives in that fog but here we are—doesn't that make you think Avril ought to know what's going on here? Isn't your job supposed to be to watch for threats? Don't you think this is one?"

Diego for his part, takes a big swallow, which gives me enough time to ask, "Who's Avril?"

Viera dashes me a look that says she's got this, and answers me only after looking back towards Diego, "I'm guessing she's taken over? Always seemed like that'd be her final play. She used to run Lunare's biggest city. Reasonable, so long as your reasons go along with hers."

"Hey," Diego finally musters a spine. "She's kept us alive. Charre and Solare too, when they came running."

Now I'm on my feet too, though less in anger than from a desire to start heading home right now, this very second.

"Running?" Viera asks the question I'm too frazzled to.

"Why'd you think we didn't come out when we saw the red lights?" Diego sputters, Viera still standing over him like she's going to kill him right there. "We know what they mean. They're everywhere back home. It's all we can do to hold the caves. The whole reason we're here is to keep this exit open in case everyone needs to run."

Nobody needs to ask what they'd be running from.

Later, after the fire's left to smolder and the wood gate's shut, with the four of us shoved into a side chamber with a bunch of food crates, I'm leaning against a rock wall waiting for exhaustion to find me. Thus far, it's failed. Thus far, my eyes have stayed wide open as I race from one idea to the next.

Damantum, gone. That's what Diego hinted at—my people, both the Charre and the Solare, have fled their homes against an impossible adversary and fled to an enemy who's done what? Provided refuge? At what cost?

And can I even be mad that my apparent empire is gone?

"You should sleep," Viera whispers to me over Vee's hissing snores.

T'Oli doesn't make a sound, but it's gone all rock over in a corner. Continuing the healing process, apparently.

Viera, though, is lying down, propped up on one arm and keeping a weary face on me, "Cave crawling takes a lot of energy, and I bet Diego's not going to go easy on you."

"He won't have to," I reply. It's not my muscles, my bones that I'm worried about. "You know Avril?"

"She's been playing on the fringes for a long time." Viera yawns. "She never had the family connections to get up to the top, but your grand defeat of all the old guard in the desert probably left a vacuum."

"You think she cast them out?"

"I think my own people did," Viera stifles a laugh. "The Lunare don't hold much with the royalty idea. Families get power till they screw up, then they're torn down and forgotten. Someone else gets a chance."

"That's... very democratic."

"Sometimes it works, sometimes it doesn't, like everything else."

Viera's lounging pose finally convinces me to lay down my own bedroll. It's nothing more than a pad, scrounged from extras left at this outpost over the years. Turns a sharp rock from a stab wound into a bruise, which, out here, is about all you can ask for. I pile up some of the packets of nutrient goop as a sort-of pillow—I'd prefer cool grass, but the stone here is too much for me.

"You said you liked adventure," I say, because I'm not quite ready to go to dreamy oblivion. "I used to wish for it. Now, I don't know."

"Because of the cost?" Viera says.

It's almost better conversing this way, when I'm staring at the craggy ceiling in the cool pink light of a patch of glowing moss. No expressions to read, just the tone, the in-and-out of breath between the words.

"Because it never seems to end."

"It does, Kaishi, but you don't want it to."

"I don't know how old I am anymore, Viera."

"What?"

"We count our age in seasons, but I don't know how long we've been gone."

"Not that long, Kaishi. Probably less than a season."

"So I'm being stupid?"

"You're being tired. Go to bed, Empress. We're going to need you thinking tomorrow."

Level 39 announces itself with a blast of steam as soon as the lift door opens. Murky red lighting lines the floor and walls, serving as guides for Sax and the Flaum as they move between huffing machinery and hissing pipes, with the constant low whine of electric energy coursing through conductors above and below them. The noise serves as more than a reminder of the multitude of actions necessary to keep Astre's Spire running on Rathfall; they serve as cover for whomever or whatever could be hiding around the next bend in the clogged level.

Which is why Sax has the Flaum lead the way, one midclaw positioned just so against the back of the Flaum's throat.

"I'm not going to run," the Flaum protests as they go. "I know you'd catch me."

"I wouldn't have to catch you," Sax replies. "You wouldn't make it a single step."

"Then how'd you know I was running?"

"I'd smell it."

Fear has a special spice to it, and the Flaum's drenched in a coating of his species' panicky pheromones right now. Without the leaden scent from the venting steam, Sax might choke on it. Flaums are legendary for their overactive glands, one of many reasons why Sax never commences an assault mixed in with the furry species; he could never concentrate under that olfactory attack.

The Flaum, though, is true to his word and navigates Sax through the winding maze until they end up at what Sax would take for an ordinary section of steel wall. The only thing out of the ordinary, really, are the spots of rust on the section they're looking at. A quick glance wouldn't give a moment's thought, but Sax is bred for pattern recognition, to find a weakness and act on it.

"Which one opens the door?" Sax says, gesturing with his left foreclaw to the seven spots arranged in a Z pattern.

"No idea," the Flaum replies. "If Fraykt wants to talk to you, he'll open up."

"That's not good enough," Sax says, and he's about to test his claws on the door when it swings open on hinges.

Actual hinges. The last time Sax had seen those was on some dirt-water planet on a mission he's otherwise scrubbed from his mind. Now he can't help wondering how old this Spire really is.

On the other side is a moldy, old yellow Ooblot. Patches of the creature are crusted over, revealing its age as far greater than Sax's own. It only has a sole eye-stalk, the other a rocky lump on its boulder-sized bulk, and it turns a red-washed iris towards Sax.

"Fraykt's willin' to talk," The Ooblot patters lightly. "Without that one."

There's no question as to who 'that one' happens to be,

and Sax tosses the Flaum aside. The creature doesn't seem to mind, picking itself up on its claws and scurrying away back towards the lift.

"You're the guard?"

"I'm Dol, and I'm Fraykt's *partner*," the Ooblot says. "Don't make that mistake again."

"Are you threatening me, Ooblot?"

"Yes," Dol replies, then the Ooblot shuffles itself around and heads back into the recess.

Sax represses the desire to carve away at the big block of rock'n'pollen-yellow cream. Not only did the Ooblot mock him, but it turned its back. Insult after insult, but there's more important things here than Sax's pride, so he swallows it and follows.

Sax thought the munching machines made up the entire utility level, but the Ooblot leads him to a small room with a flat lift tied to a simple rotor. There's a set of terminals covering the damp wall opposite the lift's platform, a metal shelf serving as a shield from the dripping water plinking from a maze of pipes above.

At first Sax doesn't get where the water's coming from, and the Ooblot must sense his confusion, because it settles its bulk in front of the lift and turns its rotating eye towards the Oratus.

"You play claws and miners, you rake and take, the rest of us have to use the scraps," Dol says. "Set ourselves up in the ditches and dives your Amigga masters leave us."

"They're not our masters."

Before Evva, before *Cobalt*, Sax would have answered that question differently. There didn't used to be shame in the thought—the Oratus are weapons, wielded to their purpose. What does it matter who's doing the wielding?

"They're not? Then your species is even dumber than I thought." Dol slides onto the platform.

That's one insult too many. Sax takes a long step towards Dol, raises a warning claw, and hears a dozen sharp tines of miners powering up. The weapons' laser-red eyes peer at Sax from between the pipes, from beneath the terminals, and, Sax notices, from a dark cavity in Dol's own massive bulk.

"Not going to work," Dol says. "Fraykt thinks you're clever, that you might be worth saving."

That stops Sax. "Saving?"

The Ooblot laughs. Slaps a button on the lift, which starts a trundling ride up. "Better get on, lizard man, or I'll shoot you."

With all the miners around him, Sax doesn't want to call the Ooblot's bluff. He leaps, catches the edge of the rising platform with his foreclaws, pulls himself up enough for his midclaws to assist and then he's over, fitting in along-side Dol as the platform continues its slow rise.

"All this houses the cooling for the Spire," Dol says as they go up. "Fraykt and I built our little empire behind the scenes, because if we'd gone out in the open, you'd have murdered him. Probably would have killed me right after."

"Because Fraykt's a commander."

"Because you're all monsters." Dol changes and flips out a gooey limb towards the encroaching wall as the platform begins its trek between levels.

Sax doesn't get what the Ooblot is meaning till the tight squeeze becomes clear as the lift goes between the Spire's outer wall and the supporting floor between levels. Sax has to squeeze tight, draping himself over the Ooblot and curling his tail across his back to fit.

"We are what we are," Sax attempts to hiss, though he's having a hard time getting enough air with his vents compressed on the Ooblot, so it comes out as a harsh whisper.

"You've got a brain, haven't you? Or did the Amigga make you all instinct?"

Sax can't even reply. He wants to get mad, but the awkward position cuts the rage to nothing. The whole thing is too ridiculous. An old Ooblot ranting at him about the state of the galaxy? Why should Sax care?

"When Plake came to us," Dol says, and Sax twitches at the name. "We thought she'd been captured, that she was leading you and the Vincere right to us out of some trade. Turns out Plake's still her same sour self."

The lift finally gets to the next level, and Sax unravels himself off of the Ooblot like a blanket falling on the floor. His vents suck in air as the lift settles into a totally different place than before. One that's lit in the normal soft whites, that's marked with clean floors and walls, and that has a pair of Flaum that Sax recognizes from his trickery down below, holding miners, their eyes tight and their little fangs bared at the sight of the Oratus.

"What do you mean, Plake?" Sax manages from the floor. Even there, he's shifting his legs, getting his talons and tail ready to strike if the Flaum decide torching him is a viable tactic. "She didn't come back to her own ship."

"Precautions," Dol says, easing itself off of the platform. "Don't worry, they won't melt your face 'less I say so." The Ooblot waits for Sax to right himself, to fall in line behind it. "Plake's one of us, ex-Vincere you might say. Had to make sure she still holds the right loyalty."

"By kidnapping her?"

The two Flaum fall into step behind Sax and Dol as

they head through another cramped hallway. One that opens, through a second hinged door, into a clean and bright living space. An apartment, going by the solid walled rectangle covered in screens showing what looks like an infinite flowing ocean beneath a clear sapphire sky.

"We live in deadly times, Oratus," Dol says as it moves into the room. "Trusting the wrong person means you wind up a corpse or worse, an Amigga experiment."

The Ooblot flattens out here, lets its yellow-creamy self relax in what Sax thinks must be Dol's home. There's not much to it—a simple nutrient goop delivery terminal, the image screens, and the wide open floor. But then, Ooblots don't need much. Even the two sisters running *Scrapper Station* didn't seem to know what to do with their luxury garden.

"You want them to lose, don't you?" Sax says finally. "You want the Amigga to fall."

"The Chorus are a bunch of overheated mudballs twisting the rest of us to pieces until the galaxy's theirs." Dol twitches and the screens shift to a sight Sax hasn't seen in a long, long time.

The Chorus live in a giant space elevator, a rising spike that lifts up from the surface of the Amigga's home planet, Aspicis—Sax doesn't know if that's where the species actually came from, or if they've adopted it. At the very top of the elevator is a round ball as large as a moon, with plenty of tendrils arcing out of it, some bristling with weapons and others with scores of antennae for sending and boosting signals. Further ribbons of red and orange light dance above the structure in what would be a pretty display if anyone else had made it—with the Amigga, the fanciful glimmers stink of calculation, an effort to dazzle the eyes while stealing the soul.

Beneath the elevator, down towards Aspicis' surface, the screens show the endless forest of thick vines, almost like Rathfall but without the pollen and extracted gasses. The day-night line, which moves ever-so-slowly on the planet, recedes away from the view, shrouding the right edge of the picture in pure dark.

"You can't mean to attack it," Sax says, and for the first time he can remember, he's quiet, in awe of the sheer audacity of what he's seeing. "You'll never win."

"It's not our idea," Dol says. "It's hers."

The central screen flips away from the Chorus and their technological wonder of a home to a feed—always pre-recorded to be sent across these distances—of a beaten, wounded Oratus who's nonetheless standing inside a large, decrepit room.

Her red scales stand out even in the low white light, which comes peeking through a hole and not through any globes. Junk scatters around her, torn curtains and broken walls frame her locked golden eyes. The scene is a far cry from every situation he's ever seen the Oratus in before, but there's no mistaking Evva.

"She's alive." Sax didn't really think she was, not anymore. Nobody survives an Amigga bounty like hers for long.

"She's more than alive, Oratus," Dol says. "She's fighting. We're fighting. It's time you joined in."

Fraykt waits in what's obviously another apartment but one that's devoid of living signs. There's only a table, too short for Sax, spanning the sole room and its white-washed walls. The walls have screens like Dol's, but they're off, leaving them blank and clear.

Fraykt himself, his weathered vyphen feathers clustered in his chair, offers Sax a dour glower as the Oratus follows

Dol into the room. The two Whelk from Sax's evasion earlier stand near the table too, miners ready. Which means there's now four weapons in the room ready to fire should Sax make the wrong move.

"So Dol told you everything," Fraykt begins.

"Where is Bas?"

"Gone," Fraykt says, the holds up a feathered hand. "Not dead, but gone. Evva's alive, our resistance is moving. We don't have the luxury of keeping lovers together anymore."

"She's my pair," Sax hisses out the sudden anger. "She's the other part of me. There is no task worth splitting us for."

"In your view, perhaps." Fraykt waves towards the table. "We don't have many Oratus on our side, so we have to use them well."

"Use us for what?"

"Sax, you haven't forgotten how the Vincere preserve their secrets already, have you?" Dol says, its bulk taking up a spot on the table's left side. "Need to know only, and right now you don't."

Sax settles his midclaws on the table. Tests its weight. Rathfall's not a small planet, and the gravity's going to provide some resistance, but Sax is pretty confident he can push this table hard and fast enough to smash Fraykt against the wall and splatter the arrogant Vyphen into bits.

"Evva wants you with her," Fraykt says then, and his words temporarily steal away Sax's murderous ideas. "They're coming close to being able to act and, in her words, they could use your talents."

Evva wants him? His commander?

"How would I even get to her?" Sax asks.

"Plake will take you. On the *Mobius*." Fraykt nods at the screen to Sax's right and it flickers to a camera feed showing Plake directing the unloading of cargo from the *Mobius* into the docking bay. "She's a good enough pilot to get you in."

"But Bas won't be coming."

"Like I said, she's gone," Fraykt replies.

"She wouldn't have left without me."

"Look around you," Frakyt says, his bulbous eyes tracking to the pair of Whelk and Flaum on either side of Sax. "Do you think we have an army? That we're ready to fight the Vincere and overwhelm the Chorus with hordes of vengeful species? We can't afford to keep you together. There is too much to do. Too many things that could use your pair's claws."

Sax is beginning to think this Vyphen won't actually bring him together with Bas. That no matter how much he pushes for details or presses to get Bas back, they're going to keep her hidden from him. Which leaves two options:

Believe Fraykt and Dol and go after Evva.

Or tear this whole thing apart.

"Why?" Sax decides to probe. "Why would you capture us? Send me outside if you needed my help?"

Fraykt settles into his chair. He thinks he's won the battle now. That Sax is coming over and there's only some formalities. Sax keeps his midclaws ready. One push, and Fraykt is gone.

"Plake promised you would both be ready to join," Fraykt says slow. "I didn't think that likely. The Chorus knows we exist. Knows that we would be tempted by a pair of Oratus so eager to help us. So I had to see whether you were true."

"By throwing me out of the Spire?"

"You were found, were you not? By Plake's own crew,

who thought you would be less likely to attack someone you knew."

"They wanted me to gather pollen-chaser parts. For money."

Here Fraykt looks confused, and glances at Dol.

"It happens," the Ooblot says. "But that wasn't part of our plan. Silver and Black were to keep you occupied until we had convinced Bas. Plake said Bas was the more reasonable one, and she was right. We would have come for you eventually."

So the Flaum wanted a bit of money for their efforts. Sax can't blame them, really. Not that understanding will keep him from issuing a stern, slightly bloody warning to the two furry creatures when he next sees them.

"And the lift? Sending all of these?"

"As we said." Fraykt takes back control. "There was some concern you'd be aggressive. That you wouldn't take this well."

"I'm not."

Fraykt waves away Sax's words. "Stunning you first, letting you hear our story without the chance of spontaneous aggression seemed like the better course."

The room settles around him. It's time, now, to choose. Trust them, and go to Evva. Or fight them, and find Bas.

She came out of the jungle, down the tall pink flowers and into the forest. She carried Sax when he couldn't carry himself. Spoke the words he couldn't say. Gave him his life when he was about to lose it. So, so many times.

Sax pushes the table hard. It slides across the floor, shoves Fraykt back against the wall. The Vyphen chokes, coughs, but Sax didn't shove it to kill. In the space of that stunned moment, when everyone's looking to see if Fraykt is still alive, Sax leans right and sweeps his tail through the Flaum's feet, knocking both to the ground.

The Whelk manage to get their miners up as Sax reaches them, as Sax tears the weapons from their grip with his foreclaws and, getting his midclaws on the triggers, fires them. The miners aren't designed for Oratus and his shots aren't accurate, but that hardly matters when he's centimeters from his targets. The blue bolts flash and both Whelk quiver and slide into mush.

A single shot manages to miss Sax, fired quick by one of the Flaum, and the Oratus makes them pay for their haste with two more blasts, knocking out, in the span of four seconds, all of Fraykt's guards.

Sax levels the miners at Dol. "Tell me where Bas is, or I'll end every last one of you."

Dol doesn't look the least bit panicked. The Ooblot has a pair of miners leveled at it, and following them, an Oratus with plenty of claws, but the only thing Dol does is shift its bulk to give Sax an even clearer target.

"You can't threaten people whose lives are already forfeit," Dol replies. "We've been working since the Vincere removed us to overthrow the Chorus. We're closer now than ever before. You kill us, maybe Evva succeeds anyway. Maybe she doesn't. We've given our lives to this cause, whether it's now or later."

"You'll die to keep me from my pair?"

"Dol," Fraykt burbles from the back wall, a watery gasp of broken ribs. "Tell him. Tell him where."

Dol's hesitation shows whether she's debating whether Fraykt's life is worth giving up Bas, which in itself makes Sax even more angry. Not only did they send Bas away from him, they put her in so much danger, in such a secretive, high level mission...

Sax can't help himself. He pulls the trigger on the miner in his left foreclaw. Sends the bolt into the wall behind Dol.

"You heard him," Sax hisses.

Ooblots can't really sigh. Not audibly, anyway. Instead, Dol collapses, spreads out like a melting ball of wax.

"Fine. You want to chase after Bas? You want to jeopardize everything?" Dol says. "She's going back to your home. To where the Oratus are made."

"Why?"

"To stop them," Dol says. "To ruin the hatcheries. To end your species."

What? Sax doesn't understand. Can't understand. Here Sax is, willing to work with those who want to subvert the galaxy's established order, and they're saying the first step is to destroy the future of his own species?

"The rest will never change," Fraykt warbles from the wall, and Sax takes the reminder to drop a miner and pull the table away, letting the Vyphen drop to the floor. "The other Oratus, they're too loyal. They will fight to stop us."

"And the Chorus will make more of you once they feel the threat," Dol adds. "They'll overwhelm us. Use you to massacre every other species in the galaxy if they have to. The Amigga think they can build a new universe for themselves—they won't mind destroying this one first."

"Bas agreed to this?" Sax says for want of other words.

"She's already gone," Dol replies. "On a light craft that left the Spire hours ago. You're supposed to go to Evva, help keep her alive."

And Sax will, eventually. His pair, though, comes first.

The *Mobius* is besieged. Sax leaves the lift alone—Fraykt's followers pulled the Vyphen to the Spire's only hospital and

Dol ditched away as soon as Sax made it clear what he was going to do.

Now he only has to convince Plake to take her ship and crew to a place crawling with angry Oratus who'll want nothing more than to eviscerate all of them.

Except finding Plake in the stacks of nutrient goop crates and the small army of loader robots shoving them around is hard. It gets even harder when a face Sax never expects to see again pops out of the *Mobius'* boarding ramp and scuttles down to meet him.

A single glance explains everything; Nobaa's wearing the vest Engee crafted for Sax, the one built to control the *Mobius* so that Sax wouldn't need to be in the cockpit the entire time. Nobaa's managed to tangle the thing around himself on hooks and hangers pounded into the sides of his carapace. It looks terrible, but then, Nobaa doesn't seem like the Teven to care about such things.

"Didn't think you'd be making it back!" Nobaa exclaims as the reedy creature meets Sax. "Thanks for the vest, by the way. Made it much easier to stake out my spot on the ship!"

"I never gave that to you."

"You threw it away right outside my apartment! What else was I supposed to think?" the Teven leans towards Sax. "I'm taking the cabin right next to Engee's."

"That's mine. Ours." Sax's claws twitch.

"Oh, Plake's moving you now," Nobaa says. "You're getting the cargo bay to yourself. It's the only space big enough, and, she says, you deserve it."

Sax takes a heavy breath. Thinks about Bas. Calm thoughts. Nobaa's not worth his time.

Sax convinces the blabbering Teven to take him to Plake, and Nobaa goes away from the *Mobius* towards another, larger, freight carrier. The kind that's designed to shuttle goods from the surface to a massive spaceship. This one's loading on slats of refined ore into what amounts to a rounded-edge nearly as tall as the docking bay's level.

These loaders don't have struts—just a reinforced hull with embedded jets that rest on the floor. The entire right side of the loader opens up and lays flat, allowing for quick moving of goods into the ship. Plake, for some reason, appears to be arguing with a burly brown Flaum near the small bubble serving as the loader's cockpit.

"She dashed away as soon as she saw the pilot," Nobaa's whispering as they close. "No idea why! But it's not a fight I want to get into, and Engee might need my help with a project, so, bye!"

The Teven pivots back towards the *Mobius* and, thankfully, blessedly, disappears. One more crew member for Sax to avoid.

Plake and the Flaum notice Sax coming well before he reaches them so they've stopped whatever they were talking about and turn to greet the Oratus with defensive stares. Sax feels like he's walked into a personal argument, but doesn't care.

"We need to leave," Sax says to Plake. "We're going after Bas."

"Shut up," Plake says, nodding towards the Flaum. "Innes doesn't need to know this."

"I really don't," Innes says, crossing his furry, and huge for a Flaum, arms. "Fact, I'd be thrilled if you took this crazy Vyphen away from me right now."

Sax catches the way Plake clenches her feathered hands, tenses her arms, and the Oratus steps between the two of them before Plake decides to start a fight. Not that

Sax wouldn't mind getting another brawl going, but he's got bigger priorities here.

"Plake, what do you need from the Flaum?" Sax hisses. "I will get it. Then we will leave."

"Whoa there, big guy. You're not getting anything from me," Innes says.

"What he owes me," Plake warbles at the same time, then points at the loader. "How much are you making off this run, Innes? How much?"

"You're an idealist," Innes huffs. "Shouldn't matter to you what I do."

Sax reaches out with his right foreclaw. Fast. Innes sees it, tries to react, but no matter how strong a Flaum gets, he's not competing with an Oratus for reaction time. Sax gets the claw up tight against Innes' throat, a single press away from ending the creature, and Innes freezes.

"Sax, let him go," Plake says, but not before waiting a long second. "I don't want him dead."

"Then he should pay you what he owes," Sax says.

Even though the Oratus hasn't ever had to deal with currency—the Vincere's limitless expenses have handled everything for Sax since he became a conscious being—Sax gets the idea of debt, of what's owed and what's not being paid.

And the idea of getting something back, rather than nothing, even if that something is just the satisfaction of knowing your enemy suffered for their choice.

"I don't owe her anything!" Innes tries protesting and the voice is tighter than usual as the Flaum tries to keep his throat from catching on Sax's claw. "It was a fair deal."

"I was desperate. You cut me out." Plake shakes her head. "Let's go, Sax. I thought once this Flaum had honor, but he's like all the other skimmers out here. Burning anyone to make a profit."

Plake turns and heads back to the *Mobius*. Sax gets his face real close to Innes, opens his mouth a slight bit, then pulls the claw away and follows.

Innes makes the smart call and says nothing to their backs.

Sax doesn't manage to get Plake alone—following her to the cockpit brings Agra-Red and the Whelk's omnipresent miner into the picture. Sax, though, suppresses the itchy instincts that come with a weapon pointed at his back . There's a conversation that needs having, answers that needs getting, and Sax isn't going to take off with Plake again until he has them.

"This wasn't a random choice," Sax says when Plake settles into the netting that supports her piloting. "You came to Rathfall and Astre's Spire so we could meet Fraykt and Dol."

Plake doesn't bother hiding it. "I could've chosen a few places. There's a lot of people that don't like the Amigga, Sax. That don't have any love for the Vincere. Fraykt and Dol, though, don't tend to trust newcomers. I figured they'd learn if you two were for real."

"After what we did on *Scrapper Station*? That didn't convince you?"

"You talk about being loyal to this commander," Plake says. "What happens if she dies? Are you and Bas going to run back to the Vincere? We need your help, Sax. You and your pair. But we had to know you'd work with us, even if Evva's not around."

"And the thinking was to separate us, capture me and throw me out?" Sax hisses. "That's idiocy. Stupid."

"It worked, didn't it?"

Sax pauses. Breathes. Thinks for a second how he would have handled it if, moments after landing on Rathfall, they'd been asked to take part in a revolution against the Amigga. Against their own species.

"We would've joined anyway," Sax says. "Where else are we going to go? The Vincere would kill us if we tried to return."

"Then we were wrong," Plake shrugs it off, her feathers remaining unruffled. "We make mistakes, Sax. At least this wound up where we needed it to be."

"Not quite," Sax shifts into a harder stance, makes sure his claws are visible. "We're not going to Evva. We're going after Bas."

For the first time, Plake actually looks surprised. "That's not what Fraykt said."

"He changed his mind after I crushed him with a table."

Plake's confusion gives Sax the excuse he needs to relay the rest of the meeting, and its results, in a steady drip of slow menace that, by the end, has Plake shaking her head and giving in to what Sax wants.

"Oratus are so much trouble," Plake mutters at the end of it. "Don't know why the Amigga ever created you."

"Because we're effective. How soon can we launch? I don't want Bas to get there long before we do."

The *Mobius* gets ready fast when Plake wants it to. Silver and Black report back not long after the call to depart goes out, returning flush with the profits of Sax's broken nest of pollen-chasers. Engee and Nobaa are already on, tweaking gadgets in the crannies of the ship. The last one back, oddly, is Coorvin, who takes up a spot beside Sax in the cargo hold as the *Mobius* warms up its jets.

"Is this what you expected when you left *Cobalt*?" Coorvin, his fur looking a much healthier white than the patchy gray it'd been under the Amigga's control. "Joining a fight against your own makers?"

"I stopped expecting anything a long time ago," Sax replies. "The Vincere sent us often enough into places where we had no idea how many we'd have to carve up, or how far the Sevora infection had spread. You learn to rely on instinct, and on those few you can really trust."

"Like Bas?"

"Only Bas."

Coorvin nods. Stays silent as the *Mobius* rumbles and rises. The quiet churn takes Sax's own loneliness at being apart from his pair and has him looking at the Flaum. Coorvin had survived on *Cobalt* for who knows how long, virtually alone and in thrall to a domineering creature that never cared one bit for the Flaum's own survival.

"You're alone." Sax says the words without a question.

"I have been for a very long time." Coorvin glances up towards the ceiling, where the cargo netting—useful here to keep them stable during the leap in a mostly-empty bay —hangs.

"The Oratus that lose their pairs?" Sax says. "Most die soon after. They throw themselves into impossible fights. Accept suicidal missions."

"Like Evva?"

"Could you call going against the Chorus anything else?"

"Meaning," Coorvin says. "That's the hardest part, Sax. With Dalachite, on *Cobalt*, I had constant goals. A drive to keep it alive, to help its experiments succeed. Without Dalachite, I have nothing."

"And now you have this?"

"Yes. Now I have this," Coorvin says. "If you lose Bas, or she loses you, this cause might help you as it's helped me."

Sax, though, doesn't find the idea comforting. Anyway, he's not going to lose Bas. Not now. Not ever.

Vee stares at the torch in his hand like Diego stares at him—an alien thing that's changing his world-view by its very presence.

"You use fire for light?" Vee hisses. "I have never seen this before."

"Now I know he's an alien," I say, watching the Oratus with a slight smile.

We'd had our nutrient goop breakfast—supplemented by a bit of cave mushroom soup for a side of 'real' food, and now Diego has us gearing up to go. The other members of Diego's watchband stand somewhere between at-the-ready and drowsy, their hands near their pistols and their eyes half-closed.

I feel the early hour even though it's impossible to tell in the cave's separate reality. Diego rustled us up before dawn, declared that we ought to get started because the further we get before the creatures start to roam, the better.

When I ask Diego what creatures he means, the Lunare just laughs. Says if I find out, it'll probably be too late.

"He's exaggerating," Viera brushes him off.

The night sleeping on the rocks seems to have helped her most of all. Viera springs up, helps me pack, and even manages some of the cooking, which I've never seen her do before. Her lips curl up often and laughs came easier for her down here.

The mark of home, I think, and I hope the jungle would bring about the same for me. If I ever see it again.

"Kaishi," T'Oli says, slurping its way over to me. "May I travel next to you?"

"Sure," I reply. "Why?"

"Because I want to be able to protect you," T'Oli replies, and while it's sometimes hard to distinguish tone in the slapping voice of the Ooblot, I get that it's being sincere.

"Protect me?" I don't mean to question T'Oli, but I kind of do. What's the slime species going to do if an attack comes?

In answer, T'Oli surges over my feet, up my legs and across my body until its eye stalks are level with my head. T'Oli's heavier than I would've thought, like wearing bulky ceremonial robes, if they were cool and wet. Then the Ooblot hardens and I'm suddenly wearing armor.

"I get it," I say. T'Oli stops its reach just beneath my neck. "Thanks."

It's a little disconcerting to have a large pair of eyes blink at me directly in front of my own, but T'Oli liquidates and drops away quick.

"You've seen masks?" T'Oli says as Diego calls for us to get moving.

"I've worn them."

"Sapphrite told me the Amigga developed them from Ooblots," T'Oli replies. "They never could perfect the hardening, though."

"Do they steal from every species?"

"They steal from everything."

What I don't ask, what I don't need to ask, is what they do with the things they steal. I know, because I'm increasingly certain that's what I am.

I'm in the middle of the pack, with Vee picking up the rear and Diego and Viera leading. From the very first step, I can hear Viera start to pick at our guide's thoughts.

"So why're you trusting us?" Viera says as we get going. "Just you, with a group of strangers, at least two of which are very dangerous."

"Two dangerous ones?" Diego's gruff growl carries back through the rocks. "I get the creature with all the claws. Who's the second?"

"You're looking at her."

Diego starts to laugh as his boots crunch along the rock, when Viera flashes a shard of stone I'd not seen her pick up. It's small, and it gleams in the torchlight, pressed up against Diego's throat.

"Don't get any ideas," Viera says.

"Same to you," Diego rubs his throat after Viera pulls the stone away. "What do you think happens, you show up at a Lunare waystation without me? They'll shoot you. And that's assuming you even find your way through this maze."

"We'd figure it out," I say up to them.

"Or, you could be thankful I'm taking my damn time to guide you, and be nice about it." Diego actually sounds miffed.

"If you get us to the rest of your people safely, I will be," I say.

Once we leave the outpost, the cave narrows until we're going single-file, black and beige rock pressing in around us. Unlike smoother caverns that I'd found by following streams as a child, these are rougher, with jagged edges and sharp turns avoiding large stones. Man-made.

Periodically, our torchlight is joined by fungal growths adding hazy colors to the scene; blues and pinks, mostly, in bulbous splotches spreading like diseases along the walls. The mood brightens every time we come across these markers of biological progress, a neon countdown to our goal.

"A week," Diego says when I ask how long this is going to take. "And that's just to the nearest village, the outer arm of Lunare territory."

"You carved a tunnel this far for nothing?"

"Not for nothing," Diego replies. "Plenty of mines and other things between here and there, and Lunare like to explore. We're not content to sit in the shade and watch the seasons pass us by."

"That's not—"

"Diego," Viera interrupts. "Answer her questions without the comebacks."

"Are humans always like this?" Vee asks T'Oli, behind me.

"Haven't been around them long, but they do seem prone to arguments," T'Oli replies. "I think they can be violent when the situation calls for it, and sometimes when it doesn't."

"We're not perfect," I say to them, almost laughing when I see how much Vee needs to scrunch himself together to fit in the tight quarters. "But we're not evil."

"Evil," Vee hisses his way around the word. "I would never use that to describe a species as a whole."

"Not even the Sevora?"

"The Sevora are prey, Kaishi. Prey that fulfill their imperative. As I exist to destroy them, so the Sevora exist to take control of others." Vee's rasping out a deeper argument, but it's hard to take him seriously when his claws are all tight together, his shoulders are hunched, and his legs and half-tail are scraping against the ground.

"You don't think taking control of others is inherently evil?"

"I don't think they have a choice, so if it is their only possible course of action, then I cannot consider that an evil act."

We have to catch up to Diego and Viera, whose fires are flickering further, so I turn away from Vee, but don't stop thinking about what the Oratus is saying. I had a Sevora in my mind once. It had lived there, spoke with me and read my thoughts, and never took control. Ignos, the Sevora, claimed it had no choice. That it couldn't direct me as it could, say, a Flaum.

Which means Vee is wrong, which means the Sevora very much could live without controlling others.

Which, to me, makes them plenty evil.

As we walk, I notice occasional spikes driven into the rock ceiling. They're cylindrical, with a mesh lining of tight-woven metal. Even when I raise the torch to one, I can't make out what's sitting inside.

"What're these?" I ask Diego when we've gone past a third one.

"Being underground doesn't mean we don't have problems," Diego replies. "You ever see one of those glowing red, you go the other way. Means there's dangerous gas, and the plant inside it can't keep up."

"Keep up?"

"No different than your jungles, Empress," Diego spits the title. "Everything either eats or gets eaten down here, even the air."

It's difficult to tell how much time passes before Diego calls us to a halt for the day. Without a sky, without even the changing temperature of the air, and only the smell of wet rock, I can't gauge where I am, when I am.

But my muscles let me know they're tired. My ankles are sore from having to keep their footing on smooth and rough stones all day. My arms ache from holding the torch, and my back's letting me know that it's not thrilled at having to carry the pack for so long. So I'm not upset when Diego slings his own pack off and sets it on the ground.

The chamber's about as large as the shuttle's living space. Enough for us all to have our own bedrolls, but not much more. There's a patch of pink-glowing fungus in the center ceiling that provides enough light for us to douse our torches. The glow also illuminates several exits.

Diego points to one, "That's the latrine. Like the other ones, you go back there if you need to take care of yourself. There's a hole, use it." Then he angles towards the middle one. "There's a spring back there, ought to be warm. Good for baths. The last one's where we're going tomorrow."

"You managed to make these every day's length away?" T'Oli asks. "That's remarkable."

"It's not precise," Diego huffs. "We use what nature gives us."

Not long after, feeling the dirt sticking to me with my sweat and more, I decide to take up the offer of the spring. Head that way with a torch and T'Oli for company. Make it about five steps into the spring's cave, before both the Ooblot and I notice something different.

This tunnel's not hard-edged like the others. The rocks are broken, yes, but these stones look like they've been whittled away, as if something's gnawed at them as opposed to using the picks and drills Diego says are the core of the Lunare digging operations.

"What do you think made this?" I ask the Ooblot.

"I can think of many things," T'Oli replies. "The most likely, though, is some sort of creature. Which, given my current assessment of human capabilities, would provide a better reason for this tunnel to be here."

"What do you mean, capabilities?" The way T'Oli said that has me raising an eyebrow.

"Compared to other species, like Vee and the Oratus, your senses seem average, at best," T'Oli doesn't put any judgment in the tone, only simple fact. "That one of your kind could smell and taste spring water through the rock from any distance away seems unlikely. Rather, my guess is that this tunnel already existed."

"Yeah, well, at least we're smart enough to use it." I counter, and keep walking towards the spring.

"That's only smart if the creature that made it is no longer here."

"I'm sure Diego would warn us otherwise."

"Yes, because, as we've discussed, humans are excellent judges of their environments."

Now I stop, glare down at T'Oli. "You don't have to keep insulting us."

"Kaishi, Ooblots are literally puddles of amorphous genetic material. Before you would feel attacked by a word of mine, consider the source." T'Oli waves its twin eye stalks back and forth and, I have to agree, the Ooblot does look pretty pathetic there on the ground.

The pool is lit in mirrored green, the plants hiding beneath the surface and shimmering their light up through the bubbling water. Steam rises from the surface, coasting towards invisible escape in the ceiling. I can feel the heat from the edge, and I jam my torch between a few rocks, slip off the dirty clothes, and dip a toe in.

T'Oli, though, races by me, slurping into the spring, where its body expands and ripples until the Ooblot looks like a lily pad.

"You like this?" I ask T'Oli, giving my feet time to acclimate to the heat.

"What, you don't think Ooblots need to clean ourselves the same as you?"

Guess I didn't. I shake my head, then lower myself the rest of the way inside the pool. After the lip, it drops off fast and I have to tread water, at least until I find the right spot where I can rest my shoulder on a stone lip.

To say that the pool's relaxing would be to rob it of its due; I simply haven't felt anything this good since Damantum's own bath houses. My soreness vanishes, I breathe the moisture into my lungs and feel the warmth excise the day's dust. Whatever dirt I have sloughs off and disappears into the depths.

T'Oli floats further, eventually disappearing towards the far end of the pool, beyond the edge of the fungus light. There's no sound save the bubbling, nothing to see except the mist and the soft green.

"You never seemed this happy in Damantum," Malo says, and I see him standing there, on the edge of the pool. Through the mist, he's indistinct, but I think he's smiling.

"Because I was always being threatened, or had Ignos telling me what to do." I take a hand, swish the water in front of me and watch the waves. "I wanted to explore the city. Try new things. Learn why you called it the greatest place on Earth."

"I would have shown you, if you'd asked."

"I know." I look at Malo again, and he's sitting by the edge of the pool. "I was scared."

"Why?"

"Because that would mean doing something for myself. I thought it would be selfish, with Ignos and so many people depending on me."

"I depended on you too, Kaishi. You depend on you."

"Wish you'd told me that sooner." I look back at the green light. It's easier than staring at that face.

"I'm telling you now."

"When it's too late to do anything about it."

"Is it?" Malo's using that same joking tone, like when he gave me the pepper-covered fish. "You might have more time than you think. Humanity's not gone yet."

"Yet." I glance towards Malo, and he's even more shrouded than before. "What should I do, Malo? You're gone, Ignos is gone. I'm just guessing."

"What do you think the rest of us were doing?"

I laugh, shake my head and shut my eyes for a second. Take a scoop of the warm water and run it through my hair, over my face.

"Kaishi?" Malo's voice is different now, more alarmed.

"Yes?" I brush the water away with my arm, clear my eyes.

"I don't think we're alone," T'Oli says, the Ooblot rushing back towards me.

I look past the Ooblot, in the darkness at the far end, and see nothing. There's no rushing water— like when some of the jungle's river predators swim towards their prey. But T'Oli's skimming towards the edge with speed, so I move too. Get out, slip on my clothes, and then yelp when T'Oli slithers onto me and hardens.

"What are you doing?" I manage to ask, glancing at the twin stalks.

"The pool vanishes into another cave at the far end," T'Oli says, its voice vibrating against me as it slaps himself to make the sounds. "Curious, I went further. There's a den."

"A den for what?"

"Have you heard of Fassoths, Kaishi?"

"No?"

T'Oli's eyestalks twitch the way they often do when it's about to launch into a long explanation of something or other. I keep my attention, though, on the water, which is now lapping against the near side of the pool. Splashing up on the same rocks that were, a moment ago, serving as my arm rests.

"I did not expect to find one here—" T'Oli starts, and then I see the shadow.

Or rather, the pool becomes the shadow. The green light goes away as a massive dark blob covers it. I grab the torch and hold it out, which lets me see, in glorious orange clarity, the sopping wet, white-haired, huge head that rises up from the water.

I immediately question if it is a head, because there's no eyes, no ears, no mouth that I can see. Only a furred oval. It's weird enough that I step back, my booted feet scraping against the rock.

Turns out that's a mistake. The oval swivels towards me. Starts moving towards the edge of the pool.

"Unless humans have a strong defense mechanism I have not yet witnessed, in which case you should immediately deploy it, I suggest fleeing," T'Oli says.

"Yeah, we've got none of those," I reply and keep backpedaling.

My running starts as soon as the rest of the creature starts to climb out of the pool. Two thick legs come first, planting clawed feet on the ground. That's when I recognize what I'm looking at.

T'Oli called them Fassoths, but I've seen them before. The Lunare used beasts like these when they fought us in the desert, when they killed the former Charre emperor. Then, we had better versions of the pistols Diego and his cohorts have. Then I had an army.

Now it's only me, cloaked in an Ooblot, sprinting and stumbling through a dark cave as death comes scrambling after.

Fassoths don't make any noise of their own. I hear the claws scrape on against the rocks, the thud as the beast's big body bounces off walls. Or maybe I'm drowning out the Fassoth with my own shouts, because my voice is going full tilt between breaths.

Which is why, when I barge into our makeshift camp, I'm expecting a host of traps set. Weapons drawn and dead-set stares trailing after me, waiting for a chance to lay into the beast.

What I get is nothing. Nobody. Even Vee, the brave Oratus, is gone. Most of our things are still on the ground, though a half-second glance confirms someone snagged the food packs.

"Keep running, Kaishi!" Viera's voice, from the tunnel Diego said leads onward. "We can't fight that thing in here!"

Great. I manage to get across the camp before the Fassoth bursts out behind me, a movement made known by the sudden flying of our bed rolls through the air as I duck and run.

"Your odds of outlasting the Fassoth are slim," T'Oli

says as I careen down the tunnel. "Find a place to hide and stay still."

"Great advice," I huff. "Let me know when you see a spot."

The tunnel's one slim pathway, carved walls giving precisely zero room to slip away. I think, though, that I'm holding my lead until I feel a push on my back that sends me flying. The torch in my right hand goes for a trip, bouncing off a looming boulder and rolling on ahead as I crash into the ground.

A dozen cuts and scrapes open in an instant. T'Oli somehow draws its eyestalks in, hardens them as I roll over, and in the process I get two Ooblot-eye-shaped jabs to my chest as its solid form clogs the space between me and the ground.

All of that pales a second later, though, when the Fassoth pins and pushes me into the floor. I feel snaps in my chest, and spiderwebs of sharp pain ripple out. I scream in there, but I'm pretty sure I black out for a hot moment too.

Survival instinct, though, doesn't let me go that fast. Neither does Viera—I assume it's her, because I can't picture Diego coming back—whose miner unleashes a different kind of crack. The Fassoth must like her as much as I do right then, because it goes charging after the Lunare. Though not before trampling me with its other legs on the way.

Then there's only me and rock-T'Oli, on the ground in the dark, my torch long gone, as ever-more-distant sounds of miner whines shot ring through the cave.

I can't move. I mean, I can, but doing so hurts so much that I don't want to. That I'd rather sit there on the floor and wait for death to find me. Maybe the Fassoth will come back and take me out of my misery.

"Kaishi?" T'Oli says. "Are you still alive?"

"Yes," I manage, though speaking feels like dredging my voice across hot coals.

"Then we should be moving. The Fassoth, if Viera and the others fail to kill it, will eventually come back for you."

"Good."

T'Oli hesitates. I can feel the Ooblot slowly liquidate itself, slide off of me and run through my hair en route to the ground in front of my face.

"Forgive me, Kaishi, but unless I am missing something, I believe the Fassoth's return would be very not good for you."

"You're missing how much everything hurts."

"Ah. Then that snap I felt was not an idle sound?"

"That was me breaking in half." I wiggle my toes after saying this and feel a momentary relief that I still can. The Fassoth didn't actually snap me in two.

"More sarcasm. I'm beginning to think this is how humans deal with difficulty."

"Now's not the time, T'Oli." I close my eyes. Start to take a deep breath and stop immediately. Only shallow gasps from now on.

I can't just lie here, right?

No.

I test my hands, both hurting from rock-scrapes, and press them against the ground. Push, slide my knees beneath me and rise up, slowly, until I'm standing, then leaning against the side. Spots burst in front of my eyes in time with the spears of pain coming from my right side.

"Standing is a good start, Kaishi," T'Oli says. "It will be easier to escape the Fassoth if you can walk."

"Yeah," I say. "Can you see anything? Cause I sure can't."

"Ooblots, sadly, are not equipped with night vision," T'Oli says. "I can, however, guide you."

"Then let's go."

I keep my right hand on the cave wall as we go. Every step sends spiking aftershocks up my system, and now that it's out of immediate danger, my body's wasting no time reading off a litany of minor wounds covering every part of me that T'Oli didn't protect. Wrists, knees, elbows, they're all beat up. I brush off a drop of what I assume is blood from my nose, but I can't see it on my hand.

There's plenty of noise in the distance beyond the standard drip-echoes of the cave. Every time I hear a miner blast apart a rock, or the crack of Diego's pistol, I get a little hopeful. Means one of them is still alive. Though I guess it also means they're still on the run.

"Kaishi, we have a problem," T'Oli says.

"Think we might have a few, T'Oli."

"There are three options here that I can feel. Which way should we go?"

"Towards the sounds?"

"The echoes make it difficult to discern where they're coming from. Can you tell?"

Hah. Can I tell. That I'm standing ought to be enough of an achievement right now. Every sense I've got is playing at half-speed as my mind slogs through an ever-present swamp of pain.

"T'Oli, pick a direction, and let's go. Worst thing that happens, we find another one of those things and get ourselves eaten."

"I don't think Fassoths would be able to eat me," T'Oli says. "You, however, they would likely find a delightful snack." I hear T'Oli oozing across the floor. "This way, I think."

And on we go.

After far too long stepping through the deep dark, I see light. Not white, artificial light like on the Sevora ships, nor the yellow heat like Ignos. But a blue halo coming out of somewhere ahead.

"Know what that is?" I say, dimly aware that I've been saying nonsense things to T'Oli for a while now as we've trudged through these endless black holes.

The Ooblot responds for a while, answering my pithy complaints with its usual straightforward commentary. It's refreshing, in a way. T'Oli doesn't indulge me, just states what's necessary to say and nothing more.

T'Oli doesn't change now.

"It's one of the fungal growths," the Ooblot says. "Nothing dangerous."

I stumble on. The pain's more or less numbed now, owing partly, I think, to my realization that I'm not going to die from my wounds. And if I'm not going to die, I might as well try to live.

We round the corner and the fungus blossoms into full bloom. It's not a small room but a vast chamber with at least a dozen natural pillars I can see stretching back, all of them coated in the plants. For a moment I forget everything as the dazzling azure sucks away my breath, draws me into the vast maps of sparkling stones coating the walls.

It's beautiful, stunning, incredible.

So much so that I don't notice the bones covering the floor until I step on one.

olis. Sax hasn't seen the small world since his birth, or, really, since he first came into consciousness. A gray rock ball with a single, jagged green scar slashing through the barren waste. A creche carved from nothing to grow a species not safe to raise anywhere else. There's a white dwarf star spinning nearby, close enough to baste Solis with enough heat to allow the Amiggas' experiment to work. The planet serves as both nursery and teacher, often a fatal one.

The *Mobius* exits its leap far enough away to see the array of Vincere ships hanging in space around the planet. Enough to make an easy landing impossible.

"This is why we weren't supposed to come here," Plake says as the opposing forces become clear. "We're not getting the *Mobius* through that force."

"Then how did Bas expect to land?"

"A single small shuttle," Plake says. "All I know is that the Flaum piloting it's on our side. Had some way of sneaking Bas through that."

"What about the far side?"

Solis isn't developed. Only a quarter of the planet, so far as Sax knows, is used for the Oratus project, with the rest of it left alone. Probably so the Amigga could add on further creations if they wanted to.

"Even if they don't chase us down, you're saying we land and, what, walk all the way over?"

"Not doing that for you, Oratus," Agra-Red says from behind. "I already think this is a stupid idea."

"Nobody asked you, Whelk," Sax fires back.

"Stop," Plake closes her eyes for a second, then looks again at the terminal. "Looks like they have a pair of smaller frigates, meant for craft like this, and then a big cruiser. Way too big for something like Solis."

"It's not meant for fighting," Sax says. "That's where they train us, if we survive that long."

"So it's a boat packed with Oratus?" Agra-Red says. "Let's not go there. Ever."

"Scared?" Sax hisses, giving the Whelk a wicked grin.

"I don't want to waste the power turning them all to slag," the Whelk replies, patting the assault miner that never seems to leave its side.

"Wait," Plake says a moment later. "You're saying that big ship is packed with Oratus? New ones?"

"A hundred or more," Sax says. "It can hold thousands, but unless they've made it easy for Oratus to earn their letters, it'll never be near full."

"Can they be turned?"

Can a weapon be twisted against its wielder? Sax himself is proof that it can, but there's a difference in the experiences he's had compared to what the Oratus on that ship, most only just removed from a harsh introduction to life on Solis' surface, have gone through. Would they turn their backs on the Vincere just after joining it?

"Unlikely," Sax says finally. "Why would they trust us?"

"Not us," Plake replies. "You."

At this, Sax laughs. "Look at me, Plake. I'm a traitor. My scales are bent and burned. I'm sitting on a ship with a ragtag group of outcasts. Why would they care about me?"

Plake looks at her own feathers, and Sax realizes she's glancing at the part of a Vyphen where medals would hang. Where rank would be established if she wore a Vincere uniform.

"I thought, when they removed us, that I was done," Plake says. "I was, I am angry. But there's something you get when the Vincere stop controlling your life. Freedom. Independence. I could choose where to go. My failures were my fault, not because I'd been thrust into an impossible situation without support. Not because the equipment I had wasn't up to the task."

"Or you weren't good enough," Sax says. The Vyphen weren't removed only because they were less pliable than the Oratus, but also because they were less effective.

Plake acknowledges this with a slight nod. "Now, though, I get to make my own choices. I don't do the bidding of anyone but myself unless I want to. Sax, your species hasn't been given a choice. They never have, and as long as the Chorus exists, they never will."

"That's the message you want me to send? That we should fight against the Chorus because otherwise they'll control us?"

"I think that's the only message we have. If we can't turn these Oratus against their creators, then as soon as the Sevora are gone, the Chorus will use them to kill every last one of us."

If the plan is to get the Oratus to fight back against their creators, they first have to find a way to get Sax onto that large ship. A plan pushed to the forefront when the Vincere frigates take notice of the *Mobius* hanging out on Solis' fringes and send a few fighters to investigate.

"Use the escape mod," Coorvin says after Plake explains the dilemma, over intercom, to the entire crew. "Send Sax. He can say that he managed to escape."

"They'll never believe that," Plake says. "And Sax is wanted. He's a known traitor."

A traitor. Sax hasn't thought of himself like that, but Plake's words aren't wrong. He's actively working against the creatures that made him, working against the society that's given him life and, at first, a purpose.

The term, though, is freeing. Sax *is* a traitor. He's cast off his chains. He has no obligations anymore.

Except to Bas, of course.

"I'll do it," Sax hisses. "Only I'll need a hostage. Like Coorvin says, they won't trust that I made it away without one."

"They'll still imprison you immediately," Plake replies.

"But if there's a bit of doubt," Coorvin offers. "Even a little, that might give Sax another chance."

A beeping noise sounds from the cockpit—Vincere craft are getting closer.

"I'll do it!" the squeaky voice coming from the intercoms has Sax wincing. "I owe Sax that much. Wouldn't even be here if he hadn't found me!"

Nobaa. Why?

Sax doesn't have the time, unfortunately, to argue and none of the other crew volunteer, so it's a swift scramble to get Sax a miner and squeeze him into the escape mod with Nobaa.

"After we kick you, we're leaping away," Plake says.

"Send a message to Astre's Spire when you're ready for pick-up and we'll come back."

"We're going back there?" Agra-Red grumbles. "It's the most boring—"

"Quiet." Plake jerks a feathered hand towards the Whelk, though Sax can't see Agra-Red's response from inside the cramped mod. "Can't believe I'm saying this, Oratus, but good luck."

Sax gives the Vyphen a flash of his teeth, then presses the panel to seal the mod. The door slams shut, the vacuum seals activate, and Sax feels the slight judder as the mod kicks away from the *Mobius*.

"Do you think Engee will think I'm brave?" Nobaa says. "This is pretty courageous, right? Giving myself up for your grand mission?"

Sax sighs and closes his eyes, waits for the pick-up.

It's strange being stuck in a capsule with little view of the outside. All Sax can see, in fact, is dark space. There's too much ambient light from Solis' nearby star to get a glimpse of a nebula or other twinkling dots, but even a blank black is better than staring at Nobaa and his endlessly blathering mouth.

Rescue comes partway through Nobaa's seemingly endless iterations on how the Teven's going to undermine the Vincere ship's control systems and use them to confuse, frustrate, and drive the ship's crew insane with blaring alarms, randomly locking doors, and food dispensers set to continuously spray nutrient goop onto the floor.

"Evac mod, we're tracking you. Who's inside?" the intercom buzzes with the stern, light voice of a Flaum pilot.

Sax feels the Oratus should be given the chance to fly fighters too, but they're too big. Creating a craft that could hold an Oratus in comfortable position yet still be able to twist and turn in heavy atmosphere isn't a problem the Amigga think they needed to solve. So instead the Vincere trust their space acrobatics to the most prevalent and, until he'd met Nobaa, what Sax thought was the most annoying of species.

"This is Sax," the Oratus says, right foreclaw pushing in the panel for a response. Now that he's said his name, though, Sax isn't sure where to go. So he falls back on instinct. "I broke free of the Vyphen traitors holding me, and I'm ready to come home."

It sounds weak, but then, that might be what they're expecting; an Oratus who played with rebellion, found it wanting and forced to fight his way free without his pair? Yes, that could mean a tired voice. A sad soul.

The Flaum pilot takes her time in responding, and then only gives an acknowledgment that Sax is going to be taken in.

"That worked!" Nobaa exclaims when the intercom cuts. "They believed you!"

"I'm too valuable to kill outright," Sax hisses. "At the least, they think I have information to give. Either I'm being honest, which means they'll interrogate me and, probably, waste me for being disloyal, or I'm lying, in which case they'll waste me for being a traitor."

"Neither of those sounds like the outcome we want."

"Neither of those is the outcome they'll get," Sax says. "Just remember your role; get out, get access, and clear a path for the *Mobius*. If we can't get a full on fight started, then we need to get down to Solis and find Bas."

"Of course! It'll be easy. I can hack..." Sax stops listening to Nobaa's drivel and lets his eyes drift back to the window.

There's a shiver as something latches on to the escape

mod and redirects its path. After a moment, the big Oratus ship swings into view, a monstrous oval spiked with antennas, and coated in glowing docking bays. They're heading towards it.

At least, that's what Sax gets to think, for a moment, until one of the two frigates swings in front of the viewport, its docking bay looming large and close. Too close to miss now.

They're going on the wrong ship.

Through the viewport, Sax watches as the escape mod settles into the frigate's empty bay. Clear bluish-black floors meld with yellow-aged walls and white lights to make for a sterile Vincere appearance.

"Why's it so empty?" Nobaa says. "Are they that scared of us?"

"They think this might be a bomb," Sax replies. "Suicide or otherwise."

"Do Oratus do that? I thought you were too valuable?"

It's weird to think of himself as some sort of commodity, but Sax supposes that, yes, there's a price for him and every other Oratus. Sending one of a limited species on a bombing run against a low-value target wouldn't be smart. Wouldn't be profitable.

Then again, the Chorus doesn't deal in profits. The galaxy they've built serves as a mechanism to support their experiments, their ambitions. They wouldn't care how many Oratus have to destroy themselves so long as the Chorus comes out ahead.

Sax and Nobaa are separated the moment the mod arrives on the frigate. Stiff Flaum and Whelk shuttle Sax through the docking bay and towards the bridge—Sax has been on plenty of these sterile frigates before, and knows where he's heading. What he doesn't understand until he's stalking through the halls—flanked by miners on either side, in front and behind, is just how bland these ships are. *Scrapper Station*, Astre's Spire, and, most of all, the *Mobius* teem with the evidence of life; stained walls, nicked surfaces, littered junk and half-finished projects. Stories told in the ambiance.

Here, though, the Vincere keep things clear and clean of the past. Sax can't tell what lives have been shared in these hallways, and the silver sheen on the walls tells no tales. Even his vents pick up only the most mild scents from the creatures around him—tasteless goop to eat and plenty of showers mean his captors are blanks.

Before, Sax would have thought these things meant perfection and order, essential traits for a military force. Now, now it reminds him of the Chorus' ultimate objective; a universe they control.

The distaste must show in his stance, because when Sax is brought into the small bridge and face-to-face with the ship's Oratus commander, a brilliant gold-scaled one who introduces herself as Rav. The second thing she says is:

"You don't look like you belong here."

"I lived in these ships for a very long time." They're no longer his home, though.

Rav doesn't bear the scars of long-time war—her scales are too perfect, her claws unbent and sharp. Sax suspects she's never been on the front lines, relegated to back-water command posts like this one. The question is, why?

"I'm not supposed to interrogate you," Rav hisses, throwing a glance towards the Flaum manning the bridge's Q-Net communications array. "They're sending a transport to pick you up. Apparently you're going to be torn apart, mentally and physically, so they can find what's wrong with you."

"They?" Sax asks the question knowing the answer.

"The Chorus."

"What do you see in front of you, Rav?" Sax says, trying to think like Bas. "A damaged, broken thing, or another Oratus?"

Rav tilts her head, bares her teeth slightly. "I see a traitor."

"To what? The Chorus? Because I choose to do something other than their will?"

"Because you choose to be yourself," Rav gestures with her foreclaw around the bridge, to the pair of Whelk standing—as much as a Whelk can stand without legs—behind him with their miners ready. "The Vincere needs loyal soldiers, or else how can we keep the galaxy safe? What happens if every Oratus takes your path, if the Sevora are given free control to spread themselves throughout every inhabited planet."

"So choosing to think for myself means I'm letting the Sevora win?"

Rav locks eyes with Sax. "Yes." Then the looks past him. "Take the traitor to his room. Keep him there until the transport arrives."

The frigate isn't equipped for much in the way of prisoner transport, much less one the size of Sax. So instead they stick the Oratus in an empty, square cabin without much inside except a long bench on the right. One that could have been covered with a cushion but, for Sax, is left hard and bare.

There's a screen occupying a wall opposite the bench, one that could be used to show calming landscapes, watch entertainment, or a dozen other things but that, for Sax, remains black and dead.

Yet, when the door shuts behind him, Sax relaxes. He

didn't realize how tense it would be, confronting his own side, dealing with the accusing stares of lowly soldiers and staff that, before, would've been legitimately concerned with becoming his next meal. Now, Sax isn't something to be feared, he's something to be scorned.

The cabin's door sits flush with the wall behind him, and the panel controlling it's been overridden from elsewhere. Sax taps a couple of the buttons just to see what might happen and each one greets his attempt with an indignant buzzing. The screen does the same when Sax experiments a second later.

So they expect him to sit and wait. Stew, perhaps, in his own decisions.

Instead, Sax hunts for the cameras. Finds one hastily latched onto a wall above the door, peering down at him from its black nub.

What would they do if Sax attacks it? Would they open the door, miners in hand, and try to stun him enough to repair the thing? Or would they let him sit, hope that Sax doesn't do anything rash as they're unable to see him?

Sax opens his mouth at the camera, crouches and jumps, swiping with a foreclaw and shredding the camera off the wall. As soon as Sax lands, he rakes the door's panel with his claws, knocking it off its perch and sending it sparking to the ground. A couple hard swings with his tail and the wall screen is coated in cracks, which has to make any camera looking through the glass a distorted affair.

"Why?" Rav's voice snarls through an overhead intercom a second later. "What's the point, Sax?"

Sax takes a bit of smug satisfaction from knowing they're using the frigate's alert system to talk to him—the cabin's private intercom was on the door panel. Sax can't exactly talk back to Rav here, but at least he knows she's frustrated.

"You're not getting out of that room," Rav continues. "I'm ordering the outside guard doubled. The Chrous transport's already leapt into the system, so your pointless destruction will get you nothing."

But it's satisfying.

And now he knows they're blind.

The dull pearl bones carpet the floor, and at first I want to panic, push away the pain and run. The bones aren't human. Not all of them anyway. Even the one I just stepped on is longer than my own leg. Thick, with a knob on either end.

"T'Oli, do you know whose bones these are?" I manage to ask.

"Given the size, it seems plausible that these belong to other Fassoth," T'Oli says. "Unless your planet has other large predators with a predilection for dark, damp environs?"

The Ooblot surges ahead of me, rolling over the bones and deeper into the cavern, around those blue-coated pillars. I don't really try to keep up, instead focusing on my awkward shamble, trying not to fall into what would be a nightmare.

"If the bones are here, though, doesn't that mean it comes back to eat?" I ask.

To the right, as I pass by the first pillar, I see the grand sphere of a Fassoth skull, almost perfectly unbroken save for a crack in the upper right temple. I only guess it's a Fassoth because there aren't any holes for eyes or ears, or a mouth.

"I don't know much about how Fassoths live, Kaishi," T'Oli replies from up ahead. "But your thought seems likely."

"Which means we shouldn't be here."

Two choices, then. Either we turn around, hope that Viera and the others took a different path and that they've killed the Fassoth chasing us, or we keep plunging ahead this way. Hope that the Fassoth or whatever lives here doesn't decide to come back. Or isn't waiting behind the next pillar.

The bones thin as we go deeper, where a small stream makes its burbling self known. It cascades along the left wall, filling a small pool before vanishing through some unseen crack in the rocks. I can picture this as a Damantum house—the boneyard being the dining area, the stream marking the kitchen.

Which means we're coming to the bedroom.

Beyond the stream, the fungal growths dwindle as the cavern closes together into a dead-end. A smooth, rounded closure whose ground is coated in soft-white hairs. T'Oli's waiting for me there, its eye stalks scanning the area.

"I can't find another way forward," the Ooblot says as I wander up, right hand on the wall.

'So we chose the wrong way."

"Depends on what you consider wrong," T'Oli replies. "We didn't find the Fassoth, so, in some ways, we chose the right one."

"What I don't understand, is you said you found the Fassoth's den on the other side of the pool. And I can't imagine Diego and the others taking up this close to two of these things." I glance back towards the blue pillars. "It's too dangerous."

"A full day's walk away is distance enough, and Fassoth would be wary of attacking a large party," T'Oli says. "They simply may have hid while Diego and the others moved through."

"Still doesn't explain the two dens."

"Do human families stay close together?" T'Oli asks.

"Generally," I reply. "Why?"

As I finished the answer, there's a clear rustling from back up the cavern. The sound of many thick feet pounding on the rock, and heading this way.

"Fassoth," T'Oli says. "Are the same."

I press against the den's back wall. T'Oli starts to sluice up me, to form its armor again. Not that the Ooblot's protection saved me the last time.

Of all the ways I thought I might die, trapped in a cave with a monstrous beast wasn't on the list until this moment. I'd pictured growing old in my village, possibly going out through disease or a hunter's spear. Maybe getting sacrificed to Ignos.

But this? No.

So when the Fassoth shows up, as it picks through the bones, kicking some aside and, using one of its eight legs, handling others, I try to think. Try to ponder some way out.

The Fassoth doesn't seem in a rush to get to me, so I watch it move. It looks larger than the one that emerged from the pool, and there are gaps in its white fur where scars make themselves apparent. Some of the bones it puts down are snapped, or have grooves cut in their smooth surface, as though the Fassoth is somehow sucking out the marrow through its feet.

What I don't see, though, is a weakness. A way around

the creature and out of the cavern. Especially when moving faster than, oh, a slow walk would make me pass out from the pain.

So when the Fassoth finally finishes with its inventory of the bone hoard and ambles towards me, I feel around my feet for a loose rock. Figure that, if nothing else, I'm going to go out with a short, pitiful fight. T'Oli twitches against me, but says nothing.

Not like the Ooblot has to worry—it'll live through this. T'Oli can go all stone and it'll be fine. Maybe T'Oli can take my bones when the Fassoth is done with me, bring them to Viera and the others so they know.

The Fassoth, so close now, dips a foot in the creek's pool. I can smell its sweaty stink, hear its thick breath. It's made no motions towards me, though. No aggressive gestures as I keep myself pinned to the wall.

No eyes. The thought hits me hard. No eyes, and no visible ears. The Fassoth might not know I'm here. I haven't made a sound, haven't moved.

Only now the creature's moving away from the pool, towards me and its bed of white fur. If it gets so close, it might be able to hear my breathing, or the rapid-fire beat of my heart.

So I throw the rock. Launch it hard across the cavern to the left side, where it strikes a pillar and rattles into a pile of bones. The Fassoth jerks immediately, tracks the rock as it flies and then shifts towards where it lands.

Then it bursts.

I've seen juar—large, predatory cats—do the same, but the Fassoth is larger. Has more legs. The Fassoth I'd first seen used by the Lunare were tame, controlled. This one leaps through the air, legs flailing out, and it crashes into the bones, scattering them everywhere.

"Go," T'Oli pats quietly.

And I do. Push off from the wall and run. Towards the right.

I make it all of two steps before the side of my chest breaks me with stabbing pain. It's like I can't feel my legs anymore, can't focus, can't land the next step and I wind up falling. Splashing into the end of the creak, and the icy cave water soaks my clothes, and me.

At least it numbs the pain.

The Fassoth isn't fooled. I see the creature wheel around towards me, and as the rock I threw fails to keep moving, the Fassoth begins creeping my way. I crawl, dragging myself forward, trying to get my legs beneath me, but they're half-frozen from the water and I'm half-stunned anyway.

I can't outrun this thing.

Which means I have to fight it.

"T'Oli," I say, causing the Fassoth to start, to lift its eyeless head and point it towards me. "Can you form a point? On my left hand?"

T'Oli, to its credit, doesn't ask questions. The Ooblot just goes. Slimes away from me, disintegrating my armor and going, instead, along my left arm and over my hand, then, building off of itself, T'Oli extends my hand until it ends in a hard-rock spear.

The Ooblot's two eye stalks fold back along my arm, turning to look at me.

"Yeah, like that," I say to the stare.

The Fassoth rumbles over, standing over me. It raises its front right leg and there, between the claws, I see how it eats. How it survives. In between those deadly points, there's a mouth. A slit filled with jagged, broken teeth.

"Stay away from me," I growl, and punch up with my left arm, right into that mouth.

The pressure, the strength of the hit ripples along T'Oli's form, to my arm and along my body as the Fassoth rears back from the strike. There's no roar, no angry call as I'd expect from anything else getting such a wound. Only the shuffling of dirt and bones, only the *drip drip* of the creek.

Life or death determined in silence.

"Having never been a weapon before, I'm not sure I like it," T'Oli says by thawing a small portion of itself near my elbow. "Awfully brutal."

"Welcome to life for the rest of us." I use the seconds bought with the strike, while the Fassoth changes its calculus on its prey, to get to my feet.

I back against the wall, the creek running just in front of me, and watch as the Fassoth heads around the pillar, careful to keep its wounded leg off of the ground. I, though, keep my Ooblot spear raised in front of me, ready.

"You know any way to scare these things?" I ask T'Oli.

"They're trainable," T'Oli says. "If you have the right tools, and catch them young."

"Thanks." I edge along the creek, towards the boneyard and the cavern entrance.

Not that I think I have any chance of outrunning this thing, but if I can knock it away, make it hesitate, that might be enough to flee.

The Fassoth, for its part, seems to be content waiting. It paces me, following along the middle of the cavern. At first I wonder what it's doing, but then I recall the fight with the juar, in Damantum's Pits. The Fassoth is a predator, I'm it's prey, and it wants to figure me out.

Well, it's not the only one learning.

When my boot brushes the first bone, I reach down, press away the pain in my side and pick it up with my right hand. I throw it back across the cave, towards the wall near the fur. It clacks off, hits the ground, and sure enough the Fassoth jerks its head back that way.

I stay perfectly still. Don't even breathe. And in a second, the Fassoth takes a couple of steps towards the thrown bone.

I toss another bone. Then a third, without taking another step. When the last one bounces with a hollow clack, the Fassoth can't resist anymore and it launches towards my trick.

And now I have it.

It's a lumpy, lurching run but it's the only one I have. T'Oli waves through the air—attached to my left arm—as I scatter bones with every step. With my right, I scoop up and throw one after another, flinging them at random around the cavern.

Clattering noise from everywhere, and I'm hoping it confuses the beast.

For a moment I think it's working. I hear the Fassoth jump after the last bone I throw, hear the beast bounce off of a pillar and see the light change as blue fungus goes flying. But apparently the Fassoth isn't as easy to fool as I thought—the very next second brings clattering claws racing up behind me.

"Now!" T'Oli says, its eyestalks peering over my shoulder, behind me.

I turn, swinging my left arm in a wide slash. T'Oli manages to harden itself into a razor's edge, and the cut goes right across the front of the Fassoth's head. The slash leaves a bright red line in the fur, and the Fassoth rears back.

What it doesn't do, though, is run.

Instead it plows forward, even as I get T'Oli oriented so the charge costs the Fassoth another gash. The beast plows into me, pushing me back and knocking me to the ground. The world blurs as my nerves overload at the impact, and I'm thankful, because now I can't really see as the Fassoth's toothy foot descends towards my face.

I feel a cold flash from my left arm. As the Fassoth's foot crashes in, T'Oli slides in front of it. The Ooblot catches the strike, wrapping itself around the Fassoth's foot. The creature stops its attack and stumbles back, probably wondering why its front right leg is covered in hard rock.

My head sits back against the stone floor—I can't keep it up anymore—as the Fassoth commences to panicked battering, hitting its front leg on the ground, whacking it into the pillars and the walls to try and get T'Oli off.

I want to help. Want to find some way of rescuing T'Oli. Only I can't move, and my head's blowing up with pain.

So I do the only thing I can.

I scream.

The sound surprises everyone; the Fassoth, who pauses its crazed whacking of the Ooblot to turn towards me, T'Oli, whose rock eyestalks flip my way, and even me, as I didn't think I had that much air left in my bruised lungs.

I guess fear can do amazing things.

T'Oli's the first to recover, climbing up the Fassoth's leg. I sit up as the Ooblot makes its way towards the fassoth's monstrous neck. The beast, though, isn't fooled and rolls. Bones fly everywhere as the Fassoth wriggles on its back before continuing upright. When the white-furred creature stands again, T'Oli's nowhere to be seen.

Stand up, Kaishi. You're not going to die lying down.

I don't really succeed. The best I get is a stumble against

the wall, near the cavern's exit. I try to throw another rock, and this time actually hit the Fassoth, which ignores my efforts completely.

The beast grumbles towards me—still favoring that right foot I cut—and I start to pray. There's nothing else to do. Nowhere I can run. So I call to Ignos, and ask, if not for his help, then for his courage.

I don't hear an answer.

The Fassoth raises its left foot, and I try to duck, but it catches me with its claws and throws me to the ground. The foot lands on my back, cutting into me, and I fall into the pain.

I'm coming to you, Malo.

"Not her." A crack—impossibly loud—shatters the cavern after the words.

The Fassoth's foot jumps off me as a second crack breaks out. Then a third and a fourth in quick succession. I brush my face against the floor to look up, to see the Fassoth back-pedaling as shot after shot pours into the thing.

Viera comes into view, a pistol in each hand, unleashing one crack after another until both weapons click empty. She holsters the left one, then reaches into her pocket and pulls out a handful of bullets. Starts reloading the pistol in her right. The Fassoth, for its part, is moving around, trying to keep the pillars between it and the Lunare.

"You still alive, Empress?" Viera says without looking back at me.

"For the moment."

"Try to keep it that way." Viera snaps the chamber back. "Vee, you're on her."

"As ordered." The hiss comes from above me, and I twist further to see the Oratus, bleeding from plenty of his own cuts, missing a pair of claws from his right foreclaw, and holding two torches, standing over me.

Viera begins a dance with the Fassoth, keeping her distance while slowly reloading her second pistol, bringing both weapons back to ready. She makes enough noise, kicking at rocks and bones to keep the Fassoth on her, but the creature's not quite so reckless anymore. Its fur is blossomed with red, and it's moving slow.

At least, that's what I think until the Fassoth bursts forward, scrambling on its back four legs while raising its front limbs to bat towards Viera.

I shout. Vee hisses.

Viera pulls the triggers. Both pistols work again. One after another. Four cracks, five cracks, their fiery flashes sparking over the blue glow. I see her face, her set, grim, look beneath her white, tangled hair.

And then she's gone, buried beneath an unmoving Fassoth as it collapses onto her.

"Go! Help her!" I manage to croak, though Vee's already moving.

The Oratus goes to work, pressing with his legs, with his claws, and then Viera's there, crawling out from beneath the beast and coated in the results of her handiwork. She's as beaten and battered as all of us, but Viera's able to stand. Able to walk to me and, after putting her pistols back, help me up.

I point, then, towards the spot where the Fassoth ran T'Oli into the ground, and Vee goes to check. Retrieves the stone slab of the Ooblot. Still in one piece, T'Oli's eyestalks are flattened into the surface of its body. None of us knows if T'Oli's alive, so Vee settles the stone Ooblot into his midclaws.

"I'll carry T'Oli until it's ready," Vee hisses.

"And Diego?" I ask.

"First one took him," Viera replies, pats the pistols. "That's where these came from."

"How?"

"He didn't run fast enough." Viera throws a look at Vee. "Then he held its attention long enough for me to take it out. Thankfully, Diego was a bit paranoid, so he brought a ton of ammunition."

Losing Diego is a hard blow. Not because I have any fondness for the man—he was, generally, a jerk to all of us— but because we're now lost down here. We've got no guide, and no way to convince any Lunare we come across that we're friendly.

"How about you?" Viera asks. "How bad are you hurt?"

Rather than list off my injuries, I break into a half-hearted laugh. "I'll survive. May need new ribs, though."

Viera nods. "Then we should head back. They'll have medical supplies at the gateway."

"No." I almost fall over, but Viera catches me. "We keep going. We've lost too much time already."

But we do go back a little, to our ditched campsite, where the rest of the food and other supplies sit. I'm tempted to return to the pool, but instead hold still while Viera wraps cut up clothing around my ribs. Tries to keep them in place. It doesn't help much, but I appreciate the sentiment. The effort.

"You didn't give up," I say to Viera as she finishes the wrapping.

Vee looks like he's asleep already, T'Oli still cradled in his claws.

"We fought through space, through other worlds, Kaishi," Viera says, using her torch to set the fire pit, full of dried fungus and other random growth, alight. "Dying to a Fassoth now would be a stupid way to go."

"We were close."

"But we're alive." Viera steps back from the small fire. "That scream, you know. That's what let us find you."

"I was trying to scare it. For T'Oli." I tell my version of the fight.

"You used T'Oli as a spear?" Viera asks when I'm done. "Clever."

"Don't know if T'Oli liked it, but we didn't have much choice."

"You could have chosen to die," Viera says. "But you didn't give up."

I catch the sentiment. Offer up a smile. "No. Though I think I might pass out now."

"Do it. I'll keep watch."

Part of me wants to offer to do the same. Or tell Viera to wake me in a bit to take her place, but the truth is that I can't bring myself to say the words. My body's demanding sleep, and as soon as my head hits the mat, I'm gone.

Our progress is achingly slow, but the nutrient goop is filling and we have a lot of it. T'Oli wakes up by the second night, more or less the same as always, though the Ooblot mentions no desire to become my spear in the future.

At first I'm afraid we'll be stuck lost in the tunnels forever, but it seems Diego exaggerated the difficulty; the Lunare didn't carve a dozen routes through the Earth. There's only one main path and a number of tiny diversions, most leading to pools or small storage caches with emergency supplies.

We avoid any smooth tunnels, anything that doesn't

bear the telltale marks of Lunare picks and their crude hacking. No further Fassoths come to hunt us down, though we're also quiet, keeping to soft murmurs as we move so that the cave's natural rumblings tend to be louder than we are.

My damaged ribs never fade, but familiarity turns the pain manageable and I gradually pick up my pace. We're all hurt, though, so speed is never a serious concern. We won't be much help to humanity if we die en route, anyway.

Viera, more than myself, Vee, or T'Oli, takes over the lead as we go. She holds a pistol in one hand, a torch in the other, and strides with confidence I haven't seen before. Maybe because Viera feels this is, more than any of us, her home. Maybe because she knows nobody else is willing to take up the leader's burden right now.

I'm certainly content to let her have it.

Especially when, late in the third day, we stumble upon a small village, built around a lake that would have been considered tiny if we were in the jungle. Our tunnel spits us out over the lake, where a man-made path leads us across the water and towards a dozen houses and a few accompanying buildings.

I've never seen Lunare homes before, and these are built from the ground up to the ceiling, the structures blending into the rock at both ends.

"They're support and shelter," Viera says when I ask why. "We have to hollow most of these areas out, so the buildings help keep the ceiling from falling in."

There are other pillars cast around too, including a few lunging out of the lake, rising to smash into the top of the cavern. They remind me of trees, in a way, only deep gray rock instead of wood.

The first Lunare to notice us are a pair of fisherman, casting their nets into the lake. I can't imagine what fish make it down here, and how they manage to reproduce if they do, but there's a woven basket between the two men, so I assume they must catch something.

When they see us, though, their net comes in fast and the closer one reaches for a pistol holstered around his belt, keeps his hand on it as we draw near. I'm expecting panic when he notices Vee, but the man's eyes only widen a little. His partner takes the gear and makes a speedy walk away, leaving his friend behind.

"You came from the other side," the man says once we're in conversational range.

"We did," Viera says, then nods back at us. "We're tired and hurt. Is there a place to stay here?"

"You think you're just going to walk in with that thing?" the man nods to Vee.

"Yes," Viera replies. "We are."

"Viera," I interject. I'm too tired for another fight. "Please, I don't know your name, or your home, but we've come a long way and only need a place to rest. We mean you no harm."

"That's what they said too," the man replies. "The ones we're fighting back to the west. They said they came with nothing to hide, no reason to hurt. Didn't last long. How do I know you're not with them?"

Viera sighs next to me, brushes away a dangling bang with the back of her wrist. "What lies beneath?"

I'm about to ask what she's talking about when the man squints at her. "Our truest self."

"Why do we go?" Viera continues.

"To find what we must."

"And who do we carry?"

"All who carry us." The man relaxes his pistol grip,

shakes his head. "Been a long time since I've heard that one."

I'm looking back and forth between the two, and notice Viera's wearing a small smile.

"It's been a long time since I've said it," Viera replies. "Good to know the old verses haven't been forgotten."

"Not yet. Not by all of us." The man seems to see us again for the first time, only now, instead of suspicion, he gives a steady look of trust. "Head to the common house. They'll have room for you. Refugees haven't made it this far yet. Tell them you talked to Anjo."

Leaving Sax alone in a room designed for rest and not, say, keeping a dangerous weapon captive, leads to poor results; Sax takes a running leap, bounces up the door and makes it to the ceiling, his claws catching in the slats of the air vent. With a kick, Sax digs his talons into the silver tiles on the ceiling—punching his sharp feet through the thin metal.

With his foreclaws, Sax tears the vent away and sends it rattling to the floor. The duct behind it isn't nearly large enough for Sax, at first, but when the Oratus peers through his new-made hole, it's clear the small duct intersects with the much larger, main one feeding this portion of the ship with sweet, sweet air. What's life-sustaining for the crew is going to bring them a very fatal surprise.

Sax rends the small duct sides to widen the path, pushing away streams of wires. He tucks in his midclaws close to his chest vents as he starts climbing up, stretching his talons and tail out behind him to create as thin a form as possible.

If Bas saw him now, half-stuck in this mess of metal,

she'd laugh so hard. Sax can't quite suppress a hiss of his own at the situation—he'd never have thought he'd be scrambling through the innards of a Vincere ship.

But he squirms anyway, because knowing the circumstances are ridiculous doesn't help Sax get out of them. It's a centimeter by centimeter crawl, with Sax's foreclaws doing the work of clearing the way. He has to test every pipe, every section of wire for give so he doesn't damage or break something that might burst hot liquid or fiery electric sparks all over him.

"Sax? What are you doing in there?" it's a Flaum voice this time—Rav probably has better things to do than babysit a prisoner. "We're hearing a lot of noise."

Sax doesn't try to respond. If they burst in now, they'll know where he is in a moment, and have stunning bolts blasting his tail in the next. And if Sax gets on that Chorus ship, he'll never see Bas again.

So Sax picks up the pace. Scrabbles forward towards the wide duct. He leaves plenty of claw marks on the ship around him, and the frigate leaves a bunch of small cuts on Sax's scales as his body bends and warps.

There's no warning when the door to his cabin opens. Just a beep and a shunt—guess destroying the door's panel didn't help—and there's a half-dozen footfalls as the Vincere guards run beneath Sax into the room.

"Sax!" One of them shouts, as if calling his name is going to get Sax popping out from behind a curtain, laughing and declaring the whole thing a joke.

What Sax does instead is finish tearing his way into the breezy main duct, where warm air rushes by and an infinite silvery corridor goes both to his left and right. He has to make a choice now, as the Flaum have performed the minimal detective work to figure out where Sax has gone and are attempting to climb up into the vents.

Problem is, Flaum are small creatures and Sax doubts they've brought a ladder with them.

Which way?

There's only one thing on this ship that really matters, only one way Sax can come close to completing his original mission. Rav. Sax bets she's still on the bridge, so that's where he goes.

Sax doesn't have a map, has no easy way of telling the layout of the frigate, but he knows Vincere ships and knows, too, that the heat keeping the ship warm comes from the bank of batteries back by its main engines. The bridge, kept far away from those same engines—a means of keeping the commander at the farthest spot from the area most likely to blossom into a fiery death at a malfunction or well-placed shot—is at the opposite end.

The Oratus follows that warm breeze and clambers through the ductwork. Here it's plenty wide for Sax, though it's short enough he has to keep crawling. Small and medium offshoots dot his path as Sax moves, and he manages to ignore almost all of them until, bouncing off the walls, comes a voice that makes Sax wince.

"You're running old systems! I could do better, if you give me just a few minutes!" Nobaa's speaking to someone. "The Oratus used me as a hostage. I love the Vincere. Love you guys!"

It's coming from Sax's right; a cramped offshoot that's still larger than the one he tore up to get here. Navigable. But is Nobaa worth risking his mission for?

No.

Sax turns back to his path, is about to go on, when the

tiniest flicker of a flash makes its way up into the vent. Followed by a panicked yelp.

"You can't kill me! That's not fair!" Nobaa's shouting.

"Why not? This isn't a prisoner ship, and you don't have anything to trade," a Flaum voice says. "If word gets out that more Oratus are turning traitor, that wouldn't be good for us. Others might get the same idea. Rav told us you're not going to leave here, and I've got other things to do. Make peace with yourself, Teven."

Sax tears his way through the duct before he really thinks about what he's doing. As soon as he hits the vent staring down into the larger room—apparently made for medical evaluations—where Nobaa's backed against the wall, Sax uses his head to smash the vent down. The metal grate crashes into the Flaum aiming his miner at Nobaa and, with his foreclaws tearing a wider hole, Sax squeezes through and lands on the captor.

Sax rips away the miner, lifts and throws the Flaum against the room's walls. The red-furred guard hits the wall hard and collapses to the ground.

"You rescued me!"

Sax takes a deep breath. Looks back towards the duct, then at Nobaa. Maybe...

"Let's go," Sax starts, moving towards Nobaa. He figures he can throw the Teven up there and Nobaa can pull himself the rest of the way.

"No, wait!" Nobaa's carapace looks strange now, covered in empty hooks and belts. "I need my things."

"Your things don't matter."

"You want to survive this?" Nobaa counters. "Then I need my gear so we can take this ship over the right way."

Nobaa's idea of the right way is a lot more complicated

than Sax's—for one, as Sax understands it, there's not even a need to slash and tear through any Flaum at all.

"If you really want to murder some things, I'm sure you'll have the chance," Nobaa says as Sax opens the door out of the medical room where they'd been holding the Teven. "This ship is full of people."

The frigate doesn't have an expansive med bay, only a dozen rooms, most of those smaller than the one Nobaa was in. They're clustered around a single monitoring station currently occupied by a robot that, after a flash scan from across the room declares Nobaa and Sax to be in good health, ignores them.

"Kind of small, isn't it?" Nobaa says. "For a ship this size?"

"Not a lot of space combat that leaves you alive," Sax replies. "Better to give the rooms to more weapons, more energy, than beds that won't do you any good."

Nobaa doesn't have a response to that other than a twitch of his arms as he turns his carapace to get a good look at the place.

"Where's your gear?" Sax hisses after a moment. "They'll find us soon."

"I don't know," Nobaa says. "I thought it would be out here. They took everything after bringing me onboard."

This frigate doesn't have cells, so it probably doesn't have a designated spot for a captive's gear either. Which means they'd toss Nobaa's electronics in the same spot as the rest of the general junk the frigate's maintenance people might need. Or it's near the docking bay, waiting for the Chorus' transport to take it back with them.

Sax tosses these options at Nobaa, who doesn't have a suggestion.

"You're no help," Sax hisses at the Teven.

Before Nobaa can properly describe how hurt he is by the insult, there's a shout from outside the med bay. Alarms bang suddenly, the harsher tone indicating everyone should find immediate shelter. The robot acts on it—whirling into activity and calmly calling for everyone in the med bay to seal their doors.

Sax takes a couple long lunges and gets to the med bay's entrance, a double-wide sliding door leading out to another corridor in which Sax can see plenty of armed Flaum and Whelk heading their way. Sax hits the panel to close off the med bay, which, so far as he can tell, is going to buy them a second of time.

"We need a way out!" Sax hisses back to Nobaa.

"You're talking to me like I know this place! Wasn't this one of your ships?" Nobaa replies.

It was, but med bays weren't a space Sax frequented. That's what the masks—and his raw talent—kept him out of. The Oratus runs his eyes around the space, and falls on the only thing that might make a difference.

"Take the miner, buy me time," Sax hisses to Nobaa, passing off the Flaum guard's miner to the Teven, who, at least, holds the weapon like he knows how to use it.

"Shouldn't you be the one doing the fighting?"

"I wish I was." Sax blows by the Teven, heading for the terminals left vacant by the robot.

There's several of them, showing bars and numbers that, Sax guesses, have to do with the occupants in some of the rooms. What he's looking for, though, is a channel to the bridge, and he finds it on the right terminal. Taps the icon with his right midclaw.

"Rav," Sax says as soon as the terminal beeps that a connection's been made. "Call off your force."

There's hissing laughter on the other end. "You're better

than I thought, Sax, but the Chorus's transport is docking now. Give yourself up. Don't hurt the Vincere more than you already have."

Rav didn't go for it the first time Sax made his pitch. She refused to play the part of traitor with him, refused to turn on her own troops or try to convince them to join Sax's cause.

"They're going to kill you," Sax hisses. "All of you. All of us. I've seen it, Rav."

Behind him, around the wall, the med bay door judders open. Nobaa, standing near Sax and using the corner, immediately lets loose a pair of bright-blue stunning bolts. Smart —stuns use less power than deadly shots, and everyone they don't kill will be one less reason for Rav to despise them.

"The Amigga are making better versions of us, just like we were to the Vyphen. Then we'll be replaced. But Rav, we can't reproduce. We're not a natural species. When they decide we're done, we're done."

"And you think that by fighting the Chorus we can live somehow?"

"If we take Solis, yes! That's where the hatcheries are. Where the Oratus can survive!"

There's a heavy hiss on the other end of the line. Nobaa unleashes a few more bolts, and Sax sees a couple return shots burn blue into the far wall past them.

"Rav?" Sax asks.

"Even if I believed you," Rav says. "Even if there's a chance you might be right, then what? The Chorus would destroy us all before they let your plan succeed."

"They've been trying to destroy me for a while now, Rav, and I'm still here."

There's another blue blast and Nobaa falls back from

the corner, his little limbs slinking limp to the ground, the miner beside them.

Sax is out of time.

He can't wait for Rav. Sax reaches down, grabs Nobaa's fallen miner in one midclaw and the Teven in the other. The med bay goes in a ring around this terminal bank, with the single open door directly behind Sax, through the back wall of a supply room.

"Oratus! Give up!" It's the skittering, stern voice of a Flaum soldier. "No reason you have to die here!"

Sax glances left, right. Only patient rooms. And above is a flat ceiling—no time to crawl up into a vent even if he wanted to.

"We're coming around to get you in ten seconds!"

That means Sax really has five. He spies his answer in one: the medical robot, moving from one room to the next and now passing by them on the right. Sax raises the miner and uses his left foreclaw to adjust the miner's power, pushing it to maximum. Turns, and aims at the robot's power supply, housed within its base, between the metal balls allowing the machine to get around.

Fires.

The bright red bolt strikes a robot never meant for combat duty. The heat burns through the robot's shell, strikes the big power supply, and overcharges it. Because Sax is ready, because he's gouged his talons into the floor and has his tail bracing against the same, the explosion doesn't send Sax flying.

It does, though, splash his eyes with heat, burn his claws and set all the lights in the med bay to a deep yellow warning glow. Alarms—true alarms—start off like wailing monsters as smoke pumps out from a dozen small fires, smoke that's as quickly shunted towards the vents as the frigate's systems take charge of preserving itself.

As Sax acts now to keep him and Nobaa alive. He twists around the corner to the right, talons pounding. The squad coming to capture him is in disarray, blown about the entry. Some are trying to help others, plenty more are lying still.

Sax hopes he didn't kill any, or at least too many. Every death hurts his cause here.

Back in the main corridor, Sax turns away from the bridge and runs. There's plenty of people there, mechanics and medics dashing towards the explosion and plenty more pushing to get away from it.

Nobody bothers to engage Sax, who towers over most of them and uses his foreclaws and tail to clear away anyone who doesn't notice the Oratus trampling through.

Lit signs show up at intersections, signaling what lies which way. Sax goes by a cafeteria, a fitness center, and a simulator section before hitting what he's looking for— cargo. The frigate's not going to be hauling freight, but there's a good chance that Nobaa's gear would find its way there.

The Teven's still not conscious and Sax has no idea how long it's going to take a small creature like Nobaa to wake up from a heavy stun, which means even if Sax finds the Teven's things, it's going to require hiding out on the frigate for a long time.

Time Sax doesn't have.

Sax hisses away some of his anger, drawing plenty of frightened looks and a couple of squeaks from the crowd, who add distance from Sax as the priority to their paths through the ship. It's a problem, as Sax is getting farther away from the aftermath of the explosion, and the panic isn't following as far.

As Sax nears the frigate's aft and its massive engines, he hunts for a place to drop the dead weight in his midclaws; Nobaa isn't helping Sax unconscious and there's a good chance the Teven's going to get shot hanging limp in the middle of a big target.

And Nobaa's body is far too small to make a good shield.

In this, the constant overhead announcements tracking Sax's progress and ordering all non-combat personnel to stay out of the Oratus way serve as an advantage. Hallways are clear, rooms are empty, and nobody accosts Sax as he barges into a storage room and stuffs the Teven in a food locker. Nobaa doesn't exactly blend in with the crates of nutrient goop, but he's not likely to get blown apart in there either.

Back in the main corridor running from bridge to stern, Sax catches some more shots from another cadre of Flaum and Whelk guards. The fire doesn't come all that close to hitting Sax, and the bolts are a dim blue—low power. The reason's clear—there's plenty of valuable equipment in the frigate, and Sax is running out of places to go. Why risk damage when they'll have the Oratus trapped soon anyway?

Soon, though, isn't now.

Sax takes the opportunity to jump and dart along the corridor towards the engines, past all sorts of glowing lights and locking doors showing ways to cafeterias, crew quarters, and maintenance bays. As the Oratus moves, the crystal white lights shift to red spectrums, adding to the constant warning drone to hide.

The corridor ends in a wide, locked and sealed entry to the engines. These are thick silver shields, meant to cushion and even block any explosion if the frigate's big thrusters decide to end themselves in a fiery death. It means Sax has run out of room.

There's a single panel near the doors, one that Sax uses to call the only place he can. To act on the idea that's made its way into his mind as his talons have scrapped and scratched their way this far.

Sax taps to call the bridge and there's a blip as the Oratus on the other end clicks into the line.

"Rav," Sax hisses. "You don't have to trust me."

"I don't have to trust you? That makes it easy."

"Trust Evva instead. She's a four-letter Oratus. A Vincere commander. She's abandoned her post. Why?"

"Because she's insane? A traitor?"

"Because she learned the truth, Rav."

The Flaum and Whelk soldiers have caught up with him. They're arrayed across the corridor, miners raised. Sax keeps talking, because as soon as he stops, he's not getting another chance.

"That the Amigga are all evil, and we're all being played for fools?"

"Exactly."

There's a heavy silence on the other end of the line. Sax keeps his eyes on Rav's guards. Why haven't they shot yet? Sax hasn't heard Rav give an order for them not to.

"Sax, even if I wanted to believe you, even if I wanted the Oratus to rise up and take their destiny into their own hands," Rav says. "There's a problem."

"What problem?"

"The Chorus has already won. I'm sorry, Sax."

The line clicks off. Sax looks back at the guards, raising his claws. They'll fire in a second, but if they don't, Sax isn't going to wait. He tenses his talons, looks to the right, where a set of lower pipes would provide grip for a bounding jump into the side of the Flaum line. Strike there and limit their field of view and maybe, maybe in the chaos there'd be a chance of survival.

But Sax doesn't get his chance to act, because there's a sharp hiss from behind the line, an order that causes the guards to split apart—Flaum stepping rapidly, Whelk sludging along the floor—to show something Sax didn't think was real. Something he's never seen before.

The Amigga created the Oratus to be weapons. Grew and designed the species to take the reins of war. That, though, was a narrow view of what Oratus could be capable of. There'd been plenty of rumors, gaps in new Oratus joining the Vincere, that suggested the hatcheries on Solis were being used for purposes less clear, less about keeping order in the galaxy and more about cleaning out what the Amigga didn't like.

Its scales aren't a single color. Instead, they shiver and shift as the Oratus moves, their surfaces reflecting the red and black lights, the glow of the dozen miners primed to fire, so that their owner appears less as a physical object and more as a wavering line, a reality-blending blur.

"They sent you?" Sax manages to say, which is all he can think to speak to a legend brought to life in front of his eyes.

The mirrored Oratus aren't supposed to exist. Everyone assumed they were a tale told in the shadows, the price paid if one considered disobeying the Chorus' orders. If one ever turned on the Vincere.

Yet, Sax and Bas hadn't ever seen one. Hadn't heard of one. How could they be afraid of what didn't seem real?

"Your charges are clear," the Oratus speaks, and even its voice is a reflection of itself, distorted and chilling. "You are a traitor to the Vincere, to the Amigga, and to your own species."

Sax moves to the left, watching the blur go opposite him. Sax has to keep a little distance, give himself a half-second to adapt when the mirror Oratus decides to strike.

"You'd trust the Amigga over one of your own?" Sax replies. "Who's really betraying their species?"

The mirrored Oratus doesn't reply. At least, not with words. It leaps up, high enough to catch the ceiling and hook onto a vent with its foreclaws. The Oratus swings forward, red lines playing over its scales between darker reflections of the watching Flaum and Whelk, and lunges at Sax with its talons.

Sax dives forward, tucking in his tail as he rolls and feeling the shift in the air above him. Sax twists as he comes out of the somersault, winding up on all six claws and talons, crouched and ready if the mirrored Oratus makes a quick attack.

"What is your plan?" the mirrored Oratus asks instead, keeping on its talons.

Sax realizes its eyes are mirrored too—probably covered by a mask helping with the imaging.

"My plan?" Sax hisses back a reply. "You're asking that now?"

"It will save me time," the Oratus says. "Tell me, and I can deliver you a clean death now, rather than a slow one later."

If there's one thing Sax can't stand, it's mockery. He rises up, matching the mirrored Oratus on his talons.

"Our plan is to end the tyranny the Amigga have over this galaxy," Sax hisses. "Starting with the Chorus."

"Then they were right," the mirrored Oratus hisses a laugh. "I've received more briefings than you can imagine, Sax. Removed all manner of traitors to the Chorus. Incompetent officials to high level Vincere officers. Even other

Amigga deemed a risk. But never, never have I encountered any with such lofty ambitions."

That isn't what Sax expects to hear. He's thinking the mirrored Oratus has a mask that's recording everything, and as soon as it gets the information it needs, the Oratus will just signal to the guards who'll burn Sax down in a blaze of miner fire. This is all just a show.

So why is the mirrored Oratus bothering to have a real conversation?

"I've risked my life many times for much less," Sax picks a path. "About time I took a chance for something greater."

The common center that Anjo directs us to is about the only bustling part of town that I can see. It's set against what must be the town square; a circle of packed earth with a large stalagmite rising up from the middle. Like our Tiers in the jungle, the stalagmite is covered in drawings and various dyes.

One stands out—a black and white version of a Fassoth, its many legs chasing after what looks like a pack of Lunare. Even the simple drawing sends a chill and I look away, over towards the warm fires glowing in the common house windows.

"Been a long time since we've seen human civilization," Viera says to me.

"I thought you said it's only been a season?"

"Feels a lot longer than that."

I nod. Even though these cavern towns are far different than the Solare and Charre villages, there's a lot about them that's familiar; the low hum of human voices rather than the hissing and clattering of the other species I've been around, the simple smells of cooking food rather than the stale purity of nutrient goop, and the ramshackle dirtiness, the imperfections of everything around us.

Humanity, I realize, is not rote perfection. It's not refined and coated with the sheen of eternal tweaking. We're rough, but strong. Stupid at times, but we try.

"It's good to be back," I finally say as we head towards the common house's doors.

Rather than the wooden portals of Damantum or the hanging cloth shields of Solare villages, these doors look like sheets of light stone, set on hinges along the sides. The opening itself is square, and on the borders, Lunare script reads that any looking for food, for company, will find it here.

"Will we be welcome inside?" T'Oli asks us.

"No idea," Viera replies. "But I think you can handle yourselves."

"I have little experience in human combat." T'Oli squirms up and onto Vee's shoulders. "What should I do?"

"Let me handle it." Viera turns back to the stone door, pushes it open, and we head into a wash of warmth and laughter.

The common house floor is dominated by a set of six stone tables, each big enough to seat ten or more, laid out across the main room. In the center, a large black-rock hearth burns coal bright, with the chimney heading up and disappearing into the ceiling. Behind it sits a long counter lined with crude-sculpted stone stools, on which sit a variety of Lunare laborers.

Beverages and food—cooked meats and roasted root vegetables, from the smell—spin by us as a pair of wait staff keep the small crowd fed and drunk. The place is, at best, half full. But it feels like far more than that when everyone turns to look at us. When even the sole musician, a man playing a simple drum near the fire, stops his beat and stares.

Even Viera seems frozen by the response, as if she's never been the target of so many different inquisitive and suspicious looks before.

I have.

"Hello," I start. "We're not your enemies." Figure that's a safe way to begin. "We came from the far side, and we're looking to get back home. A man named Anjo guided us here, and said we would be welcome for the evening."

"You, maybe," shouts someone from behind the counter. "But not them!"

I find the man, and he's a grease-coated cook staring dead at Vee and T'Oli . I notice too that there aren't many surprises sitting on the faces of the guests. They're not stunned at the presence of a tall, beaten-but-scaled and clawed creature standing in their doorway. Interesting.

"They're here to help fight against the other ones." I'm not sure if the word 'Sevora' holds any meaning here, but I have to try it anyway. "They want to fight the Sevora as much as you do. As much as I do."

"And who are you?" this time it's the musician asking, the cook in back resigning to a huffy glower. "Why should we listen to what you have to say?"

"Because I lost everything to be here," I reply. "Because I have everything to gain from helping you. Because I used to be the Empress of the Charre, and now I'm nothing more than a wounded woman who knows what we have to do to survive."

Now faces are turning to each other, questions are being muttered, and I feel the spotlight turn bright on me. So I think back to when I first stood on the Vaos with Jakkan, to where the high priest taught me how to sell myself to a populace.

Especially one in fear of an advancing, hostile force.

"You have questions. You have fears." I take a deep breath. Father said cadence was everything. "You have every right not to listen, not to trust us. But if you hear what we have to say, then maybe you'll understand. Maybe you will see that we mean to help, not hurt."

The words pour on from there. I stand past the entrance and tell stories, talk about *Cobalt*, the Oratus and the Sevora. Every time I see the audience starting to drift away as unfamiliar terms and strange ideas roll over them, I slide back to direct appeals. To the idea that humanity must stand together against massive threats. Against things that don't care if we, as a species, live or die.

When my throat is parched and I feel I can't speak anymore, it's the musician that brings me an earthen mug full of bitter stuff. I nearly spit it out after the first sip, but force it down. Beer, I think, and recall Malo's warning about the Charre peppers; you must be able to eat and drink what they do, if you want their help. If you want to be seen as one of them.

At the end of it, I don't know if I've convinced anyone, but the looks are more curious than cautionary now. One of the waiters, a young boy who seems enthralled with Vee, directs us to an empty table, and that's where we sit, at last. If not entirely accepted, at least we're not being attacked.

"Nice work," Viera says as we sit down. "I thought I'd have to shoot at least three of them before they'd leave us alone."

"This place doesn't seem so strange," T'Oli remarks as we sit down. "Though it has been a long time since I've enjoyed this sort of beverage."

"What sort of beverage?" I ask the Ooblot, who coils up on a stool and hardens its lower half so that its eyestalks and a small puddle spill onto the table itself.

"The one you're holding. If I might have a sip?"

I glance at the mug. Look at T'Oli's puddle. "How?"

"Like anything else," T'Oli patters. "Pour it on me."

I lift the mug, tilt it a little bit so that the beer runs up to the lip, and then let some pour over. I'm expecting it to hit the Ooblot and scatter all over the place, but instead the beer simply dissolves into T'Oli's skin, leaving a faint amber spot against the white.

"Not so bad," T'Oli says. "Though it could use cleaner water. More pure ingredients."

"You're drinking beer in a cave," Viera says. "What more do you want?"

The way T'Oli's eye stalks turn to regard Viera with earnest clarity, I know the Ooblot's about to answer the Lunare's question literally. I try to stop that disaster before it starts.

"Vee, what do you think?" I ask.

The Oratus hasn't stopped moving his head since we came in here. He's watching for something, and I'm curious about what.

"There's fear here," Vee hisses. "It's a strong smell." Vee turns back to me, sets his four claws on the table. "We should not stay."

"What, why?" Viera asks. "After Kaishi gave that speech? They're not going to hurt us."

"Look at them," Vee hisses back. "They are desperate. I do not know the density of your human settlements, but this seems like a large concentration for one this small?"

"Is it?" I ask, taking another stock. Sure, there are about twenty people in here, and maybe a dozen houses in the entire village. That number doesn't seem too ordinary.

"He's right," Viera says, and her voice has a different edge to it now. "Look at them. They're not locals."

I can't tell. Most are wearing the same sorts of loose clothes, boots. Some have bandannas on, others have pistols holstered around their hips. All of them are dirty—and so are we. There's not an obvious look I can pick out.

"I don't see it?" I finally say.

Viera's about to speak when the boy comes by again, asks if we would like anything to drink. Viera orders a round, and when I'm about to ask how we're going to pay for that, she pulls a small pouch of stones from her pocket.

"Diego didn't need this anymore," Viera says at my look, and now that the boy's gone, she nods towards the cook. "See how he's acting? How the rest of his staff are keeping eyes on everyone?"

I shrug. "Yes? So?"

"It means they don't know these people well," Vee hisses. "A small place like this, every person should be known. This should be comfortable. Instead, everyone is on edge."

"Why would they be?" T'Oli says after the boy deposits a set of four mugs in front of us. "They have food, shelter, and drinks?"

I'm thinking here. What would make a Charre town this worried? What would disrupt a normal village of Solare?

The answer comes walking over after we get our drinks, a gruff woman flanked by seven men.

"Name's Celice," the woman says and I'm struck by how gravelly, how deep her voice goes. "You're from the wrong side of the mountains?"

I feel Viera move her right hand to her pistol, and I tighten my grip on the beer mug. It's full, but the mug itself is hard. If I had to throw it, the mug could probably do some damage. But for now, I try not to start a fight.

Especially as I'm still in a world of hurt, and none of us are feeling ready to swap fists with this crew.

"Further than that," I reply. "We came over there from space, from beyond the sky."

Celice doesn't look fazed by that at all. "That's what they said too. You know what's happening back the other way?"

"We've guessed."

Vee, for his part, hasn't moved except to help T'Oli pour more beer on itself. The Oratus seems unconcerned by Celice and her crew. Which, if I was a scaly death-beast, I probably wouldn't be too worried either.

"It's worse than whatever you're thinking," Celice leans over, plants her hands palm down on the table. "Wouldn't be surprised if Avril's lost the first tunnels by now, even with all your Charre and Solare friends trying to help."

"We're trying to get there. What we know could help them."

"If you had thousands more with you, like that one, maybe," Celice nods at Vee. "Otherwise, all you're doing is marching to suicide."

"What's your point?" Viera interjects. "You didn't come over here to warn us away."

"No," Celice replies. "I didn't. We left the front on orders. Keep an open chain of Lunare control through the mountains, so that we could retreat all the way out if we have to. Which is where you all come in."

"What do you mean?"

"We want to go back," Celice says. "The fighting's

there. The enemy's there. We're tried of sitting around this place, waiting. You're going to be our reason. Our way home."

I blink. That's it? They want to escort us?

"Sure?" I say. "That's fine."

Celice flicks her eyes to Viera, who shrugs. "Whatever Kaishi says."

Celice nods, stands up from the table. "Then we're going tomorrow. Better see the town's doctor, too. You're all looking a little beat."

She's not wrong. After T'Oli and Viera finish their drinks—I let mine languish—the four of us arrange for a room at the common house and head towards the only sort-of clinic this town has, which amounts to a house with an older couple inside.

What they have, though, are supplies. Wraps and poultices for our cuts, which they wash out and bandage. Ointments for our blistered feet and soaps for our dirty hair. Sandy paste for our teeth to keep them from falling out. Afterwards, we head to the bath house and its spring, thankfully Fassoth-free.

When I finally fall asleep that night, on a hay bed next to Viera, with T'Oli puddled on the floor and Vee curled up on our mats in the corner, it's the first real rest I've had in a very, very long time.

Celice and three of her guards meet us in the morning. She leaves the rest of her force behind as a garrison, and we spend the next few days venturing through tunnels far better lit, signed and marked than before. They're wide enough for cart trains, for all of us to walk abreast, and even, occasionally, have carved art and paintings on the sides.

I do find myself wishing for the sky, for Ignos to shine, but the closest we get to that are the periodic ventilation shafts, through which, if I listen carefully, I can hear the whistling wind far above.

Celice gives a dire account of the war as we move. The Sevora appeared not long ago in the skies overhead, seeming first like black smudges high above. Then came shuttles packed with creatures nobody had ever seen before.

Here, Celice stops for a second to thank me.

"Why?" I ask. "I wasn't even here."

"Because you showed us what was coming," Celice replies. "You brought the first ones, like him, here."

I'd forgotten that Sax and Bas visited the Lunare hunting for me. They'd exposed Earth to the new threats from space.

"We weren't entirely unprepared," Celice continues. "Avril had contingencies. We were already overtaking the jungle, about to assault the Charre themselves—"

"Wait," I say as we walk beneath a glittering, magenta-glowing ceiling. "You were attacking the Charre?"

"Of course," Celice says, as if such a move is obvious. "You were gone. Their leading general, gone. They were in disarray. What better time?"

I want to fire off some insults, spit a bit of fire at the cruelty of taking advantage of people, but then I remember the Sevora in my own head. Ignos, constantly telling me when to push others, to use them and twist their goals to suit my own ends. I'd done that, which is why I became Empress in the first place.

"So the Sevora come and you what, run?" I finally say.

"We offered them shelter," Celice says. "Damantum's too wide open, especially for an attack from above. The

Charre aren't stupid—they listen to their priests and come rushing in, along with the Solare tribes we've taken."

"So charitable," Viera says. "That's not like Avril."

"When you're facing annihilation," Celice replies. "Every body counts. Those that could wield weapons got them, others we sent deep into the tunnels to secure routes like this one. You might not like Avril, Viera, but she wants humanity to survive as much as you do.

"And it's a good thing she did, because we didn't hold long on the outside. Nothing we can do about their... fliers. The ones that come out of the sky and send burning death into us. We've been in the mountains ever since, waiting and holding and hoping for a miracle."

Celice's expression as she says this shows she doesn't think we're it.

I can't disagree with her. A wounded Oratus, an Ooblot, and a couple of battered humans aren't going to swing the tide of this fight. At least, not without some help.

S ax charges as he finishes the words. His talons slash the metal floor and he dives at the mirrored Oratus, who doesn't see it coming.

At least, that's what Sax thinks for the fraction of a second before the mirrored Oratus shifts ever so slightly, his blurry, flashing scales throwing Sax off his line, making Sax's claws slide off scales rather than cut deep. The mirrored Oratus takes advantage as Sax flies by, gouging the Sax with his foreclaws.

The Oratus body is all weapon, though, and Sax whips his tail as he falls, gets it underneath the enemy's talons and sweeps the creature from his feet. Sax's momentum carries him into the far wall, and the gray Oratus grips, spins, and turns with his midclaws before leaping back at his downed target. Sax lands on the mirrored Oratus, claws raking, mouth biting, and receiving equal treatment in turn. Slashing, stinging pain cuts through Sax, he feels the muscles in his arms and vents tear but Sax doesn't care—he's in the bloodlust now. Everything is red and raw energy. Sax going to die, so he's going to give everything he has for this.

Which is what?

For the first time in his life, a thought stops Sax, and the mirrored Oratus takes advantage, pushes his talons beneath Sax and kicks him off. Sax flies from the middle floor and rolls into the left wall. He feels his energy draining away, his blood pooling on the floor and all he can think of is that he's given himself for nothing. If he dies here, his mission ends. Losing it all in a fight with a creature that, even if he wins, would cause the Flaum to burn Sax down where he stands.

Sax can't die for nothing anymore. He has a cause.

"Surprising, but stupid," the mirrored Oratus hisses, and there's a slurping sound in his voice now. Sax must have clawed the Oratus deep in the creature's vocal cords. "You didn't need to hurt yourself that way. Now I'll have to fix you up for them to kill you all over again."

Sax stares at the mirrored Oratus, feels the cold metal floor against his head. He wants to talk back, but the act of opening his mouth feels like lifting a ship off the ground. Instead, Sax thinks about Bas. What she's doing, where she is. If she's even still alive.

The mirrored Oratus blurs over to Sax, glares down at him.. "For the last time, tell me your plan. Why are you here?"

"I told you," Sax manages to croak. "The Chorus must be stopped."

The mirrored Oratus takes his right talon, presses Sax's throat, and he can feel the claws pushing in. "That's not enough."

"That's all you're going to get."

The mirrored Oratus pushes further with his talon, but Sax doesn't care. What's more pain to what he's already endured?

"I thought you were taking him prisoner," this hiss

comes from someone strong and new. Rav. "What do you think murdering an Oratus on my ship will do for morale? They need to listen to me, not think I might be a traitor."

"I don't care about your sensitivities," the mirrored Oratus hisses back. "This creature *is* a traitor. You should be proud that you facilitated in his capture."

"Then take him away," Rav replies. "I won't have him killed on my ship."

The mirrored Oratus hesitates, then lifts his talon off of Sax's neck. "Fine. Help me drag him to mine."

Sax can't see her, but he feels Rav look at him. "I don't think your prisoner's going to live long enough for a leap. We'll patch him up, first."

The mirrored Oratus snorts, but doesn't refuse.

Rav orders a pair of Flaum to help Sax to his feet. Three more keep their miners trained on him, even though Sax isn't going anywhere, and they all know it. Sax knows it too; he's focusing on breathing, and standing and on not giving the mirrored Oratus any more satisfaction. They take Sax along through the hallways, away from the engines and Sax's last idea. The medical bay's ruined, so instead they sling Sax into an empty crew cabin, where a Flaum patches Sax's wounds with handful of bandages and injects him with just enough Stim to keep Sax alive.

All the while, the mirrored Oratus watches over Sax. All the while, the mirrored Oratus talks. Tells Sax all about the various horrible treatments he'll be receiving at the hands of the Chorus. At the end of it, when he's concluded any number of options for how Sax may meet his gruesome end, and when Sax has had himself pieced back together, the mirrored Oratus leans in real close.

"I'm not telling you this to scare you," mirrored Oratus

hisses. "I'm telling you this because you deserve to know the ways in which you will end."

From there, with Sax barely awake, they take him to the docking bay, floating on the transport. A pair of Chorus pilots, red-furred Flaum wearing special armor and patches bearing a singles white spire jutting through black space, start launch procedures. Sax is locked into a couch at the back end. The mirrored Oratus sits across from him, giving Sax an endless dead-eyed look.

At least until the transport fails to start. At least until its microjets don't fire.

Sax manages a weak, toothy grin.

The mirrored Oratus drips contempt at Sax and his smile. Because of the refracting scales, Sax only gets the outline of the sneer, which deepens into a dead-lipped frown as the transport doesn't lift.

"What's going on?" The mirrored Oratus throws his voice towards the two Flaum in the cockpit, who are busy squeaking at one another..

"The power's cut," the right Flaum replies. "All readings are negative. I'm not getting anything from the jets."

"Looks like you'll be staying here a while longer," Sax says. "Good thing you made friends with everyone on this frigate."

"They're not my friends. They're servants, like me. All of us, even you, must bend to the will of the Chorus."

"Is that what you say to yourself?" Sax says. "All of this is the will of a bunch of blobs in a tower? You could tear any of them apart in a minute. Why take their orders?"

The mirrored Oratus exhales a heavy sigh from his vents, stands, scales shifting to match the yellow light in the shuttle's interior. "Because I believe in something called loyalty. In paying back my creators for giving me life."

"That was their choice," Sax says. "You should make your own."

The mirrored Oratus doesn't reply, instead stepping around to the panel controlling the boarding ramp. With a claw, the mirrored Oratus opens the transport's door and, after giving the ramp a moment's head start, descends, leaving Sax onboard and captive.

But only for a moment.

The two Flaum continue their rapid-fire chittering, with one on the left eventually jumping up from the pilot's chair and heading back towards Sax. The Flaum makes it near him, keeping well back from Sax's claws as it heads to the door, when there's a bright flash and the red-furred creature drops to the floor.

Sax hisses in surprise, seeing the other Flaum holding a pocket miner that it's pulled from somewhere. That Flaum dashes through the shuttle quick and slaps the boarding door's panel, sucking up the ramp and slamming the door. A moment later, after unlatching Sax from the net, the red-furred Flaum steps back behind its former colleague, miner aiming Sax's way, though the twitching hands show cautious fear more than malice.

"What?" Sax manages to ask.

"The Chorus has fewer friends than you think," the Flaum says. "The Resistance has more allies than you know."

"And the jets?"

"He'll find them working," the Flaum glances towards the door. "We should leave."

"No," Sax says. "I have a friend on the ship. I'm not leaving him. And I have an idea; open a channel to Rav."

Sax felt a shift in the last conversation he had with the frigate's commander, and he's going to bet everything that another push could sway her over to his side. With the frigate, Rav would be able to force a way for Sax to get down to Solis, to find Bas.

The Flaum gives Sax a wide-eyed side-glance, a look Sax recognizes well from his own experience. It's wondering if he's crazy, if it made a terrible mistake in choosing to help him over just following orders. But Sax is still an Oratus, and his damaged body is plenty able to handle the furball, so quick enough the Flaum decides a chance of life is better than a quick, certain death. They retreat to the cockpit and the Flaum opens up a channel.

"Why haven't you left?" Ravs voice scratches through. "You're clear. The bay is open."

"There's been a change in plan," Sax says.

Dead silence on the other side. Silence that's eventually broken by the hard thump of something crashing against the outside of the transport. The scrabble of claws digging into the hull.

"He's figured it out," the Flaum says, his voice dulling into the tone of the doomed. "This ship's not meant for combat—he'll tear his way in before long."

"What are you doing?" Rav's voice comes back. "What happened to the Oratus?"

"He's clawing his way into his own ship," Sax replies. "I'd be grateful if you stopped him." Then, to the Flaum pilot. "Start the engines."

"Why?"

"Do it," Sax orders. "Rav?"

Rav cuts a dire, lost laugh. "You want me to stop him? How?"

"Tell your Flaum he's the true traitor. That their race as well as ours depends on stopping this Oratus."

There's a ripping shriek from outside, and Sax turns to

see bright light from the docking bay filtering in through a long gash. In a second, the mirrored Oratus will rend a hole big enough for itself and Sax is in no condition to fight. A quick scan of the shuttle shows no miners here either, save the small one clutched tight in the Flaum pilot's hands. Such a small weapon, unless perfectly shot, wouldn't do anything more than annoy the mirrored Oratus.

Sax teeth and claws will have to do.

"Last chance, Rav. Last chance to choose your own species." Sax is kind of proud of that, thinks Bas would be proud of him too. Here he is, talking like someone who knows something outside of the ways of war.

Or maybe Bas has rubbed off on him over all this time.

Sax sees a pair of claws, their edges visible as black lines against the silver gray skin of the shuttle's inside. They close across the gash and tear, peeling the hull back like it's simple paper. Its entrance created, the mirrored Oratus pulls itself inside.

"Seems like we've lost power?" The Oratus growls at the Flaum pilot, sparing barely a look at its downed companion on the shuttle floor. "It seems like Sax is not the only traitor the Chorus is dealing with."

Sax spreads his patched and bandaged claws out wide. "Maybe I am a traitor to the Chorus, but at least I'm fighting for something."

"But you'll die for nothing," the mirrored Oratus says, stomping towards Sax.

Sax doesn't feel like dying quite yet though, so as the mirrored Oratus stalks closer, Sax, using his tail, smacks the flight stick behind him, sending the transport lurching forward, its microjets very much alive.

The mirrored Oratus realizes what's about to happen, realizes it has no time to get to cover, and neither does Sax, nor the Flaum. The transport rams into the back of the docking bay, the impact throwing Sax backwards, into the crumpling windshield of the transports front as glass bursts around him. The mirrored Oratus completes the crash a split second later, barging into and over Sax as they fall, with the ship, to the bay floor.

The impact sends Sax's head for a loop, the universe splitting and blacking out even as the shrieks of rending metal and sparking snaps from snapping wires fill every available audio space Sax has. He lands on wreckage, the shuttle's ceiling crunching close but not collapsing, with the smell of leaking energy ozoning the air. Smoke pours from batteries rent apart too close to food stores and the flammable fabrics coating the couches in the transport's back half.

Consciousness doesn't flee Sax entirely, though. Instinct survives, and pushes Sax up. He's hurting, his left foreclaw and his tail, so recently burned is again bearing the hallmarks of too hot, too close flame.

Sax staggers away from the wreck through the same hole his enemy's claws created, but doesn't it make it more than a few steps before the haggard hiss he's waiting for emerges.

The mirrored Oratus pushes his way free, tilting over and crashing through the right wall shielding the shuttle's cockpit. The slab cracks down on rubble, casting up a shower of smoke and dust as it hits, which frames the Oratus in the evidence of his own escape. The creature's mirrored scales no longer the glisten, their reflective array now a battered black, coated in dirt and oil and grease. Chemicals drip off of its tail, while long scars across its chest show it landed hard on the exposed batteries powering the transport's microjets.

It's a dark, broken thing now. It stumbles towards Sax, its roiling green eyes the only bright thing it has left.

There was a moment, a time when the mirrored Oratus would have taken Sax back to the Chorus. Delivered Sax to its Amigga overlords: Sax would be readied for trial, for sentencing and eventual damnation. But this one is past the point of reason now. There's only vengeance, eyes full of only anger and rage. Things Sax knows. Things he understands.

The mirrored Oratus is beyond conversation and it leaps towards Sax, flying through the air with too much strength. There's no way the creature could be that hurt and able to fly that high, until Sax realizes the Oratus must have been wearing a mask. One no doubt damaged by Sax's claws, one that gave its last protection in the crash. Doing enough to keep its wearer alive and deadly.

Sax can't fight that, so he doesn't.

Instead, he goes the other way. Dashes beneath the mirrored Oratus' charge and blitzes back towards the wrecked transport. Claws-on-metal tells Sax the Oratus has landed, but he's focusing on one thing sticking out of that inferno; a long burnt-metal shard that, moments ago, stood as the top bar holding the cockpit's windshield. The crash sheared it off, but half of the bar juts out of the fire like a spear.

Sax gets the first burn on his foreclaws as he scrambles to the wreck when he feels a hard yank on his tail. A light stab as claws break through his scales, and then Sax is getting whipped around, flung through the air. He's too heavy to fly far, and Sax hits the floor hard and rolls on wounded shoulders. He manages to stop himself and looks back towards the approaching mirrored Oratus, that scarred black form looking even more horrible in the bright bay lights.

"You'll never win," Sax hisses as the Oratus comes closer. "You'll kill me, it's the Amigga who get the victory. You're hurting your own kind."

"You think I care." The Oratus goes for a kick at Sax's face, but gives it away with a rippling tense of its strong legs.

Sax snakes out his foreclaws, catches the talon—at the cost of another gash on his left foreclaw, but at this point there's too many to count—and Sax yanks the Oratus forward. Here the sharp grip of claws embedded into metal wind up hurting the mirrored Oratus, because his back talon doesn't give and let Sax trip the creature. Instead, he holds steady while Sax yanks the Oratus' leg forward. The bone pops above the constant crackle of the burning freighter, and the mirrored Oratus roars as Sax uses the pulled leg as leverage to swing himself around and tail-whip the mirrored Oratus across the face.

The impact and the sharp jerk that follows lets the mirrored Oratus free itself, and Sax is plenty gratified to see the enemy fall into a deep limp. An emotion that quickly dies when the Oratus twists and sends its own tail crashing into Sax's head. The impact kaleidoscopes the bay and sends Sax skidding across the floor until he comes to rest against a set of empty fuel containers. They're bulky cylinders, old and probably permanent fixtures of this frigate until Rav manages to pull an assignment on somewhere inhabited.

Right now, though, they're what Sax needs to pull himself to his talons. To give the mirrored Oratus one last level stare. If he's going out here, in this ruin of a bay, bleeding out from a dozen deep cuts, he's going to do it standing up.

"You do our race proud," the mirrored Oratus hisses as it limps towards him.

"And you betray yours." Sax keeps his tail wrapped around the spent fuel container—his legs are mostly numb and Sax is sure he'd collapse without it.

"We all choose our masters," the mirrored Oratus replies.

He gets close to Sax, and Sax can't help but try, with his fore- and midclaws to get in a rake, but the mirrored Oratus catches all of them. Twists and snaps each of Sax's wrists in turn, leaving his claws broken and limp. The pain's immense, but Sax lets it all flow into the giant black hole that's formed in his mind; a calm, endless void that grows as Sax's hold on life gets more and more tenuous.

"I deny yours," Sax manages to hiss.

The mirrored Oratus gets closer. Then, with a sudden jerk, all four claws knife deep into Sax's vents. The mirrored Oratus leers close as it strikes, the hot air from its own vents blowing against Sax. Who responds in the only way he can.

He bites.

A quick, darting snap that gets Sax's teeth around the throat of the mirrored Oratus. Sax rends the scales, stabs beneath and tastes every part of the burnt grease and the warmer, softer stuff beneath. Every ounce of strength Sax has goes into his jaws then, digging harder and further.

Sax doesn't think he'll live, but neither will this thing.

The mirrored Oratus breaks into a frenzy, tearing and stabbing with its claws. Each cut takes away more of Sax. His vision goes spotty and dark, he loses the feeling in his legs, his tail. Keeps his whole energy in his jaws.

Tighter, harder.

For as long as he can.

Celice doesn't mince time or words. She moves with an angry purpose that fuels the rest of us. Up till now, I saw the Sevora and their invasion as an abstract, a menace we were going to confront eventually, but Celice embodies its effects; she wants to fight, to win, to save her home.

I do too.

After the first day's journey, which ends in another village, bigger than the last, we see the wrong signs. This one's common house is more crowded, and not only with soldiers. Carts litter the streets, and Lunare with them, curled up in makeshift tents and blankets. Others set off back the way we came, muttering talk of getting away, saving themselves.

"This isn't going well," Viera says to me as we continue the next morning.

"I thought we might stand a chance," I reply. "I hoped that if the Sevora couldn't take us as hosts, that they would leave us alone."

"You weren't empress long enough to learn empires kill what they're afraid of."

"I am still the Empress, Viera. I've just lost my empire."

"You think we can take it back?" Viera throws the question out with zero hint of sarcasm, and with plenty of exhaustion.

"You don't believe we'll win, do you?" I reply. "You think this is it for humanity?"

Viera pats the pistols on her belt. "I've got a pair of these. That's it, Kaishi. Avril might have a few tricks too, but nothing much better. The Sevora have ships that come from the sky and burn us away before we even see them. How do you win that fight?"

It's a problem I've been pondering as we've stalked through the caves. One I've been talking to T'Oli, to Vee about too. There's one solution we all keep coming to. One answer.

"We need help." I nod at Celice and her men, parting another refugee train to let us through. "They're going to fight to the end, and they don't deserve to do it alone."

"Kaishi, we're not the help they need."

"No. Remember Sax? Bas? They hate the Sevora. They said there's a whole army of them. Vee says the same thing."

"So you want to call in different monsters to fight the ones already here?"

"It's either that, or we die," I say.

She doesn't have a reply to that, and we keep on moving. The tunnels blend together, and my heart aches at not seeing the sky for so long. The stream of fleeing people thickens until it's a torrent. They squirm back from Vee and T'Oli, and a few bother throwing insults their way, though a sliver of teeth from the Oratus shuts them up quick.

At night, the four of us toss strategies around. Ways we could get in contact with the Vincere, the force Vee says might be able to help us. T'Oli says sending the message is simple, provided we get a shuttle. Which, of course, is the hard part.

Until we get to the Lunare capitol, Marilo, in its vastness, and everything changes.

You can read a lot in a person's expression, but I get a lot more from the way the refugees are running now, the way they're pulling along their children with little else strapped to their backs. The carts are mostly gone—the ones that do rumble through, pulled by tamed Fassoth, are full of dead-eyed people—and rather than the low murmurs of the lost, the caverns ring with the shouts of the panicked, the afraid.

Celice starts cursing to herself as we get closer to the opening into the Marilo's huge underground lake.

The view from the tunnel lip provides all the reason Celice needs for her epithets. All of the dark-forged glory of the Lunare is laid bare before us, and half of it, or more, is engulfed in bright-burning flames. Streaks of hot red laser pour out of several craft, hovering above the city near the cavern ceiling, but even that doesn't hold my attention for long.

Because I can see the sky. And it's clear blue.

Somehow, in some terrible way, a giant hole has been carved in the mountain under which the Lunare settled. It's uneven, with slicing cuts in the rock, and some of the edges still glow a molten orange.

Down through this opening pour more shuttles, disgorging what look, from this far distance, like Flaum. The troops disappear down into the city, vanishing into the smoke or behind buildings.

"How do they land?" Celice manages to say as we watch another dozen dive into her home.

"Oh, they have magnetic boots," T'Oli says. "They'll drop a landing pad or two, and then it's like jumping into a soft bed. They'll bounce off and be ready to go. Quiet efficient, really."

"Quiet, T'Oli," I say. "Celice, where's the army? I thought you said Avril had assembled a massive force?"

"They came behind," Viera points at the hole. "I bet they didn't want to deal with pushing through Avril's army, so they created their own back door."

I'm about to ask another question—namely, what now—when Vee flashes past us. The Oratus makes his own path through the fleeing populace simply by showing up; nobody wants to stay in his way.

"What are you doing?" I call after him.

"Hunting!" is the hiss I get in reply, and then he's gone.

"Can't keep an Oratus from his purpose," T'Oli says. "Literally, you can't. It's programmed into their DNA."

"I don't know what that means, but we have to help him," Celice says, then looks at me. "You said you're the Charre Empress? Plenty of these people are yours too. I hope you find a way to save them."

Then Celice and her men, pulling at their pistols, push forward after Vee.

"Going into that's only going to get us killed," Viera says.

"So will staying here, just more slowly." I look at the hole again.

The shuttles seem to be coming in, going low enough to

drop their complement of Flaum, and then zooming back up and out of the hole.

"If we get on top of that building there," I say, pointing at what looks like a bricked tower looming over the lake. "We might be able to get on one of those shuttles."

"On? How?" Viera says. "You want to jump on them?"

"I have an idea," I glance down at T'Oli. "You ready?"

"Always, Kaishi. An Ooblot never lacks for energy."

We run towards the city too, then. Or rather, walk fast. My ribs still hurt plenty if I try anything faster than a jog, but the crush of people heading against us means it's slow going anyway.

I just hope we make it in time.

A red flash bursts the ground in front of me as I skid to a stop, my heels sliding on the cobblestoned street leading into the city. That bolt is followed by others, tracing a line across the path and stitching up the side of the building to my right. At first the shots only melt stone, but then one strikes something more and the inside breaks open in fire and black smoke.

"C'mon, Kaishi, out of the open," Viera says, pulling me to the side, underneath the awning of what looks to be a bakery.

"We have to get there." I point out ahead, not quite to the center of the city, but to the tall, arched building that's high enough. "That's not going to happen by hiding."

"There's a middle ground between getting yourself vaporized and getting where you need to go," Viera replies.

We edge forward to the last bit of the faded green awning. There are three more buildings—the middle one mostly a melted ruin—before we hit the next cross street. Smoke burns up and out, clouding the area and making my lungs itch, but I take a deep breath anyway and make a break for it.

"Go!" I say, as if I have a clue when the Flaum are going to shoot next. "Use the smoke as cover!"

Viera and I hug the walls, moving behind the belching fountains of black smoke. T'Oli's wrapped himself around me, providing armor and some small support to my ribs. Every time I pass beneath a burning window, heat washes over my hair and ash blows into my face, but I keep going. Stopping means death.

In front of us, a man dives out of another building, holding what looks like books in his arms. He takes a wild look at us, starts to move in our direction, and then vanishes in another flash of red. Nothing's left of him save a few burning pages floating to the ground.

I can't stop though. Have to keep moving. Horror at one death means I'll fail at stopping thousands more.

We hit the cross street as a pair of Flaum round the corner in front of us, one covering down the street, one turning our way. Wearing Nasiya's Sevora badge on their armor, their brown-black fur puffs out. They're moving with miners raised, but with an easy pace. It's a slaughter, and they know it.

So Viera gets the first shot off. Takes the lead Flaum between the eyes, sending its partner swiveling towards us.

Too slow.

I'm already running, and I push off with my right foot to the left, then rebound off the building wall as the Flaum tries to track me. I tackle the smaller creature and drive it to the ground as T'Oli flows up my right hand, shifts into a sharp point that lets me finish the job.

By the time I stand up, Viera's already holding the first

Flaum's miner, playing with its triggers. She nods to the other one.

"Let's make the fight a little more fair," she says.

I can only agree.

We slip through more broken alleys, past burning markets and crumbling buildings. There aren't, thankfully, many bodies—Avril must have started evacuating the city before the raid began. The Sevora, though, don't seem to care; the Flaum expend plenty of energy zapping anything and everything.

The Sevora want to destroy us. Not conquer, not take over, but obliterate.

So when we reach the tall building, I'm coated in soot, my lungs burn from breathing in so much smoke, but I've still got the Flaum miner in my hands, and it's still ready to fire. Viera's right at my back, and I wonder if my breathing sounds as bad as hers. Or maybe that's just the continuing ripple of explosions, scattered cries, and the whine of shuttle engines.

Our target rises up in front of us, and I think it must be some sort of government building, or a temple like the Vaos, only tall and square until sharpening to a flat spire at the top. The front of it—the parts not blackened by laser-fire, anyway—is a mesh of intercut designs. Gemstones are interspersed in the pattern, coming together at the nexus of various grooves.

"I'd call it beautiful if this was any other time," I say to Viera as we crouch in the shadow of a half-shattered wall.

"The Siamante," Viera says. "Where Lunare commerce begins and ends."

"You confine your trade to one building?"

"The major deals." Viera nods at the building. "Any party wanting to get themselves established here has to make their case in this building, in front of the government and other big Lunare players."

"They used to, anyway," I reply.

"I was in there once," Viera whispers. "For a Solare tribe that wanted to supply jade."

We shouldn't be talking about this now. We should be rushing across the road, into the Siamante and finding our way up, a way to take one of these shuttles and stop this madness. And yet, right here in this ruined city, I want to hear more.

"Did they?" I ask. "Did we help the Lunare?"

"Yes," Viera says. "We approved the deal. Gave that tribe plenty of black-glass for their weapons and their ceremonies. Not that it helped them—the Charre wiped them out not too long after."

"We're always the targets." I stand. "Come on. Let's go."

I glance up, look for a shuttle and see none. There's no Flaum on this street—they're pushing out from the city center now, establishing their front. Then, I have no doubt, all of these buildings will burn.

But the Sevora push means we can run over the cobblestones to the wide stone doors, pull on the rings bolted to the tall gray portal and open our way in. Once Viera slips through I pull the door shut behind us, sealing us into the Siamante.

The sounds rumble through the wide room, a space with rows of padded benches on either side of a central rectangle dominated by a pair of desks. At the far end, set against the back wall, is a single throne-like chair with a thick shelf in front of it. I can picture a hundred squabbling Lunare in here, shouting at each other over the price of sapphires or who has the right to mine a particular mountain.

What I don't have to picture are the three Flaum above, wandering through one of the overlooks. They're hunting, at least going by their searching eyes, by the occasional human shouts shortly followed by a bright red blast.

At the sound of the shutting door, those Flaum turn and see their new prey.

"Split!" Viera yells and I jump towards the right side.

A pair of walls on either side of the door hold stairwells leading up, and Viera goes to the one opposite me. The steps are short, marbled stone scuffed with long years of boots to which mine add their prints. Above me, the grooved patterns—absent any gems—continue their meanders on the ceiling.

"Did you mean to leave Viera with the Flaum?" T'Oli asks me as I jaunt up the stairs.

"Leave her?" I huff. "This is strategy."

"A rather convenient one."

I get to the second floor and ignore the continuing steps, choosing to crouch and make my way into the long rows of hard benches. Across the way, I see dust and rock flying as Viera engages in some drawing fire with the Flaum. Their whole trio is set up around the stairwell, taking potshots at my friend.

None look my way.

I rest my arms on a bench, line up my aim, and pull the trigger. There's no kick, no sound other than the slight hiss of the miner's gas ionizing and launching forth in blazing power. Power that streaks across the chamber and hammers the wall above the Flaum. My surprise attack has the valuable result of showing them in pebbles.

"Good shot," T'Oli says as I dive away from a few fast returning shots.

"I've never fired one this large before!"

"I suggest you try again."

"Thanks," I try to think like I'm in the jungle, avoiding enemy hunters.

The key is never being where they think you are, which means either moving, or making them think you're moving.

"T'Oli, go three benches over. Make some noise." I nod to my left, my back against the bench.

The Ooblot flows off of me, careens its liquid body and a pair of stalks across the floor until it hits the distance I asked for, and then T'Oli proceeds to bang its body back and forth. The Ooblot sounds like something's slamming the stone benches with a giant mallet.

But it draws fire. Which lets me turn, put up the miner, and see that there's still a single Flaum pinning down Viera while the other two, who've spaced themselves out, take their shots at my Ooblot friend.

It feels vaguely wrong to blast someone in the back, but I shoot the Flaum anyway, and this time my shot hits the Sevora-controlled creature in its shoulder, causing it to drop its weapon and howl a high-pitched curse. One that's cut off a half-second later by my second shot, adjusted and lethal.

I duck back behind the bench, which is getting smaller as the other Flaum blows one chunk after another off of it. When I feel the piece covering my back burn away, I throw myself towards T'Oli as the Ooblot heads towards me, expanding itself to act, again, as my only defense.

Then I poke my head up, swing the miner around, and see Viera top the stairwell as the two Flaum center their weapons on me. T'Oli sweeps over my face as I duck back down, as intense heat follows the close-cutting lasers.

"T'Oli?" I say as the Ooblot flops off of me, curdles up on the ground.

"I've felt better." T'Oli's body, even hardened, is blackened in ways I haven't seen before. As if the rock-like skin has been melted together. "This, this is going to take a while."

"Stay down," I say, crawl a meter away to the next bench and try another pop-up.

Turns out I don't need to. Turns out Viera's reduced the Flaum to smoking ruin. Turns out we have a clear path to the top.

After confirming the Flaum are down, we keep climbing and pass a few huddling packs of Lunare who take one look at our miners and shrink away.

I want to tell them to run, but seeing as the Siamante still stands, it's probably better if they stay hidden here. So that's what I say; hunker down, hide, and hope for a rescue. Viera tells them to take the miners from the fallen Flaum below and, with a few flicks of her fingers, shows the humans how to fire them.

"That's how a resistance starts," Viera says to me when we're done, when we're climbing the steps alone.

"A dozen scared traders?"

"A dozen desperate ones," Viera replies.

"How would you know that?" I ask. "You've always been with the Lunare. Part of the strongest nation on Earth."

"We crush these insurrections all the time." Viera doesn't seem the least bit troubled by this. "A town decides they want to govern themselves instead of taking the latest decree. Some mine owner doesn't want to pay taxes. It's easy to start a rebellion, hard to make it last."

"Clarity's Dawn survived by hiding," T'Oli interjects. "Staying in the shadows, waiting for the right moment."

"Patience helps." Viera makes it to the top landing, where the left and right stairwells meet far above the

Siamante's front door, and nods towards the roof. "That's our way out. Won't be much cover out there, so now's the time to make a plan."

"There's not much to plan." I look at T'Oli. "You can fly one of those shuttles, right?"

"Not in this condition." T'Oli swivels its eyestalks to look at the hard-charred part of itself. "I need to be flexible enough to get all the levers, the toggles. Can't do it like this."

"Which means it's you," Viera says to me. "Think you can do it?"

"We don't have a choice," I reply. "If we don't send that message, then we're all dead anyway."

The rest of the moves are simple; go out, wait for a shuttle to dip low to drop off the next set of Flaum, and dive on it. Burn our way in and commandeer the craft.

Viera leads the way up onto the roof, and the first thing I notice as she flings open the thin slate door is how much darker, how much thicker the smoke is up here. It's as if I'm standing in the middle of a fire—Viera and I start coughing right away, and I notice T'Oli press its large eyes shut.

Even in that ashy black, it's not hard to track the shuttles. Their engines give off a light-blue glow, and the whining sound carries above the scattered screams and crackle-burst of crumbling buildings. Red flashes blink in the distance, muted bursts carrying through the dark like far off lightning. I try not to think about what each flash means, another life snuffed by the Sevora.

"There, beneath the spire." I wave and realize it's pointless—I can barely make out my own hand, and the spire's only visible because it rises over most of the smoke.

We gather at the edge, feet balancing on the stone ledge, and wait.

The Sevora shuttles look like, well, the Sevora themselves. Long ovals, with what looks like a wrap-around windshield over the front. A series of bays open alone the bottom of the shuttle, from which ladder-like tentacles extend, and the Flaum drop from those, magnetic boots flashing as they land.

We watch a pair let off a new squad of twelve and start their journey back up before we decide the next one is the target. So far, the tops of every shuttle look like sealed armor, impassible. Which means the tentacles and their open bays are the only option.

"They pull back slow enough," Viera says as the last shuttle soars by the Siamante and up into the sky. "If we time it right..."

"If we time it wrong, though, we end up smashing into the ground," I say. "There's no recovery."

"Failure means death? Seems like we've been here before."

"T'Oli?" I glance at the Ooblot, a blob on the floor next to me. "Any advice?"

"Don't miss."

"Always inspiring, T'Oli. Always."

Another shuttle's approaching whine draws away my sarcasm. Time to track our ride up and out of here. T'Oli hears the cue too, and it slithers up my back, perching near my shoulders. I notice T'Oli's not playing the armor dance anymore—apparently getting shot's robbed T'Oli of its guardian drive.

Guess I'll have to dodge this time.

The shuttle coasts by us, Flaum standing on their perches, and after they drop off onto the street, the shuttle does a slow rotation.

"Easier than that sewer tunnel on Vimelia," I say to Viera. "Easier than the trees back home."

"Just jump, Kaishi!" Viera echoes her own words, pushing off of the ledge as the shuttle picks up towards us.

I'm surprised at how little I hesitate, how quick I press off and fly into the air. How quick I fall towards that rising shuttle and its array of retracting tentacles. Barely a second passes before I hit the smooth metal bar and its cross-section pieces. My knees bang off of one, my hands reach out and snatch.

My left hand slips—the momentum's too much—and my right wrist flares as my whole weight pulls on it, as my legs dangle off, towards the diminishing city beneath us. Then I feel something cool form around my right hand. T'Oli—swirling around my arm and sealing me to the rung. The Ooblot gives me a chance to pull up my feet, get myself situated even as the tentacle pulls back into the bay.

The small door slams shut behind me, and I'm inside.

Lemon-yellow globes flash to life as all the doors shut, and I see Viera, miner already slung from its strap over her back and in her hands. She raises it towards me as I look at her.

"Viera—" I start when she fires.

The red bolt flashes over my shoulder and I hear a chittering scream, then a thump.

"Nice shot!" T'Oli warbles from my shoulder, where it's currently reforming itself. "I thought that one would definitely get you both."

I shake my left shoulder to bring my miner around as I press my back to the shuttle's outside wall. The only thing behind Viera is the sparse end of the crew bay, which consists of nothing more than hanging handholds. The Flaum don't get to ride to their assaults in comfort.

Back towards the cockpit, though, there's more than the smoking ruin of the pilot. Viera and I step over the downed

Sevora into a spectacular view over the mountain range as the shuttle clears the cavern and heads for the skies.

Browns and grays spread out beneath us, merging eventually into greens and blues as the mountains meet the jungles I know so well. Somewhere across that horizon is Damantum, or, at least, what's left of it.

There's a bank of terminals set across from the netting the Flaum occupied, with a single flight stick locked into its autopilot position.

"Where do you think it's going?" I venture to ask, moving around to get a better look at the screens.

"Nowhere we want to be," Viera replies.

T'Oli launches itself off of me as we continue our flight. The Ooblot swarms over the terminal, hunting and searching until T'Oli finds something it likes. Flapping its cream-colored skin, T'Oli flags us over to what looks like a dusty, small-screened terminal with a wide set of lettered keys.

"This is what we're looking for," T'Oli says. "It's an emergency broadcaster. It'll send out a signal that can be caught by the Amigga's Q-Net. Then they'll come find us."

"None of that makes any sense to me," I say, and confirm that Viera's equally confused.

"Light and sound can only travel so fast," T'Oli's going all teacher-voice on us now, and both Viera and I take looks out the windshield to see how close we are to a Sevora ship. None visible, yet. "If we sent a message from here towards, say, an inhabited planet, we might be long dead before they even received it. The Amigga knew there might be a need to talk across vast distances quickly, so they developed the Q-Net."

"Ok, T'Oli," Viera interrupts. "This is fascinating and all, but we're going to need to shift plans here. There's a big

Sevora boat up there now, and we're heading right towards it."

"Grab the flight stick and get away," T'Oli replies, as if this is the most obvious solution. "It's going to take them some time to realize we're actually running."

"On it." I settle into the netting, put my hands on the flight stick and judder it out from the autopilot position.

Immediately the shuttle swings as I angle it down and away from the Sevora ship and black space. Back towards the mountains, towards the jungle far below.

"The Q-Net is made up of small satellites scattered all throughout the galaxy." T'Oli drones on as I try to figure out where all the buttons are.

Some are similar to the Amigga shuttle we flew over here, but the Sevora change other things around, and it takes a few random guesses, which result in a few sudden lurches and one half-roll before I feel like I've got a good idea on how this thing flies.

"And that's how quantum computers work." T'Oli's voice fades back into my concentration as my concerns about crashing our ship die down. "Essentially, if we can get a message to the Q-Net, they'll learn about it almost instantly at the Chorus, and since leaping folds a ship across space-time, the Amigga could get a Vincere force here fast."

"Sounds great," Viera says. "Kaishi, any guns on this ship?"

"My miner's right there." I point to my weapon, lying on the ground next to me. "Why?"

"Because I think they've noticed we're not friendly anymore."

A couple of the terminals have started flashing red, but it's not till a couple of blue-lit beams shoot by overhead that I realize Viera's serious. I immediately twist the shuttle into another roll, leveling it out over the mountains, and the craft shudders and groans as I make the move. Almost as loudly as Viera, who's cursing up a storm as I send her bouncing around the inside.

"Watch that wind resistance," T'Oli says. "You're not in space. Too sharp a turn and this shuttle will snap apart like a tree in a tornado."

"Just get that message sent, will you?"

"Oh. I have to find a Q-Net satellite first. It might take a while."

"We don't have that. Go faster." I risk a look back—Viera's cursing is getting farther away—and I notice she's back by the bays again.

"Open up the doors, Kaishi!" Viera calls. "If this boat doesn't have any weapons, we'll have to improvise!"

As if I know how to do that. Thankfully, though, the Sevora aren't completely obtuse when it comes to the icons on their shuttles. I tap at the terminal that has six glowing squares, each one with a small line descending from it, and Viera's happy shout comes back my way.

"Now you just need to get us near one of them!" Viera says.

Near one? The shuttle rattles suddenly, and the terminal to my right, showing what I think was the battery's power, bursts out in a spray of sparks. I juke hard, sending our oval ship to the right and down, closer to those mountains. I keep looking up through the windshield, but I can't see anything, only blue sky and a few clouds.

"They're following you!" Viera yells. "Can you flip us?"

"I wouldn't try that, Kaishi," T'Oli says, but it's too late.

I pull back on the flight stick as T'Oli delivers the warning, and the Sevora shuttle veers back, replacing mountains and ground with horizon, sky, and then mountains again, only on the other side of the windshield.

For the first time, I see what's chasing us: a pair of three-pronged, rock-like craft whose ends glow bright red against the soft blue of home. Fighters, Ignos called them.

Well, I'll give them one.

Solis hangs against the stars. Sax watches through his own eyes, through the screen hanging against the ceiling. Thick green-purple fluid laps around him, over and across his scales. Some his natural gray, others a decidedly more metallic color. The patches cover his body, mar it like an infection. Each one a product of haphazard surgery, of the frigate's limited resources.

Then again, the Oratus are an unnatural creation. A product of engineering. This, perhaps, is the only course that makes sense.

Sax wouldn't mind so much if the patches didn't itch. Supposedly the fluid, in addition to helping his nerves, his muscles repair, is also suppressing his body's reaction to its new additions. He's to stay in the bath until the Flaum doctor—the frigate's sole medical officer—and its robots determine Sax's cells won't commit genocide against their new brothers.

He's alive.

The thought keeps coming back like his heartbeats. Sax marvels at it.

"The Chorus have asked if their transport arrived," Rav says as the door to Sax's cell shifts open.

Behind the red-gold Oratus, Sax can see tufts of Flaum fur and the points of miners on either side of the door. Rav may have kept him alive, but she's not exactly trusting him.

"What did you tell them?"

"That it never showed," Rav says, standing over Sax.

There's plenty packed into that statement—for one, it makes Rav, and her crew, traitors. They'll be attacked and eliminated by the Vincere, and with another frigate and the massive Oratus-housing ship in orbit around Solis, saying that a ship any of them could have seen didn't arrive is a huge risk.

Sax's eyes must say what he's thinking, because Rav nods towards the door and the Flaum guarding it, "I already spoke with my crew and they agreed. I've asked to meet with the captains of the other two ships here, and they're coming over before communicating with the Chorus."

"How did you manage that?" Sax is stunned, though perhaps he shouldn't be—loyalty to the Chorus doesn't seem to be all strong anymore.

"By showing them the recordings," Rav replies. "Your fight, the words you said. We all have crews, Sax. Hundreds that depend on us to make the right decisions. If we plunge blindly ahead and let the Chorus decide whether our species survive, then we deserve to die. It's time the Amigga share their control of the galaxy."

Oratus are trained to work in pairs, at most in sets of four to accomplish missions. They're not expected to share a common bond with their species, or with anyone outside their immediate chain of command. Sax has only ever cared about himself, Bas, and defeating the next enemy.

And yet, now he has a larger focus. There's a bigger goal

out there, larger than destroying the next ship or even saving Bas from her mission on Solis.

Her mission.

"I need to get down to the planet," Sax says.

"Why?"

"My pair is on a mission that shouldn't succeed. Not if there's a chance the Oratus can turn against the Chorus."

"You're not well enough," Rav hisses. "Not yet. Tell me what she's doing, and I'll have her stopped."

Does Sax trust her here? Does he have a choice?

"You won't hurt her?" Sax says.

"Why would we?" Rav reaches in with her left midclaw, into the healing broth, and grips Sax's right. "I swear, Sax, we're in this together. Every Oratus we have is valuable. Tell me where to find her, and I'll bring her back."

Sax weighs the options and decides to trust this Oratus. Rav's repaired his body, and she isn't shipping him back to the Chorus. So she must be on his side. So he speaks, tells Rav what he knows, and the frigate commander declares she'll go back through the logs of ships recently come to Solis, find the little craft Bas came in on, and track it down.

"Now, heal," Rav says. "I'll need you when the other captains come by so you can convince them to join our cause."

Rav, though, isn't quite done. "There's someone else who wants to talk to you. Someone we found wandering a corridor, that you stashed away."

Sax doesn't have to see the little Teven making his way into the room to know it's Nobaa. Rav shifts to the side to let the Teven up to the edge of the bath, and Nobaa immediately starts throwing his spindly arms from his carapace towards Sax's metal patches.

"You both know, too," Rav says. "That you owe me quite a lot for destroying most of my med bay."

"Guess you'll have to help us, then," Sax says. "Because we have no money, and no power."

Rav doesn't laugh. "You have your claws. This little one has his mind. I'll take those."

With a swish of her tail, Rav leaves the room, though the door stays open. No doubt those Flaum standing guard will tell her everything said in the room, but at this point Sax doesn't care. He's too tired, too changed to worry about keeping secrets.

"Do you like them?" Nobaa asks after he's looked at each of the metal patches on Sax's chest and legs. "They were my idea."

"Your idea?"

"They thought you were dead. With the med bay gone, they didn't have enough supplies to heal you up and repair the muscle," Nobaa sticks a small hand from a hole near the top of his carapace and waves it around the room. "Plenty of metal, though! We grabbed some scrap, sterilized it, and used the engineering equipment to put it together."

"Will it work?"

"If I'm right, you'll be even stronger than you were before!" Nobaa giggles. "We reinforced the patches, so you can take more hits. They should even stop a miner's bolt, at least the first one. You want to know the best part, though?"

Sax closes his eyes briefly. Nobaa is so exhausting.

"Your claws, Sax! They were all broken and burnt, so we replaced them."

His claws? Sax didn't notice this. Now he looks and, instead of the dull-and-dirty white they'd used to be, Sax's most prized possessions are now the glinting silver of shined, unnatural stuff. Sax can't help it, he tries to lunge for Nobaa, a snapping bite that can't get there because, well, Sax can barely move.

The Teven jerks back anyway, his eyes cowering in the carapace holes and his hands waving high in the air. "I know! I know! It's not easy to take but you have to believe me, they're stronger this way."

"Those were mine," Sax manages to hiss. "From birth."

"Yes, but these are better. They'll never break, Sax. I mean, not unless you try with a combination of—"

"Nobaa. Stop." Futility and growing resignation drain away Sax's anger to a simmer. "Leave. Now. Or I'll figure out a way to leave this bath and devour you."

"Sure, sure!" Nobaa waddles back. "Just, trust me Sax!"

All the Oratus can do is glare until the Teven is out of the room and the door is shut behind him. Sax, alone with his fabricated claws and patches of metal skin, tells himself that these are the wages of war. That these are the sacrifices required for his species to survive.

What settles in his mind most of all, though, is who took his body away from him.

The Chorus.

The next time Sax wakes up, he feels weighed down by a thousand bricks. Healing without the right creams, the right baths with true molecular repairing liquids rather than stabilizing ones is a mistake Sax refuses to make again.

Now, though, time is passing and Bas is either in danger or about to make a move that could end future Oratus forever. Sax doesn't have the luxury of waiting anymore. Rav hasn't said whether she found Bas or not.

The door to his room is shut, and while Sax could probably call for help, he's not going to. Not now. He starts first with his talons and his tail, pressing them through the thick fluid towards the tub's floor. The move comes with aches, pains, so Sax buries them beneath an avalanche of frustration and determination.

An Oratus is meant to move, not to sit.

When he strikes the bottom of the tub, Sax pushes himself back. His head strikes the wall first, hard enough to jolt, but not enough to hurt. Sax keeps pushing, pressing with his talons and swimming with his tail until, with his neck and back using the wall for support, he's standing.

The gooey stuff drips from his arms and away from his vents. His new metal claws gleam in the room's white light. Sax keeps himself from looking at his own body, at the strips of scales sliced away and replaced with bands of knitted metal.

Instead, he focuses on his right leg. The lift is slow, as though Sax is shoving up a body ten times his own size, and his muscles quickly burn like neon fire. There's a point, a singular moment where the pain intensifies and it feels like his leg might tear apart when Sax could give in, when the cool relief of failure is right there.

He falls. Presses with his tail and left leg and throws himself over the edge and out of the tub, landing on the hard floor. The impact rattles Sax's teeth, shudders up and down his arms, and Sax feels the metal plates, his skin wrapping and roiling as it moves them. None of them, however, pop. Nobaa's work holds.

The door opens a moment later, two Flaum standing there, miners at the ready. They take a long stare at Sax, before the lead one, a patchwork project of gold and brown, speaks, "We heard a roar?"

"A roar?" Sax manages to hiss, and at their look, the

Oratus realizes he just might have bellowed out when he hit the ground. "An accident."

"Do you need help?" the Flaum asks. "To get back in the tub?"

"No," Sax says. "To both."

With his foreclaws, Sax rolls onto his chest and pulls himself the rest of the way out of the tub, which eventually requires all of his limbs working together to get to a standing position, as the room's too thin for Sax to lie across on the floor.

The two Flaum stay right where they are, miners still ready.

"What are you trying to do?" the gold one asks.

"I'm going to the bridge," Sax says.

"No you're not," the Flaum replies. "Orders are to keep you here till you're healed and, uh, you're not looking good."

Sax takes a step towards the Flaum, keeping his right claws against the wall for support. His muscles are weak, his vents tired, and a faint itching pain has started up around the metal plates in his body. All of these are inconsequential. All of these are pushed away.

"I will do as I wish," Sax hisses, his mouth hanging open a fraction too long as the energy to close it doesn't come quick enough. A big splash of spit leaks from his mouth and hits the floor, the Flaum paying it rapt attention. "You can choose to die, or get out of the way."

The Flaum opt for a combo package instead, backing out of the room and placing a call to Rav.

"You're a stubborn one," Rav's voice comes over the intercom moments later, as Sax is about to reach the room's doorway.

"You already knew that." Sax keeps moving, keeps his eyes on the next step.

The corridor here isn't a main artery; it's thin, and the outer walls shift translucent as various species walk by. Black space and the stars speckling it cover the view, with the edge of Solis visible off to the right, its reflected light shedding misty rays. The two Flaum guards establish a perimeter, waving by any passing crew member and making sure they keep out of the range of Sax's claws.

Not that Sax cares. It's one step at a time, and now he shifts to his left claws and leans on the inside wall.

"What are you trying to prove?" Rav asks over the next intercom. "You'll just hurt yourself."

"I'm done resting, Rav." Sax is about to reach the next door when one of the guards darts in front of him, swipes a badge at the panel and locks it, which lets Sax use the door as a crutch a moment later. "You've brought me back, and now I'm going to find my pair."

"Even if it kills you?"

"What better thing to live for?"

Sax keeps moving, and he realizes he's attracting onlookers. Crew members and soldiers, Flaum, Whelk, Teven and more who cluster to watch this wounded, mismatched Oratus struggle step after step towards the bridge.

For Sax, every step brings with it pain, but it's as nothing to what he earns, what keeps him moving forward. Bas is on Solis, and when he gets to the bridge, he'll make Rav get her meeting, get her support, and then go planetside.

When the big bridge doors slide open, Sax nearly falls in. Only through the sheer weight of his tail is Sax able to keep himself up. He doesn't want to, hisses at himself to keep standing, but Rav moves forward to help him anyway. If before, during their conversations, Rav looked at him with mistrust, or calculated concern, here there's only open respect.

"You made it." Rav says slow.

"I had to."

"You had to?" Rav asks, her tail flicking behind Sax, and he notices most of his following horde scatter back into the ship. "You took most of my crew away from their posts. Caused all kinds of disruption, including to yourself."

"I'm ready, Rav," Sax hisses. "By the time you get your commanders here, I'll be ready. Call them."

Sax, though, isn't looking at Rav while he speaks. He's staring out over the bridge, through the giant screens at the world glowing in front of them.

"I want to go home."

As the fighters get close, I can see they have no windshield. Like flying rocks, all mottled stone and sharp angles.

"More protection that way," the Ooblot says when I ask why.

That's the end of the conversation, though, as I yank the shuttle into a flip-turn, giving Viera a chance to play tag with her miner. She spews red fire at a fighter as it rockets past, and a couple of the bolts bite into the ship's side without any apparent effect.

"Nice shooting," I offer anyway.

"For all the good it did," Viera shouts back. "Don't know if this is going to work, Kaishi."

We're bigger, they're faster. Two of them, one of us, and I'm not sure how long the shuttle's going to keep taking punches without plummeting to the ground in pieces. We have to change the game.

So I dive at that big hole in the ground, back towards Marilo in all its ruin. The fighters are already looping around to follow me, but their turn takes time and I manage to scream past a couple more descending Flaum shuttles before my pursuit gets oriented.

Then we're plunging into smoke, between the rocks and into the massive cavern.

"I'd slow down," T'Oli says. "At this speed, you're likely going to turn us all into mush."

"Working on it." I'm pulling back on the flight stick, sliding down the speed on the control terminal.

"You know I can't send the message to the Q-Net from within here?"

"Some things have to wait, T'Oli," I reply. "You won't be able to send the message if we're blown apart, either."

With the slowing speed, I guide the shuttle out from over the city, passing above the lake, where, once the smoke clears away, I can see squads of Sevora Flaum pursuing the refugees along the road we ran not long ago. They're gunning down the fleeing humans, and the sight of it lights a fire in me.

"Viera, we're going strafing," I yell back to her. "Be ready off the right side."

I bring the shuttle around low, trying not to wince as humans dive and cower when we swing near. If I could yell to them to keep running, I would. More frustration to add to my fire.

Ahead, walking along the wide rock path split on either side by the large lake, ranks of Sevora move forward with miners raised, spraying red fire at the humans. None, yet, seem to think we're anything other than support.

"Get ready," I shout a warning, though I doubt Viera needs it.

I pull the shuttle to the right, then twist it as we go over the water, flipping Viera's side towards the Flaum. I slow the engines, so that we're hovering as we pass over the bridge. Viera, with our moment's surprise, goes to work. A steady stream of red flashes out from her miner, laying into the packed Flaum troops who, until this point, probably hadn't faced any counter attack.

They take it exactly the way the Lunare took Malo's surprise assault on them so long ago—with stunned immobility. Viera's miner goes through its energy quick, and she drops it to pick up mine, and only in that brief pause do the first Sevora start to counter, start to send a few hasty bolts our way while others realize they're in a tight space without cover.

The panic that takes hold is not an asset.

When the second miner runs out of juice, most of the Sevora forces on the bridge are ruined, and those that aren't flee back towards the city.

Right in time for those fighters to find us again, as we're hovering dead in the air.

The two fighters home in on us, emerging from the smoke. They're flying cautious in the tight quarters. I do a quick consideration; we're too slow, too big to get away from them, and Viera has no firepower left. If I move forward and we crash into the lake, we do nothing. But if we stay here? The shuttle's going to smash onto the rock bridge and maybe destroy it or, if not, serve as an obstacle for the pursuing Flaum.

One more refugee might live another day.

"T'Oli, it's been an honor," I say as the two fighters settle in close to us. "Glad I got to know an Ooblot."

"And I'm happy to know a human," T'Oli replies, shifting itself to hard stone.

The fighters unleash their first salvo, a trio of crimson bolts that crash into the shuttle and send lighting racing across the terminals. I squint and block sparks with my hand, feeling their heat in my palm. Any moment now.

I'm expecting the crackling roar of an explosion, but what I get instead is a loud boom. No, a cascade of deep cracks banging in the air, and something strikes the left fighter hard. The Sevora ship lurches forward as its rear caves in, and the craft plunges down into the lake. The second fighter doesn't fare much better as the booms continue and a pair of large, rounded metal balls bang into its sides, send the fighter spinning into the cavern's wall, where it crumples and slides into the water.

"Where did those come from?" I'm ecstatic, confused, all together.

"Avril's come home," Viera shouts from the back. "And she brought help!"

I remember that I control the shuttle, so I use the flight stick to turn us, pick us up from the ground, so we can see. Pouring into the cavern from the far side, barely visible through the smoke, are Lunare and Charre soldiers. Trundling with them, some already breaking into the back side of the bridge, are those land boats, pulled by chained Fassoth, with their cannons roaring.

The Lunare have made modifications since we last fought them; the cannons aren't just fixed to the sides anymore, but sit on raised platforms, giving the Lunare manning them the option to swing those cannons around, even to aim them up, where they're now firing at the Flaum shuttles. Pistol and long-gun cracks mix with red flashes of Sevora laser.

"Why haven't they shot us?" T'Oli asks. "Not that I'm disappointed, but we look like the enemy, right?"

I'm wondering the same thing, until I hear cheering coming from behind us, through Viera's open bay.

"The refugees," I say. "If they miss, they might break the bridge, or hit their own people. Avril's making a safe choice."

"Then you'd better stay right here," T'Oli replies.

"Viera, go!" I yell to my friend. "Tell them we're friendly. Then T'Oli and I will take off and deliver the message."

Viera doesn't hesitate, and I'm glad, for even if the Lunare manage to win a small victory here, it's only going to last until the Sevora get tired of fighting, until they decide to simply immolate everything. These caverns, the jungle and all of Charre could wind up like the blowing ashes on the other side, and I will not let that happen. The faster we get that message out, the faster we get help here, the more of my world we'll save.

"How high do we need to go for this message?" I ask the Ooblot. "All the way up to space?"

"I nearly had a link established before we abandoned the sky," T'Oli replies. "Just outside of the hole should do. Which is good, because I don't believe this shuttle will fly much longer."

"What do you mean?"

T'Oli points out the broken terminals, shorted by the fighter's laser fire. On the screens still working, plenty of graphs and meters blink in reds with bars near their bottom lines. I learn which ones mean power, which mean shielding, and which mean life support, and how all of them are close to failure.

"So you don't think the Sevora will take this back when we're done with it?"

"As scrap, maybe," T'Oli says.

I settle back into the netting, watching the burning, broken city. The Sevora aren't sending any more shuttles in through the hole—after losing three, they abandoned that tactic—which means the Lunare should eventually triumph. With the space that'll give us, I'm thinking we might actually get this message off.

"Which means what, Kaishi?" Malo's voice whispers in my head. "What do you think the Vincere are going to do when they come? You think the Amigga's army will save you?"

I blink. Glance at my wrist. The Cache.

"T'Oli, give me a moment." I stare into the bracelet, see that green flash and vanish into its endless library.

What I'm looking for are species, ones left by the Amigga, ones destroyed and saved. What I find is complicated; this is a Sevora Cache, and the parasites don't know everything, so I get half-formed entries about strange creatures, ones the Sevora might have hosted for a time before they're eliminated and never encountered again.

A couple stand out. Ones the Sevora infected and spread through quickly, until, according to the Cache, most of the population had been turned into hosts. These, once the Amigga found them, were eliminated. Turned to ash.

So the Amigga aren't afraid to torch a species that's lost. It's not great, but I see the point. If something's useful to your enemy, you take it away. What's worse, though, is that the Amigga don't even try to save them. The Sevora records show an orbital attack, burning the planet to obliteration, including those small factions that weren't yet enslaved.

Is that what they'd do to us?

The go-ahead doesn't come from Viera making her return to the shuttle, but rather from Vee bounding onto the bridge and up through our bay doors. I've pulled myself out of the Cache, and the Oratus' return gives me a welcome reprieve from the repercussions of our plan's potential success.

Vee himself isn't looking all that bad for his hunting expedition; a few new burn scars on his scales, some bits of fur sticking from his teeth and a face full of satisfaction.

"I bring you assent from your people," Vee announces as he stalks to the cockpit. "They will not fire at you if you fly."

"You bring assent?" I look past him, glance out the windshield. "Where's Viera?"

"Telling your story," Vee hisses. "She did not think I would add anything, and said the amount of blood on my scales was distracting." When he notices me looking, Vee laughs. "I took a dip in the lake to spare your soft heart the trouble."

"Glad to have you back, Vee," T'Oli says from the Q-Net machine. "I must say, it's been dicey without your natural killing abilities around."

"Yes? You must tell me."

T'Oli launches into a recounting of our venture up the Siamante as I lift the shuttle up and towards the ceiling of the cavern. As we rise, it's clear that some of the fires are being put out. The red flashes have disappeared, and the large cannon boats are taking up positions around the city, with all of their cannons aiming towards the very hole I'm flying to. It's an impressive, if useless display.

Nothing the Cache told me suggests the Sevora, or the Amigga, will bother with another land invasion. Unless something changes, they'll cut their losses and blow everything apart from space.

We lift out of the hole, into the bright light of Ignos. It's nearing evening, and traces of orange and purple slant into the sky. It's lovely, and for a moment it lets me ignore the dark Sevora ships hovering far overhead.

I don't get near them, instead following T'Oli's suggestion to park the shuttle on a crumbled, frost-bitten plateau not far from the hole.

"Will this work?" I ask T'Oli.

"Perfectly," the Ooblot replies. "Already on it."

"Great. I'm going to step outside for a moment. Get me when you're ready to head back."

The ground is hard and frozen, a few sparse weeds fighting for survival up here as wind whips my hair around. It's cold and cutting, and I love every second of it. Mountains spill out around me, wild and ferocious. The jungles of my home are behind me, hidden by the peak. Ignos hits my face, and his slight warmth is everything.

Home. This is what we're trying to save.

I hope we don't destroy it at the same time.

HUMANITY RISING

THE SKYWARD SAGA BOOK FIVE

I catch the black-glass spear, duck under the flailing claws of the furry creature and jab. The Flaum's armor, meant to guard against the fiery death of miners, does little to keep the spear's point from striking home. My enemy's skittering hits a halt as I withdraw the weapon, and before it reconsiders whether to live or die, I hit it with a kick and knock the Flaum off the mountain cliff.

"Nice catch!" Viera calls from my right as she whips out one of her silver pistols and fires.

The bullet cracks over my left shoulder, and I whirl to see another Flaum, just landing on its magnetic boots and about to deliver a shot to my back, stumble away as red blooms across its chest.

"That's your fault!" I shout, this time keeping my eyes on the landing craft above, but the attack's reaching its end, and this shuttle, along with the other three scattered along the wide cliff, are turning and heading back to orbit.

They'll return, though, in a few hours with a fresh supply, while we count our wounded and wonder how much longer we can last.

"If you stop breaking your spears, I won't have to congratulate you for catching them," Viera, in her deep blue-dyed leather armor, short-gray hair snapping in the breeze, says to me as I climb back to her level.

"Tell that to the blacksmiths," I reply, glancing up to make sure the Sevora continue their retreat. "The armor we're cutting through doesn't break as easy as our leather."

I take a quick count of our losses, and while we have a hundred warriors out on the ridge, more than a dozen are being helped away, with another four or five unmoving on the cold gray rock, between drifts of snow. They won't be sent down the rope hammocks to Marilo—their bodies will be pitched off, same as the Sevora. You can't bury someone in rock, and it's too much risk to burn them.

"It's always too many and too few at the same time," I say, then shiver despite my own attempts not to. Ignos is heading towards darkness, and the mountaintops are always cold. "Does Avril have any idea why they're not attacking at full strength?"

"I haven't asked her, Empress," Viera replies. "Maybe they're scared?"

"They could raze us from orbit." I start the walk to the ladders down.

It's the duty of the Empress, or so I tell myself, to be the last one off the battlefield, but even as I leave the next shift of soldiers climbs their way over the lip. These warriors are tightly wrapped in animal skins, and bear packs of firewood on their backs. Ready to wait out the night.

"I'm grateful they don't," Viera says. "While this isn't the best life, it sure beats death."

"So far as you know."

"Exactly."

At the edge, with fighters streaming in and out beside

me, I look into the burning forges, the bustling fortress of Marilo, capital of the Lunare and, at the moment, all of humanity. Heat rises up through the massive hole punched in the mountainside by the same aliens we're now facing on a daily basis; the Sevora, creatures that take the minds and bodies of other species and bend them into slaves.

I had one in my mind once and thought it was a god. It couldn't control me, and never figured out why. Now its friends are here to find out.

Or kill us all.

The rope ladders hang for a dozen meters, hooked in with long grapples bored into the stone. We lost a few brave fighters on the first expedition to set them up, but we couldn't give the Sevora the option to camp out above the city, even with all the captured miners we have being used to defend that hole.

At first the climb was daunting—stepping up over and over again as sure death from the fall lies below, but it's hard to be afraid of dying when it's so often around you. We've all become numb by now.

At least the blisters on my hands have calloused over.

Viera insists on following me and not the other way around, so I make the descent, staving off the bone-weariness that comes after every shift. A responsibility I don't have to take but do because when the survival of your race is at stake, rank isn't something to abuse.

Marilo's adapted to the life of wartime the way a warrior culture does; by tightening diets, getting the old, the young, and the unhealthy out of the city to one of the distant towns networked by caves to the Lunare capitol, and by coming to grips with the grim reality that they're fighting to delay the inevitable.

"Another caravan left today," Avril tells me when I meet the Lunare leader in Marilo's capitol building, a spiraling feature with many levels overlooking a wide central space where, in more normal times, people like Avril would be proclaiming this or that to a listening throng of governors and officials.

Now it's all but empty, save for our Shadows—guards appointed to follow us while remaining as inconspicuous as possible—and a few officials drafting orders or delivering reports. Avril's sitting at the central table, looking just as tired as I feel, though her battles have been with logistics rather than invading aliens.

"Have we heard from the others?" I reply.

Avril shrugs. "Yes, and no. They're making progress, but none will get to the boundaries for days yet."

By then, who knows if we'll even be around to receive those messages. We've been pulling together caravans of artisans, farmers, and what people we can spare and sending them to explore. To go to the edges of the map and draw it further, hunting for new places for humanity to take root if our current hold is pulled up.

Neither Avril nor I would see our species destroyed.

"Otherwise?"

"The city continues," Avril says, and I think her hair's even whiter than before, as if the stress is turning the Lunare leader slowly to snow, and when she suddenly smiles, the pale pink of her lips seems at terrible odds with the fire-lit dim of Marilo. "There's even some hope. Several more merchants came in today, traveling back and selling wines. I bought a bottle. The hope is to open them when the fighting ends."

"Or when the Sevora finally choose to break through."

"Still no sign, then?"

The daily ask, and my daily reply comes with a shaking head. "The Vincere haven't shown yet."

If humanity is going to survive, we're going to need outside help. A week ago, I'd sent the signal. T'Oli, a Ooblot who'd traveled across the stars to bring me back home, said the Vincere would hear the message and respond, but even it has no idea how long that might take. We might be flattened, or we might be saved.

"Then why are the Sevora playing with us?" Avril says. "They attacked with so much ferocity before, but now it seems like they're just testing our lines, making sure we don't forget about them."

"I've asked the same questions," Viera cuts in—she never leaves my side anymore, and I don't mind. "Their corpses, though, don't talk."

"Does that have anything to share?" Avril points at the thing on my wrist, a dark emerald bracelet.

The Cache holds more information than I'd ever be able to peruse, and using it draws me into a kind of trance, as the knowledge I'm searching for floats like projections around me. It's incredible, and dangerous, and I only use it when I'm alone or under tight protection. The Cache is also the reason my eyelids droop and my muscles sag—too many recent nights spent swimming through its endless oceans.

"It has no clear answer for why the Sevora are behaving like this," I say slow. "But I'm still looking."

The rest of my night passes in much the same way; passing discussions with other officials, an unsteady wander through the city to the haphazard room that's been designated as my quarters, with my Shadows and Viera watching me the entire way. Eventually I collapse on the mat of clotted straw that serves as my bed.

It's a far cry from the grand treatment I received when I was an Empress in more than name, and falls well short of the comforts I had in the various space ships and alien cities I've seen during my bumpy journey across the galaxy. The mat is, though, human. Made by human hands, with no hidden purpose other than relaxation, other than giving me the opportunity to lie down and, for just a moment, shut my eyes.

"Empress," Viera's voice, coupled with the grimy smell of scrappy coffee, brings me blinking awake.

Viera doesn't need to add anything more than that. Routine kicks in and I'm up, reaching for and pulling on my own light suit of armor, pulling the leather over the Cache, which never leaves my wrist. I don't wear a cape, but one of the priests from my old city, Damantum, took my emerald necklace with them when they evacuated. Last time, I left the jewels in the city because I was afraid of losing them.

Now I fasten them around my neck, the glittering ensemble the one concession I make to my rank, the one luxury I give myself.

T'Oli, a surprise guest, is waiting outside the apartment this morning. The creamy Ooblot looks mostly like a puddle with a pair of rounded sticks jutting out of it, though these sticks have eyes and the puddle follows me as we walk towards the rope ladders.

Marilo in the morning is the same as Marilo in the evening—a bevy of cookfires, moving bodies, and the occasional hawking of wares, though the trade now is less in gold and more in necessities. Up ahead, I can already see the shift changing underway as warriors climb and descend.

No hammocks this time, I note; either there's no wounded, or there wasn't an attack last night.

"They're pulling back," T'Oli says as we walk.

"The Sevora?" I allow myself the slight flutter of hope. "Why?"

"Panic," T'Oli replies. "Something's going wrong on their homeworld. They're being careless with their communications, leaving them open and I've been able to listen on the shuttle. I'd say there's no clear leader left up there."

"I didn't think the Sevora were supposed to panic," Viera says. "Isn't that their whole deal? Order and control above everything? Boring as dirt?"

"They like to act that way, but the Sevora are as full of passion as we are," T'Oli replies, its Ooblot skin forming the sounds by smacking against itself, as the creature has no mouth. "On Vimelia, Clarity's Dawn saw more success playing the slugs against one another than pushing forward by ourselves. A rival is a rival, no matter the species."

"If they're losing control," I speak slow, thinking through the possibilities. "What happens if they give up on us?"

"Oh, they'll probably burn this entire planet," T'Oli says. "It'd be trivial, and safer."

"Then we need to evacuate," I start to speed up my walk. "Get everyone deeper into the caves."

T'Oli laughs, a strange, barking slap. "I wouldn't worry about it—they'll superheat the atmosphere. We'll all die, no matter where we go."

Well, so much for that hope.

They were made. Grown, one by one in hanging hatcheries, to the designs of beings who sought to, who did, use them. Claws, talons, tails and razor teeth, all chosen for their murderous efficiency. A plan that has worked well, has instilled the creators with all the power they could want.

Yet the Amigga want more, and the Oratus, their creations, would give that to them.

Except for Sax. Except for Bas and the growing numbers realizing that a galaxy under the control of a species with no respect for natural life makes for a dangerous, deadly place to live.

Sax stands, with his midclaws resting on a long, round silver table in the middle of the frigate's sole meeting room. The table itself is polished clear, and it's hard enough that even the unnatural metal of Sax's claws doesn't scratch it. The sound of those claws, though, makes Sax wince. Reminds him of who, of what he is not anymore.

Around the table, white circles align every one-and-a-half meters, waiting for their occupants to give them life.

Sax's own rises all three meters with him, supporting his legs and meeting his back while leaving a gap for Sax's tail. It's a gesture that shouldn't be necessary, but given that Sax's gray scales are routinely interrupted by patches of interwoven titanium, there's plenty of reason for the Oratus to be tired.

Across Sax's chest, six vents separate wide and gulp in recycled air, touched with a bit of flowered scent from the surface of Solis, the planet not far beyond this ship's hull. As he finishes his deep breath, a circular door on the left shunts open, revealing a sole guard and her miner. The Flaum, small, furry and with her two claws hands wrapped around the handle of the weapon she holds, leads in a trio of other Oratus.

The first, golden-scaled and confident, gives Sax a nod as she enters. Rav's the lead officer on this frigate, a three-letter Oratus like Sax who chose command over getting her claws dirty. She's the only reason Sax is still alive, and Rav is probably hoping Sax can convince the two Oratus following her not to destroy this ship and everyone on it.

The second Oratus bears deep blue scales, except for a series of scars cutting across his chest that have since healed into ridged black lines. His beet red eyes catch Sax's, and while they widen in recognition at the face that's been blown across the galaxy's wanted screens, the Oratus doesn't pause or demand Sax's immediate arrest.

The third, and oldest, bearing weathered brown scales, does stop when she sees Sax. Her look, though, and the slight baring of her razor teeth, is long and thoughtful. She keeps her claws at her sides, her tail placid on the floor behind her. Sax is looking for signs, but sees none.

"So you weren't lying," the brown one says to Rav, still standing in the doorway.

"Please, Cacia, sit," Rav says.

Sax freezes. A five-letter Oratus? He's never met one before, and knows there has to be less than a dozen in the entire galaxy. What Cacia would have done to earn those letters, he can't...

"Stop," Cacia says to Sax, and the Oratus catches himself, lowers his tail back to the ground. "I'm not worth getting all worried about. Just like you, I earned my letters doing my duty. Unlike you, I plan to keep them by doing the same."

"I told you that's what she'd say," the deep blue one, who's made his way to the white platform across from Sax and sat down as it conformed to his body, says. "Cacia's never going to turn on the Amigga."

Rav, seated on Sax's right, giving the nearest seat to Cacia, shakes her head. "I think, Hul, she's going to surprise you."

"Nothing surprises me anymore," Hul hisses. "I'm too bored sitting out here by Solis to get surprised."

Cacia ignores what they're saying and heads to her own platform. Unlike the other two, which sit like Sax, Cacia's platform billows out around her, letting the Oratus recline such that she's almost lying on her back. It's an incredibly vulnerable position, but once she's in it, Cacia's expression relaxes, her claws lie flat, and her eyes close.

"Sax," Rav says after a moment. "Go on. Tell them what you told me."

Sax isn't much for speeches, unless it's a battle-cry or an order to eviscerate his enemies. Here, though, he's fighting for something more than himself, which lets Sax reach deeper into an oratory he didn't know he had.

"We're winning the war against the Sevora," Sax begins. "Which is only the start. The Amigga brought us, the

Oratus and the Vincere, into existence to fight the battles they never wanted to. We have done that. We have kept the galaxy safe from anything the Chorus has deemed a threat for a long, long time."

Sax watches his audience as he talks; Hul is interested, Rav looks a little bored, and Cacia still has her eyes closed, as if she's sleeping.

"What happens, though, when the threat is the Chorus itself?" Sax continues. "What happens when they decide we've served our purpose, when they decide we're more trouble to keep around than we're worth? Do we let them end us?"

"How?" Hul interrupts. "They're a bunch of Amigga. Only the best of them can even wield a weapon, and they don't do that very well."

"I barely survived a mirrored Oratus that came for me on this ship," Sax counters. The encounter with the light-bending Oratus, a version of Sax's species bred to handle the sort of dark-edged, shadow missions regular Oratus had little taste or knack for, left Sax ruined and needing metal plates grafted across rent gaps in his scales. "It claimed the Chorus had branded me a traitor and that my only possible end was death."

"As a traitor deserves," Cacia hisses from her seat.

Sax takes another long, slow breath. He wants to take his claws and shake them all. He wants to tell them that, right now, his pair is on her way to sabotaging their entire race because the galaxy's other species think the Oratus can't be trusted. Anger, though, won't work with these three —if Sax gets too dangerous, they'll just kill him and move on.

So he tells a different story instead.

"As part of a mission, I delivered a Sevora specimen to

an Amigga station, called *Cobalt*." Sax says. "On this station, the Amigga was growing a new species. Ones they could control on their own. That had no free will."

Hul laughs, a hissing snort. "Yes, yes, we've heard the rumors. We're all going to be replaced by slime creatures from a tube?"

That's unexpected, but just because the target's discovered his gambit doesn't mean it won't work.

"They were more than slime creatures," Sax hisses. "The familiars, as the Amigga called them, were deadly, and they were getting better. It was working on disguises, so that you'd never know if the Flaum beside you was real or an Amigga slave. How long do you think the Chorus will keep us around when it can crew its frigates with endless hordes of blind followers?"

"And how, Sax, can we stop them?" Rav says. "Even if we believed you—and I'm not sure we do—would you have us take our small fleet, leap to the Chorus and fight them? Die for nothing?"

Sax blinks. He'd been focusing so hard on persuading them to see the truth that Sax hasn't spent any time on what to do when the other Oratus actually saw it.

"Help us," Sax says finally. "There's groups spread across the galaxy, working in small ways to grow our numbers, to find ways to take down the Chorus. Cacia, with your ship, you could help break the Chorus' hold on the current batch of new Oratus. Hul and Rav, you could keep Cacia safe, keep Solis safe until the Vincere as a whole can be turned."

Sax never planned on giving a speech in his life, but having his first and only, thus far, attempt at it greeted with a dull silence isn't what he expects. Rav responds to the quiet with a slow look at the other two Oratus, judging their reactions. Which aren't much: Hul takes a long breath through his vents, and Cacia keeps up her lounging. Not a word comes from either.

Silence heats quick to anger. Sax's blood pulses. Why aren't they talking? After all Sax fought for to get here, to earn a spot at this table, their reaction is to do nothing?

After another second passes, Sax slaps the metal table with his midclaws. The metal from his claws makes a ringing noise that echoes around the room, and it's weird enough to draw the eyes of Rav and Hul. Even Cacia cracks a single iris.

"I'm not giving you a choice," Sax hisses. "You either agree, now, to save our own species and the galaxy in which we live, or Rav and I will end you and find someone more willing."

Threatening a five-letter Oratus. An instant death, at least by Vincere protocols. Sax, though, isn't in the Vincere anymore. This meeting, in fact, is about as far from the Vincere as he can get. The question, now, is whether anyone else in the room feels the same way.

"Sax, I didn't—" Rav starts before Sax issues a loud growl to cut her off.

"I'm asking them," Sax hisses. "Accept, or die here."

Perhaps Rav realizes she's gone too far to take any other course but Sax's, as she stays quiet. Her claws are tight, as are Hul's, though the latter's keeping his gaze on Cacia. Whatever course the five-letter takes, he'll follow.

As for Cacia, she finally decides to make a move. At a twitch from her tail, the platform beneath her folds back into the ground like melting snow, leaving Cacia standing tall on her talons. She swings her head towards Sax and bares her teeth.

"I will not be led by a three-letter," Cacia says. "Your argument has merit. Your plans have none."

Sax has been in enough fights to know when he's in one, even though this is being fought with words instead of claws.

"It is what I have," Sax says. "We're reacting, now. Trying to stay alive until we can strike at the Chorus."

"That might have worked when you were in hiding. When your only members were of lower species," Cacia gestures a foreclaw towards the Flaum guards at the back of the room. "Now the Chorus knows you exist, and as soon as they finish with the remnants of the Sevora, you will become the Vincere's sole target."

"I already know the situation," Sax says. "Either help us find a solution, or don't."

"If the Chorus is removed, there will be a vacuum," Cacia says. "New leaders will be necessary. New commanders." Cacia's tail begins to swish back and forth, making a scraping noise as it glides along the metal floor. "I'm tired of sitting around this planet, Sax. I long for bigger, brighter things. I can begin to pull the levers that will bring the Vincere itself into our grasp, and in exchange, I would lead it."

Sax has no right to make the promise, no power to give it. Cacia's words, though, hint that they think Sax must be a high-ranking member of this resistance, that he must have some sway. So Sax says the words and gives Cacia what she wants.

Bas always says he needs to become a better liar.

I climb the rope ladders for my shift, making it to the top and into Ignos' light on another clear, windy day. Snow drifts, growing thicker as the seasons trend towards winter, gather in the gray rock crevices, burying sprigs of grass. In the distance, beyond the smaller foothills arrayed in front of me, I can make out the slightest shade of green on the horizon.

My true home. Somewhere in that deep jungle, my parents might still be alive. My tribe, my people might still struggle. The Sevora took that area first, with the refugees fleeing to the Lunare and their mountain shelters to survive. Many of my own former subjects made the long trek too, crossing plains and desert before the woods.

Many more did not.

So now I stand with unfamiliar allies, wielding bows, spears, curved kukri knives and flintlock rifles. Nothing compared to the arms I've seen, the weapons I'd made in Damantum, lost in the rapid escape. Yet for all their primitiveness, these tools have served us so far.

"That's not usual," Viera points up and I see what she's looking at.

The Sevora normally send a few shuttles through the atmosphere, buzzing down and hitting our cliffside position with plenty of laser fire. We duck and cover, using the rocks for protection, then burst out and engage in a sloppy melee that lasts until the Sevora decide they've had enough and retreat.

This time, though, instead of four shuttles, there are dozens. Behind them, too, greater shapes are descending through the clouds; larger spike-like shapes, coming towards us with their round bottoms shimmering as reflected light bounces away.

"Looks like they're done playing with us," I say, then turn towards one of the warriors. "Send the signal—we need everyone ready to hold here, and the city needs to empty."

Avril's going to wake up to a thrill, but better that than not waking up at all.

"Cover positions!" Viera shouts as the first shuttles scream closer.

Everyone, myself and Viera included, dive into carved out niches in the rock. Some hang over the hole's edge back towards Marilo, resting their feet on notches made for the purpose. A hundred fighters disappear in a moment, and good thing too, because the Sevora start shooting in the next.

Lasers don't make noise when they scream down. There's no crackling, no whistling from an arrow's feather. There's only a flash and a spray as rock fractures and bursts. The hiss as snow vaporizes. Explosions, like when the Lunare use their cannons, don't erupt—rather, small fires start as the ground literally melts.

I see several fighters on the unlucky end of a near strike —the laser superheats the air around where they are enough that their fur-lined armor bursts into flame, prompting a frantic roll-around. My own shelter, beneath a thick slate slab, keeps Viera and I safe, and I try to ignore the screams of others less lucky than us.

"Think this is the end?" Viera says as the flashes continue.

"I don't think we've come all this way to die here," I reply.

"Hope you're right," Viera says, and I see her glance at her pistols. "There are so many cool weapons out there I haven't used."

I can't stop the laugh.

The fire dies away as the shuttles get close. Once the flashes stop, it's a sign to burst out of our hideaways, and I go, black-glass spear in my right hand and a kukri looped at my waist. Viera has her pistols ready, a more conventional Lunare sword hung over her back.

"For Malo?" Viera says as we leave cover.

"Always!" I call back.

The spirit of my friend, who fell getting us off of the Sevora's home planet what feels like years ago, guides my spear as I rush towards the first quartet of Flaum dropping from the shuttles overhead. Their boots flare and catch each of the furry creatures, about my height, though of slighter build, as they land.

My first target sports clotted amber fur, which blows across its face as it's exposed to the mountain wind. Those distracting strands offer me the opening I need to slip the point past its guard, which amounts to a thrown up arm with a small hand wrapped around a miner's trigger. The stab connects and I start to pull back for a second jab when the Flaum pinches the spear into its side, pressing the point in further.

It's a move that has to be incredibly painful, but when you're being controlled by something else, something that can ignore your suffering for its own ends, such maneuvers become viable. I'm not expecting it, so when the Flaum twists away from me, the spear's torn from my grasp.

I draw the kukri, a knife that bends along the blade, ending with a heavier, flat point ideal for the more mundane tasks of life like chopping fruit or clearing leaves. Here I use it to perform a slashing cut, one that doesn't so much hurt the Flaum as force it back, giving me a meter's space to adjust.

On either side of me other warriors engage with the rest of the Flaum, using our numbers to drive them back towards the cliff's edge. Viera works her pistols, along with other Lunare marksmen, to keep other Sevora shooters from picking us off from the shuttle doors. This is the instant stalemate I've come to expect, and one that gets thrown awry as more Sevora shuttles blow in above and behind us.

The amber-furred Flaum makes its move, ignoring its wound and the spear sticking out of it to aim the miner towards me. In that instant, though, I jump forward, kukri swiping at the Flaum's weapon-wielding arm while the rest of me barrels into the lightweight creature.

I'm not a large person either—most of the warriors on this cliff face have me beat handily in height and weight— but Flaum are more fur than anything. The kukri's swing gets the Flaum backpedaling, and my left-shoulder charge hits its chest, knocking the Flaum into a falling stumble. With my left hand, I grab the handle of my spear as the Flaum chitters out a panicked screech, and draw back my weapon.

The Flaum, and the Sevora inside it, tumble over the cliff. There's a chance those boots it has can find enough metal in the mountainside to stabilize its fall, but I'm willing to live with that risk; there's more pressing targets.

"This isn't working, Kaishi!" Viera's yell cuts above the madness, and I see her wielding her sword in her left hand, a pistol in her right.

Viera ducks under a Flaum firing as it descends to land near her, then sweeps with her blade, taking the creature's legs out from under it. A quick finishing shot at the tripped Flaum buys my friend a breath, which she uses to tell me to run.

"There's too many!" Viera calls.

I rush back to the line, which now is more of a circle around the long hole back to Marilo, getting pressed in on all sides by the Sevora forces. Miners flash their bolts and our warriors fall, the Sevora forming a defensive line and allowing the ranks behind to lay down covering fire.

I'm passed back, Viera pulling me along. I try to turn, to stand with my own forces, but my friend won't let me, until I shake her off, twist away and look in the faces of the creatures gunning us down.

"Kaishi," Viera protests over the screams, the shouts and rings of metal-on-metal. "We run now, or we die!"

I've run before. Left my people to fend for themselves against a hostile galaxy, and I'm not doing it again.

"Then I die with them." I push back, get back to the front when the warrior in front of me, a bulky man in a white-furred fassoth cloak, bursts into flame and collapses.

The fighter's death reveals a grim line of Flaum with their buzzing blades drawn, the edges glowing with the same laser-light shooting from their miners, and behind them, aiming weapons, are the true killers—the Sevora gunning us down.

There's not enough of us to win, but there are enough of us to buy Marilo a little more time.

"Together!" I shout, thrusting the black-glass spear high, where it catches the light of Ignos.

And the shuttle above our heads explodes in a shattering boom, the shockwave sending all of us, human and Flaum alike, to our knees. Shrapnel rains among us, scattering burning knives into the crowd. That first boom is quickly followed by two more; another pair of shuttles immolated out of the air.

Before I fully process what's going on, the Flaum in front of me are erased as rock explodes and a great ship—larger than the Sevora shuttles, with a pointed, glimmering front—drives into the side of the mountain. The sides of the vessel slide up and open, and creatures I never expected to see again leap out.

Oratus.

Four of them, followed by more furry Flaum and sluglike Whelk, though the latter species are accessories to the brutal show the Oratus put on. The three-meter tall lizardlike monsters, with their four clawed arms, two jagged talons and long, whipping tails deliver mortal punishment to the Sevora force at a speed I can barely comprehend.

The Sevora shuttles continue to detonate from a series of fast-moving slivers shrieking by and delivering concentrated fire. The aerial squad travels in a line, each in sequence firing at the same spot on their way by, eventually boring a burning hole in the Sevora ship until it explodes.

The response to the events comes in flavors—there's my numb, stunned analysis of what's going on, there's my soldiers, who alternate between cheering and retreat, and the Sevora, who abandon what composure they had and resort to panicked flight. They leap from the cliff, diving off the mountainside and running away.

They don't get far—the Flaum and Whelk that came down with the Oratus set up their longer miners and clean up the cowards, leaving us, after a frantic series of moments, in a blood-soaked, burning battlefield bereft of enemies.

"I don't believe it," Viera says, and I'm thankful she's found her way back to my side. "They actually came."

All I can do is nod and turn my eyes upward, at the light show continuing in Earth's upper atmosphere as the Sevora force that's haunted our every waking moment since I came home burns in systematic, fatal fashion. Like watching flowers burst into bloom on a spring day, the gray-black ships pop into oranges and whites against the blue sky.

I wonder if Ignos, the Sevora that once lived inside my head is up there.

I'm surprised to find I hope it's not.

The clean-up goes by quickly, with me spending most of it watching as the Oratus go about their bloody business. Our warriors quickly find their own efforts outmatched and settle back, watching their enemies both nearby and up above obliterated by these new players.

"Stay back!" I shout eventually. "Don't engage. These are..." 'Friends' seems the wrong word, but I need to say something, so I go with, "Allies!".

One of the Oratus, with glinting green scales and looking cleaner than the others after the carnage, finds its way to me once the Sevora threat is eliminated. I've forgotten how tall the creatures are—this one is nearly twice my height, and it stares down at me with its teeth visible, those vents lining its chest opening and closing to suck in the air.

My Shadows—the three left, anyway—step up around

me, and Viera, behind me, has her hands on her pistols. I hold up a hand, telling them not to start something stupid.

"You are the leader?" the Oratus asks, its light hiss mingling with the whistle of mountain wind.

"I am," I reply. "Thank you for coming."

The Oratus cocks its head to the side. "We should thank you. This was the last Sevora fleet. With its destruction, their ability to expand is ruined."

I'm not sure how I feel about that, so I settle for a stare. The conversation, though, has passed beyond the easy introduction, and treads into awkward territory. The Vincere came, destroyed our enemies, and the only thing I want from them now is to leave and let us recover.

Diplomacy, however, requires compromise. Requires being polite.

Then the Oratus speaks and turns my plans to ash.

"You do not seem surprised to see us," the Oratus says. "Unlike the others of your kind, you do not shrink away. Tremble in fear." The emerald creature glances at Viera. "Neither does she."

A second Oratus, a darker blue in color, steps up behind the first. "They ought to be scared."

"Gar," the first Oratus says. "Stop. You've had your fill."

"Always ready for seconds," the blue one, Gar, replies. "These don't look so furry either, with more meat on their bones."

Even as my warriors shift around me, I know a joke when I hear it and crack a smile. "I've seen Oratus. Once before, two of you stole me from here."

I'm expecting a question or two, but what I get instead is a sudden tightening from both Oratus. Their tails touch, and then the green one crouches low until its eyes meet mine.

"Who stole you?"

"There were two," I say, feeling like this is a bad idea, but that lying would be even worse. "One with gray scales, called Sax, the other a pink-gold one named Bas. They took me and a couple of my friends to a station called *Cobalt*."

The emerald Oratus straightens, looks at Gar, who offers a slight baring of teeth. That seems to send a message, one that causes the emerald Oratus to expel a lot of air from its vents in a heavy sigh.

"We did not expect to find our ambassador so quickly," the Oratus says. "You will be returning with us, human. Gather your things, and pack carefully, for I don't know how long you will be gone."

The surface of Solis comes through as the shuttle breaks the heavy clouds. It's a sight Sax hasn't seen in a very, very long time. A long stripe of verdant green, a gash on an otherwise dry and rocky brown landscape. On one end of the scar, a giant mountain rises, and on the other, a low-lying lake marks the destination of the wide streams and rivers running through that strip of jungle. A kilometers-wide valley carved between two rising cliffs.

What catches the eye most, though, are the series of arches spanning that valley, rising up over the jungle from cliff to cliff and covered with stone-like armor. They look natural, brown and weathered by the often and turbulent storms that break and flush from one end of the valley to the other. Adorning each of these arches, and hanging like ripe blackberries, are the bulbous chambers that brought Sax to life.

"You have a particular target in mind?" the Flaum pilot, an ashen-furred one with scarred ears, asks.

Sax leans over her, staring out the shuttle's windshield.

Crash netting hangs behind him, forgotten in the moment. Like how Sax is going to find his pair. Her mission was to exterminate the source of the Oratus, to prevent the Chorus from making newer, more loyal versions that wouldn't hesitate to cut Sax down. A task like that doesn't lend itself to being conspicuous.

"I... don't know," Sax hisses.

"You're going to have to make a choice soon," the Flaum replies. "I can't just dawdle up here. Cacia's entry code's only going to work for so long."

"They wouldn't shoot us down."

"Solis doesn't play around, Oratus," the Flaum says and Sax gives a low warning hiss, but the furrball doesn't flinch. "Can't scare me—if they think we're not normal, they'll blow us apart and figure it out later. Which makes your threats all kinds of worthless."

The Flaum has a point, and so Sax chooses the farthest arch, the one closest to the lake. It would make sense for Bas to start from there, work her way up, rather than go to the Mountain and deal with all the Oratus-in-training coming her way.

Sax expects the shuttle to land at one of the hatcheries, but instead the Flaum targets the near side of the third arch, settling in for a landing at the very edge of the rocky mass. As they draw in closer, the ground beyond the arch, devoid of plants and anything other than gray dirt, shifts aside to reveal a small docking bay. One that, going by the speed of the door and the lack of lights inside, hasn't seen visitors in a very long while.

Yet, when the boarding ramp lowers and Sax sets foot on his homeworld for the first time since his birth, he's not alone. Another Oratus, the deep green bracelet of a Cache wrapped around his teal-colored left foreclaw, waits for him. What little lights there are frame the only exit, a single large door clearly meant for hauling small amounts of cargo. The Oratus stands in front of it and watches as Sax descends.

"You're wounds mark your status, Oratus," the greeter says. "What business do you have on Solis?"

"I'm looking for someone," Sax replies, talons settling into the packed-dirt floor of the bay. "Though if you'd seen her, you would be dead."

If this surprises the Oratus, there's no sign.

"You doubt our own skill? Solis has remained unconquered for its duration," the Oratus says. "We've trained thousands and thousands here. Any one seeking to attack this place would find themselves both over-matched and out-skilled."

"She doesn't want to fight you," Sax says. "She wants to kill you. I need to tell her not to."

That gets the Oratus to cock his head. To puzzle for a moment. Then, slowly, he speaks, "If what you say is true, then you should come inside. Leave your pilot out here. No other species is allowed on Solis, save with our consent."

Sax has no problem with that. Flaum are always more trouble than they're worth.

Sax follows the Oratus down the dim, rock-ridged corridor. The air's cool and still, and it's nice to walk, for once, without the clack of talons on metal floor. Hard-packed dirt might be primitive, but it feels soft on Sax's feet—the sand brings back brief memories of his start.

His birth, if Sax wants to call it that.

The next room, the main one for this hatchery, is huge. Like the top half of an onion, the room's sloped walls rise to a point far above them, the section anchored into the arch itself. Spaced throughout the chamber, both on the floor next to them and sitting in honeycombed creches along the room's sides, are large purple-red sacs. Each one has a small machine—no larger than Sax's midclaws—attached to it, showing a gradually-greening ring.

"This is your first time back, isn't it?" his guide says. "Most never return to Solis."

"I'm not here for the memories," Sax replies. "Have you seen her? Bas?"

"You're in such a hurry," the Oratus says, pausing near a bulging sack, its ring almost fully green. "Part of the problem of our species, I think, is that we're always running to the next conflict."

"What else is there?"

The Oratus laughs at this, but Sax picks up plenty of disappointment in the low hissing. "Do you know how they choose us? The ones who watch the hatcheries, who guide the new-formed Oratus?"

Of all the topics Sax has never once considered in his life, this has to be close to the bottom. What use would such a thought be? Knowing how these hatcheries are maintained won't help him beat the Sevora, won't help him destabilize the Chorus.

Sax is about to tell the guide to take him to Bas and be quiet while doing it, but there's something in the Oratus' expression, a light in its eyes and an eager twitch to the creature's tail that tells Sax this one's gone a long time without real conversation.

"I have no idea," Sax finally says.

"We're the failures," the guide hisses. "The ones that survive, but crash out of training. We don't make it through the wheels, don't find pairs or lose them. This is an exile, when it should be an honor."

Sax takes a step back, more at the tone than anything

else. There's genuine anger coming out of this teal Oratus' mouth. The same sort of frustration Sax might express if he were left to rot on a background planet doing nothing but watching Oratus grow day after day.

"Don't you wonder how we stay sane? What they do to keep us happy?" the Oratus continues.

Sax, though, realizes now how quiet it is in here. Aside from the shifting of the occasional sack, there's no noise. No other Flaum, and Sax recalls plenty of those when he first emerged.

"I don't have time," Sax manages a reply as the strangeness twists in his gut.

Sax adjusts his stance, widens his legs and loosens his claws. He brings his tail down to the ground, subtly pressing it into the earth so that, if necessary, Sax can use it to push off.

"Nobody ever does, for us," the Oratus says. "So when she came, when she explained to me how forgotten I am, how unappreciated we are, I heard the truth."

"What truth?"

"That we need to spare them all," the Oratus gestures around the hatchery. "All the Amigga give us are lives of violence and death. Why should we allow that to happen?"

"Where are the Flaum, Oratus?"

"Gone, Sax." The sac next to the Oratus shifts along the floor, and the Oratus gives it a dire look. Raises a talon, as if to destroy it. "They aren't necessary anymore. I don't need their help for this."

Sax springs forward, tackles the Oratus and drives the guide into the ground. Pins the guide's claws back against the dirt, making sure to keep his own head high enough, away from the guide's sharp teeth.

"Their lives are not your decision," Sax hisses.

Sax expects resistance, struggle, but the guide only looks confused.

"When Rav sent the message you were coming, Bas said you would support us?" the guide says. "You want to end our pain as much as she does?"

"Change of plans," Sax says. "The Oratus need to survive, so we can make sure the Chorus does not."

The guide twists his head on the ground to look at the sac, almost ready to hatch. "So you would give us a new purpose?"

"We're trying to give you freedom to choose."

"Then Bas? Why would she?"

"Because at the time we thought you better dead than fighting against us," Sax says. "Turns out you can change an Oratus mind."

Sax makes a quick calculation that the guide isn't ready to fight anymore and slowly stands up, lets the guide get his claws back. The guide, for his part, takes his time climbing to his talons, shocked in more ways than one.

"Bas doesn't know," Sax continues. "I need to find her."

The guide shakes his head. "She's not here. By now she's probably on the farthest arch." The Oratus stares at Sax, raising his foreclaws up as if only now realizing what he's done. "Bas was... very convincing. She made sure we took care of our own assistants. You have to stop her."

"Call the other arches. Tell them what I've told you," Sax hisses, though he's already turning to run back to his ship.

The Flaum pilot hasn't raised the boarding ramp, and she's napping at the controls when Sax's heavy bounds startle her up from her sleep. In moments Sax has the story told and they're lifting off, out through the doors and up into Solis' sky.

To the first arch.

They're barely aloft before the shuttle's communications array crackles through the speakers embedded in the front line of terminals.

"Coming from the ground," the Flaum pilot says. "They're hailing."

"Answer it." Sax checks the screen—the identifier's blocked, which, in a way, identifies who it is.

The Flaum taps the flashing orange screen, which shifts to a lighter green to show the connection's been made.

"Sax, you came for me," Bas's hiss comes through the terminal. "You weren't supposed to do that."

"I made a different deal," Sax hisses. "We're keeping the Oratus alive."

Bas hesitates. "Nobody told me."

"I'm telling you," Sax says. "Where are you?"

"The first arch."

"Wait for me? And don't kill anyone?"

"You're the one who can't control himself, Sax." There's a bit of laughter in Bas' voice, but a tinge of uncertainty too.

She's looking for something.

"I'm not a hostage," Sax says. "I'd die first."

That gets a happy sigh through the call. "Glad you don't have to," Bas says.

They meet not long after, on the ground outside the first arch. Sax descends the ramp to find his pink-gold pair standing in the small bay waiting for him, Bas' own shuttle making the space crowded. It's the longest Sax has gone without seeing his pair since they've met. Days passed, either on Rathfall, trying to find his way back into civilization, or on Rav's frigate, nearly dying and then being pieced back together. That's the first thing Bas notices, her yellow eyes going wide as her midclaws touch the missing sections in Sax's glinting gray scales. She runs those eyes up and down her pair, and Sax stays quiet for a moment as he does the same. Their foreclaws clasp and the tips of their tails wrap around each other on the floor.

"I hoped, but didn't think we'd ever see each other again," Bas says first. "They said you would go to Evva and try to bring down the Chorus. From here, I'm supposed to go up and try, somehow, to destroy the Oratus training ship."

"You don't have to do that anymore," Sax says. "They tried to get me to do what you said, I refused. Violently."

"You didn't kill them all."

Sax cracks his razer mouth open in a smile. "They're still alive."

"Then what now? Evva?"

Sax nods. "That was the deal. I'd come here and stop your part of the mission, then we'd both head to the Chorus and tear them apart."

"You almost took too long," Bas flicks a glance behind her. "I never realized how close all of these caretaker Oratus are to losing their minds. All I had to do was explain how we were being used, and they were ready to cast it all away."

"They'll have a better purpose once the Amigga are gone."

Bas laughs. "It's that easy? Once they're gone?"

"Bas, I managed to get the Vincere leaders orbiting this planet to join us," Sax says. "If I can persuade people without using my claws, then we're destined to win."

Bas asks more questions and Sax answers, then they swap roles and talk more. Eventually the Flaum pilot comes down and asks whether they'll be staying long, as she's getting hungry and they didn't pack much food in their craft. That serves as enough of a cue to grab a snack, climb back in their shuttle, and pack off to orbit.

On the way up, Bas dishes one more long communication to the caretakers she'd just turned against their own race. It's a short one, an ask to stay their claws, to keep the new Oratus growing, a promise that they'll be hatching into a better future.

A promise Sax knows they'll keep.

"Right, except I'm not going anywhere." I don't flinch away from the Oratus, despite the fact that its claws could eviscerate me before any of my Shadows could intervene. "I just made it back here, and my people have been under attack."

The Oratus stares at me. Regards me as I would a particularly interesting plant.

"Human, you are a new species," the Oratus hisses. "You are, right now, apart from the rest of the galaxy. Do you know of the Chorus?"

I've heard the term, mostly back on Vimelia, the Sevora homeworld where the Chorus was mainly mentioned with disdain. Supposedly a group of Amigga—those round, strange creatures—make up the Chorus, and use these Oratus to force the galaxy to do what they want.

There's also the fact that one of those Amigga, one named Ignos, may have created humans.

"I've heard of it," I finally say.

"They will need someone to speak for your species. If that will not be you, then who?" the Oratus says.

"I'll do it," Viera announces from behind me. "She doesn't have to go."

"Viera?" I look back at her, confused. "What?"

"Told you, Empress. I'm a traveler—that's why I left the mountains for the jungle so long ago. If we're not going to get attacked, then it seems like all we'll be doing is putting humanity back together," Viera shrugs. "That's not what I'm interested in."

Could I let Viera go as the ambassador for humanity? Alone?

"Come back," I tell the Oratus. "Tomorrow. When the light rises again, we'll be back here, ready to go."

The Oratus delivers a low hiss, "Acceptable."

Once the declaration is made, the Oratus wastes no time; it roars a command, and its troops pile back into the craft. Its doors slide shut as we back away, and I'm wondering how the shuttle is going to break free of the rock it drove into during its landing, when a loud grinding noise begins. The ground beneath our feet shakes, loose rocks rattle and snow slips from its perches as the ship drills itself free.

I expect the shuttle, as its front loosens away from the rock, to fall over and slide down the hillside, but an array of small orange circles across its bottom hull spark to life and let the shuttle straighten out while hovering in the air. It rotates, floats a small distance away, and with a smoking burst of crackling sound, the craft roars up into a sky still spotted with the fading remains of the Sevora fleet.

"You don't want me to go?" Viera says later, as we're back down in Marilo sharing large glasses of wine.

The city's turned itself out in celebration. Nobody cares

to consider that the Vincere could turn and attack us just like the Sevora did. Instead, the streets are full of people in drunken revelry. Runners riding the great white Fassoths have been dispatched to every corner of the mountains, and those Solare and Charre tribesmen who wish it are making ready, between dances and songs, to return to their homelands.

I'm watching a band of them right now from our balcony in Marilo's capitol building, a band of several dozen; Warriors, children, priests and more. Solare preparing to see if anything's left of their home. They're taking weapons too—nobody's assuming the last Sevora on the planet died on that mountainside today.

"I can't let you go," I say, taking another sip. The wine's acidic, harsh and stressed, but still welcome. "Not alone."

"So you don't trust me."

We're sitting in soft woven chairs, and mine crinkles as I lean back in it and toss Viera a smile. "I don't trust you to keep your hands off your pistols."

"Did that fine when I was staying with your tribe."

That takes me back, briefly. Avril's already sent scouts to see if my parents, if my home village still stands, but I'm not clinging to it. They never appeared in the mountains, and the Sevora struck first at the jungles and plains.

"We didn't threaten you," I say. "These things, you saw what happened on *Cobalt*. They'll try to bend you, break you. They'll want humans to accept them as masters."

"So?" Viera nods at the bouncing happiness over the edge. "If that's what we get, does it matter?"

"Dalachite, the Amigga on *Cobalt*? It was making copies of us. And you know what's on the other side of these mountains—evidence that the Amigga made us, and tried to destroy us. What's to say they won't again when it's convenient?"

"Do you think we could stop them if we wanted to?"

There's the truth I've kept from telling myself. No. No we could not win a war against those Oratus or their army they call the Vincere.

"That's why I have to go," I say, and now that the words are out, it's obvious. "You and I are the only ones that know the truth. We have to present ourselves as equals, we have to guarantee our future."

"You're going to fight for your people by leaving them again?" Viera laughs, but it's a sad sound. "You're the only Empress I've known who spends all her time avoiding her domain."

Not because I want to.

Avril doesn't object to the plan, and I wonder if it's because, again, I'm handing her all the power she wants. The Lunare, now, have every advantage over the other tribes and while Avril says she's not going to embark on an immediate chain of conquests, I'm not sure I believe her.

I came back to my people and found them ruined once, and the next time I might find them gone entirely.

There's one more person I need to talk to before the morning: Vee, an Oratus that we found when we returned to Earth, trapped in the desolate remnants of the Amigga base that led, I think, to the human species.

Vee's been taking turns during the night, preferring the cold dark to the bright day, and his presence up there, I've heard, has saved countless lives. Even so, I'm nervous opening the door to the squat building whose highest floor, at one point a series of apartments, has been given over to him.

Vee's already awake by the time we get to him, standing ready.

"T'Oli, you want to explain?" I offer to the Ooblot, who joined Viera and I after our glass of wine.

"Oh no, I think you'll do a far better job," T'Oli says. "I have no gravity for these sorts of things."

I sigh, but T'Oli's right.

"What things?" Vee hisses.

"The Vincere are here," I say.

"So that's why it's so loud today," Vee nods towards the small windows.

They have no glass, so the sounds of happy drums and celebration bleed through. Probably quite the change from the dead quiet, doomed atmosphere that's hovered over the city before now.

"They want Viera and I to leave with them," I say, after describing the Sevora's destruction. "I thought you might want to come too?"

Vee takes a long moment. Closes his eyes.

"I lost my pair in the attack on the base," Vee says finally. "The Vincere left me down there. I assume they believe I'm dead. I had nothing to live for until you found me and gave me a purpose."

The Oratus takes a long stride towards me and sets its right foreclaw on my shoulder. It should be comforting—I know Vee's not threatening me—but the sheer strength even in that one limb forces me to suppress a twitch.

"I have friends here now, the ones I've been fighting with," Vee says. "And as you say, there may yet be Sevora on this world, in the jungle."

"You want to stay here?" Viera blurts. "Really?"

Vee laughs, a rumbling, hissing thing. "Is that so surprising?"

"Frankly, yeah."

"I understand," I say, shaking my head at Viera. "Tomorrow, I won't tell them. They'll never know you survived."

Vee gives me a nod of thanks, then looks over at the Ooblot. "What of you, T'Oli? Are you staying, or going with the human?"

"Oh, I'd prefer to leave," T'Oli says. "Humans are awfully fragile, and after I've gone through this much trouble keeping Kaishi alive, I want her to stay that way."

"It's not easy," Viera mutters.

"Hey," I say to them both. "I could order you both to stay here, you know."

"We wouldn't listen," Viera replies.

I know they wouldn't, and I'm glad.

The next morning comes faster than I'd like, especially with the results of several more wine glasses dancing in my skull. Viera's in even worse shape, and she spends most of the walk to the rope ladders with her eyes shut, hands pressed to her head.

"Why do you humans consume things so obviously harmful to yourselves?" T'Oli says, oozing along with us.

"Because we have to listen to you," Viera says.

I don't bother to say anything, because, really, I don't want any more noise. Not even my own voice. Every sound brings with it another knock of my headache.

Climbing the rope ladder, though, does some magic to make me feel better. Maybe it's the exertion, or the requirement to focus my unwilling body on a life-or-death task. Hitting the mountainside, with its blistering chill air, banishes the remnants of the hangover, and I face the brightening sky with steady face.

The dozen warriors we stationed up here—because Avril refused to trust all the threats were gone, and I agreed—wave at us, but don't approach. I return the gesture, and I'm not offended they're not coming over—there's a shuttle swooping down towards our section of the cliff, and the open doors show the emerald Oratus is waiting. Nobody would want to get any closer to that if they don't have to.

The emerald Oratus jumps out of the shuttle, which stays hovering about a meter off the rock. With its claws, the Oratus helps us board, lifting first me, with T'Oli riding on my back, and then Viera into the craft.

The inside, like the first Vincere shuttle I rode in, gives its own definition to the words 'sparse'. There's simply nothing in the back save netting, though I notice the shuttle seems far taller on the inside, with a series of bars stretched across the top. The cockpit on this one is situated to our right, at the rear, where a pair of Flaum sit in tight quarters above the engines. To the left, the translucent view shows the shrinking mountain as the shuttle begins to withdraw.

"This is all you need?" the Oratus asks, staring at our small packs.

"We haven't been in one place long enough to gather possessions," I say, though I bring my hands to the emerald necklace. This time, I want to keep it, and I figure a little sign of royalty won't be a bad thing when I show up in front of the Chorus.

The Oratus nods. "We keep nothing for ourselves, either, except those weapons we deem most fit for our abilities." There's a pause as the Oratus sucks in some air, and Viera settles into a section of the hanging netting. "My name is Lan, and I welcome you, ambassador of humanity, to the Vincere."

I gather there's supposed to be something ceremonial in the sentiment, but right now I'm leaning against some draping black net as I leave my home far too soon, and I can't quite get there. So I ask a question instead.

"You know Sax?"

By the way Lan twitches, I know I've surprised the Oratus.

"We served together," Lan says, slow. "For a time, until he became a traitor to the Vincere and to his race."

"That doesn't sound like Sax." What I remember of the Oratus is his dedication to the mission, to the destruction of any threat. "He did everything he could to keep us alive."

Those words prompt more questions, and the rest of the shuttle ride is spent swapping stories of the Oratus, first of Sax, then Bas, and finally of the four of them, the last being Gar, who's waiting for us on the lead cruiser in the Vincere fleet above Earth.

If there's one thing I get from the conversation, it's that Lan isn't quite the soulless machine she makes the Oratus out to be. Regret and confusion permeate her memories as she tells them, and I sympathize; every night I turn over the time with Ignos—the Sevora—in my mind, wondering whether anything it did was out of concern for me or humanity, or whether it was all in self-interest. Whether the Sevora could care about me or my people.

Nunilite is the cruiser's name, supposedly, so Lan tells it, because that's also the name of the Amigga who discovered and designed leaping technology. As for why this specific ship gets the noble name, that's because of the giant bulb built on the front end of the cruiser. It's visible from the shuttle as we approach, largely because its bright copper shading sticks out from the bright-white of the rest of the hull.

"Leaping sends a ship through folds in space-time," Lan says, and the excited hiss in her voice tells me she prefers this to the sad discussion of her former partners. "This technology inverts the science." At my vacant look—Viera's asleep and who knows what T'Oli's thinking—Lan pauses for a moment, then tries again. "Rather than pushing a ship through a wrinkle in the universe to move from one place to another, the *Nunilite* can create a new fold between two points. It can bring them together."

"Why?"

Lan stares at me. I must have said something dumb. The Oratus opens her mouth to explain, then shuts it.

"Perhaps it's better if you don't know," Lan says. "You're not yet on our side, after all."

If Lan's expecting me to push the issue, to pester her about what sort of cosmic miracle the *Nunilite* can unleash on the universe, she's disappointed. Right now, I'm looking at Viera and feeling awfully jealous about her trip to the world of dreams, and with a simple statement I tell Lan I'm going to the same place.

The Oratus says she'll wake us when we arrive, but I'm already asleep before she finishes the sentence.

I've now landed on three places apart from Earth—*Cobalt*, a nightmarish space station where an Amigga tried to turn my species into carbon clones for its own ends, Vimelia, the Sevora homeworld where two factions tried to use my friends and I to inflame a war or end it, and now the *Nunilite*, which becomes my first glimpse of the Vincere in their element.

The shuttle doors open and Lan is the first one out, her emerald frame serving as a guide in the bright lights of the docking bay. Unlike some of the others I've seen, though, this bay is empty of other ships. It's not large, either, with deep black floors, steel-slat walls, and a cross-section of Flaum and Whelk soldiers waiting for us to exit.

What's more surprising is the amount of artillery present for our arrival. Miners aim in our general direction, and at least two of the Flaum are encased in larger... suits that give them longer limbs and larger cannons through metal extensions.

"Is this a threat?" I ask Viera as we slowly exit the shuttle.

"Maybe they think we're the danger."

"You're an unknown," Lan hisses as she steps back from us to remove any chance she gets hit by a stray shot. "The Vincere do not like to take unnecessary risks."

"That's right, we might just go crazy and blow up your ship right here," Viera says, shaking her head as she does it, a motion that stop as soon as all those miners snap to attention and the low whine of charging weapons fills the bay.

"I would not make jokes." Lan nods towards the docking bay's only exit, a thick clay-red door that appears very much shut.

"Touchy," Viera whispers to me as we follow Lan towards the door.

"The Vincere have never been known for their cheer," T'Oli states from my back, where the Ooblot's adopted its customary perch. "Some say you have to murder your sense of humor to join."

"We save our laughter for the battlefield," Lan says without turning back. "Where we mock our enemies as they fall."

"Remind me not to invite them to our next party," I say to Viera.

Beyond the red door, which opens only after we've been scanned and Viera's had her pistols and sword confiscated, there's one of what I gather to be many, many hallways. It's a wide one, and full of shuffling troops, floating platforms covered in crates, and the occasional buzzing drone shooting by above our heads.

Messages ordering individuals, squads, or other nouns I don't know echo overhead, and nobody bothers paying us any attention. At first, given our reception, I'd have thought we'd be the stars of the ship, but Lan informs us that as we've been cleared, we're no longer worthy of note.

"Where are we going?" I ask Lan as we keep walking and I lose myself in the maze.

"We're taking the long way to the bridge," Lan replies.

"Why the long way?" Viera asks.

"So you understand the scope of the ship, and your place within it."

I could choose to take the words as a threat, but our slow pace and the endless activity around us give me a chance to mull them over. We're on a military vessel, part of the so-called 'Vincere', and Lan's told us the point of coming with them will be to present humanity to the Chorus as a species worth having in the galaxy. Around us, Flaum and Whelk, along with scattered few of other species whose names I don't know—stick-like ones with tiny limbs, and large, lumbering things that look like living rock—yet all of them defer to Lan's presence. They move out of her way, don't meet her eyes, and generally act like my own guards do around me.

Where would humans fall in that hierarchy? Lan's words seem to say we'd be right in that same mix, clustered among the species meant to serve and support the Oratus and their force. Assist the Amigga in any way they desired.

"Just what place is that?" Viera asks the question as I reach the conclusion.

Lan hisses a laugh. "Whatever place is chosen for you. The Chorus sets the galaxy's purpose, and the bounds of the lives within it."

The cruiser's bridge is unlike anything I've seen before —the triple-wide doors open onto a raised platform that splits a broad, silver-blue pit in which dozens of Flaum and other species work at various stations. Overseeing all of them, at the end of the platform, is rust-colored Oratus whose scales are so scarred as to make me wince at all the pain it has to have felt.

Beyond the leader, as the rust-colored Oratus, by its straight-edged stance and slow panning gaze, makes clear that it is, sits a vast transparent shield showing, in its lower right corner, the soft blue edge of Earth. Coming into view dead ahead is the bulk of Nomis, her gray surface looking pocked and dark from this distance.

Lan leads the three of us out onto the platform, then bids us to stop about halfway to the end while she continues on.

"Maybe our species isn't good enough to go all the way," Viera says.

"We've been discounted before," I reply. "We proved them wrong."

"Undoubtedly, your past results will be indicative of future success!" T'Oli says, though only through the quietest of tapping talk.

"Are you being sarcastic?" Viera says the words to the Ooblot on my back.

"Yes." T'Oli shifts up onto my shoulders, so its less like

a pack now and more like a cloak. "The odds of a species with your level of technology making an appreciable mark on the galaxy are slim."

"Yeah, well, you're a living puddle. So there."

I can't quite suppress a laugh, which causes a smile to spread across my face when Lan and the rust Oratus stomp up and stand over me.

"Lan tells me your name is Kaishi," the rust Oratus says. "I am Kolas. Welcome to my ship, my fleet, and our galaxy."

I don't know what the protocol is here—if this were, say, a leader of a Solare tribe back home I would bow. However, I'm also an Empress. I'm here representing all of humanity. And our species should bow to none.

So I give Kolas a nod instead, and hope that's sufficient. When I look back up at the Oratus, I notice Kolas has steel-colored eyes, an unnatural blue-gray shade that seems as hard as the metal. Its mouth is full of sharp teeth, though many of these are jagged or broken.

"You're an ugly one," Viera says from behind me. "Lan here's saying that we're low down on the species pecking order. Thing is, I don't know how we can be beneath something like you, seeing as you're all beat up and broken."

I close my eyes tight. Sigh. Hope that Viera's words don't get us eviscerated right there, right then.

Instead of death whistling towards me, though, what I get is a loud hissing laugh. Kolas, when I open my eyes, is nodding, still laughing, towards Viera.

"What is your name, little human?" Kolas says. "Your bravery does your species credit."

"Viera," my friend and current exasperation, says. "Figure we ought to start negotiations off strong."

"If only it were I that you needed to persuade," Kolas says. "I am the Chorus' vessel to lead the Vincere, but I am not the Chorus itself. Keep your courage for them, and they will treat you well."

"Will they?" I ask. "Because I don't think they wanted us to exist."

That prompts the first surprise I've seen on an Oratus face. Lan's mouth pops open slightly, her vents sucking in a bunch of air. Kolas, though, only gives me a dead stare, what remains of its humor dying away quick.

"You were a failure," Kolas says. "A species far more independent than the need called for. Look what we already have—Flaum, Whelk, Vyphen. All of these are as capable as yours, and more pliable still. That is why you have a tough trial ahead. You must prove the galaxy needs you."

Kolas' answer doesn't tell me why the Chorus made humans at all, what that need was, but before I can ask the question, the Oratus turns and barks an order down to the pit of Flaum. A call to prepare the cruiser and the fleet for a leap. Kolas glances back at us.

"Lan will take you to your cabin for the leap," Kolas says. "When it's done, you can return here to witness the end of the longest war in galactic history."

A familiar ship floats beyond the pair of frigates. The *Mobius*, coasting in space like the head of a trident, waits for Sax and Bas well out of range of any surprise Vincere attack. Before they dock, Sax manages to send one last message of thanks to Rav, though when the commander asks where they're going next, Sax keeps quiet.

"The next mission," Sax hisses through space to Rav.

"There's always another one," Rav replies. "Good luck, Sax. I hope I don't have to rescue you again."

"You won't." Sax doesn't add that if they need rescuing where they're going, it'll be too late.

The Flaum pilot doesn't bother asking either, and the creature seems relieved when the airlocks open and the two Oratus make their way out of her ship. Knowing the bloody chaos that tends to follow him around, Sax doesn't blame her.

Standing on the other side of the airlock is a familiar site: Plake, her rainbow feathers furled around her arms stands center, with Agra-Red, a crimson, jelly-like Whelk whose body holds a gigantic miner embedded into its side, armed and ready beside her.

"Engee and Nobaa are busy back near the engines," Plake says when Sax looks around, curious. "I left Silver and Black on Rathfall." Plake winces for a second. "Really, they left me. Apparently your bug-hunting strategy is earning them more than running cargo ever would."

"Coorvin?" Sax asks.

The older Flaum is the only one of that species Sax likes. Coorvin's long tenure under the vice-grip of a psychotic Amigga has made him an infinitely preferable companion to the chattering madness of his brethren. That, and Coorvin's uncanny ability to slip around unnoticed through the side ways of spaces would make him a valuable asset for their mission.

"He's gone ahead," Agra-Red speaks for its captain. "The little guy is quiet, but I think he's burning for a bit of revenge. Wouldn't like to be an Amigga caught alone with him."

"He's a Flaum," Bas says. "What could he do?"

"Species have been killing each other long before your claws ever showed up, Oratus," Agra-Red replies. "Coorvin's clever enough to find a way."

Rav was kind enough to give Sax and Bas a couple of miners and a pair of masks, but that's all the gear the two Oratus bring onto the *Mobius*, so after a minute's worth of prep, the airlock breaks from the Vincere shuttle and Sax's former pilot takes no spare time in jetting back towards the frigates.

The rest of them form up in the cockpit as Plake powers up the engines for a leap. The captain makes a quick call to Engee and confirms they're good to go. Crash netting falls down around them and Sax straps himself in.

"Anyone ever been to Aspicis?" Plake asks as she hovers a hand over the terminal.

"Never," Sax says and Bas echoes his sentiment. "Nobody would dare attack the Chorus, so we were never called there."

The Amigga's home and, by default, the galaxy's capitol world; Aspicis is almost a place of myth. Sax figures the limited information is by design—to even get onto the planet takes a whole set of clearances. Even Caches, those stores of knowledge kept on ships and, occasionally, individuals were generally wiped clear except to list what had to be done to gain entrance to the planet.

"One time," Agra-Red says, and Sax jerks his heard to the Whelk, surprised. "Before I knew you, Plake."

The captain removes her feathered hand from the launch button. "Anything we should know?"

"We wanted revenge," Agra-Red said. "The Sevora ruined our planet. So we went to Aspicis to plead for a place in the Vincere, a chance to get our own vengeance. It worked, more or less. That's why you've got Whelk in the Vincere now. I was packed into a freighter, and what I know is that we never made it to the surface. The Vincere stopped us well outside of orbit and we did everything over long range communications."

The Whelk's burbling story matches what little Sax knows. Aspicis isn't so much a place to visit as a fortress that only opens for a few.

"So we can't expect to be let in." Plake closes her eyes for a second, then presses the intercom button. "Engee, Nobaa, change the leap target. I want to get as close as possible to the planet itself."

"What?" Engee's voice comes back high and bright. "You know that's dangerous, right?"

"This whole thing's suicide," Plake says. "If we're going to run a blockade, we might as well start as far through it as we can. You like puzzles, Engee. Solve this one."

The Teven says they're getting to work on it, and Plake turns back to the stars. "Funny thing, I never thought I'd do anything worth anything after they took us out of the Vincere. Guess I was wrong."

Sax threads his tail through the netting, wraps it around Bas'. "We will never part again."

She hisses a laugh. "Sax, don't make promises you can't keep."

"I'll keep this one." By the slight shake of her head, Sax knows Bas doesn't believe him, but that doesn't matter, because it's his promise to keep.

Engee beeps back, says the calculations are done. Plake's good to launch.

"If this goes wrong," Plake says. "We won't get a chance to say goodbye, so make your peace now."

The countdown starts at ten, but drops to zero faster than Sax thinks possible. Mere heartbeats and then the universe twists and warps around them, the leap folding the *Mobius* through space to the exact point Engee has them set to go. A point that could be occupied by an asteroid, by a passing ship or any number of things. Normally, worlds kept leap corridors clear of incoming vessels and debris, but here they're dodging the designated route. Here, they're going right into the teeth.

When everything snaps back into focus, the only thing Sax can see out the front of the *Mobius* is a huge, glittering hull. A battle cruiser, more than double the size of a frigate—the analysis runs through Sax like instinct—and more than capable of blowing them to bits in moments. Plake, though, gets this too and sends the *Mobius* into a spiraling dive, pulling the deep green world of Aspicis into view.

"Stations!" Plake shouts as the crash netting sucks back up into the ceiling.

There's no gravity on the ship, so Sax and the others depend on hand-and-foot holds to get around. The *Mobius* has a few weapons scattered about its hull, and the two Oratus and Agra-Red head to the respective spots. Sax launches himself towards the rear, where a claw press against a single large terminal at the back of the cargo bay sets up some stabilizing crash netting and sets Sax into place. The terminal shifts to a clear view out the *Mobius'* aft, where scrambling Vincere fighters show as blips between the five-cruiser phalanx extending back into the distance.

At least their leap gives them a bit of surprise. The Vincere fighters are slow turning around towards them, and Sax has plenty of time to settle on the closest trio. And pauses. These aren't the normal Flaum claw fighters, essentially three-pronged hooks, that Sax is used to. These, rather, look like needles. Their profile is long, thin and tiny. They also don't seem to have any weapons.

"Are you seeing these?" Sax hisses through the intercom in the terminal.

"I don't recognize them," Bas says, she's on his right, on the edge of the hull. "They must be new."

"Don't care if they're new or old," Plake says. "Get rid of them!"

The first bright flashes of hot energy lance out towards the *Mobius* from the nearby cruiser, though the shots are wide and travel above and below their ship. Sax isn't surprised—the cruiser would have a hard time hitting the tiny target, but if it could keep the *Mobius* trapped into a narrow lane, the Vincere fighters would have an easy job taking it down.

So Sax focuses, aims and starts a stitching hot fire through space back towards those needles. Behind the first trio, there are another dozen and they're closing fast. Too fast. Sax can barely see them, and the terminal's having a hard time picking up those small profiles on its scanners, so the Oratus is essentially shooting into the dark and hoping.

On either side, Agra-Red and Bas open up too, their streams having a harder time getting close to the needles, which are doing their best to stay right behind the *Mobius*. Sax can't tell if he's getting hits until one shot gets lucky, nails one of the needles in its cockpit and sends the fighter into a sparking, swirling dive away from them. Only the strike comes at point blank range, with the needles so, so close.

The needles haven't fired a shot, and they're still coming closer.

"They're going to ram us!" Sax hisses as he realizes just why these fighters have those long, pointed shapes.

"What?" Agra-Red manages to say before the first needle fighter punches into the back of the freighter.

There's a wrenching, sucking sound as the housing around one of the *Mobius'* engines tears away and the pointed end of the needle rips through. A hot second later, as high-pitched Teven shouts come through the intercom, a steady whine fills the freighter and Sax's terminal sparks and dies. It's not hard to tell what's happened, and the sucking sound of vacuum makes it clear the *Mobius*, with a single strike, is done.

"Get to the evac mods!" Plake's yelling as she comes running out of the cockpit.

Her voice barely carries over the noise of the *Mobius*

pulling itself apart. There's two of the escape craft, both latched onto the cargo bay like leeches. Sax talon-and-claws his way to the first one, slaps at the panel to open it. Hard-wired to the evac mod's own batteries for issues just like this, the panel still works enough to open the escape mod's door. Bas crashes against Sax, and together the two Oratus tumble in.

Agra-Red joins them a second later, and the Whelk slaps shut the door and sets the evac mod to ready for launch.

"They're all in the other one," the Whelk says as Bas and Sax hiss questions at him. "We're going."

An evac mod is weaponless, essentially a floating tank with a rocket on one end. If they spit out into space filled with lasers and fighters, they'll be easy targets.

"Don't launch yet," Plake's voice comes over the intercom—short-range communications between the two craft. "Wait till the last minute. I put us into an unstable dive towards the surface."

As if playing to her words, the evac mod begins to shake as Aspicis tugs against its fall. As they descend, the rumble increases until the evac mod jolts hard, too hard for atmosphere. Agra-Red does something then that Sax doesn't think is possible—the Whelk gets even redder, as if the blood in its gel body literally boils.

"That was the *Mobius*," the Whelk oozes. "Plake and I spent a long time earning that ship, running cargo for other idiots and saving our scratch till we could get her."

Sax, whose been a part of many Vincere ships lost to the explosions of war with the Sevora, can't empathize. He's never put much value in any craft—there's an inevitability that they're going to go up in a burning fireball someday.

"You'll find another," Sax hisses.

"You've never had to earn anything in your life," Agra-Red replies. "What would you know?"

"I earned my name," Sax says.

The pair glower at each other while Bas watches out the front viewport as Aspicis fills every available view. Sax follows his pair's eyes—no sense waging a war of wills with the Whelk, as Sax could shred the creature here in a second, and the ability to end, permanently, an adversary is the most important calculation in any argument.

What Sax does notice, though, as he looks out into space is that there aren't any other shots streaking past them. The Vincere fighters aren't, apparently, following them towards the ground and the cruisers aren't attempting to immolate them either.

"Why?" Sax says to Bas. "They should be able to destroy us before we hit the ground."

"Two evac mods," Bas says. "That's it. This can't be an invasion, and no doubt they're tracking our landing zone. They'll be waiting for us."

"They'll be getting more than they expect," Agra-Red burbles, its floppy arms wrapped around its miner.

"Interrogation?" Sax asks the only reason that comes to mind.

Why let an opposing force make landfall on your own turf unless you'd benefit?

"Either they don't know who we are, and they want to understand what would make someone try to leap that close to Aspicis," Bas says. "Or they do, and want to make an example of us."

Ah. The last makes sense. Sax has been party to plenty of those. Little pockets of resistance; planets or species that decide they'd like to make their own decisions rather than abide by the Chorus' demands. Those bursts of independence live until a few sets of Oratus show up and the sky bleeds as Vincere cruisers obliterate cities from orbit. Then, with video broadcasting everywhere, Sax holds up the leader of the cause with a claw to whatever part is going to make the most compelling demonstration and either extracts a loyalty pledge, or exacts the costs of refusing one.

"They won't have that chance," Sax says. "If the situation is impossible, then we must prevent them from taking us alive."

"I'll do the honors," Agra-Red says. "Wouldn't mind getting to blast a couple of Oratus before I go."

If there was any way Sax could make the Whelk's demise in this evac mod plausible, he'd act on it, but since there isn't, he settles for a glare at the crimson blob.

The evac mod postpones their fight, though, by entering the heavy part of Aspicis' atmosphere. Outside, blue-orange fire rings the viewport while, inside, the three occupants jostle on their benches. Sax uses his claws to grab holds, except his left midclaw, which is reserved for Bas. Agra-Red simply bobs with the motion, its wide, sticky base serving to keep the Whelk set on the bench.

They're silent for a while, listening to the roar and pop of the world coming into place around them. There's something about being so close to instant death that stays Sax from any cutting commentary, any tactical considerations for when they land. It's one of those things that happens on every atmospheric insertion, and on most ship-to-ship assaults; the point where, if a species has a god, they ought to be reaching out to them.

The Oratus have no deities, worship at no altar save the bloody one of survival. Sax doesn't mind this, even here.

With Bas beside him, and a purpose waiting on the planet's surface, Sax has all he needs. Though that doesn't keep his vents from issuing a small sigh when the rumbles quiet and the stress of diving through an atmosphere fades away into a bright, clear descent towards the tangle of giant vines that shroud Aspicis' surface.

Like Rathfall, but without the flowers and many times the size, the Amigga have nurtured Aspicis into a perfect genetic generator of everything they need. Every one of those vines, behind the thick green skin, holds the nutrient goop that fills the ration crates on every Vincere ship. Other planets have been cultivated to serve as forward-based 'farms', but none reach the production of the Chorus' home.

From this high up, Sax can see a few other patches too, clusters of vines adopting shades other than the dominate emerald. Bluish vines the color of morning skies and purple-red ones, like falling leaves at twilight, appear in blots, and serve as crops for the healing gels and weaponized chemicals proliferating more and more through the Vincere forces.

"They'll cover the whole galaxy, eventually," Bas says, staring through the viewport.

As they plummet, the evac mod grows warmer and warmer, equalizing as the horizons disappear and the gnarled knots of green fill the entire view, to a temperature not far from that of Solis. Sax can't smell anything of the planet, though, as the mod itself stays pressurized. Which, considering how fast they're dropping, is a good thing.

Evac mods carry enough juice for their microjets—provided the escapees aren't surfing the galaxy for too long before their descent—to make it through a bumpy landing even on high gravity planets. Aspicis isn't particularly large, but it's big enough for the evac mod to make a hard lurch when its jets fire up.

"Plake?" Agra-Red says and Sax turns to see the Whelk's using the evac mod's short-range communicator. "You still with us?"

"We're toasty, but here. Don't think they bothered to shoot at us."

"The Oratus think that means they're waiting for us on the ground."

"We don't think," Sax says, loud enough for the intercom to pick him up. "We know."

"I agree with the uglies," Plake replies. "Be ready for company. I've got a set of coordinates for Evva, or at least a safe-house, so if we can get that far without them tagging us..."

The rest of her words fade into a burst of static as the evac mod pushes all of its power into the final stages of the fall. If the first minutes seemed to take forever, floating through space on a slow slide into the planet, the last couple pass by like lightning, the vines swarming towards them and, with a half-second warning from Bas, slamming into the mod.

The escape craft is study, though, and it batters through the vines like a miner's blast through a thin wall. The viewport goes from a small window into the outside world to a useless smudge of purple and green sludge as their crash makes soup of Aspicis' foliage.

At least, until they hit the ground beneath.

It's soft, loamy soil—everything on Aspicis is controlled for optimum conditions—and it catches the evac mod like the pillow Sax wishes he has behind his head, which bangs into the side of the mod as it tilts over and stops.

A hot second later, having confirmed the atmosphere

breathable, the evac mod pops its hatch open and lets Aspicis' humidity flood in A safety feature in case the mod's passengers are incapacitated or it's landed in a sinking lava lake, the quick open lets Sax slice away his small netting and bound out of the craft.

Onto a world he never dreamed he'd see.

Our quarters are little more than a few scraggly nets hanging from the ceiling. One for Viera, one for me, and T'Oli weaves itself through and then uses its Ooblot genes to harden itself around the bands. The room we're in is thin and featureless, with a panel on the outside of the entryway and none on the inside. As soon as Lan shows us in, the Oratus retreats out of the room and the door shuts in a final way that says it's only going to open when someone whose not us tells it too.

"Guess I shouldn't have expected better," Viera sighs as we slip into the netting.

A voice interrupts her, playing through an intercom embedded next to the door, beginning a countdown to the leap.

"Why, because we're on a Vincere ship?" I ask.

"I thought these were the good ones," Viera replies. "We fought so hard to escape, and then beat back, the Sevora. Seems like we're owed a break by now."

"Clarity's Dawn survived for a very long time in the depths of Vimelia," T'Oli breaks in then. "Every one there deserved a break, a chance to leave and make something of themselves, and we never did."

The mention of the rebel group takes me back. We'd barely escaped Vimelia because of the large raid the group of freed species staged. Their goal had been to get a signal to the Vincere, to tell them the location of the Sevora's home-world so the Chorus could use their military might to end the war.

Clarity's Dawn hadn't pitched the thing as a suicide mission.

"No," T'Oli says when I ask it. "But just because you don't come right out and say it doesn't mean it's not true. Few of us expected to live through that day."

"Well, I'm glad you did."

The leap comes hard and fast, a sudden lurch followed by the twisting, bending and almost breaking of reality. My senses go haywire as colors splash across my vision, my stomach heaves and roils, and waves of ice-cold numbness play touch-and-go with extreme heat. It lasts a few seconds and feels like years.

"I'm never going to get used to that," I say when the universe rights itself.

"It's not the easiest method of travel," T'Oli says, "but it is the fastest."

Viera expresses her feelings through the contents of her stomach, which make a splashy entrance on the room's floor. Lan, who opens the door a moment later, doesn't spare the residue a look. As the three of us head back out into the corridor, small cleaning robots, looking like whirring disks, hover into the room.

Lan doesn't speak as we head back to the bridge, even when I ask her a few questions, like where are we, when can I get a meal, and how high rank is Kolas. Her mind is obviously elsewhere, and eventually we all join that soft silence.

When we get to the bridge, I understand why: out that massive windshield is a shape I've seen before. A large, beige sphere, the home of the Sevora is awash with flashing light. Out here, what must be dozens and dozens of ships swirl around each other in deadly dances—shapes that I think would be invisible save for the red and blue outlines the windshield places around all that come into view.

Kolas no longer stands free and clear in the middle of the platform: four struts have risen out of the edges of his station, and the Oratus' head is wrapped in what looks like a half-sphere of pearl.

Lan keeps us well back, letting us take in the constant stream of voices from the pits below, the intercoms around us, and the overhead announcements. Those last sound like orders, demanding this and that group report to this and that section.

"You're attacking their home," Viera manages to say. "Didn't think that'd ever happen."

Now Lan hisses low and slow. "We never knew where it was, until an anonymous signal came through one of our listening beacons not long ago. All it had were these coordinates, and what they were."

"Then we succeeded," T'Oli says, but the Ooblot's slapping voice hardly sounds jubilant. "There were no others?"

"Not that I know of." Lan asks T'Oli what the Ooblot means, and T'Oli goes into Clarity's Dawn.

I tune out their discussion, instead focusing on Vimelia, and how the planet is coming closer as our cruiser approaches it. I've picked out the color scheme now too, and the vast amounts of red indicating the Vincere forces have the blue-tinged Sevora in a slow collapse. A tightening vice around the planet.

"This isn't just a battle," I say to Viera. "This is an extermination."

"The Sevora killed Malo," Viera replies. "Exterminate them."

Without the Sevora, without Ignos, I wouldn't be here. Viera and Avril's people, the Lunare, would have rolled through our jungle and destroyed our tribe. Their weapons would have proved too much for Malo's people, the Charre, as well. Only with Ignos, a Sevora that crashed to Earth, did we put up enough resistance to save ourselves. And yet, all of that pitched against the horrors the Sevora deliver to the galaxy, that they delivered to me... I'm not lifting my voice to save them.

We spend a long time watching the slow-moving destruction. However hungry or thirsty I may have felt before, the thought of leaving the bridge and the view of the constant explosions, the burning death by fire, and the inexorable advance of the Vincere, doesn't cross my mind.

Only when Kolas emerges from the sphere, striding its gleaming, scarred rust-colored self up to us do I shake out of the battlefield trance.

"So you see," Kolas says. "At last, we have them trapped. Not a single Sevora ship has escaped the system since we arrived, and not a single one of them will live out this fight."

"How can you know?" I say. "There might be more of them throughout the galaxy."

Kolas gives me a slight nod. "True, and one may create their entire force again someday, but without Vimelia's resources behind them, the Sevora will need many miracles to threaten the Chorus again."

"Are you going to burn every inch of the planet, then?" Viera says.

Kolas points out the front of the windshield, towards the bottom of the viewing area, where a hint of the golden oval on the cruiser's front peaks through. "Vimelia has a large satellite moon. With this ship, we can break its orbit. When the moon descends into the planet, the impact will do our work for us, and ensure any Sevora buried deep in Vimelia's crust die as well."

Viera's speechless. I'm not so impressed.

"You're claiming they're all guilty," I say. "That they all deserve to die?"

"Of course," Kolas says. "The Sevora are the only advanced species left that is not bound to the Chorus. They have refused to accept our terms and join the galaxy. As such, they are a threat and must be obliterated."

Kolas finishes speaking, inhales as though the Oratus is going to continue its listing of reasons why the Sevora must die, but a sudden call from one of the Flaum below kills the idea.

"Admiral, we have an incoming message from one of the Sevora factions," the Flaum, a scruffy white-and-tan one, announces from its terminal. "I wouldn't bother sending it to you, but it's a strange one, sir."

"Stage it," Kolas says, nodding towards the windshield.

"For everyone?"

"These are the last gasps of a dying species," Kolas hisses. "We all deserve to know how they would end their lives."

The Flaum argues no further and turns back to its terminal. I'm staring at Kolas, wondering what the Oratus could be thinking—as an Empress, I heard plenty of private messages that would be both interesting and entirely inappropriate for other ears. Apparently the Vincere, or at least Kolas, operates in the open.

There's a flicker across the windshield, and then a large part of Vimelia disappears beneath a wide black rectangle. One that fills in with a vast, crowded chamber. Species sit in rows, pressed in among each other. Flaum, Whelk, Teven, and others I can't name are all staring stiffly back at the window or at the other, miner-armed guards caught on the edges of the frame, aiming at what are apparently prisoners.

"Do you see all of these innocents?" Jel's warbled voice comes through, slightly garbled in the transmission. The creature and its Whelk host lead a faction of the Sevora that wants peace with the rest of the galaxy, but that have never had the power to force it. "If you continue your assault, all of them will die. Their blood will be on your claws. Or, you can negotiate. Work with us to find a solution that does not require genocide!"

As Jel's warble dies away, the window pans to the far end of the lines of species and begins a slow crawl through them. I'm expecting to see anger, fear, on the faces there, but all that shows is a steady resignation to the fate consigned to them. Many of the species look old, with falling clumps of hair, blotches of broken skin or even lost limbs. Hosts rejected and unwanted by the Sevora.

"Kaishi," Viera says.

I know. I see him too.

"Malo," I say his name and it's a ghost coming back to life, a spirit I never thought I'd see again made flesh right there on the windshield.

It's easy to identify the Charre warrior, my friend and leader of my armies, as he stares straight back at us. Always courageous, always defiant, Malo nonetheless looks closer to the edge of death than when we left him. I see cuts running along his skin, bruises along a frame that's thinner than I remember. Still, those eyes pierce across the distance to me.

"Reach out, and help us save the galaxy!" Jel's final plea dies as the window fades and vanishes, putting Vimelia back in its center frame.

The Flaum manning the bridge don't seem to have noticed—they carry on their chittering commands the same as before. Lan, though, has her eyes on me, as does Kolas as soon as the admiral turns around.

"They have a human?" Kolas asks as it approaches.

The question prompts a recapping of our last trip to Vimelia, one I speed through with as little detail as possible, because every second that passes, I feel, brings the Vincere closer to their moon-crashing moment.

"Then you would have us save him?" Kolas asks. "You would have us negotiate with the Sevora to save the life of a single human?"

I know what the Oratus is doing. I know Kolas wants to trap me in a terrible argument—the one that every ruler must make at some point: how much is a single life worth?

To me, though, Malo is worth whatever it takes.

"You're not going to destroy this planet," I say. "Not with Malo still on it."

I make the gamble. I don't think Kolas will give up on torching Vimelia or eliminating the Sevora entirely, but I might be able to persuade the Oratus on this one life.

Kolas folds its four claws together and gives me the sort of toothy grin I've come to associate with predators who know they've caught their prey.

"Do you know why we brought you here with us, human?" Kolas says.

"I thought it was about witnessing revenge," I reply. "For what the Sevora did to Earth?"

"In part. Yet, we need to see your resolve. The galaxy has no place for species unwilling to make sacrifices for its progress."

"Saving Malo is a sacrifice?"

"The Chorus would say that your ties to a single person make you weak," Kolas says. "However, as an Oratus, bound by the strength of the pairing, I think a single person may be the thing most worth fighting for." The Oratus reaches out with its left foreclaw claw towards me. "You want to rescue your Malo? Then I give you leave to do so. I cannot, though, risk any Vincere lives in the process, and the Sevora planet will be destroyed, with or without you on it."

The evac mod's crash has punched a hole through the tangled ceiling of vines, a hole which now casts the only light Sax can see into the space. Aspicis orbits a white dwarf star, and its pearl sheen has Sax wincing as he scans for any immediate threats.

If there are any, they've been coated by the dirt thrown up by the crashing mod. Beyond the shower of deep brown —almost black—dirt, there's evidence of what Aspicis looks like when it's not serving as a landing pad; a thick coating of browning, old vines and the mosses intent on consuming them. Even these have probably been constructed by the Amigga to grind dead vines and refresh the soil.

The mosses, though, aren't making the noises Sax hears. Namely, the constant stream of vicious cursing coming from his right. the light, burbling voice of a Vyphen.

"Sounds like the captain made it," Agra-Red says as the Whelk emerges next to Sax, hands guiding the heavy miner embedded in its chest.

The slug-like creature slides out of the mod, its red look turning almost pink in the white light. The Whelk moves by shifting its skin around itself, like a tread, and as Agra-Red hits the soil, the dirt sticks to its body so that by the time the Whelk hits the edge of the clearing, it's a mottled mess

By then, though, Sax and Bas are out of the mod too, carrying a couple of emergency ration packs, along with a pair of small miners holstered by their masks. The masks don't have real belts, but instead form themselves to the handles of anything pressed against them, sealing the item against their body until Sax or Bas decide to reach for it.

"Who wants to lead?" Agra-Red asks, its two large eyes peering out from its new dirt goggles. "Don't pick me. I do better when I get a chance to aim."

Sax lets a hiss loose and steps around the Whelk. Unlike Rathfall, these vines are too thick to cut—not that Sax can't, he just doesn't want to spent the time—so instead he climbs over, through, and between. No thorns, at least, and the vines are soft enough so that Sax can grip them. Bas follows his path, occasionally picking up and lifting the Whelk through any areas Agra-Red can't slime through.

They follow Plake's loud noises for a few minutes until they come to the second evac mod, only, instead of the Vyphen captain and the pair of Teven, all Sax sees is an empty mod and a deserted clearing. A quick hop to the craft confirms Plake's voice is coming out of the intercom, and is looping through a recording.

"She's not here," Sax says.

"Then why?" Bas says behind him. "What's the point of making the noise?"

"To draw them out," the voice matches the continued cursing on the intercom, and Sax looks back towards the edge of the clearing to see Plake perched up on a vine. Now that he's watching, Sax sees the Teven pair as well, opposite Plake. All of them are holding miners.

"They're going to be here soon," Plake says. "I don't want to fight them on the run."

Sax doesn't need to ask who *they* are—it's plenty evident from the rising hum that something's approaching, and odds are low that something's going to be friendly.

"We can't fight them all," Bas calls up to Plake. "We have to run!"

Sax is briefly thankful it's his pair calling for the retreat—he's not sure he has such an order in him.

"Not yet," Plake replies, and Sax catches a sneaking smile on the Vyphen's face, resting on her folded feathered arms up on the vine. "They don't know who we are. There won't be many. We can knock out this force, then disappear before they can call any reinforcements."

"Not a bad plan," Sax says, and anyway they're out of time, so the Oratus breaks for the edge of the clearing.

Bas follows and the two of them climb up to a spot in between Plake and the two Teven, who are nestled together with their miners sticking out like weaponized thorns. Agra-Red, emphatically unable to climb, sludges its way inside the evac mod.

"I think I like the Whelk," Bas hisses as she settles on the vine next to Sax.

"It's deadly," which is the highest praise Sax knows how to offer.

The hum grows louder, then splits into two. A pair of shuttles. Sax and the others came down in a pair of evac mods, so that makes sense, but it means they won't be fighting the whole Chorus contingent at once. Plake's plan depends on speed—if they take too long to eliminate the Chorus forces, they'll be running away under fire. On a planet run by the enemy, finding a hiding spot in that condition would be difficult.

Sax taps his tail against Bas', and she understands what he's getting at. The two of them break from the clearing, Sax getting one quick nod towards Plake, and dash through the upper layer of vines back towards their own mod.

The Chorus shuttle hovers over their original clearing, a deep blue vessel bearing the orb-and-lines sigil of its owners. Side slats fold out, giving clear view of the armored Flaum squad dropping down towards the ground. Unlike on more industrial planets, these Flaum don't have magnetized boots to catch their fall on metal floors. Instead, the boots on the scrawny, furry creature's small feet pop as they near the soil.

Kinetic packets—they store up energy with motion, release it when called for to provide just enough thrust to break a fall or give a jump the boost to get the Flaum where it needs to go. Crucial for lesser species to keep up with an Oratus.

Not that it's going to help them here.

Six Flaum, all armed with miners and wearing light vests glittering with reflective coatings meant to disperse laser fire. Better equipped than a casual inspection, yet still hopeless.

Sax flicks his eyes towards the shuttle, then down to the Flaum. Bas makes a slight gesture with her foreclaw towards the sky. Sax grins. His pair always prefers the more interesting challenges. Then again, Sax has gone a while without a good bit of gristle between his teeth.

The sign comes from behind them; chittering shouts and screams as Plake, Agra-Red, Nobaa and Engee get to work blazing away at their team. The noise puts Sax's targets into a frenzy, reaching for various communication devices and then raising their miners in the direction of the noise.

Where they don't look, though, is up.

Sax descends, a hissing missile. All claws, teeth, and talons. The Flaum squad is already in disarray; their encircling of the evac mod disrupted by the chaos with their sister squad. Thus it's not a formation that Sax tears into, but rather a scattered group of furry soldiers that likely haven't seen a real fight in their entire lives.

This, too, doesn't check that box; Sax takes out his first two targets, the only pair near each other, in an opening leap that manages to dedicate a fore-and midclaw to each Flaum, driving them down to the ground with enough of a stab to make sure Sax's victims are more focused on survival than counterattacking.

Using his talons, which get a luxurious grip in the soft, crash-churned ground, Sax bursts to his right, leading the way with his toothy maw to the next Flaum in line. His angle of attack keeps the bulk of the evac mod between Sax and the Flaum he's not ripping into, meaning the first shot that comes his way is courtesy of the fourth Flaum, who's just seen a third comrade tackled and driven into the earth.

As shots go, Sax has seen better. It's a spray of bluish bolts—meaning these forces really were intent on stunning whomever they found—and the shots nail the ground in front of Sax as the Oratus leaps off his latest casualty into the air. He gets high enough for the Flaum's eyes to go wide as they track Sax going up and then, in an unfortunate turn for the soldier, directly down on his reflective vest.

The Flaum's armor offers good protection against an energy assault. It offers nothing more than paper against Sax's claws.

Still, Sax is taking care to avoid mortal wounds. Slaughtering the very forces you want to bring to your cause is a poor way of getting their support. So Sax goes for a light maiming instead, enough to prove that the Flaum's best interests lie in staying down.

Four taken care of still leaves a pair of targets with miners aiming his way, and Sax manages to get his eyes on them as they get around the evac mod. As they raise their weapons, Sax angles to the one for the right, and braces himself to absorb a blast or two.

The blast that comes, though, isn't from a miner. Instead, it's a rain of broken metal and burning terminals pouring from above. A sharp whine cuts between the shouts and shots from both this clearing and where Plake's band is playing its murderous tune as the shuttle's engines struggle with a cockpit that is now nothing more than a shredded, sparking victim of Bas' tearing talons and claws.

Bas leaps clear as the shuttle settles on a crash course into the top of the evac mod, prompting Sax and the two Flaum to perform frantic dives to get clear. Twisting metal shrieks and the gurgling slow-burn of batteries unleashing their pent up energy in fiery gouts works in the background as Sax scrambles along the outer edge of the clearing towards the nearest, still-armed Flaum.

This one's barely recovered from its dive by the time Sax hits, and the Oratus tears away the miner with his fore-claws, takes a soft bite out of the Flaum's leg to ensure it won't be moving anywhere fast, then clinches the fight with a head-side smack from Sax's tail as he wheels towards the last one.

Only, when Sax gets around the wreckage, the Flaum's already taken care of. Bas stands over her prize, breaking the miner into fragments while her right talon presses the Flaum further into the dirt. Sax comes up beside her, gives Bas a quick tail tap acknowledging an assault well-performed, and then they burst off back towards Plake's clearing.

If Sax and Bas fought with some intent on keeping the Flaum alive—Bas even mentions the shuttle she brought down was holding its place on auto-pilot—Plake and the rest of her crew blitzed their enemies with more final means. Sax doesn't need to look more closely at the burned out Flaum to know they won't be getting up again.

"They're never going to join us," Plake says when Bas asks why they didn't go for stuns. "Better to make a statement than play cute with them."

"That's a way to make friends," Sax hisses.

"We're not here for friends," Plake says, then points her miner up towards the second hovering shuttle. "Mind giving me a lift?"

Sax takes the Vyphen in his foreclaws and, with a burst from his legs, gives her a boost up towards the open shuttle. It's a good ten-meter toss, and it gets Plake up to the lip of the open cargo door, which is enough for her to grip and pull herself in.

"Don't start feeling sympathy for these things now," Agra-Red says, slithering up next to Sax and Bas. "If they'd taken us, we'd be stunned then skinned alive in front of the entire galaxy. Guess how many would feel any pity for us."

Zero's a good answer to that question. Sax, though, thinks about Rav and the rest of the Vincere forces back over Solis. If he'd hit those ships like a raging whirlwind and torn as far as he could through their ranks, Sax would never have made it to Bas, would've been gunned down by soldiers who are now allies.

"It's not that simple," the Oratus manages to say.

"For you, maybe not," Agra-Red says.

Any further deep dives into the pros and cons of

keeping your enemies alive vanishes as the pair of eager Teven hit the ground from their vines and make their spindly way over to Sax. Nobaa, whose carapace is littered with pegs and hooks holding all manner of small gadgets, is chattering at Engee, whose own lighter carapace is equally adorned with nicks and knacks.

"The plates, see, transmit the neuro-signals through fiber lines I wove into them," Nobaa's saying, and Sax notices the Teven poking at one of the several breaks in the Oratus' scales now occupied by a layered metal seal. "There's no nerve interruption."

The Teven's limbs slip in and out of holes dotting their carapace, eyes on little stalks included, and Nobaa reaches towards a metal plate dotting the back of Sax's leg, the Oratus jerks it away from the fidgety creature.

"Hands-off," Sax says.

"I only want to show Engee how they work!" Nobaa cries, excitement bubbling out. "You're my creation!"

"He's what?" Bas says.

Sax's pink-gold pair stands tall over Nobaa, whom Sax realizes she's never really met. Going by the look on Bas's face, which sits somewhere between amusement and *I'm going to carve this thing up for dinner*, the first real meeting between the two could be going better.

"The Teven saved my life on the frigate," Sax says. He's already told Bas all about the mirrored Oratus, about barely surviving with the help of Nobaa's metal grafts. "He's more useful than annoying. Barely."

"Hey," Nobaa manages to say, but in the face of eight sets of claws, doesn't push the issue.

"Did they work though?" Engee asks this question. "If they do, that would open a whole new world of—"

Engee's revelations are blessedly cut off by the harsh

wind of microjet air as Plake brings the shuttle down. She can't land it—the clearing made by the evac mod doesn't have the room—but the Vyphen brings the craft low enough for the five on land to climb into it. Sax and Bas take turns helping the less-mobile creatures inside, then clamber up themselves.

It's a tight fit—Sax and Bas adopt a permanent hunch, the backs of their necks pressing against the ceiling—and the shuttle is too bare to offer much in the way of other comforts. Instead, Plake takes the narrow cockpit to herself and the rest of them squeeze together in a back bay that gets even more cramped when Plake shuts the sliding exits.

Agra-Red's gooey self is stuck on Sax's right leg, while Engee and Nobaa stake out a central spot in the shelter of the Oratus' large forms, conveniently making it easy for the two Teven to go on about Sax's metallic additions.

"Evva, or someone working with her, dished us the coordinates to a small village," Plake says over intercom. "We aren't exactly close, so get comfortable."

"How long till the Chorus realizes this ship isn't their's anymore?" Sax asks as the shuttle lurches up and forward, gliding out over a sea of swirling vines beneath a very light blue sky.

"I've been ignoring their calls since I took the controls." Plake doesn't seem concerned about it—she's had a fatal bent to her words ever since they leapt out here, as if this whole thing is destined to flame out into disaster and she knows it.

Plake's worries don't play out right away, and they surf the lower skies over Aspicis for what feels like a long time without the slightest alarm. While they're zipping along,

Sax notices the daylight staying constant, and so Plake pulls up Aspicis' record on the shuttle's computer. The words spill out on the cockpit terminal, and, with the Vyphen pushing another button, a monotone rendition of the text plays over the shuttle's speakers.

Aspicis turns slow on its axis, but the nearby star is cool, so the side getting drenched in light for such long periods doesn't wind up burning away. The opposite, darker half of the planet gets incredibly cold, which is a process that winds up helping those vines turn their insides to the nutritious jelly feeding the galaxy.

As for the Chorus, their Meridia sits on the planet's northern pole, jutting up and out of the atmosphere as it spins.

Plake isn't taking them anywhere near the day/night border, so when she starts hitting the shuttle's microjet brakes, they're still in as bright a world as the one they landed on. Sax can't see where they're setting down; he only gets a picture of vines as they descend, and he thinks they've found a random jungle hideaway until he notices colored lights shining between the big green tendrils.

"Opening in three," Plake says. "Not picking up any welcome, but let's be ready for one."

After her countdown hits zero, the shuttle's side doors slide open and Sax bursts out, his midclaws reaching around his mask to pull off the pair of miners he's carrying. What he earns for his trouble is one very scared, and very young, Flaum. The small furball scurries back from the shuttle, with what looks like some sort of snack bar in its right hand.

Beyond the child, Sax picks up plenty of eyes looking back at him, and soon enough one of those blinking pairs resolves itself into a frantic parent, wearing not a Chorus uniform but standard dirty, tan civilian robes, dashing out and swooping up the child in her claws.

There's no miners, though. No barked orders to surrender or commands to shoot the new arrivals.

"Clear," Sax hisses, and a moment later Bas does the same.

The Teven, along with Agra-Red and Plake, shift out of the shuttle. They form up around Sax—Bas included—and stand, weapons ready.

"This is all I've got," Plake says as they keep their eyes crawling over the shapes hidden behind the vines around their landing zone. "Evva's supposed to meet us here."

"Maybe she doesn't know we've arrived," Sax says, then he sucks in a deep breath through his vents. "Evva?"

The roar carries, though Sax isn't worried about others overhearing. Anyone loyal to the Chorus probably already knows they're here, and with the stolen shuttle being plenty trackable, this is only going to be a quick stopping point anyway.

"Very subtle," Plake manages to say, but Sax isn't listening to her.

What he's listening for, and not getting, is any sounds of welcome. Any recognition or invitation. Even hostility would show they've at least made it somewhere Evva's known. Instead, there's nothing. At least, not till the the same frazzled parent, her child wrapped tight in her arms, comes back out to the clearing.

"You aren't coming to kill us, then?" she says.

"That's not the plan," Plake replies as the whole group levels stares at the only Flaum brave enough to talk to them.

"Everyone says that, and we died anyway," the Flaum sniffs. "There's only one left for you here, and he's not well."

"He?" Plake's keeping her captain role going.

"If it means you'll leave, I'll show you where he is." The Flaum turns around, walks back towards the vines she came from.

Plake glances at the rest of them, gets no opposition, and they start to follow.

"The Chorus will track that shuttle," Bas says what Sax is already thinking.

"Let them," Plake replies. "We'll just have to be quick. Besides, what can we do about it?"

Bas hisses a laugh. "Wait a moment."

She clambers back into the shuttle, which restarts its microjets a moment later. The craft hovers up and out of the clearing, though its bay doors stay open. Bas reappears, hangs down, then drops right into Sax's arms. A moment later, the shuttle blasts off, rocketing away through the sky.

"It'll keep flying until it runs dry," Bas says.

"They'll just trace it back here," Plake replies. "The last spot it stopped."

"After it goes down, yes, but that won't be for a long time."

Plake nods at last, giving Bas the point. Sax finds the whole thing tedious—Bas shouldn't have to explain herself, especially not to a Vyphen. Instead, he plunges forward past Plake, into the vines and to the village itself.

Beyond the landing zone, it's dim. The white light from the star is blocked by the thick vegetation, but the remedy from the village strikes Sax as beautiful; tear-drop lanterns, painted in arrays of purples, blues, and greens are strung up along the vines. The colors shine together, and give view to the damp streets of a real town beneath the growth.

Single-story buildings rise out of mounds in the earth, or

look to be carved from hardened skins of older vines. Doors exist as cotton curtains, which makes Sax wonder how these places survive the long cold that no doubt comes as Aspicis rotates through its slow seasons.

Scurrying through the whole ensemble are families of Flaum. It's been so long since Sax has visited somewhere that's made for actual living and not a military vessel or a place for society's desperate castoffs to find work or refuge that he spends more time than he probably should staring at species just having fun chasing each other, throwing round things back and forth, or playing with various toy figures.

Aside from the lanterns, there's a decided lack of technology here. Sax can't hear the whines of generators, though the smell of cooking fires lingers. Metal seems absent, with some Flaum carrying clay-formed cups and crates made from the rough skin of dead vines.

"This is different," Sax manages to say as they walk.

"It's weird," Agra-Red grumbles. "Not my kind of place."

The two Teven, though, seem to enjoy it. Now that the threat of immediate death has departed, Nobaa and Engee devolve into jabbering scientists, racing from place to place and asking to poke this, taste that or get some explanation as to what a Flaum's doing.

"Are there only Flaum here?" Bas asks their guide, who pauses long enough to turn back towards them.

"Then you're not with the Chorus?" the Flaum says, and must get her answer from the looks they give her. "The Amigga don't allow other species on the planet without strict permission. Not on the surface, at least."

"Why?"

"Because they think you're dangerous. All of you."

The Flaum doesn't sound like she's joking as she says

this, and Sax learns why when they round a particularly large, knotted mound covered in red lanterns. On the other side, nestled against a cluster of vines, is what was another home. Now, though, all that's left are shattered lights, broken chunks of vine and split rock. At the center of it, with a pair of Flaum spreading some purplish gel over his wounds, is a traitor Sax never expected to see again.

Avan both is and is not the Oratus he appears to be. Inside the black-scaled head, covered with more scars and scratches than the last time Sax saw it, is a Sevora. At least, Sax assumes the parasite is still there, still leaching off the life of a Vincere soldier.

Sax realizes he's hissing low and soft when he catches Plake and Agra-Red staring at him. Bas touches his tail with her own, and together the two of them walk past their team-mates and have a closer look at the traitor they once rescued from a Sevora seed ship. At the time, Avan had promised he had valuable information, and not long after sending him back to Evva, her resistance had started.

In a way, Sax realizes, the decision to let Avan live, to send him to Evva, is the whole reason they're standing here right now.

He's not sure whether he regrets that move.

Avan, though, probably does; the Oratus is in bad shape, bearing a vibrant assortment of cuts and laser burns. The loser in a fight that started at range, then progressed to get close and deadly. A quick look at the destruction around them confirms the soil and stone building crumpled inward, no doubt succumbing to an onslaught of energy that boiled away its integrity.

"He lives?" Sax asks the pair of Flaum taking nominal care of Avan.

They glance up at Sax, freeze for a moment before one

nods and they both make a break for it. Sax doesn't chase—the caretakers aren't the target, and it's not worth trying to thank creatures too afraid to handle an Oratus' direct look. So he turns his attention to the traitor.

Avan's eyes are shut, but they open quick when Sax dabs a bit of Stim—a heady mix of adrenaline and other drugs the two Oratus keep in small vials—into the traitor's mouth.

"Where's Evva?" Sax doesn't bother with niceties. Eventually the Chorus is going to find them again, and when that happens, Avan's opinion of Sax isn't going to matter. "Who did this?"

"You made it." Avan's harsh rasp cuts a flash of memory, a bad one where the traitor tricked Sax out of his mask deep in enemy territory.

The Sax of that day might have taken a talon to Avan's throat as he lies there, but this one, the newer one, holds back. Decides to play a longer game. Besides, there'll be plenty of chances to kill Avan later, when the Sevora's no longer useful.

"Answer the question," Sax says.

Avan blinks. Takes a breath, the pain of it evident in the sudden tightening of the Oratus' razor mouth.

"The Chorus tracked us here, or someone sold us out," Avan says. "An Amigga actually came, along with a pair of mirrored Oratus. They took Evva, probably thought they'd killed me."

"Do you know where they went?"

"You think I was still standing when they left?" Avan tries to laugh—it's a hopeless croak. "Ask them. They'll know."

Sax has a thousand more questions for the traitor, but he holds them back. Evva's the priority. So instead he turns and rifles the questions at the Flaum who brought them here, who's still standing with them, like she's waiting for something.

"They're gone," the Flaum replies.

"Where?" Sax says.

"Before I show you," the Flaum says. "I need you to make a promise. The other did, Evva, but in case she does not survive, I want you to make the same one."

"Promises?" Plake interrupts. "You'll tell us where they took Evva, or we'll—"

"Stop," Sax hisses at the Vyphen. "What do you want?"

The Flaum flicks her eyes at the village around them, then down at the child still in her arms. "Promise that you won't destroy this world. Evva said she would not, that destruction was not her goal. If I help you, promise that you will not ruin what we have."

The Amigga run the galaxy, have run it for so long most species can't recall a time when the Chorus wasn't dictating what could and could not happen. Sax isn't so blind to see there isn't a comfort in that, even if the result isn't always good for a species, a city or a planet. Plake, when they first meant, spoke of how the Oratus coming had ruined her life, had forced the Vyphen out of the Vincere and distorted their purpose.

Change is devastating. Sax only has to look at his own claws to see that. Not changing, however, can be equally so. Plake would be dead if she hadn't adapted. Sax would be dead without Nobaa's metal plates holding him together.

"I cannot make that promise," Sax says. "But I can promise that we will try. That whatever change comes when the Amigga no longer control our fates will not be made without thinking of what you have."

Bas touches his tail. It's all the acknowledgment he

needs, and the Flaum's resigned nod is all the reward.

The Flaum leads their small band through the rest of the village, to another landing site. The fight clearly came this way; numerous buildings, vines, and even people bear scorch marks, holes and worse. Piled robes and sheets cover what Sax assumes are bodies, though none seem large enough to be an Oratus.

"How many?" Sax asks as they walk.

"They killed them all. A dozen maybe," the Flaum says. "They only took Evva. She told us to hide, and the Chorus ignored us."

The second landing site is smaller than the first, and bears the signs of at least one small victory for Evva's force: a wrecked shuttle coats the mossy undergrowth, broken and still smoking from one of the microjets.

"So the Chorus didn't fly away," Agra-Red says.

"They're running," the Flaum replies, and points across the clearing.

There, some of the vines are cut, creating a narrow path.

"Why didn't they just call for help?" it's Engee's voice this time, going for the logical question. "We're on the Chorus' world?"

The Flaum shakes her head. "I don't know. Once they had Evva, they took her, and left."

Which means every second they stand here talking, Evva's getting further away. Sax issues a sharp hiss, cutting off Engee's next question.

"Bas and I are going after her," Sax says. "The rest of you follow if you want."

With a quick touch of their tails, and ignoring Plake's command to wait, the Oratus pair break into a run, barging through the undergrowth in pursuit of their commander, and their friend.

The planning goes quick. Despite Kolas saying no Vincere lives would be risked, Lan volunteers to pilot a shuttle down to Vimelia for us. Because the Sevora are holing up within their own atmosphere, the journey down is going to be a dangerous one, and as such, we're stuck with a small, swift craft.

Our crew is five: Lan, her pair Gar, T'Oli, Viera and myself.

The Ooblot, when I tell T'Oli that it doesn't need to come, simply laughs and suggests Viera and I would be dead in a moment without it there to save our hides. I don't bother telling T'Oli that I think the Ooblot's right.

What I do have time for, as we slip on our masks, as we gather up miners and small laser-edged swords to bring down with us, is wondering how Malo survived. I never reached him during our flight out of Vimelia's spaceport. I can see him there, still, lying on the ground by the rock wall, burned, cut and unmoving.

I tried to get to him and failed, and assumed he was dead.

Now I know he's been alive all these weeks I've spent fighting the Sevora, traveling through tunnels, and trying to keep humanity from extinction.

"I don't know," I say when Viera asks me how I'm taking it, as we sit in the shuttle while Lan runs through the pre-flight tests. "I should feel guilty for leaving him here, but what if I had tried to get him and failed?"

"Everyone would be dead." Viera is, as ever, not one to mince words. "You made the right choice, Kaishi. I'm sure Malo would say the same."

"I hope we get to ask him."

Not even the most optimistic of us believes we can simply fly down to Vimelia and, with Viera, T'Oli and I, burn our way into where Jel's keeping Malo and rescue him by ourselves. Kolas has the Vincere establishing a blockade around the planet, content to let the Sevora keep their own atmosphere under control until Kolas decides to smash Vimelia's moon against its surface, something the Sevora apparently don't know the Vincere can do.

I pitched Kolas, there on the bridge, to make a distraction. Just like my Solare tribe would do—keep the boar's attention focused on one hunter while the others prepared the fatal strike. A Vincere raid or bombardment would disguise their coming annihilation attempt, and would give our little shuttle a chance to sneak down to the surface.

Which is why Lan is hissing curses as our shuttle breaks into the atmosphere. Even though Viera and I are strapped in back in the main hold, Lan has the wall screens making it seem like our shuttle is translucent, and Viera and I get a full shot at what a Vincere assault looks like:

Kolas' cruiser is the star of the dozens and dozens of ships, ranging in size from smaller than the shuttle to twice as large as *Nunilite*—a hulking behemoth Lan calls a carrier

—and all of them seem to sparkle at once as they unleash their devastation against Vimelia's surface.

Normally a miner's blast comes only as a flash, a moment that passes with deadly results in less than a blink of an eye. The distance these beams travel, and their sheer size, traps the shuttle in what look like long waves of blue, red, and yellow light. Space is washed out by the brightness, and the fringes of the screens glow as the heat from the lasers brushes against the shuttle's shielding.

"We're going to die now, aren't we?" Viera says, and there's a tight fear in her voice I've not heard before.

"They know what they're doing," I reply. "They won't hit us."

"Always thought I'd die in a fight, or exploring somewhere new," Viera says, and she's not really talking to me anymore, her eyes staring straight out at the cascading shots of light. "Never expected I'd go without control, stuck in something I don't even understand."

"Try to believe you'll *survive* because of something you don't understand," I say.

I realize I'm not afraid, and it's because Ignos, while it took up space inside my head, placed my life, for a long time, on the line of things I didn't understand. Couldn't understand. After a while, I learned to simply let go and trust that I'd make it out the other side. And thus far, more or less, I have.

Vimelia's atmosphere envelopes the shuttle, clear air replacing the black void, the reflected beige of the surface catching the laser light and making the space-black walls of our survival corridor fade. Now those bolts look like glinting flashes, harmless in the cheery daylight. Death all around us and I can't even see it.

Lan, though, who banks the shuttle hard to the left

and out of the fiery rain, can. Jel's communication included coordinates for a meeting, and that's where we're going, hoping that it's where the prisoners are being kept. Until we know for sure, Kolas said their bombardment would avoid any buildings matching the profile in the video.

That leaves plenty of targets, though, and the devastation is evident as we swing around, giving Viera and I clear looks through the shuttle's side down towards the planet's surface.

The great cityscape burns. Buildings crumple and fall as laser strikes burrow deep within their sides, while other beams slice through tube transports or hit Sevora ships still buzzing through the skies, erasing them in fiery pops. Black smoke erupts in plumes, as more and more blasts torch the city.

"It's... awful," I say. "I don't like the Sevora, but this is wanton. They're not targeting—"

"They're going to erase all of this with the moon anyway," T'Oli interrupts. "All of it will be gone, sooner or later. It's not worth feeling bad about it—the Sevora would have done the same to Marilo and your cities if they had the time."

Not worth feeling bad about the demise of an entire civilization? Then again, the Sevora may have obliterated all of the remaining Solare villages back on Earth. The Charre too. An existential threat uniting all of humanity, just in time for me to pledge it to a greater, deadlier force. One that apparently won't hesitate to squash an uprising with extinction-level assaults.

"You can't fight this one," Viera whispers to me. "We're not strong enough. Yet."

Yet. I suppose there's comfort in the idea that, if we're

left alive, we might grow strong enough to avoid the Sevora's fate.

It's something to aim for, anyway.

"Get yourselves tightened up," Gar, Lan's pair and the other Oratus on the shuttle, hisses from the cockpit. "We've got some attention."

The Oratus' warning barely comes in time for me to grab onto the netting before Lan throws the shuttle into a spiraling dive. Outside, I can see we're nearing one of the city's gaps, where the constant carpet of buildings gives way to wider, sparser spaces of sand and the occasional garden. Mountains rise in the distance too, and it looks like Lan's trying to take us closer to their deep brown peaks. Trying, here, being the key; to my right, I can see a trio of black wedges coming straight for us. We're away from the flashing stream of Vincere bombardment now, so the Sevora are free to glide in. At least, they are until red laser bursts from the top of the shuttle, sending burning bolts after our pursuit.

The Sevora pilots begin a weird dance, their ships jerking and swirling around, yet always maintaining their same approach towards us. The fight resembles the clawing, grasping struggle I've seen between jungle birds, where each side swings up and down, trying to get in a strike.

Here, though, we're outnumbered. The Sevora split their trio as they close into the shuttle, breaking up, down, and straight on. Gar, manning the shuttle's defense, unleashes a mighty stream of hissing curses, frantically sending bolts everywhere.

The Sevora, finally, decide to attack.

From three angles, hot energy pours into the shuttle. At first, with blue-white fizzles, the lasers appear to dissipate before striking the hull, though the sudden cascade of bright alarms says the assault wasn't without impact.

"That's just letting us know our shields are gone," T'Oli says. "Every hit takes some energy, and before you know it, you're out."

"I'm guessing that's not a good thing?" I manage to say.

"Not if you're a fan of being alive."

"Told you we're going to die up here," Viera adds.

This time, I can't really deny her. The Sevora fighters swing back around for another blitz, and suddenly the shuttle lurches and I feel my stomach try to fly up and out of my mouth. We're weightless, free-falling, the rapidly approaching ground flowing up to us outside the shuttle.

I'm screaming too, along with Viera, but our voices disappear into a grand clashing of other alarms.

Just before the shuttle strikes the ground, though, it bounces. The netting strains as it catches us, and when my stomach slams back into position, I let loose the remnants of my nutrient goop breakfast.

I don't get a chance to recover, as Lan drives the shuttle forward fast, pressing me away from the nets and pushing out what little air's left in my lungs. Bolts pepper the ground around us, super-heating the sand and bursting trees, hedges and other greenery into flame. There's a flash-pop from above and I hear Gar roar, and see why when the cinder wreck of a Sevora ship slams down to our left, breaking into a thousand pieces.

The other two, though, find their zone. It's easy to tell because the hull above us literally burns away as the Sevora lasers pound into it. First the metal glows orange, then it peels back and a single shot gets through, slices the netting between Viera and I. Without the netting's support, we both fall to the shuttle's floor as more shots stitch the interior.

"Take us down!" I shout up ahead, though with smoke

filling the shuttle's body, I'm not sure Lan has any other choice.

"Get close together," T'Oli says, the Ooblot sliding off the nets over to us.

Viera and I, as the shuttle rocks towards a swift crash, slip close. T'Oli thins itself out, moves over us and, like a blanket, wraps its cool cream skin around our legs. A moment later the Ooblot hardens, giving us some protection as the shuttle begins crashing through gardens and low walls.

If we'd still been in the city, we would have smashed and burned through a building by now.

As it is, I watch through the cockpit, mouth open in an endless scream, as the shuttle buries itself into dirty ground. Sand and stones spray up around the craft, around us, with plenty falling inside, into my hair and sliding off the mask Kolas gave each of us before we left.

Then silence. Loud, terrible silence.

I run a quick check of my body—I'm breathing, so there's that. My eyes can see the broken and sparking cockpit ahead, though the increasing smoke makes it difficult to know whether Lan and Gar are still alive. A couple twitches confirm my arms and legs made it through the crash intact.

"You all right?" I ask Viera.

"Oh yeah. Completely fine." Viera's brushing dirt off her face, her hand moving automatically. "Let's do that again."

"I'd say our odds of surviving another crash like this are very, very low," T'Oli adds.

"Joking, T'Oli," I say. "She's joking. Can you get off of us now?"

The Ooblot complies, softening and sliding off. "What a strange time to tell a joke."

I stand slow, my muscles still freaking out. "Humans are strange, T'Oli." I try to wave away some of the smoke, realizing we probably don't want to stay in the downed shuttle any longer than necessary. "Lan? Gar?"

There's a soft hiss, and then Gar bursts through the smoke, Lan held in his four claws. Lan's emerald skin is burned black all over the place, but I see her vents still open and close.

"Leave, now," Gar hisses, and then he clomps over to the shuttle's side and slaps at the wall panel.

The door doesn't open.

"Of course," Viera says as she stands next to me. "That'd mean something would have to go right on this mission."

T'Oli flows up my side, along my arm and to the edge of my hand. I feel part of the Ooblot harden to latch itself to my wrist, its eye stalks poking out to the sides. The rest of its body extends out from my hand, adjusting its shape to have very fine, very sharp edge.

Guess we're getting out of here the messy way.

"Move," I tell Gar, and the big, deep blue Oratus steps aside as I make for the door. "Hope you're sharp enough for this."

"Easily," T'Oli replies.

I swing the Ooblot, slashing into the side of the shuttle. Every cut peels apart the metal like I'm cutting grass, and in moments we have a makeshift exit. Which is good, because small fires are springing up—at least our attackers did us the favor of burning an exit for the smoke—and I feel another minute inside would leave us burned and baked.

Instead we make it out into a burning field of what looks

like some form of stalk-grown crop. Thanks to our laser-filled crash, though, I'm in the middle of an array of candles. Gar, with Lan, and Viera follow me out, and gradually our eyes are drawn to the approaching whistle of the two Sevora ships.

"They're lining up a run," Gar says. "We have to leave now."

Both of the black shapes look like slivers against the sky as they curl around towards us, and for a moment I wonder if I can pull the miner from my mask and start shooting.

"Don't bother," Viera says to me. "You won't hit them."

I don't get a chance to reply, because Viera pulls me, with T'Oli's now-dulled self still wrapped around my wrist, away from the burning shuttle and after Gar's loping form. The Oratus, even carrying another of his kind, outruns us easily, dashing away into the thicker plants.

"Isn't he going to wait?" Viera huffs as we move.

"Why?" T'Oli replies. "Does Gar owe you something?"

"Is this entire galaxy full of greedy murderers?" Viera replies.

"I'll submit myself as evidence that it is not," T'Oli says.

"What's that?" I say, as much to cut into their aimless conversation as to point out the slim, soft-yellow building rising up ahead of us.

Before anyone replies, there's a skittering boom from behind us, and a quick look confirms that what's left of our shuttle has been sent to whatever afterlife awaits spacecraft. The Sevora fighters tilt up, then their aft jets turn a white-blue and they rocket off back towards the city.

"I think it's what we came for," T'Oli says, its eyestalks angling towards the building. "Kolas had the communication traced, and Lan tried to get us as close as she could."

"Do you really think they didn't see us?" Viera's still

watching the plume trails left by the speeding fighters. "These stalks aren't that tall."

"Either they did and don't care, or they didn't see us at all," I reply. "We shouldn't stand here, though. Let's go."

What none of us say as we walk through the tall stalks towards the building, though, is that we're trapped here now. Stuck on a planet that, whenever Kolas decides our time's up, is going to get very hot, very fast.

As we get close to the building, I notice that its roof keeps changing color. It's not just yellow, but a swirling mix of shades that dart and dash around each other. Jel, and her Sevora faction, had paintings like this on the walls of their base that we saw on our first trip to Vimelia.

"At least it looks like Lan took us to one of Jel's bases," I say.

The word 'base' oversells the building. It's not much larger than the shuttle, and spouts adorn the outside, linked to hoses that are, in turn, stretched to floating drones spraying water over the crops. They don't seem to care that half their field is burning up from our shuttle's explosion.

"There's no door," Viera says a couple of minutes later as we circle the structure. "What's the point of a building if you can't get into it?"

"Maybe we don't have the right key?" T'Oli says.

"Can you make your sword again?" I say. "Then I'll just cut a hole."

"That only works on thin metal, like the shuttle's hull," T'Oli replies. "I'll break if you try to slash rock with me."

I stare at the squat structure. There has to be something we're missing. I'd ask Gar or Lan, but the two Oratus have disappeared. Instead, I run my hands along the soft gray surface. It's cool to touch, and the building as a whole vibrates with the amount of water rushing through it.

"Lan tried to fly us here for a reason," I say. "There's got to be a way in."

"Maybe we need to see the way out first," Viera says, and I see her looking at T'Oli.

"I don't like those eyes," T'Oli says.

"When's the last time you had a bath?" Viera replies, smiling for the first time in a long while.

Using one of the energy blades, we cut a hole in one of the hoses leading to one of the watering drones. The hoses themselves are half as wide as I am, and the amount of water they're spewing is immense, but it's also not constant. The drones shut off their spray if they have to shift across a wide spread of watered crops. It's during one of these short moments when we stuff T'Oli, or as much of the Ooblot as we can, into the tube.

"You're both terrible people," T'Oli says, its voice coming back up the tube in an irritated patter.

"Can you block it?" I ask.

"Already did," T'Oli says. "I went a ways down the hose too—if this works, you'll see a big pop in that corner there."

The drone doesn't seem to notice there's an issue and makes its way to a section of merrily burning crops. There's a burst of rushing pressure, and then the building shudders.

"You both owe me for this one," T'Oli says.

"Whatever you want," Viera replies.

"You don't even have any money."

"We'll get you something better," I say. "A title. Empress's Ooblot."

"Stop it."

The blocked water makes itself known first by the rapid rattling of the spout attached to the building, the spout that T'Oli's blocking with its Ooblot body. Then metal starts to fly as holding rings pop, seams burst, and the entire corner of the building, like T'Oli predicted, crumbles away as the pipe bursts.

Water explodes around us and, as the tube forces its way wide around T'Oli, the Ooblot goes rocketing away too. T'Oli lands a dozen meters away. Viera and I, though, have our miners out and are already walking through the expanding puddle, past Vimelia's newest geyser, into the leaning building.

In the middle of the building's floor is the reason there's no door—there's a platform, big and metal, with a panel on a stand about the height of my head. It's clearly meant to go down.

"Guess we found our way in," Viera says.

"Question is, to where?"

T'Oli catches up with us as we play with the panel. It's not that hard to parse—there's a big arrow pointing down wrapped in a green square—but every time I try to press it, the panel gives an annoyed beep and the whole screen flashes red.

"You know how to work one of these?" I ask the Ooblot as T'Oli slimes its way onto the platform.

After I show T'Oli what's going on, the Ooblot swivels its eyes to me and blinks, then turns its gaze to the back part of the platform, behind where Viera and I are standing. There, wedged into the narrow gap between the platform and the rest of the building's floor is a piece of one of the spout's binding rings.

I glance at Viera and she takes a step over to the piece, reaches and, with a bit of effort, pulls it out of the gap. She throws it away as I press the panel again. This time it flashes green and the lift's motors start revving up.

"Sometimes it's the obvious solutions," T'Oli says.

"More often than not," I reply.

The platform sinks below the surface, into a shaft not much larger than the platform itself. White lights speckle a deep blue-painted wall. Apparently this lift doesn't warrant the kind of spectacular paint job provided to the building's roof, but it's plenty pretty anyway. If I make it back to Earth, I'll advocate more for this kind of thing—life's hard enough, it may as well be pleasant to look at.

"Oh no," Viera says suddenly, and I follow her eyes up to see a pair of massive forms falling towards us.

Gar and Lan land on the platform, their huge bodies causing the lift to rattle, the motors to whine, but apparently the Sevora design their elevators well, because it doesn't stop. I look at Lan, mouth slightly ajar at the sheer scope of the injuries running along her body; burns, broken scales, and a long, dark scar running down her neck.

"A close shot," Lan says as she sees me noticing. Other injuries have clear creams spread across them, stuff that seems to be wriggling. "Nanobots, performing miracles. My mask kept me from dying, and these will keep me useful."

"Why did you run?" I ask Gar, because I don't know what nanobots are, and I'd rather figure out if we can still trust the living weapons that just landed in our midst.

"I needed space to help her," Gar hisses. "You were a good distraction."

Viera has her miner up and aimed as Gar finishes. "Say what we are again, you overgrown lizard."

For once, I agree with my friend, even though I'm sure the two Oratus could kill us without a second thought. Gar, though, just falls into a fit of hissing laughter.

"Overgrown lizard?" Lan says. "I've never heard that description before." The Oratus turns to Viera, who swivels her miner to track Lan. "I don't think you can be picky about your allies here, human. If we leave you, who's going to fly you off this planet?"

"T'Oli and I can fly," I say. "Viera's right. If we can't trust that you'll stick with us, then you should leave. We're in this together, or not at all."

Gar stops his hissing for a moment, and both Oratus look over at me.

"This human is brave," Gar says. "She thinks she can survive on her own."

"But she won't have to," Lan hisses. "Kolas asked if we wanted to help, and we volunteered. We will see your friend returned, or we will die trying."

When Lan says the words, a weight I didn't know was there lifts off my chest. Deep down, I know that Viera, T'Oli and I won't be able to rescue Malo alone—there'll be too many Sevora, and too little time. But with two Oratus? There might be a chance.

It's been a while since Sax has chased anyone, and running through the thick vines of Aspicis makes for an exhilarating rush. He operates on instinct and the tiny shafts of light that manage to poke down from the sky. Each one is a signpost, pointing Sax towards the next bend, the next spot to sink in his talons as he and Bas rocket along the carved trail.

The two Oratus hold their silence during the run, saving their breath for breathing. There's no telling how long it might take to catch up to Evva's captors, or how far the Amigga and its Oratus guards need to get before they'll find another way to fly.

As if sensing the magnitude of the moment, Aspicis itself is quiet. Aside from the *scritching* sounds their talons make as they dig into the ground, there's little other noise; no bird calls, none of the hiss and growls of a jungle, nor the heavy mechanical shunts of technology. The Amigga have constructed their homeworld to their own desires, and Sax finds the result boring.

The smells, too, are bland. The vines don't flower, and

the only scent they bring is a lukewarm nuzzle; a soft, ill-defined layer in the air that tastes of dried grass. The Amigga have embarked on a quest to make the least interesting mix of sensations possible.

That thought ends when Sax reaches the trail's conclusion. It's not clear how far they've run, but they've arrived at another village. Or, no, something else.

What sits in front of Sax is a large cylindrical dome, made from vines that still look alive, but directed to grow like this. The dome itself is huge, several times Sax's own height and long enough to be a space station wing. At the far end, where the dome looks to have been chopped off, sits the greatest concession to mechanical necessity Sax has seen on the planet.

A mag-lev rail.

It's a single shimmering silver bar, and it's raised almost a meter off the ground. The track extends back from the dome away from Sax and Bas, vanishing into the dark jungle.

The dome and the area around it dazzles with brightness, as the overhead vines have been cleared away. Sax can make out other trails leading away from the dome too, and these are occupied with groups of Flaum making their way to and from the station. Some wheel cases behind them, others pull long carts stacked with crates and floating on microjets.

"So Aspicis isn't always obsolete," Bas hisses as she stands next to Sax.

"The war," Sax hisses. "I bet they couldn't keep the planet sacred anymore, not if they needed supplies."

Regardless, what they don't see as they look around is Evva and her captors. The Amigga and its bodyguards aren't anywhere here. At least, not in sight.

"Think they're hiding in there?" Bas says, guessing what Sax is thinking.

"If they are, they'll know we're coming," Sax gestures towards some of the moving Flaum. Plenty of the furry creatures have thrown looks their way, their faces twisting into shock or confusion, then retreating into fear and a quickened step. "Not that it matters. If we can't save Evva, then this is all worthless."

Bas doesn't argue, so together the two Oratus stride across the clearing towards the dome. The entrance to the station is, apparently, on the other side from their approach, so their first sight of the Amigga comes when it rounds the near, slope-sided end of the station.

Unlike Dalachite, the last Amigga Sax's seen, which had grown itself literally into the space station built under its direction, this one has a more typical arrangement: encasing its round, flesh-colored form is a clear shell, with a pair of white-metal bars sticking out from either side. Each bar splits into a variety of appendages, with one jutting straight to the ground and ending in a low-powered microjet that keeps the Amigga off the ground.

What's really important, though, is how many of this Amigga's 'arms' end in miners or edged blades. Sax counts a half-dozen weapons, all of them angling towards the Oratus. Two of the miners, one on each side of the Amigga, loom larger; high-energy models made to devastate and destroy. The ensemble makes clear how the Flaum village wound up a flattened mess of broken homes and burnt bodies.

"You're not cleared to be here," the Amigga announces, with plenty of slime in the words. The voice comes translated and piped through its speakers, so there's no mouth for the Amigga to pull into a caustic grin. "In fact, you're no longer cleared to be anywhere, traitors."

The Amigga doesn't wait for a response—as soon as it finishes the sentence, those big miners on either side start spraying molten energy at Sax and Bas. The two Oratus, though, weren't expecting a friendly chat and manage to dive out of the initial blast. As he jumps to the side, Sax uses his right midclaw to grab one of the miners off his mask and, when he lands, snap-aims the weapon and fires.

His shot strikes home, melting the front of the Amigga's right-side miner, as Bas does the same to the cannon on the creature's opposite. The Amigga's only reply is to laugh and bring its set of four smaller miners to bear.

These don't even get shots off. Apparently the Amigga's not used to facing Vincere-trained, three-letter Oratus, because every time one of its miners takes aim, Sax and Bas blow it to red-hot pieces. Sax has miners in both midclaws now, and they don't stop shooting until the Amigga's left without a single weapon on its rig.

"Where's Evva?" Bas rasps at the Amigga when it realizes it's weaponless and finally stops trying to spin to an armed end.

"Inside," the Amigga says. "Waiting for the train. You can join her if you like. We're happy to take all of you."

The Amigga wouldn't leave Evva alone in the station, which means the mirrored Oratus must be in there, so that's where Sax goes. Or rather, tries. He gets one long stride towards the Amigga, meaning to go around the harmless blob, when something slams into his side and drives Sax to the ground. Then lifts him up and throws him back towards Bas.

"Kah, you didn't need to come out here," the Amigga says as Sax shakes his head to clear away the blurriness. "I had them."

Bas is by him now, helping Sax stand up, and together

with his pair, they turn to see the Amigga's broken and sparking defenses complemented by a massive mirrored Oratus. Sax can't tell much of Kah's features, exactly, as the reflective scales only give a rough outline where the light seems to bend.

"This is what you fought on the frigate?" Bas whispers. "I didn't think they existed."

"They do, and they hurt."

"Traitors!" the Amigga calls. "I ask again—surrender, and perhaps your deaths will come swiftly!"

Doesn't the Amigga understand that a Vincere Oratus will never surrender? That they've been trained to do everything except give themselves to an enemy? A list of things that, as it happens, includes fighting back.

"Finish the Amigga," Sax hisses. "Then help me."

Sax digs his talons into the dirt, fakes a burst forward towards the mirrored Oratus, firing both miners as he moves. Kah doesn't stand still and take the fire, but leaps up and forward, lunging towards Sax just above his firing line, biting on Sax's move. So Sax digs in hard, leans back and brings up the miners as Kah's leap doesn't meet the charge the mirrored Oratus is expecting.

To his right, Sax catches a passing pink blur as Bas heads for the Amigga. Without its weapons, the monster shouldn't be much more than a snack for his pair.

Kah, too, isn't much more than a target for a hot moment as his momentum carries the mirrored Oratus right into Sax's fire. Blistering burns light up on the mirrored Oratus' chest, melting vents and scoring gashes in the creature's reflective skin.

Then Kah's ramming hard into Sax, pushing him back and tearing away the two miners. It's an aggressive call for any Oratus, particularly one that should have been able to engage Sax with something other than its claws. Now, though, they're in a clenched duel of slashing talons, biting teeth, and raking attacks from all four arms.

On Rav's frigate, Sax hadn't been enough. The mirrored Oratus had overpowered him, gashed and sliced Sax to pieces. Here, though, Nobaa's additions prove their worth; the metal plates provide protection, and Sax maneuvers himself to catch the mirrored Oratus' attacks on those pieces while his own claws rake at a body whose whole advantage comes from being hard to see at distance.

Kah realizes quick that this isn't a fight he wants to have, and with a tail sweep, the mirrored Oratus forces Sax back. Bleeding and burned, Kah's having a hard time standing straight, while Sax bears his scratches with an open, hissing mouth. Ready for more.

At least until he sees a second shadow crash into Bas and knock her away. The Flaum back at the village had mentioned two mirrored Oratus, and the second one begins to thrash Bas, pinning her to the ground and going for a mortal strike with its talon. The Amigga, behind it all, crows again for the impossible surrender.

Sax reacts. He falls into the bloodlust, that instinctual do-or-die state Oratus enter when survival leaves no other options. He charges Kah, then feints right, as if he's going to run by the mirrored Oratus towards the cackling Amigga. When Kah goes for it—apparently Kah's not used to tricky fighters— Sax plants his right talon and jumps.

It's a tactic that wouldn't work against a fresh adversary, against one that could leap up to meet him or grab Sax's tail and sling the Oratus back to the ground, but Kah's hurt and tired and misses his chance. Sax lands beyond Kah and, with a hard shoulder charge, bowls the mirrored Oratus off of Bas.

And Bas doesn't burn the moment, getting herself up and pulling free her two miners. Aims one at Kah and the second at the mirrored Oratus Sax has just pushed away from her.

"You said it," Sax hisses towards the Amigga in the suddenly still moment. "Surrender."

"We will not," Kah rasps, moving in slow, unsteady steps towards the Amigga. "Either kill us, or let us go, traitors."

"That's an easy choice," Sax says. "End them, Bas."

"Wait!" the Amigga says, and its voice, for once, isn't drenched in haughty superiority. "You're after us for the Oratus, right?"

"She's inside the station," Bas says. "We'll take her back after we take care of you."

Not that he's deviating from the conflict at hand, but Sax is picking up some rustling in the air. Vibrations in the ground. Paying slight attention to his peripheral, Sax notices that the Flaum moving around the station have all disappeared—not entirely surprising given that miners were firing constantly moments ago, but to have not a single one venturing to and from the station?

"You won't find her there," the Amigga says. "Not yet, anyway."

Amigga have no facial expressions. No tells, especially when their limbs are grown into their exoskeletons. Sax has no idea if this one's lying, but the way the mirrored Oratus stay still mean it's not trying to give them cover for a surprise attack.

"Give me a reason not to fire." Bas gives a slight shake to her miners.

"Now," the Amigga begins. "There's a conversation—"

Bas presses in on the trigger and her left miner fires,

scores a deep blast into the lower abdomen of the left, less wounded Oratus. Neither one, to their credit and Sax's respect, move.

"She's in the station," the Amigga blurts. "I was lying. We stunned her and left her there once we saw you coming. Let us go!"

There it is. The cowardice Sax believes sits at the core of the Chorus, of the entire Amigga species. Why else build a species to fight your battles for you? Why else try to remove anything that threatens your power rather than work with them to find a mutual solution?

Bas nods at Sax, who hesitates. He doesn't want to leave Bas out here with these three. She takes away the choice, though, with a simple touch of her tail, a promise that she'll be fine.

Though he doesn't say it, Sax makes a promise of his own—he'll find and end all three of these monsters if they touch any part of his pair. And with that, he makes a break for the station, looping around the outside of the vine structure towards the entry, which isn't a door so much as a wide arch without a seal of any kind.

Inside, with cold electric globes providing the light, there's a large platform for the mag-lev train. Lying on the ground, unconscious, is Evva. Bunches of Flaum occupy the walls, pressing back to get away from Sax as he moves forward, picks Evva up in his claws, and carries her outside.

As he leaves the dome, the rumble he's been feeling grows, and now it's accompanied by a shrill whistle. Turning his head, Sax can see the bright purple and blue front of the mag-lev train swing into view. It's moving fast, and mostly silent, that rumble coming, Sax realizes, from the pumping of power from somewhere deep beneath him up towards the track.

"Let us on that train," the Amigga's saying as Sax rejoins Bas, who's still holding her miners and her targets dead. "It's the least you can do."

"They tried to kill us," Sax hisses. "Do the same to them."

"Go," Bas announces. "Get on the train, and get out of here."

The Amigga and its escorts don't wait, moving slow and gingerly as Bas guides them towards the train with her miners. The train cars open wide, their entire sides swinging up and letting Flaum come and go, though Sax sees more than a few elect to stay seated rather than get off on the same platform as a quartet of bloodied Oratus and one Amigga who's looking in dire need of a new suit.

Still, space is made. The mirrored Oratus board and help the Amigga join them. The train cars shut, and with another hissing rumble, the mag-lev shunts into reverse and vanishes down the track.

"Why?" Sax asks, finally. "Why let them go?"

"Because I don't know if I could have killed them all before they got to me," Bas says, her eyes tracking the departing train. "You're holding Evva. We achieved the objective. Why risk it?"

His pair makes sense, and yet...

Sax would've taken the shots.

The platform ends its descent by stopping next to a copy of itself. The two platforms sit flush, the second one angling along a straightline tunnel that follows the white globed lights into the distance.

"Guess the ride doesn't end here?" Viera says.

We transfer over to the new platform, which is a tricky process when you've got a pair of three-meter tall Oratus maneuvering all their limbs in the small space. Apparently the Sevora never expected to use hosts like Gar and Lan for the kind of maintenance work these plain platforms are meant for.

The second platform has a panel like the first, and soon we're whooshing along the tunnel towards a dark ending that eventually turns into a massive space. It's as big as the spaceports I saw earlier on Vimelia, but rather than ships buzzing in and out, the giant rectangle populates itself with streams of fresh crops funneling in from one of many openings. Other tunnels with other platforms echo the one we're on, and all of them connect to a grated catwalk that circles the upper section of the chamber.

"Every time I think we've done something right, I see it's being done bigger," I say, thinking back to Damantum's granaries. I thought our storerooms were huge, with enough space to keep our entire city fed for a season. This place, and the amount of food getting shunted into the chamber's lower level, divided by steel walls to sort the crops, makes our best efforts look feeble. "We have so far to go."

"Don't compare yourselves to this place," Gar says. "It will be erased before too long."

It's almost sad, because the sounds of so much plenty pouring in, the sight of so much food that could end so much hunger, shows the Sevora aren't entirely evil. They clearly care enough to keep their own fed, to invest in constructs that support their civilization.

If you're going to keep billions prisoner, I suppose you have to feed them somehow.

There's nothing to our right except more portals to more platforms, and none of them look any different from ours. To our left, the walkway continues a long ways to what looks like a more permanent dividing wall, with an outline of a door. Platforms line the outside this way too, but at least there's something different at the end.

"As much as I'd like to take more rides," I say, nodding to the left. "Let's head that way."

We make it all of a dozen steps before the door we're heading towards slides open. A pair of Whelk, both a sickly blue, slither out, miners raised. I'm about to ask them where the prisoners are when they open fire.

Viera dives into one of the open platform tunnels, with Lan following, while Gar takes a leap to the right, using his claws to grip the catwalk railing and scramble towards the Whelk. Before I can move, T'Oli wraps itself around my chest and hardens to its impenetrable self—just in time, too, as a bolt blitzes into the Ooblot a second later, leaving a hard black scar.

"Any time you want to fire back!" T'Oli says.

I'm on it; I yank my main miner from my mask, raise the weapon and pull the trigger. Bright red bolts lance out, stitching a line well above the short Whelks.

"Sorry!" I say, diving towards the left wall, trying to get inside Viera's tunnel. "I don't really know how to shoot!"

Bows, yes. Miners? No.

"That's what I'm here for," Viera says, reaching out and pulling me into the tunnel.

I'm surprised the Whelk didn't get me with more than one shot, but after peeking back outside, I suppose I shouldn't be; Gar not only drew their attention, the Oratus took care of both Whelk entirely, spreading the sloppy remnants of their bodies all over the catwalk. With a couple of bites, the Oratus snaps their miners into junk.

"It's what he's good at," Lan says as we look at the destruction.

"Apparently." I say.

Gar didn't get through the encounter free from harm—his mask is splintered on his legs and in the middle of his chest, where direct miner shots disintegrated the armor, but the Oratus doesn't seem to care.

We join Gar at the dividing wall, and I take the lead in looking through the door the Whelks opened. On the other side is the reason why those guards were here in the first place; the prisoners we saw on the video are all clustered on the bottom floor of this half. The crop walls have been removed, allowing all of the prisoners to sit on the ground in a giant crowd, along with the dozen guards watching them, miners ready.

There's another quartet up here, on our level, and

they're watching our doorway. I have to jerk my head back as a couple Flaum send fiery shots at me.

"Prisoners and guards," I say and describe the setup. "Lan, Gar, you've got the most experience with this. What do you think?"

"Attack and devour?" Gar hisses.

"Yeah, except we don't want to get shot doing it," Viera says.

"Capture the top level, and the guards below won't have position." Lan takes over. "They'll either surrender or, without cover, we'll finish them fast. As for how to beat the four guards up here, we'll need a distraction, and then some sharp shooting."

Lan finishes the plan with a look at Viera, who nods. "I'll hit them, don't worry."

"Then what's the distraction?" I ask.

The Oratus points her scaled green foreclaw at T'Oli, still wrapped around me. "The Ooblot should be able to draw fire without risking itself."

"Just what I like hearing," T'Oli slaps. "Send the Ooblot out—it's basically a puddle anyway!"

Lan's expression doesn't change. Neither does Gar's. I glance at Viera and she shrugs.

"T'Oli?" I say.

The Ooblot slithers off of me onto the catwalk, slithers over to the door. Its eyestalks swivel back towards us as we cling to the sides, out of sight.

"If I die for this, I'm holding it against all of you." T'Oli says, then the Ooblot slithers over and out of sight through the door.

"Now!" Lan hisses at Viera, and my friend quick-steps over to the door.

Watching Viera working is mesmerizing—the Lunare

grips a miner in each hand, spins with her shoulder against the dividing wall to look through the doorway, and even though I only see her ash-white hair and the edge of her set face, I know every bolt that leaves her miners hits its target.

After the cascade of flashes, Viera steps through the doorway and we follow. The results of her handiwork are the smoking ruins of the four guards, in addition to the sporadic and rapidly dwindling return fire from down below as Viera continues her cleanup. By the time I reach the railing, my own miner and lack of ability in hand, the five remaining Flaum guards have tossed their weapons to the floor.

"Nice work," I tell her.

"I know." Viera doesn't look over at me, keeps her focus on those guards.

I'm a lucky Empress to have friends like her.

On the far side, against the end wall, there's another platform that takes us down to the floor level. Viera elects to remain up top and provide cover, so T'Oli—thankfully fine after its decoy duty—and the two Oratus accompany me.

What I see are thirty or forty prisoners, mostly Flaum and Whelk, lined up against the wall to my left. They're packed against one another, and they all look broken and miserable. Like the remnants I'd met who served in Clarity's Dawn, but without any spark of hope. Center among them, though, is who we came here to find.

"Malo," I say his name and there's more than a bit of disbelief as I do. "You're alive."

He looks up slow as I approach, and the damage I noticed during the video is worse up close. Malo's thin, with cuts and bruises across his body, and he's clothed in the same rags as the rest of the prisoners. His eyes are red, and though his mouth forms a half-smile at the sight of me, I can barely keep myself from crying at the sight of him.

"Hi, Empress," Malo says, his voice a whisper.

"What did they do to you?" I ask, and I stretch out my hand, run it along the side of his scruff-covered face.

"Tried to break me," Malo says.

I shake my head. What would be the point of breaking Malo? He's not with the Vincere, he wouldn't know anything useful.

"Humans, we must leave," Lan hisses from behind me. "These Sevora say they're the dregs, that all the rest of Jel's forces are trying to get on the only good ship left on this planet. The ship we need."

I glance back at the Oratus. "They never expected to trade the prisoners for their lives?"

"I don't think they believed," Malo whispers behind me. "They hoped the Vincere might care, but they didn't believe they would."

I close my eyes for a second. This might not be the time for politics, for morals. We have to escape the planet. Now. And we're taking all of them with us. "The prisoners coming too. As long as we made this journey, we may as well save who we can."

Gar hisses something I don't catch before Lan cuts her pair off with a twitch from her tail. She doesn't object, though, and instead points a foreclaw at the five remaining guards, lined up and looking defeated.

"Can one of them lead us?" I ask Lan.

"They will," Lan says.

"Even though they're Sevora?"

Lan bares her teeth. "If they get us to that ship, we'll take them. Ask Kolas to, perhaps, give them a chance." Lan's looking at me, so the guards behind her can't see those yellow eyes, those black slits in her pupils. None of those Sevora are getting off this planet, regardless of what they do.

And I don't care.

I thought they took Malo from me. I thought he died in that cavern as T'Oli flew us away. Now he's standing behind me, and if he's not dead, he's plenty close to it. Turning away from Malo turns my sadness, the pity and blighted hope at seeing him alive into anger, rage. The bleak force that comes when you failed to save someone you care about.

I walk past Lan to the row of five Sevora guards, all of them Flaum, and all of them wearing the dark blue armor of Jel's faction, whose name I don't even remember. I meet each of their eyes, and their beady blacks stare back at me. Of course they don't know. Of course they weren't responsible for what happened to Malo that day.

"Viera?" I call, not breaking eye contact with the Sevora.

"Empress?" Viera answers from above.

"If any of these five do anything without my permission, I want you to end them," I say. "Don't wait. They get no second chances."

"You got it."

I nod towards the Sevora, to let them know I'm talking to them now. "You heard the Oratus. Take us to the ship, so we can leave this miserable world."

I march at the front, with Viera, T'Oli, and Lan. Gar volunteers to hold the back, hissing that he'll enjoy eating anyone that falls behind. The Sevora guards point us to a secondary chamber off of the large one, a space packed with terminals monitoring the crop flows and water supply, and that has a single transport tube.

Moving such a large group on one of these seems like

it'll be a problem, until the Sevora use the panel on the side of the tube—at my order—to request a larger transport. We watch as the single pearl platform, which can mold its surface to match our seating needs, is joined by ten more. They don't sit as separate platforms, but instead form two-meter long white links from one platform to the next.

"Climb on?" I ask the Sevora, and, in particular, a red-brown furred Flaum that's taken position as their leader.

"They'll all stay together," the Sevora says. "We should go to the front."

Viera, with her miners out and aimed, follows me as we climb ahead to the lead platform. The five Sevora cluster with us on the lead platform, with Lan on the one immediately behind, along with the first set of prisoners. I let Malo, who seems increasingly tired, stay with Lan, and he leans on the Oratus like she's the only reason he's standing.

I want to talk to him. Want to tell Malo how sorry I am, but there's no time, so I bite back the words, and focus on the Sevora, on the platform, on getting us to the ship.

The platforms lurch forward, then pick up speed faster and faster until we're shuttling underneath the ground at a blinding speed. Overhead lights blink by so fast they look like a single white stream amid the gray-black tunnel sides. The stream, though, vanishes in a moment as we shoot out from beneath the ground and into a clear tube that soars through a scorched sky.

The two Oratus stand just outside the station with a third, unconscious, Oratus settled on the ground by their feet. Rescue was the plan, and now that they've done that, Sax isn't sure where to go. The Flaum certainly aren't helping—most have outright fled, and the ones who haven't shrink back every time Sax looks towards them as they cling to each other in the station's corners.

"I don't think we thought this through," Bas says.

Sax looks at her and suppresses a smile. She still looks radiant, even after the scuffle with the mirrored Oratus and the Amigga, even after dashing through a dark and grimy jungle. Here, while they court disaster, he's with her. Bas, and the mission. Nothing else matters.

The mission, though, is currently stunned, and Sax guesses it won't be long before that Amigga returns with a larger force to reclaim it's prize.

"Look at these two uglies," the voice comes from the right, the slimy one of Agra-Red. "They found themselves a prize, too!"

The crimson Whelk nudges its way fully around the

station, aiming its embedded miner with its left hand while holding a smaller shooter in its right. Ready to blast anything Agra-Red doesn't like into molecular oblivion. Behind it, armed and ready, are Plake and the two Teven.

"She's stunned," Sax offers when Plake gives Evva a concerned glance, and the Vyphen holds both her feathered hands over Evva's chest until she feels the Oratus' vents sucking in air.

"Then we have to get her out of here," Plake finally says.

"You say that as if we haven't been thinking of a way to do that," Bas replies.

"Have you?" Plake rounds on her. "Thought of a way? Or is standing here the best you've got?"

"I was thinking we'd carve you up, disguise Evva in your feathers," Sax offers, coupling the words with his toothy mug.

Engee, the Teven, steps between the bunch of them. "While you were all chasing after them, Nobaa and I talked with Avan some more. Evva's force had to get to that village somehow, and he says they have skiffs back there. Ones we can use."

The rest of the group, Sax included, stares at the Teven.

"You couldn't have mentioned this earlier?" the Whelk says.

"There wasn't a reason for it, earlier," Engee replies.

"Skiffs aren't safe!" Nobaa adds.

"Neither is staying here," Plake says. "Let's go."

There's no question who gets the joy of carrying Evva's paralyzed self. Sax starts with it, then hands it off to Bas when his arms go numb from the weight. Together, the two play a weird passing game with Evva until they make it back to the Flaum village.

Avan's there to meet them, looking better, if still on the wrong end of recovery.

What Avan can do, though is point them in the direction of the vine-runners, small skiffs barely enough for a single Oratus, and that look like sleds coated in microjets. A small windshield curls up from the front, with a pair of microjets on its top to help with sudden drops.

"I suppose that none of you know how to drive one of these?" Avan says as they stand in front of the ten skiffs Evva's crew used to get to the town.

The Oratus leader is leaning against Sax now, coming into coherence but unable, yet, to stand on her own power or do more than slur a few words at a time. They must have zapped her with a strong blast to keep Evva, a large, red Oratus, stunned for this long. Then again, why take chances with the most wanted creature in the galaxy?

"I can figure it out," Plake announces.

Engee and Nobaa say the same—and proceed to climb into one of the skiffs, laying down side by side and slotting their small limbs against the edges of the sled. On either side of the sled sit small sticks which go either up or down, allowing for an ascent or a dive as needed. Nobaa takes one, Engee takes the other.

"It's fine," Avan hisses when Agra-Red wonders if the Teven will keep themselves in sync. "The two levers are tied to each other. They'll go wherever the push or pull is strongest."

That leaves a skiff for each of them, plus a few left over that Avan has no trouble donating to the village. A small repayment for the damage they've caused, but Sax agrees it's better than nothing.

Thinking so much about how others see their actions is

frustrating; far easier to carry out the mission with eyes on the results and nothing else.

"Who's taking Evva?" Sax asks as Avan mounts his own skiff.

"I'll take her," Plake says. "I'm the only one small enough."

The Whelk's not large either, but Agra-Red's still carrying that monstrous miner, and together the two would make for a tight fit. Sax and Bas definitely can't fit a second Oratus on either of their skiffs. So the choice gets made without a struggle, and the group loads up.

The skiff makes for a weird fit, as Sax has to drape his midclaws over the side and then essentially hug the sled with the rest of him. He follows Avan's example and tucks his tail in by his side, its tip up near his head. A glance at Plake confirms she's in the worst spot, though; Evva's bulk is pressing Plake's feathered limbs hard into the craft, and the Vyphen's stretching out her neck as far as it can go to keep her eyes where they can see.

"The skiffs are set to follow mine," Avan announces, his hissing still light from the wounds. "You'll just need to hang on for the ride."

Sax is happy to hear that—they don't train Oratus to be pilots, especially not small skiffs. Bas has spent some time with shuttles and the like, but Sax prefers his knowledge focused on weapons and the ways to use them.

With a synchronized hum, all six skiffs start up with a bit of levitation, rising a meter over the ground. Sax hunkers down on his, peering through the glass windshield at the glowing purple lamps of the village as the microjets spool up.

"Take a deep breath!" Avan shouts above the whine.

A deep breath? Sax opens his vents, sucks in air on instinct, and it's a good thing he does, because the skiff lurches forward into a blindingly fast launch a moment later. The windshield keeps the air from blowing Sax clean off, but he clamps his claws tight anyway as the vines blow by beneath him.

The warm light of Aspicis' star proves ideal once Sax gets comfortable with the skiff's hurtling speed, giving him an easy view across the vast emerald expanse of huge, curling vines. Puffy pearl clouds and drifting wisps of fog break up the cerulean horizon. It's beautiful, though Sax finds the sheer lack of landscape disorienting; there's not a single hill or mountain pushing the vines up above each other, no valleys or plateaus. Just a relatively even canopy forming where the vines get too heavy to keep pushing themselves up.

It's a world tamed entirely to suit the species that owns it.

The skiffs stick true to their programming and they all fly in formation behind Avan for what seems like a long time before the traitor begins to slow. Then, Avan leans his skiff forward and dives towards what looks like a thick cluster of vines. Sax isn't expecting the shift and thinks about jumping free from the suicide course, until they get close and he realizes it's light playing tricks on his eyes.

The vines aren't quite as close as they looked, and Sax, along with the others, shoots through a series of tight gaps, eventually coming through into a burrow lit by the same dangling, colored globes as the Flaum village.

While that place held families and all the pieces of a real, civilized life, this one has the makeup of a military camp. The skiffs settle down in the middle—where plenty of other skiffs rest on the ground—and Sax sees tables carved from vines and random debris covered with weapons, tools, and spare Caches, those all-encompassing bracelets of knowledge.

Terminals are strewn around the place, hanging from slap-dash connections bored into vines. Sax traces the wires and they all slide through to a circular plate—the only true metal section on the ground—which glows ever-so-slightly orange.

Staring at the new arrivals are an assortment of Flaum, of course, but also a variety of other species. None of these wear any Chorus uniforms, and most look like they've spent a long time living on the edges of society; patched fur, scars or even missing appendages, mismatched clothes that go hard for function over fashion.

And no fear.

Evva's found herself a hardened crew, and Sax's hope for success rises high as he untangles himself from the skiff and takes his first few steps around. Something more delicious than nutrient goop is cooking on a rack of grills off to one side, a lime-green Whelk covered in a dirty brown apron standing guard over what's presumably dinner.

"Welcome to Quell," Avan says once the group's off their skiffs. "It's as close as you'll come to a home on this planet." The traitor—Avan will never be anything else in Sax's mind—points around the circle, giving basic names to places like the kitchen, showers, and various spaces for mission planning, engineering, and more.

Quell is well organized, which is exactly what Sax would expect from Evva's camp. What it's not, though, is exciting enough to keep waves of exhaustion from rolling over him. They've been on a non-stop rush since leaping away from Solis what seems like an eternity ago.

Evva still needs to recover, and they don't seem under any imminent threat, so Sax gets directions from Avan, then he and Bas wind their way along a short trail through more vines to a cluster of hammocks strung up. They come in all sizes, and they're made out of stiff, woven vine-skin.

"Think they'll hold our weight?" Bas hisses.

"I'm willing to try," Sax says. "Or I'll sleep right on the ground."

They choose the largest ones that happen to be close to each other, then climb inside and fall asleep—claws touching in the space between—to the slow breeze and steady sounds of a camp moving into its evening meal.

Morning finds Quell and the people within it the same as when Sax vanished to sleep. There's no change in the light, the temperature, but the smells are different; namely, there's no hint of cooking food, no ozone-stinging scent of batteries being repaired or plugged into miners. When Sax enters the main clearing—Bas is catching a few more moments of rest—there's a small cluster of fighters, all of them armed and all of them standing silent.

Evva's there too, and she raises a single foreclaw to her mouth. It's a universal signal and one Sax respects, slinking back under the cover of a nearby vine and holding his questions. A moment later there's a loud buzzing that comes from above, whining like a giant bee and then passing almost as quickly as it arrives. Only when the sound vanishes do the fighters relax, does Quell return to its normal quirks.

"They comb the planet constantly," Evva says as she meets Sax in the middle of the clearing.

The great red Oratus, all four letters of strength, leadership, and poise looks not too worse for her long stay in the unconscious. Still, Sax notes some of the luster is gone, Evva's no longer quite as clean, as polished as she was when she stood commander of a Vincere cruiser. Her scales are often scratched, her neck bears a long, puckering gash from her face to the top of her torso, something that could have been healed on a Vincere ship but has instead hardened to a scar.

"They?" Sax says.

"We call them buzzers," Evva replies, and at Sax's questioning look, she goes on. "I've not seen them used outside of Aspicis. They hunt for irregularities in the vines, in the villages, and catalog anything that stands out."

Makes sense that the Amigga would devote paranoid resources to keeping their planet as they like it.

"They can't detect your machines? The power?"

"If they have, we don't know it," Evva says, then nods over at a metal plate embedded in the ground. "Power, here, isn't drawn from a generator. We steal it, like the Amigga do, from Aspicis' core. This taps into a through-line, and we siphon off what we need."

"It doesn't look like you need much," Sax replies, then gives Evva a hard stare. There's a question he's been waiting to ask for a long time. "What did Avan tell you that changed your mind?"

Evva sniffs at the question, then sweeps her claws across the Quell members doing their work. "You understand, now, that the Amigga have no interest in keeping this alive. Us alive. As soon as we've played out our usefulness, they'll replace us with the next creation. You found them already, I believe?"

"The humans?"

"Avan told me the Sevora had sent one of their few remaining seed ships to that space just for Earth. The mind he took had notions of a species made there, one that failed, but came too close to abandon entirely," Evva says. "One meant to deliver a fatal blow to the Sevora, but also keep the

Amigga from our lethal claws should we ever turn against them. I needed to see if Avan was right."

"So you sent us."

"I sent the two Oratus I thought I could trust." Evva says. "When you shared what you discovered of the species, I dug further. Found the order to eliminate the humans, and the analysis recommending a new version, with changes. The Chorus isn't going to stop, Sax, until we're all pacified or dead. The Amigga aren't interested in a shared galaxy—they want it for themselves."

One of the Quell members, the lime green Whelk who hovers around the stoves like they're its most treasured possessions, approaches with a pair of browned, thick green circles. It hands one to Sax, and Sax stares at it.

"Vine cakes," the Whelk burbles. "Get used to'em."

The creatures slithers away after Evva takes her share, and Sax takes a bite. It's crunchy, the browning adding some flavor, but otherwise bland filler. Marginally better than nutrient goop, but Sax had hoped for better. Nowhere in this galaxy actually has good food anymore.

"What happens if we win, Evva?" Sax says. "When we take apart the Chorus, destroy the Meridia?"

"First, we convince the Vincere to back us. Then, we push for representatives from every species to come together and draft by-laws, like the Vincere itself uses. Hopefully, from there, we can find some common ground to begin a new civilization."

"I've been to places governed by themselves," Sax says. "They barely survive, Evva. Their people fight for daily food, they destroy each other for the smallest profit. There's no higher cause, no grand vision to strive for."

Scrapper Station and its tangled webs of power, and

Rathfall's delusional blend of hunting, profits, and castes of gas miners and executives stick tough in Sax's mind.

"At least, this way, we make that choice," Evva says. "It might not be better than now. It may be worse, but at least it will be ours."

A ruined city stretches before us across the horizon. Towers that rose once as sparkling diamonds or sharp spears to the sky are broken and burning as the Vincere continue their long bombardment from space. Strikes hit like lightning, blasting down from the sky, breaking into buildings or immolating streets in flash-fires.

Except for one huge structure that stands above the others, a sphere whose bottom vanishes into the ground. We're speeding towards it now, past interchanges with other tubes where the platforms can twist and swerve to other corners of the city or beyond.

The whole time we're moving so fast that speech is impossible—aside from the roaring wind, the only thing I can hear are my own thoughts. Around me, the Sevora guards stand straight, the platform molding around our feet to lock us in despite the speed. Their eyes are straight ahead, their arms loose, as if the Sevora have resigned themselves to their fate.

I risk a look back to see how the prisoners are doing, and they're the opposite of the guards. They're not composed, but rather squeezing back from the edges as much as the platforms will allow. They're hugging and holding each other, like mothers and children, even across different species. I suppose the end of the world would be frightening, even if the only world you've ever known has been a horrifying one.

Up ahead we're approaching the edge of the city itself, and those flashes are getting brighter. This close, I can see that the huge sphere isn't standing because Kolas hasn't tried to bring it down, but rather because the flashes that do hit it fizzle out against what looks like an invisible bubble; a shield, like what our shuttle used, before the Sevora fighters overwhelmed it.

The thought has me look around for more of those fighters, and while there's plenty of craft blitzing through the sky, none seem to be on patrol, but rather zipping towards one destination or another. Even as I look, a pair of ships slam into each other as they try to avoid an orbital shot, their debris sprinkling down to the avenues of the city in shrapnel rain.

The platform shudders as we cross into the urban landscape, and I jerk my eyes straight ahead. It's a straight shot from here to the sphere, and I realize that huge building must be Nasiya's own headquarters, and what better place to keep your last escape than your home?

I'm ready for it too. Ready for the fight. My mask has two miners on it, two razor swords I'm far more comfortable with, and I have Viera's sharpshooting and a pair of very deadly Oratus ready to spill some more blood.

What I'm not ready for is a second, longer shudder. One that pushes me from side to side and makes the whole tube shake before it stabilizes. A building already damaged by blasts ahead and to our right tilts to the side and crumbles. At first, I think it must be an earthquake—something we had from time to time back home—but a shape in the corner of my eye draws a longer look.

Vimelia's moon is a large, gray blob. My first time to this planet, I noticed it's circle resembled our own, but now it's a stretched thing, as if someone's pulling on its right side, causing it to warp. And it's stretching towards Vimelia, the distorted part expanding into a ghostly white slate as the moon comes closer to the planet.

Our time is running out.

A bright flash breaks the ice-fear of what a crashing moon means, and the platform's sudden jerk has me twisting forward, catching myself on the alabaster-white railing as our speed slows. The tube in front of us is ablaze, split apart by a blast from above that's rent it in two. The platform's not stopping fast enough either—we're getting closer and we're a dozen meters above the ground.

"Viera!" I shout as the roaring wind from our travel dies along with our velocity. "Get off the platform!"

"It would be a good idea if we moved too," T'Oli says, the Ooblot sealed tight to my back.

But our feet are locked in. I try to move, try to scramble away as the platform skids along the glassy tunnel towards the jagged opening. I'm looking at my feet, trying to pick them up, when a green-scaled claw slashes down and carves me free.

"Go!" Lan hisses as she continues hacking away at the others on our platform, even the Sevora.

I press back, trying to get away, when things shift beneath my feet, when my stomach lurches as gravity takes hold of me.

I'm falling.

The platform drops away beneath me and I jump,

reaching for Malo, locked to the second platform, and my warrior, my general, manages to catch my hand with his. I hang for a moment, feeling his warm fingers on mine, his eyes tired and red, mouth creased with the effort of holding me, and then we plummet.

And land in a burning, milky mess. I hit, and my back explodes into bruising pain, but I'm cushioned, as if hitting a heavy mass of water. Then I bounce off, rolling onto the hard street amid fiery ash and flickering flames, the end state of Kolas' bombardment. Malo's beside me, and I dive on him immediately, brushing away burning flakes from his skin. He doesn't have a mask, has no protection.

Only when I've cleared the warrior do I look around at the cascading clumps of people and platforms falling around us. The glance provides the reason I'm alive—the platforms, when they hit the ground after the fall, lose their form, becoming instead soft, blob-like pillows. The cushion is wide enough to keep most from landing on each other, though the clumps of prisoners aren't so lucky. Most are rolling on the ground, or lying still.

"You survived," Viera says as she limps over towards Malo and I.

"One of the few, apparently," I say, looking past the Lunare.

Both of the Oratus look fine, as if the large drop was nothing more than a normal jump for them. Which, maybe it is. The first few Sevora guards seem all right too, standing clumped to the side, though their furry faces are tight with pain.

"Guess our rescue isn't going so well," Viera joins me in the survey.

"We gave them a chance," T'Oli states. "It's better than they had."

The Ooblot's not wrong, and I'm not going to ruin what little chance the rest of us have by waiting in the avenue.

"Let's go!" I shout, getting the attention of those able to hear me. "We don't have much time!" I help Malo up from the ground, notice the warrior's breathing hard. "Come on, Malo. It's just another day for us, right?"

"Just another day," the warrior echoes, giving me a slight smile. "I missed you, Kaishi."

I toss him a scratched, exhausted smile back. "Missed you too."

The wreckage around us makes for a bad spot to share a moment, though, as aside from the soft platforms, the intersection that's become our landing spot is full of the burning casualties from Kolas' bombardment. Looming over and around us are further remnants of the transport tube and the bare lattices of buildings with the glass blown or melted out of their windows.

The sky, I notice, is getting ever more orange, and while I can't see the moon from where I stand, my guess is that our time is getting close to being out.

Those still alive and able form a shambling group walking beneath the tube transport and towards the great sphere. Before, on my first trip to Vimelia, most of the streets were deserted, with the crowds choosing to cluster in transport tubes or ships shuttling around the surface. Walking isn't efficient enough for the Sevora, apparently. Now, though, with all normalcy blown to shreds, panicking Sevora join our motley assortment of recovering wounded, Sevora guards, humans and Oratus. Many, with their hosts, take one glance at Lan and Gar and assume we're a raiding party and run the other way—screaming out warnings to the wind. Others hope that the Vincere won't fire on their own and trust their lives to our band, joining as stragglers behind, where Gar keeps a toothy eye on them.

"Have to say, this is like a dream coming true," T'Oli says as we walk down the devastated street. "I've wanted to see Vimelia burn for a long time."

"With you still on it?"

"Can't let perfect get in the way of good, Kaishi."

"The Ooblot's losing it," Viera says behind me. "Surprised a living puddle kept it together this long, really."

"I'm far saner than any human," T'Oli replies.

"You're both crazy as far as I'm concerned," I say, ducking beneath a broad metal beam that's fallen, crossing the entire street from one side to the next.

I want to move faster, but forcing the Sevora into a run would mean abandoning the prisoners, and someone would have to carry Malo. Glances at the moon when ruins allow seem to show our doom progressing slow, but then, I've never seen a planetary annihilation before.

"Malo, what'd they do to you?" Viera asks our rescued warrior friend.

"Everything, and nothing," Malo replies. "Little food, a lot of questions. Attempts to infect me."

"Did it work?"

Malo does some combination of a laugh and a cough. "I'm here, but every time they failed, they tried again. Until the Vincere came."

I clench my hands. I remember that—when the familiars on the space station *Cobalt* sucked the Sevora out of my head, then let it back in after I'd taken a good long look. To say that experience was unpleasant would be underselling it. To say I'd had more nightmares than I can count...

"We're here," one of the Sevora guards announces, and I

look up enough to realize that yes, we're nearly at the foot of the sphere.

This close, it's larger than I thought, and appears to be covered in row after row of dark slats that shimmer in the daylight. At the ground level, the circle curve melds into the landscape like a mountain, a smooth transition to a patchwork stone pattern beneath. Poles adorned with banners showing Nasiya and its Oratus host stand in the courtyard, though most are at some degree of bent and burned by this point, even if the sphere itself looks untouched.

As we watch, another bolt from above strikes the sphere and sparks the shield, the slight blue wave cascading around the structure and fizzling away to nothing.

"Does the front door work?" Viera asks, gesturing with her miner towards a line of ground-level slats angled vertical instead of to the side.

Each one of these has a peppered line of green lights around the outside. It seems friendly enough, but when none of the Sevora guards respond to Viera's question, I repeat it.

"We don't know," the one that's been talking, with its red and brown Flaum fur singed from the crash, responds. "Nasiya and its faction have never been our friends, we've never been here."

"You're invited now," Viera says. "Get to it."

I nod, seconding the command. The guards glance at each other, hesitating, until Viera raises up her miners at all of them. Lan seconds the threat with a hiss.

If Nasiya's base has some sort of defense, better to have the Sevora trigger it than one of us.

But there's no explosion, no scattering of Sevora and Flaum parts as the quintet approach the slats. Rather, when they get close, those green lights flash and all of the slats slide to the side, open and free.

"Well, that's disappointing," Viera says next to me.

"We still might need them," I reply.

"They said they've never been inside," T'Oli interjects. "Their usefulness to the mission is likely minimal at this point. It would be safer to eliminate them."

All five of the guards have their backs turned towards us, at least until their lead looks around to see if we're coming. I'm standing with Viera and Malo to my left, Lan to my right, a couple dozen random prisoners, Gar and his trail of Sevora hangers-on. Viera could burn down all five guards, I have no doubt.

"Not yet," I say. "We can still use them as bait."

Why am I keeping the Sevora alive? Maybe it's because we're surrounded by so much death that I can't bring myself to order more right now. Maybe it's because these five are probably going to die later, anyway, by Lan's claws.

And if I wait until then, I won't be responsible.

"Whatever you say, Empress." Viera lowers her miners. "Guess that means we're going in?"

"Yes," I reply. "Weapons ready. We have no idea what's going on inside."

When we go through the slats, though, it's clear that we've missed the main event. Nasiya's headquarters opens with a monstrous lobby that rises taller than our Tiers at home, higher than the tube transport. It's full of color too—though these murals don't shift and are, rather than scattered paints, picture-perfect images of various planets. The lobby itself arranges like a miniature version of the building its inside of—curved walls conclude in an arched ceiling, from which those images hang like banners.

Along the walls, too, flow glass-sealed rivers of the ink-purple liquid I remember well from the very first night I found the Sevora crashed into my jungle home. The rivers are spaced and come together into pools on either side of the silver center, a space that might be beautiful if not for all the bodies.

Every species I can name is represented among the casualties, from the charred, colored sludge of Whelks to the broken carapaces of Teven. Flaum fur is plentiful, and some bits of the stuff still burn.

"This was a big fight," T'Oli says.

I wait for Viera's cutting remark, but for once she doesn't say anything as we walk through the graveyard. Even the Lunare is silenced by the sight.

"One I'm glad we missed," I say finally, then turn to Lan. "Where do you think Nasiya's keeping its ship?"

"At the very top," Lan hisses. "Where Nasiya itself spends the most time."

The idea makes sense—keep the escape where you're going to be.

"There's a lift back here," says Viera, who's kept walking as I talk to the Oratus. "Going to be a tight fit for everyone though."

"Then we send the most important first," Lan says to me, and I know what she's suggesting.

This is the point we ditch away the riders, the leeches and the Sevora. I look over at the prisoners. The ones that've made it this far seem to only have eyes for the corpses, and I'm sure they're imaging themselves in that role.

"Then we send the lift back down," I say. "For the rest of them."

Lan nods, and in another few seconds we've assembled the star strike team; Malo, Viera, myself and T'Oli, and the two Oratus. Nobody questions the arrangement, because we're the only ones with weapons.

Viera's right; the lift isn't meant for a bunch of Oratus, but we solve the puzzle and manage to squeeze everyone onto the platform, the same white material and tube as the rest of Vimelia. As we're getting in, another quake rattles the ground, this one longer and deeper than the others, prompting a few sharp squeals from the huddled prisoners in the lobby.

"Better hope they built this place well," Viera says.

"It's the strongest building on the planet," T'Oli replies. "Clarity's Dawn tried to crack it many times, even tried using explosives around the base. Nothing, and we lost some good souls on that one."

We might lose some good souls on this one too, but the platform isn't going to be where that happens. After we're all on—Malo adopts a truly weary pose, crumpling down onto the platform's floor—T'Oli and I set the destination on the lift's panel. All the way to the top.

"What do you think those guards will do now that we're gone?" Viera asks as the lift starts its ascent. "Take those species prisoner again?"

"They don't have weapons," I reply. "What does it matter? Nothing here is going to last long anyway."

"I hope they fight each other," Gar hisses. "That would be a better way to die than by moonfall."

"Moonfall?" I catch the word. "You have a term for this?"

"While this technology is new," Lan hisses. "More gradual planetary destruction has been attempted. Conducting a moonfall can help break apart an icy world, add land to a smaller planet, or grant access to difficult minerals."

I shake my head. Again, this galaxy is proving itself a place far beyond what I thought possible.

For now, though, the lift's slowing and the panel's beeping that we're about to reach our destination, which means it's time to see if this fight's still happening, or if Nasiya's already gone.

Which means we're dead.

The true surprise comes later, after Sax and Bas have had their meals and accustomed themselves to Quell and how it works. There's not a lot to the base, though Nobaa and Engee immediately find themselves fascinated with the terminals and the core lines that Quell have managed to tap into.

"So we have access to their logistics data?" Sax hears Nobaa exclaim at one point.

Sax isn't so dour as to believe that such knowledge isn't useful, but Evva's Quell isn't built to last through a long war of attrition. There's not enough fighters here, for one, and, according to Evva, they only have a few other safe houses. Meaning, if the Chorus finds this base, the whole initiative is doomed before it ever really starts.

So when another skiff lowers its way into the base with a familiar Flaum piloting it, Sax feels the first real tug of hope he's had since arriving on Aspicis.

Coorvin, with his ash-black fur looking better than Sax has ever seen it, gets off the skiff and is mobbed by a bevy of

Quell members asking for information on this and that. Sax, though, turns to Plake with a different question.

"How'd you get him here?" Sax assumes the Vyphen's responsible for it somehow, and Plake's shrug confirms he's not wrong.

"Wasn't hard," Plake says. "Coorvin has a reason to be here—he was on *Cobalt* when it blew up, and the Chorus wanted to talk to him about it. He's also Flaum, which, if you haven't noticed, is kind of a requirement to get onto this planet. So he reached out to the Vincere on Rathfall, said he'd been kidnapped and needed an extraction. They came and got him, brought him here."

"And he escaped?"

"If they even tried to hold him," Plake gives Sax a skeptical look. "You think *you'd* devote a lot of effort to keeping a Flaum jailed if there's no evidence against him?"

Sax thinks he'd probably eviscerate the creature if there's a chance it could do him harm, but that's probably not appropriate to say, so he agrees with Plake.

Coorvin, though, makes the Chorus pay for their ignorance; while in the Meridia, the vast construct rising from the surface of Aspicis up into near-space above, the Flaum took careful notes of just how the Chorus keep their security running. It's a spicy setup: plenty of guards, pass-codes and timed accesses, more the higher you go. To even get in the front entrance, they would have to get past an Amigga-only bio scanner.

With every observation of the Meridia's impenetrable security, Sax sees the morale deflate among the people present. It's one thing to believe in a cause when there's a chance, a whole other thing to keep believing when failure's a certainty.

Coorvin, though, keeps them hanging till the end,

where he gives them a bit of hope: even though the lifts are staggered, so no one can shuttle all the way to the top, even though the security measures are vast, once inside the Meridia an insurgent force would be hard to take down. The key is getting into the tower's base.

"The levels themselves are crowded, with easy points to defend," Coorvin concludes. "You'll have to find ways to work the lifts, but once you're inside, you should be able to find ways to get up to higher levels. The hardest point is the entrance. You have to be an Amigga to get in, or with one. And unless something's changed, we don't have an Amigga on our side."

"We don't need one," Engee pops in here. "Bio-scans can be defeated. If we can get access to the scanner, or to the control…"

Coorvin nods. "Thought of that too, but I couldn't start asking questions about that without looking suspicious."

"I can take a guess," Evva says, her eyes ordering the rest of the Quell forces back to their work. "The Vincere has a protocol for sensitive securities, one I would guess the Chorus follows: never keep the control next to its target."

Yes. Sax knows this one—it's why every Vincere ship has its bridge as far away from its most vulnerable parts, the engines. It's why the power source governing those same engines is housed in a different part of the ship, meant to force a strike team to traverse all across a cruiser before it can get full access to its systems.

"You think the control for the Meridia's security systems lives outside of the Meridia itself?" Coorvin says.

"The Meridia is a giant target for anyone looking to attack Aspicis." Evva says. "The Chorus has the Vincere, the strongest military force in the galaxy on their side, which means any attack would have a short time to succeed.

Would you take a chance that a single, focused raid could break your system and get to the top, just because you housed your own keys in the same place?"

"If the controls for the bio-scan are somewhere else," Bas says. "Then where?"

"The place least likely to break!" Nobaa says. "Your vital systems ought to be where there's the least chance they'll get interrupted, and that means power."

All eyes turn to the metal slat. Energy from the planet's core: un-ceasing and un-interruptible.

The plan flows quickly from there; Nobaa and Engee take charge of designing a defeat program, one that should swap the bio-scan to see any species as the right one, not just Amigga. Sax and the others use Quell's terminals to get a good idea of the target.

Cavignum: Aspicis' largest power plant, the one closest to the Meridia. A massive thing that is, essentially, built around a giant hole bored deep into the planet. The construct saps the heat pouring out of Aspicis' core and uses it to generate the energy that powers the Meridia, that charges up a quarter of the entire world.

For that reason, Cavignum is plenty well defended. The few images they can pull up make it clear there's surface and air turrets, plenty of guards, and all the usual security measures like locked doors, sections that can be sealed off, and more. All of that gets coupled with the fact that moments after an attack starts, an endless stream of deadly reinforcements are only moments away.

Short of an orbital bomb, Sax isn't sure how they're going to get in. Especially when Nobaa and Engee say that they'll need to get to the right terminal in the power station itself.

"It's not as simple as just running the program," Nobaa

says. "We need to get access to the bio-scanning system. Literally get into how it operates and change what it does. That can't be done remotely, not that we can see."

"So we have to get the two of you into the power station," Evva says. "And leave you there long enough to run your program, then get you out?"

"That would do it!" Nobaa says. "Of course, there's no sure telling how long this might take. The system might be easy to crack, and we'll be ready to go in a few minutes. Or, it might be a day."

"That's not going to work."

The discussion ebbs and flows from there, eventually driving Sax close to insanity. There's too many variables on hand, too many unknowns to make a plan capable of success. What they need, really, is more information. What they don't have is time to gather it.

That desperation forces a compromise: Nobaa and Engee, along with their program, will try to get as close to Cavignum as possible so that when Sax, Bas, Plake and Agra-Red figure out a way to crack it open, the two Teven can take advantage. Evva, Avan and the rest of Quell will work on creating diversions and, if possible, get ready to hit the Meridia once the two Teven open up the front door.

It's a loose, fractured plan with plenty of holes. It's also the only plan they've got.

So Sax, Bas, and Plake board the skiffs not long after. Coorvin has a contact for them, someone who should be able to get them close to, if not inside, the power station. The problem, as Coorvin states, is that this contact operates on greed and greed alone.

They'll have to convince it that bringing down the Chorus is going to bring up its profits.

Coorvin delivers the coordinates and Sax, Bas, Plake

and Agra-Red drop the numbers into their skiffs. Their miners have been charging all night, they're stocked with arms and provisions, and both Sax and Bas have their masks on and ready to go.

It's as prepared as Sax has been in a long time and his claws are itching to take advantage.

Plake offers to take the lead, and they link their skiff to the Vyphen's so that when she starts her ascent, Sax's ride lifts up with hers. He sneaks a glance back down to the Quell base and notices not a single soul is busy watching them—they're all getting geared up for their own assignments.

As it should be.

Their target is a city, one of the few on the planet not directly linked to the Meridia. Called Terrodyne, it's a the planet's manufacturing center. Powering all of those factories is Cavignum, built around a hole burrowed into the planet's core. Set far north of their current location, it's going to be a long ride.

As the skiff start to accelerate, Sax gets his head beneath the windshield, where the noise of rushing air dies down and it's possible—barely—to speak. Plake's out in front as they blitz across the vines, leading a diamond formation with Agra-Red as the rear point. Across from Sax, he can see Bas, hunkered down like him, looking beautifully pink in the bright light.

It's a peaceful ride. There's no sign of storms, and the endless vines beneath them break up occasionally to show mag-lev train tracks or signs of small habitations. Sax would almost call it pleasant, except that it grows boring. There's nothing to do except sit and take in the same view as the minutes pass.

"Eyes up," Plake's voice warbles through the skiff's

small intercom. "We've got skiffs coming in from the left, and it looks like they're on an intercept."

Sax tries to look that way, but Bas cuts between him and the view. Raising his head up high might blow Sax off the craft, so he has to trust what the Vyphen can see.

"They're armed," Bas hisses. "Do we have any weapons on these things?"

"Not seeing any," Agra-Red says, and Sax hisses in agreement.

There's nothing on his skiff except the pair of levers to control the craft's pitch, the right one with a trigger for acceleration and the left for braking. A small display on the windshield gives coordinates against a geographic map of the world, highlighting the path to their destination. No sign of a weapons system, of shields, or anything of combat relevance.

"We'll have to out-fly them, then," Plake says. "I'm unlinking us. If something goes wrong, meet up at the target however you're able to."

"Don't lead the enemy there," Sax says. "The mission above yourself."

He wouldn't have said the words if only he and Bas were here, but Plake and Agra-Red are mercenaries. They can't be trusted to make the sacrifice.

"Unlinked!" Plake says and Sax immediately feels loose in the skiff.

He's fading to the right, because Sax is leaning that way. The Oratus stabilizes himself, the skiff helping ever-so-slightly to keep Sax level. He nudges himself left, then back right again, getting a feel for how much he has to move to get the skiff turning. Then he pulls back on the levers, sending the skiff angling up, above the other three.

Now Sax gets a clear view of the pursuit—a half dozen

skiffs coming closer by the second. They're in two uneven lines, a W spread, and they're homing in on Plake's lead. Sax's ascent puts him behind his own party, which gives the Oratus a chance to take the initiative.

Sax leans left and pushes the levers down, turning the skiff into a dive towards the approaching group.

"What're you doing, Sax?" Agra-Red manages to ask. "Getting yourself killed?"

"Maybe," is all Sax bothers to reply.

He plunges towards the oncoming skiffs, and Sax sees they're all piloted by Flaum wearing the same deep blue Chorus uniforms, including thick, visored helmets. Not elite, then. Not expecting resistance like this. Each skiff, though, looks like it has a pair of assault miners strapped to the front of it, sticking out like needles.

They're not caught off-guard, though. As Sax gets close, the Chorus skiffs scatter, some heading up, others right to cut beneath Sax, and the last pair cut their acceleration hard to try and keep Sax from hitting them.

A tactic that would work, if not for Sax's tail. The Oratus boosts his speed to the maximum, leans hard left, pulls back on the levers to sweep his skiff over the two braking hard. The Flaum glance up at Sax, just in time to see the Oratus, his skiff flipped on its left side, slap down with his tail and nail the first Flaum across the face.

The impact ripples pain along Sax's body and throws the skiff into a wobble that has Sax spinning over his second target. Apparently going that fast and striking another object isn't what Oratus tails are made for. Sax, though, manages to pull left again and swing around in time to see the results of his strike blooming into an orange fireball below.

"Juke right!" Plake cries through the intercom and Sax

flips his weight as blue-white fire streams where he would've been.

There's two options here—Sax can either focus on evading the pursuit, or finding a target and, in attacking it, hope he loses that pursuit. Sax, of course, takes the second one.

As he's already juking right, Sax leans into the turn, wrapping himself around and coming into a collision course with the second skiff he missed during his first tail-whipping assault. That skiff is just accelerating, and the Flaum has no time to react as Sax's skiff shoots towards it. Sax himself only manages to jerk the levers back on his ride, slanting up the nose just as it strikes the Chorus skiff.

Sax's own harder hull crashes through the windshield of the other skiff, including the Flaum behind it. The impact makes an expected end of Sax's enemy, but a pair of bleeping red lights and a constant shower of sparks from the front of Sax's skiff indicate he didn't exactly make out unscathed. In fact, his skiff seems to be in a constant, gradual decline, and those vines aren't too far away.

"Going to need a new lift," Sax hisses, though at least the enemy fire is gone.

Apparently everyone can see Sax isn't a threat; the Oratus sends his skiff left, corkscrewing his decline, and catches a swirling mess of a fight; Agra-Red dives and twists frantically as a pair of skiffs cling to its tail, filling the air with lasers. Bas seems to have a momentary advantage on her opponent, beating the Flaum through a tight loop and getting behind it, though Sax isn't sure what she'll do, seeing as their skiffs don't have weapons.

Plake, though, has her target in her sights, and has a miner held tight in her right hand. She's taking pot shots over her windshield, though every time she raises the weapon, the wind seems to knock her aim off course.

All told, Sax's two-for-one victory is the best the group has going for them right now. It's also bought Sax some isolation, so he uses it. Rather than keep the forward thrust, which forces the skiff into a dive, Sax pulls the air-brakes and locks the levers into their hovering position. The skiff isn't perfect here—those dead front jets mean Sax is still sinking at an angle—but now he's stable enough to pull out his miners.

"Line'em up for me!" Sax calls through the comm.

Agra-Red takes first advantage, swinging its now-smoking and sparking skiff into a line above Sax's firing angle. Because Sax is low, the Chorus Flaum don't see him, continuing their straight pursuit after the Whelk. Sax holds down his triggers, lets the energy fly free, and delivers a staccato set of shots to the closest skiff, skittering the bolts into the underside of the craft.

The shots melt away the microjets, leaving the Flaum in a skiff that has no upward thrust. The creature's smart enough to realize it's not surviving here and takes a hard tack out of the fight, leaving Sax to aim for the second one.

Only this Flaum isn't oblivious to what's happened to its friend, and it's looping up and over, turning down into a dive at Sax. The Oratus raises his miners to greet the descending skiff and its two heavy cannons. There's not a hope of winning this firefight, but Sax pulls the triggers anyway.

The Flaum's bolks spray around Sax, belting into the skiff. Sax's own shots burrow into the front of his target, and then Sax leaps, because to stay would mean death. As Sax flies, he twists, keeps his miners focuses, and pours laser into the descending enemy. His own skiff explodes, superheated into a mini-nova, followed moments later by a smoking, burning second skiff as Sax melts his target past the point of control.

The Oratus, though, is now in free fall, plummeting the rest of the distance into the vines. Sax has long enough to take a breath, to speak one name.

There's a bite of pain, then, and the world goes dark.

The lift opens into a top level entryway that may have been beautiful at some point, but that is now a wreck of shredded furniture, with a great, broken hole where I think a door once stood. The colored walls—bright blues and yellows—of the rounded atrium are pocked with scorch marks, and the light above, a bronzed flavor coming from a full, somehow whole sphere dangling from the ceiling, washes the scene in a hazy cast, as though we're stepping into a memory and not the full, deadly now.

"Looks like we're a little late to this party," Viera says as we leave the lift.

"Unfortunately," Gar adds.

"I prefer not getting shot," I say. As soon as we're all out of the lift, its doors shut behind us and the thing starts its descent. Soon we'll have prisoners and more Sevora arriving up here. "Let's keep moving, before this gets complicated. Viera, Gar, you two take point."

Which leaves me with Malo, and Lan bringing up the rear guard. I figure an Oratus on either side is going to keep us safest, especially as we move on from the atrium into a wide hallway—big enough for the four-clawed lizards—with plenty of side rooms. There's more evidence here of a crawling battle, with miner burns etching staccato patterns into the sides, floor, and ceiling around us.

Something larger detonated not far ahead either; its orange plasma burns marking a halo around our path and leaving a once-molten groove across the ground.

"Jel's forces came with firepower," Lan hisses as we go, slowly. "Be cautious. One explosive thrown back our way could kill us all."

"They're fighting for their lives," I reply. "They'll use everything they have."

I know I would. I know, if I was fighting for the last bit of humanity, I would throw every weapon, every soul I had into the battle even if there was no hope of winning.

The hallway ends in a full-width door, one that's also been forced open. Apparently Nasiya's forces weren't able to use the tight quarters to finish the fight. We stalk up close, bunch up and look through into the vast space on the other side.

Big enough to be the other half of the sphere, with the neat translucent wall effect going on through the entire ceiling and along the downward sloping side away from us, Nasiya's private docking bay has plenty of size. And plenty of bodies.

We're too late to see most of the action; like the lobby, smoking corpses litter the ground both directly in front of our doorway and at the boarding ramp of the ship, a great diamond of a thing with a hull that shifts colors even as we stare at it. At first I think the changing is random, but then I realize that it's playing to the surroundings, and the yellow-orange streaks appearing are the result of the ship catching the flashes of the Vincere bombardment outside.

"Beautiful," Malo says softly.

"Sure," Viera replies. "If you want to call it that. What I'm worried about, though, is that there's nothing left alive in here."

She's right. There's racks of batteries and cannisters of things I don't know littered around the docking bay, along with crates of what must be emergency supplies, but nothing's moving, and there's no sound. At least not out here.

The ship's boarding ramp, though, is down. It, too, is wide enough for an Oratus. Apparently Nasiya's had its host for a long enough time to have this built with its size in mind.

"If the fight is over, then whomever won will try to leave," Lan says. "We have to hurry."

Obeying her own command, Gar and Lan break into a clacking run across the docking bay towards the ship. I pull Malo with me, while Viera shrugs her way into a rear guard, watching the bodies with her miners drawn.

"Don't get too far ahead!" I try to say to the Oratus, but they ignore me, hitting the ramp at a run and vanishing up.

"They were never really yours to command," Malo says.

"Oratus only belong to the Chorus," T'Oli states from my shoulders. "Anyone else is an ally of convenience."

"Then let's make sure we keep it that way," I say and pick up the pace.

The ramp is a silver, slotted thing, the gaps providing grip for talons like those I don't have. When we get to the base, I let Viera take the lead, as now there's plenty of noise coming from inside the ship; hisses, bangs and snarls. Something's alive in there.

"Can you stand on your own?" I ask Malo, and the warrior nods. "Then cover us."

I hand the warrior one of my miners and take up the

other—I might not be accurate, but in the close confines of the ship, I bet I can hit something. Besides, with T'Oli sliming down to my left hand and sharpening itself into a needle-sword, I think I'm well-covered.

Even so, Viera takes point, and together we clomp up the ramp. Nasiya's ship is several times the size of the shuttle, and so when we get to the top, we walk into a large space, the fat end of the teardrop ship's shape. Here, at least, Nasiya's concessions to luxury are still apparent; those color-shifting paintings are everywhere, and jewels line them, providing glinting divides between the changing scenes.

Rather than netting, the floor of the ship is the same alabaster as the tube's platforms, and it changes at our touch, firming up to catch our feet and, I'm sure, ready to mold over and keep us stable should the ship decide to launch. Light doesn't seem to come from anywhere, but rather a soft illumination reflects off of everything, as though we're walking into a morning glade.

The noises come from our right, so Viera takes a turn that way, tossing her eyes at me for quick confirmation. There's a shut circular door to the left, across the alabaster room and towards what I assume is the rear of the ship, where, by now, I've learned the engines are likely to be. There's no sounds from there, though, and no signs of struggle, so I let Viera lead and keep my miner ready as we head towards the bridge.

Nasiya's craft splits itself in the same way as the underground crop granary—big dividing walls split the main room off from the next section of the ship, with domed doors serving as the ways between. The one closest to us, leading towards the front, is open, and as we get close, words begin to pour out.

"No Sevora can match an Oratus," Gar's hissing voice says. "No matter how long you've been in there, you're nothing."

There's a rasping laugh at that. "Nothing? I defeated an entire army. Me! Almost alone!"

"And you're still nothing, and now you're alone," Lan replies.

I nod at Viera, and we both pass through the door, into the second, and final, chamber of Nasiya's ship.

Nasiya's bridge isn't designed for a full crew—towards the front of the ship, everything inside the space narrows down to a single point; a swath of netting towards the very end, with two long screens sliding across the crystal-blue windshield on either side. The very apex, where I can just see around Nasiya's huge body as it leans to the side, houses the flight stick.

Lan and Gar have Nasiya cornered, though on first glance it looks like the Sevora isn't putting up any fight. Nasiya bears more burns than I've ever seen on a single body, so that its yellow-gold scales are more a mash-up of ash-black and bubbling pink blisters. Its left foreclaw is simply gone, and Nasiya's tail lies limp on the floor, with some deep cuts around where it joins to Nasiya's body.

None of the damage has stopped Gar from putting his right foreclaw up to Nasiya's throat, and his midclaws into a lethal pressure position around Nasiya's abdomen. If the Sevora tries anything more than a twitch, I have no doubt Gar would destroy the Sevora leader, and that Gar would love every moment of it.

"You're alone?" is the first thing I say. I'd been expecting some sort of shootout, a ragged struggle against Nasiya's most battle-hardened troops, but apart from the bodies outside the ship, there's nobody here. "Lan, Gar, you didn't find anyone else?"

"Who would still be here?" Nasiya hisses in reply, and plenty of wet flows up with the words. "Every Sevora that can fight is already dead, or is flying what few fighters we have left. If my species is dying, what's the value in protecting me?"

I can concede that point.

"So you were going to fly out of here alone?" I reply. "Leave the rest of your species to die?"

"I was waiting," Nasiya says. "Some of us know about my ship, I thought they would come. As you can see, they did not make it."

Lan glances at me. "Human, we need to go."

I want to ask Nasiya more questions. I want to understand how the Sevora leader came to this, and who did such damage to its host body. But I also want to avoid a moon slamming into me.

"Fine," I nod at Gar. "Get rid of it. Outside."

Gar might slaughter Nasiya right here if I don't specify, and the last thing I want in our small bridge is the remnants of Gar's favorite pastime. Nasiya, for its part, doesn't struggle as Gar drags the Sevora out, doesn't say anything beyond its low hisses. I hear the weight of the bodies on the entrance ramp as Lan goes forward to take the ship's controls.

"Can I take off?" Lan asks me.

Malo and Viera are in the shuttle. Gar's going to be coming back soon. Lan could leave now, and we'd ditch all the prisoners and the Sevora guards behind. We would be safe.

Outside the windshield, as if hearing my thoughts, the first set of prisoners bursts into the docking bay, running towards the ship. There's another rattling shake, harder and longer than any of the others, and I'm forced to catch myself on the side of the bridge's back wall as my knees buckle. T'Oli catches the struggle, slides down and forms itself around my feet, keeping me in place. Viera, with no such luck, holsters her miners and braces herself against the wall.

"Can we scan them?" I ask Lan. "To see if any are infected?"

Lan blinks at me. "Not here. On one of the cruisers, yes. But going that far is a risk, human. One Kolas would not have us take."

"Kolas isn't here."

There's a roar from the boarding ramp, and Lan taps at the left monitor, and it shifts from its clear view of the docking bay to a feed of the ramp's base. Gar's standing there, his claws wide. I don't see Nasiya, but the prisoners and Sevora guards are surrounding the Oratus, chittering and yelling for a spot on Nasiya's ship.

"You must think of the galaxy, human," Lan replies. "These few dozen are not worth risking everything."

I look down at T'Oli, but the Ooblot only blinks its eyes at me. Malo's back in the passenger section of the ship, so I look to Viera.

"Make the call, Empress," Viera says to me. "But do it fast."

Do I accept the cost of innocent lives as necessary, or do I fight for every single one? Before, back in the intersection, I'd made the call to leave behind the wounded, those who couldn't keep up. In the moment, I felt we didn't have a choice. If we hadn't made it here, all of us would have died.

Now we do.

"We're taking them," I say.

Lan shakes her head, hisses low, then begins to tap away on the two screens. A gentle whine fills the craft, and, in the feed, the ramp beneath Gar begins to recede back into the ship.

"Apologies, Human. I cannot allow that." Lan says.

I raise my miner, point it at the back of Lan's sizeable head. "Lower the ramp, Lan."

Threatening an Oratus. I might be making the worst, and last mistake of my life. Yet as I hold the miner steady, aimed directly at Lan, I don't regret it. I don't question it.

Father let Malo and his Charre warriors take me away from my tribe in order to save it from what might have been a bloody extinction. He took the easier way, let me go rather than risk a greater loss.

I am not my father. I will not make his mistake.

"Don't make me say it again, Lan."

The Oratus makes no move to tap the terminal and stop the ramp. "Human, these are the creatures that tried to destroy your entire race. You wish to save them?"

"They're not all Sevora," I flick my eyes to T'Oli, who's got its eyestalks split between Lan and I. "T'Oli, stop the ramp."

"Think she might eat me if I try," T'Oli replies.

"I'll shoot her if she does."

The Oratus stands up from the net, though she has to bend her green neck to keep her head beneath the ship's low sloping ceiling. As she rises, Lan's left midclaw taps at the monitor and the ramp pauses, leaving Gar standing just above the shouting crowd. Lan turns all the way towards me, takes a single step my way. T'Oli's binding keeps me from retreating, but Viera, with her right hand still keeping her stable, aims a miner with her left, backing up my threat with her sharpshooting.

"One more step, Lan," I say, and I'm impressed at my own voice for being this steady.

"Trillions," Lan hisses. "Trillions have died due to their efforts. They devour species, they steal freedom. You're willing to risk their return for a paltry few?"

"I am."

Lan opens her mouth slightly, the sharp teeth glinting. I know that if she decides I'm not worth keeping alive, I'll never get more than a shot off. Viera's probably wouldn't kill the Oratus either.

"We head straight for the *Nunlite*, for Kolas," Lan says finally. "Nobody leaves the ship without a scan. Any with a Sevora inside die. You must tell them. They must agree. Then we must leave."

I can tell that's as far as I'm going to get with the Oratus. Lan's already staring—and breathing—pure disgust at me, so I nudge around her and, with T'Oli guiding me, activate the ship's external speaker.

"Prisoners and Sevora," I begin. I've never made a speech asking a group to decide which of them ought to live and die, but I don't have a choice, so I plunge ahead. "We cannot allow any Sevora-hosted species to leave on our craft. If you are free of infection, board. If you are a Sevora, you will be found out and eliminated, so I advise you to seek your survival elsewhere."

As I say the words, Lan lowers the boarding ramp, so that by the time I finish, Gar's back on the ground dealing with a flood of bodies. The Oratus steps aside at the push and lets the crowd up the ramp. The tired prisoners manage to move fast, and help those couple that fall making their way up. The only ones that don't try to board, the ones that turn and run back towards the lift, are the five Sevora guards that came with us all the way from the compound.

"They're not even trying," I say as I watch them run on the monitor.

"A sure death at Gar's claws is more frightening than an unknown chance at life," Lan says. "They may not yet understand their moon is crashing down on them."

Once the crush of prisoners finds their way inside, Lan retracts the ramp for a final time, with Gar taking up supervising duty with Viera over the cluster of prisoners clogging up the ship's main bay.

With the engines primed, her claws on the flight stick, Lan lifts the ship up from the ground. T'Oli locks me into place by the back wall, where I brace myself as we start to move.

"Thanks," I tell the hard, ceramic-looking mass beneath me.

T'Oli blinks its eyes my way. "Brave thing you did. They'll thank you. Clarity's Dawn would be proud."

"Even Sapphrite?"

The Amigga had lead the rogue faction of un-hosted species beneath Vimelia's surface. Neither T'Oli nor I have heard anything about their survival after our escape from the planet the first time, which I take to mean Clarity's Dawn died in doing their final mission.

"Sapphrite would have said it wanted revenge above all else," T'Oli replies. "But it did all it could to nurture our band, and give us a mission. I think it would be proud of you."

T'Oli's words, delivered through the strange slapping of smooth skin against itself, and with all the emotional feeling of a clacking branch, don't puff me up with happiness, but they do calm the buzz of nauseating fear that I've made a terrible mistake.

Lan taps away at the monitors at her sides and, ahead of

us, a gap slides open in the sphere building's wall, showing a different world from the one we were in moments before. Where a vast city once stood, smoking ruins now exist. As we leave the cover of the docking bay, I see that the fires are only partially caused by Kolas' bombardment; the now-constant quakes from the moon's approach makes the ground beneath us appear to ripple. Cracks split open the streets, and break apart batteries, pipes, and whole buildings burst into flame, explode or just collapse into great ash clouds.

Up above, what had been a great white streak of stretched moon has expanded to fill most of the sky. The moon's shape is still distorted, and plenty of fissures line its surface too, breaking the big ball into different fragments, which drift apart from one another slowly, but nevertheless in motion as I watch. The first, a pointed crescent, begins to make initial contact with Vimelia's upper atmosphere, igniting in a blue-orange flame across the entirety of its shape.

"Hold on," Lan says, and I hear the Oratus' voice echo from behind us as the order gets relayed to our passengers.

The ship bursts forward and up. The acceleration is so hard, so sudden that the air leaves my lungs as my body presses back into the dividing wall behind me. Even though there's no wind in the ship, my eyes start to water as the force compresses my head.

Beneath us, the city ruins dwindle. I realize we're not making any evasive maneuvers around Kolas' big lasers and manage, once I get a breath, to pose the question to Lan.

"They needed to get out of the way," Lan says. "The moon could damage the fleet as well as the planet. Now they're watching for anyone trying to escape."

"Like us?"

"I hope so." Lan's voice sounds tight, so I stop my questions and let the Oratus concentrate.

Above us, the cracking moon fragments even further as the fire burns its way through the gray-white surface. Bits and pieces scatter off and begin to tumble towards us as we climb to meet them. Flames burn around the meteors, and smoke trails mark their scars as they slice Vimelia's dying sky.

"Now we see if the Oratus can really fly," T'Oli says to me.

I only nod—any words might distract Lan.

The Oratus, though, looks to be in total concentration. She sends Nasiya's ship to the left around the first fragment, a tower-sized block of rock breaking up into smaller chunks as it slides by. Then Lan swoops the ship up and around, tracing the outline of a larger piece, using the big rock to block faster, smaller boulders blasting through around us. With a quick right cut, Lan pushes us around the outside of the big one, leaving us in the path of a hill-sized ball careening our way.

I can't help it—I shout. It doesn't help, but it's all I can do.

A bright red stream fires out from the point of our ship, striking the ball with pure energy and super-heating it. Coupled with the burn from the atmosphere, the rock melts and bursts, and instead of flying through solid matter, the outside of the ship crackles as thousands of pieces fry in its shield.

"A point for me!" Gar's hissing laugh comes over the intercom.

On the other side of the debris field—as I gasp for breath —there's another series of boulders that, thankfully, keep themselves well-spaced enough for Lan to loop her way around. Then we're in the upper atmosphere, its fires licking at the sides of the ship. Around us, instead of the blue-black of space touching the sky, floats an endless descending minefield of moon rock. Like fruit from a tree, the moon's fragments take turns succumbing to Vimelia's pull, dipping out of their gradual decline into sudden bombing.

"We're going to make it," Lan says, and the Oratus' words are the first clue I've had that she didn't think success was assured.

"Thanks to you," I say.

"This is a good ship," Lan replies. "The shuttle we flew down here would not have survived that ascent."

We coast our way through the rest of the moon, until at last we break to the other side. The Vincere fleet, even larger than when we left it, shows itself through the occasional blast and explosion of a Sevora ship attempting a futile, last ditch attempt to get away.

"They have to get far enough away to leap," T'Oli says as we watch a species go extinct in little pops before our eyes. "Or else, when they try, they could fold part of the planet, or the moon, into their leaping space with them. A very fatal mistake."

T'Oli explains this matter-of-fact, and I take it in, but what I'm thinking, really, is that we survived. We did it. We made it down to Vimelia's surface, found Malo, and got off alive.

Flashes; blinks and moments come and go. Sax gets the impression he's lying on the ground, the light above carved apart by thick black lines. He breathes, but the rest of him lies at a distance, untouchable, apart, so Sax sleeps.

Oratus dreams are like any other species—fragments of life and wishes spun into visions of futures past. There are endless hours spent with Bas in frenetic missions against Sevora scum, odysseys through jungles of Sax's distant memory, the neon-lit caves of Earth where the humans lead him to the den of an angry horde of Fassoth.

When the last one fades, Sax opens his eyes again to see a familiar face staring at him, rose-gold and wonderful.

"Found you," Bas hisses lightly.

"You did," Sax manages to say. His throat is dry from too little water, his head throbs—no, his entire body aches. "How long?"

"It's still light, if that helps," Bas says. "It's been over thirty hours."

The announcement prompts a dire laugh from Sax. "Thirty hours? It took you that long to shake the skiffs?"

Bas sighs. "I was overruled."

Sax, though, is finding his connections to his muscles are still intact. It's a slow process, standing, but with time and effort Sax gets there. Notices, as he looks up, that there are a number of deep indents on the vines above, marking the passage of his fall.

"Plake?" Sax says.

"The mission," Bas replies.

"You chose the mission over me?"

"I didn't want to, my pair," Bas says, and she uses her claws to help Sax stay upright. "But we couldn't know if you survived. Agra-Red and Plake drove away the last skiffs, but more were coming. Even if you lived, we had no way to carry you."

The reasoning makes sense, and it's impossible for Sax to be angry with Bas. That would be like becoming angry with himself.

"Yet, you came back?"

Bas beckons towards a pathway obviously cut with her own claws. The vines there are torn asunder, their pieces littering the ground as they walk towards a small clearing similarly sliced open, though the charred ends here show a miner's handiwork.

Sitting in it is a small shuttle, barely larger than the evac mod they took down to Aspicis. Place and Agra-Red wait outside of it.

"Managed to survive?" Agra-Red says as Sax walks into view.

"Looks like you owe me," Plake says to the Whelk.

"When don't I?"

"One of these days I'll collect."

"And that's the day you'll find out I have nothing to give you," Agra-Red warbles a wet laugh. "All I've got is this miner and a bit of loyalty."

Plake shakes her head, takes a harder look at Sax. "You still able to go on this?"

"The mask shaped most of the fall and the vines did the rest," Sax says. "I'll be sore, but still better than you."

The Whelk laughs again, and Plake just points to the open shuttle bay. Sax creaks in first, expecting cramped quarters and finds it's even worse than he thought. There's no actual cockpit inside—there's only cargo space and it's already filled with what looks like racks and racks of dead power cells. As it is, squeezing in requires Sax to reassess his flexibility and bend himself into a mess of limbs.

Bas doesn't get any better treatment, generally placing herself on top of the path Sax defined between the racks of dark batteries. Plake and Agra-Red get the small open area directly around the bays, the Whelk settling its assault miner so the point aims right out the door.

"Where's the pilot?" Sax asks once they're inside.

"Don't have one," Plake replies. "Apparently Cavignum has such tight security they don't let much manned cargo in. Our contact says our only chance is going in by drone shuttle."

As if to emphasize the point, Plake pulls out a small device and taps a couple of signals on it. The drone begins to power up, rising from the ground on the strength of its microjets.

"How'd you convince them to take us?" Sax asks.

"I used my claws," Bas replies. "And, we promised the Flaum a position heading all of the power on Aspicis."

Sax hisses a laugh. "I thought the point of this was to remove corruption?"

"Nah," Agra-Red says. "We just want to change from corruption that destroys galaxies to the usual, grifting sort."

There's not much to say to that, though Sax feels a bit of sadness worm its way into his body as the shuttle flies along. Evva certainly had more noble aspirations than replacing the Chorus with a wheeling-and-dealing set of greedy paws, but what does Sax know about governing? He couldn't run a planet, couldn't even run a ship.

So instead he focuses on things he knows; namely, rehearsing the plan of attack. Their mission's pretty simple, now that they're on the way to Cavignum. Once they land, the group needs to break in and cause a diversion large enough for Nobaa and Engee to find a way inside. Then, of course, get out alive and, if possible, reconnect with Evva at the Spire.

Simple.

"Have you two ever done anything like this?" Sax asks after they've run through the plan twice. "An actual assault on an enemy position?"

"You're talking to a merchant and her thug," Plake replies. "We've assaulted plenty of enemies, but not like this."

"Usually it's one or two, up real close," Agra-Red adds.

"Then let Bas and I do most of the work," Sax hisses. "Cover us. Keep your eyes open for anything we miss, and clean up anything we leave behind."

"You're making it sound real glamorous," Agra-Red says.

"This has nothing to do with pride," Bas says. "The only thing that matters is the mission."

"Then I think we have a problem," Plake says, her voice running up high with concern. "Because we're not going to the right place."

Lan sets the course towards Kolas' cruiser, the *Nunilite*, as we clear the last bits of the moon. Beyond Vimelia's atmosphere, the gravity in our ship drops to zero, letting my black hair float around while T'Oli does work keeping me gripped to the floor.

"So we glide on home?" I ask the Oratus. "Then what?"

"Kolas will have the ship scanned for any Sevora before we're allowed to leave it," Lan replies. "Then, after some time to rest, I imagine you will be sent to Aspicis, to present your species to the Chorus."

I suppose that was the original purpose of Lan's mission.

To my left, the door splitting the bridge from the crowded rear of the ship slides open and I'm surprised to see Malo glide in, followed by Viera. The Charre warrior still looks ill, but he manages to give me a weak smile.

"Sorry," Malo says. "It's really crowded back there, and once everyone started floating..."

"And the vomit," Viera adds. "If you think humans

getting sick is bad, try a bunch of Flaum. It's disgusting. All in their fur, and—"

"I guess I'll stay up here then," I cut off Viera before her descriptions send my own stomach tumbling and the two of them settle in against the side opposite me.

Viera nods towards Lan, sitting in the netting. "How's the pilot doing?"

"Fine," Lan hisses.

"She did well," I say. "Didn't panic at all."

"It helps when you don't fear death," Malo says, and the warrior coughs out a half-hearted laugh.

"What?"

"Them. The Oratus. You're not afraid of anything, are you?" Malo says to Lan. "Not like us, like humans."

Lan turns a yellow-black eye towards Malo. "The only thing we fear, if you want to call it that, is losing our pair."

Outside, we're heading into the outskirts of the Vincere fleet. Open space fills in with smaller ships buzzing around, larger freighters and what must be battle-ready cruisers move past us, heading towards the ruin of Vimelia. Probably to make sure nothing survives Kolas' plan.

"Humans are like that too," I say. "With those we love."

"I love these miners." Viera gestures with the weapons in each of her hands. "Wouldn't want to lose them, either. Can't say I'm afraid about it though."

"You're terrible at these conversations," Malo says to her.

"I choose to be terrible, Malo," Viera replies. "Because it's funny, and that's how I cope with this madness."

Lan, at least, gives Viera a slight hissing laugh for her trouble. The conversation ebbs and flows from there, with Malo giving us a rundown of his time on Vimelia after we jetted off-world and left him collapsed in the docking bay cavern.

At first, Malo woke without any idea of where he was, only that things were dark and the air smelled thick and rotting. His whole body was sore, and Malo couldn't really move, so he sat there in the dark until he realized the smell was the same as the sewers we'd all been running through not long before. Malo figured if he was back there, then maybe he'd been taken by one of the Clarity's Dawn members, and started trying to make noise.

"It's tough to scream when your throat is dry and your lungs burn," Malo says. "But I kind of growled out a call for help, and someone came."

That someone turned out to be Rackt, a Vyphen member of Clarity's Dawn, and Rackt said he was surprised that Malo still lived. Nobody knew how a human's body worked. All they had were experiments, medical cream meant for scales or furry Flaum skin. But humans aren't so special after all—or so Malo found out when he didn't die.

"I stayed in the dark for a while, getting better," Malo says. "I thought we'd won at first—Rackt said that you had made it away, and I was happy about that."

The Sevora, though weren't as thrilled with Malo and the rest of Clarity's Dawn. They struck on what Malo thinks was the third day, hitting Clarity's Dawn's headquarters beneath the surface. They took some prisoners, the ones that didn't fight back too hard, the ones who might still be useful as hosts. Others, like Rackt and Sapphrite, vanished in a hail of burning laserfire.

"By the time I realized what was happening, it was already too late," Malo says. "I managed to get out of my chamber, and that was the end of it. They stunned me, and

I've spent every day since then with these prisoners, waiting to see what the Sevora were going to do."

By the time Malo finishes his story, Lan announces that we're closing in on Kolas' cruiser and the back edge of the fleet. With T'Oli loosening its grip on my feet, I manage to float my way over to Malo and wrap the warrior in a tight hug.

"We're not leaving you behind again," I say. "Promise."

"Shouldn't promise things you can't control, Empress," Malo says, but I think he's joking, even if his eyes have a wary look to them.

He's still recovering, still putting himself back together. I would be cautious too.

Gar's roar surprises everyone. We're in the final approach, and the crashing, hissing, pained noise comes out of still air. I jerk apart from Malo, just in time for Lan to push me out of the way as the Oratus streaks away from the net to the call of her pair. I try to look through the door, but Lan blocks it and when she's through, the only thing I see is a roiling mass of chaos as the prisoners throw, cut, and bite at the Oratus.

"Are they insane?" I say. "What are they doing?"

"A case of the space crazies?" Viera says, and she pulls up her miners.

Speaking of, a pair of flashes blitz through the door, followed by another hissing roar, this time from Lan. More surprise, more pain.

"Viera, go," I tell her. "Help them. I'll hold the bridge with T'Oli and Malo."

"You want me in that mess?" Viera eyes me. "I don't know..."

"If Lan and Gar get hurt, Kolas might not let us back on board," I reply.

Viera takes the hint, pushes off from the floor and heads through the entryway back into the ship's main area. I tell T'Oli to follow her and keep a barrier between the bridge and the rest of the ship—the last thing we need is whoever's causing the problem back there to get their claws or whatever they have on the flight stick.

"Empress," Malo says, and I turn to see him drifting into the cockpit's netting. "You might want to hold on to something."

"What?"

Malo reaches, grabs the flight stick, and shoves it forward. The ship lurches down, away from our landing path with the *Nunilite*. The new velocity pushes me back against the wall, and I hear more frustrated hissing and a single, angry yelp from Viera.

"What are you doing?" I yell as Malo boosts the ship's speed, faster and faster as we launch out beyond the end of the Vincere fleet.

"Saving my species, Kaishi," Malo says. "What I tried to do on Earth. What I won't fail to do now."

"Sevora." T'Oli slaps the word as I put it together.

"Ignos?" I say a name that I thought dead and gone. "You're alive?"

"Barely," Malo, no, Ignos says. The Sevora is sending Malo's hands tapping away at a feverish pace. "Like your warrior here, I nearly died in your escape."

"You crashed the transport shuttle yourself!" I shout. "You chose to come after us!"

"No, Kaishi," Ignos replies. "I chose nothing—everything I've done has been forced upon me by the Vincere, by your Oratus friends. Do you think we wanted to escape our home like this?"

The prisoners. We'd never had a scan to search them for

Sevora. Jel or Nasiya could have infected all of them. The thought makes me sick, but I push the nausea away. No time for that now. Instead, I press my legs against the wall, and push forward, flying towards the pilot's netting.

"How many?" I ask as I head towards Malo, towards Ignos. "How many of them are Sevora?"

"Every last one," Ignos says, and the Sevora doesn't turn his head until I catch the netting. Then Malo's face, twisted in a sad, steady stare, looks at me through the netting. "It's the only time Nasiya and Jel ever agreed on a plan. One that would have failed utterly if you hadn't come through for us."

I try to get around the netting, but Ignos shakes Malo's head. "Don't try it, Kaishi. Touch me, and I'll kill you." With Malo's right hand, Ignos brandishes a small, shining knife from beneath the ragged folds of his clothes. "I'm going to leap in a moment, before those Vincere fighters decide we're not worth the risk. Find somewhere to strap yourself down."

Ignos glances back at the monitors, and his right hand lets go of the knife, leaving it to float in space, to punch in a command. I start to let go, to drop back to the wall where I'd rode out the acceleration, then I pull myself around the netting, this time to Ignos' right, reaching for the knife.

And catch an elbow in my stomach. It's a hard hit, one that blows the air from my lungs and, with nothing to hold me, sends me floating back along the same way I'd been faking a moment earlier.

"The human body is not a bad one," Ignos says, and now, outside, I can see the barest few flashes as the Vincere start shooting. I hope they hit us. "It takes some time to get hold of the nerves, but with Malo stuck in our facilities, and with my experience from your own body, we had that time."

"You stole him."

"Kaishi, don't be naive. You are fighting for the survival of your species, like us." Ignos taps one more green-outlined box on the right monitor and the ship's alarms go off, announcing a short leap countdown. "Just because we've won, doesn't mean you're any better than we are."

The hissing and roaring from behind us has died down, and I don't hear any sarcastic remarks from Viera. T'Oli has its eyestalks split, one back into the mess, one towards us.

"They're all stunned," T'Oli says when I look its way. "They kept small, microstunners beneath their rags. Ingenious, really."

No. A desperate attempt that only succeeded because I ignored all advice. Lan, Kolas, even Viera tried to warn me. I tried to do what Father would not, and because of that, I've lost everything.

The leap is both instant and long, a warping of everything I am that goes handily with the mind-wipe I'm going through. The back of Malo's head, covered in scraggy black hair, seems to split into a dozen copies of itself that spill around a prism. I look left and instead of that side of the bridge, I see T'Oli spread out across the cosmos; an infinite expanse of cream blending with the stars.

Then the universe snaps back to itself and I'm there again, trapped with a bunch of my worst enemies. Outside, dead center in front of us, I can see a ship that's definitely not part of the Vincere fleet: it's huge, for one. Larger than *Cobalt*, though they share their round exterior.

"A seed ship," T'Oli says from its spread position across the bridge's sole doorway, though whether the Ooblot is telling me or whistling its own surprise I'm not sure.

"Where did you take us?" I ask Malo, pushing myself off the wall.

Part of me wants to go to the door, to check on Lan, Gar, and Viera. T'Oli says they're stunned, a fate I think I'd share if I went that way. So instead, with Malo and Ignos still staring towards the front, out the windshield, I wave to T'Oli, tell the Ooblot, with my hand, to come over, and T'Oli complies.

"Deep space," Ignos says. "Well off any charted course, near no habitable planets or points of interest. An ideal place to park the last sanctuary for our species."

T'Oli wraps its cream self around my left arm, sharpening its edge into a blade. I glide towards Malo, a warrior that I'd given everything to save, one that I wanted desperately to be alive, and that desperation blinded me.

Time to fix that mistake.

"Kaishi," Ignos says as I get close. "Don't—"

The Sevora doesn't finish. I stab forward with T'Oli, drive the diamond-hard point of the Ooblot towards my friend. But it's hard getting momentum without weight, and instead of the decisive slice I'm hoping for, my stab barely gets through the net. Malo has plenty of time to wheel out of the way, to press his back against the windshield as my swing falls short.

"Put it down," Ignos says, raising Malo's hands, palms up, to me.

"No." I slice the netting away. "You've betrayed me at every turn. Used me, like you're using Malo now. I'll never do what you say again."

"Your friends will die if you kill me," Ignos says, and there's not an ounce of fear in its voice, even as I draw my arm back for another strike.

Ignos has no room to move this time, nowhere to send

Malo's body to get away from my Ooblot sword. Yet, I know why it's not afraid. I know why it's simply staring at me now, taking a slow, deep breath.

I can't. I can't kill Ignos if it means the rest of my friends will die.

"What happens now?" I say, keeping T'Oli level, ready. "What are you going to do?"

Ignos points towards the huge seed ship, towards the docking bay that's opened up for our approach. "We're going to begin again. The Sevora will grow, we will find a new home, and we will spread."

"Until the Chorus finds you, and this whole process repeats itself."

Ignos laughs. "As it has before, so it may again. We are learning, though, and the Amigga, I think, are beginning to lose their grip on the galaxy."

"What do you mean?" T'Oli asks the question, pattering away from a patch between the eyestalks, up near my elbow. "The Chorus is as strong as ever."

"Ooblot, you've been buried under Vimelia's rock for too long. There's a rot within your civilization, one that's growing too fast for the Chorus to contain. Even if the Amigga survive this revolt, they won't be strong enough to fight us."

Seeing Ignos turn Malo into a gloating clown only makes me angry, and I push the sharp tip against Malo's body, pinning Ignos to the windshield. Nowhere in Ignos' plans was there anything for us, which means the only way out we have is the same way Malo's taken; through the mind of a Sevora.

I'd rather die than let another one of those creatures into my head. Viera, Lan and Gar would too.

"Wait," Ignos says, and now, at least, there's a leak of

fear in that voice. "Kaishi. We can make a deal here. A good one."

"Make it, then," I growl.

Outside, our ship drifts into a wide, blue-lit docking bay. It's huge, and there's a smattering of other craft around, but unlike every other bay I've been to, not a soul moves in it. There are no robots, no scurrying Flaum or any sign of life.

"I'm sure Nasiya and Jel will agree with me," Ignos says. "If we promise you your lives. You, Viera, and this one. Malo. I will give him back to you."

"What about me?" T'Oli says.

Ignos shrugs. "Go with them."

"Gar and Lan?" I ask.

Now there's hesitation as the ship settles to the ground, the whine of microjets coming in clear. As we land on the seed ship, I feel some slight gravity return, pressing my feet to the floor. If I had to swing now, the cut would be quick. Deadly.

"We can't risk them getting away," Ignos finally says. "They'll head back to the Vincere and tell them what we've done."

"I could do that too."

"But you won't," Ignos replies. "Before you managed to figure out where, who to speak to, we'll be gone. And if you betray us, then before too long, your precious Earth will see another Sevora seed, and another tribe will find their god. Only this time, I'll have full control."

My species for the Sevora. A trade.

There's only one thing to do. One way to go.

"I agree."

The drone shuttle's bay doors are shut and there's no windows to speak of, so the first glimpse Sax gets of where they're going is after the ship lands with a thud on something distinctly metallic. The shuttle's doors open with a whoosh. There's a lot of loud shouting, orders for Plake and Agra-Red to drop their weapons.

From his squashed corner, Sax can only see a little, but what he gets is a deep blue metal enclosure, far different from the vine-wrapped spaces he's seen elsewhere on this planet. He can't make out the enemies, but they must be dangerous, as Plake drops her miner and Agra-Red ejects the power pack from its own fixed weapon. Both items are swept up by furry Flaum fingers as soon as they hit the floor.

Chances at surprise are few, so Sax and Bas wait, with the latter positioning herself so that she can curl off of Sax towards the shuttle's doors, claws out and at the ready.

"Either you two leave now, slowly, or we melt the shuttle where it sits," the voice is the mechanical whine of an Amigga. "We scanned the ship for heat sources on the way in. We know you're in there."

"This is the last time I trust anyone other than you," Sax hisses to his pair.

"It's just another adventure, Sax," Bas says lightly, then climbs off of Sax and heads outside.

His muscles are still sore, so Sax takes a bit of time extricating himself from the shuttle's cramped confines, but when the Oratus manages to get himself out into the chilly, northern air, the first view tells him why it's dark: the camp's on the very edge of Aspicis' night line, with the white dwarf setting oh-so-slowly on the far horizon.

Around them rise daunting metal walls, above and over which bits of tangled vine drape. None of the greenery, however, makes its way far inside the enclosure, which, Sax notices, is covered by a wispy laser shield, the kind of screen not visible except for the small insects and occasional bits of dust that strike and, in turn, are immolated by it.

Plake and Agra-Red have already been hustled away from the shuttle, where a quartet of Flaum watch over them. The Whelk is forced to take the battery pack from its embedded miner, ensuring the weapon is nothing more than an unwieldy club. Another dozen or so of the furry creatures aim miners of their own at Sax and Bas, while an Amigga bearing a taller, treaded and apparently weaponless exoskeleton stands over them all.

"Plake, when this is done, I'm going to find your contact and eat them," Sax says across the yard to the Vyphen.

"I'll serve them up to you," Plake snaps back.

"Stop," the Amigga commands, and Sax resists the urge to take a running leap over to the thing and destroy it right then and there.

The Oratus is wearing a mask—albeit a damaged one—and with Bas there, the two of them stand a decent chance of taking out all the Flaum. However, Plake and Agra-Red have no such defense, and sacrificing their companions for a risky move seems like a poor choice.

"You've arrived at Fenebris, and it will be your new home until the Chorus decides what they would like to do with you," the Amigga says. "First, of course, we will gather your names. Then, we will submit them for your fates to be decided. My guess is that you will all die horribly within the next twenty-four hours. Any resistance will only confirm that fate."

Flaum step up to Sax and Bas, reach for their masks and for the equipment hung therein. Sax catches his pair's eye—do they fight back? She shakes her head slightly, and the decision is made. No resistance for now.

"You can take away my miners," Sax says to the Flaum as they pull the weapons away. "I'll still have my claws, and that's more than enough for you."

The furry creatures glance at each other, and Sax enjoys their quick steps away from him a second later. A little fear goes a long way.

The escort from the landing area is a short one—Sax is expecting cells, some form of detention center, but what they get instead is a shift from the wide area of the landing pad to a wider and far more sloppy yard where the ground, instead of paved stone, is mostly muddy dirt. Sticking up from the earth every so often are four-meter high heat sticks with glowing-orange bulbs throughout their length and soft fans on top to blow the heat down, and clustered around those sticks is the saddest collection of creatures Sax has seen since *Scrapper Station*. Flaum, Whelk, Teven and more huddle around each other, talking quietly or just seeming to sleep on the ground.

In the middle of the space is a large, circular trough. A few species linger there, picking at what looks like a flood of nutrient goop moving slow through the container, flowing up from one end and down on the other.

At the far end of the space, set against another large wall, stands a gate slightly taller than Sax, and aside from the way they came in—a similar gate—looks like the only way to go in or out of this space.

Altogether, the vibe Sax gets is a depressing one.

"The best part of being here," the Amigga's saying when Sax tunes back into its endless haranguing. "Is that you'll never have to worry about leaving. There's no more dreams to have, no more problems to solve. It's just this space, the nutrient goop, and the glimmer worms."

Glimmer worms?

Sax isn't the only one with questions, as he catches a shrug from Plake and similar cocked-head confusion from Bas. The Amigga, though, doesn't seem interested in going further; the creature, along with the Flaum guards, retreats with miners out and ready back through the gate, which trundles down and settles heavy on the ground.

"Can't say this is what I was expecting," Agra-Red announces in a huff. "Always thought I'd die in a firefight, not crumbling to dust in a labor camp."

"I didn't think the Chorus had these?" Bas says. "The Vincere never mentioned them."

"I guess if you break the law on Aspicis, they're not much for due process." Plake sweeps a winged arm across the space. "Look at all these miserable things."

The Vyphen's not wrong. Sax would normally see a bunch of defenseless creatures as food to have, prey to hunt, but nothing here gets his hunter's instinct going. The nutrient goop means none of the species he sees are shriveled or malnourished, but they're dead in spirit. There's no fire here.

If Plake's right, though, and these are criminals, then they must not be grievous ones. The Chorus tried to kill all of them in the skiffs not long ago, but now they're content with leaving dangerous captives in a labor camp?

"Your contact," Sax says. "They didn't tell the Chorus who we were."

At Plake's look, Sax goes over his reasoning. Namely, that the four of them should have been shot on sight, or stunned and used as an example. Why leave a dangerous quartet with outside friends alive?

"So they didn't completely screw us," Agra-Red burbles. "I'm still going to disintegrate them."

"And I'll eat whatever's left," Sax hisses. "What I'm saying, though, is that we might have a chance to get out of this. If they don't know who we are, then we might have time."

"Until they decide to look," Plake replies. "I'm not trusting for a moment the Amigga here won't run our images and see what it gets. I say we find a way to breach these walls now."

Which is how they spend the next few hours. Sax and Bas, Agra-Red and Plake split and circle the wide walls of the camp, drawing wandering looks every now and then as they brush up to the barriers. They're hard rock, though Sax feels his claws could pierce them.

"If we climbed over, then what?" Bas says when she notices Sax run his metallic claws across part of the stone, leaving a white-chipped line. "They either shoot us, or Plake and Agra-Red."

"Then what, we wait?" Sax asks, and he can't keep the derision from his voice. There's nothing worse than waiting, especially when you don't know how long. "I prefer doing something over nothing."

Their conversation—the heated tones, more likely—attracts the attention of an older Teven, its mud-brown carapace chipped and cracked, that Sax didn't even notice until the stick-like creature rises up from the ground near their feet.

"You ever hear of sleep?" the Teven announces. "It's a practice where those of us who've worked our hides all day get back a scrap of energy so we can do it all again."

Sax bares his teeth at the creature. Wants to take a swipe with his claws because Aspicis, on the whole, has been a giant crap pile for him, but Plake moves in front of him and talks straight to the Teven.

"Hear what we were saying?" Plake asks.

"How could I not? You're all talkin' like there's some big thing you're missing cause you're here."

"You know much about this place?"

The Teven laughs, always a strange thing, as Sax can't see their mouths, so their flute-chuckles pop out from their carapaces at a seeming distance from the creature itself. Like hearing an echo.

"I've been here almost my whole life," the Teven replies. "Tried to fix a way off this world, got caught for it, now I've caught so many glimmer worms it's all I see when I sleep."

"So there's no way out?"

"Didn't say that," the Teven replies. "Just no ways for an old Teven all alone. Crew like yours, there might be options. These folks aren't used to resistance. Push back, maybe you'll find they break. Or maybe you'll find yourselves fried and dead on the ground."

"One of those options sounds good," Agra-Red says.

Sax, though, is done listening to the Teven. Done standing around here. There's not a single Oratus in this yard, which means it's plausible this prison isn't designed to hold a creature like him.

"Watch," Sax hisses to Bas, and then he breaks into a long-loping run towards the nearest wall, one of the long side ones without a gate.

The sparse light makes it hard to make out anything other than smooth stone rising six or seven meters before ending in a rippling series of what look like small spikes. Sax jumps before he gets to the wall, his leap carrying him nearly halfway up before his metal claws punch into the stone. His fore- and midclaws cut right through, and Sax scurries up towards the top without hesitation.

He'll have to thank Nobaa for the claws next time he sees the Teven.

Sax hits the top of the wall and there's no alarm, no streaking bolts from one miner after the next. Over the edge, Sax sees plenty of the vines, sure, but there's something else. Something huge, glowing orange that spans half the horizon and rises up into the sky. Lights glow in the long purple twilight as dozens of skiffs and other transports flit into and out of the structure, the departing ones vanishing in all directions.

Cavignum.

Sax places his left foreclaw in between the nubs, glances back down towards his crew to tell them what he's seeing, when his foreclaw goes numb. The icy blankness spreads along his arm, into Sax's torso and all along every part of him, until even his eyes go limp and his lids close halfway.

Then, with no strength holding him back up, Sax plummets back to the ground.

At my words, Ignos nods behind me, and I whirl to see a red-patched Flaum standing in the doorway, a pair of miners in its claws hands pointing at me. "She won't be trouble," Ignos says to the Flaum.

"That's what you told us the first time," the Flaum replies. "I'm inclined to destroy her right now."

"You can try," I reply. T'Oli takes my tone, broadens and hardens its shell so that I have what amounts to a shield on my left arm.

"Nasiya," I get the sense that Ignos says the name for my benefit as much as the Sevora leader's. "This isn't the place, and you don't have your Oratus host any longer. You're not a weapon. She could kill you easily."

Nasiya's body keeps the miners steady for another heartbeat, then drops them to the Flaum's sides. "You made a deal, Ignos. I will honor it."

We disembark the ship in silence. Not even T'Oli has words for the still forms of Gar, Lan, and Viera as the Sevora Flaum and Whelk carry them from the ship. I can see Viera's chest rise and fall as she breathes, but her eyes are closed. Her hands empty, dangling from her sides as she's carried down the ramp I, back on Vimelia, ordered down for these monsters.

Like a ramshackle ceremonial procession, Nasiya leads us out through the docking bay and into a strange, huge section full of windowed buildings that rise from floor to ceiling. They're smaller than the towering heights of the structures on Vimelia, but they make every other ship I've been inside feel tiny. Yet, unlike Vimelia and the underground dwellings in Marilo, home of the Lunare back on Earth, all of these windows are dark.

The avenues splitting the buildings are dim too, with only the occasional glow coming from tall poles dotted with hooks and branches. I'm not sure what those are for, but Ignos and Nasiya, who walk near me at the head of the group, each spend a few footfalls looking at the empty roosts.

What is clear, though, is that this seed ship is meant for far more than the few of us that are here. Thousands and thousands could fit in these spaces, and that docking bay had the resources for dozens of ships.

"A last resort should be empty," Ignos says to me as we walk. "Still, these streets should throng with Sevora. This ship should hum with the possibilities of our species."

"Isn't that the plan?" I reply. "If the Vincere don't blow you up again?"

Ignos ignores my jab. "It is the plan, but first we need to decide who to sacrifice."

"Sacrifice?"

"Sevora do not breed like you," Ignos says as we near a large half-moon door that Nasiya calls a *gateway*. "One of us will need to mature, and from them, we can spawn a million more."

"That doesn't sound like a sacrifice."

"At the center of this ship is a prison," Ignos says. "It is couched in glory, but it is a prison nonetheless. The Sevora that takes residence there will never leave it. They will control the seed ship, and nothing else."

The next area we enter is again filled with buildings, but rather than the block-like utility of the last section, these are laid out in vibrant, twisting designs. As if someone had shrunk and transplanted a part of Vimelia's great city to the ship. Except this great city is empty. It's one thing to stare at the dark windows of unoccupied homes, it's another to look at a grand square, with a curling crystal spear sticking out of a dry fountain. Benches sit alone, pristine and never used. Terminals aligned in banks against the walls look back at us with blank screens.

All of us, even the Sevora, hurry through the section.

The next area grips my chest like a vice. I haven't seen a literal seed since finding Ignos so long ago on that jungle night, but here they're hanging row after row around a great ring. Their sharp noses point down, towards a gray metal floor far beneath us.

"It will open," Ignos says when it catches me looking. "When it's time for us to spread, this is how. A single seed can carry a Sevora for many, many light years until it hits its target."

"How long did you travel to get to Earth?"

"Comparatively short," Ignos replies, gesturing for me to keep walking with them as they circle the ring. "We already knew of Earth, that the Amigga were conducting some sort of test there. I was sent to see about the results, to corrupt them if I could."

"You succeeded."

Ignos laughs. "Succeeded? Here you are, despite my

every effort to turn your species into slaves for mine. If anything, Kaishi, I helped your people achieve technological prowess sooner than they should have."

"But if you hadn't, you and all of your kind would be dead now."

"Maybe, maybe not," Ignos says, then the Sevora gestures with Malo's left hand towards a thin metal bridge going over the gap beneath the seeds to a squat square door. "That's what we're looking for. The final bridge. The Sevora that crosses over will never come back."

I'm expecting Ignos to explain why, but it falls quiet after saying the words, and I realize Ignos itself is thinking about making that choice. The Sevora walks Malo forward, joining Nasiya's Flaum host and a third, a small lime-skinned Whelk at the foot of the final bridge.

"They're choosing," T'Oli says.

"I gathered." I look around at the other Sevora. Most are watching the trio discuss, and those that aren't are hovering over Viera, Lan and Gar. The carriers have set the Oratus and the human down, and they rest on the floor, stiff and still. " T'Oli, we have to find a way out of this."

"I don't think the two of us can beat all of them."

"If we can't, they'll take us too," I reply. "I don't trust Ignos at all."

"Right. That seems logical. That Sevora has betrayed you at every opportunity."

"Thanks for the reminder." I shift, with T'Oli around my wrist, closer to the stunned bodies. If any of them are close to waking up, I might be able to distract the Sevora long enough to get an ally...

"I will claim the honor!" Nasiya's voice is high, skittering, and, beneath the bravado, trembling. "I will walk the final bridge, and become the founder of our new beginning."

The words seem ceremonial, but the buzz, and even angry replies Nasiya gets from the rest of the Sevora show the proclamation isn't a certainty. The entire pack of Sevora, even the ones watching the Oratus and Viera, descend on the trio, pushing and shouting at each other.

"I suppose the factions haven't ended their fight after all," T'Oli says.

"They're giving us a chance." I look at the bodies. The seed ship's gravity isn't as high as a planet—an aggressive run and I feel like I'll float off the ground—but I don't think I can carry an Oratus alone.

Viera, though, is much smaller.

While the Sevora struggle with each other, T'Oli slips off of my wrist as I squat down and slide my arms beneath Viera's back. With my legs, I try to lift my friend. I strain, lift hard, expecting resistance and I don't get much. Viera doesn't float, exactly, but I'm able to tilt her upright and forward, where, as she begins to fall with her face destined to smash into the ground, I catch her, bringing up my arm to keep Viera's chest pressed against my own shoulder.

It's probably not comfortable for her, but as Viera's in stunned oblivion at the moment, I'm not too worried.

"They're noticing," T'Oli says.

"Then distract them," I reply, starting to run around the ring.

Viera's feet and ankles drag on the floor as we go—she's taller than I am—but my floaty jog gets us some momentum. Some of the Sevora yell, but no miner shoots at my back, no weapon strikes me down.

I wonder if they don't want to damage their last ship.

After a few steps, with the seeds hanging like spikes up

above me and the shining outer walls of the central ring to my right, I hazard a glance back. T'Oli's taken control. The Ooblot's swimming around a quintet of Flaum chasing after me, using its liquid and solid changing to trip and irritate the pursuit. Every time one of the Sevora tries to pull a miner, T'Oli liquefies its way up their body and slurps itself into the crannies of the weapon, then solidifies to burst it into pieces.

Still, T'Oli is only one Ooblot, and eventually a couple of the Flaum break past it and come after me. It's a foot race I'm not going to win, but I'm close enough now to the open door of my destination; the empty entertainment quarter.

"Stop!"

Ignos yells the word. I keep moving.

"Kaishi stop!"

The doorway's there, Viera's in my arms. All that's left is one foot in front of the other.

"We'll shoot!"

I reach the ramp heading up to the gateway. Risk a quick look behind me and see the two Flaum scrabbling my way, with T'Oli close to them. See Ignos with several more well back, with miners raised in my direction.

"I trusted you!" I shout back to Malo, to the Sevora inside his head.

And I run. Carry Viera through the gateway and back into the dark, empty mess of the entertainment section. No miner bolts blaze through the spot I leave behind. The two Sevora Flaum don't even crest the gateway.

Which means I'm free to carry Viera through the dark, running between buildings, trying to find a place to hide.

The place must be a restaurant. The only clues to that are

the large pieces of equipment in a separated room on the lower level, bulky metal pieces that look well-suited to cooking. Staying on the ground floor is a poor plan, though, so I drag Viera—whose starting to feel awful heavy even in the low gravity—to what looks like a lift.

It doesn't move.

Of course not. The Sevora won't turn this section on, not till there's a reason to, and my needs definitely aren't a reason. I chose the restaurant because the outside lacked the flair of the other buildings, only a nameplate in curling white on a black banner labeling the place "Verdant". I figure they'll search all the buildings eventually, so I might as well be caught somewhere with a name I like.

If I don't get this lift moving, though, I'm going to be found way too soon. The idea is to get some weapons, defend myself and give humanity one last good showing before the Sevora devour my species or the Chorus grinds them into galactic dust.

"Having problems?" T'Oli's slapping voice is a relief in the lonely dark, and I look over towards the entrance to see the Ooblot slime in.

"How did you get away?"

"The thing about Ooblots, they're very hard to kill," T'Oli replies. "I managed to slime a miner away from one of them, this beauty here, and your friend Ignos decided to let me go rather than get in a firefight."

"I guess we take that. Any ideas?" I sigh, glance at the platform around me. "I want to get up to the second level, but I can't get Viera there."

T'Oli oozes up the side of the wall next to me, gets a little over my head, and then solidifies part of itself. "A new handhold. One of my many talents."

"Nice. Viera goes first."

Together, the Ooblot and I lift Viera higher and higher up the lift shaft, with me using my legs and all the energy I've got left to push Viera up one meter at a time. T'Oli wraps itself around Viera's body, stabilizing her for my next push. Until, with one more jumping shove, I get Viera's shoulders level with the next floor's gap.

Just like in the sewer depths of Vimelia, T'Oli forms itself into a lever, pulling Viera up and over the edge.

"Have another jump in you?" T'Oli asks me a moment later.

I nod. Gather my legs, and leap. Doing this in low gravity is a freeing sensation that brings a momentary belief that I might never come back down. With T'Oli catching me, I never actually do. Climbing with the Ooblot isn't at all like climbing a tree—it's more like sticking your limbs into an immovable vice, then using that vice as leverage to pull yourself up and reach out with the other hand into T'Oli's stretched out body, and repeat.

"Do you ever get tired of being used?" I ask T'Oli when we're up on the largely-empty second level. Whereas Verdant's ground floor was full of tables and cooking appliances, this space appears dedicated to a different type of gathering—long, wide tables split the area, and each one is surrounded by cushioned couches.

"Are you asking if I dream of doing more?" T'Oli says. "Don't you think I should enjoy being useful?"

"Well, I..." I start, but T'Oli's right. My idle question gets to a deeper point—what does T'Oli want? Why is this Ooblot tagging along with me?

"If I said I wanted to see the Sevora dead, would that work?"

"No." I lift Viera onto one of the cushions, then step over to the broad windows on the second floor. The dim yellow lights in the section's ceiling provide the little light we have, and all I see on the street are static shadows. Bent corners of buildings, rounded sidewalks aligning streets meant for bustling crowds. "You're too calm for that. I've seen things driven by hate before."

Sax, as the Oratus went after the Amigga on *Cobalt*. The Fassoth that tried to devour me in the caverns beneath Earth's surface. Even the assassins after the Emperor's death, who believed I would be the end of their entire civilization.

"What if I just live?"

"I don't understand?"

"I don't dream, Kaishi," T'Oli says this like it says everything—without sorrow, without emotion, just as a fact. "I spent so long underneath the ground on Vimelia, seeing so many drive themselves to death chasing impossible goals, that I lost my own need for them. Instead, I do what I believe is best, and help those I choose to."

"You're choosing to help me?"

"It's quite entertaining," T'Oli says, the Ooblot sidling up near me. "I don't have any grand motives. You're here, you're kind, and helping you has brought me to places I would never have seen otherwise. That's quite enough for me."

B as kicks him awake, laughter in her eyes as Sax blinks himself alert. He's lying in the muddy filth beneath the wall, and the rest of their group stands around him. What's clear, too, is that he's been out for longer than a few seconds.

"It's time to go," Bas says. "I would've let you sleep longer, but..." His pair nods over to the far gate and Sax stands up to see a phalanx of armed Flaum standing outside of its open portal. "Apparently we need to gather glimmer worms."

This seems to be the purpose of the prisoners here, as all the ones previously lying about the courtyard are now shuffling towards the open gate, with no excitement whatsoever.

As Sax gets up, he notices a few new aches joining in with the bruises from his earlier plummet through the vines. He's putting the mask through its paces, and even with its protection, Sax makes a note to avoid far falls in the near future—he's not averse to pain, but dealing with it every second gets tiresome.

"Does anyone even know what glimmer worms are?" Agra-Red asks.

"My guess?" Plake says. "The Amigga made everything on this planet, so they have to serve a purpose."

Before any of them can follow up on the idea, a loose, low musical blast pours out of the speakers embedded in the corners of the prison walls. It's loud enough to stifle any conversation, and the prisoners around them pick up their pace heading towards the gates.

"Come on, my friends!" the Amigga's voice rings out in its tightly-synthed glory. "It's another opportunity to earn my respect, another opportunity to power the galaxy whose gifts you so ignorantly spat upon. Hurry, now, to the Glimmer mines—as you know, any laggards will be melted once the final trumpet sounds!"

Sax winces as the Amigga's booming voice makes his head hurt even more. The point, though, is made and they tromp beneath dark clouds in the dim light towards the open gate. They're the last bunch through, and the Flaum guards don't hesitate to toss Sax and the others sneers beneath their visored helmets.

"Should I eviscerate them?" Sax hisses, loud enough, to Bas. "There's only a few."

Two dozen, actually. All armed and skittish. Sax wouldn't stand much of a chance, but that's not what he's going for; when the Flaum slip to slight panic, when they back away and a few squeak and raise their miners, Sax gets his laugh.

"You're going to get us all killed," Agra-Red grumbles. "Don't want to die so you can have your fun, Oratus."

"I don't care what you want, Whelk," Sax replies.

Then they're through the gate, which opens into a wide tunnel slanting immediately down. Like the prison yard, the

Glimmer Tunnel, as Sax decides to call it, sports the bare minimum of supports holding the slick, black rock walls up. The tunnel's floor is made of mixed rock patches and slippery sand, and with every breath, Sax's vents pick up the stale scent of hundreds of unwashed, sweating species.

So far as experiences go, this isn't going to be a pleasant one.

The tunnels spiderweb quickly, breaking off into larger corridors and tiny cracks. The pair of Oratus, three meters tall, find themselves with very limited options. Plake and Agra-Red, in the interest of following the trails of the other prisoners who, presumably, know more about where these glimmer worms are hiding, split off and leave Sax and Bas alone.

They have two options in front of them—one, lit by the usual glow lights jammed into the ceiling, seems the more traveled route. The other, with a few light spikes driven into the walls, jerks and twists out of their view a few steps along.

"Neither of these paths are going to take us out of here," Sax says. He's delaying partly because this crossroads is the only spot he's been able to stand up straight for a while, and his sore back is luxuriating in the stretch.

"Sax, my pair, have the falls broken your mind so much that you only state the obvious?" Bas hisses in reply. She cloaks the words in a soft smile, though, so Sax doesn't feel the cut. "We're not escaping while we're down here, so we may as well try and find one of these creatures."

"You mean, a hunt?"

"It's been a long time."

Since a real hunt, of an animal and not a criminal, or a Sevora. Yes. Every so often with the Vincere they'd been lucky, been sent on a mission to a wild world that, after the objective had been secured, offered the chance to revel in their instincts. If being imprisoned by the Amigga is going to offer them anything, Sax will take the chance to fall inside his true self and the delight in the hunting that follows.

First, Sax opens his vents and catches another deep whiff of the cave's many smells. There's the already-mentioned stink, and beneath that the loam of growing plants, the dripping twinge of wet dust, but beneath all of those things, there's something else. A jolt hanging at the tail end of every breath.

The scent comes from his right, down the twisting tunnel. Sax turns that way as Bas takes a step in the same direction. Their tails touch—no words necessary here.

As they set off, Nobaa again makes his modifications worth their efforts. Sax's talons and, when he places them against the rock walls, claws pick up vibrations. Like scents, each tiny shake carries a pattern that Sax sorts through to find what he's looking for. There's the steady footfalls caused by the many pounding feet under the ground here, and in between those, a steady wriggling, a constant shiver in the earth.

"I can't read it," Bas says, her claws next to Sax's own. "There's too much clutter."

"These can," Sax says, pulling his metal claws away. "A snake lies this way."

Sax takes the lead then, stepping through the tight tunnel. They bend around corners, duck beneath leering rocks and jump across small streams. The further they go, the less frequent the light, until the glow-sticks disappear entirely and the two Oratus use their masks to cloak their eyes in low-light vision. What was black and brown shifts to green grades, allowing the two of them to keep making their way.

Every so often, Sax touches the wall again and confirms he's on the right track. Every time, the vibrations are there, only more pronounced as the extra noise from the other species fades. Bas catches it too, now.

Not a word's spoken until the tunnel hits a new, wide chamber whose walls are perfectly visible to Sax because of the wriggling thing hanging down in the center. That the neon-blue-lit thing is a glimmer worm is obvious—not just because of the blue-white light the thing emits, but because it's carved a hole through the ceiling and is now in the process of munching its way through a large, sparkling geode resting on the cavern's floor.

With a blink, Sax gets rid of the blinding night-vision and takes in the glimmer worm, which appears to be taller than Sax, if thin. Its skin, pulsing with light, is covered in tiny hairs, each one occasionally launching sparks to another. The worm doesn't have any feet, and the head devouring the geode is the only dark space, where small blue tongues lance out and take tiny chunks from its meal.

"Found it," Sax says.

"Remember what I said about the obvious?"

"Not at all," Sax says the words as he moves into the cavern, slowly making his way to the opposite side of the chamber.

Most prey can run. Best to cut off any escape before the battle starts.

Sax, though, doesn't get halfway across the room before the glimmer worm pauses its crunching meal. The creature turns its rock-black face, with the tips of its blue tongues barely visible in the worm's own light, towards Sax. They both hesitate, then Sax flicks his tail ever-so-slightly.

Alive. That's how they're supposed to deliver the glimmer worms. Dead, they're worth nothing. So when Bas reacts to Sax's signal, she leaps at the glimmer worm with every intention of tackling and driving the thing to the ground.

Instead, the worm sucks itself back up towards its hole, causing Bas to blow by beneath it. Sax takes his leaping turn as soon as the glimmer worm retracts, aiming to grab the thing's head, and manages to snag it. The glimmer worm's face is just as rock-like to the touch as it is to the eyes, and Sax's heavy weight pulls the worm from its hole, the blinking body piling out and onto Sax as the Oratus lands on his back.

Any thought of victory goes up in a bright flash as the glimmer worm takes its sparkling blue light and flares. The cavern washes out in white, and Sax closes his eyes, yanks his claws back to cover them, and by the time the glow fades, the worm's wriggling away further down the tunnel.

"That, that was terrible," Sax manages to say.

"We don't know anything about these creatures," Bas hisses. "These Amigga are playing with us, sending us after prey without preparation."

"They'll die for it," Sax says. "But now I want this worm. Set the masks."

Sax flips his vision to infrared, a spectrum that runs on heat. He doesn't leave it there—chasing the worm through the tunnels is going to be impossible if they can't see any of the twists and turns—but now the mask will flip between the low-light vision and the infrared with barely a twitch of Sax's eyes.

Then, with talons scratching on the rocks, the Oratus give chase. Running down prey is exhilarating—every step, every breath in pursuit of something using its every moment to get away. There's no more pure comparing of strength, skill, and intelligence than a hunt.

Unfortunately for the glimmer worm, the Oratus are great hunters, and the caves don't give the creature many options to get away. As Sax and Bas catch up they begin to pace the worm.

"It must be going somewhere," Sax says as he and Bas settle for keeping the worm's blue-lit tail end in view.

"Or it's just running from us."

"On Rathfall, I found a nest that let me survive," Sax replies as they vault over a spiky set of rocks and splash through a stream on the other side. "If this worm has its own lair..."

"We couldn't grab one of them, and you're already thinking of more?"

"Planning ahead, Bas."

"This new you is strange." Bas, though, doesn't sound all that upset.

The clue they're waiting for comes soon after in the form of a rising glow further ahead. Going from night-vision dark to the bright green warning that it's too bright is jarring, but Sax blinks over to infrared just in time to see a boiling mass of pinks, blues, and oranges.

There must be a dozen worms or more here.

The one they're chasing dives into the pile, but the wriggling mass doesn't make any moves to get away. The worms could be flaring constantly, for all Sax knows—it's not going to help them here.

"Take the closest?" Sax says.

Bas touches her tail to his in agreement, and they take a few steps forward, reach out with their claws, and grip the first worm. It struggles, but once Sax and Bas get it free from the rest of its group, the worm seems to realize it's captured and falls limp.

"Playing dead?" Sax says, holding the flopping body in his midclaws.

"This is an Amigga creature," Bas replies. "Any instincts it has are programmed into it. If they truly want these worms, then my guess is they're primed to become passive once caught."

"Then why would they flare?"

"Because you don't want just anyone taking your glimmer worms," Bas hisses. "Only those who know, with your permission, how to do it."

As fun as the hunt was, an ending without a fight, without blood and carnage, fades the excitement from Sax's two hard-beating hearts.

Still, at least they caught one.

They don't get to hold on to the worm for long—after Sax and Bas carry the thing back up to the tunnel entrance, they're directed to deposit the worm into the back of a large cargo skiff, where a Flaum pilot sits in front of a rectangular bin. As the worm slides in, joining three others, the skiff powers up and a soft purple sheen appears over the top— one that would no doubt give a nasty shock to anyone trying to breach it.

The Flaum guards watching Sax and Bas drop off their catch give the Oratus plenty of space, more than before, to which Sax attributes his constant flexing of his claws and baring of teeth. Keeping Flaum on edge is too much fun to stop.

"Batteries," Plake says later when they've reformed in the crowded yard. "That's what the glimmer worms are for."

This time, Sax and the others have their own heat lamp. Nobody wants to tangle with a pair of Oratus, so they're given plenty of space. With their masks, Sax and Bas aren't cold, but Agra-Red's skin is dull with chill and Plake has her feathers held in tight. If it's going to take their entire crew to get out of here, Sax might as well help keep them comfortable.

"Why don't they just use normal batteries?" Agra-Red replies. "Like everyone else?"

Plake shakes her head. Sax doesn't know either, but Bas gives a low hiss and they turn her way.

"It's all vanity," Bas says. "The Amigga built species to solve other problems, so why not this one too?"

"That's a lot of trouble to go through for pride," Agra-Red says.

No one disputes that, and nobody knows otherwise, so Sax turns the conversation to ribbing the Whelk and Vyphen for failing to catch a worm of their own.

"We can help you with that tomorrow," Sax finally says, once he's earned steady glares. "We found a whole nest. Even you two should be able to catch one there."

"A whole nest?" Plake says, and the way she turns her head towards Agra-Red has Sax reading layers into the words.

"Might be enough," Agra-Red replies. "I've never tried with a glimmer worm. Might just explode."

"What?" Bas and Sax hiss at the same time.

Agra-Red jiggles its loose, gel-like skin. "I'm a Whelk. What I've got for organs float around in mostly water. If we can get a glimmer worm out of the tunnel without them collecting it, I should be able to pass its current along into the gate, short it out."

"Couldn't any one of us do that?" Bas asks. "We're all organic."

"Yeah, if you want to dilute the current," Agra-Red

replies. "I've done it before, to help jump start machines on the *Mobius*."

"And it doesn't kill you?" Sax says.

"Stings a bit," Agra-Red laughs. "There's a theory Whelks came around because of lightning strikes hit the wrong puddle. Stick us into a power source and we'll pass the energy through like a wire."

The Whelk's plan, though, requires them to get a glimmer worm out of the caverns without getting detected. Given the worms are well over a meter long, that's going to be a trick in and of itself.

"We'll cause a diversion," Sax hisses. "They're already scared of me—they won't look away if I start showing some claw."

Nobody objects, though Bas gives Sax an eye roll. She knows as well as he does that Sax wants the chance to slice a bit, bite a bit. He knows she wants the same, even if she won't admit it.

"I need you to stay here," I tell T'Oli as I turn back from the windows.

The Ooblot's twin stalks look back at me. It's unnerving that there's no expression, no face to read on the slime creature, so after a second I start the walk towards the other side of the room, towards the lift shaft leading down.

"You're going to need weapons, you know," the Ooblot says to my back.

"I'll find some," I reply. The Sevora took the gear I had on Vimelia, and while I'm still in my mask, I'm not foolish enough to think I can do what needs doing with my hands.

"Why don't we start with these?" T'Oli oozes over to me, goes up along my arm and hardens itself into a blade again, and points with its eyestalks towards one of the tables.

With three quick slashes, I cut apart one of the legs and slice the rounded end to turn it into a jagged point. I make a second one, and then set the pair of makeshift short spears into my mask, where they hang as though I'd set them into glue.

"You'll keep her safe?" I say to T'Oli as I head to the shaft, armed and slightly dangerous.

"An Ooblot's not going to stop much by itself," T'Oli replies.

"Keep her alive till she wakes up, then come find me."

"What are you going to do?"

"Lan and Gar are the only things on this ship that can stop the Sevora," I reply. "I'm going to rescue them."

"A suicide mission? Clarity's Dawn had plenty of martyrs. They never accomplished what they wanted."

I quirk a smile. "It's my fault we're in this. I told Lan to let the Sevora on the shuttle. I have to try."

"Or we could try and make it back to the shuttle," T'Oli says.

"You and I both know that's where they'll think we're going."

Ooblots can't sigh—that I know of—but the puttering pops that come from T'Oli then seem awfully close to it. "Then do yourself a favor and stay alive. The galaxy is much more fun with you humans in it."

Going down the shaft is easier than climbing up—I hang from the edge, then push off into a roll, just like dropping from a jungle tree, though the floor here is harder than the leafy dirt I'm used to. My haphazard spears scratch against the tiles too, something to note if I'm trying to be quiet.

From there it's back into the dim dark entertainment section, where I spend my time slinking back towards the ring gateway. There's still no sign of the Sevora in here, and I'm surprised that Ignos and the others think I'm so little threat as to not warrant even a couple Flaum.

But then, Ignos has been around humans. Its been inside my head. If anything can judge how dangerous I am, it's the Sevora.

So I try not to take the lack of interest personally as I make it to the gateway, which is shut. I try to do what Ignos did and walk over to a black nub. Ignos had stared into it from Malo's eye, and I try to do the same, but get no response. There's no panel in sight either, which means I'm stuck.

No, it means I have to look for another way in.

I retrace my steps quick—behind me, there's the entertainment district. Then the empty and even creepier residential area. Following both of those is the docking bay. That last is the only place I'm sure the Sevora won't leave me alone—if I get to the shuttle and toss a message out to Kolas and the Vincere, their new civilization is going to end quick.

Now, I've never sent a message through space, but Ignos wouldn't know that.

I backtrack, my boots treading soft on the metal. Alone, the entertainment district goes from being a curiosity to a cavern of shadows. The emptiness takes on an ominous tone, and the faint whir of electronics bustling beneath the surface permeates everything, a continual whine that sets me on edge. What I wouldn't give for a singing bird or a rippling breeze through some trees.

What I wouldn't give for a bite of food too—I haven't had anything to eat since before our assault on Vimelia, and my stomach's considering that an emergency on par with being a solo insurgent on a seed ship.

The gateway on the other side of the entertainment district is open. There's a black nub here, on the right side, so I don't think it's a different setup than the ring-ward door. Both of them opened when I came through with the Sevora, so if only one is open now...

The Sevora are setting a trap.

I quickstep to the side of the gateway and peer through back into the residential district. While it's not a bright oasis, there's been a change since I was last here: the lights along the avenues and in some of the buildings are glowing, and they're casting a green-blue glow through the space. Doorways into those same buildings, dark and closed when we first went through here, now stand open, beckoning to soft-lit interiors full of screens.

What I don't see are any threats—no Flaum, no Whelk, nothing. So I take a cautious step through. The glow of a building to my immediate right, a five-story sloping affair that looks like a mountainside turned domicile, draws me towards its orange fluorescence. It's not the flickering fires of home I'm seeing through its jagged, curled entrance, but the similarity is enough that I can't resist going closer, holding my short spears at the ready.

There's a whistling bang from behind and I whirl, jabbing at air. Nothing there. Except, I notice, the gateway. It's shut.

I have no way back.

For the gateway to close now seems too suspicious to be coincidence. I turn back to the gravelly building, but instead of fascination, I hunt for traps, tricks, eyes in the dark. A vice holds every nerve.

Breathe, Kaishi. You'd be dead already if they wanted you that way. You've made it this far—beyond the skies of your own home, on a ship of an alien species, one of whom has taken over the mind of the man who took you on this journey to begin with, a man you're realizing you...

It's all too impossible to be scared.

But I can't let that distract me.

The deep breath does help. As does my grip on the spears, the light feel of the mask on my skin. I'm way beyond what I know, but I'm an Empress. I've survived this long.

When I walk through the archway into the building's entrance, I see the imitation fires burning in glass cages dangling from a close ceiling. Their source, rather than dried wood or brush, are little discs set in the bottom of the cages, and their gouts of sporadic orange and red glint through the enclosing prisms to dance along the walls.

I say walls, but as soon as I recognize them as such, as soon as I step into the middle of the entrance, they shift, fading from the rocky brown to a deep blue that draws in the fake-fire light. In large, block letters, a question appears:

What is your name?

I stare at the image. What is my name? What kind of question is that?

"Are you going to answer it?"

Ignos' words have the telltale verve of a transmission, a wired tone that says the sound isn't entirely natural. It's a twisted version of Malo's voice and I hate it. There's nobody in the room, though. Ignos must be watching me—from outside my mind this time.

"Kaishi, you have to play along."

There's no nub to look at. No direction I ought to stare. Only the screen. Only those words.

"I will not *play*."

The screen doesn't change. Ignos doesn't appear out of some hidden door. But there's a hint, a whisper of a sigh making its way through the magical channels that tie Ignos' voice to my ears.

"Kaishi, we are closing in around you at this very moment. Even if Malo or those Oratus gave you enough training to evade us, I'll seal you in this section. This ship is huge. You'll starve before we need to think about opening it up."

The door I came through is still shut, so if those Sevora are coming, they're not here yet. There's no other way out of this chamber, though. Only the blue screens. Ignos is calling it right—I don't have much leverage.

"Then what's the point?"

"The point? Kaishi. The point is you. Imagine what might happen if we sent a seed back to Earth with you inside of it? How simple it would be to take humanity at a single stroke? You and I had nearly completed the birthing pools in Damantum. We could finish what we started."

Insults die in my mouth along with defiant proclamations. Those won't do any good here.

"You still want to take humanity?" I stay in the middle of the room, my short spears ready.

"All species, Kaishi. All of them ought to have the chance to join the Sevora," Ignos replies. "Look at Malo. He lives because I allow him to. Without the Sevora, he would have died in that spaceport, where you left him."

"You caused all of that."

"Because you would not open your eyes. Now choose Kaishi. We want to come in. Nasiya and Jel, they do not trust you. I do. I know you'll see. Let the Sevora into your world, and your people will never lack for miracles. They will survive whatever evils the Chorus designs for them. Humanity will prosper."

I point my spears to the floor. Let them hang loose in my hands and give the door a slight nod. My shoulders slump, and I take a deep, hanging breath as my eyes close.

The door shunts open, and standing there is Malo, is Ignos, and my warrior-champion is flanked by a pair of

Flaum holding miners. They're straight, quiet. Resolute in the way of total Sevora control.

Ignos walks into the chamber, Malo's arms reaching for the spears, and the two Flaum come behind. Malo's eyes are a defiant blue, even as the rest of him is still gaunt, starved and weak. Somewhere behind those irises is my friend. I left him behind once. I will not do so again.

"Humanity will be free," I whisper.

Ignos cocks Malo's head, and I move. My right short spear carries with my lunge, sweeping up even as I duck under the snap-quick turn of the Flaum's miner. When it fires, the Flaum's shot scores over my head. My short-spear does not go beneath its stomach.

Ignos, with Malo's body between me and its second guard, grabs at my left arm. Rather than trying to fight the pull, I let go of my short spear, let Ignos stumble back with its own strength. The Sevora clears the line for its ally, just as I brace and swing, with my right short spear, pulling the Flaum stuck on it to the left. It's body blocks the second miner flash, which fills the air with the stinging scent of burning fur.

The seed ship's lower gravity helps me push my Flaum shield forward, and the Sevora host takes another pair of miner hits to the back before I crash into the shooter. Before I drive my spear through one victim and into a second.

Before my own gets driven into me.

It's a numbing lance, a sudden wrongness in my back. There's pain, yes, but it's white-cold with shock. Ignos drives me forward with the attack, helping me impale the two Flaum and driving us against the wall. Warmth doubles up with the chill, and it feels as though my stomach is leaking, spreading itself around me.

The mask isn't made to stop short spears.

Ignos withdraws the weapon and the three of us, the two silent Flaum and I, collapse on each other. The burned fur of my first one brushes my face—a desert yellow color, though now spotted with red. It is, though, the first soft, comfortable thing I've felt in a very, very long time. I could almost sleep...

"Stop it," Ignos says behind me. "Quit fighting."

No. I blink. No.

I hear Ignos backpedal. "We know your species. I am your mind."

Ignos is... my mind?

The question cuts through the pain's haze. The Sevora and its host are leaning back against one of the flames, still holding my short spear, its dark metal glistening with red wet. Malo's cerulean eyes see mine, and even from across the room, I know them.

I left Malo behind once. I will not do so again.

My fingers find the miner, pry it free. It hurts, it tears to turn myself, but I need the shot.

"Hey," I say, and my voice doesn't sound like me. It's soupy, strange and thick and it runs down my lips.

Malo looks at me. Ignos grips the spear, opens its mouth..

"Do it," Malo says to me.

I pull the trigger.

The journey to and from the nest the next day goes smooth, though Sax enjoys the jaw-dropping awe that comes over Plake and Agra-Red when they come to the glowing ball of lightning swirling in the back of the cavern. The nest has grown overnight too—there's a dozen or more of the glimmer worms here now.

Sax and Bas take one, reaching in and pulling it out from the swarm, then hand the limp worm to the Whelk and Vyphen. They take a second for themselves.

"Look at this, the Oratus find the treasure," says a voice from behind them, a squeaky, old one that belongs to the elder Teven from the yard. The creature's not alone, though; there's a pack of Flaum, Whelk, and others crammed behind him. "Told all of you it'd be smart to follow these two. The Amigga didn't fool around when they made Oratus. Not at all."

A moment hangs while both parties, the four and the two dozen, decide what happens next. With no weapons between them, it'd be a trivial exercise for Sax and Bas to rend their way through all the prisoners. What benefit, though, would such a massacre serve?

"We have an offer for you," Bas strikes first, and when she lays out the terms and conditions, there's not a single dissent from the bedraggled crowd.

The offer, though, requires the two Oratus to lead the flash-blue train of worm holders up to the cavern's front. At first, the half-dozen Flaum guarding the cargo skiff are shocked when the worms begin to appear, then, when every pair of emerging prisoners comes out carrying another, they get suspicious.

So Sax makes his move.

The Flaum guards are watching the next batch unload their worms into a suddenly-packed cargo skiff when Sax steps up behind them, takes his claws, and taps two of the guards on their shoulders. They turn, and start to stumble back at the sight of him, when Sax tightens his grip on their shoulder pads. With his foreclaws, Sax slams each of the Flaum against each other, mashing their miners and helmeted heads together and dropping them, limp and unconscious, to the ground.

This gets the attention of the other guards, who, launching into chittering alarm, start to bring their miners to bear on Sax. The Oratus is already moving to the next pair, while Bas, who's positioned herself behind the two closest to the cargo skiff—and farthest from Sax—neutralizes her targets.

The prisoners break into their own part of the play, lunging forward and grabbing at their oppressor's miners. A pair of Teven jump onto the cargo skiff and knock off the pilot, smothering the shrieking Flaum to the ground, where a stunning blue flash numbs it a moment later.

A bellowing horn rolls through the courtyard as the

resistance expands, and the far gate leading to the landing pad shunts open a moment later, with another dozen armed Flaum pouring out of it and into the yard.

And everything goes wrong.

There's no warning from the Amigga, no call to surrender—the Flaum guards simply advance beyond the gate and begin firing. The bolts aren't blue either, but the burning, killing red. Flaum, Teven, Whelk begin to drop as they're struck.

Sax reacts with instinct. Before, he'd been trying to keep Chorus Flaum alive in hopes they would change their sides. Now, the stakes are mortal. Preserving life means taking it.

While some of the prisoners who've taken miners from downed guards take scattered shots back, the Oratus goes for a direct route; he takes two long lunges towards Bas, who kneels, sets her midclaws, then catches Sax as he jumps. The boost gets the Oratus high enough to catch the top of a heat stick.

Oratus are huge creatures, tall and heavy with endless cords of muscle beneath their scales. When Sax slams into the top of the heat stick, it bends, breaks and sends Sax riding back towards the ground. What the heat stick also does is blow bright, a shockwave of compressed light and energy suddenly loosed on the yard.

It's a blinding flash, accompanied by a burst that launches Sax, claws clinging to the heat stick's top, across the wet, muddy yard towards the Flaum. The momentary stun from the flare has the Flaum bringing their hands down from their eyes in time to see Sax leaping from his ride into the middle of their formation.

Mud, fur, torn armor flies into the air and skips across the ground as Sax whips and snaps. His claws tear, his tail trips, and with every bite of his mouth, Sax disarms an enemy. Bas joins in seconds later, crashing into the Flaum ranks from the other side. The enemy is outclassed, outgunned, and it's only moments before the prison's guards are nothing more than shredded snacks set upon by the remaining prisoners.

Sax meets up with his pair in the middle, her scales, like his, coated in all the evidence of their victory. After a quick confirmation that neither one of them bears anything more than the lightest of burns, they head through the open gate into the prison's landing zone.

The sole tower and barracks that makes up the prison's living space sits on the far side of the clearing. The Amigga's going to be in there.

"Ready?" Sax hisses to Bas.

"Very."

They lope across the landing pad, and are almost all the way across when a growing microjet whine has them stop, wheel around, ready for some new threat.

Instead, it's Plake, sitting at the controls of the cargo skiff. Agra-Red, assault miner re-acquainted with a power source, sits in back on top of a pile of pacified glimmer worms.

"Time to go," Plake announces.

"There's still an Amigga here," Sax protests. "It deserves the same as those Flaum."

"Oratus, now's not the time for your bloodlust," Plake replies. "Think bigger for once in your scale-brained life. We have to get out of here before that Amigga's reinforcements arrive."

Plake's right, of course. They ought to be jumping into that skiff and letting the Vyphen carry Sax and Bas away into the sky.

But.

"This prison ends now," Sax hisses, and he breaks towards the barracks as Plake fills the air with curses behind him.

The barracks and its tower have a wide double-door blocking the entrance, but it's not reinforced like the gates. There's no guards on the outside either, which lets Sax hit the barrier with all the force of his charging, tearing self. The metal rends, the door caves inward, then falls off its supports entirely.

Inside, there's a wide room, a mess hall and rec area coupled into one. A lift wide enough for the Amigga and its exoskeleton sits at the far end, and Sax makes a line for it. There's other people inside, more Flaum, but these are either the prison's support staff or they've decided getting mauled isn't in their interest, because they press back against the room's walls.

Sax is content to let them live. For now.

Someone's watching upstairs because the lift jolts before Sax can reach it, the doors shutting as it starts a journey up towards the second level. Sax keeps moving, digs in his talons and leaps, turning his shoulder as he flies so the Oratus crashes through the wall and the lift's doors, sprawling into rising lift. Sax sweeps his tail in before it gets caught by the lift's movement, then swings himself around so that he's ready when the lift hits the next floor.

He's covered in mortar, dust and broken bits of metal. So far, though, the mask keeps his scales intact, and aside from the constant aches in his bones from the falls, Sax is ready to go.

The feeling lasts until the lift's doors open and the Amigga, fully suited up, sprays laser through the opening doors. The fire stitches a line in the back of the lift, missing Sax, who's hugging the ceiling. After a few seconds, the steady fire stops, and the Amigga's tuned laughter spills down the hallway.

"Are you going to cling up there forever?" the Amigga says. "Reinforcements are coming, Oratus. They'll put down your little uprising without difficulty."

An overconfident Amigga? Impossible.

Sax hisses, then uses his foreclaws to tear apart the lift's roof tiles, sending them cascading to the lift's floor.

"You won't even slow us down!" the Amigga continues. "I'll order up new collections and we'll have plenty more broken Flaum here collecting glimmer worms before another day is out. You'll have accomplished nothing, except killing innocent soldiers!"

Sax barely catches the last bit as he scrambles out of the lift and into the tight shaft around it. There's not much room above him, save the magnets keeping the lift stable. Sax, though, doesn't need much. The walls in this place are thin, clearly meant for convenience and not for standing up to assaults. He presses himself against the back of the lift's shaft, then slams forward, crunching through the wall.

As Sax breaks through, he pushes forward with his talons, leaping as the wall collapses before him. The Amigga stands before him, wearing its exosuit, with this one sporting a pair of rudimentary miners attached to gimbals on the sides. Nothing like the fancier assortment sported by the Amigga Sax and Bas encountered outside the mag lev station.

Not that any equipment could make a difference here.

The Amigga tries to adjust its aim, tries to backpedal on those treads, but all it gets is one quick, missing shot off before Sax collides with its exoskeleton. Sax gets his talons into the tiled floor and pushes, shoving the Amigga—now shouting, pleading with Sax to stop—across the floor, through the line of terminals the forest of sparks they create as the Amigga's armor suit obliterates their fragile screens, and out the windows.

The Amigga plummets down, cracking against the ground in a shower of mud. Prisoners, having broken free of their yard, descend on the creature, beating and breaking apart its protection with the mad intensity of species knowing their lives are forfeit and wanting to spend their last moments in revenge.

"Ready now?" Plake cries as she swoops the cargo skiff in front of the shattered window.

Sax meets his pair, sitting in the back with Agra-Red, and Bas gives him a nod. That's all he needs. With another leap, Sax lands in the back of the skiff and Plake shoots them away. The Vyphen keeps them low, keeps their running lights off in the darkness.

It's easy to see, though, the Chorus shuttles descending towards the prison, and the night's broken when their heavy lasers start to flash into the yard.

At least they're too far away to hear the screams.

Ignos set its trap close to the gateway. The one that had closed behind me, the one that Ignos came through, that's wide open as I drag Malo's body towards it. Ignos said it was locked, that I was trapped. I shouldn't be surprised at another Ignos lie, and it just piles onto the rest of me.

Every footfall, even in the soft landing of low gravity, comes with pangs. My body's slowly going numb, and I stumble, but manage to get a leg out and catch myself. Not sure I could pick myself up again, after the bloody pool the first—and last—attempt produced.

My left hand hangs behind, clamped tight around the stone-frozen wrist of Malo. The warrior's still breathing, which means the Sevora inside his head is still alive too. Lan showed me how to swap between a miner's modes, and the blue flash worked as the Oratus said it would. Malo's alive, even though I might not be for much longer.

The gateway's a broad doorway when it's open, at the top of a ramp that's getting stained as I limp up it. I have my spear in my right hand—the miner's useless for me unless

I'm within a meter of the target—and as I hit the top of the ramp, my right leg decides it's done and I catch my fall on the butt of the weapon.

"Guess we're crawling from here," I say to my friend.

Not that I have a plan. Maybe get back to T'Oli. In truth, I know I'm not going to make it that far. I hope, though, I can get close enough for T'Oli to find Malo. Maybe the Ooblot can find a way to remove the Sevora. Do what I couldn't and save my friend.

I crawl through the gateway. Across the threshold to the gold flickers of the dead entertainment district. The low lights blur and stretch, winking away and whisking back to a beat of their own. The ship itself seems to tilt. Have the Sevora turned the seed ship on its side? Is this what would happen?

No. I've fallen over, that's what. And I'm not alone.

Four Flaum crest the ramp, each one carrying a miner. Two raise their weapons and point them at me, as if I'm somehow going to summon the energy to fight back. Every breath takes a toll, requires weaving through a tangled web of broken nerves and rattling bones. All I can do is stare as they rip Malo away from me. With Ignos safely clear, the two executioners set their sights for a mortal volley.

I tried, Malo. Viera. I tried.

My ears are ringing, my hearing shutting down too, so the flashes play out like a dream. Heavy crimson, the shots wash out the darkness. The two Flaum aiming at me go first. They're hit from behind and their stringy fur catches fire as the beams cascade into them. The other two, by Malo, barely get themselves turned around before the assault falls on them.

Smoke surrounds me as this district gets its first real show.

"Still alive?" T'Oli says, though the sound comes from another body.

Viera cleaves through the scattered smoke, lurching forward as the Ooblot moves her limbs, bends her knees and arms, though I notice her eyes blink of their own accords. Her mouth falls into a tight frown too when I offer her a smile, though since my face has gone numb, I don't really know what I'm doing.

"Unfortunately, I cannot carry three humans," T'Oli says, and the Ooblot lets Viera down gently next to me. "It does look like you're very hurt, Kaishi. I'm not an expert in human anatomy, but that is a lot of blood."

I open my mouth—I can tell I'm doing this because my chest isn't yet numb, and the whiff of air leaking into my body gives my motion away—but only manage a cough.

"Yes, that's the situation." T'Oli forms back into its creamy puddle, both eyestalks dodging around me, getting in for closer looks. "How about we plug the hole right here?"

A sudden, paralyzing cold hits me from my lower back. My eyes pop open, I suck in air, try to scream and only half manage it. Before I've come down from the polar sting, though, T'Oli laces itself along my body. I feel the Ooblot knead through my fingers as it spreads itself thin.

"You're going to have to help me, all right?" T'Oli whispers—a light slapping sound given most of its body is coating me. "I'm not much good at moving humans."

I want to tell the Ooblot I can't help myself, but then my hands shift a little; a push from T'Oli's hardening, contracting body. I go with it, lending my tiny strength to the effort. It's enough, somehow, to get me to my knees. From there, T'Oli pools itself beneath and behind me, then slowly hardens and shoves itself up, shifting me to a stand.

All the while, Viera blinks at me from the floor. I think I see her legs and arms twitch, but then T'Oli has me lurching around back into the residential district.

"Nobody's going to have first aid in the party town," T'Oli whispers. "But where they live? That seems more likely."

I thought I'd be dead by now, but T'Oli's support gives me energy, gives me hope, and I cling to it. The dark fuzziness still lingers on the edges, my muscles spasm and ache, my lungs feel like I'm underwater, but we go. Past the orange place where Ignos sought to trap me, to the next building, an ordinary square structure with oval windows and a dark door.

"Going to lean you here for a moment," T'Oli says, and the Ooblot does just that, pressing me against the side of the building near the door.

The Ooblot slimes over to the door itself, a smaller, squat one I could barely fit through standing up, and presses itself against the metal. After a moment, T'Oli shivers, and the door shakes. There's a sound of tearing metal, and then something bursts in the far side and the door falls back inside the house with a loud thump.

"Good thing there's so few Sevora on this ship," T'Oli says as it returns to me. "Else we'd be overrun by now. Between us, though, I think we've knocked out a third of them. Not bad for a squishy species like yourself."

Unlike the home Ignos led me to, this building looks more ordinary. Straight halls with doorways lining the sides. Unlike the entrance, these are wide open in the lightless hallways. Ignos may have sent power to its chosen structure, but this one isn't turned on yet. In a way, I'm thankful for the dark.

I've made it this far, and now, I try to tell T'Oli, I'm

done. My legs can't seem to rise anymore, even with the Ooblot boosting every step. T'Oli gets the idea, and we swerve into an open room where I collapse, with T'Oli's gentle assistance, onto what appears to be a large reddish sponge.

"Be back soon!" T'Oli chirps and the Ooblot vanishes.

With it, so goes my consciousness.

I wake with a rush, in the same dark room. The only light comes through the window, flicks of the scattered blue lamps throughout the section. The first thing I do is breathe, and it's amazing. Incredible.

I'm alive.

Somehow, I'm alive.

"Empress," Viera's voice is soft, and she's leaning against the wall across from me. "Kaishi. I'm sorry."

"Why?" I try to say and it comes out a scratchy, hoarse mess.

"I failed you," Viera looks down at the miners she has in each hands, as if admonishing the weapons too for their own failures. "I should have stayed on the bridge."

"It would have ended the same," I say. "How long was I out?"

Viera shakes her head. "There's no way to tell time here, but I don't think for long. T'Oli found some powerful creams. They woke me up the rest of the way too. I told the Ooblot not to give any to Malo."

"He's still taken."

"I figured, seeing how panicked his eyes were when I looked at him."

"Where is he?"

"Locked across the hall."

"And T'Oli?"

"Keeping watch," Viera says. "That Ooblot's vicious. After getting you back here and reviving me, T'Oli skewered each and every one of the Sevora inside those Flaum bodies. Said the only way to be sure is to get the little suckers themselves."

After what the Ooblot's been through, a genetic experiment forced to flee into the sewers beneath the Sevora city on their homeworld, T'Oli's probably got rage to spare.

"Good," I reply.

Trying out my arms and legs is a cascade of miracles. Each one works, and while there's plenty of itchy, poking pain, I manage to roll myself out of the bed. Viera catches me as I fall off of the sponge, and she helps me stand. I'm wearing, now, a set of loose-fitting clothes, the vests and pants meant for a Flaum, and one of the legs slips beneath my feet and nearly trips me.

"Have a knife?" I ask Viera, and she produces a strange-looking blade, a serrated edge against a silver-black haft.

"Careful with it," Viera replies. "I took it off one of the Flaum. When you press this button here, it gets interesting." She does so, and the edge buzzes, soft and sharp.

I am careful, and I use the blade to cut away the clothes so they're less like a stifling, messy collection and more a set of functional, if ugly, rags. Nobody is going to confuse me for an Empress, but at least I won't trip and fall on my face.

Now there's two priorities. A few meters away from me sits the warrior I've been trying to get back since the moment I lost him. Farther afield, somewhere in this ship, are a pair of deadly Oratus being taken, every second, closer to their own capture by the Sevora.

I want to ask Viera what to do, but I already know.

There's only one choice I'll regret if we don't make it out of here alive.

"Let's go see him."

Ignos, and Malo, are still stiff and stunned. Their body, Malo's body, is laid flat across another of the sponges, which must be what passes for beds around the galaxy. Malo's eyes flick towards me as Viera and I go into the room, though I can only tell they move because Malo's pupils catch the sliver of blue light from the window. Otherwise the room's too dark to tell much.

"Go and get T'Oli," I say after we stare at Malo for a moment. "It's time we gave Malo his body back."

Viera puts a hand on my shoulder for a moment. Squeezes. Then disappears away into the building. I adopt her stance, leaning against the wall and looking at Malo.

"Ignos, I could hear people while I was stunned, so I assume you can hear me," I say. In a way, the darkness makes it easier—it feels like I'm talking to Ignos like we used to, in the caverns of my mind. "You told me I was destined for greater things. That I would be the source of miracles, that I would save my tribe. You were lying, but you were right. You told me that Viera would be a good friend, that Malo had possibilities. You were using me, but you were right."

I stand, move over to the sponge. Place my hands against its soft surface as I lean over and try not to wince at the lingering pain.

"You stayed with me through the sessions on *Cobalt*, you told me not to be afraid, and even though you were only saying those things so I wouldn't leave you behind, you were right." I stare into those eyes and I don't know whether it's Malo or Ignos who looks back at me. "Because of all that, on

Vimelia, I chose to spare you. I did the thing you would have warned me not to—I gave my enemy another chance."

I hear a pattering, slithering noise from the hallway. Times' almost up.

"You taught that final lesson when you came back for me. Thank you, Ignos. And goodbye."

T'Oli doesn't need a command to know what to do, and the Ooblot catches the vibe of the moment and says nothing as its creamy self sluices up the sponge, surrounds Malo's head, and slivers a piece of itself inside.

I force myself to watch. To see every small bit of the Sevora as T'Oli pulls it, struggling, out of Malo's ear. As T'Oli sets the squirming nest of pointed tentacles on the floor. The miner's barrel is almost larger than the Sevora itself.

I can't miss.

The three of us meet in the building's entryway. Malo's still flat on the sponge, nerves fried by the heavy stun I delivered not long ago. As such, my war council consists of three: me, wearing robes meant for another species and still weak from a mortal wound barely healed. Viera, the healthiest of us, holds a pair of miners in her hands and stares out the doorway behind me, eternally searching for the next threat.

Then there's T'Oli, a pearly blob decorated with two eyestalks. Out of any of us, I suppose the Ooblot has the most reason to be here. Made by the Sevora and abandoned by them, T'Oli's been on a slow path to vengeance since its creation.

"You're going to take Malo to the shuttle," I say to T'Oli. I'm not so much standing as leaning on my short spear, the ache in my side sapping strength from my legs. "The two of you need to get away and leap back to Earth."

"If you think warning the rest of the humans will help them survive," T'Oli replies. "You are overestimating your species. Any Sevora raid will overtake them."

"We fought them off last time," Viera says.

"We were lucky, and the Sevora were distracted by the Vincere's assault on Vimelia," T'Oli replies. "With their survival at stake, they won't play games. They will infiltrate, destabilize, infect and destroy."

"I preferred it when you weren't so depressing."

"That's why you need to get Malo back." I steal the conversation. "He's had Ignos in his head, he knows the Sevora, like you. And our people will follow him."

Like they followed me, when they needed to.

"We could all go for the shuttle, you know," Viera says. "We'd have time to get another message off, let that big ugly Kolas and the rest of their lizard friends save Lan and Gar."

I've thought about that option. Followed it to the possible ends—what happens if Kolas doesn't catch this ship? If the Sevora get away and restart this war that's been going on for so long?

"There's a chance to end it here," I reply. "If we stop them and take this ship, then the Sevora are done. There won't be another war, another species won't be lost."

"Since when did you get so grand?" Viera asks me, but she says the words with a slight smile. "The girl I remember only wanted a part to play in her own tribe."

"My tribe's a lot bigger now."

T'Oli doesn't put up any more resistance, though the Ooblot does help me break apart some more metal so I have a full-length walking staff to go with my short spear. Viera has her miners, and after we say one last goodbye to Malo, who blinks up at us, Viera and I head off.

Only one place to go, and that's back towards the central ring. From there we have to get lucky and find where the Oratus are. Then we have to get really lucky and catch the Sevora before they turn Lan and Gar into the deadliest slaves imaginable.

We trade the blue lights of the residential section for the soft gold of the entertainment district, and I try not to pause as we pass by the bodies of the Sevora Flaum.

"Guess nobody's looking for them yet," Viera says as we move past. "T'Oli really helped. I could barely move, Kaishi. Without that Ooblot, I wouldn't have been able to even pull the trigger on this thing."

"We picked the right sewer to dive in, back then."

Crossing the entertainment section takes a bit of time, as Viera takes the lead and scouts ahead, while I limp behind her with my staff. Whatever T'Oli used to get me on my feet, it's definitely not a total miracle. Maybe I should have gone to the shuttle and sent the Ooblot with Viera on the rescue mission.

But I'm not one to send someone else to clean up my own mess.

"Gateway's shut," Viera says when I catch up to her on top of the small rise leading back towards the central ring. Like the others, there's a black nub next to this one that doesn't react at all when I wave a hand towards it. "Tried that too. Either there's nobody watching, or they're content leaving us here."

"Well, I'm not content staying."

It doesn't take a long brainstorm to find a path through the gateway; Viera swiped two miners, but across all the burnt Flaum, there's several more. We take the extra weapons, stack them against the gateway and get well back. Viera sets up the aim, takes a look at me.

"Ready? Because there's no more secret mission after this. They'll know we're coming."

"I don't care."

Viera laughs. "Liar."

She's right, and she shoots straight.

The fireball is loud and short, full of warping metal and the starved crackling of momentary flames with nothing but steel to bite into. The smoke is momentary, a mist whisked away by unseen, unfelt breezes that leaves behind a blasted hole in the center of the gateway.

"These doors don't stop much, do they?" Viera says.

"Are your heavy doors deep inside your own home?" I reply, then heft my staff and walk forward. "Let's go. Lan and Gar need us."

"Yeah, you've made that clear," Viera replies, keeping her miners up and ready. "Just promise me one thing."

"What's that?"

"When we save their scaly butts, you'll get them to admit they needed our help."

The ring is more ominous when it's empty. Bright and silver, but all the seeds hanging above look like teeth out of a nightmare. That the vast corridor extends in both directions without end also adds an eerie side, as if we've stepped into a mirrored universe where things just go off forever.

"I think we have two options," I say to Viera as we stare across black-steel floor. "We either try to get into the seed ship's core and hope we draw their attention, or we try and find which quarter has the Oratus."

"Or a third," Viera says, stepping in front of me. "We just start shooting."

The sound of booted feet on metal clanks towards us

from our right, and a trio of Whelk, come slithering around the corner. Two of them have miners, and one bears a pair of what look like short black sticks.

Their momentum carries them into view even as Viera opens fire, blitzing down the first two in a hot second, their gel-like bodies super-heating and bursting into gouts of gooey liquid. The last, with its miner, attempts a scattered retreat, spraying shots that manage to etch a nonsense pattern of burns into the walls around us.

"Don't shoot it." I put my hand on Viera's arm. "What do you bet that thing's going right where we want to be?"

"I like the way you think, Empress," Viera replies, and then we're off.

Or, at least, Viera is. I tell her to go ahead, keep on the Whelk's trail as I stumble along. I'm not much use in a chase—no idea how good I'd be in a fight either—but my utter uselessness in this momentary encounter prompts me to ditch my short spear for one of the blasted Whelks' miners. I may not be much of a shot, but I might be able to distract someone long enough for Viera to finish them off.

The Whelk goes halfway around the ring—bypassing one large, closed gateway—before scuttling through a wide open portal leading to someplace new and different. I'm surprised to see, from the ring as I catch up, breathing hard, to Viera that this section isn't shrouded in dark like the others. It's even brighter than the ring itself; an almost scalding white.

"Together?" I say to Viera as she gives me a look that speaks volumes about how battle-ready she thinks I am.

"Kaishi, you can stay back," Viera says. "By my count, there were only a couple dozen Sevora on that ship. We've taken out almost half. Maybe more. I can handle this."

"I'm not leaving you."

"Then don't get me killed, either."

This time I grab her arm tight, make Viera look at me. "The Oratus are the priority. Not me. You get them out and they'll make sure the Sevora are finished."

I search her eyes, catch that lock of increasingly dirty and frayed white hair hanging down over Viera's forehead. Back in the jungle, so long ago, the constant humidity kept Viera's hair frizzy, at least until she caved and used the same ointments we'd cultivated from plants for years. Now, in the dry, dull air of these ships, it's almost perfect.

Minus the dirt, the sweat, the scattered flecks of blood and ash.

Viera doesn't have to reply. A simple, slight nod shows she understands.

Cavignum, during Aspicis' long nights, looks like a frozen fireball expanding into the sky. An orange, roiling glow somehow kept constrained into a mostly perfect sphere. The bottom cuts away into a mammoth structure lit by a glittering army of lights. Skiffs blitz in and out, though Plake hesitates, hovering low and nestled in some vines before adding their own stolen ride to the bunch.

"We can't just go in," Plake says. "We don't have any credentials, and I may be a smooth talker, but the rest of you are going to get us straight up shot."

"There's another problem," Bas says. "We need to let Nobaa and Engee know when to get into the station."

"Hope you remember the channel they're listening on," Agra-Red grumbles. "Cause I don't. Not after they took everything away from us."

Sax hisses a laugh. "I've had to remember so many codes and coordinates. Don't worry, Whelk. When we have the diversion created, we'll be able to send the message."

"Grand." Plake, dimly visible in the ambient light,

waves a feathered arm up at the skiffs going by. "Any ideas on how we get inside? I'm not going to ask about a diversion because I know your answer's going to be 'destroy stuff'."

"Can we use these?" Bas holds up one of the glimmer worms. "You said they might be batteries?"

"Maybe," Plake replies, and the Vyphen takes a long look at them. "If nothing else, you could hide beneath them and let me get us inside."

"Or I could," Sax offers. "That way, if it goes poorly, I can fight."

"If you have to fight right away, we're all dead," Plake says. "If nobody's got a better idea, grab some worms and get cozy."

The cargo skiff isn't large enough to hold two giant Oratus lying down in it, at least not with any degree of comfort. Sax and Bas have to wrap entirely around each other, fitting arms and legs into any possible cranny, and encircling themselves with their tails. Plake and Agra-Red set about covering the two of them with the glimmer worms, each one hitting Sax like a squishy package of nutrient goop.

Agra-Red, then, squeezes itself down in between some of the worms, resting like a coating between the two Oratus. Whelks don't quite have Ooblot levels of flexibility, but they're pretty close. One advantage, Sax notes, is that Agra-Red can't talk when it's this spread out.

"Hope you're all comfy," Plake says.

Squeezed in the back of the cargo skiff, Sax can only tell what Plake's doing by the feel of his weight as the skiff drops, thanks to the slight breeze that manages to make it through the layers. He's not thrilled at being packed away like some piece of, well, cargo, but there didn't seem to be any alternatives, and—

"Sax," Bas says to him, and her hiss reminds him that their heads are actually touching. "Are you all right?"

"Perfect," Sax replies, which is both far from the truth and close enough that it doesn't matter.

"Good," Bas says. "It wouldn't be fair otherwise."

"What wouldn't be fair?"

"When it starts? I don't want to feel like my score doesn't count, just because you're hurt."

It's been a while since they took a count. Casual missions feel so long ago; when their set dropped into a war zone or a Sevora facility with simple search-and-destroy orders. It'd been easier then to find some extra fun in the carnage. Not so much now, not when the consequences seem so much higher.

Then again, maybe the stakes mean their games are even more important. What would it matter if they came out of this conflict alive, but having lost themselves?

"I'm already winning," Sax replies. "I took at least seven Flaum down back there. And the Amigga."

"You didn't kill the Amigga, the prisoners did."

"But I—"

"The rules, Sax. I took five Flaum back at the prison. So you have a slight lead, for now."

"For now."

The skiff moves slow for a long time, with Plake telling all of them to keep quiet as they pass by another vessel. It's a dull ride, but Sax isn't disappointed by the soft moments with Bas. Before, with the Vincere, Sax always felt invincible. That he and Bas would always make it through to the next one.

Now that feeling's gone, replaced with a grim fatalism. The odds of success are so low, the importance so high, that

Sax feels better assuming he's not going to make it to the end, replacing fear with a macabre determination.

"Coming up on the first gate," Plake says. "Looks like the landing platforms are beyond. Keep still."

The skiff slows, then stops.

"Manifest?" announces a squeaky Flaum voice.

"Uh, glimmer worms," Plake replies.

There's a moment's silence, then Sax sees a crawling blue light pass over their cargo area. It's a slow crawl, detailed.

"You hear about the other prison?" Plake says suddenly, loud.

"What prison?" the Flaum guard replies.

"Back that way, guess the prisoners rebelled?"

"You're a Vyphen, aren't you?" the guard says after hesitating. "Pretty strange to see one of you here, and running cargo?"

Plake's going to ruin it. Sax tenses, ready to burst up from the glimmer worm cover and take out the guard. Not that they'd make it very far after, but dying in a fight would be better than getting gunned down lying in the back of a cart and covered in worms.

"You see what's going on in the galaxy?" Plake says. "Everywhere's a mess. At least here, you can get a stable job. Running glimmer worms is a lot better than dying up there."

That, somehow, gets a laugh from the Flaum. "True. I was with the Vincere for a while, and I thought every day I'd be fodder in another attack. When the chance came to transfer here, I jumped on it."

The light hovering on their cargo hold clicks off.

"Looks like a good haul," the guard says. "Head to platform B, drop the worms there."

"You got it." Plake gets the skiff moving again, shifting its angle lower and to the right.

"I did not think we'd get through there," Plake says a minute later. "You all owe me your lives."

"After we saved you at the prison?" Sax hisses back. "We're even."

"Saved me? The Whelk and I were just fine. We didn't need your claws."

Sax knows Plake's playing with him, and he doesn't bother to reply. The skiff's slowing down now for the landing, which means their disguises are about to be ruined.

Sax can't wait.

"There's guards and staff everywhere," Plake says. "I have a new plan. Hold on."

"What?" Sax manages to say as Bas offers a questioning hiss.

Plake sends the skiff suddenly into a tight right slant, and a second later Sax hears a startled squeak followed by the crunch of metal-on-metal collision. Pops sound from their own skiff, which wobbles in the air as microjets try to compensate for their now-non-functioning fellows. The shaky moment gets cut short, though, when Plake throws the skiff forward, bending it into a hard acceleration.

"Cut out, now!" Plake yells.

Sax doesn't understand, but Bas does. His pair uses her claws to slice at the back of the skiff, breaking apart the thin railing into a shower of sparks. Sax twists his head so he can, for the first time, actually see out the back, and he catches the wide bronzed expanse of the landing platform, the various skiffs alighting on it, and all the people running towards another skiff that's apparently crashed and is burning away on the ground.

"Kick!" Bas hisses, and Sax follows her lead, pushing with his talons and scurrying out the back of the skiff.

On the way, with his tail, Sax scoops Agra-Red, pulling the Whelk behind them as they fall the few meters down to the landing pad's surface. They've barely landed when the cargo skiff strikes something behind, bursting into crackling flame. Alarms sound out immediately, though the disastrous procession of events seems to have Cavignum's guards confused.

Plake, well back from the other three, is already running up to the nearest guards, throwing her feathered self around and exclaiming outrageous threats about the skiff that allegedly hit hers.

"She's buying us cover," Bas hisses, though Sax thinks the gouts of smoke and fire are doing a better job than the Vyphen.

A look towards the explosion shows Plake didn't aim at random either—around the bent, broken wreckage of their skiff is the similarly destroyed shape of a loading gate leading into Cavignum itself. It's an opening that Sax and Bas are only too happy to take advantage of.

"Carry me?" Agra-Red says as the Oratus turn to move. "I can't keep up with your giant legs."

After a derisive snort from Sax, Bas takes the honors, scooping up the Whelk as they sprint towards the door. Sax closes his vents, holds his breath as they dash through the smoking sparks, and then they're through to the other side.

Into the largest power plant in the galaxy.

They have two objectives—find a way into the base that Nobaa and Engee can access, and then make sure that way is open when the pair of Teven try to make their escape.

"Does Cavignum have a control center?" Sax asks as

they dash through the wrecked door and into a wide cargo corridor.

It's a silver space, metal tweaked and polished to handle the heat extremes possible in what amounts to a giant hole sucking heat from the planet's core. The temperature inside is plenty warm already, especially compared to the chilly night outside, and the corridor's ceiling is peppered with holes leading to vents top-side.

Sax gets this information from the mask without feeling it, as the transparent suit does its best to keep Sax's body at prime operating temperature. The mask also blunts the smell of burning things, letting Sax focus on what lies ahead —namely a forest of branching paths, doors, and ramps leading to other levels.

Nearly all of these entrances and exits have shifting signs next to, hanging over, or imprinted on the floor. Only a couple appear to be on, and that's because cargo sleds are heading their way, with the signs displaying shipment names and directions.

Except everything's stopped now, and dozens of eyes stare down the corridor at them.

"Are you always this obvious?" Agra-Red says. "Of course it has a control center. We just have to find where that is."

"I liked you better when you couldn't talk."

"I've never liked you at all."

Bas has no time for them, apparently, as she takes off running. Sax follows, because what else can he do except chase the one he loves? Behind them, Agra-Red yells for them to slow down, but every second means more guards, and the Whelk's not worth mission failure.

"Where are you going?" Sax hisses ahead to his pair as

she pads past the first split in the corridor, with ramps on either side moving up and down.

"The Amigga are obsessed with being at the center of their creations," Bas says. "If this place has a control, it's going to be as close to that middle as we can get."

"What about the Meridia?" Sax asks. "The Chorus sits at the top."

Bas skids to a stop, glares at Sax. "They live in the middle. Trust me, Sax."

He's never had a problem doing that, and doesn't have a problem now, so when Bas resumes her run, Sax follows.

They pass by those cargo sleds, and the Flaum piloting them don't bother to shout. Neither do the uniformed workers moving from one station to another, nor the delegation of what looks like inspectors, leading their furry Flaum selves around the station in all-white uniforms.

No, the first obstacles come as they near the end of the corridor. A trio of Flaum, but ones in heavy exo-suits. Sax almost laughs—these are Vincere relics, used before the Oratus came to power to give Flaum some combat advantage. They're black-metal and give the Flaum an extra two meters of height, made for exploration and hostile suppression.

Normally, Sax would expect to see a wide shoulder rack sporting miners on the exo-suits. These don't carry any laser weapons, though, and instead look to have had those racks melted and refined into large hammers, making a pair of them per suit. Sax supposes they might have industrial applications, but these three are clearly lined up to prevent the charging Oratus from getting through the smaller door behind them.

It's hard to know what's funnier—the idea that three

Flaum could stand up to the Oratus alone, or that they thought these exo-suits would give them a chance.

"Left," Sax hisses as they get closer.

Bas takes the hint, and when they're a dozen steps away from the Flaum, who are raising their slow fists to do... something, the two Oratus leap onto the walls, their talons and claws biting through the sides as they keep scrambling forward.

The Flaum in their iron workhorses don't, can't respond fast enough. Sax is on the left, and his target makes a clumsy, lumbering step-and-swing at him. The aim is low, and would be barely enough to clip Sax's lower claws if the Oratus didn't jump from the wall and land on the outstretched, punching arm. With a twist as his claws tear through the metal, Sax rips the construct's arm out of its socket.

Unfortunately, the Flaum's machine has a second arm, and it backs up its fallen partner, swiping down at Sax, whose ridden his victim limb to the floor, as the Oratus throws away the busted first arm. Lying flat on his back, Sax digs in with his talons and kicks, scooting himself out of the way of the hammer blow, towards the Flaum and its suit. When the Flaum's fist hits the floor, it splinters the chromed tiles like they're made of glass. What the fist doesn't do is stop Sax from planting his foreclaws on the ground behind his head and using the momentum and their leverage to flip himself up and over.

Sax flips onto the exo-suit's chest, with the Flaum getting a terrible view of Sax's talons. The Oratus commences tearing, aiming for any wires. Sparks fly and pop into Sax's mouth, each one stinging with victory. He feels the exo-suit slant to the side as the right leg loses power, and Sax is about to scale up and go for the pilot when something slams into the back of the exo-suit and tips it forward.

Sax can't get away—his claws are all caught mid-rend—and the whole suit falls on top of him, pinning the Oratus to the ground. The glass shield blocking the Flaum shatters, pressing the furry creature against Sax's torso as the Oratus tries to breath. The exo-suits, it turns out, are heavy, and Sax isn't in position to move it.

The pressure on Sax's vents is too intense; all his air's going away. Sax snaps at the exo-suit with his mouth, but it's a futile gesture—all that's there is metal, and there's no way he'll be able to get himself free before he suffocates, even if the mask keeps the weight from crushing his bones.

Of all the ways to die. Killed by a Flaum.

Heat burns through the exo-suit, and Sax feels the Flaum pilot eject itself, run through the metal cage that had been stabilizing that glass windshield. The heat, though, doesn't die away, and suddenly the exo-suit feels lighter, a clanging bang sounding through the hallway as its other arm drops away to the floor.

"C'mon you dumb Oratus," Agra-Red's voice carries. "I don't have enough power to cut the whole thing apart. Lift!"

A bit of inspiration can go a long way when it comes to strength. Sax takes the prodding of the Whelk and pushes. The exo-suit moves slightly. All four claws, talons and tail, though, aren't enough to get himself clear. Still, that tiniest of spaces is enough for Sax to open his bruised vents and suck some much needed air.

"Can't!" Sax manages to hiss.

"Your pair's busy with the other two," Agra-Red counters. "You want her to die? No? Then get yourself going."

There's another blast of heat, and the foot of the exo-suit falls off near Sax's head. Those few kilograms, coupled with the adrenaline-fear for Bas and the breath of fresh air, give Sax enough motivation to try another heave. This time, rather than lifting the suit straight up, he goes for a squeeze, sliding himself along the floor as he tilts the suit ever-so-slightly. Just enough for him to slip out.

Enough for Sax to stand, look and see Bas leaning against the far wall, laughing, while the Whelk is shaking its head, its heavy assault miner glowing from its own heat.

"She told me you have to learn to be patient," Agra-Red burbles. "You're diving right in without playing the battle-field. You could have waited for me to burn down each of those things from a safe distance—or did you not notice they only had big clubs?"

Bas... watched him? Sax nearly died there. He looks at his pair, knowing frustration, betrayal's showing on his sharp, gray-scaled face.

"Stop it," Bas hisses when she notices. "You almost got yourself killed this time. Next time you go leaping in without thought, you might risk all of us."

"What was I supposed to do?"

"See the strategy!" Bas roars back. "Communicate with me, with our allies. Work as a team, for once."

Sax shakes his head. Teamwork? Bas is his pair. They *are* a team, always. He takes a breath, is about to tell her exactly what she can do with her suggestion, when Agra-Red wheels around and takes a pot-shot with his miner into the heavy door blocking their way forward.

"Anyone have an idea for this one?" the Whelk asks. "If you're all done with your relationship problems, I mean. Otherwise I'm happy to wait until the hordes descend upon us."

Sax has a usual method for getting through doors; namely, his claws and hacking and slashing with them until an opening presents itself. This door, as Sax discovers with a few trial swipes, is both chrome-plated and full of thick, reinforced metal behind. There's no way they're getting through.

A quick glance back down the wide corridor shows a bunch of Flaum heading their way—Cavignum's guards finally catching on and coming to defend their station. Which means there's only one way for them to go: up the ramps.

"Follow me!" Sax hisses, and starts off.

Once again, Bas gets to play carrier for the Whelk, hustling the gel creature as the two Oratus run and leap up the cargo ramps. The first jump brings Sax up to the slanted surface of the ramp, then a couple of steps gets him to another corridor, similar to the first but instead of a soft orange glow from pulsing energy, this bears a blue tint from the translucent cables lining the hall—the power starting to pump into battery packs and outbound connections.

Coupled with the chrome, it's a beautiful array of colors shifting between the cold spectrum. One that Sax could watch for more than a second if doing so wouldn't result in him being turned to molten mush by a pack of angry guards.

There's one more set of ramps, though, so Sax makes another leap, hearing the shriek of Bas's talons as they grip the metal behind him. Then they're at the top level, and here the light's a standard, dull yellow-white; the energy by this point refined to its usable level. And, like the lower levels, there's a door.

The difference? This one's open.

Standing next to the control panel, with a small miner pressed to a Flaum guard's head, is Plake.

"Took you long enough," Plake says. "Let's go."

"How?" Sax manages to ask.

"Everyone went chasing after you, so I made a friend here who told me which doors would be the last to lock in an emergency," Plake says. "So we came to this one, and once I heard your manic hissing, I figured you'd be coming my way."

There's plenty of noise coming as the guards make their way around and up the ramps, so Sax, Bas, and Agra-Red—whom Bas dumps on the ground as soon as they stop—dash through the door. Plake slips through after them, dragging her hostage with her, and tells the Flaum to shut and lock the door.

Then they take a look at what's around them, and Sax's hearts fall.

Batteries stack in front of them, the sapphire ends of the piled cylinders indicating they're charged and ready for shipping. This section is a vast ring, one that starts its curl as Sax looks to the left and right, a curl that slowly shifts in color, the stacked batteries showing less charge as the ring goes 'round.

The walls behind the batteries are massed cables, shunting energy refined on prior levels from pure heat to the batteries meant to store them. Above, through what Sax assumes must be meter-thick glass, glows Cavignum's great orange ball. This close, Sax can make out the thin lines holding together the nano-netting meant to capture and hold the font of heat coming from Aspicis' core.

What this technological wonder doesn't have for them, though, is terminals. Wherever the control center might be, it's not here.

"We need the control center," Sax hisses at Plake's hostage.

The Flaum cowers at first, but finds its spine somewhere in its dark blue uniform. "You're three levels too high. It's underneath, where it's safer."

"Any good ideas on how to get there?" Agra-Red says to the hostage. "Think hard, cause your life depends on it."

And, given the sudden banging on the door behind them, their own might too.

"Think while we move," Bas says, a suggestion they act on.

Unlike the earlier corridors, though, the central battery ring isn't lined with doors. As they move, Sax catches the battery colors fading from blue to green, and eventually to yellow and still no exit. Finally, with only an endless chromed wall on their left and infinite batteries on their right, Sax hisses for them all to stop.

"Is there a way out of here?" Sax asks the hostage, who lets loose a chittering cackle.

"One way in and out," the Flaum says. "The batteries funnel up here, and then they're taken out the door we came in."

"Funnel up from where?"

The Flaum, though, shakes its head. Plake shoves the miner against its side, enunciates the threat with a deadly whisper, but the Flaum only replies with another brisk shake.

"Not telling you anymore," the Flaum says. "I'm going to die anyway for getting you this far."

"We're trying to help you all," Plake tries, shifting to diplomacy from her more aggressive means. "Taking down the Chorus is going to help the galaxy."

"That's what you think? That taking away the only security we've ever known is going to help us?" The Flaum chitters another weak laugh.

Sax tears the creature from Plake's grasp, tosses it down

the ring, back the way they came. "We don't have time for this."

Plake takes a look back towards the hostage, as if she's thinking about getting the Flaum back, but then the furry creature gets to its feet and starts to run. Plake raises the miner, then shakes her head, holsters it.

"Let's go," the Vyphen says. "Some people will never understand."

"They will, when we win," Agra-Red adds as they get back to their run around the ring.

It's not hard to find the funnel the hostage mentioned; it's a wide gap in the line of batteries, filled partly by chromed scaffolding and a lifting mechanism. A look down shows a dead batteries being loaded far below by precise conveyors.

"It's a tight fit," Bas says, peering in.

"You see another way?" Agra-Red says. "Cause I don't, and I'm not wearing a mask, so I'd rather not get shot."

As if hearing the Whelk, the rapid pounding of feet on metal echoes around the ring. Agra-Red slimes its way closer to the gap, starts to look at how it can fit in there. Plake draws her miner, covers behind them, while Sax and Bas look the other way.

"Can you make it?" Plake asks the Whelk.

"Not a problem for a gooey thing like me," Agra-Red says. "You're tiny too, captain."

"Don't call me tiny."

"Facts are facts," Agra-Red replies. "As for the big monsters, don't know about you."

"Go," Sax hisses. "We'll figure it out."

Adding to the mystery, the rapid footsteps have stopped, seemingly just around the ring's bends. There's a heartbeat or three of nothing, then a very clear scratching of a heavy nail on metal. A sound Sax knows, because it's one he's been making this entire time.

"Leave," Sax says. "Now."

"Don't have to tell me twice," Agra-Red says, and the Whelk disappears down the gap, slipping and sliding its slimy self along the bars.

"Get through this alive," Plake says as she follows the Whelk. "Never thought I'd say this about a pair of claw-mongers, but we need you."

The Vyphen, winged arms fluttering, disappears, leaving Sax and Bas alone in the hallway. The scratches are coming, deliberately loud now. Sax uses the threat to take his own look down the battery gap.

There's no question—the Oratus, standing three meters tall, with thick tails, are never going to fit through there. Not unless Sax gets to carving a wider hole, and there's no time for that. There's no time for anything, anymore.

On either side of them, standing alone in the center of the corridor, are two mirrored Oratus'. Their scales reflect the batteries and white lighting, giving them a shimmering appearance, with their outlines showing as slight distortions in what Sax can see. With their every move, the light bends and twists around them, so Sax can barely tell where the creature is, much less where it's going to be.

"Only two of you?" Sax hisses, looking at the one facing him, knowing Bas is doing the same to the one looking at her.

Their tails touch, ever so slightly.

"More than enough to deal with a couple of Vincere traitors," says his Oratus, and Sax recognizes the voice, the same one from the train station. "Where's the rest of your band?"

"I told them we didn't need their help to take care of you."

Kah hisses a laugh—unlike Sax's own, it's a strange thing, distorted and mechanical. These creatures might be alive, but they are designed just like the machines moving the batteries around them even now.

"At least you still have your confidence," Kah says. "But do you still have your intelligence? The Chorus has an offer for you: in exchange for what you know about your leader, Evva, and her plans, the Chorus is willing to see you sent back to your former post."

"Not going to happen."

"No? We have a lead on the Sevora homeworld, Sax. Come back to us now and you can still make it to the end of the war you've been fighting your entire life."

The Sevora homeworld? Sax wasn't sure that even existed—he'd resigned himself to finding the last of the little slugs on some drifting seed ship somewhere. How the Sevora had managed to keep an entire planet hidden this long...

No. That's not the point. He's not fighting that war any longer.

"I'm not fighting for the Chorus anymore," Sax says. "I'm fighting for our species. For the lives we deserve to lead."

Sax expects another laugh, or another offer. What he gets instead is a slight bow.

"I respect a warrior with a cause, even if they are a traitor to their own," Kah replies.

"Can you kill him already?" Bas whispers. "Every second we're talking here, Plake and Agra-Red are in danger down there."

A single mirrored Oratus nearly cost Sax his life. Now

there's two, and Bas doesn't know what she's up against. And unlike the train station, there's no space for a miner standoff. It's going to be up close and brutal. Before Sax can give her any warnings, though, their enemies burst forward, striking with a long swipe of their sharp claws as they dart in.

With slight pressure on his tail, Sax knows which way Bas is going to go, and he leaps right, dodging the swipe and ending up against the ring's outer wall. Bas clings to the inside, hanging above the empty hole for the batteries, while the two mirrored Oratus sit in the middle, each one turning to face their respective target.

Sax catches Bas' eye from across the ring, and goes low. He launches himself from the outer ring, aims for the ground and catches the floor with his left foreclaw, then his left midclaw, pulling hard to whip his body and, more importantly, his tail around towards the two Oratus. Kah, watching Sax, sees the strike coming, but the one watching Bas is busy ducking from her own leap, her high strike. Sax's tail sweeps the other mirrored Oratus to the floor, while Bas slams Kah, who jumps to dodge Sax's tail. Bas tackles Kah from behind and drives him forward into the outer ring, her claws and mouth putting in work.

It's a mad scramble then, as Sax tries to take advantage of the downed mirrored Oratus, grabbing its shoulders as the creature tries to get up and, using his talons to grip the ground, wheels and launches the Oratus into the outer ring, next to where Kah has just shoved himself away from the wall. Kah's trying to pin Bas back to the ground, but Bas disengages, sidesteps the push-back so that Kah stumbles with no resistance, allowing Bas' follow-up tail strike to slap Kah left across the face.

The blow pushes Kah towards Sax, who delivers a

talon-kick to the mirrored Oratus' right knee, knocking Kah to a kneel, then Sax bites in with his left claws and funnels the mirrored Oratus into its companion, just peeling itself off the wall. The two of them collapse into a pile against the outer ring.

"I forgot how nice it is to fight with you," Sax hisses towards his pair.

"Because you're always going off on your own."

"I'm here now." Sax says the words as they both turn, claws ready, while the two mirrored Oratus extract themselves from each other. "Ready?"

Bas nods. Sax tenses to leap.

And the floor explodes beneath them.

Through the gateway is a deep red and violet section. At first, I think the light's a cause of some alarm we've set off, some Sevora security mechanism alerting anyone here that a pair of rogue specimens are loose.

Then I see the vines.

They're cased in huge tanks; glass enclosures that rise from the floor and halt well short of the ceiling, where each separate tank joins with its fellows to create one large space where the vines snarl and twist among each other, an occasional large, purple flower blooming out. The red and purple lights crisscross between the thick stalks, casting shadowed versions of the plant patterns on every surface.

"Look," Viera says, pointing her miner at the base of one of the tanks. Each one is lined with a silver basin, and each one is full—some have overrun their sides, spreading the deep purple liquid across the black-metal floor. "Nutrient goop. Seems like nothing in this galaxy eats real food."

For now, I'm happy not seeing Flaum. Even though this space is big enough to match the entertainment and residential sections combined, there's not a single Sevora running through towards us. No miner shots coming our way.

"If you're worried about food now..." I start, and Viera waves my words away.

"Just joking, Empress."

"Then let's keep moving. The Oratus have to be on the other side of this section."

I don't know for sure, of course, but it's a feeling. It's a hope. Which is all I have right now.

Walking beneath the giant plants, I find myself re-evaluating a little about the Sevora. They clearly don't hate all life, and they're cultivating food here for their hosts. They have an entertainment district, and places for their species to live that seem viable, if not luxurious.

If it wasn't for the whole 'take over your mind' aspect, I'd find the species similar to our own.

We're getting close to the end of the section when I feel a sudden burst of pain from my abdomen, right where Ignos stuck its spear. I press my miner-wielding left hand to the spot for a moment, and the feeling subsides.

Viera, though, notices. Her nervous eyes give something else away.

"What are you hiding?" I say.

Her eyes flick to my wound. "T'Oli asked me not to tell you. The Ooblot said half the treatment relies on the person believing they're going to be all right. I, for one, think it's better to know."

"Know what, Viera?"

"It's a patch, Empress. T'Oli's boosted you with something it called stim, it found a packet on one of the Sevora Flaum and said it would keep you together for a little while."

Her words clear things up. Viera didn't argue when I

suggested Malo go with T'Oli. Even the Ooblot didn't put up much of a fight. They know Malo's going to need to rally humanity if we fail, not because I *might* die, but because I'm going to.

"How long do I have?"

"T'Oli didn't know. It's never done this to a human before." The dim light makes it hard to tell, but I think there might be tears in Viera's eyes. "It doesn't matter, Kaishi. Let's focus on the mission."

"Easy for you to say."

"No, it's not easy for me to say."

I believe her, and respect her, so I turn away from the conversation. Shove away thoughts of a fragile mortality and reach forward with my staff. Go one step and then another. If my life's ticking away, then I plan on making the last moments of it useful.

The next gateway, like the one we went through to get here, is open. And again it stands clear, without sentries. Either the Sevora that escaped Vimelia with us are not soldiers, or Ignos took the only ones who were.

"Or it's a trap," Viera says as we head up the crescent steps towards the entry.

"The last section had plenty of good spots for an ambush. If they'd wanted to kill us, they could have attacked then."

"Maybe they're waiting for the perfect moment."

"Maybe you're giving the Sevora too much credit. Haven't they been losing this war since it started?"

Viera concedes my point as we reach the top of the steps. Here would be the ideal point for a stream of miner fire to cut us both down, but instead all we get is a great view of something I've seen before, though because this section is so empty, it takes me a moment to fit the memory to the place.

When we escaped Vimelia the first time—that I have to add that qualifier makes me shudder—we did it through poisoning a Sevora hosting center; a place for hosts to be given up and new ones gained. This new section spreads forth in white and blue, a hard change from the darker shades we're leaving behind, and the colors pair, illuminating various pools. Each one, whether lit in sky blue or white, has metal poles leading to and from it, the angles making it obvious which direction is preferred.

Almost all of the pools, though, are empty. Except one, right in the center.

"They're not hiding very well," Viera whispers.

A dozen Flaum and Whelk, including our escapee, surround the pool, the only one full of the inky liquid I've felt too many times on my own skin. Nearer to us, splayed out inside the Sevora ring and still, apparently, stunned is Lan. Gar is nowhere.

Which means the Oratus is probably beneath those purple waters.

All eyes are on the pool. Given how many fighters they've sent away towards us, I'm not all that surprised. Who could imagine a couple humans and an Ooblot would stand a chance against the almighty Sevora?

From here, though, neither side will be doing much destroying. Viera might be able to land a couple of shots this far away, but I'd probably hit Lan. Or shoot the ink and zap Gar. Instead, I gesture with the staff towards the only other things in the room; racks and racks of clothes, armor, and weapons.

What's the first thing a Sevora would want to do with their new host? Outfit them in the right gear.

There's hundreds of miners lining tall stacks, and dozens of hanging robes, vests, and shells clinging to hooks on spindly structures whose base struts sport control panels that, I'm sure, could rotate a preferred item to Flaum height. A central gap leads through to the pools, and it's what Viera and I stared down when we first entered the section. Now we form up on the left side of it, on the backside of a miner rack. Viera takes point, peeking around the corner.

"Gar's still not out," Viera whispers to me. "We have a chance."

"Then let's take it."

Strategy sits back and lets instinct run with our attack. Viera slides around the rack, lifts her miners and opens fire, red bolts blitzing off towards the Sevora pack. I follow, my left hand aiming, squeezing the trigger, and adding to the chaos without hitting a single soul.

But that's fine, because what our onslaught buys us is panic. The Sevora try to scatter, but Viera's picking them off, or at least she is until one clips her with a return shot. My breath catches as the right side of Viera's chest burns, but my friend never stops shooting.

If she can fight through her pain, I can fight through mine.

One of the Flaum breaks to my left, heading towards one of the empty pools and fires wildly along the way. I set my staff on the metal floor, brace my arm against it, and rest the miner on my right forearm. The Flaum reaches the next set of railings as I settle my sights, and the Sevora's choice to scramble over rather than dive under gives me the target I'm looking for.

This time, I'm blasting red. This time, I strike true.

Viera pushes me to the side and we both tumble behind a line of hanging battle suits not unlike the one

Viera's wearing—all different sizes, all looking artificial and stiff.

"Are you all right?" I push myself back from Viera, keeping my eyes hunting for movement. I don't know how many Sevora are left, or whether they'll try to attack us, but I'd rather not die for lack of attention.

"I might be joining you in death's corner," Viera says, and there's plenty of tight pain in her voice. "But I'm not there yet."

"Then why did you push us?" I settle onto my chest, ignore the cutting sting my abdomen gives me, and aim beneath the vests. There's feet moving out there, looking like they're circling around us. Between the clothes we're next to and the rigid miner rack to our right, it'd be easy to trap us. "I'm counting at least four of them left."

"Because we were about to get torched." Viera gets up to her knees, still holding miners in both hands. "Setting your staff and standing still isn't the way to survive a firefight, Kaishi."

"Shooting the air isn't going to help either."

"Then go for the Oratus and leave the Sevora to me," Viera replies.

I'm a little surprised at the heat in her voice. The stress. She thinks I need taking care of, watching over. Heat hits my face as I realize here, well, she's right. I'm not going to be much help, but I can, at least, take care of myself.

"They're all yours." I crawl beneath the vests, get to the other side, and with the clothes hanging above me I set the miner against the ground and pop off a couple shots at the only Flaum I can see.

I miss, striking the white-washed far wall and leaving burned circles as evidence of my spectacularly bad shooting.

The Flaum raises its own miner, and I reach up with my staff, snag a pair of the vests and pull as the Sevora gets ready to shoot. The clothes fall over me as the bolts slam in, the heat sifting through to my right shoulder but not quite getting to my skin.

Chitters and screeches echo from elsewhere in the section, so at least Viera's doing work while I hide beneath the vests. Hoping, waiting... and there it comes, the telltale clacking of claws on metal as the Flaum comes closer. The vests laying over me shift as the Flaum pulls at them, and as soon as the last one goes, as soon as I see the furry face peering at me, I fire.

Turns out even I can hit at this range.

Lan looks untouched, still and perfect on the floor, her green scales glittering against the white tiles. Her eyes are open, and they track me as I walk up. Before I left the cover of the vests, I waited until the shots died down, until the squeaking shouts stopped, and until Viera wandered back into view, her eyes casting about with her miners following.

"She's still alive?" Viera asks me—she's keeping away from the Oratus, staying where she can cover both the gateway into this section and the spaces between the other racks.

"Still alive."

"You can't tell if she's infected, can you?"

"Because I had one in me once?" I crouch down next to Lan, look hard into those eyes. "No, I have no idea."

"It would be easier now, you know," Viera trails off.

Execute Lan before she gets her potentially possessed self back. It makes sense, if you're heartless. Or hurt, tired, and fighting for survival.

"No." I straighten, turn to the pool. "We're not giving up that easily."

I expect Viera to protest, but she just wheezes out a laugh. "You never really change, Kaishi."

Any reply I'm thinking of goes away when the pool shows signs of life. The deep purple-black ink shifts, ripples going towards the edges. I back away, and briefly consider dragging Lan with me, but my wounded self issues a pang in protest, so I leave the stunned Oratus where she is. Viera levels her miners towards the water.

"Don't wait," I say. "As soon as it's obvious Gar's taken, you have to kill him."

"No sympathy for this one?"

"Not this time."

Lan's still a question. A hope for the future. I know Oratus can be controlled by Sevora, and if Gar's been down there for that long, he's probably well in the hand of whatever parasite won the lucky lottery to take his mind.

A pair of thin claws appear over the edge, their points biting into the floor and leaving silvery scratches. Then a head. Gar's. Eyes open and blazing as the ink drips off of his scales.

"Stop," I shout to him. "Come up any further and we'll shoot."

"Then what am I supposed to do?" Gar hisses. It sounds like him, but Sevora don't change a host's voice. "Hang here forever?"

It's a sudden riddle—how am I supposed to determine whether a Sevora's inside of Gar? Is there a giveaway? Ignos could dig into my mind, my memories, and build up a knowledge of humanity. There's not a question I could ask that would give it away. I had hoped some plan would come to mind, that there'd be an obvious way, but I can't think of one.

So I go with the only sure thing I have.

"Viera, stun him."

The Lunare doesn't give any tics or tells, doesn't announce her shot with some battle cry or flourish, but Gar explodes out of the pool, leaping high enough that Viera's shots skate by beneath the Oratus.

But the gravity that gave Gar the boost betrays him now —the fall back is slow, and the Oratus is helpless in the air. Viera slides her weapons up, aims, pulls the triggers.

They click. Harmlessly.

"Viera?" I say.

"I knew I was getting low—you're up!" Viera says to me, then turns and starts back towards the other rack of miners.

I think mine still has power, and level the miner as Gar hits the ground. My shot goes, but Gar twists on those talons and I miss to his right, over the pool and into the section's back wall. I think Gar's going to come for me, but instead the Oratus darts towards Viera.

"Watch out!" I yell, stitching a line of blue bolts behind Gar and cursing myself the entire time.

Then Gar's gone from my view, down that center line. I get there with my staff, in time to see Gar catch Viera as she pulls miners from the rack. In time to see those claws dig into Viera's armor and launch her, flailing, across the section until she slams into the wall above the gateway we came through.

Gar turns to me, then. Stares my way, his mouth spreading in a razor grin.

"You're not Gar," I say, aiming the miner straight at the Oratus.

"But you know me, Empress of the humans," Gar replies, his hissing voice a rasp.

"I do?"

"I invited you into my home, once," Gar replies. "A

home that you tried to destroy when we offered you peace. Now, we will go to yours and take what you would not give."

Jel. The Sevora leading the faction opposite to Nasiya, someone Ignos said was also on the ship. Of course, Jel's rank would give it first choice of new hosts.

"We should've killed you back on Vimelia." I fire the miner again.

This time I hit. Strike and burn into Gar's chest. The Oratus stumbles, but Jel keeps Gar on his feet. I try again, but, like Viera's, my miner clicks. Nothing, and I can't get past Jel to the miner rack. The Oratus is stumbling towards me, Gar's right side twitching and dragging as Jel keeps the body moving.

I'm hurt, I don't have a miner, but I do have a staff.

"Your species is a mistake," Jel rasps through Gar's mouth as the Oratus comes towards me. "You were meant as a cure to our 'problem', but the Amigga failed. You saw Ignos. We learned how to take your kind, and we will take all of you."

"You tried that already." I shift the staff to both hands, holding it across my body. "You failed."

If Jel is crushed by my words, the Sevora and its Oratus host don't show it. Instead, Jel leaps at me, four clawed arms set wide, as if the goal is to crush me in a sharp, deadly hug. I can't match the Oratus for strength, I'm not faster, so I set my legs and jab the staff forward, trying to keep those nasty claws away from me.

Jel simply barrels through the charge, grabbing my staff and pushing me back until I trip and fall to the floor. Me, the staff, and a looming Oratus mouth, all teeth and leering anger. Jel hisses low and slow, giving me the full glimpse of my soon-to-be-doom.

All I can think of doing is buying time. Hoping that Lan or Viera will get up and fight. Even if I die, that one of them will finish Jel off.

So I push the staff between us. Fix my arms against its gray-metal line and interrupt Jel's snapping mouth. Until Jel bites the staff and snaps it in two. The bite comes through hard, and for a second the Oratus is right up against my face, Gar's smooth scales rubbing my skin.

In my hands, though, I now have two pieces. Two jagged pieces, and a target in the right place. I might not be all that strong in the galaxy's scale, but now, with all the desperation and anger and fear pulling me tight as a spring, I push and send each pointed fragment into Gar's head. Where those small dents, those tiny ear cavities, and a Sevora sit.

Jel jerks back, hisses loud and long, stumbles for a moment, and then collapses to the floor, snapping off one of the fragments while the other sticks up in the air like a terrible grave marker.

An instant of free-fall through a cloud of fire and rubble, a moment where Sax's stomach tries to leap out of his body, where he's thankful the mask keeps the shards of fracturing metal from stabbing into his vents and eyes, and then Sax hits the ground.

The mask can't blunt all the discomfort of landing on rubble, and Sax turns himself mid fall so his right fore- and midclaws suffer the brunt of the impact, but the explosion gives Sax the adrenaline he needs to push past the pain and force himself up with a swish of his tail and a dig from his talons.

Sax's first glance confirms Bas is alive and picking herself out of her own pile of cables and chromed floor tiles. His second looks for the source of the explosion and finds Plake and Agra-Red near a wide door leading out of the room. They're staring, though Sax finds Agra-Red's heavy miner aimed up towards the ceiling, suspicious.

The mirrored Oratus, though, didn't fall. The hole in the floor collapsed the center of the battery ring above, but left the edges for their enemies to peer over.

"We going to run, or you want to wait for those things? I didn't detonate those batteries for nothing." Agra-Red says.

"They were going to lose." Sax barely holds himself back, keeps his claws at his sides. "We had them."

"Probably a trap," Agra-Red shakes off Sax's glare. "You don't fight a mirrored Oratus. You run."

"Next time, leave us."

"This time, we're going. Now." Plake issues the order, and with the mirrored Oratus above apparently checking their wounds, Sax decides to follow it.

"Remember the mission," Bas hisses as she comes up behind him.

Why does that phrase keep getting in the way of his fun?

Beyond the battery room, it's clear they've entered a different part of Cavignum. No longer over the flowing energy source, the floors bear a design less suited for heat and more for pleasure; curling green and purple lines mimicking Aspicis' landscapes cover the floor, and the walls, between doors, are broken up with pictographs that Sax recognizes as sights from around the galaxy; various planets, highlights from the realms the Chorus controls.

"I'd almost call it beautiful if I didn't know what it represented," Plake says as they move.

Theoretically, they'll find some indication of the control room, but Sax isn't seeing anything other than locked doors with blaring red lights. A low-tone alarm starts up too, declaring Cavignum under lockdown. That it's taken whomever runs this place this long to call their insertion an emergency tells Sax just how confident they are in their forces.

Not that Sax hasn't proved a lot of people wrong on that bet.

"It's still beautiful," Bas replies. "We're not trying to destroy this place—if we take down the Chorus, this planet, this galaxy is still going to need Aspicis."

"They can have it," Agra-Red, sliming its way along the ground, says. "This planet is garbage."

As if hearing the Whelk's insult, the lights in the corridor flicker and die, plunging them into an absolute darkness. Sax flicks the mask over to night vision and scans back and forth. Finds the reason why. The doors they've passed are opening, with Flauma and other species breaking into the corridor and running back the way they came.

Evacuating the hostages. The alarm blots out the sounds of footfalls, and there's no talking.

"Stop for a second," Sax says. He's not interested in the fleeing workers, but rather in the rooms they left behind. "Form up."

"You going to guide us?" Plake asks. "Because Vyphen can't see in the dark."

"Hold on to Bas' tail," Sax says.

He'll die before he lets the Vyphen hold onto his body. Bas gets it, releases a quick laugh, but doesn't argue. She knows Sax too well.

It's a quick sprint down the hallway and into the first open room on the right. The lights are still out, but the doors opening means Cavignum's not entirely without power. Terminals in the room still glow, and they're showing the kinds of graphs that make Sax think this is one of the places that controls the flow from beneath the surface.

Not what he cares about, but terminals are flexible.

Plake catches the idea too—which is good, as Sax has about as much trust in his own ability to use a foreign terminal as he does in Plake's chances one-on-one with a mirrored Oratus. While the Vyphen sets to work, Sax sets up watch at the door, taking the occasional chance to spook passing species with a low hiss.

Other doors along the hallway are open now too, with more and more staff streaming away. Sax could reach out and tear them apart. They shrink away from him as they pass by, running quick. A calculated gamble—Sax and the others haven't made a point of attacking random civilians, but they've caused plenty of destruction. Get out, save some lives.

Sax almost respects the Amigga running this place—he's sure there's one of the orb-like monsters here somewhere: saving lives always seems to be their last concern.

"Found it!" Plake announces with a thrilled bubble. "Close to here actually. Just down the hall, on the left." There's a pause, long enough for Sax to turn his head, about to ask why they aren't moving. "And Bas was right. It's in the center—only the center's not where the hole comes up."

"Great," Bas says. "Can we go?"

Plake gives the affirmative and they're back in the hallway. The remaining staffers turn and run back the other way at the sounds of Sax loping towards them, vanishing into side rooms where nobody cares to follow them. Eventually they make it to the door, the only one still locked shut.

"You have another battery bomb?" Sax asks the Whelk, knowing full well the creature has nothing.

"If any of you'd thought to grab another miner, I could make one," Agra-Red shoots back. "This thing packs a punch, but there's no way it's getting through a thick, heat-shielded door like this."

Sax places a claw against the door. It's hard, well-forged and constructed to stand against even normal Oratus claws. Then again, he doesn't have normal Oratus claws, not anymore.

"Cover me," Sax says, and gets to work.

The first scratches don't seem to make a dent—it's hard to tell in the dark if he's making any progress. One swipe, two, three and all Sax is wondering is whether his claws are going to break off, when there's a sudden change in tenor, a strike knocks off a long strip of the door's protective shell.

And his next swing bites. Tears off a good chunk of the metal.

"Finally found something you're good at," Plake says.

Sax doesn't get to reply. The hallway's lights come on bright and blinding, causing Sax to stumble back from the door, which works out well as the space he's been standing suddenly fills with red laser.

Apparently breaching the control room is a step too far for Cavignum's security, as they've sent a squad of Flaum— and Sax catches the telltale shimmer of the mirrored Oratus behind them—to the hallway, which they're now filling with deadly laser.

Agra-Red takes a couple of return shots as Bas hammers her weight and claws at a less-protected door on the oppo- site side of the hallway. A few swipes at the thin barrier and it breaks in, allowing the four of them to tumble inside the side room. Sax earns himself some burns, largely deflected by his increasingly-damaged mask, as the prize for last one inside.

"Nice choice," Plake says as they get a better look inside.

It's a break room. There are a couple of tables, a scat- tering of chairs, a large wall-screen showing some sort of local Aspicis news which currently features a meticulously groomed Flaum talking over an aerial shot of... Cavignum.

"We're famous," Agra-Red gives a hopeless, warbling laugh. "Never thought I'd die with a billion eyes watching."

"Not dead yet," Sax hisses, looking back out the door, across the hallway towards where they need to be. "If I can get another two or three swings in, I can open that door."

"You'll be charred slag before you get one." Plake doesn't offer a better solution, instead staring at the broadcast. "Are you all seeing this? They're saying repair crews are waiting outside as soon as this place is secured."

"Isn't that normal?" Sax offers.

"It's the solution for the Teven," Plake says. "We just need to make sure they're in that crew, then get out of here."

Before the glimmer-worm prison, they'd had communicators. They could've called Nobaa and Engee and told them the plan. Now, though, all Sax has is the mask, and its narrow-band wave isn't going to carry his words more than a few dozen meters.

The break room doesn't have any of those devices around either, but it does have a single terminal connected to Aspicis' global network and, beyond that, the galaxy at large. It's a small screen, and Bas looms large over it, her claws tapping away at the icons as they appear.

"I can reach them through this," Bas says. "Buy me a minute."

Sax knows how he can buy her several. He heads back to the doorway, peeks his head out of the hallway to see the security squad advancing towards them. A quick burst of miner fire has Sax ducking himself back inside as bolts strike the frame and ceiling around his head.

"Trying to get yourself killed?" Agra-Red, set up with its miner behind Sax. "How's that going to help?"

"Shut up." Sax hisses, then sticks a single foreclaw out, waves it up and down. "I have an offer!" Sax roars this loud enough to carry into the hallway.

When nothing tries to incinerate his waving hand, Sax tries sticking his head out again—at a different height than before, just in case—and he sees that the two mirrored Oratus have taken spots at the head of the Flaum column, with the furry creatures holding their miners ready behind them.

"What is your offer?" Kah asks. "Know that you have no other escape, and we could easily kill you should we choose."

"That didn't go so well for you last time." Sax steps into the middle of the hallway.

He's an easy target here, but he's hoping giving himself up is going to buy Bas the time she needs to send the message to the Teven. It also gets him closer to the control room door; even if this tactic fails, Sax figures he can get in one or two good swats before the mirrored Oratus or the Flaum burn him down.

That'll have to be good enough.

"Regardless," Kah says, and Sax likes the annoyance in its hissing tone. "Give yourselves up. Aspicis and its energy shouldn't suffer for your cause."

"I want the lives of my friends guaranteed," Sax says. "They should be allowed to leave Cavignum. This was my idea, and I made them do it."

Kah laughs and it echoes up and down the hallway. "Your idea? Sax, we have your records. You're not a mission planner, a commander. You're a set leader, a weapon made to carry out the tasks of those above you. Don't act like we're stupid."

Sax stiffens his spine. They're right, of course. Sax is a weapon. He's never been much of a bluffer anyway.

"Sent it," Bas hisses softly from the room to his left.

"So is that a no?" Sax asks Kah.

"We'd much rather have you dead," Kah says, stepping to the side of the hallway.

As the words come out of the Oratus' mouth, Sax lunges towards the control room door. Gets a strong swipe in that tears the uncoated metal to shreds. Flashes fill the hallway, and Sax expects, even as he continues flinging his claws, to get torched, but the fire doesn't come. There's plenty of flashes in his peripheral, and a couple glancing hits send burning pain up his side, but Sax lives.

"Keep cutting you big lizard," Agra-Red cackles from behind him. "I've got them ducking for now, but they'll find their spines someday!"

Sax gets in another slash, then another, until the door is a series of metal ribbons. He raises his claws again when something very heavy crashes into him from behind, breaking Sax through the remaining strips of metal and rolling them both into the control room.

"Couldn't stay away from you any longer," Bas hisses as she scrambles off of him, towards the big bank of terminals.

There are dozens of the screens in the big, empty space, along with chairs and netting to keep various species assigned to monitor them comfortable. Even the ceiling sports a projected, swirling display showing the current core temp of Cavignum. It is, as expected, very, very hot.

"Don't touch anything!" It's the monotoned voice of an Amigga, translated through its intercoms.

This one, an amber color and looking like a dried out piece of old fruit, sits in a chair at the room's far end. It's not so much a suit as a cradle, and Sax can't see a single weapon on it.

"If you destroy the wrong thing, then this whole plant could explode," the Amigga pleads. "Not only would you kill yourselves, but many, many more on Aspicis could die."

"Maybe that's what we want?" Bas says, her claws hovering over the screens.

"If so, then there's nothing I can do to stop you," the Amigga says. "But I refuse to believe Oratus would commit themselves to a mission of pure destruction with no other end. We did not fail so badly with your species."

Sax wants to strike the creature down for those words, but a yelp of Whelk-pain from the hallway reminds him they don't have much time here. Agra-Red's miner will run out of power eventually, and then they'll be swarmed.

Yet, they need to damage this place somehow, if Nobaa and Engee are going to have an excuse to come here as part of the repair crew. So Sax turns and slashes at the screens of the terminals. Cuts the glass, shreds the housing, but leaves the inside alone. Bas gets it, does the same to the screens next to hers.

"What are you doing?" the Amigga asks. "Please, if you cut too deep!"

"Find us a way out of here," Sax says. "Or we will destroy everything."

The Amigga has no eyes. No visible senses whatsoever, but Sax gets the sense that the creature is staring at him, trying to decide if the Oratus is serious.

"We've made our message," Bas adds. "Shown that we can strike anywhere, if the Chorus doesn't give in to our demands. Let us leave, and you'll keep your station."

Lying. Bas is so much better at it than Sax is, and her reasoning shoves the Amigga towards action. The creature's suit buzzes, and suddenly its voice blares out of speakers from everywhere.

"Hold your fire!" the Amigga shouts. "Allow the intruders to leave, or they'll obliterate Cavignum entirely."

The command does its job, and Agra-Red's shooting halts a second later.

"They'll escort you to an exit," the Amigga says. "Please, don't damage anything else. You've made our lives difficult enough."

"We don't care," Sax replies, though he doesn't move. "Bas, go with them."

His pair hesitates, looks at Sax. "What?"

"The only reason we're getting out of here at all is because these threaten the entire station," Sax says. "I stay, they won't hurt you. If we all leave, they'll take us the moment they've secured this room."

Her look only lasts a moment but it's a moment Sax holds constant in his mind as Bas sweeps out of the room, as she takes Agra-Red and Plake with her through some combination of passageways and out into the jungles of Aspicis.

Those pink-gold scales around her golden eyes. Sax saw in them the acceptance, the understanding of the mission. That it comes first.

Except, here, it didn't. Sax made the offer, Sax gave himself up not for the mission, but for her, because nothing else matters.

I wait, at first. Simply lie there with my head propped up and watch the body. Jel must be getting back up. It can't be dead. I've never seen an Oratus fall, aside from Sax's surprise blasting on *Cobalt* courtesy of Coorvin, the station's captive Flaum. Mostly, I can't believe I'm the cause.

Around me, the section buzzes. The ship hums. These throngs, the vibrations, are new. As if the Sevora ship is coming to life around me. Ignos said it would take time to get the seed ship up and running again. That it would happen gradually as the chosen one, the Sevora elected to helm the ship, began to merge with the craft itself.

The noises, though, remind me that we're not done yet. So I pick myself up, slow and gradual, first to my knees, and then to my hands—palms flat against the tile—before with a last push I get to a sturdy stand. Gar is still down. No motion. I look back towards Lan, and she's twitching. Her claws beginning to flex, her tail swishing ever so slightly.

Gar is her pair. What happens when an Oratus' pair dies?

I can't answer that question so I move past Gar's body and beyond. Past the racks of vests and clothes, past the weapons all neat and glistening. Ready for a war that I hope is over. Along the way I see the bodies of Viera's earlier victims. I would want anything than to be on the other end of her rage.

They're all down, all of them. Smoking, motionless.

But then, so is she. Viera lies flat on the ground, sprawled out, but breathing. There's a gash on the side of her head, turning some of her white hair pink, matting it. Her left arm hangs at an odd angle away from her body. And her eyes are shut as I get close and kneel down over.

"Can you hear me?" I said to her. "Viera?"

I get nothing from her, so I set about tearing strips from her the robes she's wearing beneath the armor and making bandages. I don't want to move her arm, because I don't know what's wrong with it, so I do the best I can get her turned over. Staunch the bleeding, and lay her back down. I look back across the section, making sure nothing else is moving, and see I'm still the only one up.

Which means I'm the last one of us. Which means it's up to me to stop the seed ship.

First, I go back to the weapons rack. Take a pair of miners, take up the short half of the staff that popped out of Gar's head when he fell. And then I go. One miner slung across my back, the other in my left hand with my right wielding my half staff and using it as a crutch when I have to.

I go back to the ring, which feels emptier than ever before. For a hot second, I think about going back, finding the docking bay, Malo and T'Oli. We might be able to escape, the three of us. But no, that would only delay what needs doing.

I have to stop the Sevora. For Viera, Gar, Lan and all the others.

So I orbit the ring and walk beneath those glistening seeds pointed down like daggers over my head. I breathe steadily cleaner air as recyclers, newly activated, cleanse the ship of the musk of what must have been years and years of floating here abandoned in the black, waiting to be called upon. The last hope of an evil race.

I find my goal on the far side of the ring, near where the Sevora had nearly fought each other earlier. When Nasiya claimed its right to the center of the ship.

The silver walkway across the ring leads to a wide, square door in the deep gray central core. A door that Ignos said would be sealed. A one-way crossing for the Sevora that would give its life for the rest of its species.

"I guess you're too slow," I mutter, taking my first step on the walkway. Around me, beneath me, the ring extends down into the black void of space. I can see it all, infinite. It makes me dizzy for a moment and some part of me feels like I should just take a jump. Glide down and out and forget all of this.

And maybe I would have, except the walkway shakes. Something starts a process which cannot be undone. Behind me, at the edge of the ring, the walkway begins to recede. Pull back towards the center. I move. Hustle across the metal towards the door with no control panel. One that may not open, that may leave me stranded on a vanishing edge.

So as I stumble forward, the pain in my sides keeping me from moving too fast, I aim with my left hand, flip the miner to the third mode, one Viera showed me once but that I've never used. The trigger on the miner is light, built for smaller Flaum hands. When I press it, instead of scattered shots the miner bursts forth its energy in a solid beam as I run, racing my own plummeting doom towards the door.

The pattern I sketch, the opening I roast is not pretty. It's not large. But the elongated oval is enough, its edges burning orange with heat, for me to fall through and land on the inside. I've arrived right never thought I'd be. In the heart of my enemy.

It's a strange look, when I stand up. Pick myself from the floor and stare as, behind me, the thin door I cut through is replaced by slamming outer plates. A seal too thick for any miner to ever pierce. In front of me is a tall, black, walled cylinder. It's perfectly rounded, smooth. Without any way in that I can see.

I walk around the outside. Looking for an entrance and finding only what must be bins for nutrient goop, for food and drink. There are links to pipes coming from above, narrow and slight. Too small for anyone to sneak through. Except maybe another Sevora.

What I also find, though, is a total lack of an entrance. There's no door, no control panel. No waving flag saying here, here is what you're seeking. In the absence of all that, with only the thrum of the ship for company, and feeling so alone, I collapse against the outer wall and sit. One miner in my left, my short staff in my right, and my second miner looped over my shoulder harness. Armed, dangerous, hurt and pointless.

"What would you do?" I ask the air. I ask Viera, Malo.

Viera would probably just start shooting. Claim that there's no reason to fret as long as you have energy. As long as you can burn your way through. Who knows if that wall can be penetrated by a simple handheld miner? Who knows what's on the other side? If I burn through all my energy here, what happens? Would Nasiya simply tear me limb from limb? Could I beat a Flaum controlled by one of the most vicious Sevora with only my staff?

Malo might be more strategic. Hunt around for another way, but I didn't find anything obvious and I'm running out of time. I can feel it, as Viera promised I would; T'Oli's temporary cure is starting to fade. The pain's only increasing, and the edges of my toes and my fingers are growing weaker, more numb. I have to end this, and I have to do it quickly.

And T'Oli? What would the Ooblot do? Rattle off some facts about... No, wait. I look at my left wrist. It's right there, the answers I need. So I take what's left of my weakened spirit and send it into the Cache. Dig its depths to find the seed ship, and how I can destroy its core.

The answer is simpler than I'd realized: The central Sevora is protected by the main core walls. The only thing that's going to bring them down is a great force or, if necessary, provisions. The need for food and water, especially early, when the Sevora is still maturing. That's it. All I need to do is make sure the food arrives, and those walls will come down for me.

I leave the Cache and its emerald flash, and hope that Ignos' gift to me will be the end of its species. I stand and go back to the basin with the little pipes leading to it. Next to them is a small panel with only a very simple request. A green button covering the entire screen. I press it and there's a rumbling, a whooshing noise as deep purple sludge begins to drop from the pipe and into the bottom of the basin, collecting into a puddle. A trap being set by the Sevora's own ship.

I hear it then. The clicking, winding and whirring of gears out of sight. The black walls slide down one after another as I turn to see what a Sevora finally given a chance to grow looks like.

A younger me, more naive, would have screamed. Would have run at the sight of this thing in front of me. That it was a Flaum is evident, but it, very much, is no longer one. The furry body stands at a set of terminals and, springing from that fur, as if pores had opened into new life, stringy red and yellow and green tentacles arc up and down, clinging to the computers, lodging into spaces beneath the Flaum and the grated floor it stands on. Yet, the Flaum still lives. I see it tapping away, I see it breathing and I see those blood red eyes turn towards me as the walls finish descending.

"The human," Nasiya says. It's a voice far from the squeaky skitters of a normal Flaum and trending more towards a scratchy broken noise. Like a person in the morning after a too late night with too little water to drink. Muscles frayed and at the end of their purpose.

"Yeah, I am human," I say. "And I'm here to stop you. To stop your species. To stop this war."

"I don't care why you're here. I just care that you die." Nasiya punctuates the reply by stepping back from the terminals.

As the Flaum moves, the tentacles coming out of its arms and back and shoulders quiver and withdraw, until they arrange around the Nasiya's Flaum like a halo of scraggly hair. It's strange, but I'm too angry, too tired and hurting to be scared anymore.

I aim the miner and fire.

A long bolt of energy launches forth – I realize I forgot to switch the weapon from its single-beam setting – and cascades into the set of terminals next to Nasiya. The screens and their metal housings burn, exploding in sparks and raining fire across the central cylinder. My shot gets to Nasiya, who growls a hoarse, low noise as I leave a black burning scar across its chest, and heads towards me. But the Sevora has weakened its own host, and the Flaum lurches, stumbles even as those tentacles head my way. Even as my miner sputters out of power.

I use the basin and push myself to the side, continuing around the ring as Nasiya lurches out of its grated home after me. For every step the Flaum takes, its tentacles move even faster. They seem to be growing too, chasing after me like weeds, growing along the ground in my direction. With my left hand, I drop the dead miner and swing my shoulder, pulling my backup weapon around my chest where I catch it even as my right hand and the short staff keep me up and stumbling away from the creature.

"Stop and fight," Nasiya says behind me.

"It's not my fault you're slow," I reply. I give the miner a quick glance to make sure it's going to fire the quick bursts of bolts, and twist. I plant my feet and turn, ignoring the sting of pain that I'm so used to already, and pull the trigger. Hold it tight as red bolts stitch across the inside of the chamber.

Most miss as Nasiya crouches, but a pair strike its body, burn holes into its shoulders and Nasiya falls forward. But the tentacles don't stop. They wrap on my legs, crawl up my calves and over my knees and I swipe at them with my staff. A pair of green tendrils latch on to the gray metal stick as I strike, and while they don't pull it away, they stop its momentum. I have to let go to get my hand back, to push away another set of yellow vines getting close to my throat. I kick and push, but can't get away from the things as they multiply, seeming to come from everywhere and cover me like a net.

They're at my neck now, climbing around my throat. In a second they'll get to my eyes, my mouth, or choke the life out of me. I do the only think I can think of: aim the miner lower and pepper more bolts, more hot red, into Nasiya's body. Into the Flaum until it catches fire.

The tentacles climb over the bottom of my chin, I feel them in my hair, around my neck.

Now, finally, I scream. But it's not fear. It's anger, determination, desperation all coming out because I'm holding that trigger and I'm shooting my enemy. Not for me, but for my friends, for my species, for this galaxy that has apparently suffered so much at the hands of these evil creatures.

I just want it to end.

And even as the tendrils use the scream to climb into my open mouth, it does.

Nasiya has no final battle cry. There's no grand proclamation, no evidence of my triumph other than the harsh crackle of flames and the smell of liquefying flesh as the tendrils begin to shrivel black. They die away and I spit them out of my mouth, brush them from my legs and back and stare at what had once been the leader of the Sevora. At the last remnant of a species so hated by so many.

"Viera, Malo, I did it," I say to myself. There's no one else here. There's only me, trapped inside the central core. Any terminal I might use is burned and broken.

So instead I make my way to the basin of nutrient goop. Try a bit of the substance just to get the taste of Nasiya's tentacles out of my mouth. As my body gets looser, as the pain grows and my eyes start to water, as every breath gets harder than the last I press myself against the wall and watch as the Sevora's last fire burns out.

They stun him, of course. Barge into the control room with miners firing and they don't stop until Sax is a burned, disabled husk on the floor. Kah tears away Sax's mask, pausing only to sneer and offer up some insults at Nobaa's metal patches. Then they pick Sax up and haul him away.

Sax gets the whole experience fed to him like a dream; it's a series of blurry images as what's left of his senses struggle to piece together the scrambled feed. There's a mag-lev train in the basement of Cavignum that he's brought to, both mirrored Oratus taking point on his escort. They clear a whole car for Sax, giving the Oratus the most prized ride he's ever had on a transport.

The train shoots fast through the endless nighttime vine forest, and the inside is light only in the low blues of a deep ocean, as their attack on Cavignum apparently carried into sleep cycle time. Not any anyone in Sax's car—except, maybe, Sax himself—gets any.

So everyone sees the Meridia as it comes into view. To say that the Meridia is a shaft of light would be too simplistic; it's a living space, a fortress, and a center of public governance all in one. There's all manner of blinking lights, yes, but each one sends a different message: the constellations of steady red mark countermeasure turrets, the wider, broader whites and yellows give hints to residents, while greens and blues illuminate docking spaces for messenger drones, small ships, and more.

The other defining feature of the Meridia is that, from the ground, there doesn't appear to be a top. The atmosphere and darkness of space beyond muddle away the definition of the construct well before it actually ends, like a mountain vanishing into clouds. As such, to Sax, it's as if the horizon's been split by an ax, rising thick and strong from the surface.

Like parasites clinging to the host, there's a vast city surrounding the Meridia, with plenty of other buildings shooting high and always, always looking miniature next to the galaxy's premiere structure. These, too, glitter in the night, and their lights peek in through the train windows or shine up from beneath as the track passes overhead.

The train isn't the only thing moving in the skies either —despite the apparent hour, skiffs, shuttles, and ships maxing out the limits for atmospheric entry clog the skies above the buildings, though again the Meridia acts like a filter, with only a few allowed to slip within the mandated perimeter.

The train isn't one of them, and it slides into a massive, slab-like station near, but not too close, to the base of the Meridia. Sax, numbed again with a couple more courtesy stuns, is loaded onto a waiting cargo sled and, with the two mirrored Oratus continuing their escort, walked along a broad avenue towards the Spire.

Sax doesn't think his eventual end-point is all that high

in the Meridia, but without windows, it's hard to tell. He's shuffled into a room, lowered through a ceiling to a cell, which is where his escort finally leaves him.

The Oratus doesn't bother moving—he knows what's coming, he's seen it plenty of times before; when the Chorus decides, Sax will have a simple death, sent out across the galaxy, to mark the end of yet another futile attempt to change the set course of the universe.

THE LAST CYCLE

THE SKYWARD SAGA BOOK SIX

Do you know the dreams you have when you think you're dreaming forever? They're slow at first, an endless series of stories, each one less and less real as you begin to find the flaws.

Flashes of leafy canopies, my bright-lit home mingle with the fantastic. I share dinners with Father and Mother. Hunts with Malo and Viera through dense jungle and damp caves. Even T'Oli, the creamy Ooblot joins me as we climb through the sewers of a now-dead planet.

I know none of this is real.

Because I'm supposed to be dead.

And yet.

I'm not me anymore: the way you become intimate with your body over time, one season after another of touching your muscles and moving, jumping, thinking. Those connections are gone. I am adrift in an unfamiliar sea of strands. I cast out, trying to find parts of myself.

Answers come slow. Tentative. Like a flowers blooming after the first rains, each connection is beautiful. Fragile.

A voice from everywhere, nowhere tells me they will get stronger with time.

The voice echoes in my dreams. Changes, too. Sometimes its Malo saying the words, veering away from our hunt to offer an explanation of why I can't speak, or see yet, even though I'm right there with him in the forest.

Other times, the voice fills a void of nothing. I'm between selves, a break in the stories and words of comfort come. The sounds of friends whispering to me wishes, compassion. Things I hold on to in the dark.

Nerves had to be repaired, the voice tells me as I wander through the ash wastes of Earth's far side. New strands grown and connected. Organs made using what limited examples exist of human biology. I don't know what it's talking about, but I hold on to the last thing the voice says: I am still a human.

When I see for the first time, a phantom centers my eyes. My friend. One who, last I checked, was barely conscious. Had just been loosed from the clutches of a creature so evil that it took the very freedom away from Malo's soul. But there he is, in front of me, his head wearing short black hair, still gaunt but smiling anyway. His shoulders show the long arc of ash-inked tattoos across his chest and arms as he leans over me. As he brushes my forehead.

"Empress," Malo says and his voice is slow, soft, as if I'm made of glass that might shatter should he talk too loud. "Welcome back."

The welcome comes with a barrage. I'm greeted first by Malo and then a parade of others, most straight from my dreams. A healthy Viera, though she still sports a bandage around her head. Lan, the emerald-scaled Oratus who keeps her four claws clasped and head bowed, who offers her thanks in a low hiss. Lastly, with Malo still by my side, the huge bulk of Kolas, commander of the Vincere force dedicated to the extermination of the galaxy's enemies.

With each of them comes bits and pieces of the story that brought me from the end of the Sevora War to a long and wide red sponge bed on Kolas' cruiser, the *Nunelite*.

Malo and T'Oli had made the docking bay on the seed ship. Ignos, the Sevora that had at one point been inside me and that had, back on the seed ship, been so determined to return to its place of power, had left the shuttle we arrived in undefended. T'Oli and Malo took the craft, lifted off, and made the leap back to Vimelia, the Sevora home world where Kolas and his fleet were still cleaning up the remnants of their enemy.

Kolas came back with them, and a seed ship left empty by Viera and my efforts presented little trouble. Eventually, a Vincere strike team cut into the center and found me.

"You were dead," Malo says.

"Actually," T'Oli, who's oozed its way up Malo's side and rests on his shoulders, both eyestalks bobbing at me. "She was in the state called a coma. A living paralysis. Not really dead, but not really alive. Catastrophic failure of several organs. She would have died, though—"

"She gets it," Malo says to the blob, then looks back at me. "We put you back together."

I try to ask what that means? Only my voice doesn't work. Not yet, anyway. But my hands do, and when they get the message, I write out the words. The questions.

It turns out there's an advantage to being a species grown by experimentation. An advantage to being designed by another. Kolas has an Amigga with his fleet. One who is able to pull up the secret records of humanity's existence. One able to find out how I function, and with that information put me back together. The Amigga wove new organs, new nerves and cells from vats of biological material and built me back. As I hear all of this, I can only think of what Ignos told me when it first crashed through the sky and took up residence in my mind: *I will bring you miracles.*

"Kolas says we'll be leaping soon to the Chorus," Malo says some time later—I'm drifting in and out of consciousness, and as T'Oli puts it, time has little real meaning in space. There are no days, no seasons, only Cycles; major events marking the passing of eras. Despite that unsettling description, I know Malo has barely left my side. Only when I order him to sleep does he leave. "Apparently they want you to be the emissary for humanity," Malo flashes me a smile. "I can't think of anyone better."

"I don't want to," I manage to say – my voice is coming back in spurts, what I'm told is the result of new muscles. Ones that need to grow and train. I won't be able to run far for a while either, or breathe too heavy, or eat too much. All the result of organs learning their place in a new body.

"I don't think you have a choice," and there's real sadness in Malo's eyes. "I wish you did. I wish we could just go home. But Kolas says we're needed now."

"Why?"

"Apparently we need to prove the Chorus is to be trusted. We need to stand up and proclaim our allegiance to them."

"Why? I know I just asked, but what does the Chorus need from us?"

Malo shakes his head. "Kolas would not tell me. He only said, since you owe the Chorus your life, you must do this."

I close my eyes for a moment. The last time I owed an Amigga a favor, the last time I had to do what an Amigga said, it nearly ripped me apart. Dalachite, on another space station an eternity ago, threatened to use me as a project for its own research. Getting involved with the Amigga is a quick way to die, or worse. Why would I help them now? My life or no?

"Kolas also told me," Malo continues and now his voice is even sadder, as if not only what he's saying is tragic, but ugly and distasteful. Exposing a weakness in himself. "They'll destroy Earth, Kaishi. If we don't give the Chorus what they want, they'll send the Vincere to complete what they tried before."

That's more like the Amigga I know. Pose generous, and seal the deal with a threat.

Well, I've seen worse.

As if waiting for Malo to complete setting the stage for my new life, the door to my room swishes open to reveal someone new. The Amigga. Unlike Dalachite, the one that ran *Cobalt*, or Sapphrite, the leader of Clarity's Dawn and the resistance beneath the surface of Vimelia, this one is different. This one is smaller, a healthy gray-blue color that does nothing to stop the queasy shifting of my stomach as I look at a ball without eyes, without arms. It's encased in a translucent sheath, one with the barest hint of yellow on the fringes. The Amigga floats on a set of micro-jets around the base and sides. No mechanical arms, but strange, pocked circles evenly space along a stripe around the Amigga's suit.

"Interfaces," the Amigga says as it notices me looking, as it floats into the room. "Bring me near a device, and I can interact. Form a connection and control. Useful on ships, when the more crude methods of metal arms and legs have less value."

I blink at the Amigga from my sponge bed, and notice Malo sitting rigid. Neither of us like Amigga. Neither of us enjoy the thing's presence, but I swallow my distaste. I put the crown on – not a real one, of course, but the one I have to wear at all times whether or not I'm in my palace or among my people. As Malo and Viera have told me; *Empress* is not a title to be worn and taken off at will, but rather bonded and lived with forever.

"I'm told you saved me," I say. My voice is getting stronger now. It has the volume, if not the flavor, of how I used to sound. "Thank you."

The Amigga hovers closer and Malo tenses, as if he's going to get up and punch the thing. I want to reach out and touch him, tell Malo no, don't worry. I don't think the Amigga is here to kill me. I don't even know if it could.

"I was glad to do so. Partly because no Amigga has helped a human before, and new intelligent species are so rare. A scientific first, which my name will forever be associated with," It's hard to know where to look when the Amigga speaks. There's no eyes, no mouth to focus on. The words come from the thing's suit, from speakers that cause the speech to reverberate through the small room. "My name is Ferrolite. I am the lead Amigga assigned to this fleet. It is my job to ensure that Kolas and his forces carry out the Chorus' demands. It is also my job to make sure I preserve those things of interest to the galaxy. Like you."

"Now you want something in return."

The Amigga has no capacity, that I can tell, to show surprise. Shock or disappointment. There's no emotions to read and since its voice comes through a mechanical synthesizer, it lacks the emotional tones a human might be able to put in. As such, with Ferrolite hovering before me, I have no idea whether the Amigga is happy or sad that I move immediately to business. But I'm tired, and if someone is going to ask something of me I'd rather know and be done with it.

"Human, Kaishi, the galaxy runs on a stable framework

of species working beneath the Chorus to live fruitful, happy lives. We would welcome humanity within our community. But every species needs an ambassador, every species needs someone to bring it to the galactic stage. After what you've done I can think of no better."

"Because I destroyed a Sevora ship?"

"Because you demonstrated the capacities civilization values," Ferrolite says. "You are brave, courageous, intelligent and kind. Lan told me how you tried to rescue her and her pair, rather than escape and save yourself. Kolas told me how you gave everything to retrieve this one here on the Vimelia. These are laudable traits. These are valued. The Chorus is always looking to improve the make-up of the galaxy and if humanity is a reflection of you, then your species would be well appreciated."

It's hard not to like the Amigga's words. Hard not to feel a slight blush of pride, of embarrassment at being so singled out for something I thought was only the right thing to do. Yet, here I am, ready for more. I think it's because, having gone so long, across so many places, there hasn't been any outward acknowledgment of what we've done. My struggles have been made apart from the world I love, mostly apart from my species. Finally, here, as I claw my way back from death, I'm recognized.

"Will you?" Ferrolite gets to the question. "Will you add humanity's voice to the Chorus?"

I don't like the Amigga, I don't trust Ferrolite, but I can understand its motivations. I can sympathize with its goals; the Sevora are gone, the galaxy is on the brink of peace and prosperity. Any Empress would want to bring her people into that oasis. I have to think of everyone, not just myself.

"I will serve," I say. "Humanity will join your galaxy."

If there's any congratulations to be had for promising

humanity's part will be played, Ferrolite doesn't give any. No fanfare bursts through the speakers, drinks and feasts don't appear. The Amigga only gives the briefest sound of approval, then floats away as if the only thing I'd agreed to is a moment's peace.

"You trust that thing?" Malo says.

"I don't have a choice, do I?" I reply. "Ferrolite put me back together. Without it, I wouldn't be here."

"That was its choice, this is yours."

"Then what should I say, Malo?" I look at my warrior, propped up in my bed. "What should I tell Avril, or all the refugees of Damantum when the Chorus declares them a threat and now, instead of scared Sevora, we're facing an Oratus army descending on Earth?"

Malo leans back against the side of the room. Stares across at the nothing on the far wall. "I just found freedom. I don't want to lose it again. Not yet."

"We won't," I say, though I don't know for sure. Another promise pledged in the dark. "I'll make them respect us."

Malo laughs, and the hollow bark cuts me. "Kaishi, we were pawns to the Sevora, and we're no different now. The Chorus doesn't need to respect us, because we aren't a threat, and we have nothing to offer them."

"That's not true. They made us, remember? An Amigga built us, created us because they wanted something better. The Chorus knows we're valuable."

Those words mollify Malo a little bit; he offers a half-hearted nod. Then his eyes go down to the tattoos on his chest. "All of these are lies, you know."

"Lies?"

"Ignos didn't create us. The Amigga did. All the gods, all of our society is based on lies."

"Now you're being sad," I fight back. "You don't know

whether our Ignos had a hand in our creation or not, and even if the gods didn't directly control anything, the idea of them helped us survive. Helped our people grow, love, and learn."

"And when the Chorus arrives and starts telling every human they're a product of the Amigga? Like the crops we grow in our fields?"

That's a harder question to answer. I don't know how my own people would take that, the Ignos-worshiping Charre. Avril and her hardy, logical Lunare beneath the mountains might absorb the discovery in stride, but the society I lived in... would it stand up to such a revelation?

"It's still a secret, right?" I say. "We don't need to tell anyone. There's no point in it."

"The Chorus will."

"Not all of them know," I reply. "I don't think Ferrolite knows—it said we're a new species."

"Then we keep this a secret, for now?"

"When the Chorus comes to Earth, there'll be enough changes. I don't think we need to doubt our gods at the same time," I say, wanting as much to keep a hold of the rituals, the sayings and the beliefs I've held since my beginning as to keep my people from falling apart.

We keep at it, discussing, playing with our past as though it's something to be chosen or tossed aside depending on our whims. Until my own body catches up with me and I start missing words, start closing my eyes, and Malo does the nice thing and lets me claim victory by falling into a deep, deep sleep.

The four of them, a true set and a terror to the Chorus' worst enemies. Sent across the galaxy on more missions than Sax can remember, each one a dizzying array of objectives, attacks, and merciless slaughters of species who dared defy the command of the galaxy's rulers. Each and every one of those missions plays, dragging Sax through a life lived at the fringe of sanity for far longer than he had any right to expect.

Starships crash, miners misfire, or an ambush catches a pair off-guard. There's a million ways an Oratus can die in this galaxy, and most of them don't live all that long for it. Yet Sax has seen enough to learn his way of life is wrong. Or, at least, it's in the service of the wrong thing. The wrong species.

Being alone with his thoughts is the worst thing Sax can imagine. Well, not the *worst* thing, because where he's at now, sequestered in a holding-tank of a cell, with a white ring-light up top for company, undercuts the awfulness of his imagination with the slicing knife of solitude. Not that Sax minds being alone—he prefers it to most company—but these tight walls, forming up square around the large Oratus, compress his single self until Sax is overcome with the impossible urge to

GET OUT.

The hissing roar goes nowhere. Bounces around the cage, makes Sax sick of his own voice. Still, it feels good to yell, to do something. He sticks out his foreclaw, running it along the chromed sides of his cell. There's not enough room for Sax to extend his arm fully, so the strike, when he makes it, is haphazard and awkward. Even so, an Oratus' strength should be enough to make a mark.

The walls remain unblemished. They show Sax's distorted reflection haloed in the light from above. Four arms sporting clawed hands, though his razors are no longer the organic originals. His claws gleam like the walls, like patches of his gray scales, ones stripped away and replaced with metal plating. Surgeries hiding the scars of his near death and giving evidence to the same. Sax's tail wraps around his squatting talons, its tip twitching on occasion as an outlet for fraying, frustrated nerves.

You gave yourself up for them.

That's the thought that keeps coming back. It calms Sax down, opens a mental gate to his pair and what Bas might be doing. Sax isn't much for fantasy, for dreams beyond what he can see and kill, but in here he doesn't have much choice, so when his hearts slow, Sax wonders.

With the Cavignum, the planet Aspicis' great power plant and the source of energy for his current prison, compromised, there's a chance that right now Bas is launching an attack on the Meridia, which Sax is trapped inside. Evva, an older, larger Oratus and the leader of the force both Sax and Bas joined, would be acting on her plan, throwing her forces into an assault that could change all of civilization.

The attack will likely get everyone killed and change nothing at all, but Sax can't take that stance. He's been bred not to fail, not to consider losing once a mission begins. He must fight to the last end, always striving for the goal. Before, the Chorus dictated that objective, and Sax, as a member of the Vincere, carried out the orders without a thought to a mission's broader purpose or its affect on the galaxy at large.

Now Sax centers himself on his pair. Factions change, worlds and space stations trade out for one another, but there is only one pair.

He has to get out of here. For Bas.

As if hearing his thoughts, there's a light clicking and a series of hisses from above as the locks sealing Sax inside decompress and the hatch, the only way out of this room, swings up and open. Sax looks, not knowing what to expect, and bright light keeps him blinded. His vents, the slits in Sax's long torso that feed his hungry muscles with air, take in the smells of life. Creatures are up there, and they don't smell of dirt, of sweat and service. Higher officials, then, coming to gawk at their prisoner.

The white glow shifts to a cerulean shade, the color of Aspicis' sky, and a low-glowing band around Sax's waist changes to match. As it does, Sax's metal plates and claws tug too, a change in his localized gravity that sends Sax floating up from the floor and towards the opening on top. Sax is an awkward monster, and he has to help the ring bring his body through the hatch, but with scrabbles and contortions, the Oratus gets himself through.

Most Meridia levels are tall, four or five meters high to allow for the variety of species, including Oratus that come marching through its halls, and this level is double that to account for the prisoners. Sax emerges from his cell into a black and red space, the latter's bright color sectioning the various cells that Sax is now hovering over. Most are dark, but a few, like his, have a white-blue halo around the top.

Sax's view of the other cells vanishes quick, however, as sealing walls rise to cut Sax off from the rest of the level. Escape prevention, private interrogations, all sorts of devious deeds would be possible without prying eyes. The walls are the same black, shiny tile used everywhere else, and Sax bets the Amigga can run current through those tiles to stun or kill anyone stupid enough to try an escape.

The first priority in a new, hostile space is target identi-fication, followed by target elimination. Sax figures his death is imminent, and making that death expensive is the best move he's got.

The ring around his waist keeps Sax moving until he's closer to the level's ceiling, which leaves his talons a meter off of the floor. Without leverage, all Sax can do is wave his tail around, and when he sees his target, he stops. A single tail whip isn't going to do much to the mirrored Oratus waiting with a miner drawn and ready to deliver an instant execution.

"I beat you already, didn't I?" Sax hisses at the Oratus, whose scales would blend in more fully with the light, but whose recent scars leave long lines of puckered red and pink through his reflective coating.

Sax gave Kah those scars, and it's always fun to remind your enemies that you won. Sax would go even further, remind Kah about every thrashing blow delivered outside of the mag-lev train station in the vine jungles of Aspicis, but it seems like a waste of energy. Kah's not worth it.

"Is that why you're floating in our prison?" Kah hisses a reply.

"I gave myself up."

"Nobody cares," Kah says, but there's a sigh that whistles out of his vents. "But as you surrendered once, perhaps you'll consider doing it again."

A deal. This wouldn't be Kah's idea, then. No three-letter Oratus would strike a bargain with a captive. Better to eliminate the threat and move on to other things, especially when that threat is Sax, who, given an inch of freedom, will take every possible measure of revenge.

"Speak," Sax hisses.

"I was going to," Kah replies. "You don't have any right to command me here."

"They've kept you locked up in here too long. You don't know how to threaten someone properly."

"I don't need to threaten you." Kah gestures with the miner, as if the weapon's going to do his job for him.

"If you're just going to shake that miner, then at least give me a Flaum to scratch. I've gone too long without a real meal."

Kah gives Sax a hissing laugh for his trouble. "Your pair and that mass of prey are preparing to launch an attack on the Meridia. They will lose."

The words clear up Sax's fog. He didn't know whether the attack had started yet, whether Bas and the others had made it free from the Cavignum after Sax's gambit. Kah just confirmed both. Sax hopes a razor grin he can't repress doesn't give it away.

Kah, though, isn't watching him. Instead, the Oratus is glancing further back through the level. Kah's looking through the one side of the square cell that didn't rise, and while Sax doesn't have a view to what Kah's looking for, he can guess.

Mirrored Oratus always have masters.

"If you come out against the assault, if you help us turn their forces to our side." Kah turns back to Sax, his voice a low rasp. "The Chorus is willing to guarantee your life, along with your pair's. Your crimes will be forgiven, and you will have a choice of returning to Solis or choosing a planet of your desiring on which to retire."

Retire. Few Oratus get that chance, and the ones that do only receive it because of crippling injury. Any Oratus that can fight would, will, wants to fight. That is their purpose. That is their calling. Despite his life being tied to the idea, Sax snorts at the word before he considers what Kah even said.

"Perhaps," Kah allows at Sax's sound—he would understand, too, the insult in the idea of retirement. "We could arrange for a strategic post. Someplace where you could find plenty of entertainment."

Meaning things to slaughter. This would be better, except Kah's offer comes with a deal-killer: Sax isn't going to turn against his pair, against his former commander Evva and the cause he's joined. Not to go back to the Chorus and their pack of traitorous manipulators.

"You already know my answer," Sax says.

Kah glares in response. Matches Sax's eyes for a long moment before the mirrored Oratus dips his head in a nod that, Sax thinks, carries a tiny bit of respect with it.

"There is no other offer," Kah replies, though the words come rote; a question whose answer is known, which must nonetheless be asked. "Accept, or you will never see Bas again."

Her name this time. A sweetener, and if Sax were a

weaker species, he might fall into the trap of possibilities; imagined futures laid out before him with a single, simple *yes* dividing their brilliant promise from his miserable present.

"There is no other answer," Sax says. "I will not betray her."

Again the nod. This time, though, Kah's motion is joined by a whirring noise from beyond the cell. The sound of micro-jets pulsing up, sending their cargo this way. Sax has sent the signal, and now he's going to see what the Chorus cares to do in response. Maybe they slaughter him here. More likely the Chorus will use the opportunity; a staged execution for all the galaxy to see. It's how traitors ought to be dealt with.

Sax has seen plenty of them himself. And cheered along with the rest of the Vincere when those dissidents were brought to fatal justice.

Kah steps across the room, behind Sax, as a pair of Flaum guards enter through the opening Kah's been glancing toward this entire time. These aren't average Flaum, small furry creatures with a penchant for squeaky conversation. No, these are armored in Chorus blue, carrying assault miners in their hands with secondary weapons attached around their waists. They stare at Sax with fierce focus that impresses the Oratus. If the average Vincere Flaum possessed this level of grit, it's possible the Oratus wouldn't be needed at all.

"So you *are* bringing me dinner," Sax hisses anyway, because it's more fun to keep the prey unbalanced.

"Quiet," Kah hisses slow from behind Sax. "This isn't time for games."

And when what's following the Flaum, when the source of those micro-jets, slides into the room, Sax can only agree.

"What was it like?" I ask Malo later, when it seems like the two of us will go uninterrupted for a brief speck of time. "With Ignos, and the Sevora?"

Malo's slow in answering that question and I understand why—back when I'd been the only one with a Sevora in my mind, even coming up with the words to describe how it feels to have something else inside you was a struggle. And that's when Ignos was trying to help me.

"At first it was like this," Malo says, and he's looking away from me, over towards the wall, but he's not really seeing the cold steel there either. "I woke up in a strange room with Flaum coming and going. I noticed their badges right away, and knew I'd been taken."

The furry Sevora captives had made sure Malo was healthy, to some degree, before doing anything else. Malo expected to be taken right away, but instead they ran him through strange machines. With miners and guards, Sevora scientists had poked and prodded Malo until, one morning, a green-shaded Whelk oozed into his room and told him it was time.

"I wanted to fight, but Kaishi, there was nothing I could do," Malo says, his fists clasping and releasing. "Every time I tried to do something they didn't order, they'd shoot me. I spent a lot of time stunned, waiting to die."

That's not what happened, though. Instead, the Sevora hustled Malo off to one of the big birthing centers, where rectangular pools full of dark ink swirled as lines of captive species waited to receive their Sevora hosts under heavy guard. The Flaum took Malo to one end, to a smaller pool with no line.

"Meant for special Sevora, or so they told me," Malo continues. "I went right up to the edge and looked over, said a prayer, and with their miners aiming at my back, stepped in."

The first touch of a Sevora on the mind is like the fading remnants of a dream—something else present in your consciousness, something that isn't quite real. Unlike the dream, though, the Sevora never go away. With me, I could feel Ignos' thoughts, its frustration as it tried and failed to crack my neural code and take complete control of my body. With Malo, the loss of himself was almost instant.

"As if I was a series of locks, and I could feel it picking me apart one by one," Malo says. "My arms, fingers, legs, then my eyes and mouth. Then I was a visitor in myself."

I want to continue, because I can tell that Malo's still broken from that experience and I want to fix him. Or at least try. When my room's door opens, though, and Viera's there, her face tells us our time is up.

"Can you walk?" Viera says to me.

"I think so?"

"Good, because Kolas says it's time to say goodbye."

Getting out of the sponge bed is my first big test. After fighting my way onto and off of the Sevora homeworld, into and then through an entire seed ship, it's disconcerting to try and stand only to fall over when my legs fail to balance. Malo catches me, holds me steady while Lan watches from the entry.

"We'll wait for you," the Oratus says. "Take the time you need."

"Suppose their sense of urgency is gone now that the Sevora are dead," Malo says.

Maybe, but I get a different feeling from the lingering stare Lan gives me before she leaves. I was the one, after all, who killed her pair. Who drove a metal shaft through the Sevora that'd taken up residence in Gar's mind. I don't feel hate from Lan, but then, I don't feel much of anything from her.

"What is an Oratus like when they lose their pair?" I ask Malo as we make our way from my room.

"I think they'd be like us," Malo says. "When we lose someone we love."

We're in a medical wing, as there are plenty of other rooms near mine whose occupants are making a variety of groaning, gasping, or chittering noises. Drones flit and wheel across the floor, trundling into and out of those same rooms, with a sharper shout or sudden, happy sigh as evidence of their work. Outside of each chamber, covering the spaces between, are large panels showing names and colored bars with values for things I don't understand.

I look at mine, and it's all blank. Only my name, in luminous green, sits at the top. All of my bars are deep black and gray. Zeros abound. According to this thing, I'm dead.

"Won't be like that for the next one," says a gravel-squeak behind me, and we turn to see an older Flaum looking around us to my screen. "We learned a lot about humans from the three of you. All about your insides, how they're juicy. Plenty of things would be happy to have you for a snack."

"Uh, thanks?" I offer as Malo recoils. "Who are you?"

"Your doctor, such as it is," the Flaum, who's wearing a soft blue mask around his fur, shrugs. "All I'm here for is to make sure the robots keep things on schedule, lend a hand if one of'em loses their minds."

"Robots can lose their minds?"

"They can rot like anything else," the Flaum says. "Throw a new situation at them, like you, and they'll have no idea what to do. So I step in, teach'em that you're a carbon-based creature and need some good old red blood to survive."

I've already thanked the Flaum, so the best I can think of to do is give the creature a nod. The Flaum, though, doesn't seem to want to stop and reaches out with his clawed hand, tracing a line across my stomach and up towards my heart until I grab the offending limb and hold it.

"Sorry," the Flaum says, looking at his trapped hand. "Just remembering where we fixed you. The new parts should be better than your old ones. You're welcome."

Before I can respond, the Flaum slips his hand free of mine, wheels to another room and stomps away, leaving Malo and I staring after him.

"Better than the old ones?" I ask Malo, hoping the Charre warrior paid attention when the Flaum was fixing me.

"Like Ferrolite said, they grew everything," Malo looks away, shakes his head. "I don't understand how, or what happened, but they said you were dead and now you're back."

I could press him for more, but there's pain in those eyes, frustration. I know it too—ignorance breeds anger, despair, and worse. So I drop it, resolve to ask Ferrolite later, or maybe T'Oli. The Ooblot seems like it would know about this.

We leave the medical wing through what appears to be a sheet of glass, one that shimmers as we approach and, when we walk through, leaves my skin, mouth, and eyes with a tingling feeling.

"You get used to it," Malo says as we continue on. "They're everywhere on the ship. T'Oli calls them purifiers, says they keep us all from infecting everyone else."

One more miracle to add to the list.

"If we can get things like this, the Chorus might not be that bad," I say slow. "I don't trust the Amigga, but this would save so many lives. Every summer, we lose so many to sickness."

Malo doesn't reply as we walk down the long hallway. It's wide and crowded with passing drones and myriad species. While the Sevora leaned into Flaum and Whelk, species I assume they could control, maybe even breed with little effort, the Vincere are a more diverse bunch. Groups of trunk-like Teven pass by, their carapaces ornamented with all sorts of designs, and larger, rock-like monsters roam, carrying materials or sporting large harnesses covered in what look like tools.

Noises abound too—from overhead commands issued in all manner of slang to general chatter to the hissing, whooshing of doors, machines, and generators hidden behind wall panels around us.

I'd thought Damantum, the capitol of my chosen people and home to teeming thousands with their markets, cookfires, fights and celebrations, was noisy. Here, though, in the metal confines of Kolas' ship, the sound presses around me, close, constant, compressing.

Before long, a floating drone not much larger than my head whips out in front of us, a fire-blue light glowing on its top. It darts our way fast enough for Malo to slide himself in front of me, only for the drone to hover to a sudden stop a centimeters away from Malo's nose.

I look at the machine over Malo's shoulder as it runs its light across our faces.

"Kaishi, Malo," the drone says our names, munching over each syllable in its monotone. "You're requested on the funeral deck."

"That's where we're going," Malo says.

"I'm here to make sure you go the right way," the drone replies. "Follow me, please."

"Apparently I'm too slow," I whisper to Malo as we pick up the pace, shuffling after the drone.

"It's my fault," Malo says. "We should have been going faster from the start. I just didn't want to rush you."

"It's not like Gar is going anywhere."

Malo gives me a look that says he's not a fan of casual conversation about the dead, but at this point, with what I've been through, politeness is not at the top of my agenda. Gar, through the Sevora taking his mind, did try to kill me, after all.

The drone doesn't take any detours or linger in front of other diversions, instead shuttling us to the rear of the ship, where a lift whose doors are coated in a mournful blue-black and speckled with stars awaits. Past the lift, our grand corridor closes in on a huge set of sealed, thick slabs plastered over with alarming signs beneath inset gold lettering claiming the engines lie beyond.

"Funeral Deck," Malo reads the control panel outside the lift. "Guess this is the place."

"Thanks, uh, robot," I say to the drone, which gives a quick beep and blasts away, no doubt motoring to some other lost souls.

The lift pushes us a short way up, and the doors open into the quietest place I've been on the ship. The Funeral Deck isn't a large space; Lan and Kolas hunch with their three-meter height, but it's wide enough to hold the members for Gar's last goodbye.

What the Funeral Deck does have, though, is a somber wonder. All of the panels—floors and walls—are painted over in deep blues, so close to black that the difference shows like a secret: subtle, slight. Whirling across these panels are faded yellow swirls, spinning collections of starbursts tracing out long patterns around us.

Viera's already here, and her eyes light up with a suppressed smile when she notices we've arrived to give her some company amid the two Oratus and a smattering of other species, all of which are decked out in uniforms and gear that make my simple hospital shift seem small. Guess being the envoy for humanity still can't get me a good outfit.

Beyond the crowd stands the real highlight; a shielded window into sparkling space itself. Along the window's bottom edge, a white-orange glow flickers, a light whose origin perplexes me until Viera whispers that it's the engines, that she'd stood staring at it, brows raised in an unasked question, until Kolas told her.

"Thanks for sparing me the question," I reply.

"Everyone's here?" Kolas glances around the chamber, lingers his imposing, scarred, rust-colored visage on us for a long moment. "Then begin."

There's no hint as to who Kolas is talking to; nobody

jumps to attention, there's no affirmative or beep of acknowledgment, but from the way everyone starts to move, I gather Kolas pulled some trigger.

I don't know what an Oratus funeral entails, and given the ferocity with which the creatures fight, I have to believe there's plenty of these that go on without bodies of any kind to say goodbye to. On Earth, in Damantum or the jungle, we would bury or burn those who fell, depending on time and ceremony.

Without any guide, I follow what the Oratus and others do. First, we crowd up to the window, staying silent. Lan stands apart in the center, with Kolas cloaking her and using his bulk to guarantee her space. We line up on their right. Lan's not crying—if Oratus are even capable of such things —instead, she stares ahead resolute.

Outside, there's nothing to look at except the black. Then a small white-silver shape drifts into view. It doesn't take a close-up analysis to figure that it's Gar. The Oratus is tiny from this far away, but clear. Someone's coated Gar's scales in the white, and his claws have been clasped in front of his body, his talons folded up and in. His tail, though, is free and frozen in the vacuum.

Words don't come. Silence sits heavy as we all watch the figure, until some timer hits its mark and the ship's engines flare. All of a sudden the low, steady white-orange burns into a galvanized alabaster blaze that engulfs most of what we can see, Gar included.

Except, no. The Oratus is there. First as a black outline in the white nova, then as a fluorescent rainbow of color. Gar's glow hollows out its own place in the engine wash, like a star against a monotone sky.

The engines die as suddenly as they come up, and Gar's luminescence has its own stage to shine on. His body blinks between shades, crossing from deep pink to bright red to blue and back again, and as it does so, Gar's shape diffuses and spreads. A cloud that gradually grows and dims, floating away into eternity.

"For all the miracles they have," Viera says back in my room. "That was the most impressive thing I've seen yet. When I go, that's the kind of send-off I want."

"If I can make it happen, I will," I say, without adding that I'd want the same for myself.

"You think I'll go before you?" Viera's leaning against the wall near my door, as if she's wanting to ditch out at the nearest moment. Malo's back at his usual post next to the great red sponge. "Lots more people want your head than mine."

"Who wants my head? The Sevora are all dead."

"Just wait," Viera says. "Once word gets out you're the Amigga's new favorite, somebody's going to want you gone."

"Then they'll be disappointed." Malo has his steadiness back.

On the seed ship, I'd thought him broken, but it seems like he might come out of this intact.

"Malo," I interject. Then stop. Why come out against that? Why chide my friend for being protective? "Thank you."

Viera's nodding too. "I don't like conceding points to a Charre, but Malo's right. We've already taken on an entire species and won, Kaishi. Anyone that comes after us, they'll lose."

Though with the Sevora gone, I'm not sure who that's going to be.

. . .

"You didn't have a choice." Lan meets me in the ship's mess hall, a wide space where the floor is dotted with white splotches that rise up to accommodate whomever moves over them. "Gar died fighting."

It's crowded in here; everyone getting their last shot at nutrient goop and other food before Kolas' leap countdown hits zero. By my guess we have about an hour, which I hope is enough time to talk with Lan before folding the galaxy in two makes mash of my insides.

Father always made the effort to talk, to reach out to any member of our tribe that dealt with loss. He would bring gifts to their home, promise help collecting a harvest or cooking their meals if that was necessary. The acts were small, but I always caught the appreciation on those faces when they saw Father afterwards.

I also saw Father himself, how he seemed more full, more sure of his choices after making peace.

But what Lan says confuses me. Gar did die fighting, but it was me the Oratus was going after, and I don't think Lan means...

"The Sevora," Lan continues, maybe realizing that I'm not following. "Gar would have resisted every attempt by the Sevora to control his body. The only reason you survived was because the Sevora hadn't won. Not that early."

I'm a little offended that Lan doesn't think I could win that fight, but she's probably right, and I'm here to offer support, not talk up my own combat prowess.

"I'm still sorry, Lan. If there had been another way, I would have tried it."

Lan hisses, and I'm not sure if it's a laugh or a sigh. "Oratus are weapons. We are designed to fight until we break. It's always a matter of when, not if."

"Like all of us."

Lan nods, then cocks her head to the side, fixing me in her left eye. "Do you know how an Oratus finds their pair?" Lan says, her yellow iris sharp against her glittering emerald scales.

I shake my head and Lan launches into a story that's as much catharsis as anything. I listen, though, because it's also fascinating: there's a stretch of land on a planet, hatcheries, and only those Oratus that make it to the top of a mountain together find their way to the Vincere. Gar and Lan sliced and slashed their way through a jungle, up that mountain and through a ruined base to make it there.

"He chose my name, as I chose his," Lan says. "Everything I am, he made. Everything he was, came from me."

"What will you do now?"

"Serving the Vincere is everything I know," Lan replies. "Oratus are rarely freed from that obligation, the debt we owe the Amigga for our lives."

"So you'll stay here, with Kolas?"

"For now."

Lan shoves the rest of the nutrient goop in her mouth, rises and gives me a silent goodbye with her eyes. The countdown continues in the background, and it's getting low enough now, so I wave Malo over—I asked him to let me have this moment with Lan alone—and my friend helps me back to my room, where we set ourselves up for the leap.

Coreward. To the Chorus.

It's hard to get around if you have no limbs at all. Amigga, being large sensory orbs with acidic skin, have no legs, no arms, no way to propel themselves from place to place without the assistance of some sort of device or unlucky species. Sax isn't sure if Amigga evolved or modified themselves to be like this, or if they subsisted on their own planet through their ability to grow and intertwine themselves into just about anything. Go to a space station run by an Amigga, and you'd find the creature at the center, its nerve tissue wrapped around every system keeping the station running.

Go to the center of the Chorus and you'd find the First Chair, the Amigga dictating what comes up for discussion, which species get annihilated, and what to do with traitors like Sax.

The First Chair has an exoskeleton worthy of its position: nine black-gold rings loop around its body from a few millimeters away. Those spaced rings are matched by a set pressed against the First Chair's skin, ones Sax guesses provide the magnetic latch keeping the outer rings in place.

Those outer bands aren't for show either—fixed to them are a series of micro-jets keeping the creature aloft, and, if Sax is guessing right, pin-point miners. As if the First Chair is a planet orbited by tiny, deadly moons.

The living array floats into the room behind its Flaum guards, moving slow enough for Sax to analyze, dissect, and dismiss the creature. The miners seem too small to pack enough power to kill Sax, and a single tail whip would interrupt the flow of those rings and send the mighty First Chair crashing to the floor. As is often the case, an impressive presentation hides a weak core.

The First Chair heads in front of Sax, stopping before the open hatch to the cell. Its whirling parts face the Oratus and Sax wishes the Amigga would give themselves mouths already, or at least eyes. Something to clue others in on what the Amigga might be thinking.

"Traitor," the First Chair's voice comes in hard, metallic. "Why have you failed your creators?"

Ah. So it's this line of inquiry. The Amigga: always hunting for easy answers to questions that don't have them.

"Because my creators failed me," Sax hisses.

"Did we? I thought we gave you everything; life, purpose, and all you needed for support."

"You gave me *your* purpose. You never let us find our own."

Sax is hissing these replies, but the words feel strange. Ever since meeting Rav in orbit above Solis, Sax has had to use a different sort of vocabulary. Speaking in terms not solely focused on killing, on destroying the enemy. Talking about things like purpose and reason is easier now than it was, but every sentence still tastes wrong coming off of Sax's tongue.

"Your own? Is that what this fighting is about?" the First

Chair says. "Your species trying to find a new reason for being? Why should a tool need a purpose greater than the one given it by its wielder?"

"Because our wielders are a collection of conceited monsters," Sax hisses.

The First Chair's bands whir faster, the little pieces zipping around the Amigga at blurring speed. "Clearly, if we allowed the Oratus to degrade this far, we *are* conceited. However, I would say it is you and your ripping claws that are the true monsters. The creatures that come in the night and tear apart families, civilizations. That was your purpose, Oratus. To be a monster." The Amigga floats to the side, circling Sax. "Even the changes you've elected to make for yourself are in line with our designs—metal claws? Patches of steel armor in your scales?"

Sax doesn't bother answering. He's waiting, watching, hoping the First Chair gets so involved in its own speech that it floats within range of Sax's tail. One slap at the Chorus leader would be a good way to go out.

"You won't give Kah any answers about your friends, which I understand," the First Chair continues. "But perhaps you can solve a riddle for me. One that's bothered us since the very first iteration of your species, when we found it impossible to keep some small part of your Oratus blood from turning towards independence. We devised countless ways to suppress that urge, from more genetic editing to Solis itself and the way the Vincere operates, and yet here it rises again. What, this time, prompted your awakening?"

The First Chair's stopped moving, hanging behind on Sax's left. Not seeing the Amigga makes the answer easier, as if Sax is confessing to the dark.

"*Cobalt.* A space station where we found our replacements. Familiars with our likeness being made with the intent to overtake us, to eliminate us." Sax makes sure to say this loud—not that he thinks Kah or the Flaum guards might turn traitor, but he may as well give them a chance. "The Amigga there wanted us to die."

"And your response to this was to kill the creature and assume all of us were on its side?"

"Weren't you? Aren't you?"

The First Chair hesitates. Sax considers it a minor victory that the creature is thinking about what the Oratus said. Coming up with a response an Amigga doesn't anticipate is always a win.

"Look at the Flaum that work with me," the First Chair continues, its silver tone continuing to sound like a status alert from a dying ship. "Their species is inferior to yours in most respects. Yet, they still serve. Through the galaxy, species we have made or modified survive. We do not eradicate those who we pass on the path to the perfect species, and we will not start with the Oratus."

"I'm thin on trust at the moment."

The First Chair moves again, this time coming around Sax's right side. There's a point, when the Amigga gets past Sax's right talon, when it's just close enough to...

There. Sax has little momentum, nothing to push off of, but he still leans, still whips with his tail and cracks it from left to right. Those gravity rings pull back, fighting to keep Sax positioned in place, but the Oratus is strong and he gets movement. His tail arcs towards the First Chair's spinning bands, and hits nothing.

The Amigga jolts itself above the strike as all of its bands pause for a hot second and its array of micro-jets shoves the Amigga up at once. Without another pause, the rings run back into their rotation, keeping the First Chair at its newer, higher level.

The Flaum guards whip their miners towards the Oratus, but at a command from the First Chair, the furry critters hold their fire.

"A program," the First Chair says. "Technology even faster than you, Oratus. We've been hesitant to go back to such methods, seeing as computers are easier to steal than the minds of loyal servants, but they are useful." The Amigga continues its orbit, stopping again in front of Sax's face. "You, Oratus, continue to be a failure. The only insight you've provided me is that, as is ever the case, your species does not survive contact with fresh ideas. You are weapons, nothing more."

"At least I'm not you," Sax rasps.

The Amigga lowers itself to the floor. "Yes. Thank goodness for that."

A snide dismissal. The First Chair still isn't that far away, so Sax tries again. Pushes against those rings and lunges with his claws, with his mouth, and this time the First Chair doesn't flinch away. Doesn't even move as Sax manages to break the ring's hold enough for a swipe.

The attack never hits. Instead, one of the miner-covered rings lets loose a precise, small stunning bolt that strikes Sax's swinging mid-claw. The shot robs Sax's arm of its strength, its energy, and allows the gravity ring binding it to pull Sax's arm back. The Oratus didn't get close to hitting his target.

"Another try?" the First Chair says.

"Persistence is a virtue," Sax manages a hiss, venting his frustration in the words.

"Stupidity, however, is not. Wasting your energy on the impossible is a poor choice."

"Then why are you trying to convince me to turn?"

The Amigga floats silent for a moment, rings twirling. "You make your first good point, Oratus. I thank you for your honesty." The First Chair rotates back towards the door. "Kah, take the traitor and perform the standard execution. It seems we must remind the galaxy, again, what happens when some choose to refuse our guidance."

Sax watches the First Chair float away, leave the room with those two Flaum guards trailing it. Then his limbs tighten, the rings pressing his body close together until Sax feels like he's going to pop. His vents barely have enough space to squeeze in air, and his arms and legs are going numb as blood fails to get through. The Oratus sinks, until Sax hovers a millimeter above his hatch.

"Guess you didn't give the First Chair the answer it was looking for," Kah hisses, and as the mirrored Oratus stalks by Sax, a brighter, red ring glows around Kah's right foreclaw. As Kah walks, Sax begins to float after him, tied to that glowing ring. "Too bad. Your record says you're good."

"I beat you." Sax's voice comes out high, almost yipping with the compression.

"But you're going to die anyway," Kah replies. "And everyone's going to see it."

From the bridge, where Kolas has called us to watch the approach to a world he calls Aspicis, a great green ball fills in the void. It's a deeper, darker emerald than the bright leafy colors Earth shows off from space, and it's backlit by a shock-white star that, whether by Kolas' intended approach or sheer luck, hangs just behind Aspicis, haloing the planet in a holy glow.

"Beautiful," I say.

Our platform extends in a thick line over a deep-cut U shape, inside which bunches of Flaum and Teven work at terminals or circle around projections displaying what look like maps of the galaxy or sections of the ship, *Nunilite*, that we're aboard. It's a bustle of activity that gets no interruption from the approach to Aspicis.

I suppose once you've seen a thousand worlds from space, the next one isn't all that remarkable.

"It is beautiful," Ferrolite states. The Amigga is floating off to my left. Absent during Gar's funeral, I'd forgotten the Amigga existed, but now that we're arriving at its home, it makes sense Ferrolite would be here to brag. "What you're looking at is the most magnificent world in the galaxy, home to the center of progress, of civilization."

"For you, maybe," Viera cuts in.

"For your species as well," Ferrolite replies, and it's impossible to tell if it reads Viera's reply as an insult. "Once you join the Chorus, everything we decide will chart your path as well as ours. The benefits we provide will be yours."

"So will the costs."

I hold myself back from intervening. Viera's being who she is, and while nobody makes a move, and the chatter from the others on the bridge continues, I think Kolas is listening to the exchange just as Malo and I are. Though if Viera oversteps her bounds, I don't think the Oratus would take her side.

"Your civilization, compared to the rest of the galaxy, is primitive," Ferrolite's monotone voice sticks to its low, mechanical pitch. "Everything your society uses, depends on, and desires will be improved by joining the Chorus. Even if we call on humanity to assist in a larger endeavor, its costs will be negligible next to the gains your people reap from our relationship."

"We keep hearing that." Viera folds her arms. She wants to lean on something, no doubt, but there's nothing that can give her that dismissive slouch on the bridge. "The Sevora said the same thing. Didn't deliver."

"Human, without us, you will fall prey to some other species. Refuse us, and the Chorus will not protect you next time."

Ferrolite floats forward after the words, ending the argument. I'm not sad about that, as Viera wasn't going to get us anything more than a bad reputation, and besides, we're drawing closer to Aspicis and I'd rather watch what's going on outside.

"She's going to get us killed," Malo whispers to me.

"If a bit of chaff gets the Amigga angry, humanity won't last long anyway." I nod forward, out beyond the massive windshield, signaling to Malo I have other things on my mind.

Like the collage of starships appearing out of the black folds of space in front of us. From the far distance, I couldn't see them at all. Great ovals and tiny slivers dancing and darting around. Others look like skeletal spheres, hanging around Aspicis with wide bars connecting focal points. As we get closer, colors burst out too—these aren't the common gray-black I've seen elsewhere, but painted in reds, blues, and golds.

"The Chorus' Cradle," Kolas announces as we begin to pass by the outer ranks of the ships. "If the Vincere is the hammer of the galaxy, then this is its shield. These ships are the outer band, and the spheres the wall to any threat. Aspicis herself lies nestled within, a reward only for loyal visitors."

"Every color shows the ship's proper placement in a fleet," Ferrolite says. "Align every one in a parade formation and you will have the Chorus colors, leading, of course, with our chosen blue."

"Who are you parading for, if the whole galaxy is yours already?" Viera asks, refusing to cut the venom out of her voice.

"Discipline is never a bad thing to encourage," Kolas answers, forestalling any comeback from the Amigga and getting another positive point from me. I'm starting to see why Kolas is running this ship, this fleet. "Reinforcing a ship's proper position, how to pilot in a formation, show our soldiers and our commanders that we are not a wild force but a deliberate tool."

Viera, for once, holds her tongue at the massive Oratus' response, and that's without Kolas flashing a single razor tooth.

After we pass by most of the fleet, our ship slides beneath one of the spherical structures with its gold shading. I notice the large turrets dotting the ship twist and track us along our route. The Cradle isn't much for trust, apparently. When I point it out, Ferrolite tells me each of these structures scan incoming ships, looking for abnormalities. Anything suspicious, and they'll attempt to disable the ship for a closer inspection.

"Abnormalities?" I ask, thinking we, humans, might be one.

"Mass above normal," Ferrolite says, taking over guide duties as Kolas strides away from us to direct his staff from the end of the platform. "High power usage. Weapons or shields ready. More than a few have attempted to attack Aspicis, including the Sevora. We will not be surprised."

Once we're past the Cradle's outskirts, we trace an orbit around the planet, falling into a line of other ships, most smaller than ours, as we cruise above Aspicis' dark side and head towards the light. Ferrolite breaks into a long digression about the planet, explaining its long night and day transitions, and how few people are cleared to land on the planet itself.

"So why are all these ships here?" I ask. "If nobody's allowed down on the surface?"

"There are runners," Ferrolite replies. "Watch."

As we round the planet's edge, and as a filter drops over the massive viewing shield to blunt the brightness of the white star, it's easy to see the swarms of small craft shooting up and down from Aspicis' surface. The line of ships we're in comes to a congregation around what looks like a large, square stake rising from the ground all the way out into space.

The runners swarm these ships, latching onto them and breaking away minutes later or longer. Once they've all detached, the bigger ships, their missions complete, burst their engines to life and glide away from the planet, through an open, blue-sphere-lined section of the Cradle.

"So this is all cargo?"

"Cargo, and also those people called to the Chorus or that happen to live on Aspicis," Ferrolite says. "Information and technology. All of it passes through here. As will you."

The way Ferrolite says 'you' has me stick to the word. The Amigga didn't say all of us, didn't say the three of us.

"Viera and Malo are coming with me." There's no argument on that. I'm not leaving them, and I doubt either would agree to me vanishing on an Amigga ship alone.

"You are the envoy for your species, not them," Ferrolite counters. "We cannot allow unnecessary visitors on Aspicis. Security demands it."

"My security," Viera says. "Demands I stay with my Empress."

"Agreed," Malo echoes. "We will not leave her."

I stare at Ferrolite. The Amigga may not have eyes, but it's clearly seeing everything, so it ought to know I have no intention of leaving my friends.

"This will... require a conversation," Ferrolite replies. "We want humanity's support, of course. But we don't want to compromise the safety of our most valued members."

"You just finished telling us how primitive we are," I say. "Now you're going to claim we're a threat? Choose one, Ferrolite, but the only way you're getting us to your planet is as a group."

Ferrolite hovers. Kolas twists, his red-black eyes twinkling as he glances our way. Is that a quiet laugh I'm seeing in his ridged face? Maybe Kolas likes seeing someone stand up to the Amigga. Maybe he's not entirely under their control.

"I will see what can be done," Ferrolite states. "Regardless, we are nearing the connection point. You should go and get your things. Our ferry will be here soon."

As if I have anything to bring along. Malo and Viera match my expression with shrugs; none of us have weapons, or any other possessions beyond the clothes on our backs, and even those are tailored outfits designed for Flaum. Pearl-green vests and pants. No masks this time, and no robes either—apparently we're going in front of an audience that cares about presentation.

After Ferrolite leaves, Kolas stomps over in front of us, his heavy breathing from the vents lining his long torso drawing our attention his way.

"What happens next will be a momentous event for your species," Kolas says slow and deep, like a rumbling volcano. "But do not lose yourself in what the Chorus tells you. The Amigga drive civilization and the galaxy forward, yes, but they do so with their own plan. Their own goals. Do not lose sight of what makes your species unique."

"What do you mean?" I reply. "I thought we were joining a group?"

Kolas flicks a claw back towards the Flaum manning the various stations on the bridge. "You are. And you will get many things for doing so. When the Amigga find a place for you, however, be wary of becoming only that and nothing else."

"Like you?" Viera, again. "The Oratus? You sound like you're warning us against doing this at all."

Kolas regards Viera with a melting look. The kind that

says he's so far over and above Viera that it's an honor he's even considering her words. "The Cycles are covered in dead cultures. Would those same species have died without the Chorus, destroyed themselves in pathetic wars or been drowned by the Sevora? I cannot say, but I know most did not truly survive either. Maybe humanity is different."

That seems to be the end of his warning, as Kolas turns back to his command and hisses out orders to bring the ship into a blank section of space. As the cruiser turns, grass-green lights blink up out of nowhere, forming a path through the void. At first I'm confused about what they are, but as the lights move and form up, I realize they're tiny ships, directing Kolas' pilots where to go.

"C'mon, Empress," Viera says. "Time to go meet our new overlords."

I grab one last look at Aspicis' star as we go from the bridge—it's not the same color as Ignos, but I hope the god can see his way through to us anyway.

I have a feeling we'll need all the help we can get.

The Chorus shuttle is minimal—no bridge, only a simple set of white couches that rise from the floor to meet us as we settle in. Viera, Malo, myself, T'Oli and Ferrolite, who pauses a moment when it sees the Ooblot with us as well. The blob had been spending its time scurrying around the cruiser, digging into everything it could learn after spending most of its existence trapped beneath the Sevora sewers.

"T'Oli's my assistant," I say, going with the story we agreed upon. "None of us know how things work here, so T'Oli's going to keep us out of trouble."

"This was not approved," Ferrolite grumbles.

"Humans like to change our deals."

"I'm starting to see that."

The Amigga, though, doesn't protest any further and instead settles into its own side, still floating along in its microjet-boosted shell. I'm waiting for the airlock door to close, but it doesn't. A second later, Lan ducks through it, her large form taking up almost a third of the shuttle's space by herself.

"You're coming too?" Viera can't help but ask.

"There is something on Aspicis I need to do." Lan sits across from us, closes her eyes, and appears to fall asleep.

Once the Oratus is settled, the shuttle goes into a series of swift changes; the airlock shunts shut, the globe lights along the ceiling dim, and the hull around us fades to a near-translucent shade.

"Enjoy the descent," Ferrolite says as we disengage from the side of the *Nunilite*. "It's the most beautiful entry in the galaxy."

"I think you might be biased," Viera replies.

Ferrolite doesn't answer.

In fairness to the Amigga, Ferrolite isn't all wrong. As we drop beneath the packed lines of ships delivering and receiving cargo and passengers, the breathing room gives the giant bulk of Aspicis time to show itself off. And, set against that deep green, the tower, which Ferrolite labels the Meridia, makes an imposing entrance.

Our shuttle, unlike plenty of others rocketing towards the surface, aims for the Meridia's top. Unlike, say, the mirrored surfaces of the Sevora buildings or the stone roofs of our temples, the Amigga crown their achievement with a glittering red-orange spectacle.

Sashes of light layer, looping from one side of the Meridia's top to the other, folding between each other and dancing across the broad black space. Our shuttle coasts towards it, and as we do, the sashes change color, shifting to a green-blue shade that reminds me of seaside shallows back on Earth.

"Amigga are capable of art too," Ferrolite says. "I know you think we're a brutal species, but look at this and tell me that we can't make beautiful things."

"What does it mean?" Malo asks as the ribbons of light swoop around us.

"The changing shape of the galaxy," Ferrolite replies. "Every color, every ribbon is another part of our collective. Even as our nature changes, we stay connected to one another. A bond that cannot be broken. One you are joining."

As a spectacle, it's mesmerizing. The white light of Aspicis' star gives the sashes a shine that makes them shimmer like jewels. And yet. The familiars on *Cobalt* could be beautiful too, that didn't mean they were good.

So why am I doing this? Why did I volunteer if I don't trust the Amigga to do the right thing?

Because if I don't, they'll destroy humanity until someone does what they want.

"This is your home?" I ask Ferrolite as the shuttle heads further down the Meridia and the wonder work disappears behind us. "This planet?"

"*My* home? Yes. Our species? No." Ferrolite pauses. "Our home planet is long since destroyed. Too many accidents, too many costs extracted in pursuit of better things. Aspicis, though, is the result of those lessons. It is verdant, and every part of it produces what we need. So in that sense, Aspicis is our home. One we've built to our desires."

"You wanted a giant metal stick jutting out from its surface?" Viera asks.

"The Meridia is necessary."

Ferrolite tells us why in stages. The first comes when the shuttle lands, when we're unloaded into a tight, blue-metal docking bay with space only for one more of the craft. Unlike *Cobalt*, where a single familiar greeted our wondering selves as we left the shuttle, Ferrolite's assembled a quartet of Flaum guards to wait for us. They're all sporting crisp sea-blue uniforms, with a single lava-red circle etched on their chests. Each one carries a miner in their hands, with a smaller one on a belt. They stare at us without a shred of surprise or the skittering nervousness I'm used to with the furry creatures.

"This is some welcome you have for new friends," I say to Ferrolite as we head down the ramp.

The Amigga's taken the front position, gliding through the air on its microjets and seeming confident we'll follow. We do, and I pull myself in front of Malo when he tries to take a guardian's leading role for our little group. If this disembarking is going to be the Chorus' first true impression of humanity's envoy, it's not going to be one of me hunkering down behind Malo's back. T'Oli, though, takes its spot on my shoulders, ready to swamp down and harden into armor at the slightest threat.

I'm willing to sacrifice a little protection for ceremony, not all of it.

"I don't want you to feel unwelcome," Ferrolite replies. "It's been too long since we've inducted a new species. There should be some celebration."

"If this is their idea of a celebration, maybe they *can* learn something from us," Viera whispers.

Ferrolite has us form up between the guards, and they escort us from the quiet docking bay. We're weaponless and wearing soft-padded shoes made from flexible gel that molded to our feet back on the *Nunilite*. I still have, though, my emerald necklace. Malo has his tattoos. Viera, well, Viera has her attitude. We're about as ready as we can be when we reach the end of the docking bay and a pair of interlocking circular doors spin themselves loose from each other to let us inside the Meridia.

I'm expecting something sparse and metal. Efficient and clean like the Vincere ships. What I get, though, has me pausing in a breath-stealing gasp that Ferrolite probably expects. The first word that comes to mind is color—the space is awash with it, a glitz that, after a moment, I track to a hanging piece of colorized carapace. At least, that's what I assume the thing is—a shell larger than me that hangs on a pair of translucent bars descending from the ceiling. Each part of the shell, like a beehive's honeycomb, is filled with a different color that warps the light streaming through it from a mottled set of globes in the ceiling. The outcome is dazzling, and if that was everything, it would serve to redefine my expectations for the Chorus.

But no. What I'm looking at isn't a hallway, it's an entry into a wide circle, and beyond that hanging shell there are displays, screens and objects housed within floating prisms of glass. Wide terminals show cascading scenes of wonders —blue mountains, shifting tornadoes of yellow dust, a volcano spitting huge sheets of ice high into the sky—that I want to stare and watch forever.

Weaving their way among these displays are more Amigga, along with scattered other species all in various degrees of finery. A few throw glances our way—it's hard to tell with the Amigga, though some I see have those eye-like cameras on their floating suits—and freeze for a moment, trying to place us in their galactic lexicon.

I try to give them a smile. Try to look calm, and not as overwhelmed as I feel.

"I take it all back," Viera says. "This is amazing."

"I know." I'm struggling to fit the wondrous ensemble— even the air carries with it whiffs of tantalizing spice—into what I know about the Amigga, and failing. "I don't understand how the thing that created *Cobalt* could do this."

Ferrolite, hovering in front of us, rotates around until what I consider its front faces me with its onslaught of wrinkling, massed skin. "Surely every human isn't alike?" Ferrolite quivers for a moment. "You haven't developed a hive mind, have you?"

"I don't know what that is?"

"They haven't," T'Oli answers for me.

"Then you should understand." Ferrolite sounds a little relieved at the Ooblot's response. "Some Amigga prefer the strict simplicity of an austere station. The Chorus, though, wants to let the galaxy's unique creations display where its leaders can appreciate them."

"Like if you had a bunch of Charre tribal art hanging around the Vaos," Viera says. "Nothing like a little reminder of what you control."

But Viera's remarks can't sour what we see as we follow Ferrolite, along with our guards, around that circle. From the outside, the Meridia appeared massive, but it's only when I'm inside one of its levels that I understand just how big the structure has to be. We walk out of sight of the docking bay, following a path littered with glowing rocks, metal sculptures of creatures coated in what look like teeth, and what appears to be a huge, stuffed Fassoth set alongside a stretch of wall.

Every so often, on our left side, towards the center of the level, the circle breaks into small passages. Each one of these is marked by an overhang bearing a pair of numbers. First it's three and four, then five and six.

"Sections," Ferrolite says when I ask. "Every one of the dozen members of the Chorus has their own piece of the central chamber to call its own. If you wanted to visit with, say, Millinite, you would go along until you reached section ten."

"Which one is yours?" Malo asks.

"I'm not a part of the Chorus. At least, not yet." Ferrolite's statement drips with the same ambition I heard in Jakkan's voice, the same thing I heard when Jel spoke of our contribution to the Sevora, and what I felt from Ignos all those times it dove into its digressions about humanity's future.

"That's what you want us for, right?" Viera says. "Kaishi gives up humanity to the Chorus and Ferrolite gets its big bonus?"

One of the Flaum guards lets out a squeaking laugh at that, though the furry creature cuts it off quick when Ferrolite whirls around. "Achieving a spot on the Chorus is about more than simple accomplishment. You must also have timing. Right now, there is no vacant seat. Only when one is empty, would I even have a chance."

"Guessing that happens when you kill one of them?"

I close my eyes for a second, shake my head. Viera's going to get us kicked out before we even join.

"Death does happen, but it's rare," Ferrolite doesn't seem offended. "More often, we get bored. As would you, I imagine, if you spent cycles doing the same thing. Amigga leave to pursue their interests, and others take their place."

Ferrolite resumes the tour and I take the moment to drop back next to Viera, ask her whether she really wants to annoy everyone we meet.

"Kaishi, just think of how good you'll look next to me," Viera offers.

"She has a point," Malo says. "There's a reason everyone on Earth hated the Lunare."

"Humans are so strange," T'Oli patters from my shoulders.

It's not until we reach section nine that Ferrolite brings our expedition to a halt. Unlike the other sections, though, this one has a massive creature in front of it, one I don't clearly see until we're standing within a couple of meters. It's as though the light—here, mostly white—bends away from its bulk, rendering it a shimmering distortion in my eyes rather than a solid object.

"We've arrived," Ferrolite announces to the thing when we come up. "I have the humans with me."

"The Chorus has other business now," the creature replies in a steady stream of hisses. I recognize the speech and glance at Malo, whose own set face says he knows that sound too. An Oratus, but one that looks far different from what we're used to. "You'll need to wait."

"This is a new species! They wish to join," Ferrolite protests. "You can't delay this."

"It's not my choice to make, nor yours," the Oratus replies. "The First Chair is well aware of your arrival, and the induction will happen when the Chorus is ready for it. Take them to a waiting room."

Ferrolite sputters out a curse in a language I don't know, then turns towards us. "Come with me. We'll find a space for you somewhere. It shouldn't be long."

Yet we don't manage more than three steps away before the Oratus hisses at our backs, "Ferrolite, the Chorus will see your new species now."

Viera cracks a laugh, and I suppress my own. I'd seen my father, I'd seen the Charre Emperor make similar snubs. A bit of playing with pride to make sure a player didn't forget their place. Ferrolite realizes it too, yells at the Flaum guards to leave, then tells us to follow it inside.

As we walk by the massive Oratus, I feel the hot breath coming from its vents. It's both gross and alien, a reminder that we're in a place I don't understand, about to join with a galactic empire that views humanity as one more jewel in its collection.

The lift doors open to a level Sax has never visited, but has seen many times before. In front of Sax, past Kah's shoulders, a central space with a broad white circle dominates most of the level. Across from these lift doors stand a second set of the same. On either side of the central chamber are tall glass walls adorned with black-painted cameras angling towards that white space in the middle. On the glass walls themselves, which Sax sees as Kah pulls him floating into the room, a broadcast is playing.

Cavignum, the giant power plant sitting on the edge of Aspicis' long night, glows orange on the walls. Skiffs and other ships, plenty with various flashing lights, surround the structure. Apparently it's still under an emergency guard after Sax and Bas tore through it. The sight blooms a bit of warmth in Sax's ring-restricted stomach; always satisfying to see a good result.

Kah places his prisoner over the white circle in the center of the room, and orients Sax towards the glass wall with more cameras, all of which sport small red lights aiming towards his face. Sax isn't one for chills, for nervous tingles, but being here, in this room where so many traitors to the Chorus have died, nonetheless gives him an uneasy twinge. The last type of demise an Oratus wants is one of summary execution. Not much honor in that.

A shape moves behind the broadcast and one of the panels, showing Aspicis' vine-covered surface to the right of Cavignum, blinks off as the glass wall's door opens and another Amigga floats out. Unlike the First Chair, this one has little more than a simple micro-jet platform and a harness with a quartet of small, nimble-looking three-fingered hands. It orients towards Sax and stares at the Oratus without speaking for a long moment.

"It's been quite some time since we've had one of you," the Amigga says, and unlike the First Chair's metallic tone, this one bears a scratchy whine, a voice chosen to annoy, to drive away conversations so its owner could return to wanted silence. "The smaller species fit better in the frame, but we'll make do. Set him down."

Kah hisses and does what the Amigga asks. Sax sinks to the white spot, which, when his talons touch it, flows up and around his legs. Around his tail. Latching and sealing Sax. Where, with the rings, Sax could lean from one direction to the other, could swish his tail, here Sax is kept rigid. The sole advantage? With the platform wrapping him, the rings loosen up. Let Sax breathe in full.

There's a reason for this. One Sax knows because he's seen this play out before—they'll want a confession, a public acknowledgment of how right the Chorus is. Most of the prisoners refuse to give it, seeing as their death is a certainty, but the Chorus always asks. Always gives its victims one more chance to plead for their lives.

"Looks like you were part of the Vincere," the Amigga says once Sax is secure. "Not sure why I'd think anything different, except the Vincere usually does a better job of killing its own traitors. Suicide missions and the like. Still, you're here now, which means you've got a choice. The First Chair told me you have one last chance to talk. Say everything you know about the enemy and we'll leave these cameras off. Have Kah here finish things quick and private. Let nobody know your shame."

Sax glares at the Amigga. The orb does nothing in response.

"Or, if you keep quiet, as that look says you're going to, then these cameras are coming on in a few minutes. They'll tap into the Priority Beam, sitting atop this tower, which will shoot out your pathetic death to every corner of the galaxy. All of the people you served with, every planet you went to, each of the species you threatened with those shiny claws of yours will know you're getting a traitor's fate."

The Amigga's words cut deeper than anything Kah, anything the First Chair said. It's how the Amigga presents Sax's situation; as a fact. A cold, hard reckoning that Sax will be remembered as nothing other than a failure, a waste of a soldier who couldn't even serve his own creators effectively. With those words comes a certain future, where Evva's force is squashed and all of the accomplishments Sax and Bas achieved with the Vincere are erased by their reckless choice to aim for something higher than their orders.

A traitor's fate.

Is Sax ready for that?

There's a flash on the glass that catches Sax's eye, a quick spray of words as the focus shifts on Cavignum. Tilts in closer to say repair crews are on site, that engineers are working through the software and other mechanisms to make sure operations are unaffected. The words shift again to warn that brief power outages may be necessary as Cavignum resets itself to proper working order.

"What're you thinking Oratus? Don't watch that. It doesn't matter to you." After the Amigga says the words, the broadcast dies away. "Tell me what you want. It'll be your last choice in this life, so make it carefully."

Yet Sax is distracted by the now-gone image of Cavignum. Those flashing lights and the panicked broadcast a sign that his struggles haven't been an utter waste. They *have* accomplished something, though the sum-total of the result is still being determined.

Nobaa and Engee, a pair of Teven engineers, ought to be inside Cavignum by now. Their reedy bodies would be making a beeline for the power station's command center, where they can, where they could, control access to the Meridia's outer locks. Kill the power, and Evva's team has a chance to enter. Black out security alerts, and reinforcements will be slow in coming. A chance that's only possible because Sax gave himself up.

That's why he's here. That's why Sax can accept his fate: he's not a traitor, he's a fighter. A believer in something better than the universe he was born into.

So Sax flashes his teeth at the Amigga and gives a long, low hiss. One that says exactly what's coming to the Amigga if, when, Sax breaks free from this white mold.

"Right. That's all I can expect from your type," the Amigga says, then laughs. One of its metal hands raises up, and from behind Sax another one of the doors opens and a pair of ever-present Flaum come out. Unlike the First Chair's guards, these have no weapons, no armor; a simple green-blue vest with the Chorus patch gives away their position. "Set the frame and let's get ready to show this Oratus out of his life."

The Amigga vanishes back through its door, and the Cavignum broadcast returns, while the two Flaum burst into chittering motion. Using small, handheld terminals, the Flaum circle around Sax and align the cameras, which chirp to acknowledge the commands as they shift their shots. The action is both boring and infinite, as Sax stews in the thoughts of his own demise while publicity needs stall it further and further.

Until, at last, the two Flaum form up again to Sax's right, between the glass wall doors, and announce their work complete.

"Then get back to your stations," the Amigga announces from its hideaway behind the glass wall. "Swap the Priority Beam from Cavignum to this room and let's go."

The Flaum disappear and, seven seconds later, the image on the glass in front of Sax changes. He sees himself now. Locked into the white platform, staring at the glass projection. The screen shifts, showing Sax from a variety of angles, and Sax is so immersed in his own dirty gray scales, in the scars and the metal plates, that he doesn't realize the Amigga's talking. Going on and on about how Sax is a traitor to this and that, an enemy of the Chorus and deserving of a slow and painful death.

Sax has heard it all before and tunes it out. Instead he focuses on the image, tries to look strong. Confident. There's every chance that Bas is seeing this. Every chance that this is going to be the last time she sees her pair.

He wants her to be proud. He wants her to remember him.

So when the Amigga pauses for a long second, Sax widens into a toothy grin. Brings in a deep breath.

"Stop. Cut the feed," the Amigga snaps. "Switch to the ground channel. The Meridia. It's the new priority."

And Sax is gone from the glass, replaced by a wide view of the Meridia's front entrance. A wide stone courtyard with pools of purple nutrient goop funneling up towards a set of steps, bordered by escalating ramps to accommodate other species, leading towards a large, sectioned blue gate. A giant, pressed in C is smashed into the center of the barrier, and it's right into the middle of it that the first shot strikes. A red bolt, too small and weak to do real damage, the shot burns a black mark into the Meridia's flagship doorway.

A signal.

The attack is starting.

Sax realizes the true significance of that first shot. It's not about making a mark; it's proving the Meridia's defenses are down. An energy assault should have been blocked by the Chorus' protections, should have been swallowed up by the barriers meant to keep what's about to happen from, well, happening.

If there's one advantage to getting a broadcast execution, it's that Sax has a perfect view as the assault begins. The Meridia's cameras pan wide to show a barrage of skiffs, large and small, converging. A number of Chorus guards, two dozen or so, turn and run at the sight of the force, retreating back towards the gateway. There's no weapons down here. No exterior defenses beyond the shields.

Why would there be? With the Vincere protecting the planet from orbit and the Chorus restricting the numbers of people allowed on Aspicis, assembling any force large enough to assault the Meridia should be impossible. Yet, here it is. Dozens and dozens of Flaum, scatterings of other species, and a trio of Oratus led by Evva's black and red form come streaking into the picture.

Blue flashes lance from the buzzing skiffs down at the fleeing Chorus forces, slamming into the Flaum and stunning them, leaving bodies lying on the white stones. Even as Sax himself feels the urge to lash out, to strike down the enemies, he understands why Evva isn't shooting to kill; those who serve the Chorus today might serve its replacement tomorrow. The only true enemies here are the Amigga.

Sax feels a claw touch the back of his neck.

The Amigga and the mirrored Oratus.

"A delay," Kah hisses. "Don't get any hope from your friends. We have plenty of defenses here to deal with them, and the Vincere will scramble air support. Their end will be like yours; swift, and seen by all."

"Maybe, but you're looking like a bunch of cowards now," Sax hisses back.

Kah seems to agree with his captive, because the Oratus lifts a claw and hisses out a question to the Amigga as the Chorus defenders continue to crumble in front of the onslaught. Now the skiffs are landing, and Evva's forces are running towards that big gateway. They'll be there in a moment, and if Nobaa and Engee succeed, that's when they'll take control of Meridia's power and yank that door open.

"Switch back to the execution?" the Amigga intones from behind its glass. "You're right. This isn't doing our image any favors."

The broadcast flips again, back to Sax. Kah's in the picture now, the Oratus looming over its captive, ready to deliver the blow.

"Ready?" Kah hisses, but not to Sax.

"I've been waiting," Sax replies anyway.

"It lacks the ceremony," the Amigga calls. "But go ahead."

"Goodbye, traitor," Kah says, and Sax watches the

image as Kah squats to Sax's level, the reflective scales blurring Kah's body in the light. The mirrored Oratus' jaws open, head towards Sax.

The lights don't flicker; they die. Even those pinprick points on the camera. The white mold keeping Sax in place dies too—melting to the floor in an instant as the electric current keeping its form vanishes. Sax isn't ready, but his talons are already on the ground, so they catch his fall. Instinct works next—with a snap of his jaws and a rolling, slashing move, Sax parts the loose rings from his scales before Kah manages to take control. The mirrored Oratus instead closes his teeth on air, the whoosh of the move brushing over Sax's tail.

Sax has no mask, and he can't see in the dark, so he follows the smells. The sounds of the glass doors opening and the Flaum rushing into the room. They're yelling out to catch Sax, which is about as much as they get from their mouths before the Oratus, leaping through the air like silent death, hits them and drives the furry creatures to the floor with his mid-claws. Taking a guess as to Kah's approach, Sax whips his tail as he lands and gets a satisfying *whack* out of the move. Kah takes the hit and stumbles into the glass wall, which, in a testament to the materials the Chorus used in their flagship tower, doesn't break.

In the dark, Sax grabs at the reason the Flaum came out of their room in the first place: stunning miners. There for this purpose; an execution gone bad and in need of aggressive pacification. The weapons are small for Sax's claws, but he's not shooting at range—a blast from each confirms the two Flaum, already wounded from Sax's claws, won't be moving any time soon.

Kah gives himself away with a hiss and Sax twists as, with a flash, the lights power back up and on. Both Oratus stop, because both know Sax has the position, and the weapons to make this a short fight.

"What are you waiting for?" the Amigga announces behind its glass barrier. "Kill the traitor!"

"Are you going to shoot me, Sax?" Kah asks, spreading his claws out wide. "Defenseless?"

"Yes," Sax hisses, then pulls the triggers on both miners.

Two blue bolts flash, two hit their target, and Kah crumples to the ground in frozen paralysis—even a mask won't keep you upright at this range. With a quick step, Sax closes on the fallen Oratus and bites down, severs Kah's right foreclaw. Sax takes it out, holds it and glances at the bloody appendage. Coorvin, the Flaum who'd managed to do some spying for Evva, said the Meridia operates on bio-scans, and Sax is betting Kah's claw-print is going to get him where he wants to go.

Now there's only the lifts, which Sax backs towards, eyes on those glass doors. Have to keep watch for any attempt from the Amigga, who's staying plenty quiet now that there's no one else to defend it. Part of Sax wants to go in and destroy the creature, but seeing as the broadcast is still showing the middle of the floor, once occupied by Sax in his execution chair and now by Kah's still form, the Chorus is going to know what's happening. More guards will be coming.

Sax isn't going to be here when they arrive.

I walk into the center of the galaxy's ruling organization and I can't see anything.

It's black everywhere as we leave the small hallway leading in from the outer circle. Ferrolite floats in front of me until the Amigga isn't there anymore; it just fades away into darkness. I keep walking, expecting, somehow, for everything to reveal itself. All I get is a subtle shift in the air, a wider echo of my soft steps to announce that yes, we're in a larger space than before.

"I, Ferrolite, bid you to welcome the newest species to our galactic collective," Ferrolite's voice bursts out a little ahead of me, so close that I stop moving for fear of running right into the Amigga. "The humans, from the planet previously designated Ex-Two-Five-Oh, but that, as per our new species custom, shall be henceforth renamed to their preferred title: Earth."

I hear what Ferrolite's saying as the Amigga continues through a long-winded version of our discovery in the war against the Sevora. Ferrolite seems to be speaking to an audience, but as I cast my eyes around, there's nothing but darkness. Either this is a trick, or the Chorus doesn't need light to do its business.

"What's going on?" Malo whispers to me. "Can you see anything?"

I start to shake my head, then realize Malo wouldn't see that either. "No, it's all dark."

"Maybe the Amigga don't need light?" Viera offers. "They don't have eyes, right?"

Viera's comment makes me realize the Chorus could be watching us right now, laughing as we spin around and search for light that isn't there. Demonstrating the full competence of our species by twirling like idiots in front of our new leaders.

"I can see everything fine," T'Oli patters. "What are you talking about?"

I'm about to answer T'Oli when I notice Ferrolite's gone silent and the Ooblot's last words hang in the still air of the room.

"Is there a problem, Kaishi?" Ferrolite asks me.

"We can't see," I reply. "Everything's black."

There's a beat as everyone internalizes what I've just said and comes up with a solution, then a half-dozen tuned, mechanical voices blurt out various phrases like 'spectrum' and 'light waves', ending with one louder, sharper voice, like a bronzed blade cutting off everything else.

"Salcite, adjust the room light to mid-wave," the voice says. "These creatures are sensitive."

Like Ignos bringing dawn to a new day, the room arises from nothing. Shapes begin to mold out of the dark; a long interior wall surrounding the central platform where we stand, with dividing walls separating out the sections Ferrolite described in our tour. Each section is different, presumably reflecting the passions of the owning Amigga, and I see everything from glowing terminals to hanging beasts, to a swarm of gibbering Flaum surrounding an Amigga resting on a floating dais, like a Charre Emperor of old. Two of the twelve sections are populated by hazy projections, like the ghost we saw back on Earth, with teal-colored blobs floating in space.

Unlike the ring surrounding the Chorus' chamber, there's not much here outside of the sections themselves. No fancy artwork, no homages to the galaxy's planets. Only a flat, unadorned space for us and a series of set lights in the ceiling casting a deep red across the entire room, so that it seems like everyone's drenched in a bloody wash.

"You can see now, yes?" the same voice asks.

"We can," I'm about to add 'sort of', but something in that voice tells me now isn't the time to get picky. "Thank you."

"Then, if I can continue?" Ferrolite interjects. "As I was saying, we were over Vimelia, and I was helping Kolas devise the plan to use the planet's own moon to crush—"

A short blast of static cuts off the Amigga, like the blaring of a rude horn. I try to find the source, but can't locate it before the voice that had been commanding others speaks again.

"Ferrolite, your briefing and its due accolades will come later. There are other urgent issues that we must attend to. I motion to begin the Oath of Joining at this moment, so we may deal with other matters," the voice says, and while I get that it's asking the others for their input, the tone suggests there's no option except the one it wants.

"First Chair," Ferrolite starts, but its words are washed out by another burst of static.

One by one, globes as large as my head, attached to the fronts of the Amigga sections, pop into light shades of green.

They blink to life until the entire circle fills in—a unanimous verdict. Ferrolite takes a slow turn at the lights, then floats back by me, towards the way we came in and hovers there on the fringes.

I'm thankful Malo and Viera are right behind me, that T'Oli still rests on my shoulders, otherwise I might get a little nervous standing in the center, the focus of all that alien attention.

"Are you ready to begin?" the voice booms.

An invisible weight lands on me as the Amigga speaks the words. The same weight I felt when I stood atop my tribe's Tier, Ignos in my head telling me what to say. The same weight I felt in the moments before we left Sax and Bas on *Cobalt* to strike out on our own; this is a step I can't take back.

Unlike those moments, here I'm in a wide room, red and dark, surrounded by creatures I don't know and don't understand. The consequences of what I'm about to do are hazy, with glittering benefits from endless miracles tainted with the fog of everything I've ever seen the Amigga do.

So I hesitate. And ask.

"I am ready, but first, I want to know," I say, each word pressing up against the last and then tumbling out together. "Ferrolite has promised humanity your help: cures for disease, technology that will make our lives less dangerous and more fulfilled, and protection from invasions like the Sevora one we just survived."

"All of that you will receive," the First Chair replies. "With plenty more still. Remember, it was under our order that the Vincere came and saved your species. It was under our order that the Sevora were destroyed."

I feel Malo step up next to me. His face is set straight, sturdy. He doesn't put a hand on my shoulder, but I feel the support all the same. "You didn't defeat the Sevora. Kaishi did. *We* did. You owe her, and the rest of humanity, the thanks you're awarding yourself."

Malo's charge sucks the air from the room. I wonder if the Chorus has ever been rebuked to its face, here in this chamber, before. They may decide to kill us here and now. Find a new, less confident ambassador from our species.

"Human," the voice booms. "I am the First Chair. Leader of the Chorus, the twelve Amigga responsible for the trillions of lives in this galaxy. Including, whether you wish it or not, your own. In this chamber, you will understand the measure of your minimal part to our massive one and speak accordingly."

A pause. I shake my head, knowing Viera's opening her mouth behind me, about to announce some retort that'll get us all killed. Somehow, it works. My hot-blooded friend stays quiet. My cold one does too—Malo manages to stew in the words, his Charre stoicism letting him store the moment for later.

"Yet," the First Chair continues. "You're correct in pointing out your own species' efforts. Your individual ones as well. The Chorus *does* recognize the help you have provided to the galaxy, human, which is why you are standing here now. Your species will receive all that we've claimed, and we will gladly give it. If that answer satisfies you, Kaishi, ambassador to the Chorus, we would hear your oath."

A glance shows Malo's not mollified by the words, but he does give me the slightest of nods. His arguments are done. A look back at Viera earns a shrug and little else—the Lunare glides through life, taking what comes her way and this is no different. T'Oli, on my shoulders, gives me a pair of taps as if to say *steady*, then hardens into a sturdy blanket.

Comfort for the moment I give my species' independence away.

"I'm ready. Tell me what to say."

I'm falling. That's what it feels like. I'm leaping and now I'm off, riding out the descent in all its scary numbness until I hit the ground.

"First, your associates must back away to the edge of the room," the First Chair says. "In this oath, you are the whole of your species, both yourself and every single one of them. This includes the creature on your shoulders."

Malo provides an arm for T'Oli to clamber onto, and then the warrior wraps me in a tight hold.

"I believe in you." Malo whispers, and he's gone before I have a chance to say anything back.

And then I'm alone, standing center in that ring.

"The Oath you are about to speak has been taken by dozens before you," the First Chair says, and while its voice comes through the grainy filter of a speaker rather than a mouth, the words carry a cadence that suggests the beginning of a ceremony. "It will be taken by dozens after. You will repeat the words as they are spoken, in the manner best suited to your species. Your responses will be recorded and, upon conclusion of the Oath, will be sent to every corner of the galaxy, so all will know of your commitment, and all will know of your reward."

In the gaping pause I wonder if I should respond, when the red lighting in the chamber fades away except for two halos, one around me and the other around the Amigga that must be the First Chair. It's larger than Dalachite, the Amigga that ran *Cobalt*, but lacks that one's endless fronds linking Dalachite to its chosen home. The First Chair floats like Ferrolite, but instead of a transparent shell, rings encircle its body. They rotate around each other, with the

Amigga at the center, the rings swirling over, under, and around. Their motion or something about them keeps the First Chair aloft, and while the Amigga has no eyes I can see, I feel its stare.

"State your name, and your species."

In the dark, the First Chair's words come from all around me, loud. As if I'm being spoken to by a god.

"My name is Kaishi, and I am a human." I pause. "From Earth."

There's nowhere to look except the First Chair and its rings, so that's where I stare.

"I, Kaishi, submit myself and my species, the humans, to the service of a better universe," the First Chair begins.

The reply comes out of my mouth, automatic. The words are numbing. Necessary. A private conversation, a dance between me and this strange creature. Even as I speak, though, I drift.

Back to the top of the Tier, with my father beside me and our tribe watching from below the Tier's rocky steps. Ignos falling away in the sky and yet speaking words in my mind, bidding me to unite my father's people to its will. Desperate and afraid, I cling to the Sevora's words as the only rope that can pull me to safety from my own mistakes, and my hands grip the black-glass knife, knowing what's expected of its glistening edge.

Every word I speak is for my species, every sentence binding us to the Chorus and its direction.

I'm back on *Cobalt*, standing on the platform while Dalachite's tests poke and prod at me, twist my eyes and toy with my senses. I am nothing more than a trial, a subject to be examined and explored even while, moments ago, others called me Empress from obedient lips. Alone, I lean on myself, fill the void between hot and cold, piercing pain and chilling metal touches with determination, the will to make it through.

The will of the Chorus is my will, its belief is my belief, and its dreams are my dreams.

In the caverns beneath Vimelia, I walk between ruined peoples, aliens I don't recognize doing what I'm doing: surviving. Next to me is an old Amigga, lamenting how its greatest loss is that it will, now, die. That dying, itself, could be a *choice* is beyond anything I have ever considered. Not a soul in my tribe, among my friends, thinks immortality is possible, but for this one, it is practical. Yet as it bemoans paying the highest price, I look at those around me and see so much life, so much spirit where there ought not to be any. Basking in the life they have, however fragile and imperfect.

Every effort we make, every action we take, will serve the Chorus' desires, and in doing so, our own.

Marilo bustles by me, both my people and not working together to repair damaged buildings, to forge new weapons or climb the ladders to the cliffs to defend our last city against an enemy we can't defeat. There are grim faces all around, and terror's icy grip ought to have hold of everyone, but I see no fear in our eyes. A call goes round for wine, another for bread, and scraps are given where they can to keep the city going. To keep our hope alive.

For with this oath, we become partners in a grand design, and forevermore pledge ourselves to progress.

Malo, Ignos stands over me in the shimmering gold light of the room in the seed ship, and the only thing holding back the Sevora's spear from a mortal strike is the last, desperate effort of my most trusted friend, who I thought I'd lost. Malo had been taken for days, torn apart and turned against his will into a tool. One used for the opposite of Malo's own purpose; his driving love of his people. Malo fought against the impossible, and in daring to try, succeeded.

"We serve the Chorus. Now, and forever, with bonds unbroken," the First Chair concludes.

I take a breath. A long one, and feel the slow slip of air into my body. This is it. With some simple words I'll fulfill a bargain that will deliver my people from their hardships, and all I'm giving up in exchange is our freedom. What a small price to pay for the Chorus' miracles.

Father, Mother, I hope you would be proud.

"Finish the oath," the First Chair prods.

I seek out the Amigga and level my eyes at the creature and its weaving metal bands. Open my mouth. As I say the first word, everything blinks white, a loud tone crashes over my speech, and before I can consider the rest of it, a half-dozen blurred, mirrored Oratus are standing in the center circle around me. They're not looking my way, though, but towards their leader.

"First Chair," the one nearest the Chorus leader hisses. "An enemy force is attempting to breach the Meridia, and we believe one or more of them is loose inside the tower."

I look back at Malo and Viera, but all I see on their faces is confusion. Nothing to do with us, then. Ferrolite hovers at the entrance, its expressionless body unreadable. T'Oli, though, makes one move, breaking free to slither to me, wrapping itself around my chest and shoulders and drawing a warning hiss from one of the Oratus in the process.

"Activate insurgency protocol," the First Chair says. "The Chorus will evacuate as a precaution." When the First Chair finishes the words, activity bursts around me. The mirrored Oratus leap into various sections where Amigga are floating around, pushing them and their Flaum and Whelk attendants out through their exits. The couple of Amigga appearing as images blink from existence without a sound. "Humans," the First Chair continues. "Unfortunately, this ceremony and its subsequent discussions must be postponed. Ferrolite will show you to a safe chamber where you can await our call to resume."

"We didn't finish?" I say more to myself than anyone else, even as Malo waves for me to join them over by Ferrolite's floating form.

"You never said the last line," T'Oli replies. "Right now, humans will still get nothing from the Chorus. Congratulations!"

"Why do you say that?"

"Most of my life, I was kept under the Sevora's rule. I wouldn't give up my freedom again for anything."

T'Oli's pattering isn't easy to make out over the clacks of Oratus talons, the buzzing of words and hisses, and my own pounding heart as it tries to calm down from the oath, but I get what the Ooblot's trying to say. Taken as a cold calculation, giving humanity to the Chorus would mean an endless bounty of benefits, but it would also mean giving ourselves the same treatment as the Flaum sent scurrying around me, as the Oratus ordered to guard this and that level, the Whelk commanded to ready shuttles for evacuation, and the Vyphen, not even present—disposed of and forgotten. Which role would we assume?

Ferrolite glides in front as mirrored Oratus usher us from the room, their blurred forms made more imposing by the hot breath from their vents and their hissing commands to move faster. The outside ring is chaos—species are running at random as sounds, lights, and signals I don't understand flag one Flaum to turn right into a side hallway, pull another Whelk back through the entry we just left, and send a squad of chattering, robed Teven sprinting by us without a glance.

"I should be leaving too," Ferrolite's saying to a mirrored Oratus that's taken up position behind us, playing bouncer to the Chorus chamber. "Find a Flaum to escort the humans."

"The First Chair gave *you* the command," the Oratus replies. "You must obey."

"Someone's not happy playing our escort anymore," Viera says to me.

"Ferrolite got its glory," I reply. "Why would an Amigga do anything that doesn't serve itself?"

Ferrolite's protests get nothing more than a hissing glare from the Oratus, and the Amigga's reddish brown bulk seems to sour as it decides it can't cast us off after all. As the bustle continues, Ferrolite whooshes its way back to us, then starts heading down the ring with nothing more than a single, harsh command, "Follow."

"Probably hopes we don't, just so it has an excuse to order us killed," Viera continues her whispers.

"Is there ever a time you're not joking?" Malo says.

"Not that I've noticed," T'Oli interjects from my shoulders. "Viera's attempts at humor take up more than ninety percent of what she speaks, by my count."

"Quiet, puddle," Viera says.

As we sweep around the ring, terminals that, on our way in, had been showing scenes from the galaxy have switched to various feeds from around the Meridia. I only know that much because, at the bottom part of every picture, the feed's location is displayed in wide, white lettering on a bright-blue background. As other species stop and stare at the screens, I realize the banners do more than just identify where—they tell everyone watching what places to avoid. What routes might still be safe.

One of the terminals, a large one blanketing the wall space between a pair of section entrances, blinks to show a massive interior courtyard and labels the scene *Meridia: Grand Entrance*. The place might have been grand once, but right now it's a burning, smoking mess. Laser fire occupies every open space, with a contingent of Chorus fighters hanging back near a vast bank of lifts. Fire pours in at the defenders from every angle as they try to huddle behind what cover they can find, and pop off shots in retaliation.

Even Ferrolite stops to watch, giving us all a chance to see the attack unfold. It's not pretty—the defenders are already desperate, and the attackers—I'm sure it's the force the mirrored Oratus mentioned to the First Chair—aren't content to settle into a firefight. A pair of small, bee-yellow balls arc into the picture, bouncing along the white stone near the doors, and when they burst, a bright flash knocks out our view for a moment. Like a parting mist on a sunny morning, our picture comes back slow and shows, among other newcomers, a rose-gold Oratus taking apart the defenders amid the lifts.

"Think I recognize that one," Viera says.

There's no doubting it's Bas, the other Oratus that took us from Earth so long ago. I last left her, and Sax, on *Cobalt*, stranded as the station broke apart. What she's doing here, fighting against the same creatures that commanded her to take us, I don't know. But I'm confident that letting on we're familiar with Oratus the Amigga want dead won't help us with the Chorus.

"You what?" Ferrolite asks.

"She's joking," I say. "Talking about that Flaum. We've seen a lot, and they start to look the same."

Ferrolite has no expressions, so I don't know if the Amigga buys my cover, but then the feed blinks away to some interior room bustling with more Chorus guards. The shift shakes us from the moment, and Ferrolite orders us on without another question.

We hit the safe room a moment later. Ferrolite floats aside and asks us to enter, and with quick, confirming looks at me, Malo and Viera, lets us head inside. The room's large, big enough for a few dozen people at least, and it has a wide window that looks into the upper-crust of Aspicis' atmosphere. We're sitting on the edge of space, and a constant blue-tinge to the view makes it apparent that the Meridia is spending plenty of energy keeping this level stable.

Alongside the usual white flooring, ready to form up to tables and chairs at our mental command, the room houses a pair of terminals on the far wall. A couple of what seem to be static images layer the other interior walls, depicting giant vines flowing beneath a blue sky.

"You'll stay here for now," Ferrolite says. "Someone will come for you when it's safe enough to leave. I suggest you touch nothing and enjoy the view."

The Amigga doesn't wait for questions, but jerks itself around and floats away. As it leaves, the two-meter wide doorway slides shut behind it. The whoosh-click quiets the alarms, the pounding steps, the constant voices coming over intercoms and leaves me with my friends, apart from everything.

I feel myself breathe. Marvel at it. Blink and sense my eyelids brush over my eyes. For the moment, there's nothing demanding me to be somewhere, to do something, to react or attack or run. Instead, I get to think.

"I almost gave up humanity," the words are out of my

mouth before I can stop myself. Away from Ferrolite's pressure and the parade of promises, relief takes their place. "But I didn't, right?"

"The oath wasn't completed," T'Oli says, and the Ooblot slithers off of my shoulders to go towards the window. "By the Chorus' own definition, you've pledged nothing so far. Of course, that leaves Earth open to assault and destruction by whomever desires it, but you're still free."

Malo's walking around the white flooring, raising up various chairs, tables, versions of furniture I remember from Damantum. At the Ooblot's words, though, the warrior stops, his hand brushing the surface of a simple stone bench. He looks from the Ooblot to me.

"Are you changing your mind?"

"Didn't you see what's happening out there?" Viera says as she stands by the window. "This whole place is a mess. They've got a rebellion going on. Why would we want to join that?"

"I wasn't asking you," Malo says to her.

"I am," I speak up, partly because the last thing I want right now is for my two friends in this place to fight over a decision I've already made. "I'm not going to go through with it, Malo. When Ferrolite comes back, I'll tell him that we would love to join the Chorus as partners, but not as servants."

Malo lets the bench sink back into the white as he steps over to me. "You know as well as I do that they won't accept that."

"I know. I just can't, Malo. I can't give us up like this."

I'm expecting Malo to resist. He's always been practical, and that side of this choice lies with the Chorus and their countless benefits. Instead, though, he gives me a simple smile.

"You know I'll follow you no matter what," Malo says. "The Chorus had better think twice before they say no."

"You don't think I'll be dooming us all? They won't torch Earth just because I'm being difficult?"

"They might." Malo nods over at Viera. "But they might do that anyway, because Viera's going to say something stupid."

"I heard that," Viera calls over.

"Don't care," Malo replies.

Over Malo's shoulder, I catch sight of a shifting screen; one of the terminals, flickering between feeds of the outside. A brief view of the ongoing battle gives me a thought, and Malo sees the change in my eyes.

"If we're not going to join the Chorus," I say. "Then we might want to figure out whose fighting them, and whether we should help."

When you're in a giant facility full of the galaxy's most advanced technology, assuming the enemy knows exactly where you are is the safest option. That assumption proves true for Sax when the lift locks after going up all of one level, its doors opening and dumping Sax out into what appears to be a support space for the level below. Several terminals glow among the well-organized shelves of audio-visual equipment.

The cameras, the Q-Net links for sending long-range messages, microphones and other black and gray devices Sax doesn't know nonetheless strike him as familiar. So many times Sax has been on a raid, cutting through a hostile town or assaulting a cruiser and there, some distance behind or floating above on a skiff, are Flaum holding gear like this. Taking and sending the images across the galaxy to build support for all of the Chorus' various assaults.

Speaking of assaults, Sax wonders how the one below is going. The terminals offer an obvious chance to check in, though at first glance these appear to be secured. Small blue patches below the screen indicate bio-markers; scanners to make sure the person attempting access belongs inside. Out of curiosity, Sax places his own midclaw in the bio-scanner. See if the Vincere removed his credentials.

The terminal's screen, a blank blue asking the prospective user to touch the bio-marker, shifts to show Sax's face, his old Vincere three-letter rank, and, following that, a large block set of words declaring Sax both a traitor and wanted. Sax hisses a laugh—he's not sure who those words are for, someone standing over Sax's shoulder? As if they're going to see what's on the screen and immediately attack him in the name of the Chorus.

What happens next does make Sax snort a surprise. The screen shifts black for a brief moment before brightening again, though this time into a gray, featureless box that fills with a pulsing leaf-green circle surrounded by a string of numbers. Sax stares at it—he knows this, has seen it before... somewhere. In his conflict-addled state it takes a deep memory dive to place the juddering shape into context and define the proper reaction. Something relegated to other species. To prey. Not normally worth his time.

Sax notes the number, then taps on terminal and answers the call.

"Sax? Can you hear me?" the voice is tight, stressed and yet packed with a sense of wonder. "I think I have it right. Don't I?"

There's some mumbling elsewhere that Sax catches, though the green circle is now still, with a neon-blue outline signifying Sax's answering tap.

"Nobaa?" Sax hisses the Teven's name, one he didn't think he'd have occasion to use again. That Sax says it now is, if he's being honest, disappointing. Tevens are the most annoying things. "I can hear you."

There's no guarantee that the Teven can hear Sax, but

by the series of startled exclamations, the Oratus guesses his reply came through.

"Excellent!" Nobaa says. "We've secured a room in the Cavignum. They think we're running repairs, which, we are because your method caused quite a lot of damage and without our work, this whole place—"

"Get to the point." Sax waves a claw, hoping Nobaa can see it.

"Yes. The point. We have access to the Meridia's security systems, for now. Eventually, we won't. Before then, you have to get to the top. To the Priority Beam."

That's what the Amigga below was talking about. Some sort of broadcast tool. It didn't sound like a weapon, so Sax hasn't thought about it since.

"Where I'll do what?"

"If we don't get the message out to Solis and the other Vincere sympathetic to Evva, the ones in orbit around Aspicis will crush us."

"I'm not much of a speech-maker."

"It won't take much!" Nobaa's somehow getting even more excited. "Just tell them to hold off. Give their own species a chance!"

Before Sax can reply, the signal fuzzes, the green circle goes black and the terminal's gray box shifts to red, with bold black letters stating that the terminal has been locked. Guess that's the end of the conversation. Still, Sax has his objective now. He didn't need to listen to the Teven any longer.

If, though, the Chorus are sealing his terminal, that means they know where Sax is. The sudden chiming of the lifts on the far end of the level—across from where Sax came in and separated from his position by walls of stacked equipment—reinforce the point and the Oratus jerks himself into action. The size of the lifts means a dozen Flaum, with armor and weapons, could fit inside and that's more than Sax wants to fight head on.

So as the sounds of small claws on tile floor start to patter and the first call for surrender chirps out, Sax aims one of his miners towards the lights and fires. One shot per glowing rectangle, each one melting out in a shower of sparks, and in six shots and as many seconds, most of the level is dark. The only lights left sit over the lifts behind and in front of Sax, casting enough shadows through the shelves and stacked equipment to make a world of jagged white-on-black edges.

A hunter's paradise.

Sax goes low, tapping his talons and midclaws on the ground as he slithers around the equipment, blending his own noise with the nervous approach of the Chorus guards. With one of his miners emptied of energy, Sax crouches off to the level's middle side, back against the wall. He smells, hears, *knows* the Flaum are getting close to the center, where Sax shot out the lights. As the creatures get close, Sax cocks his foreclaw back and then launches the miner in an arcing toss over their heads.

The weapon clatters into a pile of small boxes, which do their duty and tumble, hitting each other with enough clacking to draw the eyes and aims of every Flaum in the room.

Sax can't ignore that many backs, that many targets for leaps and slashes, bites and tripping tail whips.

Two Flaum go down before any shots are fired, and those red bolts lance towards noise, towards shifting shadows as Sax knocks shelves, throws bodies, and generally turns the scene into one of constant motion. To stay still is to die, so after taking a satisfying chomp of a third Flaum,

Sax burrows away beneath a falling camera stand, taking cover behind a full shelf. His vents scoop air, his two hearts race, and, with a foreclaw, Sax picks a clump of fur from his teeth and listens.

The Flaum are squeaking to each other, a high-pitched sound that bounces around the level without purpose other than to say *here I am, come eat me!* It's instinct. It's meant to tell the squad where its members are, but Sax uses the chirps to navigate, slip around behind and towards the lifts the Flaum rode as the Chorus guards congregate in the middle and form some sort of firing circle.

Numbers still aren't in Sax's favor, so he's not thrilled to see both lifts on this side glaring red and locked. Sax isn't wearing a mask, so any hit's going to give him a severe burn or worse. The locked lifts mean the Flaum in the center don't have any excuse to go hunting, either—Sax comes to them, or they wait for more reinforcements and Sax gets gunned down by a far superior force.

But if there's one thing Oratus get used to, it's being outnumbered.

Sax takes a pair of heavy steps away from the lifts, making plenty of noise. Stops just before a pair of tall shelves that look heavy, and, with a kick of his right razor talon, Sax cuts out the corner post of one of the shelves. It begins to lean, and Sax catches it, steadies it. The metal struts groan, and Sax covers the sound with a roar of his own.

"I'm over here, and I surrender!" Sax calls loud, keeping his midclaw on the precarious shelf.

Any Vincere member would know an Oratus never surrenders, but these Flaum have been in the soft comfort of the Meridia for who knows how long. They haven't been on the galaxy's front. So they form themselves up and come cautious from the center, creeping three abreast with miners raised. The second and third rows hang a bit behind the first, keeping their eyes peeled in different directions, as if Sax will appear from anywhere.

To be fair, Sax might.

The Oratus expects the Flaum to try and negotiate, but they give their intentions away by the fear and sweat streaking off their fur in pungent waves. Sax almost coughs, the stench is so strong. These aren't confident soldiers, ready to apprehend an enemy. These are scared children, who'll spray lasers everywhere before they think of another alternative. When they finish talking, if Sax so much as twitches, they'll melt him.

The moment arrives: the lead Flaum sees Sax as they head between the shelves. The miner snaps up and the Flaum starts to screech a threat.

Sax doesn't hear the words. Doesn't care.

With his right claws, Sax pulls the weakened shelf down while sidestepping in the opposite direction, using the stocked shelves as a barrier to the few panicked shots making it out as their own material buries the Chorus guards. It's a clanging, squeaking crumble that leaves half the Flaum incapacitated and the others firing madly into the shifting shadows, trying to hit an Oratus that's hunkered himself down behind a giant, un-powered terminal.

Sax waits out the flashes. Lets the confidence that comes when you embrace a futile situation fade away, waits for fear to creep back into his prey. The Flaum will search now, see if any of their wild shooting found a mark. The scuffing steps of light, booted feet bring truth to the idea, and confirm the Flaum's total loss of cohesion: they're splitting up. Two pairs, going to different sides of this part of the level.

The two coming near Sax's terminal manage to round the corner, manage realize Sax isn't dead, then they lose their miners and their consciousness as Sax slams them into each other. Killing all of them isn't the goal—no matter how fun it might be. Or tasty.

The collapsing Flaum trigger the attention of their last-remaining brethren and Sax figures to use the bodies as bait, but these Flaum are cowards. The clue comes when the lift panel beeps, with whooshing doors a moment later.

Their escape can be Sax's, too, and the Oratus leaves a set of heavy grooves in the floor as he bounds towards the open lift. One of the Flaum, stepping in after its friend, manages to whirl and get its miner up. A motion that brings the front half of its long barrel into the space the now-closing lift doors plan to occupy. Rather than shutting, those same doors freeze at the rifle's obstruction, simultaneously giving Sax the opening he needs to slip through the doors while causing the Flaum to give up its shot as its partner pulls it back into the lift.

A good description of what happens once Sax slithers his bulk through the doors would include the thwacking of the Oratus' tail, the tripping kick of his left talon and the sparking snap of Sax's jaws as they bite that fateful miner's barrel apart, rendering the weapon little more than a sputtering bit of metal.

A sufficient description would simply state that when the lift reached its destination, only the Oratus remained upright, conscious, and capable of continuing its trek towards the Priority Beam.

Outside, above the blue fringe of Aspicis' atmosphere, ships are gathering. Viera's calling them out to us, one by one, as shuttles blast away from the Meridia towards the bulks of Vincere cruisers, frigates, and more. Tiny lights glowing towards massive ovals, spindly branch-like craft, and those colored rings that make up both the defense and the safe haven for Aspicis' ruling species.

"They're all cowards," Malo's saying, next to her. "They're being attacked at their very center and their response is to run?"

"Did you see them?" Viera says. "An Amigga can't exactly fight for itself. They have no hands. No legs. Nothing."

"Then how did they take over the galaxy?"

It's a good question, but answering it isn't going to help us escape so I tune them out and focus on the terminal. T'Oli's draped itself over the top of the screen, which is a meter wide, and we're watching a small fight play out on level three, close to the surface. Bas, the rose-gold Oratus that stole me from Earth, is busy leading a quartet of battered Flaum wearing ragged, varied cloth and metal armor through a floor stocked with crate after crate of what looks like nutrient goop. Chorus forces are using the crates as cover, and it's a slow-going firefight.

"Any other ideas?" I ask the Ooblot. We've been trying to get the terminal to switch off of the broadcast to something we can use, but T'Oli says I lack the security, which is why the screen's ignoring me.

"You're sure you want to leave this room? Now?" T'Oli replies.

"If we stay here, we'll either die when the tower blows up, or the Chorus will come back and force me to complete that oath. When I don't, we're dead."

"A compelling set of options."

"It's not my fault."

"Well..."

"T'Oli, are you going to help, or not?"

The Ooblot bends its eyestalks around the sides of the terminal, hunting for something while I watch. T'Oli used to be a creamy white, but enough miner scars and other debris from our last few encounters has given the Ooblot a series of blackened scars along its surface. I'm sorry for that, but I'm not at all sorry for bringing T'Oli with us. The Ooblot's proved its worth time and again, as the recurring nightmares I have about the Fassoth caverns beneath Earth's surface remind me every night.

"The terminal's secured," T'Oli says. "So we either find the passcode, which, as it seems to be tied to a genetic scan, isn't going to work. Or we do what the Chorus doesn't expect its guests, waiting for approval and acceptance from the First Chair, to do."

"Which is?"

"Tear the terminal apart."

The Ooblot doesn't wait for me to ask how. Instead, bits and pieces of itself flow into the tiniest of cracks around the terminal, where various pieces were meshed together. T'Oli hardens its skin, and in doing so, expands those cracks ever-so-slightly. The Ooblot repeats the process over and over again until, with a hasty patter, it tells me, "Catch!"

The screen falls forward towards my arms and I rush my hands up in time to snag the glass as it falls into my grip. It's heavy and warm, but T'Oli doesn't give me much time to do anything with it before pattering at me to set it on the ground. I do, and lean it against the silver, square post that serves as the terminal's base.

"As expected," T'Oli patters from up at the top of the post. "It's entirely wireless here. If we cut the power for a moment, the terminal will reset."

"What?" I'm still watching the fight on the screen, because at least Bas leaping into the middle of the enemy, claws whirling, makes some sense.

"The screen doesn't have a life of its own, Kaishi. It needs power, like a fire. It must be fed," T'Oli stops pattering for a moment, and the screen goes black. "In this case, that power comes from a little transmitter here in this post. One I just wrapped up in my non-conductive skin."

"I have a thousand questions."

The terminal bursts into colors so bright that I sit back, hands on the ground and feeling a lot like a little girl, surprised by the unexpected. The colors fade into a default slate blue, with several small squares dominating the screen. I recognize these from *Cobalt*. Ignos called them icons. Here, one is shaped like another terminal, black and rectangular. Another, though, I recognize; an emerald-green ring, like the Cache I still wear on my left wrist.

I've mostly forgotten about the device because, as its former owner told me, it contains a library of the Sevora's knowledge. A now-dead alien species that's never been a part of the Chorus, never been inside the Meridia, probably wouldn't have much to say about the tower we're in. Still, I remind myself to take it for a look if T'Oli's terminal hijacking doesn't work out.

"As I thought," T'Oli patters as it slurps down next to me. "They set these things to run on a slave circuit to some central station in the tower, but if you knock them off, someone has to put them back on."

"Can you stop that?"

"Explaining things?"

I close my eyes for a hot second. Think of the jungle. The breeze through the trees. T'Oli is its own creature, with its own mind, history, and way of working with its world. I can't expect it to understand me, just as I don't understand it.

"You've lived all your life in a galaxy I didn't know existed until a short time ago," I say to those creamy-gray eyestalks. "What you think is common knowledge, I don't know. I don't even understand." This is the point where, if I was talking to something with hands, or even claws, I'd reach out and take hold of one to press my point. Because T'Oli has neither, I hope the Ooblot reads the sincerity in my eyes. "I want to learn all of this someday, but now? Right now? I'm too scared, too stressed and tired to worry about anything other than survival. So tell me straight. Can we get out of this room?"

T'Oli quivers. Its eyes look back at the terminal. "I will

try, Kaishi. The terminal is now unlocked. We can use it to learn about this place, and perhaps find a way to open the door."

I give the Ooblot a smile. "See? Not one thing I didn't understand."

"Don't take this as an insult, but that was harder than you know."

Malo comes over a little while later, as T'Oli and I peruse the terminal's endless secrets. The warrior crouches next to me, watches as we cascade past diagrams and pages, flashing boxes full of information, numbers and words, graphs and pictures. I'm chasing a thread, a word that appeared not long into our scouring of the Meridia's levels: *Cobalt*.

T'Oli had us looking for ways to open the door, but when that space station's label flashed up under a list of Chorus assets, flagged in bright red towards the top in its own little box titled *Potentially Lost*, I took control. The Chorus let their terminals work by touch, so when Malo gets over to us, I'm tapping and whisking away all manner of long logs and pictures that toy with nightmares just beneath my surface.

All the pieces are here, stored away in what T'Oli calls *Cobalt*'s 'file'. There's a map, like the one I saw when I was on the station. Those very same corridors are laid out, white lines on a deep blue background.

"Those were our rooms." I say as Malo sits next to me.

"This is *Cobalt*?"

"Don't you recognize it?"

"I never saw a map like this." Malo watches as I slide our view around, over towards a larger rectangle room. He puts his own hand on mine to hold the screen still for a second. "I know that place, though. Viera almost killed me there."

"Dalachite would have killed all of us if we hadn't taken care of it first." I find the chamber where the Amigga tested me, and the central core, where Dalachite's body had merged with the station itself. "It still haunts me, you know."

"We all have nightmares now." Malo's voice says he's thinking of his own demons, and I don't blame him.

I don't want to look at *Cobalt* anymore and so I swipe away the map. What comes up next is a longer document. A wall of text that would have me skipping past if not for the title. *Our Future Universe.* It's a grand statement, something I'd expect Father, or Jakkan back in Damantum to make before a litany of promises about a coming utopia. This... this isn't much different, except the Amigga version of paradise includes the gradual elimination of every competing species.

"Two paths," T'Oli says, its eyestalks reading alongside my own. "Your *Cobalt* was on one, exploring biological routes. The other is a turn back. I never thought the Amigga would consider it."

"A turn back?" Malo asks.

"Look at the terminal," T'Oli says. "It's small, it can do a lot, and it doesn't take any food or water. You don't have to teach it anything, and it will never ask you a question, or disobey an order."

"Right?" the warrior looks as confused as I am.

"Now imagine you add a weapon to this. A miner."

"Like the familiars," I say. "They took orders from Dalachite, and they used weapons."

"But they weren't very frightening," Malo says. "I could have beaten any of them."

T'Oli patters out some nonsense that I gather, from the way it closes and shakes its eyestalks, means we're not getting it. Viera announces another shuttle launch and T'Oli's eyes snap back open.

"That's it. Think of those ships. Like Kolas' cruiser, but smaller, and everywhere. They could fly, shoot you from space, and be coated in armor," T'Oli says.

"That would be... harder for me to beat," Malo replies.

"Impossible, more like," the Ooblot says. "They existed at one time, took over planets—"

"But they're not around anymore?" I ask.

The Ooblot says no and I turn back to the report. Malo's still asking questions but if these things aren't a threat right now, I don't have time for them. The report's clear, straight. Humans aren't mentioned, but it's not hard to see where they fall in with the pathways to one of the Amigga's imagined futures. We're a test, and so far as this document reads, we failed it. Other species are listed too, and all of them falter when pressed by the Chorus' standard for success: control.

"After that rogue faction, using stolen machines, took so much territory so fast," T'Oli's saying. "The Chorus forced the Vincere to strip away all A.I. from their ships, and most of the networking too. They destroyed so much of their power because the Chorus was so afraid someone could take it out of their control. One Amigga, one Flaum with the right codes and the Priority Beam could have forced every Vincere craft to self-destruct, or turn their cannons on each other."

"The Priority Beam?" I ask, because there's nothing about that in this report.

"The galaxy's most powerful communication device," T'Oli says. "That's all I know. Sapphrite told me all of this, but I never thought I'd get off Vimelia. Or invade the Meridia. Otherwise I would've asked more."

"No, it's fine," I look back to the terminal. "That doesn't matter. There's enough here to prove we can't side with the Chorus, no matter what. We'll die if we do."

"We'll die if we fight them too," Malo replies. "You know that."

"Hey!" Viera calls from the window, and I'm relieved she's rescuing us from falling into the same pit of doom and gloom we've been circling since coming into this room. "I can tell by your sad face and Malo's set shoulders that you're talking about something useless again. Know what's more fun? Counting all the ships still blasting off of this place. Everyone's leaving. I think the Chorus is afraid."

"Even if they are, so what?" I reply. "You think Bas and Sax will treat us any better?"

"They are warriors," Malo says. "They might be honorable. Better than the lying Amigga."

"So if the Chorus is scared of them and if they'd be better friends to us, I say we help them," Viera agrees. "Get out of here and do what we can to make sure they win this fight."

I'm about to endorse the plan when there's a strange buzzing sound that fills the room. A pair of panels on the wall behind the terminal slide out, and with a glopping, messy noise, purple nutrient goop slimes from some hidden pipe to fill the new basin, rushing out from behind the wall to where we can grab it. Viera's the first one there, looking at the food with a shake of her head.

"Even here, we still get the same garbage," Viera says. "You'd think they'd have something better."

"If they're feeding us, it must mean they think we'll be here for a while." I find that second wall panel that opened turns out to be a drawer full of utensils—plates, bowls, thin fabric things that I gather must be for cleaning any goop that finds its way onto us instead of into our mouths.

"Well, if we're going to join a revolution, I don't want to do it hungry," my Lunare friend says, and she takes a bowl and scoops it through the goop.

"I never like to fight on a full stomach," Malo says, watching Viera and then me take our portions.

"Better than an empty one," Viera says between mouthfuls. "Eat up, Charre. You're all bones now anyway."

The nutrient goop goes down easy as we watch ships continue to cluster outside. Smaller craft are joining, or launching from, their larger brethren now, with many streaking towards the atmosphere in formations. It's a fascinating display, and one that chips away at my own resolve to fight against the powers that created all of this. At least until T'Oli speaks up.

"I believe I have found your history," T'Oli announces. "It seems the beginning of your species occurred only a few levels down from here."

"I thought you were searching for a way to open the door?" I ask as I go over towards the Ooblot, looking at the screen.

"Oh, I don't think that's possible from here. It seems the Chorus do not trust their own guests to do what we've done, and gain control of the system."

"So we're trapped?"

"Unless you have a better idea, I think we're stuck until Ferrolite comes to let us out."

The screen shows a space some levels beneath our own, and while there's not much in the way of description—giant black boxes cover most of it, with warnings of improper security—the level's title tells enough of a story: *Alternative Species Development*. If T'Oli's right, and the story of our species begins there, then I want to know it. I want to understand why the Amigga chose to make us.

Then I want to destroy any records of it.

Like the others, this lift ignores Sax's input. The floor he selects isn't where it goes, but at least this time the lift heads up. Towards the Priority Beam, one level at a time. Once the doors open, though, Sax decides he'd have preferred to go down.

If he understood the other levels, this one feels like Sax has stepped out of the galaxy he knows. The reality he knows. Machines, at least those with any moving, walking, or talking capability have long since fallen out of favor. There's no reason to risk creating a death robot that could be hijacked from some remote location or by someone who happens to get inside its internals when you can create a genetically-modified super weapon like the Oratus.

Which is why Sax is surprised to find this level packed with eight-limbed robots. What's more, though Sax is too young to have seen any of the old warbots in action, these look glistening new. The sheen on the bright blue Chorus paint glimmers in the static white light from overhead stripes. No combat burns, no dirt or rust from action on hostile worlds.

Who would store these here? And why?

A step out from the lift gives Sax a good view of what he's looking at. The warbots sport a core, a ball that looks like an Amigga fashioned out of teal-shaded steel. Each one has a number of modules attached to it, most ending in either microjets, miners, or variations on multi-tools and physical weapons meant for either destruction or interrogation. All of them appear to be dormant, and their silent stares loosen the frozen knots forming in Sax's stomach.

The warbots hang from detachable clamps lowered from the ceiling, black-and-gray striped cords dangling like an industrial puppet-master's strings.

A return to machines like this would raise terror on other worlds, would pull recruits to Evva by the thousands, and not without reason.

The first time the Amigga built a gigantic armada of computerized soldiers, they marched from world to world, building the base of what became their empire. Sax has seen the logs, read up on the history. Required, in case the Vincere should ever run up against a similar force from somewhere else.

The warbots would stream in towards the target, an endless wave of tireless, ruthless fighters. They would decimate everything with uncompromising exactitude – targeting what was necessary, not caring at all about the morality of the situation. In other words, a perfect Amigga soldier.

At least until the warbots were stolen, hacked and turned against their creators. The first time was an anomaly, then it happened again and again and again.

All it took was one enterprising Teven, and then word spread around. Rebellious worlds started turning invasions into their own armies. Before long, and facing elimination by their own creations, the Chorus scrambled to bring back cast aside species like Flaum and Vyphen. Even then, that old version of the Vincere barely held on, and with the Sevora beginning to rise, the Chorus needed a stronger, better solution.

The Oratus proved to be the answer.

Except, apparently, the Amigga are changing their minds. Going back to how it was before. Maybe these new warbots are better, more resistant to the faults that ruined prior generations. If so, then the familiars on *Cobalt* aren't the only path the Chorus is taking to its new future. One that doesn't seem to have a place for other species.

Regardless, the warbots aren't active now, and if the Chorus loses here, none of this will matter.

Sax starts looking for a way off of the level. The lift gates are showing red—locked. No chance of getting out that way, unless he wants to carve through with his claws, and there's not enough time for that. Instead, Sax wanders past the warbots searching for an opportunity and finds a terminal in the center.

Sax tries to boot it up, but the terminal rejects his own foreclaw with an angry beep. So instead Sax uses the claw he took from Kah down below, the limb now hardening into a stiff splay. It could almost be a weapon, if Sax felt like being morbid.

When Kah's claw touches the screen, it shifts and gives Sax an array of options, including the only one Sax wants to use.

Below, where the Flaum attacked, Nobaa reached him from a safe space in the Cavignum. Sax retraces the call now, puts in the number and tells the terminal to send the signal. After a moment spent staring at a blinking gray screen, Nobaa answers.

The Teven's in a room bathed in Cavignum's classic orange-and-chrome decor, though it's ruined somewhat by the white and blue glows from all the terminals. Engee's hook-covered carapace hovers nearby, her tiny arms reaching out and tapping away commands while Nobaa rotates a hole and sticks a small eye out towards the screen.

"Sax, I never expected to hear from you again. Truly, we all thought you would die. You didn't! That's great news!" Nobaa pauses as Sax struggles not to snap the terminal in half. "But, where are you?"

Sax takes a deep breath through his vents, opens his mouth to speak when Nobaa starts up again.

"No, seriously. I'm tracing your call through the Meridia's map and it doesn't look like this level is supposed to be there. Wait. Are those warbots behind you?"

Of course Nobaa would know about warbots. Of course he'd recognize them immediately.

"I think so," Sax manages to say. "They're not running now."

"That's good news for you. Otherwise you'd really be dead!"

"That's not why I'm calling," Sax says.

"Oh, yes. I suppose it wouldn't be. What do you need? Anything I can help with?"

"I hope so," Sax says. "I need a way off this level. A lift, or somewhere to go where I can catch one."

"I can't control the lifts," Nobaa says. "But I can say that it looks like there's a long lift above you. One that could take you right to the top. That's what you want, right?"

"Yes."

"Well then, you need to get one more level up. If the lifts won't work, try going to the ceiling. You've got those fancy claws, right? Use them."

"I don't need you to tell me when to use my claws," Sax hisses.

"I was only suggesting! That's all I ever do—suggest!"

Sax is about to reply with some sort of insult when there's a low beeping noise from his left. Then a rattle, followed by the soft click of a latch letting loose. With the microjets whirring up it's not all that hard to learn what's happened. A suspicion that's confirmed when the warbot floats into view, those eight arms maneuvering weapons his way.

"Nobaa, a warbot just activated," Sax says, stepping away from the terminal and turning to face the metal adversary.

"Don't fight it! Run!"

That would be a coward's move, and Sax is no coward. Instead, Sax settles on his talons and gets ready to leap as the warbot floats at him. Sax wonders why it hasn't opened fire, until realization strikes. If these warbots were ready to go, charged and set, they'd already be active. The Chorus would've sent them against Evva right away.

Since the warbots are all still here, silent and waiting, their miners might not be charged. All their programming might not be ready. Which means the fight's going to be up close and personal.

Just how Sax likes it.

The Oratus starts with a quick step around the terminal, bringing the warbot into full and centered view. With the dead 'bots on the right and left serving as an audience, Sax sizes up his closing opponent.

At around three meters tall, Sax is larger than the warbot, though the latter compensates for its size with those eight limbs. Sax counts a pair of swords in the mix, with two more bearing the apparently-dead miners. The other four hold what look like tools or docking appendages. So, two swords against Sax's four claws and a pair of sharp, deadly talons. Those are odds the Oratus will take.

Sax makes the first bet by digging his four main claws into the hanging warbot directly to his left. Whether because these warbots aren't active, or because their armor is coming later, Sax grips, poking through the robot's metal skin and, with a pivoting yank, breaking the warbot free of its chain. Thus shielded, Sax charges forward with the dead warbot covering his torso. At the last moment, as Sax sees his target pull back the swords for a swing, the Oratus throws the dead warbot into its live companion.

The warbots crash into each other, their limbs hooking, breaking, scraping. Sax doesn't let the maneuver go to waste either, following up the throw with a leap that carries him over the top of the two. Kicking his talons—his left into the top of the dead warbot, his right into the top of juddering live one—Sax crosses behind his target and drops to the floor. As he falls, Sax uses his tail to snake around one of the live warbot's top limbs, one holding a syringe-like data-port connector.

With his tail hold, Sax bites his talons into the floor when he lands and whips the warbot free of its companion and into another one, smashing its right sword arm into a hanging bot and crumpling it. Freeing his tail in the process, Sax whirls around, ready to dig his claws into the warbot's back and finish the fight.

Warbots don't have traditional bones, joints, the usual constraints of biology. So when Sax turns around, expecting a free shot at a battered, distracted enemy, what he gets is a blazing sword coming towards him. The warbot's reversed its limb, and the swing is accurate enough to shave a long, thin slice through the surface of

Sax's torso. A couple of Sax's vents sting with the cut, but it's not fatal, not serious, because Sax's own instincts backed him up.

The warbot uses the space bought by the swing to juice its microjets and get itself untangled, while Sax looks for another approach.

What makes warbots so devastating is their ability to calculate, on the fly, the exact trajectory Sax might take on his attack. The warbot will be able to swing the sword to the perfect spot, right where Sax is going to be. Surprise, unpredictability—those are Sax's assets, and he has to use them. His adversary isn't going to give him the time, though. The warbot's moving forward again, keeping that buzzing sword front and center.

Sax back-pedals. He has no weapons aside from his claws, and Sax would rather not lose those to a swift swipe from that sword. The warbot's pressing him now, forcing Sax back towards those lifts, which he could try to open with Kah's claw, or...

Sax grabs the claw and whips the stolen hand at the warbot, who swings the blade to catch the claw and sever it. The move, though, carries the sword away from its central position, and Sax jumps quick to take advantage. The warbot's limbs are on the outside of its body, so when it tries to bring the blade back from its wide swipe, Sax catches the limb just beyond the edge with his left foreclaw. His other three claws get to work tearing off the warbot's back plate, which rips away with a second's worth of swipes. Sax's teeth attack the innards, a bite full of metal and glowing wires.

He's tasted better.

The warbot shudders, its microjets fail, and the construct collapses to the ground in a metallic screeching shamble. Sax steps over the fallen thing and heads back to the terminal, where Nobaa's still waiting on the call.

"I'm back," Sax hisses.

"Are you all right?"

"Of course," Sax says, but before the Oratus can confirm his best route to the next level is a hack-and-slash ride through the ceiling, another set of whirring jets comes to life. Followed by another, and another. "More of them are activating, Nobaa."

"How many?"

"There are dozens on this level alone." Sax puts the numbers together—even without their miners, the warbots could manage to overwhelm him, and if there's more than one level of these things, those buzzing swords could kill Evva and Bas too. "We have to stop them."

"We?"

"You're the Teven, think of something," Sax hisses, then he has to back away from the terminal as the sword from the next warbot slashes where he was.

Three warbots are coming at Sax now, gliding around the terminal and surrounding him, leaving only one option. Sax gathers his legs and jumps towards a line of still-dead warbots behind him. He lands and scrambles up one, leaving heavy grooves in the thing's body. From there it's up the latching cable, climbing with his claws until Sax makes it to the ceiling. A couple of hard strikes push the tips of his claws through the top tiles, letting Sax cling to the surface and look down as the warbots consider the best way to pursue him.

"Hold them off!" Nobaa calls, the sound tinny and small coming from the terminal. "Engee and I are thinking!"

"Think fast." Sax starts to move, because the warbots

are getting the idea that their microjets can loft them high enough to take swipes towards Sax.

The Oratus isn't moving at random, though. Sax's muscles and sharp claws let him skitter across the ceiling faster than the warbots can follow, and he circles around them back towards the collapsed corpse of the first one. When he gets there, Sax lets go of the ceiling and drops, landing on top of the downed warbot. Its metal comrades are closing quick, those swords glowing red-pink with hot energy, when Sax uses his claws to shear off the swords from the dead, grounded warbot. Because the blades are made for the machines, they don't have hilts or grips like normal swords might, but Sax doesn't have the luxury to complain.

Without an internal battery, too, the swords don't burst to life. But Sax proves their worth anyway, swinging to counter the first warbot's pair of blurring strikes. The swords are made to withstand the heat and force of themselves, so Sax's makeshift defense counters the assault, clashing, sparking against the warbot's attack. The warbot's moves aren't difficult to block at first, but these things are designed to evolve, adapt. The longer the fight takes, the more the warbot's going to target Sax's vulnerabilities, make the Oratus miss, make him lose some limbs.

Which, all things considered, Sax would prefer to keep.

So he jumps back, grabs that last bit of space between the line of warbots and the lifts, and throws one of the swords. It's a straight strike, a line-pierce that, even without the energy, carries an Oratus' strength and a super-sharp blade right through the first warbot's front armor. The sword sinks in deep and prompts a telltale crunch, a high-pitched whir as components wind themselves up without restraint, followed by the warbot's plunging collapse to the ground in front of Sax.

It's a moment of triumph stolen when more warbots on Sax's right and left spark to life, detaching from their cables and making their way towards him while the other, already active ones float over their disabled friends. Sax has one sword and his back to a pair of locked lifts. Not the best situation.

When surrounded, with no other options, the best move is to limit the number you have to fight at once. Straight ahead, Sax has at least two warbots in a line. To his right and left there's one apiece. Get through one of them, and maybe Sax has a chance to get away, buy himself some time.

So Sax feints right, flips the sword to his right foreclaw and leans that way, drawing the warbots in that direction and forcing the right warbot to raise its sword in a straight defense designed to block a throw like the one Sax just made at its companion. Already learning. Shifting his weight, throwing his tail to the right to help swivel him around, Sax pivots and launches to the left, over the stabbing charge of a warbot who thought it had an open shot at the Oratus' back. Sax's leap carries him over the warbot's blades, with Sax bringing his talons up into a tuck to avoid the scorching slices.

As Sax crashes into the advancing warbot, he uses his midclaws to clamber over the machine. With his right foreclaw, Sax jams his other blade through the top of the orb, stuttering the warbot into collapse. Sax rides the machine to the ground, then yanks the blade out with his right midclaw and breaks into a run, ducking and weaving through the crowd of hanging warbots, more and more of whom are starting up to life. Sax can move for the moment, but he's going to be overwhelmed in the next.

"We've found an opportunity!" Nobaa's screaming through the terminal rises above the medley of mechanical whines. "These warbots are still running old software! That's why they're not active—the Chorus must have known they'd be vulnerable!"

Sax, who's cutting wildly with the sword as he runs around the level, doesn't get what the Teven's saying. So what if the warbots haven't had their internal programming changed—it's not like Sax can adjust it now. The Oratus barely has time to duck and dodge sword strikes. More and more warbots are activating and the level's filling with the whir of microjets and the whine from the swords.

One of those blades will land a cut sooner or later, and Sax won't survive what follows.

Learn why we were made, and then destroy our makers. Seems simple enough, but doing either requires getting out of this safe room. The terminal's been no help, so the four of us are standing in front of the door, willing it to open.

"What if I scream for help? Think anyone will answer?" Viera asks.

"Try it." I don't think anyone will, but it's worth a shot.

Malo and I, with T'Oli coating me in its own body armor, take up positions on either side of the door, and at my nod, Viera commences with a series of truly terrifying shrieks. She howls that the window's cracking, that we're about to get sucked into space, and that I'm suffering from some sort of critical illness. It's inventive, it's scary, and I'd come running if I heard it.

Or maybe I'd head the other way.

The door, though, stays shut. Resolute.

"Guess they don't care if we die in here." Viera sounds offended.

"More likely they can see what we're doing and know

there's no real threat," T'Oli patters. "I would bet someone from the Chorus is watching every move we make."

"You could have suggested that earlier," I say. "Saved us the trouble of listening to Viera."

"I believe letting loose can be healthy," T'Oli replies.

"It did feel good to scream," Viera agrees. "You should try it, Empress. You've got to be frustrated."

I am, but it's not the kind of frustration that's helped by screaming and shouting. I look at the door again, "T'Oli, you think they're watching us?"

"I doubt there's anything in the Meridia that isn't watched, Kaishi."

"Then why don't we give them a show?"

T'Oli tilts its eyestalks, which, seeing as those stalks are resting on my shoulders, makes it look like I have a pair of gray growths spiking out of me.

"Make your sword," I suggest. "Let's try and hack our way out of here."

"I don't think the door is thin enough?"

"Guess we'll find out," I reply to the Ooblot as it forms up along my hand, its skin hardening into a razor edge. "You ready?"

"For you to hit me against a door? Technically, I am as sharp and as durable as I can be, so yes. Hit away."

"Sorry," I say as I take the first swing with my right arm.

It's an overhead chop, meant to slice the door vertically down the middle. Instead, T'Oli's edge strikes the metal and bounces off, though the Ooblot does manage to leave a small groove where I hit.

"That's going to take a long time," Malo says from his corner, watching.

"If you have any other ideas, I'm listening." I try to keep frustration from nipping at the edges of my words, but it's hard. Chipping through this door with T'Oli is going to take more time and strength than I have, and that's not counting whether the Ooblot's going to put up with the abuse.

I give Malo a few seconds, but no inspiration flies from his lips, so I lift T'Oli up for a second strike. Both of its eyes wince, and mine do too. And I swing. There's a clank, a screech of metal and another piece, a little larger, falls out to the ground. I sweep the chunk away with my foot—it's barely bigger than my fingertip—and get set for round three.

When the door opens.

There's no warning. No gradual twisting of locks or command from Ferrolite that we're about to get introduced to some new guards. Instead, from one moment to the next I'm looking at a gray metal barrier and then a pair of annoyed, black-furred, blue-uniformed Flaum. Their miners are holstered, their claws are at their sides, and their beady eyes go right to the Ooblot I'm wearing on my arm. Behind them, the once-crowded halls of the Chorus ring look very, very empty.

"Hi," is all I can think of to say.

Malo works faster, flying out from the side to tackle the left Flaum and drive the furry creature into the ground. That draws the eyes of its companion, which opens it up to a swing once my instincts kick back in. These Flaum are meant to keep us here, not help us. Yet when my right hand, with T'Oli on it, lands, I don't feel the smooth stabbing of a sharp knife but the jolt up my arm of a hammer blow. My target stumbles backward, to the other side of the doorway, and its hands go towards the matted fur spot where I've apparently punched it.

"What are you doing?" I shout at the Ooblot even as I step into another swing, this one aiming higher.

The Flaum, though, ducks the move and dives at me.

Gets beneath my swipe and hits my waist. Knocks us both to the ground. T'Oli thinks fast and slimes from my hand up and around the Flaum's left claw, then drips to the floor before the Flaum can shake the Ooblot off. T'Oli hardens as I squeeze out from under the creature, sealing the Flaum to the ground.

"Stop." Viera's voice hits loud and hard. "I hate the smell, but move and I'm torching your fur."

The Lunare stands next to us, a miner in her hand and pointing at my Flaum. The one tussling with Malo stops too, with Malo gripping both its forearms in what looks like a stalemate. That one still has its miner holstered, but mine is missing its weapon.

Viera's threat gives me the time I need to walk over to Malo's Flaum and yank its miner away. From there it's a threaten-and-move situation to get the pair of Flaum guards to walk back into our former prison. We head outside, T'Oli back on my shoulders, and Malo taps the panel to slide the door shut.

"Is it cruel to leave them in there?" Viera asks.

"They did it to us," I reply. "Fair trade."

The Chorus ring is deserted. The alarms have, thankfully, gone quiet. All the terminals now have a blaze red EVACUATION banner glowing across the bottom, followed by a strict sentence declaring said evacuation is only for Amigga and their guards. All other Chorus personnel, apparently, must fight for their fleeing masters.

"What would Damantum have done if the Emperor had fled the city and left the rest to die?" I ask Malo as we walk by the screens.

"They would have obeyed," Malo replies. "The Emperor had divine right. Some may have fled eventually, when the end was clear. But most? They would have stayed."

I take his words to mean we'll still find plenty of resistance here. The terminals showing the fighting taking place in the Meridia sport level numbers in the corners, and while there aren't signs saying what level we're on, I'm willing to bet it's a lot higher than the thirty-second floor I'm seeing on the terminals showing the constant battle.

Any Amigga, Flaum, or other Chorus troops that haven't made the long descent will still be here. Whether they'll take our escape as an assault or ignore us, I'm not sure.

"So do we descend?" T'Oli asks. "Try to meet up with the fighters?"

I want the Chorus to fall, I want to help Bas, but at the same time, Malo, Viera and I have two small miners to our names. We're far from some rescuing force blitzing to the rescue, and I'd rather not get caught in a firefight when neither force knows whose side we're on.

"No," I say as we continue along the ring. "We're not going all the way down yet. First, I want to learn about us."

"Us?" T'Oli asks.

"She means humans," Viera says. "I'm interested in weapons, if that counts. We find any, I get first choice."

"All yours," I say. "T'Oli, you said you think you know where the Chorus is keeping our history?"

T'Oli affirms it found a strange level not far below this one: a space with a spotty description that hinted at secrets I'd dearly love to know.

Back on Earth, I'd learned a little about the Amigga that designed us. It failed many times, and left its failures for us to find beneath the ash and wreck of an attempted Vincere extermination. But it was also clear that Amigga, that Ignos saved us. Took a shuttle and flew us away to the other side of the planet and let us thrive. What I want to find out is *why*? Why us? Why make humans when the Amigga have Oratus, when they have hordes of Flaum waiting to obey their every order?

"Something's coming," Malo, whose a half-step ahead of me, snaps. "Fight or run?"

From the growing clatter of boots on the ground, a fight is going to end with all of us dead or imprisoned. So I make the call and we cast around for a place to run to. Going back around the ring seems doable, but they might keep on going after us. If there's one place I *don't* want to fight someone, it's outside our old safe room, where a couple of angry Flaum reinforcements are a door panel away.

There's a dark entrance to the Chorus chamber to my left, but if there's any part of the Meridia under constant watch, I'm guessing it's there. So when Viera breaks for a small door slotted opposite the section entrance, I go with her.

Unlike our safe room, this door opens at our approach. No panel required. It's easy to see why—a store room. We rush in, crowd among the boxes and metal shelves holding all manner of supplies. No weapons that I can see. Only tools, slice of life stuff like solutions labeled for cleaning, repairs, or more. Powered-down robots linger in the corners and hang from hooks in the rafters.

As we pile in, the door closes behind us, leaving only a greenish glow from lights ringing the crease around the sides of the ceiling. It's enough to see, enough to make out that there's something else in the back of this large store-room. The bright white-blue light of a terminal screen halos its circular silhouette. Malo holds up a hand to us in the universal signal for quiet and advances. As he goes, Malo's left hand slips onto a shelf and slides off what looks like a thick metal bar with a curved end. The motion doesn't make any noise, and Malo slips the weapon into a two-handed grip as he gets closer. Viera and I watch, miners raised, and T'Oli forms its customary armor over my chest.

"If you're looking for the intruders, they aren't here," a gruff, robotic voice sounds. "You should know better than to think they'd make it this far."

Malo pauses, throws a glance back my way.

"You're not a bunch of mutes, are you?" the voice continues. "I thought that gene line died out some time ago. Turns out you Flaum go insane if you can't talk to each other."

Flaum? I'm almost insulted. Malo's confused now, and Viera's looking at me with a narrow-eyed, tight-lipped stare that's begging permission to roast this thing, but I'm a curious person, and I can't help but ask.

"You think we're Flaum?" I say, gesturing for Malo to move to the side and give Viera a clear shot.

The creature shudders for a second, and then there's a whir of a machine spooling up. With a grind of creaky metal, the Amigga turns around to face us. It's not too distinct with the terminal's light washing out its skin, but it's easy to pick out the thick, rudimentary metal legs and bars forming a cradle for the creature. Compared to what I've seen with Ferrolite, much less the First Chair, this Amigga's equipment is so basic that I have to repress a laugh.

"Humans?" Now the Amigga sounds surprised. "You're not supposed to exist."

"Yeah, we know," Viera says. "You and the Sevora both tried to make sure of that. And both of you failed."

"No, no," the Amigga replies. "Not like that. There was always something wrong with your make-up. Your species could never live long enough to be viable. That's why the experiment was scrapped. Such a shame we had to waste a great planet on your species."

"You didn't waste it," I say. "It's our home."

"Is it?" the Amigga laughs. "Of course Ignos would pull a move like that. It always was bullheaded. Never wanted to give up even when its projects failed."

Part of me wants to hear what the Amigga has to say, another part of me is getting annoyed at the Amigga's constant barrage of insults.

"Why do—" I start to say.

"Be good little failures," the Amigga interrupts. "And leave me now. The First Chair calls for an evacuation and I finally have a moment of peace to myself. Can't have mistakes like you ruining it."

"Call me a mistake one more time," Viera says.

"Are you upset by the truth, failure?" the Amigga says.

Before another word leaves its speakers, there's a series of bright red flashes tracing from Viera's miner to the Amigga. Each hit sparks a tiny flame, and at the third, a garbled groan comes from the creature. Then Malo's filling the space, striking hard and fast with his stolen tool. He breaks anything he can find on the Amigga's machine, then cracks apart the terminal's screen too.

"I don't know what's going to shoot us in here," Malo says to my raised eyebrow when the warrior's done flailing around.

"Agreed," Viera says.

"It could have told us something," I say, going up closer and looking at the Amigga. "It knew about us."

"What it knew," Malo says. "Isn't us. We're not some failed experiment, Kaishi. We're the only ones who get to decide what we are."

The Amigga's body is burned and crumpled. Whatever secrets it held, I'm not going to hear them now. So I stand, turn around to my fellow failures, and nod towards the door.

"Malo, you're starting to think like me," Viera says. "I don't like it."

"Me neither," Malo replies.

Unfortunately, the opposite side of the level isn't any better than where Sax came in from. A pair of lifts, both locked down with a glowing red panel, and without Kah's now-severed hand, Sax isn't getting out that way either. Instead, he has to jump and gouge off of the wall to dodge a series of strikes from the pursuing warbots. More than a dozen, now, rotate to watch Sax leap from the wall into another batch of still-dead warbots, using their cables to keep himself moving above the ground.

Running around in pointless circles isn't going to keep him alive for long.

"We've found an exploit!" Nobaa's yelling from the center terminal, the one voice that, as much as it bugs him, gives Sax a bit of hope. "Engee's in the Meridia's network, and all these warbots are hooked into—"

Sax misses the last part of that as the warbot he's standing on activates and pops loose from its cable. His talons keep Sax gripped on top, and give the Oratus a chance to leap before the new warbot swings its sword through where Sax was standing. With his own powerless blade, Sax blocks the warbot's second sword as the Oratus lands on the next warbot in line. He'd like to turn back and take the fight to one of these things, but several more are already swarming the position, their microjets floating them over deactivated machines and towards Sax. A sightless, implacable line of glowing swords and blue-metal orbs.

Back to the original lifts. Buying time. Buying space. But when Sax gets to those same doors, that same red panel, he stops. His vents push out air, and he hisses one long, low sound. Running isn't what he's meant for, isn't what he does. If Sax is going to die, it won't be with a sword to the back. It'll be fighting and trying, however impossible it might be, to live.

Wheeling around, Sax expects to find the warbots coming towards him, ready to slice him into Oratus chunks. What he sees instead forces a blink, then another. A sorting of the sounds, the clashing and clanging that Sax thought was the warbots forcing their way through to him but is, instead, the battering cacophony of metal smashing metal. More warbots are activating, disengaging from the thick black-white cables holding them to the ceiling and settling into a fight with... each other. Swords swing, buzzing with energy, and empty miners bash against each other as metal limbs fly and sparks set fires to cables and wires scattered around the room as the machines destroy themselves.

Sax watches. Spends a thought thanking Nobaa, Engee. The terminal's in the middle of that fiery robot struggle, and Sax figures it's not going to survive. The two Teven must have found a way to do exactly what had been done to warbots countless times throughout their existence—turn them against their creators.

It's good to have the reason for his existence confirmed.

Now Sax suppresses his own instincts. He wants to jump into the fight, to tear and bite and destroy along with the mechanical things, but Sax holds himself back. Focuses his swift-beating hearts and his twitchy eyes away from non-imminent death and towards the ceiling. Nobaa said his escape was up there, through the ceiling to another lift. One that could go higher, maybe all the way to the Priority Beam.

Sax takes another jump, scales the wall to the ceiling and digs in with his talons and foreclaws while his midclaws get to work tearing and shredding aside the tiles. Digging their way through the Meridia's guts to carve a path upwards. There's pipes and wires, unknown cabling and things that make noises as Sax tries to weave his way through them. An Oratus isn't small, so while Sax tries to shove aside what he can, he leaves more than a few snapped and shattered things left in the annals between the two levels.

Sometimes those things shower Sax's scales in sparks, sometimes in gasses or in disgusting fluids, but Sax doesn't think about it. Forces himself past the moment and into the future, to where all of this pays off. To where there is no more Chorus and the only choice he'll have to make is where, with Bas, they want to go. What things they want to hunt. The hope sticks with Sax and helps him grind his way through until he gets to the thicker flooring before the next level.

Scrunched between a thick black pipe that suggests terrible things if it's broken and a knotted assemblage of cords, only some of which bear Sax's slashing marks, the Oratus squishes up against the heavy tile. It's cool, and red. Thick and smooth, even on the underside. What light Sax has filters up from the level below, where, going by the noise, the warbot brawl continues on. He can see, he can brace, and he can push, and when Sax does, the tile buckles and breaks free of its setting, sliding up and over its neighbors.

There's one problem: the tile is small, and Sax is huge. He has to shift more, and do it before anything on this level decides to blast him to pieces. Sax works fast, kicking and pushing other tiles aside, expecting a blast to come through at any moment, but none does, and Sax gets himself out and standing without a single attack rendering him useless.

"Fascinating. I never expected to see myself here," the words are soft, slow and methodical, as if each one comes as the result of deliberate effort.

The level is lit in dim crimson from a series of lamps over the lift doors on either side of the level. The first thing Sax notices, after tracking to the light, is that both banks have red-glowing panels in front of them. Locked beyond Sax's ability to open them.

"You don't need to worry," the voice continues. "They drop the food down every now and then. Enough to keep you from starving."

Sax looks back to the sound, the weakness of which led the Oratus to discount the noise until any possible escapes could be identified. Seeing as there are none of those, Sax affords the speaker his full, clawed attention. And recoils. Almost falls back through the hole he's just made.

The voice comes from an Oratus, but it's the oldest Oratus Sax has ever seen. Scales once a metallic green are chipped and fading, curling at the edges like a flower in the cold. Dark holes sit where his eyes should be, and of his claws, only the right foreclaw remains. All others have been grafted together, their ends pulled into harmless clubs.

Teeth too, are gone, and the talons shriveled, translucent splinters.

"Age is a terrible thing," the Oratus continues. "We're not meant to grow old, you and I. Not made for it."

"Who are you?"

"Me? I was someone once, a very long time ago, but now I am only a test. An experiment for the Chorus," the Oratus glances upward with its eyeless face. "They watch me all the time. Looking for something, anything. They keep me alive, use me for what they need, and leave me here when they are done, to wait."

Sax follows the look. Across the ceiling, shrouded in shadows due to the angle of those red-eyed lamps, camera nubs sprinkle across the tiles. So many of them for one subject, for one small area.

"But what are you, visitor?" the Oratus asks. "A new subject? Have the rules of the game changed?"

"The game is ending," Sax hisses. He doesn't have time for this, no matter how curious this Oratus and his story might be. "Do you know a way to call the lifts?"

The Oratus laughs, or wheezes, Sax can't really tell what the old creature's vents are doing. "You don't call them. They do." The one claw points up. "Everything here belongs to them, including you and I."

Sax is about to go take a closer look at one of the lift banks, but the Oratus' words deliver an angry cut. This creature is wrong, broken. An Oratus should never give up. Should fight to the last, and embrace a well-earned death. This one is everything that an Oratus should never be.

"Nothing owns me," Sax replies, and instead of going to the lifts, he stomps towards the old Oratus, who is lying on the empty floor near a waste-water recycler. "The Chorus may have made me, but I am not their tool."

On the battlefield, Sax would help a downed fighter. He would bring them to their feet, administer what aid he could and call for help so that he could resume his real mission. This isn't a battlefield, and the old Oratus, aside from its age, appears unharmed. Maybe that's why Sax is so compelled to force the Oratus to his talons, to get the creature standing. The old Oratus hisses in surprise when Sax suddenly grips its arms and lifts the creature up.

"Your name?" Sax says.

"Subject," the Oratus hisses weakly, leaning on Sax. "That is what they call me."

"I don't care what they call you. What is your name?"

The Oratus lifts his head, a slow, creaking motion that has Sax wincing. It is wrong for an Oratus to be this weak.

"Rovel," the Oratus finally says, the letters marching out one after another like an opening box.

Five letters, and not a combination Sax has heard before. Not a name for an Oratus bent to war, nor one for command. Rovel. The name's surprising enough that Sax steps back—careful to keep his claws in position to catch Rovel should he topple forward—and considers the old Oratus again. The wounds, the deformations, but he can see a different frame on Rovel now. Standing, Rovel doesn't assume a combat stance. He's straight, his claws, aside from the midclaw bracing himself against the watering station, hang limp by his sides and Rovel's eyes track towards the ground.

Demure, servile.

"They've broken you?" Sax ventures to ask. There has to be some explanation for this, for why an Oratus would be so placid.

"Broken?" Rovel says, then pauses, as if considering

whether he might be. "No. No. Not broken. Defeated, maybe, but I was made this way."

Another strange word to use, and Sax ignores the pressure to get moving, to find an exit, to follow intuition down its dark path. "You're the first one."

Now Rovel looks up. Now Rovel meets Sax square. "The first one that survived."

"They've kept you alive all this time?"

"Too valuable to die."

Sax doubts that, looking at Rovel. The Chorus could have captured any number of Oratus, taken them from the Vincere and secreted them here. There must be some other reason, maybe one that could help.

"Tell me how to get off the level," Sax hisses sharp. "Now."

"I already—"

"You lied."

Rovel tilts his head. Says nothing.

"The Amigga are ruthless. They would replace something as worthless as you seem to be. Call the lifts."

Rovel gives Sax a level stare and, for the first time, bares his teeth. "I am the first, but I am also the last, Oratus. They gave me a mind to match this body, and when it proved too strong, I helped them reduce your kind to instinctual monsters. To flashes of anger coupled with just enough comprehension to make military strategy." Rovel settles as he rasps the words, shedding off the weaker stance, standing firm and glaring bright. "You are a product, and we are your maker."

"I don't care," Sax says, and it's true. He is who, what he is. Nothing this pathetic excuse for an Oratus might say can change that. "Call the lifts."

"Do you know why I'm here?" Rovel hisses again,

apparently not hearing Sax. "Because you all failed. I used to be at the top of this tower, used to stand near the First Chair. But now the Oratus will go extinct, replaced by those machines. All because of your resistance. Because you will not obey your creators."

"One more time. The lifts."

When Rovel takes a deep breath, starts in on another rant, Sax whips his tail and cracks the elder Oratus in the face, sending Rovel reeling into the wall next to the water station. It's a move that tells Sax all he needs to know—his tail came in a long arc, with plenty of time for Rovel to intercept, dodge, or even attack Sax before the strike arrived.

Oratus should be weapons, and even an old weapon ought to know how to fight.

"Pathetic," Sax hisses, then turns towards the left lift bank.

Nobaa said there was a lift here capable of taking Sax all the way up to the top. There are four on this level, and one of them is what he's looking for. Five long strides brings Sax to the lift doors and their red panel, with no way to unlock it.

Unless...

"Rovel," Sax looks back at the old Oratus, picking himself up slow from the ground. "You might have a way to serve your species yet."

On the far end of the level, opposite the docking bay where we arrived, sits a bank of four smooth metal doors. Each one is shaded a different color, and as we approach a raised panel standing front of them, the screen divides to show ranges of numbers next to small, colored squares showing those same colors.

"This makes it easy," I say as we walk up to them. Around us, the usual collection of terminals occupy the otherwise empty ring. After leaving the Amigga's corpse back in the storeroom, we've moved slow to get here, but we haven't heard another set of steps coming our way. "Where did you say the level was?"

"Only three beneath this one," T'Oli replies. "So, the green one."

Each of the doors has a single-screen panel that sits dark until I press my palm against its cool surface. This one lights up in teal, and while I don't hear anything, only a moment passes before the green doors open and give way to a wide, tall lift. The size is so absurd that I stare at it for a moment before remembering just how huge Oratus are.

"Makes me feel small," Viera says as we get in.

"That's why you're carrying the miners," I reply.

I'd given Viera my miner too, seeing as my shooting is as likely to snipe one of us as it is the enemy. Instead, I followed Malo's choice and grabbed a pair of long, thick tools to wield.

One, a half-meter long bar that ends in a near-point, comes with a strap that lets it rest on my shoulder. The other, a shorter and thicker club with a mallet head, finds an easy grip in my left hand. With either, I should be able to make some useful contribution to a fight without risking too much damage to my friends. The club, after all, is similar to the kukris. A little longer, a little heavier.

Malo does the honors and taps the button to send us down and the lift obeys with a whoosh.

Unlike the lifts on a Vincere ship, or even on the Sevora's moon-smashed Vimelia, this one isn't an austere box of metal. Rather, the side walls shift between static scenes as we move. When we entered the lift, I saw an icy sky with falling, glittering snow catching light from a distant star. Now we're descending surrounded by spinning asteroids in deep space, with splashes of purples and reds scattered around us.

The Amigga are capable of terrible things, but beautiful ones too. Just like humans.

When the lift doors open, though, there's not much of that beauty before us. Instead, the ghost-blue from terminal screens dominates a dark space. Any overhead lights are off, and the only things I can see from the doors are those screens, and the larger, shimmering projections occupying spaces between them.

There are depictions of creatures I've never seen before —things with a multitude of legs, others that appear to be blobs of gas with only a single, small ball floating in the center. Others show carved up landscapes, ridged canyons or a vast, vine-covered plain. All in that white-blue, and all floating just below the height of my eyes.

"Hold up," Malo whispers, again leading the way. "We're not alone."

"I thought they ordered an evacuation," Viera mutters. "Why are people still here?"

"Maybe they're crazy," I say. "Like us."

What Malo sees comes clear to me as I step around a giant, spinning projection of a planet. Clustered farther into the level, messing with a series of images, is an Amigga, along with a trio of Flaum. None of these, though, are carrying weapons. None are wearing armor, though the Amigga appears to float on a microjet machine like the one Ferrolite uses.

"So Ferrolite wasn't lying," the Amigga says, and its low, gravel voice echoes from speakers around us, apparently embedded throughout the level. "The humans really have come home."

With Viera keeping her miners trained on the Flaum and their spherical leader, I take the lead, weaving through the projections and the terminals producing them. White spots on the floor bear a faint, deep blue outline, allowing me to see where you might be able to create a chair. One of the Flaum already has a small pedestal next to it, where a device that looks like a Cache is resting.

The aliens watch me, silent and still. I feel like I'm some mythical creature, walking out of legends—or at least, old data logs—to appear in front of disbelievers. Still, unlike the Amigga in the storeroom above, this one lets me speak first.

"We want to know where we came from, and why," I say first. "Can you tell us?"

"I don't think you'd believe me if I did," the Amigga replies. "You're not working with that force attacking the bottom of our beautiful tower, are you?"

"Not yet." Technically, we haven't done anything to help Bas and her invaders, and I'm not afraid to take advantage of blurred lines here. "We came here to pledge our species to the Chorus, and I want to know why you saw fit to create us."

"Then I will make a deal with you," the Amigga replies. "Put down your miners and let my associates go free. They should leave the Meridia anyway, and I promise you they will not go find any guards. Do so, and I will use my access to show you the restricted records that hold your true history."

Trusting an Amigga is like throwing a black-glass knife into the air and trying to catch it; you're going to get hurt. Still, I don't think Viera can shoot us out of this situation. Given our lackluster luck with the terminal in the safe room, getting through without whatever access the Amigga's talking about doesn't seem likely. So while the six eyes of the Flaum trio and the expressionless blob of gray that is the Amigga stares back at me, I have to choose: risk our lives for a chance to see our history?

"Do it," Malo says, and his voice is closer than I expected. I feel him come up behind me, then move next and past me, towards our hostages. "Send the Flaum away. Open the logs."

"Malo? What?"

Malo doesn't glance back at me, but instead points with his toolbar across the level, through the projections and towards the opposite lift. "Go." The Flaum, though, only move when I give the nod and Viera lowers her miners by the smallest of margins. Once the furry creatures have started their exit does Malo throw an eye my way. "We broke out of that room because you wanted to learn where we came from. If you don't get the chance to see it, then what's the point?"

"You don't sound like you want to know?" I ask Malo, and note that Viera's staying back and out of this argument. T'Oli, too, is sliming away from me and following the Flaum, content to leave its pattered opinions out.

"I know where I come from," Malo replies. "My parents lived in Damantum, though I guess they don't any longer. I'm a Charre warrior, and I serve the Empress and follow the god of all things, Ignos. Nothing else matters."

The Amigga floats there, content to let us argue. Maybe it's studying our behavior, logging our every word into the Chorus' short history of the human race.

"You weren't there," I say to Malo. "When we went back and saw what was left behind, what survived when the Chorus tried to obliterate every bit of us. We were *made*, Malo. Designed and grown. What I don't know is why."

Malo only steps back from the Amigga and the terminal behind it. Waves for me to take his place. "Then learn. But Kaishi? Don't tell me. I don't care. I prefer the history I know. Our history."

The warrior can make his own choices, so I take up his offer and walk near the Amigga, who rotates around to face the terminal. It's a large one, with a trio of wide screens, each with a nub on the top that projects blue light onto a platform behind the whole setup. Right now it's showing a landscape, but with a quick buzz-whirr, the Amigga issues some command that slides several pieces out of its floating disk. The tendrils with shiny, short cylinders on the end float towards the ground for a half-moment, then snap towards the terminal and latch onto matching circles.

"We'll secure the area," Viera offers from behind me, as much, I suspect, to give Malo something to do as to hole up from a threat. We all know the Chorus could wipe us out if they cared enough. "You let us know when you're done."

"I'll be fast." It's a promise I can't keep, because I have no idea of the journey I'm about to start, but it seems like the right thing to say.

"Human," the Amigga says. "The curse of my species is that we do not care overmuch for the feelings of others, but I must agree with your friend. What you will see here will expose your past as something better left forgotten. These secrets will not win your war, nor save your kind."

"You don't know that."

The projection behind the terminal shifts as text begins to fill across the screen. Behind and beyond me, I can hear Viera and Malo start moving furniture. Blocking the lifts. Buying me time to learn, and to understand.

"Very well. Your story, such as it is, begins with an accident."

The Amigga's terminal blurs and shifts until I'm seeing another world on its screen. Behind the terminal, the blue projection changes too; into a world I recognize as my own. Earth's continents sit on the slowly-spinning globe, until they're joined by a much smaller oval, one that the projection targets and zooms in on. The terminal joins in, locking into someone's perspective. There's a manicured white-metal hallway, a few Flaum standing by holding all manner of devices and watching as whomever guides the terminal's view glides along.

Glides.

"These are an Amigga's eyes?" I ask.

"In a manner of speaking," the Amigga replies. "This device records and transmits what we might see if we had eyes. We bind our nerves to its receptors, and in doing, gain control over its abilities just as you have over your own limbs."

"Then who is this?"

"Your creator."

Our 'creator' presses on until it gets to a large, circular hatchway. It issues some even-tempered commands to other Flaum—these all wearing full masks, the sheen of them keeping the Flaum's fur pressed down—and the hatch opens. I recognize a shuttle on the other side, and soon enough our guide is in its cockpit.

"What're you going to call this planet?" One of the Flaum pilots asks. "It's not on the registries."

"I haven't thought about it." The guide holds silent for a moment. "We'll choose later on. When we know what's going to happen here."

The recording freezes. I glance up at the projection and its frozen too.

"This is the first inkling we have of Ignos's doubt," the Amigga says to me. "An Amigga should be more confident. We gave Ignos one of the most valuable remaining planets in the galaxy. Ignos told us it would create our last species, and it lied."

"You trusted Ignos, you mean."

"The Amigga don't trust lightly. Reputations are built and maintained, and Ignos had a spotless one. It helped design the Oratus, including the mirrored variant you see all over this tower," the Amigga almost sounds sad here. "So much promise wasted on a flawed premise."

"Which was?"

"That we could create something better than ourselves."

The terminal jolts into another clip before I can investigate that statement. We're in a forest now, one far different from the jungle I grew up in and more resembling those scattered sets up in the Lunare mountains; pines and bits of snow. A brown floor rather than one crawling with ferns. Yet it's verdant all the same, though the view pans through a wide array of Flaum wielding tools or driving massive, lumbering machines tearing their way through the landscape.

"We will need to dig deep," Ignos says to something we cannot see.

"Deep?" The light voice betrays another Flaum.

"Enough to bury our mistakes, and preserve our successes."

The screen shifts again and we're further along. A small brook runs along between a set of trees and a trio of creatures occupies the center, staring at the moving water. The creatures are small, shorter than me, and wear various skin tones, from brown to black and white. Some have tufts of hair sticking out from odd places, like their knees or the middle of their backs. Their hands, too, are shrunken and end in hooked claws.

"Touch it. The water will not harm you," Ignos says.

The creatures hesitate. One casts a look back at the screen, and I see that its left eye takes up nearly half its face, its pupil huge the eyelid a sagging mess. The others, though, look more normal. More human. Yet none of them move to obey the command.

"Touch it, now." The exasperation is obvious in Ignos' voice.

Still, none of them move. A different one opens its mouth, and a low, distorted chirping comes out, like a Flaum's skittering squeak mixed with the hooting calls of an owl. None of them touch the water.

"Too afraid. Increase the aggression and the curiosity in

the next batch," Ignos says. "And, please, clean up the hair. They must be adaptable, and hair adds too many complications."

"Anything more with these?" I can't see what asks this question, but it sounds like another Flaum.

"No. Dispose of them."

I blink. Keep myself from stepping back from the terminal. "Ignos just had them killed?"

"A project like this will have numerous failures on the way to success," the Amigga tells me. "Would you rather they were left to roam an unfamiliar world until some predator consumed them? Or, depending on the development stage, they may not have had the ability to eat. To speak or digest. Creating a new species is a messy business."

I'm starting to understand why the Amigga treat everyone as secondary, as tools to be used. If you'd disposed of countless iterations as nothing more than mistakes on the way to your preferred creation, you might not care all that much either.

The terminal flashes again and now we're underground. A space I recognize, though the lack of junk and presence of functioning lights give it a different feel than when I explored the ruined base. Ignos appears to be floating in front of a wall-sized terminal, looking at a lot of different graphs and numbers.

"There's been another conflict," a Flaum's voice, I think the same one from before. "That makes three this week."

"I thought we'd tuned the violence? They passed the tests."

"It's not the violence, Ignos. It's the intelligence. When we made the Oratus, we made them obedient to a fault. These humans, they have too much independence. When they get frustrated, they do not listen. They fight."

"But they can be taught?"

"Yes." The Flaum's voice gets more hopeful. "Our evaluations show, too, that the Sevora will not be able to establish full control."

"Because of that independence."

"Yes. It seems the same will that drives these humans to act in their own interests can allow them to overpower a Sevora's blocks."

"Then we will find another way to calm them down."

The terminal pauses again.

"Do you see the problem?" the Amigga says to me. "Ignos believed willpower was the key to defeating the Sevora. What it failed to realize was that same willpower could, one day, be used against the Chorus. When we saw these recordings, when we saw Ignos' continued failure to make humans happy in a controlled, defined existence like the Oratus have within the Vincere, we made the choice to end your species before it could proliferate."

"You didn't like that we thought for ourselves?"

"Not only that you thought for yourselves, but that you acted on those impulses. Ignos also had your breeding rate tuned high enough to make galaxy-wide populations a strong possibility. Oratus are controlled. Vyphen, Teven, most species have low enough birth rates to keep them manageable. Flaum are too skittish and ill-equipped for command to be a threat. Humans, though? They would be problem." The Amigga gives a monotone laugh. "You *are* a problem."

The terminal flashes again, and now Ignos is floating fast towards the base's large docking bay. Things are shaking, panels on the roof are falling in, and the Flaum around Ignos are yelling at each other and the Amigga.

"Make sure the back-up supplies are ready!" Ignos shouts as the Amigga enters the shuttle-filled bay.

When I was last there, the exit had been buried shut. T'Oli, using a stolen shuttle, crashed through the roof to give us a way out. Now, through Ignos' eyes, I can see a wide open ramp leading to bright blue sky. Grass and trees peek around the sides as Ignos takes what looks like a longing glance at an Earth it's about to leave.

"They are. We already have enough stored away." The same Flaum's voice. "Ignos, we have to leave now. The Vincere are sending shuttles down."

"Then we have one chance," Ignos says. "Set the save-state protocol. Make them lose too much, and they might leave us alone."

Ignos floats its way up a shuttle's ramp, and within moments the craft blasts out through the bay. Instead of rising into the sky, however, I watch through Ignos' 'eyes' as the ship barrels through the tops of trees and narrow passes, hugging the ground.

"Chorus, when you see this, know that I don't hold your short-sighted faults against you," Ignos says, and the recording blinks to black. "You may think I have failed, but I promise you, I have not."

"That's the end of it," the Amigga says a second later. "After that transmission, we heard nothing more from Ignos. We commenced a cleansing bombardment of that side of Earth a short time after, and it was assumed Ignos perished in that assault. Now, though, it seems more likely Ignos and its associates died a more natural death after helping your species start again."

So it's all true, then. I'm surprised at myself for the confusion I'm feeling, the disappointment. I guess I had hoped, somehow, that everything I'd suspected was all wrong. That the humans Viera and I discovered on the far side of Earth were a product of some later experiment gone awry, not the original tests for what later became Father, Mother, and me. That most of humanity worships the great yellow star in our sky as Ignos makes more sense now—the haunting ghost of where we began.

The unsettled twinges in my gut curdle to distaste quick. Being the creation of a hard-driving, brutal Amigga isn't a history I want to have. It's not an inspiring story. Not one of overcoming hardship, or creating a better world. It's one alien's idea that, through luck and some planning, survived forced extinction from the rest of the civilized galaxy.

More than all of that, though, I don't want to be the property of the Chorus. I don't want to be their creation. Their *product*.

"Delete it all," I say, and when the Amigga doesn't immediately move to follow my order, I raise the hammer in my right hand. "Do it, now."

"Human, these are sealed records," the Amigga replies. "They are not on Caches. They do not exist anywhere but here, where only those with proper clearance can view them. Humanity's origins will remain a secret, I assure you."

"Yes, they will," I say. "Because you're going to destroy them. Now."

The Amigga hesitates. I gather the creature takes the destruction of knowledge like this some sort of sacrilege, given the setting and its ability to access these secret records. I, though, see these recordings as evidence of something that doesn't matter.

Before I saw what Ignos did, I believed we came from the dust, from the magic of a god. All of the humans back on Earth believe something similar. Myths and legends, stories are told every day and night about the wondrous ways our civilization grew. These... these are nothing. A bad story told by a bad species, and one that doesn't deserve a second telling.

"Do what she asks." Malo appears next to me, and together we use our weapons to imply the consequences.

The threat can't have much weight, as I don't know how the terminals work. How the Chorus stores these recordings. If the Amigga doesn't obey, I don't think we'll be able to—

The terminal flashes. A black circle, outlined in red, appears in the center of the screen. Slowly, the solid red fills in from the outside until the entire circle is complete. Then, with a tiny chime so low I can barely hear it, the terminal goes back to its static, icon-covered screen.

"It's done," the Amigga says. "Your secrets are lost, now."

"How can we trust you?" I ask.

"I do not think I can convince you," the Amigga replies. "You would not understand how to verify. What you can do, though, is choose to believe."

"Choose to believe? That doesn't mean anything."

"Doesn't it? Aren't you making the same argument for your own people? Letting them choose to believe their own stories for their origins?"

I stand with that for a breath. The Amigga's right on all counts, though the thought annoys me. Still, the creature did say that these secrets are only stored here. Why take any chances?

"Malo, let's break these things, and then go find the others. Viera, keep an eye on this one."

The Amigga's smart enough to back away as we start swinging. It doesn't say a word as I bash in one terminal screen after another. As Malo tears apart the thick cords linking things together, prompting sparks to fly in the dark spaces of the level. Despite the size of the place, with both of us working together, we manage to devastate everything fast. I'm sweaty, but smiling at the end of it.

"Feels good getting back to what we know, doesn't it?" Malo says to me when we're done.

"I'm definitely better at smashing these things than using them." I look over at the Amigga, floating silent amid the rubble. "Thank you for your help. When the Chorus falls apart, I'll let whatever replaces them know you're worth keeping around."

"It doesn't matter who's in charge," the Amigga replies as we head towards the lifts. "The cycle's always the same. The stories are forgotten, and then retold."

"What a boring philosophy," Viera mutters. "I think you made the slimeball a little sad."

"It'll get over it." The lift panel, for the one we didn't barricade, sits in front of me. "I'm guessing we need to keep going down?"

T'Oli slithers its way onto my shoulders. "If you want to find those fighters, that's probably a good idea. Unfortunately, these lifts only go back up."

"Then I guess that's where we're heading." I put my hand out, touch Malo's shoulder. "You ready?"

"I am, Empress."

"Viera?"

"I'm ready to shoot something, Kaishi. Let's get 'em."

A battle-cry for the ages, I think.

Rovel sputters protests as Sax drags the old Oratus back towards the lift bank. The words aren't worth paying attention to; gibbering insults and petty threats from a coward. Sax has heard the same many times before, usually from his soon-to-be victims.

Not that Sax plans to kill Rovel. No, if there's anything that will serve to turn the Vincere to the side of the Resistance, it's the sight of this creature. This anathema to what an Oratus should be. If the Chorus are willing to do this to an Oratus, then there are no limits to their evils.

"Activate it." Sax pulls Rovel the rest of the way.

"You think I would still be here if they let me use the lifts?" Rovel switches tactics.

It doesn't work.

"Yes." Sax takes Rovel's last remaining claw and presses it against the panel.

As expected, as Sax knew it would even as he hoped, in some small corner of himself, that Rovel really wasn't such a servant of the Amigga, the panel turns green. The nearest lift ought to be coming now, and if Sax is lucky, it'll be the one he's looking for.

"I tried," Rovel says low and soft, defeated. "I told them I would try to turn you, when their methods failed."

"A stupid idea," Sax says.

"Almost as stupid as attacking the Chorus."

Rovel's hiss dies as the lift's doors open, revealing not an empty container that Sax could ride to the top of the Meridia but an Amigga. Or a warbot. Or both. Sax back-steps from the lift while Rovel moves to the side, giving plenty of room for the new arrival to plod out on its trio of metal legs. Those three limbs form the foundation of an exoskeleton that sweeps up and around the gray-green bulk of the Amigga, which is covered in a filmy seal that Sax recognizes as a mask. Splitting the mask are a quartet of metal braces that slide up and over the Amigga like a cage, only this cage has lethal attachments.

Unlike the warbots, which played their weapons off of thin metal limbs streaking from their floating bulks, the Amigga's artillery spreads out over its head like a canopy, with a central beam rising like a rotor sitting across the top of the cage and splaying forth glowing ends like a leaf spreads its veins.

Sax looks at this assembly, at its lethality, and does what any Oratus greeted with such a display would do.

He laughs.

The hissing sound gets the Amigga to freeze, its body settling on those three legs with a creaking halt. The miners over its head angle their points towards Sax, as if that's going to scare him. These Amigga keep forgetting that Sax is supposed to be dead—there's not much to be afraid of when every breath is already borrowed.

"Not the reaction I was expecting," the Amigga says, its

voice low and grave, and still monotone. As if a computer were attempting to intimidate Sax. "I suspect you will change your assessment soon enough."

"Not likely."

"Those warbots below are old. Artifacts. Too many Amigga believe we need to rely on others to do our fighting for us," the Amigga says. "Using those old warbots as a guide, I've designed a way we Amigga can finally take control of our own destinies."

While the Amigga prattles on—Sax suspects the words are more for whomever is watching than Sax himself—he sidesteps towards the left wall of the level. Unfortunately, Rovel hasn't outfitted his floor with anything resembling furniture, so there's no cover on the flat, plain tiles. Without something to hide behind, the best move is going to be a fast assault. And not from where the Amigga expects it.

"You had control of your own destinies," Sax hisses back at the Amigga once its speech breaks, continuing to move. "Look at Rovel. You took him and turned the next version into me, and now you've lost."

"No, we've learned."

The Amigga swivels its body and Sax realizes a second too late that those three legs are designed to go in any direction, and the Amigga can wheel itself in whatever way it chooses. As that array of lasers turns towards Sax, the Oratus jumps towards the level's left wall. Catches on it with his claws, digs in and moves fast, clawing and climbing his way up the side towards the ceiling. Behind him, Sax feels the heat and sees the flashes as the Amigga burns a lot of bolts into the wall beneath him.

When Sax gets to the ceiling, he starts towards the Amigga and stops when a cascade of hot red fire burns in waves directly in front of Sax. The bolts leave a black line scored into the ceiling, and as the whine fades, it's replaced by Rovel's rasping laugh. Sax, frozen, has no doubt the Amigga could have roasted him right there. The monsters array is focused right at Sax, but the Amigga doesn't fire.

"See? This is as easy as it gets," the Amigga says. "Not even an Oratus that has defeated your execution plans can handle my design! After I finish him, give me the seat I deserve!"

There it is. Sax's last question is answered. The lifts stopped here, Rovel's been waiting here, and Sax would bet the warbots were activated all to lead him this way. Survive this far and he'd make a worthy kill for an Amigga looking to elevate itself all the way up to the Chorus.

Sax has been used for his entire life. First by the Vincere, and now by Evva. Not once has it made him angry, not until now.

The Oratus drops from the ceiling, pushing off with his claws to fall too fast for the Amigga's array, which starts blinding the level with laser fire, to track Sax. With a twist in mid-air, using the push-off as momentum, Sax hits the ground claws-first and, ignoring the shock of impact-pain, he pushes off towards the Amigga. Sax keeps his body as low to the ground as he can, his vents pressing against the floor as his claws, talons, and tail push him forward.

To its credit, the Amigga isn't so confident in itself that it doesn't try to back up. Those three legs start their rise and fall while the array orients on Sax's charge. Unlike a micro-jet, though, there's no instant propulsion here. A sacrifice of speed for stability, for the heavy weight arms like the ones the Amigga's carrying require.

Unfortunately, Sax is fast.

The Amigga scores a couple of glancing shots far down Sax's back as the Oratus leaps, the pain washed away by

Sax's bloodlust—that unquenchable thirst for the destruction of everything lying between Sax and his goals. The Oratus hits the Amigga in the middle, and Sax drives his claws through the mask's main weakness: close, personal, devastating blows. Every part of Sax contributes—his mouth tearing away the array's attachment to the rest of the Amigga, his claws shredding apart the cage and the creature inside of it, his talons ripping away the connections to those thick legs. Sax's tail, too, gets in a good whack when Rovel makes a worthless attempt to dislodge Sax from the assault, sending the old Oratus crumpling back against the very water station Rovel sat next to when Sax first arrived on this level.

Before the Amigga can say another word, before it can fire another shot, it's gone, and Sax is gulping down the remnants. He's never actually eaten an Amigga before, and while few things compare with the delicious, furry meat of a Flaum, Sax doesn't mind the mid-mission snack.

With sparking remnants littering the floor around him, Sax rises from the kill and turns back to Rovel, who's fallen into pure groveling mode now that his apparent benefactor's met the fate Rovel deserved cycles ago.

"Please," Rovel says, his voice a sickening whine. "I had no choice."

Sax doesn't answer. There's one thing he still needs from Rovel, and he understands that the only thing this Oratus truly values is its own skin. A currency as easy to exploit as any other.

"Then let me give you one," Sax replies, pouring every bit of a real Oratus' hiss into the words. "You will get me to the top of the Meridia, or I will give you your death here and now."

"The top?" Rovel says, and here his eyes track to the

other lift panel, opposite where the Amigga came from. "I don't have that clearance. Allocite, the Amigga you just... ate, would have been able to take you there."

"Then how close?" Sax says.

Rovel pauses, again throwing eyes towards the other bank of lifts, then the Oratus gets back on its talons. "Close enough, I think, for you to go the rest of the way."

At a wave from Sax's foreclaw, Rovel leads the way to those lifts and places his claw on the control panel. Once again, it turns green. This time, though, a lift doesn't immediately open, and a series of numbers appears on the panel.

"A queue," Rovel explains when Sax gives a slight warning hiss. "No games. There aren't many lifts that can traverse so many levels. For security, I believe. I don't have a priority clearance."

Sax can agree with the Chorus on one thing—trusting Rovel with anything important would be a mistake.

"After I leave," Sax says. "Summon another lift and go down. Find Evva and tell her what you did."

"They'll kill me if I do."

"I'll kill you if you don't," Sax puts a single foreclaw against Rovel's nose. "You turned against your own species. I can't say what the galaxy will look like when the Chorus falls, but perhaps, if you help us get through this tower, there might be a place in it for you."

The traitor's access might not last long once whichever Amigga controls such things realizes Rovel isn't on their side anymore, but even if the Oratus' claws get the fighters up a few more levels, then it's worth the attempt.

"I didn't want to do it," Rovel tries again as the counter on the panel ticks lower. "You see these stumps? They were burned off. One by one. Allocite made me fight, made me try to destroy its tests."

"You failed."

It's the truth, and it's devastating. Rovel shrinks away from Sax, goes back to the wall and sits, staring sullen towards his fellow Oratus. For his part, Sax is just fine cutting off the conversation. The stakes have been laid, the deal's been made, and there's no reason anymore to suffer the conversation of someone so lost as Rovel. Maybe Evva can redeem the old one, if she cares to try.

The lift dings a moment later, arrives empty, and Sax delivers one more hard stare to Rovel. A look that ought to haunt the Oratus' nightmares. One more price for him to pay, and far from enough.

A coward.

Sax would die a thousand times first.

Despite being armed and ready for anything, my twitchy aggression, spiked after our successful destruction of my own species' history, falters when I'm confronted with what's pasted in gold-rimmed Chorus blue on each of the lift's three walls and, once they close, the two doors:

RESEARCH AND ARCHIVES ONLY

As if to confirm the words, the panel only lists ten levels, each of which is higher than the one we're just leaving. Their labels are vague enough to be interesting—one level reads out *Planets and Planetoids* while another discusses *Robotics and Mechanical Recovery*. None of them, though, seem like they'll take us to Bas and the other fighters.

"Where do you think we should go?" I ask. There's a brief silence, and then the quiet patters give truth to my suspicions: T'Oli has an opinion.

"This is a dedicated lift, and I would assume most levels have lifts like this," the Ooblot says. "Given that we're likely to be pursued, and that the Chorus will know where we are the moment we leave this lift, I suggest we choose the level that sounds like the most fun."

"The puddle's got a point," Viera says. "Let's go there." The Lunare points to the sixth one above ours, a level titled *Astronavigation and the Vincere*. "Figure, if nothing else, we can get a glimpse of what kind of weapons we'll be up against when the Vincere comes after Earth."

"You and I both know they'll blow us up from orbit." Nonetheless, I press the button. "If the Chorus doesn't die here, humans are probably done."

"They may not hold the rest of your species responsible for your crimes," T'Oli says as the lift churns to life, whisking us upward. "Humanity may yet have a chance to enslave themselves to the Chorus' will."

"Is the Ooblot always this way?" Malo asks, and Viera and I give him our exhausted affirmatives at the same time.

"We are, always, who we are," T'Oli responds.

The lift doors, thankfully, put an end to that conversation with a smooth opening. Beyond them is a level that, at first, seems similar to the one we just left. Terminals abound, and blue projections fill in most of the gaps in the dark room. Instead of landscapes, of worlds and recordings, these are floating images of ships and whole fleets. In the very center, surrounded by terminals, and down a slight ramp into the space, swirls what looks like a grid of glowing stars.

"See anyone?" I say as we step out of the lift.

My eyes aren't picking up anything, though some terminals show things in the midst of being run—one has a recording going of some battle, another is showing the continued feed from the assault below. A couple containers of nutrient goop sit half-eaten on a small table made of the same white stuff that ought to have descended back to the floor after its use.

"Looks like they were interrupted," Viera says, coming up the center with me.

"By the evacuation." Malo breaks right, stepping around a slow-spinning image of a three-pronged ship that looks like it holds a single pilot.

"Or us," I say. "If T'Oli's right, everyone saw what we were doing down there."

"And they chose not to stop us?"

"They may have other priorities," T'Oli says from my shoulders. "A small group of humans, easily defeated, may not be worth the attention of the guards at this time."

I get to the center and notice that grid of stars isn't just a nameless work of art. Instead, each one of the pulsing spheres of light has a name, and when I reach out with my hand to touch the nearest one, it flashes and rises above the others. Then it floats to the middle of the grid, before, like an egg opening from the top, spreading apart and sending out countless little images. At first I'm not sure what I'm looking at, but then the blue light resolves the blurs into tiny ships, many clustered together. Like a formation.

"Fleets," I say when the words makes its way through my awed mind. "This, this must be every Vincere force in the galaxy."

I look down at the names again, hunting for one in particular. It's not far from the one I grabbed at random— Kolas. I touch the sphere for the Oratus' fleet, and the one I'd opened retracts and slides back to its place in the grid. Kolas' ships blow into the space, and I note too that the word 'Aspicis' sits above the mix of craft. So the Chorus has the size and location of their fleets available in an instant to any of them. Back in Damantum, it would have been so useful to know where my generals were, what my hunters were doing or who was still alive after a far away battle.

"Wake up, Empress." Viera's tone is tight. "Incoming."

From the lift behind us, next to the one we came in, a set of six Flaum emerge with their miners holstered and their mouths agape. Which, seeing as I'm a classified species standing in the middle of dozens of floating ships, makes some sort of sense.

"Hi," I say to them as they shuffle out of the lift. To my right, Viera's hunkered down behind the terminals, the lowered central area giving her just enough room to hide. Malo's found a place to hide to my left. T'Oli's wrapped itself around my chest, but its eyestalks are hidden behind my head. All in all, we're pretty well set for an ambush. "Can I help you?"

One Flaum feels brave enough to take the lead and steps in front of its friends, closer to me. This one has a deep brown fur, pocked with patches of white. It would be pretty if not for the blue, over-sized Chorus vest hanging over its shoulders. Apparently it thinks I'm harmless because neither of its claws go for weapons.

"Who are you?" the Flaum's voice is scratchy, high.

"Kaishi," I say. If they don't know who I am, then my name has to be meaningless. All I'm angling for now is a trip right to that lift they came in on. If we can get there without getting us killed, well, I'll take it. "Human ambassador to the Chorus."

The Flaum sniffs. Cocks its head. "Human?"

Our stimulating conversation is cut short before I can reply. Through the ever-present intercoms, a voice I recognize in its bland monotony comes through loud and clear.

"These are the ones I ordered you to find!" Ferrolite's

command pours out around us. "Take them, and bring them to my shuttle."

The Flaum all jerk, like puppets on strings, at Ferrolite's command. The lead one, with the patched fur, is the only one that doesn't reach for its miner. Instead, its eyes widen at me as its mouth opens to ask the obvious question, "Will you come with us?"

If we go with those Flaum and get on Ferrolite's shuttle, we're dead. As it is, we're likely dead anyway, but I'd rather die fighting. I hope Viera and Malo agree with me, cause they're about to lose their options.

"Nah," I say. "I've got better things to do."

For a second I wonder if the Flaum's going to ask *"what things?"* but Viera doesn't give the creature the time to respond. She pops up from behind the terminal and lets loose with both miners. I'm surprised to see blue bolts lance out from the weapons and wonder if Viera's grown a conscience.

I feel T'Oli forming up its usual sword onto my right hand. I shift the hooked bar tool to my left and take a running step through the blue lights of Kolas' fleet towards the Flaum.

And don't make it more than a step. Malo gets there first, as the Flaum yanks a miner from its holster and aims it at me. My warrior slams his metal bar onto the Flaum, cracking its head and sending the creature crumpling to the ground. Behind it, the other furry Chorus forces dive and duck behind terminals, some sending back a shot or two our way. The lift they came in, too, snaps shut.

"We have to get out of here," T'Oli patters to me. "They'll have reinforcements coming."

"Way ahead of you." For once, I actually am. Seeing Malo down the Flaum has me reversing course, turning and heading to the level's opposite side, where another pair of lifts glow beyond more terminals and floating depictions of ships and stars. "C'mon! To the other side!"

"I'll cover you!" Viera shouts. "Go!"

I'm already moving. In the past, maybe, I'd have panicked at the idea of leaving Viera behind, but now I know what matters is getting to those lifts. Getting them open. Then we'll find a way to keep the Flaum off the Lunare till she gets over to us. So instead I run and jump, dive and duck my way towards the far side as an increasing number of blue bolts flash around me. The Flaum are getting braver, but they're losing the accuracy battle as I get further and further away.

The lift on the left is like the one we took here—pasted over with a dedicated level warning, because the Chorus value their scientists enough for two dedicated lifts. The lift on the right, though, is the same all clear gray like the first one we rode. I slap at the panel to summon the lift, then drop as a pair of shots slam into the wall above me. I'm not on the ground for more than a breath before Malo slides along next to me.

"Made it," he says, and I notice he's added the Flaum's miner to his mask. "You all right?"

"Still breathing. Viera?"

"Still shooting."

I nod towards the lift. "It's coming."

Malo jerks around the terminal for a quick look, raises the miner and squeezes off a shot. There's a sharp squeal back in the dark.

"Viera!" Malo shouts. "Go now! I have you covered!"

"Easy to say!" Viera calls back.

I, without a miner or a good way to see what's happening, sit with my legs bunched, ready to spring as soon as the lift's doors open. It's frustrating that I can't shoot, that I can't swing, but I suppose that's the job of an Empress; depend on those you trust to make your plans succeed.

The lift dings, the panel turns green. Malo's still looking back towards Viera, still shooting into the dark when the doors swing open. When I see something that makes my jump, my rapid scramble for our escape die before it ever starts; a mirrored Oratus.

It's easier to see in the dim light here than the washed-out white and reds in the Chorus chambers. Here, the Oratus' scales don't quite know how to reflect the blues and black, and as a result there's a hazy teal cast to the creature that lets me see its wicked teeth in all their glory as its head turns towards Malo and I.

"Kaishi," T'Oli says. "You can't beat this creature."

The Ooblot's talking like that because, in spite of the fear twisting and tying me in knots, I'm standing up. I'm stepping around Malo, who's just noticing what's come to find us, and I'm staring the beast full on.

"Don't tell a human what she can't do," I mutter to the Ooblot. The Oratus gets its giant self out of the lift, all three meters and more, and glares down at me. "Give me my sword, T'Oli. I'm gonna need it."

The Ooblot, at least, doesn't ask questions when I give it a command. Its cream self, blotched now because of shots taken and scars earned on our journeys, grants me my razor's edge, extending out from my hand half a meter. Sharp, deadly, and completely inadequate to the task at hand.

"Give up, human," the mirrored Oratus hisses. "You cannot win. Your species is not designed for it."

"Getting real tired of people insulting my species." I step forward with my left, stab in with my right and send

T'Oli's point rocketing in towards the bottom half of the Oratus' torso.

If there's one hope I have in here, it's that all the terminals create tight quarters for a creature as big as the Oratus. It's going to have a hard time dodging, jumping, or doing much of anything with its tail. So the Oratus does something stupid and tries to grab my strike. T'Oli does some lightning work and reforms itself as we slash, coating my wrist in its nigh-invincible skin and narrowing its blade to a needle's point. The mirrored Oratus' left midclaw closes on my wrist and its claws slide off my new armor, allowing my strike to slip past and deliver a solid stab.

The only reaction as T'Oli gets a puncture's view of an Oratus' insides is a hissing snarl, and then the thing's left foreclaw backhands me into the wall next to the lifts. It's a hard hit by an arm as tall as I am, and I bounce off the wall and sprawl to the floor, only to find that T'Oli's not on my right hand anymore. I push back, trying to force the cobwebs from my shaken head, and stand up. It takes two seconds for me to do that, which is more time than I should have.

But the Ooblot's saving my life again.

T'Oli's flowing around the mirrored Oratus like the most annoying bug you could imagine. Its Ooblot body slides along the mirrored Oratus' scales, getting just out of the way of the creature's claws or teeth. T'Oli's not just annoying the monster either—I can see bits of its fluid form changing into tiny points and biting, piercing into the Oratus' scales as they move.

"We have to go, Kaishi," Malo's at my side, and he's pushing me towards the open lift door. "Now."

"Can't you shoot it?"

"I tried," Malo replies as we move. "The shot bounced off."

I have a litany of other excuses to try, but close them off as Malo pushes me into the lift. The mirrored Oratus finally manages to snare one of T'Oli's two eyestalks and tears the Ooblot off its scaly hide, then flings my friend deep into the level. Those yellow-green Oratus eyes turn towards us next, and I slam the panel inside the lift, commanding the doors to shut. And as the Oratus' foreclaws swipe towards us, the Meridia does what we need, and the lift doors slide shut.

There's the brief sound of claws on metal, and then the lift's whisking away. To what level, I don't know.

But my friends won't be there.

Stars.

Thousands. No, millions. More.

The lift opens onto a light-less level brighter than any Sax has been to within the Meridia. Despite the inky walls, the padded black floor and the empty dark ceiling, the galaxy swirling inside this space makes it simple to see. The twinkling stars, the miniature nebulae, and the pulsing core at the center, though, make understanding much harder.

The lift's panel—the only concession to practicality Sax can see on the level—glows red, telling him his current hijacked ride won't be going any further. So Sax walks into the starry swirl. At three meters tall, Sax is used to looking down at things, but here he's in the middle of the lights. Unknown balls of blue and white fire dance by his eyes while clouds of purple and blue slide into and through his scales, appearing on his other side as though Sax means nothing in this level-sized galaxy.

What is this? The question frays Sax's drive, shunting aside the focus on the Priority Beam with a taste of the same wonder Sax felt on *Nova*, watching a star burst with Bas by his side. On that station, the point had been to relax, to marvel at what nature could create. This hits him in the same way, and Sax almost falls into its spinning spell before a voice speaks out:

"Solis."

At the words, toned in an Amigga's unnatural voice, the galaxy freezes its rotation. Then, with the slightest shiver, the stars and gas clouds blow out around Sax, vanishing into the room's black walls. The push isn't even—the galaxy's center coasts to one side and a different star, at first just the slightest glow, takes center stage. Zooming in.

The Oratus catches what's going on and snaps his eyes from the spectacle. Keeps the two far lifts in view, with a quick snap glance behind him to make sure surprises aren't using the distraction as an opportunity to claim Sax as a victim. But there's no beeps, no whooshing doors. Nothing but Sax alone here with a voice and, now, his home.

"We're evacuating," the voice speaks again and Sax catches it now. The First Chair. "I'm the only one of the Chorus still here."

Solis, a rocky wasteland of a world, spins in front of Sax, and the room itself flushes with yellow light from his home-world's star, lingering at the very edge of the projection. As Solis spins, the fertile green scar placed there by a species bent on growing another, comes and goes from view. Of the ships orbiting the planet, there is no sign. Not a military tool, then.

"Why are you staying?" Sax hisses to the air. With the lifts locked, his choices are few, and if the First Chair is willing to speak with him, then the least Sax can do is hold the Amigga's attention and keep it away from Bas, Evva, and the rest. "Shouldn't you have been the first one away?"

"The Chorus changes over only in times of crisis," the First Chair says. "I've allowed this pathetic resistance to arise. Responsibility demands I be the one to see to its destruction. If I fail, the Chorus will elect a new First Chair, one who will guide the Vincere in doing what I could not."

"So you're the only one that's not a coward." Sax stalks closer to the planet, leering down towards it. Trying, and succeeding, to pick out those rock arches where he dropped from so long ago.

The First Chair manages a laugh, a jarring series of blips that reminds Sax of a broken alarm. "If I fled, I would be executed for abdicating my duties. I stay because it is my only chance at life. Just like you, fighting when you should be dead."

"If you want to kill me, you'll have to try harder."

"I don't want to kill anyone. At least, I didn't," the First Chair says. Sax finds that hard to believe, but the First Chair drags the end of the phrase into a sigh, suggesting a truth made impossible by reality. "Part of running a civilization is coming to terms with the less savory parts of it. Learning that everyone will not understand or agree with you, and that they will hate you for your choices."

"Because your choices hurt them."

"Yes. Creating the Oratus *did* hurt many of us. Creating you may wind up being the end of our species, if we can't shut down that insurrection going on below." Solis spins away and the galaxy, or at least part of it, reappears.

Sax stands in the middle of a collection of stars. Solis's system hovers to his right, while a clustered band that includes Aspicis dominates the center of the level. The planets are too small to see, but as Sax focuses on any of the stars, the names of the systems appear like mist over the red, blue, white and yellow orbs.

"This is our home," the First Chair continues. "This small part of the galaxy holds most of our intelligent life. Without the Chorus, it would not exist. Even if space-faring technology had fallen into the grasp of every species, they would have torn themselves apart in war without us."

"You don't know that."

"We do," the First Chair delivers this edict with the tired patience of a commander pointing out the obvious. "We've seen it. Stopped the senseless destruction so many times with the honeyed gifts of our miracles. And after that technology was brought against us, we destroyed those who dared and kept only the simplest ones. Only the safest species."

Time is difficult to judge. Cycles, with their indeterminate length, give Sax little idea of how long the Chorus has been in power. The potential span twinges his mind, makes him wonder how arrogant Evva and the rest of them are for attempting something that must have been tried many times before. If the First Chair is speaking truth, then the Chorus has seen many worse rebellions, many more difficult fights.

And yet, Sax is still here. By the First Chair's own words, Evva is progressing. So something must have changed. The Chorus must be weaker. The First Chair is keeping quiet. Content to let Sax work through the implications.

"Then you made us." Sax speaks as the realization comes through. The Oratus are the difference this time. A species so strong, so deadly that the Amigga needed to keep control of them to survive. "We're the problem."

"Like the artificial intelligences we crafted before you, the solution has once again turned on us," the First Chair confirms. "All I can hope for is that we can defeat your friends here, and reduce your species to irrelevance before it happens again."

The galaxy zooms out again, expanding until the endless stars once again swirl around the room.

"Why are you telling me this?" Sax hisses. As much as he'd like to keep the First Chair talking, he's fascinated. No enemy ought to reveal its goals to its opponent, not unless victory, or defeat, was assured.

"Because, Oratus. You have a choice to make. Before, I offered you a chance to save your friends. Now, I offer you a chance to save your species."

"But you just—"

"I said irrelevance, not extinction. The Chorus will remove your species from the Vincere. You will be given worlds to control, and like the Vyphen, be allowed to choose your own destinies."

"I'm not the one who can make that choice." A three-letter Oratus deciding the fate of his species? Sax doesn't think Evva would be a fan of that.

"Your friends will not listen to me. They might listen to you," the First Chair says. "Agree, and I'll send a lift to where you can meet them. Discuss the offer, and decide."

The lift Sax arrived in blinks green and its doors open, inviting a clean, Flaum-less interior. The two guards Sax took care of must have survived. Picked themselves off the ground and crawled away to wherever the Chorus stashed the guards who lost. They were -

Irrelevant.

This fight isn't only about survival. Not just about casting the Amigga from the top in a desperate bid avoid elimination, but also to say they deserve a chance at their own destinies. Living under the weight of the Chorus, knowing their charity drew the border for the Oratus' part in the galaxy, would be as bad as a slow, creeping descent into extinction.

Better to swing the claws while he has them. Better to attack the enemy while he can.

"You hesitate." The toneless voice comes through the galaxy, as if the cosmos itself is speaking to Sax.

Behind that voice is no god. Behind that voice is prey.

"Tell the lift to bring me to you," Sax hisses. "Then we can begin a negotiation that matters."

The reply comes by the slamming of the lift doors. The flash of red on the lift panels as the lock, sealing Sax on the level, trapped within the spinning lights.

"So you're a coward, like all of the other Amigga," Sax says, prowling the edges of the room. No idea if the First Chair is even listening, but the words feel good to say.

Sax tests the dark walls with his claws, and while they're soft at first touch—a surface more adept at catching the projection's light without reflecting it in a blinding back-and-forth—beneath is the same hard metals Sax would expect to find on a Vincere ship. With time, Sax could carve his way through. With that same time, Bas, Evva, and the others would all be dead.

The center of the galaxy is the brightest part, a dense cluster of stars in myriad colors pulsing. Sax heads to it next, takes in the lights. Touches the shape with a claw, and when it doesn't react, Sax has to stop himself from getting carried away by philosophical meanderings. Maybe it's being here, at the center of civilization's power, or that he's been alone and on the edge of death so often, but Sax keeps drifting into the sorts of ideas an Oratus isn't meant to have.

Purpose, for a living weapon, shouldn't be hard to define.

The chime of another lift arriving kills the musings,

letting Sax turn and settle himself for whatever surprises the First Chair's sent his way.

Sax has never seen a single enemy more than twice. They're either dead, or, well, dead after the second encounter with Sax's biting jaws or razor claws. So when Kah clacks his way out of the lift, followed by a second mirrored Oratus, their reflective scales making the dancing galaxy all the more mesmerizing, Sax gives Kah a star-lit grin.

Time to correct this error.

"Even after all the First Chair's offering you, there's no thought of surrender?" Kah asks as he moves to one side of the galaxy while the other Oratus heads opposite, trapping Sax in the middle.

"So you can use me against my own pair?" Sax hisses. "Those aren't Oratus tactics, Kah. You know better."

"I know you're too headstrong to understand what's right," Kah replies.

The Oratus has plenty of scars from their last tussle in the broadcasting level, and the way Kah sits back on his talons, keeps his fore- and midclaws up makes it clear the Oratus has no desire to tangle with Sax.

Sax is about to fire back, but stops. The two mirrored Oratus haven't attacked him yet, and they're not supported by what should be a crushing amount of armed Flaum. Then there's the First Chair, spending time talking to Sax, trying to get the Oratus to change his mind.

"Two of you?" Sax says instead. "Two of you. In all of the Meridia, that's what you send against an enemy this far up your invincible tower?"

Kah gives a low growl, switches his tail across the floor as stars and nebulae blow through him. The reflective skin mirrors those floating sparks, making Kah appear less invisible and more a distorting curve in the swirl of this miniature universe.

"In moments, the Vincere will sweep down from above and blow apart your pair and your Resistance," Kah says. "You could save them. Tell them to give up."

"So you'd destroy the Meridia to save... what, exactly? The Amigga that have already escaped?"

Bluffs. Bluster and threats. It's hard to believe that Sax thought the Chorus a strong and immortal fixture for so long when the illusion of their power is so clear now. All of these species in thrall to their commands because the idea of rebelling seemed so impossible, but when you're actually fighting them...

Turns out the Chorus isn't quite so strong.

Kah's opening that mouth, inhaling with those vents, when Sax makes the move. He leaps through the galaxy's burning core at the mirrored Oratus. Standing straight, tall, and ready, Kah would have been able to meet Sax's leap with any number of counters. As he's mid-breath, though, Kah makes a fumbling, tripping retreat back to the galaxy's outer edges, flinging his claws up to deflect Sax's swiping charge.

Sax presses the attack for two seconds. Enough for each of his four claws to get a single rake in, then he uses his momentum to press past Kah, turning to the right and snaking his tail up and over the bracing Kah's shoulders. With a snap, Sax pushes Kah forward, right where Sax was and right where the other mirrored Oratus, rampaging from behind through the blinding clouds of interstellar brilliance, dives.

Mirrored Oratus rely on their stealthy scales to throw their opposition off balance, to make shots fire wide and security systems miss their very presence. As they're all elite servants of the Chorus, Sax figures they haven't spent much time training against each other, learning to recognize their own telltale blurs when targeting a strike.

The hypothesis proves true when Kah meets the slashing swipes and snapping bites of his supposed ally, a flurry of blows that cuts through Kah's already-unraveling defense and re-opens plenty of old wounds.

And by the time the mirrored Oratus realizes its mistake, Kah's reeling away and Sax is making his own attacking leap. Both of Sax's talons catch on the mirrored Oratus' torso, biting to the creature's chest and back, and giving Sax the one moment he needs to make lethal work with his jaws on the enemy's exposed head.

The body rides to the floor, and Sax settles with it, locking eyes with Kah the entire way. The mirrored Oratus looks at what remains of his companion, and lets loose a long sigh from his vents.

"You don't have to," Sax offers, though, with the blood-lust pulsing through him, he wouldn't mind if Kah decides to go down thrashing. "They don't control you."

"No," Kah hisses. "They do not."

There's vulnerability in those words. An opening for one of Bas' verbal snipes. A method of attack Sax would have sneered at not long ago, but that now makes an increasing amount of sense.

"Look at what's around us," Sax says, pointing with his claws at the infinite stars. "You want to give up the chance to see all of this just because some Amigga told you to?"

Kah hisses a dour laugh, runs his claws along his new injuries, as if trying to see if they're as long and bloody as they feel. "If you lose, then the Chorus will kill me and I'll see none of it."

"Do you think we'll lose? After this?"

"I wasn't lying," Kah says. "We've been herding your friends. They're going to find themselves sealed on a pair of levels soon. The Vincere will hit those two with targeted antipersonnel blasts. They'll all die, and the tower will survive."

Only one reason for Kah to tell Sax this: the mirrored Oratus doesn't want them to lose. Or, Kah just wants to get Sax focused on something else to launch some surprise assault, but given that Kah stands still, wounded, and doing nothing with those claws suggests the former.

"How can I stop them?" Sax says.

"You can't," Kah replies. "Only the First Chair could order Nalucite to go back on the plan, and that won't happen."

Sax doesn't know the name, but now he has a new objective. It won't do any good to get to the Priority Beam and send a message if Evva and the others are reduced to charred ash flitting through Aspicis' sky.

"Then help me find this Nalucite," Sax says.

Kah's already moving as Sax says the words. Stepping long and slow past Sax and towards those locked lifts. "Nalucite is the Meridia, Sax. There are other Amigga that help, that keep tabs on isolated systems, but this one? It won't be easy."

"Because it's been easy so far." Sax follows Kah to the lifts and watches as the mirrored Oratus places a foreclaw on the lift panel, which turns that beautiful shade of grass-green.

When the lift's doors open, though, Kah doesn't move towards them. Sax gives the mirrored Oratus a breath, but when Kah only stares his way, Sax gets the hint and goes inside alone.

"Tell it to take you to level zero," Kah says. "That's where you'll find it."

"You're not coming?"

"You just offered me freedom," Kah replies. "I'm going to take you up on it, and get out of here before someone decides I'm better off dead."

Sax barely gets a nod off before the lift doors close. The lift sits still, waiting for Sax to give it a command. Level zero. That sounds like it would be all the way down. A long and steep drop, and the opposite direction from the Priority Beam.

"Zero." Sax says the word.

Anything for Bas.

Gone. After I swore I wouldn't leave another friend behind, with the shutting of those lift doors I've left two. Viera and T'Oli, ditched on a level full of enemies. The glimmering teeth of that mirrored Oratus, snarling towards us in the blue-dark light, haunt me the entire lift ride, which, thankfully, is short enough for Malo to tell me we'll find them only three times.

"We will," Malo insists again as the lift doors open. "I swear."

I don't answer, because the part of me that thinks of the Ooblot and the Lunare is numb and doesn't want to process anything other than the opening stages of grief. So, when my eyes catch the terrifying display in front of us, I'm grateful for the distraction. Fear is better than loss, curiosity better than sadness.

The rows of floor-to-ceiling tubes in this level bring plenty of fear as they glow, illuminating with the same sapphire lighting scheme this section of the Meridia prefers. The lights are, this time, implanted in the tops of the tubes, and the liquid inside each shifts around as some circulating current keeps things lively. The effect makes the entire level appear undersea, shadows playing in the glass forest as I walk into it. Malo comes behind, his metal bar raised and ready.

"I recognize this place," I say mostly to myself. I've seen similar things on Vimelia, on *Cobalt*. These tubes aren't empty—half-formed species linger in each of them, some looking closer to Flaum, while others resemble mossy rocks or stringy, shapeless masses of tendrils.

"You've been here?" Malo answers anyway.

"No, not exactly," I reply, continuing to go forward. At the base of every tube is a small terminal displaying a simple read-out I actually understand—temperature, pulse, the sorts of rudimentary medical terms we'd even defined in Damantum. "The Cache showed me an entire ship full of these once. A Sevora craft. They were growing new hosts."

"Why would the Chorus have this, then?"

"For the same reason." I head over to a terminal in front of a stone-silent Flaum that looks more or less normal, albeit submerged in water. Beyond the vital signs, I flick my finger through graphs and diagrams, through code names and equations I don't understand. "Only instead of giving them over to parasites, I think these are for experiments."

Malo stares at me and I can see the disgust in his eyes. "Kaishi, why did you pick this level?"

The lifts that I can see, a similar double-bank on either side, have panels glowing a bright red. I don't need to be up close to know that they'll be locked, keeping us on this level. So I lean back against the Flaum's tube, my hands at my sides.

"I didn't choose it," I say. "The lift stopped here on its own."

"But, why?"

"Malo, who cares why?" I want to be frustrated, angry. Despairing and enraged all at once. I want to be in one of these tubes too—lifeless and floating, watching the eons pass without a single concern. "One of the Chorus did it. Or maybe the lift was already going here. They have Viera and T'Oli, and they're going to come for us too. It's over. Done."

Even leaving Vimelia that first time, with Malo gone and out of reach, I didn't feel so lost. Not even on *Cobalt*, as the Amigga poked and tore at me. Or on Earth, as the Sevora launched attack after attack and every human in Marilo knew it was only a matter of days till we died. I can't find a hold here, not in this tower with all its horrors. Not now.

But Malo, my true friend, tries his best. He picks up my sorrow and carries it back to me, putting his arms on and then around my shoulders. Maybe he expects me to cry here, but I can't bring myself to do it. This is too far past grief now; not only are we trapped, but I never finished the Oath. As soon as the Chorus deals with Bas' little insurrection, they'll carry my crimes back to Earth and deliver the punishment to my people, to Avril and all the others depending on us for safety. Waiting for the miracles we promised them.

"We can't give up, Kaishi." Malo tries talking. "You didn't give up on me. You came back."

I shake my head against his skin and watch the blue lights play on the far wall, try not to see what's in the tubes lining it. "Malo, we did give up. We were sure you were dead. The only reason we came to Vimelia was because Lan and Kolas brought us there."

Malo's silent, and for a second I wonder if he's going to let go, drop me right here and now. Instead, Malo hugs me tighter. "But when you knew, when you had the choice, you risked everything for me. This is no different. We'll get them back."

There's plenty of differences, and I open my mouth, an angry heat rising to explain to Malo just how different it is to launch a rescue mission with a pair of Oratus, plenty of weapons, and the backing of an entire Vincere fleet compared to a couple of lost humans trapped in tower full of all-knowing enemies.

I don't, though, say a word.

Because something else speaks instead.

"Why not join them?" Ferrolite's voice, like it did on the other level, echoes out around the tubes. Amused, tinged with static and echoing off the glass, the Amigga's words lend to the ethereal nature of the place. Of my current state of mind.

"You're not killing her," Malo says, stepping back from me, lifting the bar, and searching for the Amigga.

"Of course not," Ferrolite replies. "That would only hurt my reputation. I brought you humans here to bind yourselves to the Chorus, and that will happen. Your friends are alive, and they are waiting for you."

I'm too tired, too warped by the struggles of the day to play word games with the Amigga, so I glare at the ceiling and hope the creature can see my face. "No."

That's it. That's all I'm saying to that thing. Ferrolite did, though, shake me out of the black cloak threatening to suffocate me there on that level. Its cold reasoning brushes away the shroud, and I replace it with fatalistic determination: if we're going to lose, we might as well give it everything we have. So I give Malo a nod.

"Are you ready?" Malo asks me.

"I'm ready."

"Ready for what?" Ferrolite says. "Aren't you going to save your friends?"

We walk back to the lift we came in, the silver one that's supposedly able to traverse most of the Meridia. The red panel's still there, still locked. I try tapping at it, but there's no response. Malo works his bar on the lift doors, but gets nothing more than a few scratches on the smooth surface.

"You have two choices humans," Ferrolite says as I try a more blunt method, banging my bar to no effect. "Either accept my offer, or rot here until someone cares enough to send guards to finish you off."

"I don't think we're getting through here," Malo says to me. "At least, not with force."

"Then let's look around," I reply. "There has to be some way out."

So we commence the search. I look around terminals, press buttons on the ones I can find, and even take a brief detour in the Cache only to find that the Meridia exists as nothing more than a vague notion. The Sevora, apparently, never managed to get a spy in here. I should have exchanged my Cache for a new one on Kolas' ship, but then, looking at the deep emerald bracelet, I'd be leaving a piece of this whole journey behind.

Meridia's levels aren't small—each one is only a little smaller than a section on a Sevora seed ship, or almost the size of my own village. Even so, it becomes clear pretty quickly that we're not going to find an exit. All the terminals are secured or confusing, the four lifts refuse to open, and beyond the forest of tubes, there's not a single answer for our problem. Other than the one Ferrolite constantly pushes into our ears.

"You have no other choice!" Ferrolite states, and I'm

getting impressed by the sheer number of ways it's demanded we listen to it.

"Why do you care?" I say. "Is your reputation that important to you?"

"It's all we have! The Chorus members are slotted by their contributions to the Amigga species—so I need this. I need your oath. And you need it too, humans. Your species needs our protection, our technology." Ferrolite's tone doesn't change, not quite, but its tactics shift all the same. "Aren't you tired of this? All these strange things, these fights, this destruction. You've already cleansed your past of its unwanted origins. Take your victory and go home."

Malo catches my eye and he does look tired. I'm sure I'm no treat either, coated with sweat from running through this station, tired and sore. The thought of waking up to a cool ocean breeze, watching Ignos—I refuse to combine that terrible Amigga, that terrible Sevora, with the god of my tribe—rise over the horizon... maybe it's worth saying yes one more time. I've just been in the deepest despair I've ever felt, and here's a rope to climb out of it.

"You'll let us leave? Unharmed?" I ask.

"Yes. It wouldn't be right to murder an Ambassador. Even your, er, adventures can be excused as a primitive species frightened by this pesky insurgent attack," Ferrolite's cooing now, at least as much as its synthetic voice allows it. "A simple recording. We can dispense with the ceremony as the Chorus has mostly departed the Meridia. I'll even have a shuttle waiting to get you out of here as soon as we're done."

Malo's watching me. Waiting. Opinions hide behind that set face but he's playing the soldier again, waiting for his commander to say what she thinks first.

"Then tell us where to go, Ferrolite. I'll do it."

The Amigga doesn't respond with words. Instead, our chosen lift lights up, and those doors open. Waiting for us.

"It'll kill us when you're done," Malo whispers as we start to move towards the lift. "You know it's a trick."

The old me might have argued with Malo then, might have said something about how Ferrolite just gave us all the reasons why it wouldn't do that. Instead, though, I agree. "You're probably right, but what choice do we have?" I gesture at the tubes standing around us. "Do you see what they're doing here? Making more species?"

"So?"

"It doesn't matter what we do," I continue. "Whether we make it out of here or not, the Chorus will keep going until those familiars we saw on Cobalt or something like them supplants every other species. We might as well try to enjoy the time we have until that happens."

Malo laughs. It's a quirky, heartless, head-shaking laugh, but a laugh nonetheless. "Kaishi, what do you think we've been doing? All this time in this tower?"

"What?"

"This is us! Ever since I've met you, it's been one adventure after another. We've nearly died a dozen times, should have died a dozen more. We're battered, bruised, but we're still here." Malo points his finger at me. "From the moment we get out of danger, you're itching to throw us right back. I see your eyes, hear your shouts when we're in the worst of it. You're a soldier, Kaishi. A fighter queen, a spear-wielding huntress of the Solare."

It's the longest speech I've ever heard Malo give. What's more, he's speaking in his own language, the words of Damantum, the Charre. The words no Amigga can understand, a creation wholly of humans. And it gives me an idea.

"So you're saying we ought to keep this going?" I reply

when Malo pauses in his parade of names. "That if we're going to walk into Ferrolite's trap, it's because that's who we are?"

"I'm saying we're fighters, Kaishi. We'll get Viera and that strange thing, T'Oli, back. Then, we'll tear this whole place down."

Now it's my turn to laugh. "Malo, you've lost it. But I think I like this new you."

"Enjoy it while it lasts."

I will, because as the lift doors shut behind us, I'm sure we won't last long.

Plummets of an impossible range and speed are nothing new to Sax—any given assault might require the dive-bombing insertion of the Oratus and his team in conditions ranging from adverse to apocalyptic. What he's not used to, what has his stomach feeling like a flitting feather as the lift shoots down, is the solitude. Outside of these four walls there's a mission going on; his pair is fighting for her life, for their galaxy, and Sax doesn't know when he rockets past her level on what might be Meridia's sole whole-tower lift, but he feels the separation all the same.

And devours it. Banishes it into the churn of other sensations as Aspicis' exacts a stronger pull on his descending body. From the outer edges of the atmosphere to, soon, the ground beneath the surface. The lift itself is pressurized, those doors sealing tighter as the implications of Sax's command get relayed through the lift's systems and refined into a strict set of actions meant to ensure Sax doesn't burst like an over-filled balloon as his trip commences.

Doesn't mean Sax feels nothing. Doesn't mean he's not distinctly aware of his talons resting harder on the floor, or of the vague remnants of nutrient goop searching for a way up and out his throat.

He keeps it down.

Eventually the lift settles into place and a light tone announces they've reached level zero. Sax is pretty certain he's underground. The lift begins a steamy, noisy decompression that has Sax's tiny ear holes pop as thicker air floods in through the lift's loosening doors. The decompression takes time, but this is one thing Sax doesn't want to rush: he's seen what happens when you break the pressure apart on a ship.

It's the only time he's felt pity for the Flaum crew ordered to clean up the mess.

When the doors do open, the lift barks a snappy order for Sax to leave, "There are others requesting service. Please depart."

The Chorus. Always ready to sacrifice politeness for efficiency. This time, though, Sax agrees—no reason to wait in that lift any more. Not when he can step out into a space unique from the rest of the Meridia.

None of the steel walls or austere, industrialized floors present themselves to Sax as he steps out of the lift. Level Zero starts with a cavernous entry, one that makes clear this isn't just another part of the tower. Sax sees a showcase of glittering rock formations; various blacks, deep browns, and yellows. The stones are smoothed and refined, spiking up and down from floor and ceiling, or clustered together in stacks so constructed as to make clear their origins in a planner's scheme and not natural processes. Sparkles glint out from everywhere, and at first Sax thinks the twinkles are a decorative touch, but a close inspection of a jagged mustard-yellow boulder to his right makes clear those bits are circuits. Transistors. The insides of a machine.

If confronting this strange place were to give Sax the urge to flea, the lift gives him no time to act on it. As soon as Sax's tail leaves the traveling cube's confines, its doors snap shut and the lift disappears. The sound pulls Sax's eye towards the transport and he notices there's no panel here. No way he can see to call the lift back.

Which means he's stuck. Kah, or maybe the First Chair, tricked him. Sent him down here where Sax wouldn't be able to do anything. The realization trickles through Sax's nerves, maturing into a fine hot anger. One that he takes out on that same mustard stone. The first strike with a foreclaw tears through the yellow like fine paper, and the second, his left midclaw following in with razor points slashing, draws sparks and smoke and... something else.

Hot, red.

Blood?

Sax stares at the stone, at what's seeping from his slash and draining to the ground around his talons.

"Are you quite finished?" says the skittering voice of a female Flaum.

Sax turns and sees a golden—too golden to be natural—furred Flaum standing, paws clasped, in front of one of the three hollowed, arching exits from the entry chamber. Her eyes, which should be black and beady, look at Sax like flashing jade, and it takes the Oratus a moment to realize her pupils are ringed by glowing implants. That realization draws Sax into a closer inspection, and he picks out, nestled in the Flaum's fur, plenty more baubles peeking from those blonde threads.

"An ordinary Flaum? This deep in the Meridia?" the

Flaum speaks again. "Even an ignorant Oratus like yourself should know better. Your species is smarter than this."

Sax doesn't know what the Flaum's talking about, so he bets on his two strengths: claws, and threats.

"I need to make sure my pair isn't trapped," Sax hisses, dripping as much menace as he can into the words. "You're going to help me, or I'll carve you up right here."

"And then what?" the Flaum replies. "You'll drink up the blood? Oratus, I allowed you to come this far, and I didn't do that so you could threaten me."

Sax tilts his head. Blinks. The Flaum *allowed* Sax?

Rather than explaining, the Flaum guesses Sax's question, turns and strides away through the earth-toned, Chorus-crafted cave. Sax takes one more look at the slashed yellow, at the visible, wounded red-brown flesh weaving between the copper and silver circuitry. Wires poke out and vanish, and the whole thing seems to pulse to the beat of some far off heart. Ideas come and go as Sax starts off after the Flaum, all coming to rest on a singular suspicion.

Following the Flaum brings Sax into vast room, one whose base extends deeper into a machine-made basin. The same collection of rocks cluster the space, towering on top of one another and dangling down from above like bright spears. In the center, resting in a raised, golden cradle, is that suspicion.

The Amigga is massive. Easily as tall as Sax and wider still. Its skin is layered in wrinkles, and a pair of other Flaum climb over it as Sax sees the creature, each one wiping ointments or sloughing off blackened, dead parts of its flesh. Unlike other Amigga Sax has seen in this state, this one hasn't spread its tendrils all around, but looks instead to be funneling them through its massive pedestal. The rock Sax slashed back near the lifts, the pulsing piece? It all comes back here.

But to be this large? To have grown its actual body through this much space? Sax can't comprehend how old this Amigga must be. Dalachite, back on *Cobalt*, had been cycles old and still only managed a few meters of growth; thin tendrils connecting to terminals to give it control of its station. This one, this one...

"Old enough," the golden Flaum next to Sax says. "Numbers become meaningless when you've lived so long. Knowledge, wisdom. Those are better markers of experience."

"If you're so old, and wise, then why did you bring me here?" Sax asks. "What can an Oratus tell you that you don't already know?"

The baubles on the golden Flaum show their purpose now. Amigga are experts at twisting minds, but direct control, that takes some assistance. Dalachite learned that the hard way when Coorvin shook loose of its influence on *Cobalt*. This one here is taking no chances—the golden Flaum is as locked into the Amigga as any Sevora host would be.

"It's not what you can tell me that matters, but what you can *do* for me." The great Amigga in the center, with those pair of Flaums scrubbing it, quivers. "Like all Amigga, I am dependent on others for my own survival. A mistake we made cycles ago, when we believed what the Sevora could do would be easy to transfer. It turns out without direct control, a subject asserts its own will quite quickly." The golden Flaum keeps her claws clasped while she speaks for her master, green eyes staring at Sax. "Yet these Flaum will not outlive me. I will need assistance, eventually. Assistance I no longer think the Chorus will provide."

"You don't believe in the Chorus anymore?"

"They are a bunch of squabbling children. They've seen so little, and believe they know so much," the Amigga continues. "I, on the other hand, have witnessed the birth of real civilization. I have helped it grow through so many trials. I would not see it die because a group of Amigga believe they are better than every other thing in our galaxy."

"You want us to survive and win," Sax says.

"Yes. I want you to work with me. You will need my help, and I have much to offer. Not least, the control of the Meridia. I have already proved my side—your forces make their way up with my help, and your small strike force of humans has been able to use the lifts with my aid as well."

"Humans?" Sax doesn't understand.

"Yes. Three of them. Marauding along the upper levels. I assumed, as they seem to be enemies of the Chorus, that they belonged to your side?"

Unexpected allies, whomever they might be, ought to be used. So Sax firms up his gaze and offers an assenting nod.

"Then you will agree to our deal? You will help me survive?"

The thought of ceding any power to the Amigga makes Sax clinch his claws. They are fighting to get out of the Amiggas' control, not merely switch which one pulls the strings. Yet, it's clear Sax is going to be stuck down here if he doesn't say yes, so that's what he hisses in reply.

"I assume, because of the effort the Chorus has gone through with you, you do have the power to make this promise?" The Amigga says. "If I find out you don't, I will bring this tower down with all of you inside of it."

A threat. That's a language Sax can understand. A clear, straight line between life and endless oblivion. It's the same stance Sax would take, the same stance he's *about* to take.

"We fought against the Sevora for cycles," Sax begins. "We fought them because of what they could do to species. Take their minds, reduce them to something other than themselves. I don't really understand what you're doing to these Flaum, but if we win, you're going to release them."

The Amigga quivers again, this time violently enough to send the Flaum scampering down from the pedestal. "I cannot. They would have nothing left if I did. Their minds have been mine for so long, they would not know how to function."

"We will teach them." Sax is as surprised as anyone to find the fire in his voice. But he's been a captive long enough, he's been on the receiving end of too many tortures to let this go. The entire reason for this resistance has been to free species from the clutches of others. No exceptions. "We will do what we have to, to help them. No more control. Any species that takes care of you will do so because they wish to, either because you pay them or persuade them."

"Then perhaps I'll leave you here and strike a new deal with whomever survives," the Amigga replies. "Others will be more willing to negotiate, I'm sure."

"You said you are old, wise," Sax replies. "You said you understood how civilization works. How can you claim that, and still rob these Flaum of their souls?"

"Because from what I've seen, civilizations drive on necessity. Those who work hardest to get what they need survive and succeed. I need these Flaum, and I have taken them."

Sax opens his claws, sets them on the rocks nearby. Those yellow and black ones, juicy growths of the Amigga inside of them. "Then I'm doing what's necessary. Help me stop the Chorus. Then you'll survive. I promise."

The Amigga's slow to respond. It keeps Sax waiting, guessing, wondering. The Oratus keeps his eyes turning, watching for blasts to the back, a sneak attack or some other deadly ambush. An Amigga's caught him off guard before, not again. Not here, not now. Sax has no time to be stunned.

"If you guarantee my survival, I can accept your terms," the Amigga says finally, breaking Sax's thought. "I will ensure the doors remain unlocked," the Amigga twitches and the Flaum next to Sax pulls out a small handheld terminal. Powers it on and it sparks to life and shows a grainy image that resolves into clear clarity.

"The lifts will come when called," the Amigga says and in the picture, Bas and Evva climb into the frame, loping closer to a pair of lifts with a red panel looming in front of them. The Oratus pause for a moment, glance at each other, as other fighters sneak into the frame and exchange laser fire with something off-screen.

The panel flips to green and both Bas and Evva, the pink and the red-black Oratus, stare at the sudden switch. Suspicious, as they ought to be, of any good fortune. It's only after a staccato stitch of lasers crashes into the closed lift doors to their left that Bas slaps the panel and calls the lift.

"Your friends will find the lifts take them to the safest routes. While those the Chorus uses will send them elsewhere or fail to operate at all. When the defense collapses, you will have control of the tower."

"And the Vincere?" Sax says. "Won't they just destroy the Meridia from space?"

"You would not be attempting this if you had no plan

for that, I hope," the Amigga says. "If you don't, then this whole mission is folly."

So Sax mentions the Priority Beam. Shares his goal. The Amigga agrees. Provides Sax with access to the main lift all the way up. As the golden Flaum puts away the screen, showing the Oratus scrambling into their new lift, Sax does the same. Rushing back through the caves, having made a promise to a creature that should've been his greatest enemy. But he does it anyway, slipping inside the lift the Amigga calls for him.

Suction sounds as the lift pressurizes and begins its rocketing assent to the very top of the tallest tower. Towards one more chance, one more leap to save his pair, his cause, and himself.

The lift descends for a long time. Far longer than any of our other rides, and down enough that I feel heavier. I suppose if you have a tower that goes all the way out of the atmosphere, the gravity might change too. Malo and I keep our metal bars in opposite hands, and keep our others held. If we're going out, we're going out together.

This level is far different from the research ones we've been exploring up till now. A large central area comes clear as soon as the doors whoosh aside, and dominating that, standing atop a dark crimson floor that bears a startling number of scratches, is a white-formed chair holding Viera. She's tied, with some sort of metal bands, around the chair. T'Oli, its two eyestalks giving the Ooblot away, is wrapped around Viera's chest, offering its hardened armor to my friend.

Surrounding Viera, from a distance, are large glass walls behind which glow plenty of terminal lights. Machines I don't recognize loom tall in the the shadows, some throwing pinpoints of red light at us, at Viera, like unblinking eyes.

"Ready?" Malo asks, speaking in Charre.

"Ready." I take the lead, and feel a slight sadness as my hand slips out of his. "Viera! Are you alive?"

The Lunare's ash-haired head jerks up at my words. Her face has a bloody scratch on one cheek, and as I get further into the room, I can see she's sporting a few more wounds too; the clean silver suit she had coming off of the *Nunilite* has splotches of red all over to go with tears along the shoulders—she's been dragged. It's enough to make me angry.

That anger doesn't help me catch the mirrored Oratus waiting inside, to the right of the lift. I only get the smallest warning from Viera's eyes, from her mouth starting to form the words, and then the Oratus strikes. I try to raise the bar, but the creature ignores me and pounces on Malo instead. The warrior gets a single frantic swipe in, one that the Oratus catches with a midclaw. As the creature's tail cuts Malo's legs out from under him, the Oratus tears away Malo's weapon and throws it to the side.

I don't even get in a swing before the Oratus has its shimmering claws to Malo's throat.

"I think that's quite enough," Ferrolite announces, floating into the central room through a door in the glass. The Amigga's added a new array to its floating microjets—a pair of spindly metal arms, both of which end in what look like miners. "You understand the terms, human? Say your Oath, and all of you go free. Fail to do so, and your friends pay the price."

"That wasn't the deal." It's a weak comeback, but with Malo one slip of a claw away from instant death, I'm having trouble thinking clearly. "You didn't say—"

"No, I didn't," Ferrolite cuts me off. "That's the way the galaxy works, Kaishi. You always have a second plan."

The room's frozen while Ferrolite basks in its apparent victory.

"Kaishi, don't do it," Viera says this time, and her voice carries all the pain she's in. "We're gonna die anyway. Don't give that blob the satisfaction."

"Oh, you'll say the words," Ferrolite says. "Because if you don't, I'll make sure Earth gets razed to nothing. It'll burn. We can't have rogue species polluting the galaxy." Ferrolite pauses. "Wait, doesn't Earth have a moon? I think Kolas could use one more test of his little toy, don't you?"

I drop the bar to the floor. It clangs loud, which at least gets Ferrolite to shut up.

"You want me to talk? Show me where, because I'm guessing you're not the one that needs to hear it."

"Ignos really did a wonder with you humans. So perceptive." Ferrolite gestures with its miners towards the chair Viera's occupying, and as it does so, those metal bands looping between Viera's arms, legs, and the chair snap open. "Sit there, and look straight ahead."

Fine. I head over to Viera, reach down to help her up, when a red bolt from Ferrolite's miner hits the space between us.

"No helping. She can crawl," the Amigga says.

I throw Ferrolite a glare.

"Don't," Viera whispers through gritted teeth. "Not worth it. I can move."

Viera falls forward, putting out her arms, catching herself on her elbows as she leaves the chair. T'Oli, for its part, swirls around Viera to help her lift her arms, her knees, as my friend crawls over to the glass wall and sits back against it. Her face is drained, and those red marks are larger.

The chair's empty now, so I sit in it. Press my back

against the white. I keep my arms and legs, though, out of the binders. Something Ferrolite probably notices, but the Amigga doesn't bother commenting on it. Instead, the creature floats in front and to the side of me, makes sure I can still see those bright red pinpoints of light leering down from the glass wall.

"Now, put on your best face," Ferrolite says. "This is going to go out to the entire galaxy. All of civilization will hear your Oath. Are you ready?"

"Is that a question?"

"I suppose it isn't. When the little lights turn green, the words to say will project onto the glass in front of you. Repeat them exactly, or your friends will die."

My legs are loose, my palms are sweaty. I'm breathing, but it's short and shallow. This is it. This is the moment.

The lights blink green. Sharp, grass green. Like magic, wisping on the plain glass surface, white letters form up into a set of simple sentences. Five lines, and that's it. Humanity's a thrall to a species I despise, an organization I hate.

"Are you ready, Malo? Viera?" I say in Charre. "I'm not going to say the words."

"In our standard language, please," Ferrolite says to my right. "It's important we be able to understand you."

Viera, keeping her head down, mutters, "I'm with you."

"Me too," Malo echoes, his voice stretched with the claw at his throat.

T'Oli, for its part, doesn't understand what I'm saying but seems to get the gist. The Ooblot slimes off of Viera and blinks its eyes at me.

"When I say," I shout as Ferrolite continues to yell at me for talking in the wrong tongue. "I'm going to go for the Amigga. You three handle the Oratus for as long as you can.

If this is being recorded, it will show we didn't give up. We fought to the end."

"Kaishi!" Ferrolite's booming its voice from all the speakers now. "Stop, or I'll have this one kill your friends anyway!"

"Just a prayer," I say to the Amigga in words it understands. "For us, on this new journey." Then I take a breath, this one full, until it feels like every inch of me is tight and ready. "Go!"

I burst off the chair towards Ferrolite, who responds with a startled shout. I don't see what happens to Malo, but given the sudden angry hissing erupting from behind me, I gather my warrior isn't dead. That's all the attention I can spare him, though, because Ferrolite's floating back and trying to get its miners angled at me. Unfortunately for the Amigga, I'm small. Fast. And I've had plenty of practice juking around trees and out of lines of bow fire.

Ferrolite's trying to get back to its glass door. I jump and one of its miner shots streaks by me, the mask keeping me safe from any harm, and I tackle the Amigga. Hit its metal arms and shove its floating body out of the doorway and back into the glass wall. Shrieks abound as Ferrolite's exoskeleton scratches the wall's surface. I'm hanging on it now, looping my left arm around Ferrolite's right side, and my hands are grabbing for the miner gripped in its holster.

The Amigga's saying things too, threats and commands and shouts, but I don't care. The miner's all that matters. But I can't get it. I'm trying, tugging and pulling and it's not coming out from its socket. Ferrolite spins, puts my back against the glass wall, and then presses me against it. The Amigga's gray-blob form is so ugly up close, and I try to look away but it's hard when the creature has me pinned. When it's crushing the air out of me.

I bring up my knees and kick out against the Amigga's spongy-soft form. Microjets might be good for floating but they're not much for resistance, and my kick gets me enough leverage to let go of Ferrolite and drop to the floor. Almost at the same time as I hit the ground, I see Malo fly across the room, red lines slicing his chest, and slam into the glass wall opposite me. Cracks form where Malo's shoulder hits, and he's slow to get up, but he's lying near my old metal bar. As Ferrolite re-orients my way, the mirrored Oratus snatches T'Oli off its back and opens its toothy maw.

"All this fighting, and you've still lost," Ferrolite says. "Instead of your loyalty, everyone is seeing your failure."

I stare at the green lights behind the Amigga. If every one of those lights is an eye through which the galaxy is seeing our last moments, then they'll see that humans won't give up.

"Yeah, well, you're ugly." I push myself away from the wall and spring at Ferrolite again. "Slide it now, Malo!" I say the words in Charre, hoping the warrior can hear me, can still act.

To the side, I see Viera make a swipe with Malo's metal bar, knocking aside the mirrored Oratus' Ooblot-clutching foreclaw. My reward for the glance is a shot to the chest, one my suit catches, and partially absorbs. Burning pain ripples from the spot, but given how close I've come to death before now, it only makes me laugh.

This time, I go below. Duck beneath Ferrolite's shooting arms and snag the metal bar as Malo slides it towards me. Ferrolite wheels itself around, expecting me to go completely underneath its bobbing body. Instead, I back up, using my feet and their grip to get behind the Amigga and line up for a hard swing. I connect, delivering as strong a stroke I can muster. The blow sends the Ferrolite careening forward into the glass wall near Malo, and the Amigga gives off a howl of purple rage to match its bruising skin.

Advantages shouldn't be lost, so I follow up the swing with a three-step approach, raising the bar above my head and planning to bring it down on what should be a final, destructive blow. Instead, just as I catch my own face reflected in the glass, the mirrored Oratus slams me with its tail, catching my stomach and flinging me, metal bar and all, back across the room. I hit the glass hard and things go hazy for a moment, with a few crystals falling around around me.

When I shake the blurs loose, I get a grim picture: the mirrored Oratus is helping Ferrolite get itself turned around. Malo's still on the ground, though he's at least sitting up. Viera's motionless over by the lift doors, and T'Oli's sliming my way, but the Ooblot's sporting a series of new dark lines on its cream-colored skin, and one of its eyes is gone entirely, the stalk waving with nothing more than a bloody stump on top.

Looks like this is it. I get to my feet, brace against the wall to stand, the metal bar in my left hand. T'Oli gets to me and, without a word, slithers up and brings a sword to my right.

"We're not giving up!" I muster a broken shout. "You will not win!"

"No," Ferrolite responds, synthed voice tight with pain. "But neither will you."

The mirror Oratus echoes its master's words with a deep hiss. I'm ready to accept the end, and give one last look of what I hope is determination to those green lights. Let them see what I'm dying for, what I'm fighting for. We will fall, but we will fall free.

Ferrolite bids its minion to attack first, and the Oratus is happy to oblige. It reads my new weapon though, and takes a cautious approach. Its talons step near one at a time while I circle towards the center. Try to give myself enough space. Ferrolite could shoot me, but it seems content to watch as its Oratus rends me to pieces. Or maybe the collisions with the wall damaged its miners. Either way, it's me against a giant lizard.

"C'mon." I spit at the beast. "I've faced worse."

"Don't think that's true," T'Oli patters quietly.

I'm as surprised as anyone when I laugh at the words. One last joke from the Ooblot. As I wipe away a sudden set of tears, the Oratus makes its move.

Its tail comes first, snaking around my right and driving me back a step, and while I'm retreating, the Oratus cuts its strike short and jumps at me. I try to stop, try to reset my feet to stab forward, but I'm off-balance and the swing comes too slow. The Oratus clubs me with its fore- and midclaws, sending me flying back to the ground in front of the lifts. Before I can move, the Oratus jumps again, this time landing with its talons near my legs, their claws putting pressure into my ankles.

I'm trapped. I'm dead.

The Oratus hisses, looks at me and opens its jaws.

Which, for some reason, make a *whooshing* noise.

"Guess we chose the right floor after all," a second hiss, this one deeper, angrier, comes from behind me. "Get off."

The voice doesn't wait for an answer. A giant red-black Oratus flies over my face, colliding with the mirrored Oratus and driving it off of me. The red Oratus grips its enemy with all four claws and whips the creature into the weakened glass wall on the right, and the whole thing comes down in a shower of glistening shards.

I start to stand when another shape whistles by above me, green scales catching in the sparkling lights of the fallen glass. Even as the mirrored Oratus struggles up, tries to untangle itself from the mangled machines, its eyes on the red Oratus in the room's center, the new, green Oratus scales the wall behind it. I feel a gentle pressure on my shoulder and a soft hiss at my ear, "Stay down, little human."

The hiss has a verve, and as I sit back, my eyes are drawn to that green Oratus, now jumping from the wall as the mirrored enemy gets up on its talons. At the motion, a name clicks through my stunned mind, and I *know* its Lan making the dive down at the mirrored Oratus, know it's Lan wrapping her tail around my enemy's neck, pivoting and, with her momentum, flinging the mirrored Oratus out of the pile and right towards the red Oratus.

Who makes the most of the opportunity, catching and clamping down on the mirrored Oratus with her claws, holding the beast steady. Bas jumps over me, goes three long lunges, and uses a swift snap of her jaws to take care of the trapped monster. And that's it. With a clamp of those jaws, the fight is over.

Which is when I notice Ferrolite is gone.

With a hiss and the clicking clank of opening locks, Sax reaches the top of the Meridia. Gravity here lessens its pull on Sax's talons, so that when he steps through the door in the Meridia's topmost chamber, Sax floats a brief moment before touching down on the black metal floor. There's no cushion, no concession made to comfort.

Instead, effort seems to have gone into looks. The floor vanishes away beneath him, a wave of shimmering dark tiles broken only in the center where, like a perfect bubble rising from a lake of tar, sits the Priority Beam. On its curved, domed surface, small nodules jab in pinks and blues. Fluorescent, short or long and always with a rounded, metallic top. They point out in all directions including back towards where Sax stands now.

What draws Sax's eyes most, though, is the view above.

The top of the Meridia soars above Aspicis' atmosphere. Kissing space itself. As if in celebration of their hubris, the Chorus capped the Meridia with a clear shell. Transparent, and yet magnetized, electrified or in some other way the Sax doesn't know, it's enhanced to block the brutal cascade of harmful radiation and potential debris strikes. A faint white glows at the very edges where the glass comes into contact with the black walls surrounding Sax, which rise just over his head.

The Chorus use the view they've created, too. Dancing, luminous red bolts arc back and forth from one long antenna to another through the space overhead. A light show, a promise of Chorus power and resources. The display blazes and obstructs the view of the cruisers and starships assembling above the planet. Obscures the pops of fiery explosions as some of them fight each other.

It seems not every Vincere band is siding with the Chorus. Evva may even have sent a short-wave message to friends she has in the system. But that's not what Sax is here for. What he needs to do, with this beam will let him do, is tell the rest of the galaxy to come. To help them. To win.

What Sax is looking for as he goes into the room is a terminal. But there isn't one. The floor itself gives a hint of something—tiles are easy to retract and shift around, but there's no clue how.

Perhaps the Amigga down below might know. Sax casts around his eyes, looking for a camera, something that he could use to send a message to that unlikely ally. The walls of this level, though, are bare.

But, as a click and grind announces, these walls are not simple.

One of the black pieces behind Sax slides away, and then another and another until several meters worth of doors open, revealing a glaring white room opposite the lift were Sax arrived from.

Filling the new space, floating, spinning its shiny silver rings, is the First Chair. Two rings of microjets, swirling to keep the Amigga aloft, while the weapons on two others settle on Sax. Still another covered in buzzing communications devices comes to life.

"We built a bunker here for this purpose," the First Chair says in its distinct, calm monotone. "There was always a chance that the Chorus would need to call for help, and the Priority Beam makes for a good final refuge."

"Then it's serving its purpose," Sax says, turning and spreading his claws. Yet, he can't attack yet. He can't assume that he's going to figure out how to use the Priority Beam on his own.

The First Chair seems to know this too and doesn't make a move. "I don't know how you made it here. Kah and Lei vanished, and yet here you show not a scratch. That should not be possible."

"But here I am," Sax says. "Show me how to use the Priority Beam. The fight is over."

"Is it?" The First Chair says. "In spite of those few out there who choose to betray us, our forces will still win. No matter how far up the Meridia your friends get, the Vincere will still bomb it to oblivion. Nothing will be left except rubble, except your broken, shattered dreams."

"Did you forget you're still in this tower?"

"Like I said before, I don't care. I'm dead either way. The only thing that matters is making sure you and your efforts die with me."

The words are the only signal, and one Sax doesn't catch. A pair of bright red bolts lance out from the rings as the weapons spin, triggering at the precise times to send their hot death right at Sax. Who moves, but not fast enough. Nothing is faster than light.

The first bolt strikes Sax in the side, down near his waist and causes his right leg to wobble, to lose feeling. The second one hits Sax's left midclaw and shears it off at the wrist. High-powered, deadly.

There's only one way to fight an enemy that has range when you do not, and Sax closes as quickly as possible. He dives, presses with his tail, his left leg, and with what he can get from his right. It's a fumbling leap, one that falls short but nonetheless forces the First Chair to float back into its bunker.

The weapons come around again on those rings and fire off another pair of shots but now Sax is moving forward fast, digging his claws and talons in and gouging that black metal floor to propel himself along it. The shots miss. Leave smoking marks in the tiles behind Sax. The Oratus is scrambling still and now he's beneath and near the First Chair. Sax reaches up to grip with his left and right foreclaws, snagging those rings and beginning to tear when he receives a shocking reply. A heavy burst of electric energy shimmers through his metal claws and sends Sax twitching to the ground as all of his nerves lock up.

But death doesn't come.

What does come is a second sound, the clang of metal as the First Chair and its body hit the floor. The Amigga's microjets are struggling, sputtering to come back to life. For moment both of them lay there, unable to fire, unable to attack, unable to move.

"I didn't plan for this," the First Chair's voice comes through weak, soft. The power pushing to its communications array not quite enough to give the voice its full volume. "Miners, microjets, the shock shield all at once. Congratulations, Oratus. You found a flaw in my defenses."

Sax catches the words but can't do much with them. He's trying, in the same way that he might try to move an arm or leg that's fallen asleep after lying on it all night, to restore connection, to twitch, to move to bring himself to life and when he hears the telltale whine of the jets coming back, that's when the icy hand clamps over his hearts. When he realizes he can't do it.

He can't move.

But he can roar. Long, and loud.

There's panic in the sound, there's fear and anger and loss having come so close but now with the First Chair hovering above, dangling those weapons down on him... it's over. One blast to the head and it's done and all Sax has fought for is ruined.

The lights die. The bunker goes dark.

In that moment of confusion Sax knows the Amigga down below can see, can help at least to some degree. Knowing he's not alone, that there's another helping him, gives Sax the boost he needs. This is not solely his cause, but the fight for every species living in this galaxy. Every species that wants freedom and is willing to try to get it.

Just as the First Chair starts to ask what's going on, Sax pushes his tail and his left talon. He kicks himself beneath the First Chair and this time, this time, when he reaches to grab the rings there is no electric shock. There is no burst of numbing energy. Only a tremor, a taste of what might happen if Sax gives the First Chair more time.

Instead, Sax's claws dig deep. They tear the metal and rend the rings and send the First Chair rocketing away. There's a clang as the Amigga strikes the far side of the bunker, which isn't a more than a few meters wide.

At the sound, lights flash back on, blinding Sax for a hot moment, then his eyes see the First Chair covered in a flow of sparks from its broken rings; one of its weapons and one of its jets show their damage in an incendiary shower.

"Unexpected," the First Chair manages to say as it cuts

the power to those rings, restoring itself to a lopsided sort of hover only centimeters above the ground. "I didn't order those lights off."

"You're already losing control," Sax hisses, struggling back to his talons.

"You're running out of time to talk," the First Chair responds and swivels a second weapon towards Sax.

There's no room for fancy maneuvers, no time for bobbing and weaving. Instead, as a laser shoots into his chest, Sax charges forward and crashes into the First Chair, biting slashing snarling and feeling again and again the red laser gut punch as the First Chair continues to fire.

Moments flash in fire and instinct and pain.

It's broken. There's no rings left except for the one Sax meant to leave out of his hacking slashing biting. The First Chair's covering itself in the dissolving acid that Amigga's use to feed, and its presence keeps Sax from carving any more into the Amigga's body.

Not that Sax needs any help to fall back. He's burned and bleeding too. Parts of himself are hollow, though any pain that's coming is being quashed now in waves of adrenaline. Stim would be nice. Any one of a number of drugs that can keep him numb. As it is, Sax's just going to have to rely on his own strength to make it through.

"Tell me," Sax says. "Tell me how to use it."

"The Priority Beam?" Even in monotone, the First Chair's voice carries with it a quiver, and a weight, the dull sadness of terrible loss. "Why?"

"Because you have nothing more to lose," Sax says.

Going all the way back, all the way to his first moments on Solis when he first hatched, Sax's been taught, told, ordered, that the mission comes first. Ensure the enemy's defeat, or as much of it as you can, before you die. It's an ideal that's carried Sax through countless assaults, adventures to worlds enemy and friend. Yet here he is, commanding, beseeching the very core of that vision to ignore it.

"Why?" The First Chair says. "If I've lost everything, why help the ones who took it from me?"

Sax has an answer. He knows why you might help the enemy. Why you would abandon everything you'd been taught.

"Because we're not the ones who took everything from you," Sax says. "You took it from yourselves. You lost your way, and you know it, or you wouldn't be here waiting to die. Help us clean up the galaxy. Help us make this better. That's what you want, and we're ready to give it to you."

It's not Sax's most eloquent speech. It's not going to be replayed for cycles in front of classes to study how to turn someone's mind at the last moment. But it's real, it's what he has. The First Chair, who has very little, listens.

"Then promise me," the First Chair says. "Promise me you won't destroy our species. That Amigga will have a place in your new world, in your grand vision."

Another deal, another promise that Sax has no right to make and no position to guarantee. But he can guarantee it. As long as Sax breathes, just as he has here, the Oratus can fight to make sure the words he says are honored. So when Sax agrees to the First Chair's ask, he does so with confidence, with courage and conviction.

"Yes," Sax hisses, a rasp low in week as the whole of the blast are starting to take their turn. The creep along his muscles and bones stabbing, burning, aching and yet, for now, he keeps enough of it away to focus. "I will. The Amigga will not die while I have claws with which to defend them."

"Then you can have your message. You can have your

victory," the First Chair says. "Though I don't think the rest of the Chorus will lay down easily."

Before Sax can say anything, the First Chair rattles off a series of words that make seemingly no sense. Names of places and people in a specific order and cadence that suggests a code. When it finishes, there is a grinding beneath the floor of the Priority Beam and from around the circular dome emerges a series of terminals. The screens plug into the nubs, and as each one connects, the screens large and small light up and show in greens and reds when they've connected to quantum satellites far beyond the planet.

This is how it works, this is how the Priority Beam reaches all corners of the galaxy and moments. How it can transmit beyond the confining speed of light and send Sax's request, his plea.

Near the bunker, two more panels in the floor shift aside and raise a simple interface. An interface for typing words and that's all. Visual data can't make it so far, can't make it to the simple itemized connection of the quantum network. Sax claws his way to the terminal, he's glad of it. If the first message of liberation came from a bleeding, battered, nearly dead Oratus, Sax isn't sure many would sign up.

Instead, Sax taps the words on the display. Simple, and yet complete.

"A new government has taken the Meridia and a new galaxy has begun. Come to Aspicis if you can, and claim your freedom."

Evva may want to send something longer, and doubtless the various news agencies covering this attack will have their own interpretations out before long. But this message gets the point across. Once he finishes, Sax sits back from the terminal and stares at the wall of red and green the lights across the screen. As the message goes out, as those quantum points find their counterparts, each icon on the screen changes from red to green.

It's done then. At last.

We're bloody, bedraggled, and barely standing.

But we *are* standing.

Bas and Lan are using their claws to dabs bits of cold, gray cream along the various cuts we've suffered while the green lights on those cameras glow on. Apparently our fight was, is, being sent all over the planet, including inside the Meridia, which is how the Oratus knew to come here in the first place. The Meridia's own lifts seemed to know too—sending the Oratus to this level without them having to choose it.

"What?" I manage to ask.

"Perhaps someone wants you to live," Bas says, turning a couple of her claws up in a question. "Sax, maybe. Or an Amigga tired of the Chorus running things."

Bas says Evva might know too, but the commander's already left, gone off to reunite with some of their other forces. Bas and Lan, though, have a few vials of the cream and they use it liberally.

"This itches. Really bad." I bite my lip to keep from

scratching at the line on my left arm where, I gather, some of the broken glass must have made a cut.

"That's the nanobots," Bas hisses as she works on Viera's more numerous wounds. "You'll get used to it. They're putting you back together."

I don't even want to know what 'nanobots' are, and suppress any fear of the things getting inside of me. T'Oli sees my nervousness and tries to tell me that nanobots are why I'm still alive at all—after the seed ship, these tiny, invisible things put my body back together.

"Doesn't mean I have to like them," I say, then spare a look for Malo, whose getting the first aid treatment from Lan. He's going to have a couple of new scars across his chest, and his shoulder's looking stiff after Lan popped it back into place. "You doing all right, Malo?"

"I've lived through worse." Malo flicks a finger towards Bas. "First time I met her, it was almost as bad."

I'd forgotten about how Sax and Bas thrashed Malo and Viera around the jungle when they kidnapped me from Earth's surface. Back then I was still in thrall to the Sevora, back then I didn't know anything.

"Where is Sax?" I ask Bas.

"Somewhere in this tower," the Oratus hisses back at me. "Causing problems, as always. After you, I'm going to find him."

"Not alone," Lan adds.

"You're not going after Evva?"

Bas laughs. "I think we'll all wind up at the same place before this is all over."

I would ask where that might be, but my eyes float to the lift across from me. The right one of the two, a silver color and the one Ferrolite must have taken. The one to its left is shaded red, and Bas says that means it's dedicated to the media levels of the Meridia, and I can't imagine Ferrolite docking its escape shuttle anywhere this low. The Amigga's pet Oratus might be dead—Lan insisted we leave the body in clear shot of the cameras, so that anyone watching understands this is real—but Ferrolite's continued existence has taken priority on my list of things to handle while I'm here.

Apparently, a mission to join the Chorus has turned into a violent protest against most things the Chorus stands for. Guess I'm not the best choice for Ambassador.

Bas steps away from Viera, who manages not to collapse all over again. Instead, the Lunare just looks tired, and I can empathize. Without the edge-of-death boost keeping me ready to run, my own muscles are telling me it's time to grab a nap. Malo, too, looks like he's best equipped for a solid chunk of hours on one of those red sponge beds the galaxy likes.

Which is why I ask, "Have any stim?"

Lan snaps her eyes to me, cocks her head at an angle. "Why do you want that?"

"Have an Amigga to catch." I have no idea if it's possible, but if there's any chance, any chance at all...

Bas appreciates my sentiments with a low hiss of her own, then she scoops another black-topped vial off of her mask with her midclaws. "I was saving this for Sax, but I think you might be able to use it more."

"Wait," Viera interrupts. "You want to go after Ferrolite? Now?" When I don't shoot down the idea, Viera's hands go up. "Why bother? Look at these two, and that other one, Evva—they're going to have this thing won in a few minutes. Then we'll have all the time to track down the Amigga, rather than right now, when we're half dead."

"That's what we thought about the Sevora," Bas says. "Many times we thought we had them gone, so we held back. Did not over-commit. And every time, they would slip away and come back stronger than we anticipated. If you can crush your foe, then crush them."

"Or eat them," Lan adds.

"Yes, eating them is good too. Especially if they are tasty," Bas hisses. "I have never eaten an Amigga, though."

Viera's throwing disgusted looks at both Oratus, and I'm trying and failing to hold back some much-needed laughter. It's a moment that dies when I catch T'Oli slithering over to Ferrolite's chosen lift, the Ooblot's sole eye stalk a clear reminder that, nanobots aside, we're not getting out of this unscathed.

"I'm with Kaishi," Malo says. "We have to stand up for our species. Ferrolite wanted credit for bringing us to the Chorus. Let's give it what it's looking for."

"If this gets us killed, I'm holding it against you both." Viera looks like she wants to add a few more gripes, but Bas's outstretched claw coated in stim interrupts, and after that buzz, Viera's objections die away in a frenzy of distracted twitching.

Which is how the three of us, with T'Oli riding on my shoulders, wind up on Ferrolite's lift heading up. I didn't expect our options to be so narrow, but it turns out the Meridia doesn't have many levels designed for docking. There's the one we came in on, near the Chorus and meant for visitors and reserved as such. Then another five set aside for Chorus members themselves and their various entourages. Beyond those, there's only one more level on the tower, labeled for emergencies or high priority visits. I'd say Ferrolite's evacuation qualifies as both, so that's where we choose to go.

"Are you going to be ok, with one eye?" I ask the Ooblot as the lift scurries up. I have to talk because the stim is hitting every nerve like lightning, and if I don't say anything, I'm afraid I'll be like Malo, who's busy clenching and opening his fists, or Viera, who seems like she's hyperventilating in the corner.

"I will have it replaced later with a mechanical version. Until then, my depth perception will be off. Please don't ask me to aim. Or judge distance." T'Oli says.

T'Oli says 'later' like it expects to make it to some future beyond the now, and I guess I'm there too, drifting as our lift rises to what I'll do first when I get back to Earth. Maybe it's being optimistic, but, well, maybe we deserve some optimism after all this?

The lift hits its mark and the doors whoosh open into thin entryway that goes into a lobby sporting three triple-wide doors. One for each of the emergency bays, I gather. All of them are closed, and there's no clear one Ferrolite's chosen to use.

"It went that way," Viera points at the one to our right and I'm about to ask how she knows when I realize the evidence is at our feet.

Black lines lead to the left and straight ahead doorways, but an amber-yellow glistens towards the right. Of course they'd light up the floor—smoke and such climbs to the ceiling, and you might not have time to mess with terminals.

"Are we ready?" I ask, heading to the marked door.

Bas and Lan each gave us a miner, so Malo and Viera have some lasers ready to go. I'm holding my scavenged tool, and T'Oli's made a blade of itself again, putting us in as good a shape as we're going to get. That we're only standing because of a heavy dose of drugs is a fact I'm choosing to ignore.

When we get close, the door opens on its own accord, no panel push required, which I guess fits the idea of emergencies. On the other side is, indeed, a shuttle, though a smaller one than I've used before. At first glance, this resembles a cone, though without the strict separation of cockpit and passenger hold. It's been painted too, a deep blue with a small set of lime-green circles. Chorus colors. There's no boarding ramp that I can see. Only a small platform lowered from the craft's center. The rest of the space is lit in white, and decorations are non-existent. Racks of various things litter the sides, no doubt placed in case a last second fix is necessary to escape.

Floating in front of it, barking orders at a trio of Flaum guards, is Ferrolite. Its last command, to send the guards back our way, dies as the door opens.

I can imagine what the Flaum see as they turn our way: a trio of beaten, bloodied creatures from a new species, two holding miners and a third wielding a crude metal bar and what looks like a pearl sword with a single eye bobbing from it. Where that falls in terms of Flaum nightmares, I don't know, but it's strange enough that, instead of engaging, the three guards break from their frozen moment to dash to the shuttle's loading platform and start ascending.

"Cowards!" Ferrolite calls after them, and the Amigga starts to float their way, but its microjets, possibly damaged from our fight, putter too slow. The platform's gone up and in before the Amigga gets there. "You'll all die for betraying the Chorus!"

"Aren't you a little beyond those threats?" I say to Ferrolite as we walk forward in a line. Malo's on my right, Viera's on my left, both with miners raised. "I don't think your Chorus is going to help you now."

Ferrolite rotates back towards us, and before it turns, I

get a good look at the massive purple bruise across its back. Guess my strike did some work after all.

"No," Ferrolite says, and its synthed words are low-toned, somehow melancholy in their unnatural verve. "No, it won't."

"Sounds like you're giving up," Viera cracks.

"Aren't I?" Ferrolite replies. As the Amigga speaks, the shuttle starts up a whine as its jets power to full life. "I've been abandoned by my own guards. I've failed to capture the allegiance of a new species. Even if I survive this day, I'll be nothing to the Chorus. I'll never get a place."

"If you're expecting pity..." I'm almost within striking distance. Malo and Viera know to shoot if there's a risk, but until then, I want the final strike. It's my job, my duty as both Empress and ambassador, or so I tell myself.

"Reality is what it is," Ferrolite says. "For me, it is the end. For you, the same is likely true. If the Meridia is likely to fall, as inconceivable as that may be, the Vincere will raze it to the ground and burn your leaders alive in the process. Then, the Chorus will build a new one. The galaxy will remain the same."

"But you won't be in it."

The shuttle begins to move, and as it does, the slate-gray wall to our left splits apart, revealing a view of space and the plenty of Vincere ships occupying it. A blue-tinged light washes over it, and I've taken off from enough space stations now to know that's the magnetic shield, keeping our air, ourselves from getting pulled out into the infinite.

I raise T'Oli, bringing its Ooblot-sword to bear. "Last words, Ferrolite."

The Amigga, with its broken exoskeleton still hanging around it, doesn't have any eyes or arms, no mouth or shoulders with which to make known its emotions. Instead, it floats, still and ugly. "Kill me then. Do what you came to do."

Not long after I first found Ignos, I stood at the top of our tribe's Tier. After all of the promises Ignos told me to make, my own people wanted me to plunge a black-glass knife into a a captive. Like Ferrolite, the captive was helpless. Like Ferrolite, who floats still in front of me, weaponless and without hope, the captive had accepted his fate. The Amigga has threatened us, has tried to force me to submit humanity to the Chorus' will even after I'd changed my mind, and had done it all for personal gain.

And yet.

I couldn't perform the sacrifice then, because I was too scared. Too new to the consequences of power and the terrible decisions that must come with it. Since then, I'd played the merciless leader. I'd executed my share of sacrifices and enemies alike because I thought such things were necessary. Such things were expected.

But maybe it's time for those expectations to change.

A pop-bang sounds as the shuttle's boosts out of the bay, and as it soars from the room, a bright red bolt fires from the sole cannon on the shuttle's top. Compared to the massive light-shows put on by the Vincere's larger ships, the flash here is small, targeted. It's also enough, as the laser strikes the side wall of the back, to cause the magnetic shield to flicker. Sparks fly from the hit, and suck out into space as vacuum pulls at us for a moment.

"Run!" T'Oli patters from my hand. "The shield is failing!"

The blue tinge vanishes again as T'Oli's words get my legs into motion and the pull jerks me back, towards black space. Whistling air blows my hair, pulls the breath from my mouth. Viera, closest to the door, gets close and it jerks open. We're not trapped, yet.

"Kaishi!" Malo shouts. "Your bar!"

The warrior has it right—with the shield flickering, it's hard to take more than a step or two at a time, but Malo reaches Viera's outstretched arm and with his own right hand, grabs my left, holding the metal bar. Together, we pull against the failing shield. Closer, with every lunge, towards the door.

Over the random pops, another whine makes itself clear, and against my own judgment I look and see Ferrolite's microjets struggling against the vacuum's pressure. With nothing to hold onto, the Amigga jerks back a meter or so every time the shield dissipates, and only manages to stop its momentum during the breaks. The Amigga's going to get sucked out before too long.

"You can't save it," T'Oli patters loud, its sole eye following mine at the Amigga.

"No, but you can. Stretch, T'Oli," I say. "Prove we're not like them."

The Ooblot hesitates and Malo gets us another long step closer to the door.

"Ferrolite isn't the Sevora! The Amigga created us, and the Oratus. They can't all be evil!" I shout the words, and Ferrolite twitches its towards me as it fights its slow suck into oblivion. I'm not sure my argument is all that good, but now, more than anything, I want Ferrolite to live, to understand how wrong it was. To accept, maybe, that humans aren't the mistake all the Amigga seem to think we are.

T'Oli, at last, buys into my wish. The Ooblot stretches itself out from my right hand, looping and hardening part of itself around my wrist and using the pull of a vacuum beat to fly like a thrown rope through the bay towards the

Amigga. There, the Ooblot wraps itself around Ferrolite's broken exoskeleton.

"Pull, Malo!" I call to my warrior, and he does.

Viera's bracing herself against the door and together the four of us reel each other in one by one, with Ferrolite sneaking inside the door as the shield flickers and fails for what sounds like the last time. A brief alarm sounds and a harder, thicker slat slams down and covers the door we just came through, leaving us scattered around the center of the level. Safe, alive, and breathing.

"You saved me," Ferrolite's monotone fails to send any gratitude, but I assume it's there.

"Why'd they shoot the shield?" Viera shouts when she gets her breath back. "What's the point of that?"

"Disobeying an Amigga means death," Ferrolite replies, hovering just inside the door. "They likely thought killing me would spare their own lives. Now, I will enjoy taking each and every one of their souls, slowly."

"No," I stand up while T'Oli untangles itself from the two of us. "You'll do nothing except what we say. All the killing, the executions and the dominance, all that stops now."

Ferrolite doesn't say anything for a moment, until Malo, Viera and I are all standing, all facing it. "You think, because you saved me, the Chorus will strike a deal with you? I am nothing to them."

"But you could be," I say. "We're going to win this war. When it's done, the Amigga will need someone to speak for them. Someone who understands us, and who's willing to work with the Oratus."

If there's a key to this Amigga, it's ambition. It's the chance at glory, respect, and power. Now that I know how

Ferrolite operates, I think I can work with it. Bas, Evva, and the others can too.

Ferrolite, too, seems to see its path forward—it doesn't object to my offer, and with Viera keeping a miner leveled at it, the four of us return to the lift, and head higher.

He's sent the message. Very soon, the entire galaxy is going to question its allegiances. The Vincere's going to have a choose a side. Or, more likely, engage in a war with itself.

"So many are going to die," the First Chair crackles as its voice systems, apparently damaged, work to translate the Amigga's thoughts into words.

"So many already were," Sax says. He's stepped away from the terminal back over to the First Chair's bunker, where he can keep a watch on the Amigga. "Only they didn't know it."

"How many of them will you kill?"

Sax looks at the broken creature in front of him. Those metal rings are twisted and snapped, the occasional spark bursting from a gouged microjet or a miner Sax bit in half. The First Chair, for all its position, for all its supposed power, is nothing but a blob. Entirely dependent on the systems it's built. It's almost pathetic, except Sax knows he's just as reliant on those same systems. He might be a weapon, but he doesn't know how to grow his own food, repair a starship, or colonize a world.

"As few of them as possible," Sax hisses finally. "Every death will be a failure."

The First Chair absorbs the words as Sax crouches and, wrapping his tail around his talons, sits next to the Amigga. It's more comfortable this way, and Sax's throbbing body feels better against the cool hard floor.

"We started out that way too," the First Chair says. "A noble species, and one not as helpless as you find us today. We had limbs once, bodies more suited to catching prey in our watery home."

"You couldn't have known."

"We learned how to store recordings long before we decided that knowledge was the only currency that really mattered," the First Chair says, and Sax begins to realize he's listening to a confessional for the Amigga as a whole. "You can watch Amigga from before, living lives impossible to us now. Before we changed our own genetic make-up, long after we subjugated the Flaum and pushed them into service. Once you have someone to lift a glass, fly a ship for you, why worry about it yourself?"

"Or fight a war for you."

"Exactly. We chased after the one thing no other species could, and look where it brought us."

"You ruled everything. For a long time."

"And how many subjects would say we did a good job of it?"

Sax looks at his claws, metal-made. Unnatural. His tongue brushes along the inside of his teeth, still his from birth. His eyes blink, turn towards the arcing red lightning fixed to the top of the Meridia, flashing against dark space and the popcorn explosions as Vincere ships swirl and fight one another. The message is getting through, allegiances are being forged and broken in blood.

"I would," Sax rasps. "We would not exist without your kind, and until you went too far, we served without question."

Across the room, a lift door opens wide and reveals someone Sax thought he'd never see again. Bas claws her way through the chamber with a pair of long leaps, landing next to Sax and with one of her talons pressing against the grounded First Chair.

"Leave it," Sax says. "The Amigga's already given up."

"This one tried to kill you," Bas hisses. "I have no mercy for it."

"I expect none," the First Chair replies, its voice fractured now, broken as the technology driving its speech begins to fail. "You were made to be predators. Do not betray your nature."

The word that sticks with Sax, lying wounded and exhausted, is *made*. The Oratus were designed to be one thing, but if there's anything Evva, Bas, and Sax have proved with this entire operation, it's that they are more than what they were made to be.

"Sorry," Sax manages. "But Amigga taste awful."

"They really do," Bas echoes, and a glimmer comes to those golden eyes of hers as she catches what Sax is thinking. "We don't want to eat you."

"Mercy?" the First Chair says. "I would not have thought the Oratus capable of it."

"This isn't mercy," Sax hisses, air whistling through his burned vents. "You've used us for so long, now it's our turn."

Evva is the leader of their uprising, her black and red scales the visage that drives their forces forward, that frames their vision. The First Chair is the same for the Chorus, a leader synonymous with a government. Taking, and making, the Amigga turn against its former allies and speak out against the Amigga's endless cruelty, that is true justice, and for the First Chair, far from a merciful ending.

But in its current state, with its rings lying broken on the ground, its microjets powerless and shooting the occasional spark across the floor, and with Bas sticking a talon right up against its rippled, gray body, the Amigga has no options. No choices. Just like the First Chair intended for the Oratus.

"Time to go?" Bas says, her tail winding around and helping push Sax up until he's standing on his talons, his own tail doing what it can to keep him balanced.

"Yes."

Sax takes one more look at the Priority Beam as they head towards the lift down. It's still lit, still pushing Sax's message to the galaxy's corners. Strange to see a mission accomplished that didn't end in blood, destruction, or extinction. A feeling Sax could get used to. Some of the time, anyway.

Bas carries the First Chair—the low gravity up here makes it easy to hold the Amigga in her claws, and the Amigga doesn't bother protesting. Resigned to its fate, or accepting it. Not that it matters.

For once, the Oratus are in control.

This time, the lift goes where I want it to; back to where I nearly sold out my species to the First Chair. To the top of the Meridia.

We're silent during the ride. Ferrolite floats towards the back of the lift with Viera next to it, her miner ready to fire should the Amigga feel like doing anything, anything at all. T'Oli's riding my left arm, where it can monitor what the lift's doing. Malo's with me, his hand near mine but his eyes, like mine, staring ahead at the steel doors and his mind somewhere I can't place.

When we broke out of the safe room Ferrolite stashed us inside at the start of this, I had thought we'd be able to clear up the shroud around human history. I had thought that, by destroying our origins at the hands of a rogue Amigga, we'd be able to preserve some measure of dignity as a species. That maybe I wouldn't feel like a pawn. An experiment the Amigga failed to throw in the trash.

Instead we'd all nearly died. T'Oli had lost an eye. Viera, Malo and I are all hurting, and for what?

"Don't question yourself," Malo whispers as the lift climbs.

"How'd you know?"

"You close your eyes tight when you're doing that," Malo says. "And, you're kind of hurting my hand."

I didn't even notice that I'd grabbed it. That I'm squeezing it tight.

"I don't want to be wrong," I say, letting go.

"No way to know for sure," Malo replies. "I didn't know if taking you from your tribe was the right move. The Emperor was the holiest person in Damantum. Someone claiming to hear from Ignos probably ought to be seen as a threat."

"What changed your mind?"

"The conviction." Malo smiles, memories dancing around his eyes. "The way you spoke on the Tier showed you believed."

"Or that I could say what Ignos told me to."

"No Sevora could do that. Ignos may have given you the words, but you spoke them."

The lift slows, settles in for its stop. This high up, the gravity's low and as the lift comes to its rest my feet bob ever so slightly off the floor.

"I still believe in us, Malo," I say as my toes touch the metal floor again. "Humans are the equals of anyone, everyone else."

"See? That's what I mean. Conviction."

When the lift doors open and we leave, I'm smiling too. Small, determined, but a smile. One that vanishes as we enter the familiar ring around the Chorus chamber and see a trio in front of us. A Vyphen, looking battle-scarred and tired, a Whelk with what looks like a giant miner lancing straight out from its ruby-red body, and an ash-black Flaum that comes swirling back through deep memories to my mind.

"Coorvin?" I manage to dredge up the creature's name.

Before I finish, the Whelk's trained its miner on me. With the barrel in my face the weapon's even larger than I thought it'd be at first, and now I'm getting nervous. If this thing's a member of the Chorus, it might liquidate all of us before we even start to move.

"Fire and the orb gets it," Viera preempts any answer to my question with the threat from behind me.

"Why should I care?" the Vyphen replies, the creature's eyes moving from me over my shoulder, towards Ferrolite. "That thing isn't any friend of ours."

I permit myself a half-sliver of calm. Only a half. I try looking non-threatening, spread my hands out wide, and say Coorvin's name again. This time, I follow it up with, "Want to tell your friends that we're, uh, friends?"

The Flaum tilts his head at me, and I don't see much kindness in that face. "Friends? Last time I saw your species, you were leaving Sax, Bas, and I to die as *Cobalt* fell apart."

Oh. Yeah.

"That wasn't my fault! The Sevora told me to do that."

Now the Vyphen and Whelk are glancing back and forth between Coorvin, myself, and the Amigga, their expressions saying they're sliding towards shooting us all first and figuring out if we're dangerous later. Coorvin, though, doesn't let it get that far. The Flaum sighs, places a hand on the barrel of the Whelk's miner and pushes it to the side.

"These are humans," Coorvin says.

"Worthless ones," Ferrolite grumbles, and Viera gives the creature a light smack with the butt of her miner.

"Humans?" the Vyphen asks. "Should I know what these are?"

The question gives me a chance to lay out the concise version of human history, which comes out to about three sentences: we're from a planet called Earth, the Sevora landed there and brought all kinds of awful with them, and now the Chorus found us and brought us here. I don't mention Ignos, I don't talk about how the Amigga thought we were the answer to their Sevora problem, and I definitely don't mention how the Chorus decided we were better off annihilated than allowed to survive.

"Sounds like they're on our side," the Vyphen says.

"I don't trust them," the Whelk counters.

"You don't trust anyone," Coorvin says.

"I trust you both."

"Only because I pay you," the Vyphen holds up a feathered limb to forestall another comeback and turns to me. "If you're all the way up here, holding an Amigga hostage, you must have more of a story."

"I do, and I'll tell you. Later." I nod past the trio. "Where are Bas and Lan? I need to speak to them."

What I don't say is that I want to leave this place. That I want to get back to Earth as fast as possible so that I can stand with my people when the Chorus decides to send their Oratus to wipe all of us away.

The Vyphen gets the point, thankfully, and, after sending the Whelk to give Ferrolite additional assurance of its demise should any escape be considered, we walk through one of the section tunnels to a chamber I'd hoped never to see again.

The Chorus room is back to its classic red and black. Each of the Amigga booths are empty, without the faintest sign of the dozen Amigga and their attendants that cast who knows how many species to their ultimate ends. Or tried to, anyway.

Lan, and the larger Oratus they called Evva occupy the center. When she sees me, Lan breaks out into a toothy grin.

"Your hunt was successful," Lan hisses first.

"Barely," I reply. "Where's Bas?"

"Her pair needs her," Lan says, and the smallest echo of concern comes through. "I would have gone as well, but Evva must be protected. Though, it seems, not from this Amigga."

It's strange, seeing the very creatures that struck so much fear into me not all that long ago, laughing at Ferrolite. Seeing the Oratus give us a friendly greeting melts the last of the ice away from the Vyphen and Whelk as well, and conversations break out between us. I fall into a re-telling of where we went in the Meridia, and when Lan asks for the fuller story, I tell that too. Still, I keep humanity's origins a secret.

Evva stays silent as I tell my tale, I see her eyes tighten as I talk about the archives, when I lie and say we wound up there after trying to find our way down the giant tower to where the fighting was taking place. Whatever goes on inside her mind, she chooses not to confront me, and waits until I'm done to speak.

"You nearly pledged your species to the Chorus," Evva says when I'm done, her voice a stronger timber than Lan's. I recognize the weight—confidence. I'd heard it in the Emperor, in Dalachite on *Cobalt*, and even in Malo while Ignos held his body and commanded me to surrender.

"Because I did not, I think I've killed us."

"No," Evva says the word. "I don't think the Chorus will be much of a threat anymore."

"They won't give up just because you took this tower,"

Ferrolite calls, having drifted close enough to hear our conversation. "The Vincere will take it back. You can't hope to hold it."

"The Vincere no longer works for you," Evva says. "I would choose your next words carefully, Amigga. Your species may have a part to play in what comes, and you would seem to be in a good position to determine how big a part that is."

Ferrolite, a slave to ambition, falls silent. Which returns the Oratus gazes to me. It's not much of a guess to see what they're looking for.

"You want the same thing the Chorus do," I say to the dozens of teeth, those shimmering scales, those yellow-black eyes.

Evva doesn't deny it.

"The Amigga ruled by themselves," the Oratus says. "We will do things differently. A council, yes, but one made up of every species. Yours included."

Sit in one of those red-lit sections? Live in this tower, or on the world far below? This wouldn't be the servitude of the Chorus, but it wouldn't be home either. I throw a glance back to Malo and he meets me, steady and ready to accept whatever I choose.

"Kaishi," Viera's voice speaks up. "If you don't want it, I'll take it."

That has all of us turning towards the Lunare, who still has her miner trained on the Amigga.

"What?" Viera says. "Always said I liked seeing new places. No offense Kaishi, but if you're going back to those tunnels, or that sweaty city of yours, I'd rather stay here. Make sure the lizards don't get too power-hungry."

"Lizards?" Evva hisses.

And I laugh. I laugh because Viera's wearing a cocky

smile that says she's more than up for the challenge. Equipped with an attitude that would have earned her a swift death from the Chorus, Viera might be the voice humans would need here. She'd make sure we wouldn't get thrown around, that Earth would be safe.

Or she'd annoy everyone so much the Oratus would eat her.

There's a lot of eyes staring at me. A lot of teeth, too. The red light inside the chamber, all that space suddenly seems big. Too big. I'd asked for destiny and it came for me, but I never really chose it. Here, though, my own life, Viera's, and humanity's role in the galaxy at large all comes down to a word from my lips.

"Can I take a moment?" I say, and it's softer than I mean, but I want to get away, to breathe and think without all the eyes.

Malo catches my thought and takes me by the hand, guides me out as the Oratus grant my wish with a hissing assent. I'm barely out from the middle before Evva starts up behind me on some other task, so I don't feel all that rushed.

"Thanks," I tell Malo once we're outside, back in the cold metal of the ring. "It was a lot, in there."

"Even Empresses need a break sometimes."

I nod, and start walking. Without the threat of death or under Ferrolite's demanding direction, the Chorus level seems nice. Evva's troops—I'm guessing—have commandeered the room controlling all the various screens, and the terminals have reverted to their prior cascade of pictures from across the galaxy. The foreign landscapes, covered in icy vistas, rocky plains, and sprawling purple jungles, calm me down. Distract me from my own lingering pains.

"You're worried about her?" Malo ventures the question after we've gone a quarter way around.

"I feel like this is my responsibility. I brought us this far, it's not fair for me to walk away."

"I think you've earned that right." Malo's voice doesn't sound like my father, but it's something I could imagine him saying. "I thought part of being a leader meant knowing what your people could do better than you."

"You think Viera would make a good ambassador?"

"I don't think she'd let them kill us." Malo laughs. "Or push us around."

"I'm afraid she doesn't have the patience for it."

"How do you know?"

I pause. We've reached the part of the ring where our old safe room sits to my left. The door's open, the panel green, and through it I can see the fringe of Aspicis' blue atmosphere. Malo's question is a good one. I've been on the run with Viera, in plenty of danger, but the time we spent running Damantum before the Oratus arrived was brief. It's hard to pay attention to a friend when you're learning everything on the fly.

"Viera did manage to live with our tribe for a while," I say slow, feeling out the idea. "She didn't manage to offend us too much."

"Compare that with you," Malo says. "Everywhere you go either falls apart or gets attacked."

"Hey."

Malo laughs and I can't hate that.

We make it back to the red-lit center ring and I ask Viera one last time if she's willing to accept the job. Her response is a little too enthusiastic, and prompts a sigh from Ferrolite, one which Viera rewards with another swat of her miner.

"You can't do that to everyone you don't like, you know,"

I say as Ferrolite floats away from her. "You have to talk to them."

"Don't think the new government's started yet," Viera replies. "When it does, I'll be nice. Nice enough, anyway."

Even as I roll my eyes, my thoughts are turning to one place. The only one that really matters.

Home.

For once, Sax isn't thinking about prey and predators. His claws aren't raised and his teeth aren't ready to sink into an enemy. He's not wearing a mask, nor wielding miners.

Relaxed.

The word makes him laugh, a delighted hiss and gets a glance from Bas, standing next to him in front of the many meters-high shield giving view to the purple-red expanding light show in front of them. Behind and around the two Oratus, plenty of other species are doing the same thing; watching nature's grandest spectacle while robots bring food, beverages, and all manner of other pleasures to their sides.

Above and around Sax, a sound-dampening field serves to quiet every word not coming from his pair's mouth, ensuring a magical, private experience. The old Sax would have found the inability to hear what's going on around him stressful—too easy to sneak up on someone when they can't hear you coming. The new Sax? The new Sax doesn't care.

"I don't think I've ever heard you laugh like that," Bas says, and there's concern in her eyes. "Are you all right?"

"Look around us," Sax says, and he gestures to his right, where Plake and Agra-Red sit at the next circular pad. Beyond them, Nobaa and Engee occupy their own, and the various Flaum, Coorvin included, sit beyond Bas. "How could I not?"

Once they'd managed to square things away on Aspicis, Evva insisted the lot of them needed to go and leave her alone to work things out as various ambassadors, merchants, and power brokers flew in to stake their claim within the new galaxy. Sax wanted no part of the politics, and neither did the rest of Plake's mercenary crew.

"You're changing," Bas says. "I like it."

"I'll always be a hunter," Sax replies. "But this isn't so bad either."

A robot floating on microjets enters their sound-proof dome and slides, using some precise magnets, a series of bowls full of strange-looking puddings, noodles, and slabs of red-brown meat, all grown right in *Nova*'s own gardens and labs.

"Do you know the last time I had a meal that wasn't nutrient goop?" Bas says as she hooks one of the slabs with her right foreclaw.

"You didn't eat a single Flaum when you took the Meridia?"

"A little bit of fur doesn't count," Bas laughs, tosses the steak into her mouth. "The last time was here, Sax."

Sax blinks. Guess that's true for him too. So much time grinding through nutrient goop-fueled jobs for the Vincere and eventually he'd stopped remembering the meals. Now he follows his pair's lead, nabs a slab of slight-singed meat, eats it. Juicy, soft, real. Sax devours a few more while Bas starts recounting how they met, and Sax realizes they'll have all the time now for the past, for each other.

The idea doesn't scare him like it would have not long ago—his pair is his purpose, and Sax has yet to fail a mission.

In front of them, deeply nestled in the blooming red, a tiny purple blossoms. Just a speck, gas expanding out into the wide infinite. Something new in a stellar cloud older than all the cycles the Chorus ever saw.

Damantum isn't as I left it. There's a lot more metal here, for one, and the sky isn't a clear blue because it's crowded with so many ships.

I'm standing on the Vaos, that golden temple in the middle of my city and one of the few structures left intact after the Sevora started their war. I wasn't here when it happened, but I've heard from my own people that dark shapes appeared overhead, followed by bright lances of burning energy that crashed through homes, walls, and palaces alike. The Charre, my adopted people, fled the city in all directions and plenty haven't returned in the time since, with the Vincere's help, we drove the Sevora away.

"You're frowning," Malo says. He's next to me, watching my face as the wind blows my hair into my eyes. "What's wrong?"

"Nothing," I reply. "Just thinking about what happened, and what's next."

The future's everywhere in front of us, down the Vaos' many steps and stretching over a city under construction. Some of the repairs look familiar, but most are strange, with mobs of humans watching as Flaum and other species demonstrate the technologies being sent our way in all those ships. Viera sent notice that we'd be getting a surprise not long after Malo and I, courtesy of Plake and her shiny new Vincere ship—apparently it had belonged to a Chorus Amigga—made it home. After dropping with us, T'Oli had scurried off with a band of welcoming traders and left in search of Vee, noting that it was probably a bad idea to let a rogue Oratus wander free for too long.

While Evva and the new leadership of the Vincere sorted their thing out, plenty of planets and groups wanted to get in on what was now a wide open galaxy. Resources and expansion were the new thing, and Earth had plenty of the former, with possibilities for the latter. As such I'd already been invited to a dozen dinners aboard various cruisers, and had all sorts of strange bribes offered to me.

I'd turned them all down.

"You think all this generosity will melt your heart?" Malo says. "They're really trying."

Another wave came in the form of donations, of personnel coming with tools and trades to teach my people, and the Solare and Lunare in the jungles and mountains, about all the ways their own lives could be easier. I wasn't asked about any of these, but with our military still in shambles and my own appetite for a fight long gone, I'm not objecting to a little bit of charity.

"It's going to take them a long time." I put my hand on the altar next to me. There's still red there, a stain from a lifestyle dying away, but no more sacrifices. I encouraged the priests to worship Ignos, but without the bloodshed. Unity, cooperation. We'd give those a try and see how our god treated us. "And I don't mind. If everyone's busy with the visitors, then they're not asking me questions."

Malo laughs, shakes his head, and we watch Ignos tilt its way towards the horizon.

"I wonder how long this will last," Malo says after a minute.

"How long?"

"Everything's already changing, Kaishi. It won't be too long before the Charre decide they don't need an Empress, or warriors. We'll be part of all... this."

The wind picks up at the top of the temple and I relish the breeze. Too long breathing in artificial air, with the drone of a fan behind every gust. Now I get spices, the smell of baking bread and, yes, a bit of that tongue-tingling current of burning electricity.

"After all we've been through, you're worried about a little change?"

Malo looks at me, the corner of his mouth lifting up. "I suppose that sounds stupid, doesn't it? It's just that we've only made it home, and now we're losing it again."

"It's changing Malo, but it's still here." I take a step down from the top. "Come on, I can smell those peppers cooking."

START YOUR NEXT ADVENTURE!

PARAGON'S FALL

All his life, Aegis has defeated every villain he's come across, one punch after another. He deserves a break, but when word spreads of a plot to destroy the Paragons, Aegis must don the suit one more time.

THE SPEAR - PREQUEL SHORT STORY

After his band subdues an enemy village, Malo takes his eyes off a skilled captive and loses his spear when she vanishes into the jungle night. Charged by his commander to recover the weapon or never return, Malo sets off in search of the thieving girl.

A prequel to *The Skyward Saga*, *The Spear* is an action-adventure story that dives deep into the jungle to find Malo's true heart.

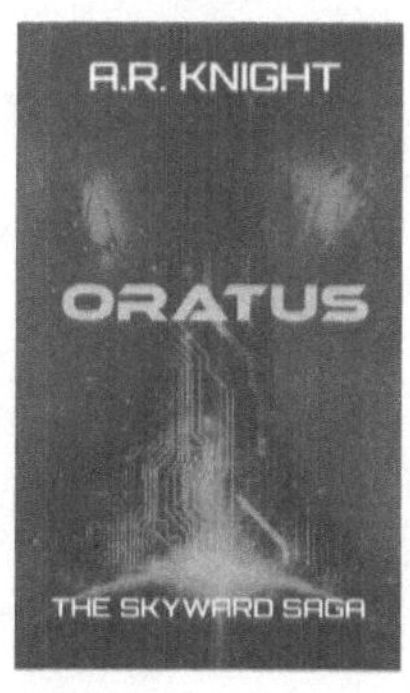

ORATUS - PREQUEL SHORT STORY

On the day she is born, Bas is expected to fight for her life.

The Oratus, a warrior species bred to bring peace and order to the galaxy, do not start quietly. From her first moments, Bas is issued a challenge: climb to the top of the Mountain. If she makes it, Bas survives. If she doesn't...

Oratus is an action-adventure prequel to *The Skyward Saga*, following the brutal first days of life for a species that knows nothing except war, survival, and the bonds forged in those moments.

STARSHOT - BOOK ONE

Caught between warring factions, Kaishi and her tribe face

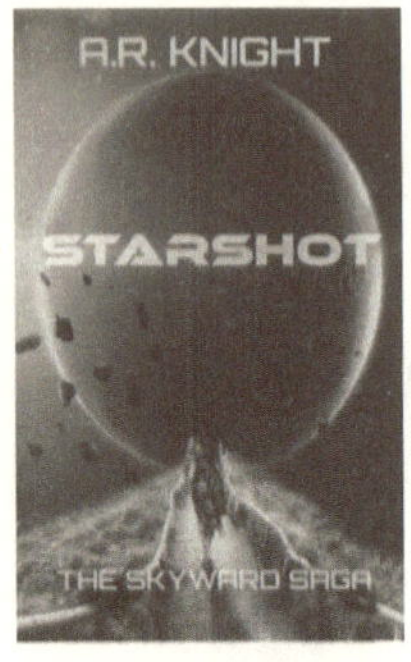

extinction. When a burning meteor lights up the night, Kaishi investigates and finds a voice with answers for everything, with secrets that could let Kaishi save her people. All Kaishi has to do is promise to follow Its orders.

But this promise carries a terrible price.

Starshot is the first book *The Skyward Saga*, a completed sci-fi adventure series that features mind-bending alien encounters, far-future action, devious villains, and a heroine that won't stop fighting.

MIND'S EYE - BOOK TWO

Kaishi embraced the gifts the Sevora gave her, but becoming an empress has attracted the kind of attention that comes with claws.

Following the Sevora's guidance has brought Kaishi and her people back from ruin and into prosperity, but as miracle after miracle pours from the voice in her head to the forges in Kaishi's great city, interstellar eyes take notice.

Mind's Eye is the second book in *The Skyward Saga*, a sci-fi adventure series filled with frenetic action, weird creatures, and a universe begging to be explored.

CLARITY'S DAWN - BOOK THREE

To survive on an alien world, Kaishi must decide whether to trust the creature inside her mind, or reject it and risk everything to fight for her freedom.

Ignos lied. The alien promised to take Kaishi and her friends back

to Earth, to home. Instead, Ignos has brought them to its own world, teeming with other parasites that see the humans as hosts, and a potential gateway to their own survival.

Clarity's Dawn is the third book in *The Skyward Saga*, a sci-fi adventure series spanning alien worlds, unique technologies, and colorful characters scrambling to survive as odds mount against them.

CREATOR'S END - BOOK FOUR

Home. Kaishi can see Earth, but between her and her family stand a hostile fleet and Kaishi only has one ship that she doesn't even know how to fly.

Her sole chance at survival depends on a risky attempt to reach Earth's far side, where nobody Kaishi knows has ever been. And the Earth Kaishi finds when they reach the surface is far different than the one she knows.

Creator's End is the fourth book in *The Skyward Saga*, a sci-fi adventure series that brings peril, heart, and fascinating technology in equal measure as Kaishi and Sax look to save their species and themselves.

HUMANITY RISING - BOOK FIVE

Earth is under assault, and Kaishi has arrived to lead her people, just in time to see them destroyed.

Hiding under the mountains with continuous attacks from the skies, Kaishi marshals humanity's remnants in a final stand against overwhelming odds. Hope resides in a last ditch effort to

call out beyond the stars for help, as Kaishi climbs the cliffs to fight one final time beside her friends.

Humanity Rising is the fifth book in *The Skyward Saga*, a sci-fi adventure series that puts the galaxy at risk as species wage wars for survival, worlds are ruined in revenge, and histories are rewritten by the victors.

THE LAST CYCLE - BOOK SIX

The Sevora have been defeated, and now Kaishi and Sax come together on opposite sides, with the galaxy's most powerful force in between.

Kaishi goes from one threat to another when the same alien army that saved Earth from the Sevora invasion demands that Kaishi submit humanity to their rule. Submission comes with gifts, peace, and a promised place at the galactic table. Resistance means certain destruction.

The Last Cycle is the final book in *The Skyward Saga*, a sci-fi adventure series that brings the galaxy to the brink of cataclysmic change, where hope rests with those brave few willing to risk everything for a better future.

THE METAL MAN - PREQUEL SHORT STORY

After a disaster on the Moon, Mox's search for strength brings him to a dangerous scientist and a choice between the life Mox knows and the vengeance he desires.

The Metal Man is a sci-fi action prequel to *The Wild Nines*, running alongside Mox as he faces the most difficult choices in his life, the crucible that forges one of the most formidable mercenaries in the solar system.

WILD NINES - BOOK ONE

For Davin and his veteran mercenary crew, running security on Europa should've been easy, and was, until a deadly mistake makes the Wild Nines the number one enemy in the solar system.

Wild Nines is the first novel in *The Wild Nines* series, a fast-paced, action-driven space opera set in a corporate-controlled solar system where laws are profit-driven, and survival often depends on how fast you are on the draw.

DARK ICE - BOOK TWO

Davin tried to clear his name, and wound up owing the most dangerous man in the solar system. And it's time that debt was paid.

Dark Ice is the second novel in *The Wild Nines* series, an action-

packed space opera where humanity's expansion through the solar system is driven by blood, sweat, and greed.

ONE SHOT - BOOK THREE

Returning to the solar system's center, Davin's crew, the Wild Nines, find worlds in turmoil as uprising against corporate control consume everything they know. The battle between corporation and citizen threatens to split the Wild Nines apart, and when the rebel's ultimate plan becomes clear, Davin and his crew may be the only ones who can stop it.

One Shot is the third novel in *The Wild Nines* series, a blistering space opera that brings colorful characters to epic battles with stakes large and small, as Davin's mercenary crew must decide what their future holds.

RIVEN - BOOK ONE

The dead belong in Riven. The living on Earth. But as war fills Riven to bursting, Carver has to find a way to keep those lines clear, or there won't be much difference between the worlds for long.

Riven is the first book in *The Riven Trilogy*, a steampunk fantasy set during a twisted World War One. With action-packed adventure, humor and a little bit of love, Carver's adventure promises to keep you turning the pages, searching for answers along with the guide.

THE CYCLE - BOOK TWO

Carver thought he'd saved the world from the endless dead, but as Earth tries to find peace, a new threat targets the guides themselves, and Carver's first on its list.

The Cycle is the second book in *The Riven Trilogy*, a steampunk fantasy set during a twisted World War One. With snappy characters you'll grow to love, a unique world, and fast-paced action, Carver's attempt to save the only family he knows will have you turning the pages all the way to the end.

SPIRIT'S END - BOOK THREE

All his life, Carver wanted to save Riven, the world of the dead. Now, to save those he loves, he has to destroy it.

With the Guides in shambles and Riven overrun with furious dead, Carver embarks on a final journey to try and keep the departed where they belong. Ending Riven's growing threat, though, requires knowing how the world works, and who made it. Carver must journey through Riven's dangerous history to find an answer.

Spirit's End is the devastating conclusion to *The Riven Trilogy*, a steampunk fantasy lost between worlds. Take one last walk with Carver and his friends as they battle ancient evils, unravel Riven's final puzzle, and come together to save Earth from ruin.

PARAGON'S FALL - BOOK ONE

All his life, Aegis has defeated every villain he's come across, one punch after another. He deserves a break, but when word spreads of a plot to destroy the Paragons, Aegis must don the suit one more time.

Paragon's Fall begins a new series exploring a world run by would-be heroes, who prove to be all too human as they clash with each other, normals, and monsters from their pasts. Explore a fascinating take on the superhero genre, and how getting everything you want might be the worst thing you can imagine.

ACKNOWLEDGMENTS

The Last Cycle closes the longest series I've ever written, consisting of six novels and a pair of novellas. It's easy to say that these stories are the product of an over-active imagination and that the only requirement to telling them was to sit in front of a keyboard and type.

I wrote this series in multiple countries, on beaches and on mountainsides. In planes and in bars, restaurants, cafes and in the corners of libraries. All of those moments came with the help of others, from my wife and her endless patience with my escapes to other worlds, to the baristas whipping up espresso or the attendant carefully handing me water across full seats in turbulence so as not to spill on my computer.

In short, a series like this takes time and effort, not just by the writer, but by those who help give that writer the time and space to, well, write. So, thank you, because without your help, I never would have met Kaishi, nor traveled the stars with Sax and the Sevora.

A.R. Knight spins stories in a frosty house in Madison, WI, primarily owned by a pair of cats. After getting sucked into the working grind in the economic crash of the 2008, he found himself spending boring meetings soaring through space and going on grand adventures.

Eventually, spending time with podcasting, screenplays, short stories and other novels, he found a story he could fall into and a cast of characters both entertaining and full of heart.

A.R. Knight plans on jumping through to other worlds and finding new stories to tell in the limitless borders of our imagination.

Thanks, as always, for reading!

For more information:
www.adamrknight.com

Oratus:
Nicole

Creator's End:
Elmer and Evelyn

Humanity Rising:
Kathy and Paul

The Last Cycle:
To Blanche and Don